History of Modern India

for Civil Services Examination

Third Edition

History of Modern India

for Civil Services Examination

Third Edition

Sujata Menon

G. K. PUBLICATIONS (P) LTD.

Title : History of Modern India (3ed)

Language : English

Author Name : Sujata Menon

Typeset & Published by :

Career Launcher Infrastructure (P) Ltd.

A-45, Mohan Cooperative Industrial Area, Near Mohan Estate Metro Station, New Delhi - 110044

Marketed by :

G.K. Publications (P) Ltd.

Plot No. 9A, Sector-27A, Mathura Road, Faridabad, Haryana-121003

ISBN : **978-93-5681-287-1**

Printer's Details : Printed in India, New Delhi.

CONTENTS

PREFACE TO THE THIRD EDITION

I am pleased to present the Preface for the third edition of this book. It has been dedicated to providing authentic and simplified content for UPSC aspirants since its inception. The primary objective of this edition is to offer straightforward and updated content.

It is a common myth that history is a static discipline; however, it has experienced interpretational and structural changes in numerous areas and themes over the years. Hence, the field of history is continuously developing as a result of the re-examination of existing information, emerging discoveries, and the integration of other domains. For UPSC aspirants, it is a challenging task in keeping up with the ever-growing changes in the subject of history. Hence, it is imperative for an UPSC aspirant to engage with the most up-to-date versions of historical literature.

Consequently, there is always a need to look out for easily comprehensible content for a subject as vast and complex as history, which is often layered with multiple interpretations. Despite the availability of some academic books on history that are simple, they tend to be difficult to grasp, particularly for UPSC aspirants, who have to cover a vast syllabus within a limited time frame.

This edition has been updated to cater to the needs and requirements of UPSC aspirants. It encompasses various topics and themes, including new interpretations and emerging perspectives on modern Indian history. For example, separate chapters have been included on right-wing organizations such as Bharatiya Janata Dal, Subhash Chandra Bose, and Dr. B. R. Ambedkar, thus providing a context for the rise of various organisations and leaders and their contributions during the national struggle.

It is now a comprehensive edition, consisting of 22 chapters that cover a broad range of topics from the 18th century to the first half of the 20th century India. At the end of each chapter, previous years' questions are given, and their solutions are easy to track from the chapter. As usual, simplicity and authenticity are the unique features of this edition. The book is composed in a straightforward and clear style, encompassing all the subjects in a brief and comprehensible manner.

In this edition special attention has been given to make the book more reader-friendly by incorporating pictures and diagrams. Some topics in this book are explained through simple diagrams, making them a unique selling proposition (USP) of this edition.

I hope that UPSC aspirants find this edition not only useful but also engaging. I wish them all the best in their endeavours.

With warm regards

Dr. Sujata Menon

June 2023

1 CHAPTER India in the Eighteenth Century

The eighteenth century was a landmark period in the history of India and was marked by three major political developments – the decline and disintegration of the Mughal Empire; the emergence of a number of independent and semi independent kingdoms and powers; and the rise of the East India Company as a dominant political power. All these resulted in fierce struggles, conspiracies, battles and wars.

In this chapter we will study the disintegration of the Mughal Empire and the rise of regional states and powers in the 18th century. The rise of the East India Company as a political force will be examined in the next chapter.

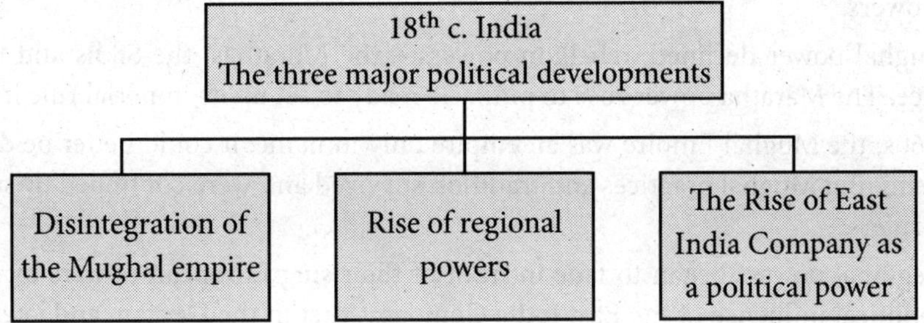

Debate over 18th c. India

The 18th century has been a subject of debate among scholars.

Following are issues of debate:

Conventionally, the 18th century has been viewed as a period of decline, anarchy, and economic decay, or simply put, as the Dark Age. This view is propagated by those historians who considered that with the decline of Mughal state, there was an an overall decline in polity, economy and society in the country. However, this view is now not accepted since Mughals power was not as widespread or deep as it was assumed. Important parts of India, especially the North East and South, remained outside it, as did several social groups.

The latest studies find 18th century India not as a period of anarchy and decline, but of growth and dynamic politics. The period is marked by the rise of several regional and local powers, which resulted in maintenance of law and order and flourishing of economy in their respective regions and areas across the country. Historians therefore find that this period was marked by reconfiguration of economic and political structure under various regional states and powers. They argued that the establishment of local power centres was the dominant feature of the eighteenth century, rather than the fall and rise of all-India empires. There was no overall decline in economy due to disintegration of Mughal imperial state. While the traditional centres of trade and commerce held under the Mughals declined, there was a corresponding rise of the regional powers that opened new vistas in the economy.

Though by 18th century the Mughal Empire had declined and disintegrated, its tradition, practices and glory continued. The emerging regional states and local rulers adopted and emulated several Mughal practices and Mughal tradition. Changes were introduced in the adopted Mughal practices suiting to the situations. Mughal administrative practices were adopted even by such states as the Marathas, which were hostile to Mughal imperial rule. These states largely copied Mughal methods of administration. According to historian Satish Chandra, the 18th century is to be presented as a separate chronological whole, rather than split into two of halves, pre-British and British.

Therefore, politically, the 18th century was beset with fragmented polity. In its first half, there was decline of dominant power like Mughals and emergence of local power centres. Then, the second half of the 18th century witnessed the strengthening of local states- the Marathas, the Jats and the Sikhs.

The Afghani invasion under Nadir Shah and the Turrani invasions under Abdali through 1740s and 1750s further deteriorated the Mughal empire, but asserted the positions of regional states and regional powers.

As Mughal power declined, rebellion powers – the Marathas, the Sikhs and the Jats rose in prominence. The Maratha power rose to pinnacle ready to set up its imperial rule in North India.

By 1760s, the Mughal Empire was an empire only in name; it could better be described as the state of Delhi. But Mughal practices and tradition survived and were continued by successive states and petty rulers.

The regional powers began to fade in front of the rising European powers by late 18thc. The growing political influence of the East India Company, first in the Deccan, and later in Bengal, led to the gradual decline of regional powers by the end of 18th century.

Debate Over 18th C. India		
A dark period and period of anarchy due to decline and disintegration of Mughal Empire	Not a dark period as there was rise of regional kingdoms and regional powers	Polity, eonomy flourished and law and order situation restored under regional kingdoms

Causes of the Disintegration of the Mughal Empire

Babur founded the Mughal Empire, Akbar extended and consolidated it. The empire continued in its splendour till the death of Aurangzeb in 1707, though symptoms of weakness were apparent even before that. The decline became very rapid after the death of Aurangzeb. Therefore the causes for the downfall and disintegration of Mughal Empire can be studied under two categories: Causes attributed to Aurangzeb and factors for which he is not responsible.

Causes Attributed to Aurangzeb

- **Aurangzeb's religious policy :** Aurangzeb reversed Akbar's liberal religious policy. He followed a rigid and fanatic religious policy. His anti Hindu measures led to the rise of several conflicts and revolts that weakened the structure of the Mughal empire. The communities that revolted against Aurangzeb were the Jats, the Satnamis and the Sikhs. These communities began to strike deadly blows at the Mughal Empire.
- **Deccan policy :** Aurangzeb spent nearly 25 years of his life pursuing his Deccan policy. He first completed the conquest of the states of Bijapur and Golconda in 1686 and 1687 respectively. These conquests were a great triumph for Aurangzeb, but soon after it proved a blunder and contributed to the downfall of the empire. The conquests of these states left the Marathas free to turn their whole attention against the Mughals. The demoralised soldiers of the armies of Bijapur and Golconda either joined the Marathas armies or began to plunder the Mughal territories. Finally, Aurangzeb had to face the major resistance from the Marathas who were organized under the leadership of Shivaji.
- **Vast empire :** After the conquests of Deccan states like Bijapur and Golconda, the territorial expansion of the Mughal empire reached its zenith. However, it became too difficult to control and administer vast territories by one man or administrator. Aurangzeb managed to administere and control such a vast empire. But soon after his death, the Mughal provinces declared their independence.
- **Long wars in the Deccan :** Aurangzeb remained in the Deccan for 25 years conquering Deccan states. The efficiency of the army was lowered due to continuous fighting. Deccan wars adversely affected the financial condition and weakened the emperor's hold over Northern India.
- **Policy against Rajputs :** Unlike Akbar, Aurangzeb followed an anti Rajput policy. He alienated the Rajputs. Although Jai Singh and Jaswant Singh had helped him to attain the throne, Aurangzeb turned against them and poisoned Raja Jaswant Singh. The Rajputs thus turned against the treacherous policies of Aurangzeb. Two major friendly Rajput states, Mewar and Marwar, came into conflict with Aurangzeb and eventually alienated from the Mughals.
- **Policy against the Sikhs :** In the times of Shah Jahan, good relations prevailed between Mughals and the Sikh Gurus. But Aurangzeb turned against them as Sikh Gurus supported his rival brother Dara Shikhoh during the war of succession. He executed Guru Tegh Bahadur in 1675 CE. His son Guru Gobind Singh vowed to avenge the death of Teg Bahadur. He transformed the Sikhs into a military force by creating Khalsa and waged war against the tyranny of Aurangzeb.
- **Policy against Marathas :** Aurangzeb followed an anti Maratha policy. He refused to recognize the importance of befriending with Maratha chief Shivaji. Being a fanatic Sunni Muslim, Aurangzeb did not accept the rule of the non Muslim Marathas. Therefore, Shivaji and his men resorted to guerrilla warfare and plundered Mughal territories in the Deccan. The Maratha attacks proved fatal to the Mughal empire as it eventually culminated in establishing an independent Maratha state under Shivaji.

Factors for which Aurangzeb was Not Responsible

- **Weak successors or Later Mughals :** the Mughal emperors till the death of Aurangzeb were all competent persons but successors of Aurangzeb were worthless rulers. (Later Mughals or Mughal emperors after Aurangzeb are discussed below.)
- **Degeneration of Mughal nobility :** Before 1707 CE, Mughal India saw great generals and administrators like Bairam Khan, Raja Todar Mal, Raja Man Singh and others. With the decline in the character of later Mughal emperors, deterioration set in the Mughal nobility also. Corruption, debauchery and conspiracies became common among the nobility in the court.
- **Economic bankruptcy :** Akbar established a sound and effective financial system which was maintained by his successor Jahangir. The share of the state was one third of the produce of the land and it dealt directly with the cultivators. This system began to deteriorate under Shah Jahan. The share of the state was raised to one half of the produce of the land in the time of Shah Jahan. The system of farming out land revenue was introduced. A lot of money was wasted on building magnificient structures during Shah Jahan's time. Wars of Aurangzeb exhausted the treasury. He was not in a position to pay the troops regularly towards the end of his reign. Financial condition became still worse under later Mughals.
- **Inefficiency of the Mughal army :** The Mughal state was a military state. But Mughal army was a loosely organized system consisting of Mansabdar army, Dakhili army, Ahadi soldiers and other soldiers. The vast standing army as seen under the sultanate was limited under Mughals. In due course the loosely organized Mughal army become inefficient. The pomp and show attached to Mughal army adversely affected it. The weakness of the army became apparent during Shah Jahan's time when it failed to recapture Kandahar.
- **Decline of Mansabdari system :** The Mughals' public services were based on Mansabdari system. Mansabdari was instituted by Akbar which became the backbone of Mughal bureaucracy and military. Mansabdari system reached its highest level under Akbar and his successors. But during the later Mughal era, the system encountered many defects due to inefficiency of the rulers and the corruption of the officials. Its decline contributed to the deteriorating standards of the Mughal army.

Later Mughals

The Mughal Empire which was brought to its pinnacle of glory by the great Mughals saw a decline in its fortunes and glory in the eighteenth century during the last years of Aurangzeb's reign who died on February 20, 1707. The succeeding Mughals of the eighteenth century, collectively called the, later Mughals, were weak and remained puppets in the hands of others.

Most of these later Mughals were pleasure seekers and neglected the affairs of the state. Unlike their predecessos, later Mughals were thoroughly unfit to rule India or incompetent to maintain the banner of the glorious Mughal rule. Most of them were victims of intrigues and faced unnatural death. Later Mughal emperors, progressively declined in power and could do little to prevent the rise of the regional powers.

In the 150 years period between the death of Aurungzeb in 1707 to the 1857 revolt when the last of the Mughals, Bahadur Shah Zafar, was deposed by the British, there were as many as 12 Mughal rulers who occupied the throne.

Bahadur Shah-I (1707-12)

Muazam, the eldest son of Aurangzeb, ascended the throne after waging a bloody war of succession. He acquired the title of Bahadur Shah. In his short rule, Bahadur Shah brought some significant changes. He **reversed the narrow minded and antagonistic policies of Aurangzeb.** He made agreements with Rajput states, **granted sardeshmukhi to Marathas,** but not Chauth. He released **Shahuji**, the son of Sambhaji, from prison . After the release of Sahuji, civil war broke out among Marathas that resulted in removal of Tarabai from power and Sahuji as the Maratha ruler.

Bahadur Shah I
— Wikimedia Commons

Bahadur also tried to make peace with Sikh leader Guru Gobind Sahib by giving him a high Mansab. After Guru Gobind's death, Sikhs again revolted under the leadership of Banda Bahadur. This led to a prolonged war with the Sikhs. Peace was made with Chhatarsal, the Bundela chief and Churaman, the Jat chief.

Bahadur Shah I was too weak to say no to his nobles. Thus, intrigues and conspiracies ruled his court. He was incapable of suppressing the forces of disintegration which threatened imperial unity. Under his rule the state finances deteriorated.

Jahandar Shah (1712-13)

He was the son of Bahadur Shah. With the death of Bhahadur Shah, a civil war broke out. Bahadur Shah's four sons waged a blood war of succession. Ultimately, Jahandar Shah emerged victorious and became the emperor with the help and support of his minister Zulfikar Khan. A noted feature of this time was the **prominence of the nobles. Zulfikar Khan** became the Wazir or prime minister, and the entire affairs of the empire came into his hands. Jahandar Shah was addicted to sensual pleasures and did not take interest in administration. He came under the influence of a concubine Lal Kunwar whose relatives he promoted to the high positions. According to historian Owen, 'Jahandar Shah was an utterly degenerate representative of the House of Timur, Babur and Akbar.' Within a year he was murdered by his nephew Farrukh-Siyar, who ascended the throne the help of two Sayyid brothers- Abdullah Khan (deputy governor of Allahabad) and Husain Ali Khan (deputy governor of Bihar)

Farrukh Siyar (1713-19)

He ascended the degraded throne with the help of Sayyid brothers in 1713 CE. Farrukh Siyar was feeble, cowardly and incompetent. The two Sayyid Brothers acquired full control of the state. Sayyid Abdullah became the Wazir and Sayyid Husain Ali became the Commander-in – Chief of the Mughal army. After his accession, Farrukh Siyar came under the influence of anti Sayyid friends, and followed a policy of conspiracy against Sayyid brothers. This angered the Sayyid brothers so greatly that they imprisoned, blinded and murdered the emperor.

During Farrukh Siyar's reign Sikhs became powerful and began to strengthen their position against Mughals under the leadership of Banda Bahadur. However, Banda was captured by Mughals and put to death cruelly on 19th June 1716 CE. Another development during the reign of Farrukh Siyar was granting valuable trade concessions and exemptions from custom duties in Bengal to the agents of East India Company.

Sayyid Brothers – the king makers

Sayyid Hussain Ali Khan, deputy governor of Patna and Abdullah Khan, deputy governor of Allahabad, were known as the Sayyid brothers and later became famous as the king-makers in Indian history. After Farrukh Siyar murder in 1719, the Sayyid Brothers placed in the throne several phantom emperors. They were Rafi-Ud-Darajat, Rafi-ud-Daula, Nekusiyar and Ibrahim. These emperors quickly disappeared. Finally, they placed another puppet emperor named Mohammad Shah in 1719, who did not like to remain puppet in the hands of the Sayyids.

The Sayyid brothers adopted the policy of religious tolerance. They abolished Hindu pilgrim tax jizyah . They **granted Marathas** the right to collect chauth and sardeshmukhi of the six provinces of the Deccan. The murder of the emperor Farrukh Siyar created a wave of revulsion against the Sayyid brothers. They were looked down as *'namak haram'*. In 1720, emperor Mohammad Shah got rid of Sayyid Hussain Ali by assassination and imprisoned Abdullah.

Mohammad Shah 'Rangeela' (1719-48)

Roshan Akhtar, or Mohammad Shah, ascended the throne with the help of Sayyid brothers in 1719. Unlike his predecessor, Mohammad refused to remain a puppet in the hands of the Sayyid brothers. He was fond of a life of pleasure with a doting indulgence in wine and women. He was therefore given the name 'Rangeela'. In his thirty years rule, the Mughal Empire dismembered into autonomous provinces as Mughal governors and other powers asserted their autonomous rule. According to historian Dr. K.K.Datta, 'Province after province – the Deccan, Oudh and Bengal-slipped out of imperial control, the Marathas established their power far and wide, the Jats became independent near Agra, the Ruhela Afghans founded the state of Rohilkhand , the Sikhs became active in Punjab, and the invasion of Nadir Shah dealt a staggering blow to the Delhi empire'.

Mohammad Shah Rangeela* — *Wikimedia Commons

The most remarkable achievement of Mohammad's reign was the extinction of Sayyid brothers who had created many enemies. Nizam-ul-Mulk, who had helped the emperor in liquidating Sayyid brothers, was offered the position of royal wazir. But he did not like the idea and retired to the Deccan, from where he hailed, and founded an almost independent state of Hyderabad in 1724. "His departure was symbolic of the flight of loyalty and virtue from the Empire". Mughal governors of Bengal and Oudh followed suit and carved out semi independent states of Bengal and Oudh. In 1739, Nadir Shah, a Persian ruler, invaded India, that further crippled the empire politically and financially

Ahmad Shah (1748-54)

After the death of Mohammad Shah 'Rangeela', his son Ahmad Shah ascended the throne. He was very young and had no experience of administration and utterly lacked leadership qualities. His court was dominated by eunuchs and women. Javid Khan, an eunuch also known as Nawab Bahadur was emperor's favourite and leader of court party. Wazir Ghazi-ud-din Imad-ul-Mulk the grandson of Nizam-ul-Mulk, and Javid Khan, were jealous of each other . Therefore, conspiracies, intriguing and plotting became the norms of the day. Administration was in shambles and prestige and power of the Mughal emperor reached an all time low. Under such pathetic state of affairs, Ahmad Shah Abdali attacked India in 1749. Ultimately wazir Ghazi-ud-din succeeded in deposing and blinding the emperor in 1754.

Alamgir II (1754-59)

After deposing and blinding Ahmad Shah, wazir Ghazi-ud-din, who was now very powerful, placed on the throne the second son of Jahandar Shah, Aziz-ud-Din, under the title of the great Mughal Aurangzeb, Alamgir II. He remained a puppet in the hands of Ghazi-ud-din. During Alamgir II's time, the Wazir Ghazi-ud-din formed an anti Maratha front, in order to expel the Marathas from Northern India. It failed miserably, because Marathas became more powerful than before. The fourth invasion of Ahmad Shah Abdali took place during Alamgir's time. Imperial city of Delhi was captured and sacked. In 1759, Ghazi-ud-din assassinated Alamgir II.

Shah Alam II (1759-1806)

Ali Gauhar or Shah Alam II was the legitimate son and successor of Alamgir. When Alamgir was murdered, Ali Gauhar was in Bihar. He assumed the title of Shah Alam II and declared himself as the Mughal emperor. However, he did not have the courage and power to face powerful Wazir in Delhi. Therefore he remained away from Delhi for 12 years. During his stay in Bihar, he joined Mir Qasim of Bengal and Shuja-ud-Daula of Oudh in declaring a war against the East India Company. The joint forces were defeated in the battle of Buxar in 1764. The East India company recognized Shah Alam as an emperor and gave him a pension. In return, Shah Alam granted to the company the Diwani (right of collection and administration of revenue) of Bengal, Bihar and Orissa in 1765. In 1772, Shah Alam returned to Delhi under the protection of the Marathas. In 1803, General Lake captured Delhi, but Shah Alam continued to hold the title of Mughal emperor and was given twenty six lacs of rupees annually as pension. Therefore, the succeeding Mughal rulers were the pensioners of the East Indian Company.

Akbar II (1806-1837)

He succeeded his father and lived on the British pension. He was a king merely in name and his authority was confined only to the Red Fort at Delhi.

Akbar II
— Wikimedia Commons

Bahadur Shah II
— Wikimedia Commons

Bahadur Shah II (1837- 1862)

After the death of Akbar II, his son Bahadur Shah II succeeded him as the Mughal emperor – the last link in the Mughal dynasty. The new ruler also was a titular emperor. In fact he was called emperor, only by courtesy. Due to his alleged participation in 1857 revolt, he was charged and deported to Rangoon as a state prisoner. Bahadur Shah Zafar died in Rangoon in 1862 . He was the last ruler in the line of Babur. With his death the Mughal dynasty came to an end.

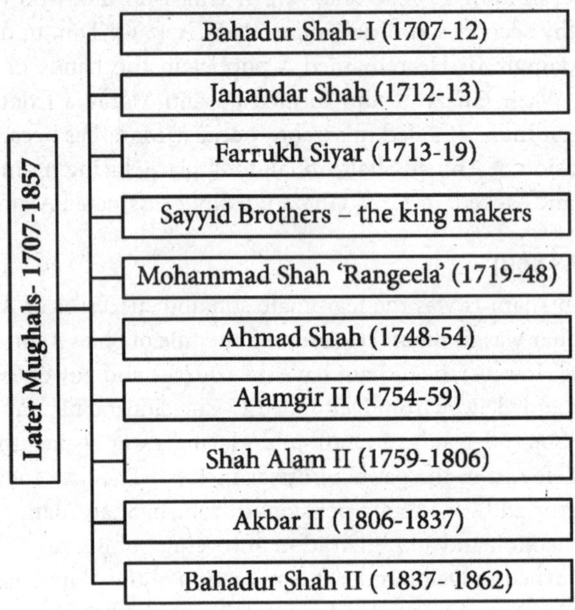

Foreign Invasions – Nadir Shah and Ahmad Shah Abdali (Durrani)

The Invasion of Nadir Shah (1739)

Nadir Shah
— Wikimedia Commons

Nadir Shah, the Persian ruler, was greatly attracted by the fabulous wealth of India and the chaotic conditions prevailing in the country due to the intrigues, corruption and disunity among the nobles and rulers. As Nadir Shah embarked on his ambitious expedition, he conquered country after country and then defeated the Mughal army at Karnal. Next, he entered Delhi in 1739, imprisoned the emperor Mohammad Shah and plundered the whole city. As a few of his soldiers were murdered on a false rumour that Nadir Shah was dead, he ordered a general massacre in Delhi. Innocent people were butchered mercilessly. Besides the two centuries of accumulated wealth of the Mughals, he carried away the famous Kohinoor diamond and the jewel studded peacock throne of Shah Jahan to Persia. He departed after 57 days leaving the Mughals politically crippled and financially bankrupt. Nadir Shah's invasion exposed the hidden weakness of Indian rulers to several powers that had their eyes glued to the throne of Delhi.

Invasion of Ahmad Shah Abdali (1748-1761)

A portrait of Ahmad Shah Durrani
— Wikimedia Commons

Ahmad Shah was a general in the army of Nadir Shah. Nadir Shah was greatly impressed by the qualities of his general. He complimented him by saying, 'I have not found in Iran, Turan or Hind any man equal to Ahmad Shah in capacity and character'. Ahmad Shah was an Afghan chief of the Abdali clan. Nadir Shah was assassinated in 1747. Thereafter, Ahmad Shah became an independent ruler of Afghanistan. He declared himself the king at Kandahar and captured Kabul. After his accession, he styled himself as Durr-i-Durran or the pearl of the age. He and his successors therefore were known as Durrani also.

After establishing his power and position at home, Ahmad Shah Durrani led several expeditions to India between 1748 to 1767. In all he led seven expeditions to India during the time of Mughal emperors Ahmad Shah and Shah Alam II. The attempts of Ahmad Shah Abdali show a revival of Afghan power trying to establish supremacy over the ruins of the Mughal Empire. The invasions of Abdali were more than mere plundering raids. He wanted to establish his rule in India. In 1761, he defeated the powerful Marathas in a famous battle- the Third Battle of Panipat. The battle is discussed in detail later. With their defeat in the battle of Panipat, the power and ambition of Marathas to set up Maratha Empire in north was crushed, and made the Mughal Empire to exist in name, only ruling Delhi and a small territory around it.

Rise of Regional states and Regional Powers

Through the 18th century, the Mughal Empire gradually fragmented into a number of independent, regional states. The previously attached groups to the Mughal authority such as local gentry, nobility and commercial communities began to part from the Mughal authority and assert power in their respective area of influence. As a consequence of this, the Mughal Empire got disintegrated into semi autonomous states such as Awadh, Bengal and Hyderabad. The other Mughals provinces came largely under the sway of rising powers of Marathas, Sikhs and Jats.

The emerging regional states and powers of this period can be divided into three overlapping groups:

1. States that were old Mughal provinces like Awadh, Bengal, and Hyderabad. Although extremely powerful and quite independent, the rulers of these states did not break their formal ties with the Mughal emperor.
2. States that were tributaries to Mughals but enjoyed considerable independence as *watan jagirs.* These included mainly Rajput principalities
3. States under the control of Marathas, Sikhs and others like the Jats. They all had seized their independence from the Mughals after a long-drawn armed struggle.

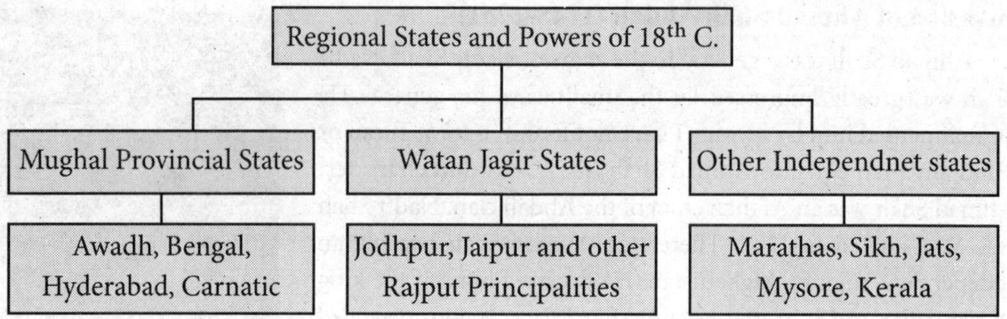

Provincial State of Hyderabad

Nizam-ul-Mulk Asaf Jah, a Wazir of Mughal emperor Mohammad Shah, founded the Hyderabad state in 1724 CE. The dynasty that ruled the state of Hyderabad came to be known as the Asafjahi dynasty, after its founder. Nizam-ul-Mulk's family belonged to a place known as Bokhara in Samarkand. They migrated to Delhi during the time of Aurangzeb. Emperor Bahadur Shah appointed him the governor of Oudh and gave him the title of *Khan-i-Dauran*. He was appointed governor of the Deccan by emperor Farrukh Siyar and given the title of Khan-i-Nizam-ul-Mulk. He was very helpful to Mohammad Shah in his efforts to get rid of the Sayyid brothers. In lieu of his commendable services in Deccan, Mohammad Shah appointed him his Wazir in 1722 CE . Nizam attempted to bring about administrative reforms, but failed to do so, as the emperor was very lukewarm to reforms. He found the Mughal court very undesirable and full of plots and intrigues. Therefore, the Nizam retired to Deccan in 1723 CE. He ruled quite independently till his death in 1748.

Nizam of Hyderabad- Nizam-ul-Mulk Asaf Jah I also known as Chin Qilich Kamaruddin Khan, Nizam-ul-Mulk, Asaf Jah — Wikimedia Commons

In the later part of the 18th century, the state of Hyderabad was constantly engaged in a struggle against the Marathas and with independent Telugu warrior chiefs called Nayakas.

Provincial State of Oudh

Burhan-ul-Mulk Sa'adat Khan (1722-39) was appointed subedar of Oudh in 1722. He was earlier a Wazir of the Mughal emperor Mohammad Shah. For his services, he was made the governor of the Oudh province. Oudh was a prosperous region, controlling the rich alluvial Ganga plain and the main trade route between north India and Bengal. Sadat Khan held the combined offices of *subedari, diwani* and *faujdari* . He tried to decrease Mughal influence in the Oudh region by reducing the number of office holders (jagirdars) appointed by the Mughals. Sadat Khan suppressed lawlessness in the state and improved the law and order. He disciplined landlords, or *Zamindars,* and won over nobles by giving several concessions. He organized an efficient system of administration. He introduced several reforms in the land revenue system which proved very beneficial to the farmers. After the death of Sadat Khan, his nephew and son in law Safar Jang (1739-54) became the ruler. His rule witnessed a period of peace, prosperity and cultural development. Lucknow, the capital of Oudh became the centre of art, culture and crafts under the patronage of its Nawabs, chieftains and Zamindars.

The prolonged period of comparative peace and economic prosperity under Sadat Khan and Safdar Jung resulted in the growth of a distinct Lucknow or Lucknavi culture around Oudh court.

After the death of Safdar Jung, his son Shujah-ud-Daula (1754-75) became the Nawab of Oudh. During this period, the interference of the English increased in the state as they were making serious efforts to bring under their control several parts of India.

Provincial State of Bengal

Bengal gradually broke away from Mughal control under Murshid Quli Khan (1717-27) who was appointed the governor of Bengal by Aurangzeb in 1705 CE. Soon, he was also made subedar of Orissa. During the rule of weak successors of Aurangzeb, he founded an independent kingdom of Nawabs in Bengal. He however regularly sent large tribute to the Mughal emperor. As an independent Nawab, Murshid Quli Khan successfully crushed all the major revolts in Bengal province. He confiscated the *jagirs* of those officials who opposed him. He tried to improve his financial position by reducing the expenditure. Nawab Mushid made the foreign companies pay the octroi duty like other traders. He collected the revenue in a strict way. He gave equal opportunities for employment both to Hindus and Muslims, and appointed Bengalis, mostly Hindus, on various civil and army posts.

Murshid Quli Khan the Nawab of Bengal
— Wikimedia Commons

After the death of Nawab Murshid Quli Khan, his son in law Shuja-ud-Din (1727-39) succeeded him in governing Bengal and Orissa. Bihar was also added to his territory and he appointed Ali Vardi Khan as its deputy governor. He continued to follow the policies of Murshid Quli Khan and maintained peace in the state.

After the death of Shuja-ud-Din, his son Sarfaraj Khan became the Nawab, but soon Ali Vardi Khan (1739-56) deposed him and declared himself as Nawab. He legalized his usurped position by securing an imperial *farman* from Delhi. Like his predecessors, he also took several steps to strengthen the state. He made all possible efforts to keep the foreign companies, mainly East India Company under his control.

After the death of Ali Vardi Khan in 1756 CE, his grandson Siraj-ud-Daula (1756-57) succeeded him. Unlike his predecessors, Siraj proved to be a weak Nawab. He could not control his conspirators, and the East India Company was emerging as a powerful political force. Under his tenure, Bengal was conquered by the East India Company, and the Nawabs of Bengal became puppets in the hands of the company's officers.

The Watan Jagirs of the Rajputs

Many Rajput kings, particularly those belonging to Amber and Jodhpur, were permitted to enjoy considerable autonomy in their watan jagirs – the hereditary jagirs, or principalities of those Hindus rulers who were employed in Mughal services and accepted Mughal's suzerainty by giving taxes and tributes. After the death of Aurangzeb, several Rajputs states declared themselves independent from Mughal rule. In the 18th century, these rulers now attempted to extend their control over adjacent regions. Special mention can be made of Raja Ajit Singh of Jodhpur, who also held the governorship of Gujarat, and Sawai Raja Jai Singh of Amber who was also the governor of Malwa. They tried to extend their territories by seizing portions of imperial territories neighbouring their watans.

Raja Sawai Jai Singh of Amber (1699-1743) was an outstanding ruler. He was a great astronomer, builder, engineer, jurist, social reformer and a statesman. Jai Singh erected observatories at Delhi, Jaipur, Mathura, Ujjai and Varanasi. These observatories are known as Jantar Mantars. He was the founder of modern city of Jaipur, commonly known as the Pink City.

The Sikhs

Under the leadership of the last Guru, Guru Gobind Singh (1675-1708), the Sikhs became a political and military force. This helped Sikhs in their efforts to build a separate state in Punjab. Under the leadership of Guru Gobind Singh, Sikhs waged wars against Mughals. After his death in 1708 CE, it was under Banda Bahadur's (1670-1715) leadership the fight continued. Banda Bahadur carried on a vigorous struggle against the Mughals for about eight years. His important victory was in 1710 CE over the Mughal governor of Sirhind. He also captured the areas lying between the rivers Sutlej and Yamuna. Banda Bahadur abolished zamindari and struck coins in the name of Guru. However, his strength could not match the strength of the Mughals. In 1715 CE, he was captured and executed along with several Sikh soldiers.

For about half a century after the death of Banda Bahadur, the Sikhs lost their glory. Mughals now followed the policy of persecution of Sikhs. However, the invasions of Ahmad Shah Abdali paved the way for the rise of the Sikhs in Punjab.

The Jats

The Jats were agriculturists who lived around Delhi, Baghpat, Tilpat, Meerut, Mathura and Bharatpur areas. Mughal persecution drove them into revolts. The Jat state of Bharatpur was founded by Churaman and Badan Singh. Under Churaman, they acquired control over territories situated to the west of the city of Delhi, and by the 1680s they had begun dominating the region between the two imperial cities of Delhi and Agra.

The Jat power reached its highest glory under the rule of Suraj Mal (1756-63). He extended the Jat kingdom till the present day west UP. Bharatpur became the centre of his kingdom. After his death in 1763, the Jat kingdom was split up among petty zamindars.

Lohagarh fort, Bharatpur : The fort was built by Raja Suraj Mal
— Wikimedia Commons

Farukhabad and Rohilkhand

The Rohilas were the inhabitants of Rohilkhand. They suffered heavily at the hands of the Jats and the Awadh rulers, and later the Marathas and the British. Muhammad Khan Bangash, an Afghan adventurer, established his control over the territory around Farrukhabad during the reign of Mughal emperor Mohammad Shah. The states of Rohilkhand and the kingdom of the Bangash Pathans were a fall-out of the Afghan migration from the 17th century. Big level immigration of Afghans into India took place in mid-18th century because of political and economic anarchy in Afghanistan. Another Afghan adventurer, Ali Muhammad Khan, took advantage of the collapse of power in north India, following Nadir Shah's invasion, to set up a petty kingdom known as Rohilkhand. This was the region of the Himalayan foothills flanked by Kumaon in the north and the Ganga in the south. The Rohillas clashed constantly with Oudh and Delhi, and with Jats and Marathas.

Other Independent Kingdoms

In the latter half of the 18th century, some independent kingdoms emerged. Significant among them were the kingdoms of Mysore, Kerala and Carnatic. In late 18th century, states of Mysore and Carnatic became the centre stage of Anglo-French rivalry that resulted in the supremacy of East India Company in India.

Mysore

In the 18th century, the state of Mysore came under the rule of Hyder Ali and later his son Tipu Sultan. Both of them were hostile towards the British, but friendly towards the French. Hyder Ali (1766-82) started his career as a petty officer in the Mysore army under the rule of king Krishnaraja Wodeyar II. The king had been reduced to the position of a mere puppet by two of his ministers. Hyder Ali, on account of his military skill and leadership qualities, became the chief of Mysore army and soon declared himself as an independent ruler after the death of the king. After becoming king he extended the boundaries of Mysore. The State of Mysore under Hyder Ali was always under the threat of Marathas, the Nizam of Hyderabad and the English. Hyder Ali fought many battles with the Marathas, Nizam and the English who formed alliances against him. We will discuss these battles under Anglo-Mysore wars in the third chapter.

Kerala

The kingdom of Travancore rose into prominence after 1729 under King Marthanda Verma, one of the leading statesmen of the 18th century. He subdued the feudatories, conquered Quilon and Elayadam. Marthanda Verma defeated the Dutch, thus ending their political power in Kerala. He organized a strong army on the western model and undertook many irrigation works, and also the canals for communication. Travancore in the second half of the 18th century became a famous center of Sanskrit scholarship. Rama Varma, successor of Martanda Verma, was himself a poet, scholar, and musician. He conversed fluently in English, took a keen interest in European affairs, and regularly read newspapers and journals published in London, Calcutta and Madras.

King Marthanda Varma of Kerala
— Wikimedia Commons

Carnatic

It was one of the Subahs of the Deccan, and therefore it was a dependency of the Nizam, who maintained his control until his death in 1748. Taking advantage of the weakness of the Nizam, the Nawab of the Carnatic, Saadatullah Khan, freed himself from the tutelage of the viceroy of the Deccan and made his office hereditary. Thus, without the formal approval of his superior, the Nizam, the Nawab Saadullah Khan of Carnatic made his nephew Dost Ali, his successor. After 1740 the Nawabship of the Carnatic became a bone of contention among the rival claimants and this provided an opportunity to the ambitious Europeans to fish in the troubled waters.

The Marathas

It was Shivaji (1627-1680) who carved out a stable Maratha kingdom in the Deccan. After Shivaji's death in 1680, the kingdom established by him could not be kept intact by his successors. His son Sambhaji (1680-89) succeeded him, but was defeated by Aurangzeb, and in 1689 put to death. Another son of Shivaji, Raja Ram (1689-1700) ascended the Maratha throne. He was in constant war with the Mughals. After his death in 1700, his widow Tara Bai (1700-07), managed the affairs of the state bravely. In order to create a divide and civil war among Marathas, Mughals released Sahu, the grandson of Shivaji and son of Sambhaji, who was in Mughal captivity for more than 18 years. Sahu put forward his claim to the throne, but Tarabai declared Sahu, an imposter.

A tussle for the throne began between Sahu and Tarabai. Sahu emerged victorious with the help of Balaji Vishwanath, a Maratha Sardar. After becoming the ruler, Sahu made Balaji his Peshwa (chief minister). All the power of the state came under Balaji's office. With this, started the rule of the Peshwa. The office of Peshwa , in due course became hereditary. The subsequent Peshwas became the real rulers of the kingdom and the king was reduced to a figurehead and ruled in name only. The Peshwas that ruled from 1713 till 1761 are considered as Great Peshwas. From 1761 to 1818, the later Peshwas ruled.

Following are the Great Peshwas and Later Peshwas:

Great Peshwas

- Balaji Vishwanath (1713-1720)
- Baji-Rao I-(1720-1740)
- Balaji Baji Rao-(1740-1761)

Later Peshwas

- Madhav Rao (1761- 1772)
- Narain Rao (1772- 1773)
- Madhav Rao Narain (1774-1795)
- Baji Rao II (1795 – 1818)

In this chapter we will discuss the three Great Peshwas. Later Peshwas are discussed in the following chapters.

Peshwa Balaji Vishwanath (1714-20)

He excelled in diplomacy. He was able to unite a large number of Marathas under the leadership of Sahu. Balaji got three concessions from the Mughal ruler which proved to be very helpful in strengthening the Maratha power. These were: the Marathas got the right to collect 'Chauth' i.e. one fourth share, of the revenue of the Deccan and southern India; the Marathas got the right of Sardeshmukhi i.e. one tenth of the revenue in other territories; the Maratha's right of control over all the territories earlier held by Shivaji was accepted by the Mughal ruler.

Peshwa Baji Rao I (1720-40)

After Balaji's death in 1720, his 20 year old son Baji Rao became the Peshwa. Next to Shivaji, he is considered to be the bravest and the shrewdest Maratha chief. He was a master in the guerrilla warfare. Baji Rao wanted to set up a purely Hindu state and this ideal was expressed by him as 'Hindu Pad Padshahi'.

Peshwa Baji Rao I
— Wikimedia Commons

Under his leadership, Marathas led many successful campaigns against the Mughal Empire. Baji Rao followed the forward policy of expanding Maratha Empire in the North. Under his leadership the Maratha Empire included Malwa, Gujarat, parts of Bundelkhand. He established Maratha hegemony near Delhi and surrounding areas. He defeated Nizam of Hyderabad and forced him to grant the right of Chauth and Sardeshmukhi. Baji Rao invaded Portuguese territories and captured Salesette and Basin from them.

Baji Rao died in 1740. He was only 40. The Maratha empire which was recently formed, received shock by the untimely death of the valiant and brilliant Peshwa Baji Rao I.

Peshwa Balaji Baji Rao (1740-61)

Baji Rao's 18 year old son Balaji Baji Rao was nominated the next Peshwa. His period saw the rise and fall of the Maratha power. He followed his father's forward policy. Balaji Baji Rao's slogan was 'Cuttack to Attock', i.e. to expand from Orissa to Peshawar. After the death of Sahu in 1749, he shifted the capital from Satara to Poona. It was during Balaji's time that Maratha state was transformed into Maratha confederacy. The Peshwa became the actual leader of the Maratha confederacy.

The Marathas consolidated their power over Gujarat, Malwa and Bundelkhand.The Nawab of Bengal was forced to cede Orissa to the Marathas. In the south, the state of Mysore was forced to pay tribute. The Nizam of Hyderabad had to part with vast territories. The Marathas in the north marched through the Gangetic Doab, reached Delhi and Punjab.They collected tributes from the Mughal emeperor and the governor of Sirhind. Thus, the year 1760 marked the phenomenal rise of the Maratha power. 'Their frontier extended on the north to the Indus and Himalayas, and on the south nearly to the extremity of the peninsula, all the territory within those limits that was not their own, paid tribute. The whole of this great power was wielded by one hand...and all pretentions of every description were concentrated in the Peshwa.'

But in January 1761, the Marathas received the severest blow from Ahmad Shah Abdali in the Third battle of Panipat. After that the Maratha power never recovered again.

The Third battle of Panipat decided that the Marathas were not destined to rule India after the decline of the Mughal power. Only for a while, after their defeat at the hands of Abdali, they could get some of their lost power, but the English proved to be very strong and they annexed most of the territories of the Marathas.

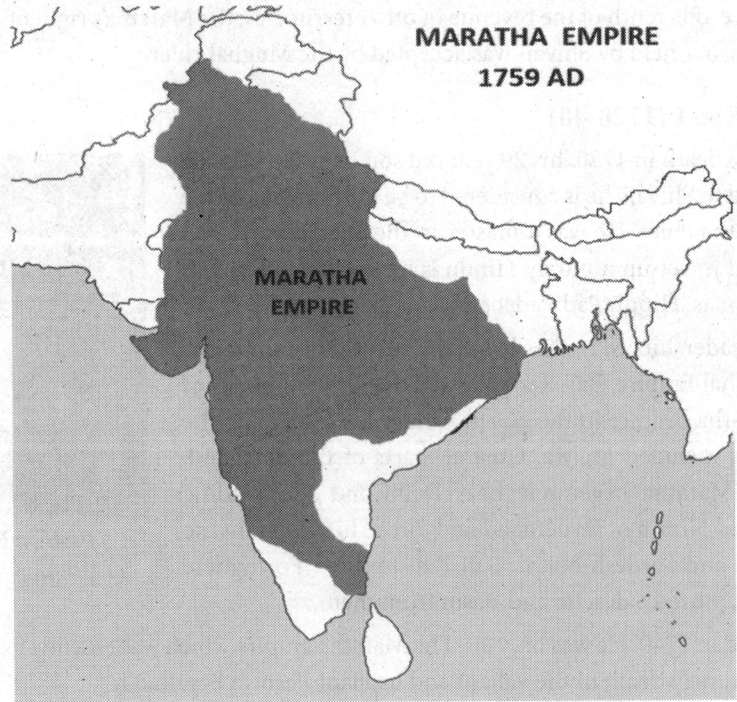

The extent of the Maratha empire, 1760 — Wikimedia Commons

The Third Battle of Panipat (1761)

The third battle of Panipat marks a turning point in the history of India. It dealt a fatal blow to the dominance of Maratha power in India.

Some of the important causes responsible for this battle were:

- Marathas' activities in North West- Maratha penetration into Delhi and Punjab was a challenge to Ahmad Shah Abdali, as he considered the north –west India his own sphere of influence due to his earlier invasions.
- Maratha occupation of Punjab was a challenge to the authority of Ahmad Shah Abdali . He regarded Punjab as a part of his empire.
- Ahmad Shah Abdali was financially deprived, as the earlier Mughal tribute was now diverted into the hands of the Marathas.
- Abdali was encouraged by the Rohillas who had greatly suffered by the Maratha raids

Finally, clashes and conflicts between the two powers became inevitable.

The Third Battle of Panipat was fought on January 14, 1761 CE. The Maratha forces were commanded by Sadashiv rao Bhau in the north with a very large army. Bhau was confident of Maratha victory and hoped to put Peshwa on Mughal's throne. But Maratha plans suffered a setback when their potential allies, the Jats, withdrew from the battle. The tide of the battle soon turned against the Marathas and by the end of the day they were killed, taken prisoner or fled.

Sadashiv Bhau the commander of Maratha forces — Wikimedia Commons

The Marathas suffered a great loss in this battle. The great debacle suffered by Marathas is described by historian J.N Sarkar in these words, 'there was not a home in Maharashtra that had not to mourn the loss of a member and several houses their very heads and entire generation of leaders was cut off at one stroke.'

However, Maratha historian Sardesai presented a different view. According to him, Maratha power did not die completely. They soon recovered and revived under Peshwa Madhav Rao. But the sudden death of Peshwa Madhav Rao in 1772 CE was more fatal than the battle of Panipat. Therefore, 'Battle of Panipat decided nothing.'

- **Mistakes of Sadashiv Bhau :** Some of the mistakes committed by Bhau was responsible for the disaster. First, he alienated the sympathies of the Jats and Rajputs. Consequently, they withdrew their help from the Marathas. Second, he overestimated the artillery of Ibrahim Gardi, which could not be of much help in the battle. Third , he dismounted from elephant to mourn the death of Viswas Rao. This was a mistake on his part, as that time more supervision was required. Fourth, he committed another blunder of plunging into the army of the enemy. This act was suicidal. Fifth, from the beginning, his war strategy was poor. He could not keep intact the supply line.
- **Lack of unity amongst Maratha cadres :** There was no unity among Maratha leaders due to their mutual jealousies and animosities. Damaji Gaekwad, Jankoji Scindhia and Malhar Rao were jealous with each other. When Bhau dismounted the elephant on the death of Viswas Rao, Malhar Rao Holkar left the battlefield.

- **Desertion of Jats and Rajputs :** The Marathas under Schindhia and Holkar, had alienated the sympathies of Jats and Rajputs. Some of the Jats and Rajputs did join with Marathas, but they fought half heartedly.
- **The well trained and vast army of Abdali :** The Afghan forces and their allies were larger in number and better trained than the Marathas. They cut the communication line to Delhi. As a result the Maratha army could not get the essential supplies and virtually faced near famine conditions. Despite the Marathas' possession of good guns, the Afghans' artillery was more effective. Besides, the Maratha forces were not well trained in fighting on the plains, as they were adept in waging guerrilla wars.
- The Rohillas and Oudh joined with Abdali and Abdali won over the sympathies of Nawab of Oudh and the Rohillas. The number of Abdali's soldiers increased when Rohillas and Oudh's armies joined with the Afghan army.
- The Marathas also spent time and resources in protecting Hindu pilgrims and other non-combatants who were caught in the siege.

Effects of the Third Battle of Panipat

- The defeat of the Marathas entirely changed the course of Indian history. The battle proved disastrous to the Marathas. They lost the cream of their army. It is said, ' There was not a single home in Maharashtra that was not mourning the death of a young man'.
- The East India Company made the best use of the defeat of the Marathas. It was now in a very advantageous position to consolidate its hold in the Deccan region. In fact , the English benefitted more as compared to Ahmad Shah, in the defeat of Marathas.
- The Mughal power received a severe blow with the victory of Ahmad Shah.

Panipat as a Site for Historic Battles

In Indian medieval history, Panipat became the site for three major battles - 1526, 1556 and 1761, that changed the course of Indian history.

In the first battle of Panipat in 1526, fought between Babur and Ibrahim Lodi, the rule of the Delhi Sultanate came to an end and Mughal rule was founded. In the second battle of Panipat in 1556 between Akbar and Hemu, the Afghans and Rajputs were subdued and Mughal empire got consolidated. In the third and final battle of Panipat in 1761, fought between Marathas and Ahmad Shah Abdali, the imperial Maratha power was completely crushed and gave a final blow to the crippling Mughal empire. The third battle of Panipat in fact gave a golden opportunity to the British to set up their dominance, as there was no major Indian political power left to challenge them. Thus, each battle of Panipat changed the course of Indian history.

The town of Panipat was an ideal battleground for those who invaded India from the North West and those who defended the country from the South. The reason behind the choice of Panipat as a battleground was its strategic geographical location. It lay on relatively high ground and between vast marshes on the West and the River Yamuna on the East. There was no good direct road to it; so it was not suitable for trade or commerce. A large tract of land on a flat plateau provides ideal conditions for armies at that time to launch cavalry attacks. As the invaders came through the north crossing Punjab, Panipat was almost the last area to be conquered before entering the capital Delhi.

Maratha Administration Under Peshwa Rule

The Maratha system of administration under Peshwas was a combination of Shivaji, Mughals, Deccan Sultanates and the changes introduced by the Peshwas.

The nominal head of the Maratha Empire was the Raja of Satara known as Chatrapati. Actual administrative and military powers were bestowed to the office of Peshwa . During Shivaji's time, the Peshwa was one of the members of the Astha Pradhan- the Council of Shivaji. It was from the time of Peshwa Balaji Vishwanath that the office became hereditary, as his son Baji Rao I succeeded him to the post. Under Peshwa's rule, new changes were introduced in the executive, legislative, judicial and military administration. The administration was a three-tier system with a central government at Poona, provincial government and the district administration.

The Central Government – the Huzur Daftar

The Peshwa secretariat at Poona was called the Huzur Daftar which was the nerve centre of Maratha administration. Huzur Daftar was a huge establishment with several departments and bureaus. All accounts and revenues of the Empire were maintained by the Secretariat. The most important departments were the El Beriz Daftar and Chalte Daftar. The former dealt with the accounts of all sorts and was located at Poona. It maintained classified accounts from all other departments. The El Beriz Daftar created a thorough index of the total receipt, expenditure and balance of the state's income in a year. This index was known as Tarjuma. Later on, during the time of later Peshwas under Nana Fadnavis, many improvements in the working of the Huzur Daftar were introduced.

Provincial Administration

The provincial administration was extremely strong under the Peshwas. The entire Maratha Empire was subdivided into Taraf, Pargana, Sarkar and Subah. The big provinces of Khandesh, Gujarat and Carnatic were under officers known as Sarsubahdars. The Sarsubahdars appointed their own Mamlatdars who acted as the Deputy of the Sarsubahdars. Next in the rank of the Sarsubahdars were the Mamlatdars. Mamlatdars were assisted by the Kamavisdar in their work. The Mamlatdar and the Kamavisdar were the representatives of the Peshwas in the provinces. Their duties were of diverse nature, namely looking after agriculture, industry, civil and criminal justice, control of local militia, the police, and revenue assessment of the districts and villages . The Deshmukh and the Deshpande were the other district officials who also performed several important duties. The smaller administrative divisions were called Mahals or Tarfs. The chief officer in a Mahal was called the Havildars. The villages were the lowest units of administration and were self-contained and autonomous. Patel was the chief village officer and was responsible for the dispatch of the revenue collections as per stipulation, to the centre. Kulkarni was the village record keeper, or clerk, who was next in rank to the Patel. In Shivaji's time, these posts were transferable. But the Peshwas made these posts hereditary.

The Town Administration

The pattern of the Maratha town administration was very much conforming to the Maurya town administration. The Kotwal was the chief administrator of the Maratha city. He performed variety of duties such as adjudicating in disputes, maintenance of peace and order, regulation of prices, settling disputes about houses, roads etc. and sending of monthly accounts to the government.

Judiciary

There was a hierarchy of the judicial officers. At the top of the judicial administration was the Peshwa, below him was the Sar-subahdar. Next in rank was the Mamlatdar, and in the villages, the Patel. In towns the judicial duties were entrusted to the care of a Nyayadhis. In the ultimate resort, and appeal could be referred to the Raja Chhatrapati. In the villages, the civil and the criminal cases were usually controlled by the Panchayats. The Peshwas, in order to maintain the peace and order in the society, strengthened the police administration. The metropolitan Police at Poona was very much efficient, which controlled the civil and social order in the state.

Land Revenue Administration

Since agriculture was the principal industry of India, land revenue formed the main source of income of the Peshwas. The Peshwas controlled the land revenue in their own way, which was different from the system initiated by Shivaji. The Peshwas gave the grant of land on long lease on a fixed state demand. To give inducements to the cultivators and to bring more lands under cultivation, the Peshwas followed a special policy. In this policy, the new lands which were brought under cultivation, were lightly taxed by the Maratha Peshwas. The Peshwas also promoted the cultivation of the rocky regions or the wasteland. In times of famine, drought or plunder of crops or failure of crops, remissions of land revenue were granted. However, the state demand, as well as the mode of payment of land revenue, was not uniform throughout the Empire. Thus the revenue system of Marathas was based on the security of the taxpayer.

Chauth and Sardeshmukhi

These taxes formed on important source of revenue, particularly in captured territories outside Maratha lands. These taxes were levied by Shivaji, but continued even under the Peshwas. Chauth was a payment demanded from enemy territories near Maratha kingdoms, and the Marathas, in return for that payment, undertook not to raid those territories. It was equal to one fourth of the produce of land. Sardeshmukhi was levied at the rate of ten percent on the same territories. It was demanded on the flimsy ground that the Marathas were hereditary Deshmukhs of those territories.

According to historian S. G Sardesai, chauth was a military tribute paid by the conquered or hostile territories. According to historian Jadunath Sarkar, the tax chauth, which was 25% tax on revenue or produce, was realized from the alien territories to save themselves from the unwelcome presence of the Maratha soldiers . Shivaji was not under obligation to guard the territory from foreign invasion or internal disorder. Since Shivaji was the hereditary sardeshmukh (chief headman) of Maharashtra, he demanded an additional levy of 10 percent known as sardeshmukhi.

But historian Ishwari Prasad put a different opinion. According to him, the term 'Desai' is the corrupt form of the Sanskrit word Deshswami, also called Deshmukh. The Sardeshmukh stood above many Desais, and Deshmukhs were under the control of the Sardeshmukh. Sardeshmukh was paid for his services and this payment was called Sardeshmukhi. Shivaji claimed to be the hereditary Sardeshmukh of his country.

In a nutshell, both these are considered as security taxes. Chauth is a kind of tax which the small kingdoms or dynasties have to pay to the Marathas in order to protect their territory being invaded and conquered by the Marathas. Chauth is 25% of total revenue generated in the State and it is paid to the Marathas Sardar. Whereas, Sardeshmukhi is a tax on Chauth, i.e kingdom has to pay additional 10% tax on Chauth collected, just to maintain the hereditary right of king on the tax collection.

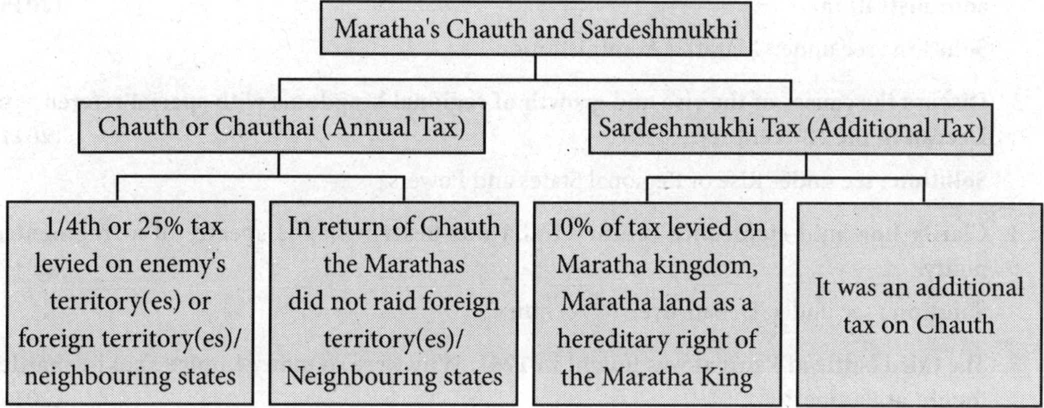

The Maratha Military System

Maratha military was modelled on the Mughal military system. Greatest emphasis was laid on the cavalry, as did the Mughal system. The mode of army recruitment, payment of salaries, making provisions for the families of the soldiers etc., showed a strong resemblance with the Mughal military system. Needless to say, Mughal expansion in the Deccan had its direct influence on the Maratha military system.

The Maratha infantry was recruited mostly from the Rajputs, Rohillas, Sikhs, Arabs and the Sindhis, since the Marathas were less willing to serve in the infantry, their choice being the cavalry. Compared to the Maratha soldiers, the foreigners, that is the Arabs, Rohillas, Sikhs, Sindhis etc. were paid a higher salary.

The Peshwas also gave up the system of payment from the treasury to the soldiers and copied the Mughal system of granting jagirs to them and thereby making the army a feudal army. Maharashtra being a hilly country, the cavalry was naturally the main strength of the Maratha army. Every jagirdar had to bring a stipulated number of horsemen for a general muster every year.

The Peshwas followed an expedient of checks and balances in order to neutralize the military power of the feudal lords by giving them jagirs in the same area so that mutual jealousy might keep them in check.

The Maratha artillery was manned mostly by the Portuguese and the Indian Christians. Later on, English soldiers were also recruited in the Maratha artillery. The Marathas also kept a well organized navy. Maratha navy was built mainly for the purpose of checking piracy, collecting duties from the incoming and outgoing ships and guarding the Maratha ports.

Previous Years' Questions

1. **Short essay on Chauth and Sardeshmukhi of the Maratha rulers.** **(2007)**

   Solution : see under 'Land Revenue administration under Marathas'.

2. **Compare the Peshwas' bureaucratic management with that of the Imperial Mughal administration.** **(2015)**

   Solution : see under 'Maratha Administration'.

3. **Discuss the causes of the rise and growth of regional kingdoms with special reference to Deccan in the 18th century.** **(2011)**

   Solution : see under Rise of Regional States and Powers.

4. **Clarify how mid-eighteenth century India was beset with the spectre of a fragmented polity.** **(2017)**

   Solution : see under 'Debate over 18th century'.

5. **The third battle of Panipat was fought in 1761. Why were so many empire-shaking battles fought at Panipat?** **(2014)**

   Solution : see under 'Panipat as a Site for Historic Battles'.

2 CHAPTER

The Advent of European Trading Companies in India

Introduction

In the 15th century, Europe witnessed an era of geographical discoveries. Many land and sea routes were discovered. In 1492, Columbus of Spain discovered the Americas. In 1498, Vasco da Gama of Portugal discovered a new sea route from Europe to India. The main motives behind these discoveries were to make profit, to establish supremacy, and finally to spread the gospel of Christianity. In fact, it was Gold, Glory, and God, that infused the European explorer with the spirit of adventure. The Europeans came to know about the vast wealth of India from the accounts of Marco Polo and some other sources. For India, it was its immense wealth that attracted Europeans to this country.

Originally, the European interest in India was primarily a commercial one. Though India had a very long history of trade relations with Europe, India's external trade was originally controlled by the Arab traders. Heavy demand for Indian commodities like spices, calicoes, silk, various precious stones, porcelain, etc. caught the attention of the European traders from the early medieval period. However, for a long time they failed to establish a direct trade relation with India as all the major land routes to this country were then controlled or blocked by the Arabs who constantly resisted the European merchants' efforts to enter into the Indian markets. As a result, the western traders concentrated more on discovering a safe sea route to the 'Golden East'. In the 15th century, Europe achieved great advancement in the art of shipbuilding and navigation. Hence, there started an enthusiastic preparation all over Europe for a long and adventurous sea voyage to reach the unknown corners of the East.

The Portuguese and the Discovery of a Sea Route to India

Background

Portugal held the most favorable position for the discovery of sea route to the east. Firstly, the country had a long Atlantic coast and her mariners got accustomed to seafaring activities. Secondly, the coast of Africa was not very far off. Thirdly, the long struggle against the Moors had developed a crusading spirit, and after expelling them, the Portuguese began to attack them on the African coast. The Portuguese, therefore, under the new impulse of discovering a sea route to India, began to move southward along the western coast of Africa. Prince Henry of Portugal (1394–1460) greatly encouraged navigation and exploration. He started a regular school for the scientific training of seamen. He is often called 'Prince Henry the Navigator'. Equator was crossed by 1471 and the Congo River was reached by 1481. In 1488, Bartholomew Diaz was carried by storms round the southern end of Africa which came to known as the Cape of Good Hope. The discovery of this new sea route called as 'Cape of Good Hope' opened the gate for European trading companies to trade further with the eastern countries, mainly India.

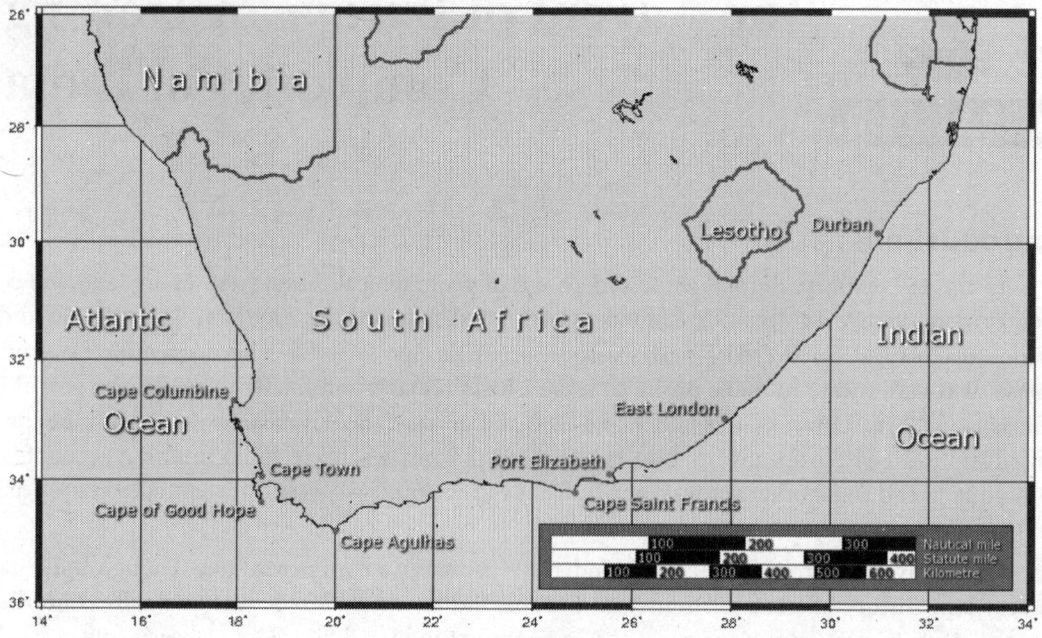

The Cape of Good Hope
— Wikimedia Commons

Vasco da Gama (1460 or 69 – 1524)

Vasco da Gama
— Wikimedia Commons

In 1497, Vasco da Gama, another Portuguese navigator, sailed to complete the work of Diaz. He sailed along the Atlantic coast of Africa, rounded the Cape of Good Hope, and reached Mozambique in the Indian Ocean. There he saw some Indian ships and hired the services of an Indian crew. On 20 May 1498, he reached Calicut where he was received by the King of Calicut, the Samoothiri or Zamorin. Vasco da Gama, thus, became the first Portuguese explorer to reach India via the African coast successfully. He is one of the most famous and celebrated explorers from the 'Age of Discovery'.

Vasco da Gama's discovery was very significant as it paved the way for the Portuguese to establish trading relations with Asia. The route meant that the Portuguese would not need to cross the highly disputed Mediterranean nor the dangerous Arabian Peninsula, and that the whole voyage was now possible by sea.

Vasco da Gama's legendary voyage to India helped the Portuguese to improve its economy that was mainly based on trades along the northern and coastal West Africa. At first, the Portuguese traded with spices (mostly pepper and cinnamon), but soon included other products, all new to Europe, which led to a commercial monopoly of the Portuguese for several decades.

For his contributions, da Gama was named in 1524 CE as the Governor of India, under the title of Viceroy, and given the newly created County of Vidigueira in 1519 CE. The Portuguese national epic poem, *Os Lusíadas*, was written to celebrate Vasco da Gama. His first trip to India is widely considered a pinnacle of world history, as it marked the beginning of the mercantilism age that initiated colonialism.

Portuguese India or Estado da India

In 1501, Vasco da Gama came back to India for the second time. He set up a trading factory at Cannanore. Gradually, Calicut, Cannanore, and Cochin became the important trade centers of the Portuguese. The rapid success of the Portuguese was envied by the Arab traders. They instrumented enmity between the Portuguese and the local king. As a result, hostility started between them. King Zamorin suffered a humiliating defeat at the hands of the foreigners. This proved the military superiority of the Portuguese over the native Indian ruler. Portuguese East India Company began to establish factories and their colonies on Indian territories very soon.

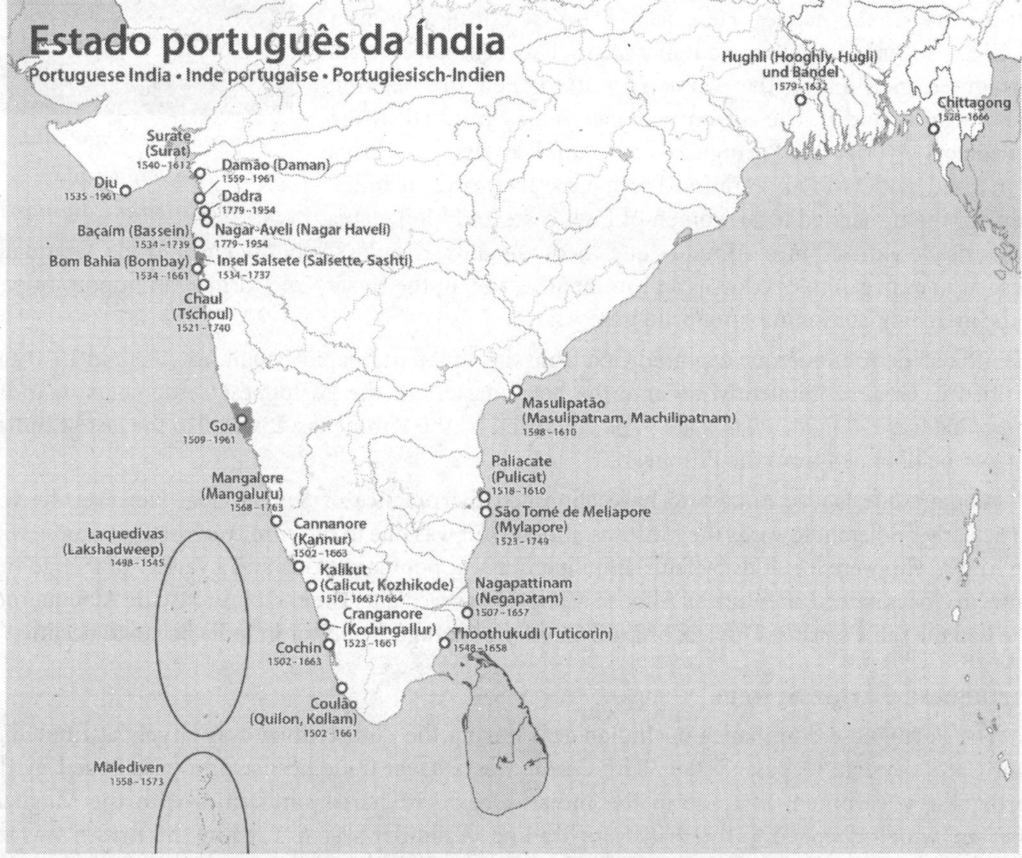

The Portuguese empire in India — Wikimedia Commons

Francisco de Almeida (1450–1510)

In 1505, Francisco de Almeida was sent as the first governor of the Portuguese possessions in India. He believed that Portugal should not extend her territories in India, since she did not have enough men to garrison the fortresses. He also felt that their factories should be confined only to the coastal region because these could be protected by their fleet. He was in favour of developing naval power and he termed his policy as the 'Blue Water Policy'.

Alfonso de Albuquerque (1453–1515)

Portuguese governor Alfonso de Albuquerque — Wikimedia Commons

The real founder of the Portuguese power in India was Alfonso de Albuquerque. In 1509, he replaced Almeida as the Portuguese governor in India. There were four aims of Albuquerque's policy to consolidate Portuguese power in India: to occupy certain Indian territories for trade purpose and to rule them directly; to colonize selected districts by encouraging mixed marriages with the natives; when either of these alternatives was not possible, forts should be built; when even this fails, native merchants should be induced to accept the overlordship of the king of Portugal and to pay him tribute.

Albuquerque was an able administrator. He opened educational institutions for the natives. He started the first Portuguese mint in Goa. He encouraged mixed marriages between lower class Portuguese men and native women to strengthen the position of Portugal in India. The mixed marriage policy resulted in the settlements of a sizeable Portuguese community known as casados or married settlers in and around Portuguese fortresses in India. Many of them married local women of high caste and high status giving rise to a mixed race. Albuquerque encouraged the *casados* to conduct local trade. Gradually, these *casados* began to develop as a prominent section of the society and formed an important part of the merchant community in Portuguese Asia.

Alfonso de Albuquerque captured Goa from the Sultan of Bijapur Ismail Adil Shah in 1510 and fortified it. Goa, subsequently, became the headquarters of the Portuguese settlements in India. Thus, Goa was the first Indian state to be colonized by the Europeans. It was also the last of Indian states to be liberated from the Europeans.

Albuquerque is also known to have abolished the practice of *Sati* in Goa. However, he was particularly intolerant towards the Muslims. Probably, it was due to the enmity of the Portuguese with the Arabs, who were Muslims by faith. Albuquerque was popular in Goa and a variety of mango that grows in Goa is named after him as 'Alfonso Mango'. However, after the end of Alfonso de Albuquerque who had the same spirit as Dupleix or Lord Clive, the Portuguese power in India began to decline.

Portuguese Cartaz System

The Portuguese dominance on Indian seas during the 16th century was largely attributed to their *Cartaz* system or pass system. The *Cartaz* was a naval trade license or a pass issued by the Portuguese government to trade in the Indian Ocean. It shared similarities with the Mughals' *farmaan,* which is issued to the British for trading. A similar system used by the British was the navicert system in the 20th century.

The Portuguese, with a view to protect their vessels and for the identification of enemy ships, introduced *Cartaz,* or a pass, that needs to be duly signed by the Portuguese authorities.

Thus, Portuguese *Cartaz* was a navigational license for safety and identification purposes issued by the Portuguese to native ships. The ships that did not buy *cartazes* were confiscated along with their cargo, and the people on board were enslaved.

Through *Cartaz* system, Portuguese were able to monopolize and control overseas trade in the Indian Ocean. They frequently attacked and confiscated trading vessels of other countries including Indians in the Indian Ocean and other naval trading centres around the Arabian Gulf. As a result of the strict enforcement of the Cartaz system, the Arab traders' and Indian native traders' overseas trade suffered during the sixteenth century.

Decline of Portuguese Power in India

The sole aim of the Portuguese was to maintain their trade monopoly in India. Therefore, they combined trade with power from the very beginning. Their held over the coastal areas and superiority in naval power helped them significantly. By the end of the 16th century, the Portuguese brought Goa, Daman, Diu, and Salsette and a vast area around the Indian coastline under their control.

However, the Portuguese ascendancy on Indian trade did not last long. With the arrival of new trading communities from Europe, there began a fierce rivalry among them. In this struggle, the Portuguese had to give way to the more powerful and enterprising competitors.

Significant factors for the gradual decline of Portuguese power were as follows:

- **Limited Resources :** Portugal was a small country to maintain the burden of a trading colony located in a far off land. She could not spare enough men and money for a distant colony like India. This prevented Portugal from strengthening her position and extending her possessions. Her resources were limited before the mighty Mughal Empire and her new European rivals in the east.
- **Piratical Methods of the Portuguese :** The Portuguese earned notoriety as sea pirates. Their cruelties and unruly nature earned the animosity of the native rulers. According to historian P.E. Roberts, 'the profits of the Portuguese were derived as much from plundering raids upon Arabian merchants as from legitimate commerce.' The piratical methods of the Portuguese discredited them in the eyes of the Indians and the people could not very often trust them.
- **Intolerant Religious Policy :** The rigid religious policy followed by the Portuguese made them the enemy of the Muslims of India. The Hindus were also not very happy with their policy of forcible conversion of the native people to Christianity. Albuquerque followed a biased religious policy towards Muslims and ill-treated them. His successors began to persecute the Muslims and the Hindus alike. Their spirit of crusading led to a fanatic desire to convert all their subjects to Christianity, even at the point of the sword. After 1540, the Portuguese colonies were flocked by numerous Jesuits and priests who displayed an intolerant bigotry and introduced all the horrors of the inquisition. This policy was one of the main reasons that they could not survive for long.
- **Incompetent Successors of Albuquerque :** Portuguese power in India made a rapid expansion under Albuquerque. His successors were weak and incompetent. Majority of them lacked the charisma of Albuquerque.

- **Defective Administrative System :** The administrative system of the Portuguese in India was characterised by corruption of a high degree. The salaries of the officers were low and they freely accepted bribes. They looked more to personal interest than to the interest of the country. The administration under Portuguese hardly took care of the local people. Corrupt administration lowered the prestige of the Portuguese in the eyes of the native Indians and they could no longer command the ungrudging loyalty of their subjects.
- **Temporary Union of Portugal with Spain (1580–1640) :** From 1580 till 1640, the Spanish crown and Portugal crown remained united under the Spanish Habsburg kings. The temporary union of the crowns of Spain and Portugal under Philip II in 1580 proved ruinous for the Portuguese cause in India. Spanish King Philip II subordinated the interests of Portugal to the Spanish interests. Spain was too much entangled in the European affairs and due to this union, Portugal also got involved in European wars. Philip did not care much for Portugal's Indian possessions. The Portugal's limited resources were exhausted in European conflicts. The English began to plunder Portuguese ships after their union. Worthless Spanish officers were sent to the Indian possessions and they tried to make as much money as they could by fair and foul means. This corrupted the Portuguese administrative system in India and made their rule unpopular.
- **Advent of European Rivals :** Finally, the coming of the Dutch and the British in India posed a serious challenge to the Portuguese power in India. The latter could not survive against these rivals and as a result, their monopoly over Indian trade collapsed. Thereafter, they remained as a second grade trading class in India.
- **Discovery of Brazil :** After the discovery of Brazil, the Portuguese began to give prior attention to their western empire in South America. It became a place of greater importance than India to them. It resulted in complete neglect of their Indian possessions. In other words, the discovery of Brazil greatly weakened the position of the Portuguese in India.

It is interesting to note that the Portuguese, who were the first to come to India, were also the last to leave this land. It was only in 1961 that the Government of India recaptured Goa, Daman and Diu from them.

Significance Of The Arrival Of The Portuguese In India

India never had direct contact of maritime trade with European nations bordering the Atlantic Ocean. Vasco da Gama's landing on the Indian soil in May 1498 CE ushered a new chapter of far-reaching consequences. Arrival of Vasco da Gama marked the beginning of colonial trade with India that encouraged and instigated other European powers to follow them.

Portuguese were the first Europeans to settle and colonize in India. By 1503 CE, Portuguese had already established trading centers and colonies at Calicut, Cochin, and Cannanore and effectively suppressed the Arab resistance. In 1509, De Almedia was followed by Albuquerque as the second viceroy. Albuquerque laid the foundation of the Portuguese power in India by conquering Goa in 1510 CE, and it became the headquarters of the Portuguese in India. With the expansion of Portuguese rule, India's trade relations with Portuguese too intensified. The *Cartaz* system or Pass system ensured Portuguese dominance over the Indian Ocean maritime trade. For the first time in the history of international trade, commercial treaties with Indian rulers were concluded by the Portuguese alone.

Portuguese gave importance to naval strength and naval warfare. De Almeida, the first viceroy, initiated the 'Blue Water Policy' or the mastery of sea by a strong naval power. He believed that Portugal should not extend her territories in India, since she did not have enough men to garrison the fortresses. Their factories should be confined only to the coastal region because these could be protected by their fleet. He was in favor of developing naval power and he termed his policy as the 'Blue Water Policy'. Hence, Portuguese's power and colonies were concentrated on the coastal regions in their expansion.

To strengthen their rule, the Portuguese adopted the policy of mixed marriage and religious intolerance. Their *spirit of crusading* led to a fanatic desire to convert all their subjects to Christianity. After 1540, the Portuguese colonies were flocked by numerous Jesuits and priests who displayed an intolerant bigotry and introduced all the horrors of the inquisition. This policy was one of the main reasons that they could not survive for long.

The age of the heroes for the Portuguese India had passed away with the end of the rule of Alfonso De Albuquerque who had the same spirit as Dupleix or Lord Clive. His legacy remained popular among the native Indians. But his policy was not continued and the Portuguese empire on Indian soil was abandoned in favour of the other Europeans. In 1612, they lost Surat to the British. In 1631, Mughals recaptured Hugli from them. In 1661, Portuguese government gave Bombay in dowry to Prince Charles II of England.

The Dutch

After the Portuguese, it was the Dutch who arrived in India. In 1602, the United East India Company of the Netherlands, or *Vereenigde Oost-lndische Compagnie* (VOC), was formed and it received the sanction of the government to trade in the East Indies. After their arrival in India, the Dutch founded their first factory in Masulipatnam in Andhra in 1605. Gradually, they established trading centers at different parts of India and became a threat to the Portuguese. They captured Nagapatinam near Madras (Chennai) from the Portuguese and made this place their main stronghold in South India.

The United East India Company of the Netherlands or Vereenigde Oost-lndische Compagnie (VOC) — Wikimedia Commons

The main commercial interest of the Dutch lay not in India but in the Spice Islands of Indonesia. They had no dream of establishing an empire in India. They were satisfied with the huge profit earned through business. They monopolized the trade in black pepper and spices. The most important Indian commodities the Dutch traded in were silk, cotton, indigo, rice, and opium.

Factors that Favoured the Rise of Dutch Power in the East

There were several factors which favored the rise of the Dutch power in the east:

- The Dutch had been taking Asiatic goods from the Portuguese port of Lisbon and distributing these to several countries of northern and western Europe. In 1580, Portugal had personal enmity with Spain and Philip II closed the port of Lisbon to the Dutch sailors and merchants. The Dutch now wanted to have direct access to those Asiatic goods.
- The attempts of Dutch to find a sea route through the Arctic Sea failed. They turned to the Cape of Good Hope route which was being used by the Portuguese. Their navy was stronger than the Portuguese navy in the eastern waters.
- The Dutch were in revolt against Philip II and the union of Portugal with Spain left them free to attack the Portuguese on the high seas and in their settlements.
- The Dutch had practically won independence from Spain by the end of the 16th century, though it was formally recognized in 1648. They were full of national spirit and vigour.

Growth of Dutch in the East Islands

The Dutch established themselves in the islands of South East Asia. They also founded a few settlements in India. In 1619, they established themselves in Batavia. It gradually developed into a prosperous port which became the headquarters of the Dutch in Indonesia. It gave them a foothold in Java and controlled the western entrance to the Archipelago.

The Dutch and the English had come to the east as friends but soon became rivals. The speedy rise of the British in the Eastern trade posed serious challenge to the commercial interest of the Dutch. Commercial rivalry soon turned into bloody warfare. In 1623, the Dutch brutally killed some English traders in Amboyna. This incident accelerated the rivalry between the two European companies. After prolonged hostility, in 1667, both the parties came to a compromise by which the British agreed to withdraw all their claims on Indonesia, and the Dutch retired from India to concentrate on their more profitable trade in Indonesia. The Dutch turned out the Portuguese from Malacca in 1640 and from Ceylon in 1658. In India, the principal Dutch settlements were Nagapatinam on the eastern coast and Chinsura in Bengal. These were the minor settlements of the Dutch in India.

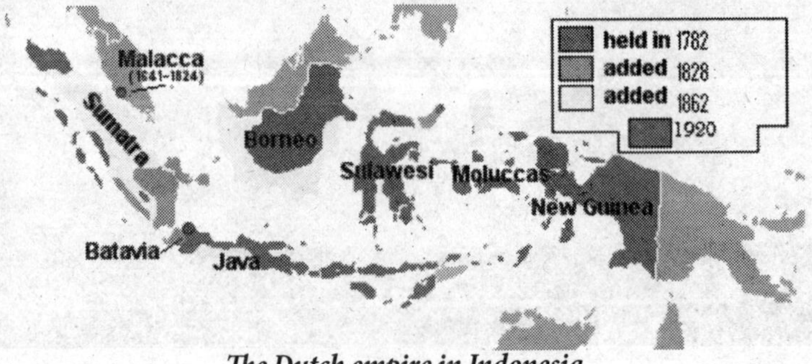

The Dutch empire in Indonesia
— Wikimedia Commons

Decline of Dutch Power in India

The Dutch never became a strong power in India and their possessions were ultimately captured by the English. This was due to several factors:

- The Dutch were primarily interested in the islands of south-west Asia. They never concentrated on the mainland of India.
- The Dutch system of administration in the settlements was defective. The salaries of their employees were low and they carried on a lot of private trade. It resulted in the neglect of the company's possessions.
- The Dutch military forces in the east were weak. These were ill-recruited, ill-paid, and ill-organized.
- The Dutch were too much engrossed in European affairs. Their resources and energy were greatly consumed in European wars.
- The appearance of the English weakened the Dutch position. British navy was superior to the Dutch navy.

The East India Company and its Growth Till 1680

The British merchants had been greatly attracted by the profitable trade of Portuguese with India. Still, they were among the last to join the race to trade with India. The main reason was the naval supremacy of other European countries, mainly Spain. British were not sure of their naval strength and therefore, did not venture into trading activities in the east. However, in the year 1588 CE, British gave a cursing defeat to the 'invincible' Spanish Naval Armada. This victory made England the foremost naval power in the world. Now this naval victory encouraged them to embark upon trade adventures with the east.

Picture depicting the defeat of Spanish Naval Armada — Wikimedia Commons

In 1600 CE, British merchants formed a company as the Company of Merchants of London Trading into the East Indies. The company was called as the 'Honorable East India Company'. It was originally a charter company and was granted a Royal Charter by Queen Elizabeth I in 1600 CE to carry on trade with eastern countries for 15 years. The Queen herself became a shareholder of the East India Company. Sir James Lancaster commanded the first East India Company voyage in 1601 and in March 1604, Sir Henry Middleton commanded the second voyage. The Company was led by one Governor and 24 directors, who made up the Court of Directors. They, in turn, reported to the Court of Proprietors which appointed them.

The Battle of Swally and Trade Expansion

At first, the East India Company tried its luck in the Spice Islands of Indonesia. But due to the strong resistance of the Dutch, it had turned its attention towards India. In India, they first arrived at Surat in Gujarat and decided to establish a factory there. In 1608, the Company sent Captain William Hawkins to the court of the Mughal emperor Jahangir to secure royal patronage. After much persuasion, Jahangir permitted the Company to establish its factories at various places on the Western coast. In 1613, first British factory was set up at Surat. Portuguese, who already had a relatively stronghold on the Gujarat coast, resisted the setting up of a British factory in Surat. Their conflict resulted in a naval battle known as the Battle of Swally that took place on 29–30 November 1612 off the coast of Suvali or *Swally*, a village near the city of Surat, Gujarat, India. This naval battle gave a major victory to English East India Company over the Portuguese. This relatively small battle is historically important as it marked the beginning of the end of Portugal's commercial monopoly over India, and the beginning of the ascent of the English East India Company's presence in India. The battle also convinced the English East India Company to establish a small navy to safeguard their commercial interests from other European powers and also from pirates. This small beginning is regarded as the root of the modern Indian Navy.

Battle of Swally — Wikimedia Commons

The Battle of Swalley reduced Portuguese influence at the court of Emperor Jahangir and the English got permission to set up a factory at Surat. In 1615, Emperor James I of England sent Sir Thomas Roe to Jahangir's court seeking more concession for the East India Company. Roe was successful in securing a royal *Farmaan* that allowed the Company to trade freely all over the Mughal Empire. The British were permitted to set up factories in various parts of India. In a short time, English factories were set up at Ahmedabad, Broach, and Agra. Sir Thomas Roe also laid down the policy for the company which was followed by the company for the next 70 years. It was unaggressive and wholly mercantile. Sir Roe disliked the military commercial policies of the Portuguese which consumed the greater part of their profit.

Sir Thomas Roe
— Wikimedia Commons

After setting up the first factory in Surat, the company began to expand its trading networks by setting up more factories in the coastal regions of the country. In 1611, Captain Hippon founded a factory at Masulipatnam, a seaport of the Raja of Golconda. In 1639, Francis Day purchased some land from the Raja of Chandragiri and built a fortified factory which was named Fort St. George. The town of Madras developed near it in a few years and became the most prosperous city on the east coast in due course of time.

Bombay Island, which was a group of seven islands on the west coast of India, was a Portuguese outpost. Bombay Island came as a gift to the British owing to the marriages of Charles II, the king of England to the Portuguese princess Catherine of Braganza. Later, Bombay Island was leased to the Company in 1668. The marriage treaty of Charles II of England and Catherine of Portugal on 8th May 1661 placed Bombay in the British possession as a part of Catherine's dowry to Charles. On 21 September, 1668, the Royal Charter of 27 March 1668, led to the transfer of Bombay from Charles II to the English East India Company for an annual rent of £10.

The English made their first settlements in Orissa and Bengal around 1650–1660s. In 1663, factories were established at Hariharpur in the Mahanadi delta and Balasore. In 1650 CE, Gabriel Boughton, a surgeon of the company, obtained from the governor of Bengal, a license for this company to trade in Bengal. An English factory was established at Hugli in 1651.

Growth of the English Settlements and Change in the Company's Policy After 1680

The English settlements grew after 1690. Job Charnock, the English agent at Hugli for a long time was trying to set up a factory at the site of modern Kolkata. However, the hostility that developed between English and Mughals under Aurangzeb prevented Job Charnock from establishing a factory. After conclusion of peace, he secured Aurangzeb's permission and established a factory at modern Kolkata in 1690. This factory was fortified in 1696 and given the name of Fort William. A few years later, the company purchased the villages of Sutanuti, Kalikata, and Gobindapur. A prosperous city grew up in that area and came to be called Calcutta.

Following is the list of English settlements and factories:

- Masulipatnam in 1611
- Surat in 1613 – Became a chief factory that governed other factories in Agra, Ahmedabad, and Broach
- Bombay – In 1668, Bombay was transferred to the East India Company by Charles II at an annual rent of £10.
- Bombay replaced Surat as the chief settlement of the English on the west coast in 1687.
- In Orissa – Hariharpur and Balasore in Orissa in 1636.
- Fort St. George and Madras – In 1639, Francis Day purchased lease of Madras from the Raja of Chandragiri and built a fortified factory which was named Fort St. George. The town of Madras developed.
- In Bengal region – Hugli factory in 1651, followed by Patna and Kasim Bazar.

Meanwhile, the company changed its policy of peaceful mercantile laid down by Sir Thomas Roe to an aggressive policy around 1680s. The weakening of the Mughal empire in late 17th century encouraged the Company's authorities to take up an aggressive stand against the Mughals. This resulted in hostility between the English and the Mughal emperor Aurangzeb. This hostility against the empire ended in disaster for the English.

In September 1695, English pirate Henry Avery captured Mughal ship *Ganj-i-Sawai* near Surat which was returning from Mecca. When news of the piracy reached Aurangzeb, he nearly ordered an armed attack against the English-governed city of Bombay, though he finally agreed to compromise after the East India Company promised to pay heavy financial reparations and promised to behave better in future.

East India Company's Headquarters

By the early 18th century, the British East India Company had three main headquarters–Fort St. George in Madras, Fort William in Calcutta, and Bombay Castle in western India. These were independent presidencies governed by a president and a council, appointed by the Court of Directors in England. For further expansion, the company adopted a policy of allying with various princes and *nawabs*, and promising security against enemies and rebels. The Indian rulers often gave them concessions in the form of territories in return for the security. By this method, the company's intervention in Indian politics increased and power struggles between the company and other European trading companies, mainly the French began. Conquest of Bengal marked the beginning of a power struggle between Britain and France.

Fort William is a fort built in Kolkata on the eastern banks of the River Hooghly in 1781. It was named after King William III of England and Ireland. Sir Charles Eyre started its construction near the bank of the River Hooghly with the South-East Bastion and the adjacent walls. John Beard, his successor, added the North-East Bastion in 1701 and in 1702, started the construction of the Government House (Factory) at the centre of the fort. Construction ended in 1706. The original building had two storeys and projecting wings. An internal guardroom became the Black Hole of

Calcutta. In 1756, the Nawab of Bengal, Siraj ud Daulah, attacked the Fort, temporarily conquered the city, and changed its name to Alinagar. This led the British to build a new fort. The rebuilding of the fort was started by Robert Clive in 1758, after the Battle of Plassey (1757), and completed in 1781 at a cost of approximately two million pounds. Fort William is one of Kolkata's most enduring Raj era edifices.

Fort William, Kolkata — Wikimedia Commons

Fort St George, or White Town, is the name of the first English fortress in India, founded in 1644 at the coastal city of Chennai. To secure its trade and commercial interests in the spice trade, the East India Company felt the necessity of a port closer to the Malaccan Straits. The company succeeded in purchasing a piece of coastal land, originally called Chennirayarpattinam or Channapatnam, from a Vijayanagar chieftain named Damerla Chennappa Nayaka based in Chandragiri. Here, the Company began the construction of a harbour and a fort. The fort was completed on 23 April 1644, coinciding with St George's Day. The fort was hence christened as 'Fort St George'. It soon became the hub of merchant activity. It gave birth to a new settlement area called George Town which led to the formation of the city of Madras. It also helped to establish English influence over the Carnatic and to keep the kings of Arcot and Srirangapatnam, as well as the French forces based at Pondicherry, at bay. The Fort now serves as one of the administrative headquarters for the legislative assembly of Tamil Nadu state. The Fort Museum contains many relics of the British era, including portraits of many of the Governors of Madras.

The French in India

The French East India Company was the last to the join the race of colonial exploit. In 1664, during the reign of King Louis XIV, the French East India Company was formed and it received the permission to trade with India. In 1667, the French East India Company sent an expedition under the command of Francois Caron which reached India in 1668. In the same year, the French established their first factory at Surat in Gujarat. In the next year, Marcara, a Persian, who accompanied Caron, established another French factory at Masaulipatnam. In 1673, the French obtained permission from Shaista Khan, the Mughal Subedar (governor) of Bengal to establish a township at Chandernagore (present Chandannagar), near Calcutta.

Francois Caron was replaced by Francois Martin as the French Governor in 1674. He obtained a village called Pondicherry from the Sultan of Bijapur, and founded a prosperous city on that site. Pondicherry, thus, became the main stronghold of the French in India. The French company established its factories in different parts of India, particularly in the coastal regions. Mahe, Karaikal, Balasor, Kasim Bazar, etc. were a few important trading centers of the French East India Company.

Following is a list of French settlements in India:

- **Surat :** The first French factory in India was established by Francois Caron at Surat in 1668
- **Masulipatnam :** Marcara, a Persian who accompanied Caron succeeded in establishing another French factory at Masulipatam in 1669 by obtaining permission from the Sultan of Golconda.
- **Chandernagore :** In 1673, the French established a township at Chandernagore near Calcutta.
- **Pondicherry :** in 1674, the French governor, obtained a village called Pondicherry from the Sultan of Bijapur and founded a prosperous city on that site. Pondicherry became the headquarters of the French in India.
- **Mahe, Karaikal, Balasor, Kasim Bazar**

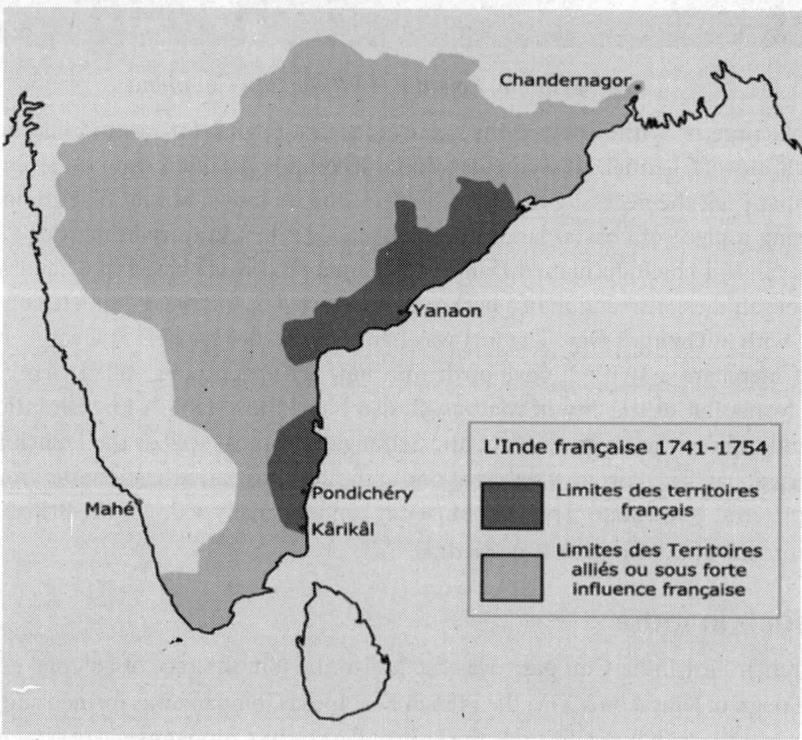

The map showing French settlements in India — Wikimedia Commons

Soon, the French company appeared as a serious rival to the English in 1740.

However, the French company suffered from the following defects:

- The English settlements were on the whole, superior to the French settlements. On the western coast, the English possession of Bombay was far superior to the French settlement of Mahe. On the Coromandel coast, the English possessed Madras, which was in no way inferior to Pondicherry. In Bengal, the French settlement of Chandernagore stood no comparison with the English possession of Calcutta.
- The financial position of the English company was better than that of the French company. Its trade was profitable. French trade was not on the same scale.
- The French company was a government-run Company but the government did not take keen interest. Whereas, East India Company was a private company and faced less interference by the government. Its employees possessed a lot of incentive and initiative. Their prosperity was linked with the prosperity of the company.
- The English government took a keen interest in the welfare of the company, though it was a private company. Some of the directors of the East India Company were members of Parliament and thereby, made the government take interest in it. The French government was too much embroiled in European affairs and it did not take much interest in the affairs of its company.

Joseph-François Marquis Dupleix (1697–1763)

In the initial years, the French objectives in India were mainly commercial. But with the progress of time, there came a change in their policies. The vision of the French power in India was further reinforced by the appointment of Joseph-Francois Dupleix as the Governor of the French East India Company in 1742.

The French Governor Marquis Dupleix — Wikimedia Commons

Dupleix was the governor general of the French establishment in India, and the rival of Robert Clive, the governor of East India Company. Dupleix made several voyages to the Americas and India, and in 1721, was named a member of the superior council at Pondichéry. He displayed great business aptitude, and made large ventures on his own account, and acquired a fortune. In 1731, he was made superintendent of French affairs in Chandernagore, near Kolkata. The town prospered under his administration and grew into great importance.

In 1742, he was appointed as the governor general of all French establishments in India. He succeeded Dumas as the French governor of Pondicherry. His ambition now was to acquire for France vast territories in India, and for this purpose, he entered into relations with the native princes, and adopted a style of oriental splendor in his dress and surroundings. He built an army of native troops, called sepoys, who were trained as infantry men in his service. He also included Hyder Ali of Mysore in his service.

In fact, Dupleix was the first European statesman to dream of establishing an empire in India. During his time, political motives began to overshadow business interests. Dupleix successfully used the mutual mistrust and weakness of the local rulers for securing more and more political benefits. By exercising his talent in diplomacy and intrigue, he earned for the French Company a respectable position in the Indian political scenario. But the French were not unrivalled in their ambition of political supremacy in India. In this regard, their dream was always challenged by their European neighbor, the British. Subsequently, both the European powers were locked in long wars for gaining political supremacy in India.

Anglo-French Conflict–The Carnatic Wars (1746–1763)

The mid 18th century saw the transformation of the English East India Company from a trading enterprise to a political power. The Portuguese and Dutch were eased out by a strategy combating war and diplomacy at the Mughal court. By the 18th century, the main foreign power remaining in the fray was the French East India Company.

Traditionally, France and Britain were rival countries. Their rivalry continued in India over trade and territories. The rivalry between the French and the British resulting in a series of military conflicts in the south is known as Carnatic Wars, which spanned from 1746 to 1763. These wars were primarily the Anglo-French struggle for domination over Indian trade and territories, but were significant for laying down the ground for British Empire building in India. It is interesting to note that one of the chief sources for the study of Carnatic wars were the private diaries of Ananda Ranga Pillai (1709-1761) . He was the secretary and chief Dubash or interpreter /mediator of the then French Governor- General Dupleix. These private diaries of Ananda Ranga Pillai cover the years from 1736 to 1761.

Deccan on the Eve of Anglo-French Hostility

The Indian Theatre of great Anglo-French hostility of the eighteenth century was seen in the south Indian kingdom of Carnatic with the capital at Arcot.

The hostility between the French company and the British company in India resulted into a series of military conflicts known as Carnatic Wars that spanned over the period of 1746–1763 CE. These wars were primarily fought for gaining supremacy over the Indian territories and directly connected to the Great Anglo-French Wars of Europe.

The conflict between the English and the French took place on account of the unstable political conditions in south India where the four powers–the Marathas, the Nizam of Hyderabad, the Nawab of Carnatic, and the Sultan of Mysore were competing for supremacy. Both the French and the British used the weak political conditions of these states to increase their powers and territories.

Dupleix Instigated Carnatic War

Joseph-François Dupleix arrived in India in 1715. In 1730, he was made superintendent in Chandernagore and the town prospered under his administration. In 1742, Dupleix became the Governor of the French company. To expand French influence in India and set up a colonial empire in India, French governor Dupleix found an opportunity in the Carnatic.

Dupleix built an infantry of Indian troops known as Sepoys. These sepoys were used by French in their conflict with native rulers. The First Carnatic War was fought with the help of sepoys.

Where Was Carnatic? What Was The Problem There?

Carnatic was one of the provinces of the Mughal Deccan and under the suzerainty of the Nizam-ul-Mulk Asaf Jah of Hyderabad. Its capital was Arcot. The Nawab of the Carnatic, Saadatullah Khan, who ruled from 1710–1732, freed himself from the Nizam's control and founded the Nawayath dynasty. Later, Saadullah Khan made his nephew Dost Ali Khan his successor, who ruled from 1732–1740.

In 1741 CE, the Marathas invaded the Carnatic. They killed its ruler, Dost Ali, and captured his son-in-law, Chanda Sahib. In the absence of any ruler of Carnatic, the Nizam of Deccan sent Anwaruddin, a near relative of his as the Nawab of Carnatic.

However, in 1748 CE, Chanda Sahib was released by the Marathas and he made a claim for the throne of the Carnatic.

In 1748, the Nizam of Hyderabad died. A power struggle started between his son, Nasir Jung, and his grandson, Muzaffar Jung.

The French and British who were looking for an opportunity to gain a foothold in the Carnatic, started making alliances with the claimants for the throne of Carnatic and Hyderabad. Both these powers supported their own allies and sided against each other.

The following tripartite alliances were formed in both the states with the help of the French and English:

Tripartite Alliances

- **Hyderabad :** France allied with Muzaffar Jung while English supported Nasir Jung.
- **Carnatic :** French supported Chanda Sahib, and British allied with Anwaruddin and later his son Mohammad Ali

In 1740, the Austrian War of Succession broke out in Europe. The English and French participated in the succession war as rival parties. The echo of this war was felt in India that resulted in the first Carnatic Wars. In the war, both the powers tried to capture each other's headquarters–Madras and Pondicherry which were in the state of Carnatic.

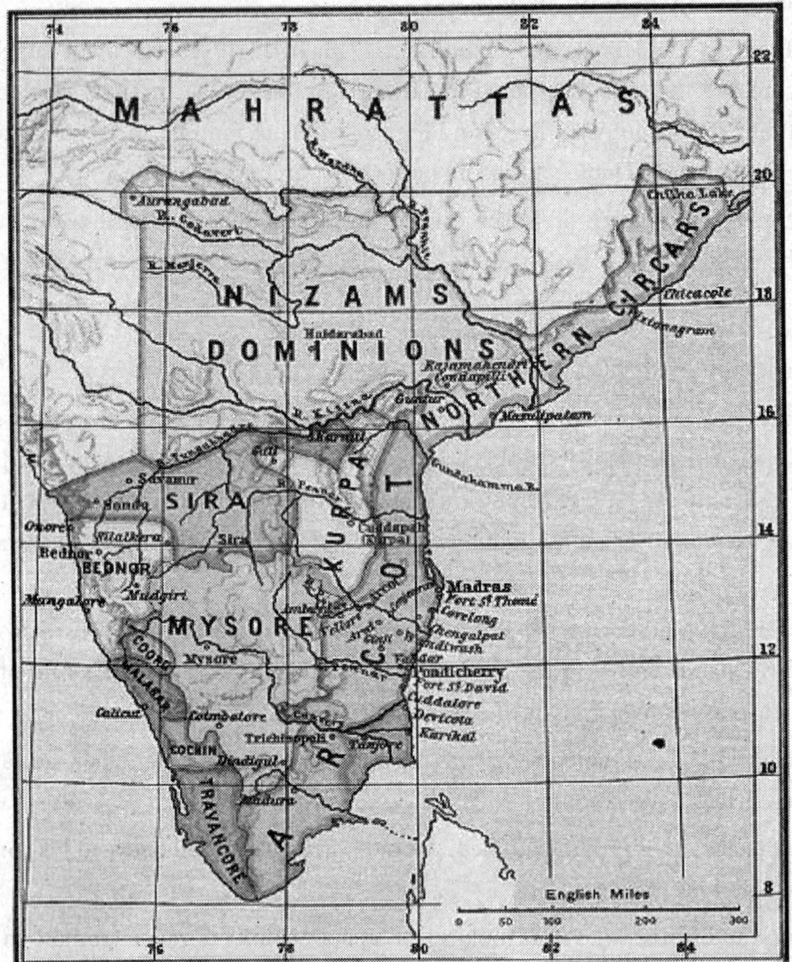

Map showing Carnatic or Arcot including Nizam's territories (Northern Circars)
— Wikimedia Commons

The First Carnatic War (1746–1748)

This war was an echo of the War of Austrian Succession in Europe.

Following were the main events of the war:

- With the starting of the war in Europe, the British Fleet arrived on Coromandel Coast and they started capturing the French ships.
- The French Governor Dupleix requested the Nawab of Arcot, Anwaruddin Khan for help but the Nawab did not respond.
- Dupleix appealed to La Bourdonnais, the governor of Mauritius, to assist him with his naval fleet.
- With the help of La Bourdonnais's fleet, Dupleix captured Madras, the English headquarters, and imprisoned many British Company servants including Robert Clive.

Battle of Adyar (Madras)—1746

Nawab Anwaruddin of Arcot — Wikimedia Commons

With the capture of Madras, the English appealed to Nawab Anwaruddin for help. Dupleix promised the Nawab that he would hand over Madras to the Nawab at an appropriate time. But the Nawab was not satisfied. Nawab sent a large army to fight against the French. But a handful of the French army routed Anwaruddin's vast army at Adyar near Madras in 1746 CE.

The war of succession came to an end in Europe by the treaty of Aix-la-Chappelle in 1748. Peace was restored between the French and English across India and America. British got back Madras from the French, while the French got back the Fortress of Louisburg in North America.

The First Carnatic War was significant for the French military superiority over Indian powers. French were able to defeat Nawab's strong army with only 500 French soldiers. Dupleix now planned to establish French supremacy in the Deccan. The First Carnatic War totally changed the commercial character of the French company.

First Carnatic war (1746-1748)

Causes

- The Austrian War of Succession in 1740
- Commercial rivalry between the French Company and East India Company
- To capture each other's headquarters – Madras and Pondicherry – which was in the state of Carnatic

Events

- British fleet started capturing the French ships
- The Nawab of Arcot, Anwaruddin Khan did not give help to French.
- La Bourdonnais, governor of Mauritius, assisted Dupleix with his naval fleet.
- With the help of La Bourdonnais's fleet, Dupleix captured Madras

Battle of Adyar 1746

Nawab's large army was defeated by a handful of French army at a battle in Adyar near Madras in 1746

The Treaty of Aix-la-Chapelle in 1748 ended the First Carnatic War

The Second Carnatic War (1749–1754)

The main cause of this war was the disputed issue of succession in the Carnatic and Hyderabad.

In 1748, the Nizam of Hyderabad (*Asaf Jah I*) died and a war for succession broke out between his son, Nasir Jung, and his grandson, Muzaffar Jung.

In the same year, the son-in-law of the erstwhile Nawab of Carnatic, Chanda Sahib was released by the Marathas and he claimed for the Carnatic throne.

Dupleix pledged French support for Muzaffar Jung for Hyderabad and Chanda Sahib for Arcot. British pledged support to Nasir Jung for Hyderabad and Muhammad Ali, the illegitimate son of Anwaruddin for Arcot.

Following tripartite alliance was formed:

- French supported Muzaffar Jung and Chanda Sahib
- English supported Nasir Jung and Anwaruddin

Events Leading to the War

The French killed the Nawab of Carnatic (Anwaruddin of Arcot) and his son Mohammad Ali fled and took refuge in the Fort of Trichinopoly. The French also killed Nasir Jung of Hyderabad. Soon, the British killed the French nominee for Hyderabad (Muzaffar Jung). French General de Bussy, quickly put his nominee *Salabat Jung* on the throne and maintained the French Influence on Hyderabad.

With both the British nominees being killed, the French influence in Hyderabad increased, and it appeared that Dupleix's dream of French supremacy in the Deccan was about to come true.

Seige of Arcot, 1751

Robert Clive, who was a clerk in the East India Company suggested an attack on Arcot, the capital of Carnatic. Clive, along with 200 European and 300 Indian soldieries captured Arcot in 1751. Chanda Sahib was captured and executed.

Mohammad Ali, an ally of the English, was made Nawab of Arcot/Carnatic.

The French prestige fell down heavily. Dupleix's hopes were dashed to the ground and he was called back in 1754. Dupleix was replaced by Charles Godeheu in 1754.

This Siege of Arcot was a heroic feat, far more important than the Battle of Plassey. It made Clive a national hero in England. The Prime Minister Pitt, the Elder, described him as the "heaven-born general".

Lord Clive
— Wikimedia Commons

Treaty of Pondicherry

French governor Godeheu signed a peace treaty with the English called the Treaty of Pondicherry in 1754. According to this treaty, both parties agreed not to interfere in the internal affairs of Indian states. Secondly, they returned the conquests made from each other.

The treaty gave British a stronghold in the Carnatic. The French were able to keep a stronghold in Hyderabad under de Bussy.

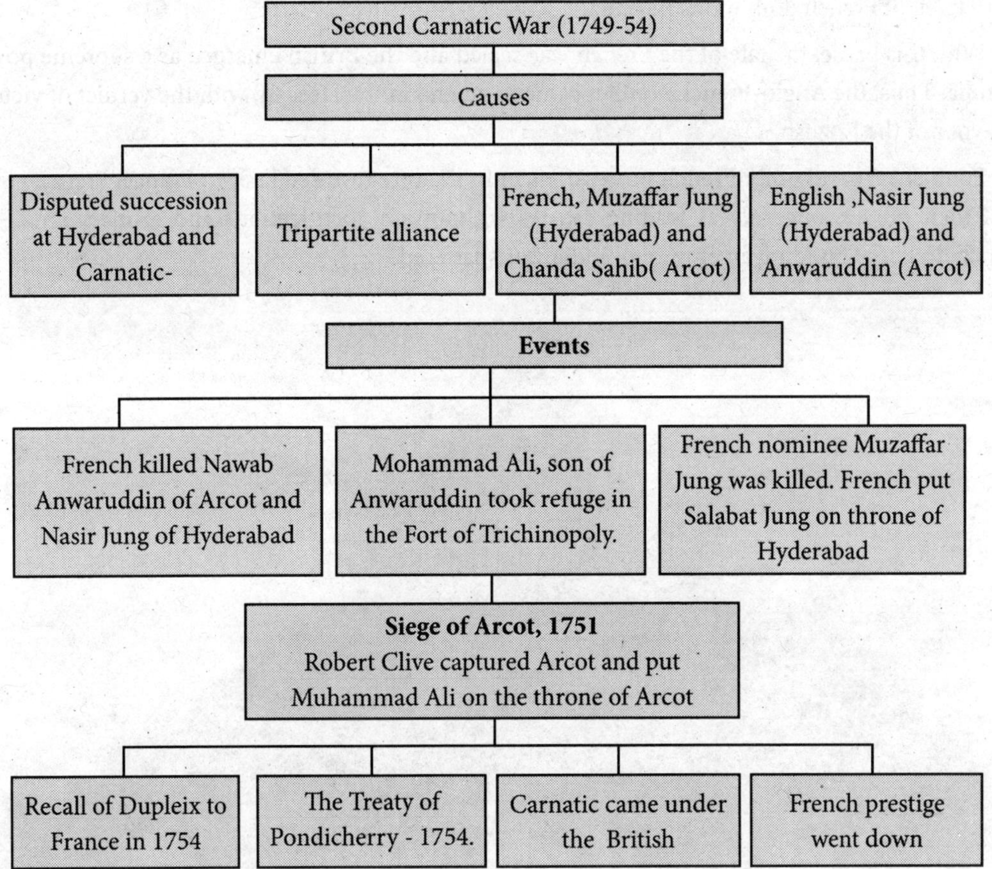

The Third Carnatic War (1757–1763)

This war coincided with the outbreak of the Seven Years' War in Europe in 1756. The French and the English joined the opposite camps. This time, the war passed beyond the limits of the Carnatic and reached Bengal as well, where the English captured the French possession of Chandernagore in 1757.

Due to financial problems and unfavourable government policies, the French remained handicapped in asserting their position vis-à-vis the English. The French fortunes in India went into a decline and they were finally defeated in the Battle of Wandiwash, or Vandavasi, in 1760.

The Battle of Wandiwash (1760)

The Battle of Wandiwash or Vandavasi, was a decisive, battle of the Third Carnatic War. The French army led by Count de Lally, lacked in naval support and funds. He attempted to regain the fort at Vandavasi (now in Tamil Nadu), but was attacked by English commander Sir Eyre Coote and decisively defeated. Lally retreated to Pondicherry which was besieged by the English. Lally defended it gallantly for some time but surrendered in 1761. The fall of Pondicherry sounded the death knell of French dominions in India.

With this battle, the fate of the French was sealed and the British emerged as a supreme power in India. Thus, the Anglo-French conflict came to an end in the Deccan, with the verdict of victory in favour of the English.

Pondicherry and other French possessions in India were restored later to France. French could hold their possessions only as trading centres without any fortifications and armies. Thus, the French dream of building an empire in India was shattered.

The Vandavasi Fort — Wikimedia Commons

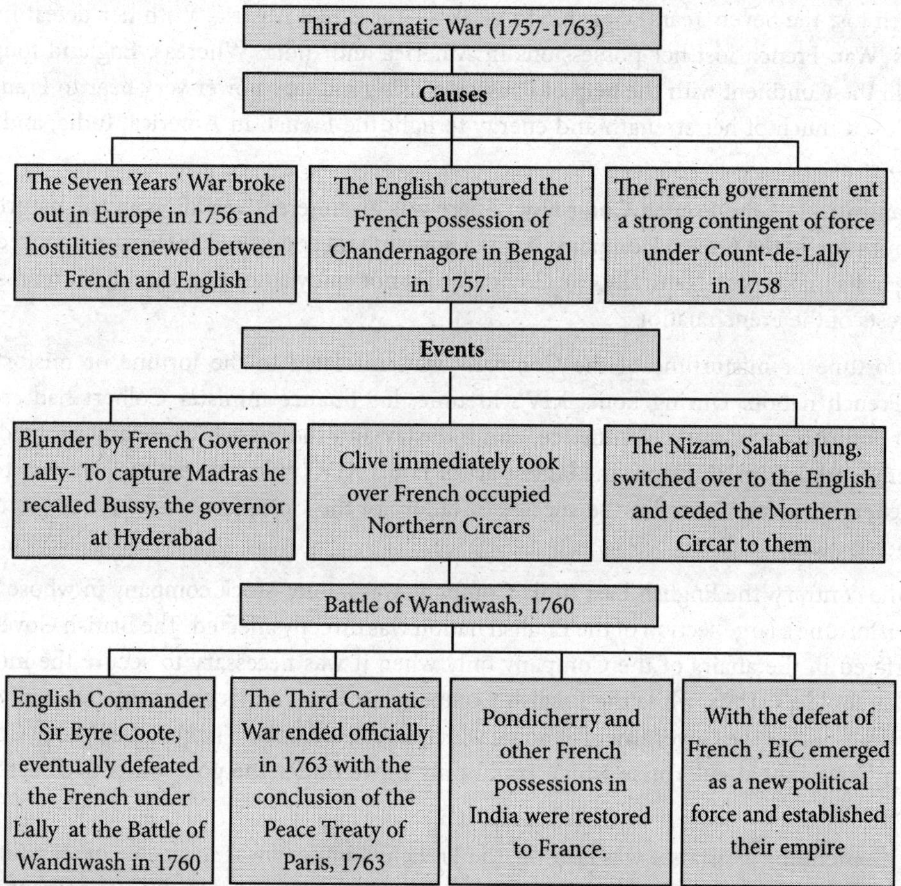

Causes for the French Failure in India

The Battle of Wandiwash sealed the fate of the French in India.

Let us examine in detail the reasons for the failure of French in India:

- **French Government :** The French Government in the 17th century and for the major part of the eighteenth (till the French Revolution in 1789) was an absolute monarchy. The policy of the Government was determined by the whims of the monarch. The French Government did not realize the importance of the colonial empires in India and America, and got her involved in the Continental War near her home which precluded her from sending adequate help to her colonies abroad.

  Historian Alfred Lyall rightly points out : "India was not lost by the French because Dupleix was recalled, or because La Bourdonnais and D' Ache both left the coast at critical moments, or because Lally was head-strong and intractable. Still less was the loss due to any national inaptitude for distant and perilous enterprises in which the French have displayed high qualities. It was through the short-sighted, ill-managed European policy of Louis XV, misguided by his mistresses and by incompetent ministers, that France lost her Indian Settlements in the Seven Years' War".

French lost the Seven Years' War due to weak alliances like Austria. With her defeat in Seven Years' War, French lost her possessions in America and India. Whereas, England fought the war in the Continent with the help of Prussia, a rising military power very near to France, and employed much of her strength and energy to fight the French in America, India, and on the Seas.

- **Organisation of the French Company :** There was an inherent weakness in the nature of the organization of the French Company. It was a government sponsored enterprise financed by the King in its major part. Naturally, the Company did not enjoy autonomy, nor did it represent the interests of the French nation.

  The fortune or misfortune of the Company was unrelated to the fortune or misfortune of the French nation. During Louis XIV's lifetime, his finance minister Colbert had created a great enthusiasm in trade, commerce, and industry and the French Company profited by the general enthusiasm. But from the latter part of Louis XIV's rule, this enthusiasm was replaced by general neglect. Naturally, the success or failure of the Company was of no concern to the French nation.

  On the contrary, the English East India Company was a joint-stock company in whose fortune or misfortune a large section of the English nation was directly affected. The British Government interfered in the affairs of the Company only when it was necessary to secure the interest of its shareholders. Thus, while the English Company moved with its own initiative and with the moral support of the Government at home which interfered only to help it, the French Company was a Government enterprise which could only move under the government's directives and assistance.

  The moment the assistance was lacking, the French Company was incapable of standing on its own. While the English East India Company was an asset to the British Government (for the Government even received loans from it), the French East India Company was a liability to the home government.

- **Conquest of Bengal :** the English conquered the Bengal in 1757. It was a rich and prosperous province. Its conquest greatly increased their resources in men and money which were used against the French in the Third Carnatic War. Clive sent Colonel Forde from Bengal and he captured the Northern Circars. The Bengal troops took an important part in defeating the French at Wandiwash in 1760 and in capturing Pondicherry in 1761. Thus, the capture of Bengal enabled the English to win victory in the Deccan.

- **Superior Settlements of the English :** The French settlements were by no means equal to their prospective rivals, the English. The English had three well-established settlements in India, namely, Bombay, Madras, and Calcutta, and had in their possession one dockyard and an excellent harbour.

  The French had only one seat of power, Pondicherry, and a harbour and sea base at Mauritius, but it was distant and ill-equipped. Both for commercial purposes and for purposes of war, the French seat of power was less advantageous compared to that of the English.

After enhancing its authority in Bengal, particularly after the Battle of Plassey, the English got vast resources in men and money at their disposal. This enabled the Bengal Council to send financial assistance as well as supplies to the Carnatic strengthening the English position there.

But French general Lally was not even in a position to pay his troops. Strategically and financially, English position in Bengal meant inordinate accession to strength to the English Company while the French position in the Carnatic was far too inferior. Historian Smith rightly remarks that "..... Neither Alexander the Great nor Napoleon could have won the empire of India by starting from Pondicherry as a base and contending with the power which held Bengal and command of the Sea". Instead of putting all its resources and men in the Carnatic conflict, English under Clive, equally focused at Bengal and got it before their Carnatic victory. Thus, historian I. A. R. Marriot rightly remarks *"Dupleix made a cardinal blunder in looking for the Key of India in Madras; Clive sought and found it in Bengal"*.

- **Recall of Dupleix :** The French government recalled Dupleix in 1754. It was a blunder. He had not been responsible for the French setbacks in the Second Carnatic War. He was a competent person and had done much to further French interests. He might have still done something to retrieve the position of the French. His unjust recall created a vacuum which could not be filled. There was no competent person to take his place. Moreover, his policy was given up by his successors. His recall greatly contributed to the French failure in India.
- **Mistakes of Lally :** Count de Lally was sent as governor general and commander in chief during the Third Carnatic War. He was a daring man and an incorruptible person, but at the same time, he was a hot-headed fellow. After capturing Fort St. David, he decided to attack Madras and for his help called Bussy from Hyderabad. It was a political and military blunder. The moment Bussy left Hyderabad, the English captured Northern Circars and the Nizam joined the English. Thus, the French influence at Hyderabad came to an end and Lally did not have the satisfaction of capturing Madras. Even Pondicherry was lost in 1761. Thus, Lally's mistakes also contributed to the French failure.
- **Naval Strength :** The Carnatic Wars proved beyond doubt that success or failure depended on the naval strength. The French success in the First Carnatic War in 1746 was due to her naval superiority. But this superiority could not be maintained by the French beyond 1748 because during the War of Austrian Succession, the French naval strength was greatly reduced.

  The naval superiority of the English in the Seven Years' War enabled the English to keep their communication with India undisturbed, to keep their settlements at Bombay and Calcutta supplied with necessary reinforcements, and to isolate the French forces in the Carnatic. The lack of naval strength of the French compared to that of the English was one of the decisive factors for the failure of the French in India.
- **Enterprising Spirit of the English :** The Industrial Revolution which was taking place in England in the eighteenth century created a great enthusiasm among the English merchants to collect raw materials for the latter. This created a great enthusiasm among the English to exploit the Indian markets for purchase of raw materials and marketing of finished goods. But the

French did not demonstrate that kind of enthusiasm in trade and naturally, they did not find trading profitable. This realization, in turn, made them more indolent and less enterprising in matters of trade.

- **Competent English Generals :** Carnatic Wars were determined by highly competent English generals like Clive who was a general and statesman, and Sir Eyre Coote, a highly disciplined general. In the French East India Company, execution was carried by only Dupleix who was a statesman but not a great general. His successor, Count de Lally lacked the foresight and statesmanship of Dupleix.
- **Lack of Financial Support :** The English Company by its trade could not only pay its way in India, and loan out funds to the British Treasury, but could also meet the military expenses of war. The French did not, or rather could not, make the trade pay for their expenses. Success in conquests or in administration largely depends on the financial backing.

Sir Eyre Coote - the general in the East India Company — Wikimedia Commons

The French Government at home or the Company, was not in a position to come out with the necessary financial help even at a time when Dupleix had succeeded in acquiring territories in India. Dupleix spent his own fortunes to meet the financial needs of the French Government in India, but this was too small in comparison to the task he had undertaken. Poverty dogged the French in India even when they were at the zenith of their power in India.

Previous Years' Questions

1. **How was Cartaz system used by the Portuguese to maintain their control over the oceanic trade? (2014)**
2. **Dupleix made a cardinal blunder in looking for the key to India in Madras: Clive sought and found it in Bengal. (2013)**

3 CHAPTER

The British Conquest of Indian States – 1757-1818

The mid-18th century saw the transformation of the English East India Company from trading enterprise to a political power. Factors such as weak political conditions in Bengal, third battle of Panipat and subsequent downfall of imperial Marathas and victory over Carnatic wars helped East India Company in establishing its political hegemony over leading Indian states. In this chapter we will look into the conquests of Bengal, Mysore and Maratha states. The conquest of Punjab and Sindh will be dealt in the next chapter.

The Conquest of Bengal (1757-1764)

Introduction

From the beginning, the British were interested in Bengal on account of its richness in natural resources and well developed industries and commerce. Rich resources and good prospects of trade in Bengal attracted various European trading companies. François Bernier, a traveller who visited India during Aurangzeb's reign wrote, "The rich exuberance of the country…has given rise to a proverb in common use among the Portuguese, English and Dutch that the kingdom of Bengal has a hundred gates open for entrance, but not one for departure." The other reason for the British gaining supremacy in Bengal was the trading concessions given to the company by the Mughals. A significant concession given by the Mughals was that of Emperor Farrukhsiyar's Imperial *farman* in 1717. The Farrukhsiyar *farman* granted the Company several privileges: the permission to import and export articles from Bengal without payment of custom duties in return of an annual payment of Rs. 30,000; the right to issue passes or *dastaks* for the movements of such goods and rights to rent more territory around Calcutta. It is said that the Company's surgeon, William Hamilton, cured Farrukhsiyar and the Emperor was moved to grant trading rights to the Company. Another story tells of a bribe to a eunuch by the Company, and a rumoured British naval attack on the Mughal navy at Surat.

The Company servants were also permitted to trade but were not covered by this *farman*. They were required to pay the same taxes as Indian merchants. However, the Company misused the Imperial *farman*. This *farman* became a perpetual source of conflict between the Company and the Nawabs of Bengal. All the Nawabs of Bengal right from Murshid Quli Khan to Alivardi Khan had objected to the English interpretation of the Imperial *farman* of 1717. The Nawabs of Bengal ignored imperial *farman* and continued collecting customs duties from the East India Company. The situation worsened in 1756, when the young and quick tempered Sirajud-Daulah succeeded his grandfather, Alivardi Khan. The new Nawab Sirajud-Daulah was opposed and challenged by many groups.

The Causes of Opposition to the New Nawab

The Succession of Siraj-ud-Daulah

In 1756, Siraj-ud-Daulah succeeded his grandfather, Alivardi Khan as Nawab of Bengal. He was the son of Ali Vardi's youngest daughter, Amina Begum. Sirajud-Dalulah's succession as a Nawab was challenged and opposed by many groups. In addition to Sirajud-Daulah's aunt Ghaseti Begum and his cousin Shaukat Jung, there was a dominant group within the Nawab's court that opposed his succession. Many nobles espoused the cause of Shaukat Jung.

Siraj-ud-Daulah
— Wikimedia Commons

Sirajud-Daulah was a young man of nineteen and a short tempered person. He is known to have been hostile to his most devoted advisers; he blindly trusted very few people and often insulted and defamed his foes and rivals including the British.

Hostile Relationship with the English

English showed sympathetic attitude towards Nawab's rival claimant Shaukat Jung. This made Siraj turn against British and became suspicious of their activities. He was also irritated by the fact that the trade privileges that English received since 1717 CE were grossly abused by the company. The English supported the enemies of the new Nawab and disobeyed his orders. A rich Bengali merchant named Kishan Das had incurred the displeasure of the Nawab. He had fled to Calcutta with his family and treasure and given shelter by the company. The Nawab asked the English to hand over Kishan Das to him but they refused his orders.

"Siraj-ud-daula has been pictured" says the biographer of Robert Clive, "as a monster of vice, cruelty and depravity."

Fortification of Settlements

Ali Vardi Khan had not permitted the English to fortify their settlements. In 1756 CE when the war between England and France was imminent in Europe, the English and the French began to fortify their settlements. Sirajud-Daulah did not like this and immediately ordered to stop fortification. The French obeyed him but the English did not care at all. This annoyed the Nawab.

Attack at Calcutta Fort, 20th June 1756

When the British refused to stop their fortification activities, the enraged Nawab captured the English factory of Qasim Bazar and then attacked and captured Fort William at Calcutta with an army of 50,000. He renamed Calcutta as Alinagar. The army at Calcutta consisted of about 515 soldiers, out of which about 230 were English. The defence of the Calcutta fort was organized by John Zephaniah Holwell, a senior officer in the company. About 146 English were taken as prisoners, and were shut in a small cell. Only 23 survived the next morning. This is incident is known as Black Hole tragedy.

The Black Hole Tragedy

The Black Hole was a small dungeon in the old Fort William in Calcutta, where troops of the Nawab Sirajud- Daulah, held British prisoners of war after the capture of the fort on 20 June 1756.

The Fort's defence officer John Zephaniah Holwell, claimed that following the fall of the fort, British and Anglo-Indian soldiers and civilians were held overnight in conditions so cramped that many died from suffocation, heat exhaustion and crushing. He claimed that 123 prisoners died out of the 146 held. Holwell wrote that after seeking a place in the fort to confine the 146 prisoners including him, at 8 pm, the jailers locked the prisoners in the fort's black hole which was 14 by 18 feet (4.3 m × 5.5 m) in size. The term 'black hole' was 18th century military slang for any military prison - similar to 'the glasshouse' in the 20th century British Army or 'the brig' in the US Navy. When the "Black Hole" was opened the next morning at 6 am, only 23 people were alive. However, the precise number of deaths, and the accuracy of Holwell's claims, has been the subject of controversy.

The Arrival of Clive

When news of the fall of Calcutta broke in Madras on 16th August, 1756, the Council immediately sent out an expeditionary force under Colonel Clive and Admiral Watson. Clive assumed command of the land forces, while Watson commanded a naval squadron. Clive and Watson then moved against Calcutta on 2nd January, 1757 and recaptured it. The fortifications of Fort William were strengthened and a defensive position was prepared in the north-east of the city.

Lord Clive
— Wikimedia Commons

The Treaty of Alinagar, 5th Feb 1757

On 9th January, 1757, under Captain Coote and Major Kilpatrick, the town of Hooghly was attacked. Clive launched a surprise attack on the Nawab's camp. The attack scared the Nawab. He concluded the Treaty of Alinagar with the Company on 5th February, 1757. The treaty had three clauses. Firstly, agreeing to restore the Company's factories, settlements privileges and rights. Secondly, allowing the fortification of Calcutta. Thirdly, to provide compensation for its losses. The amount of compensation was to be determined by the Nawab.

Clive had three reasons for making peace with the Nawab. Firstly, he feared that the French might join the Nawab. Secondly, his relations with Admiral Watson were strained. Thirdly, war with France was about to break out in Europe. Also, he might be called be called back to Madras.

The Attack on Chandernagar and the French Alliance

Concerned by the approach of the Seven Years' War in Europe, the Company turned its attention to the French threat in Bengal. Clive plundered the French town of Chandernagar near Calcutta. The Nawab was infuriated on learning of the attack on Chandernagar. He felt the need to strengthen himself by forming alliances against the British. Plagued by fear of attack from the north by the Afghans under Ahmad Shah Durrani and from the west by the Marathas, the Nawab started secret negotiations with the French. The Nawab also moved a large division of his army under Rai Durlabh to Plassey.

Discontent Against the Nawab and Conspiracy

Clive soon learnt that the nobles of the Nawab were dissatisfied and conspiring to depose him and put on the throne Mir Jaffar, commander-in-chief of the army and brother in law of the former Nawab Ali Vardi Khan. Leading members of this conspiracy included Rai Durlabh, treasurer of the Nawab, Ominchand (Amir Chand), a Sikh merchant, Jagat Seth, the richest banker of Bengal and several officers in the Nawab's army. Clive joined this conspiracy through Omichand and terms were settled. A treaty was drawn between the British and Mir Jaffar to raise him to the throne of the Nawab in return for support to the British in the field of battle and the bestowal of large sums of money upon them as compensation for the attack on Calcutta.

When these details were settled Ominchand threatened to disclose the whole conspiracy to the Nawab if he were not given 30 lacs of rupees and a clause to this effect inserted in the treaty. Clive, prepared two drafts of the treaty - One genuine document in white paper and other fictitious in red paper. The genuine document contained no mention of the amount to be paid to Ominchand. It was signed by Clive, members of the Secret Committee and Admiral Watson. The fictitious paper in red contained a clause relating to the payment of 30 lacs to Ominchand. It was signed by Clive and the secret committee. Watson refused to signed, so Clive forged his signatures. Later on, Clive was accused of forgery when British parliament set up an inquiry committee against him in 1772.

Clive had been in search of an opportunity to attack the Nawab. He accused him of violating the term of the treaty of Alinagar and without waiting for his explanations, he dispatched an army against the Nawab. The Nawab also sent an army to face the enemy and on 23rd June, 1757, both the armies fought a pitched battle in the field of Plassey near Murshidabad.

The Battle of Plassey and the First Revolution in Bengal

The Battle of Plassey took place on 23rd June, 1757 in Plassey (or Palashi) near Murshidabad, the then capital of Bengal, between the forces of East India Company and the Nawab of Bengal and his French allies. The Nawab's army consisted of 35,000 infantry of all sorts and 18,000 cavalry. The army also included a detachment of about 50 French artillerymen under de St. Fairs. Clive's army consisted of 750 European infantry with 100 cannons, 2100 sepoys and 100 artillery-men assisted by 50 sailors.

The Battle of Plassey was a battle only in name. All the generals and the commander in chief, Mir Jaffar and Rai Durlabh were allied with the British and made a show of resistance. Only a handful of Frenchmen in the service of the Nawab offered resistance. The losses on the side of the English were 23 men killed and 49 wounded. The losses on the other side were about 500 killed and almost the same wounded.

The battle was won by the British through treacherous means. It was not the superiority of the military power but the conspiracy of the Nawab's officials that helped the English in winning the battle. The Nawab was forced to flee and was put to death by the orders of Miran, son of Mir Jaffar.

The English proclaimed Mir Jafar the next Nawab of Bengal. Historians have termed the narrative of the conquest of Bengal from 1757 to 1765 as a political revolution. The Battle of Plassey is considered as the first political revolution in the history of India as an independent Nawab of Bengal became a mere puppet in the hands of the British, and the Company the *de facto* rulers.

After the Battle of Plassey, the Company was granted the undisputed right to trade freely in Bengal, Bihar and Orissa. It also received the *zamindari* of the 24 *parghanas* near Calcutta and a high compensation from the Nawab.

Lord Clive meeting with Mir Jafar after the battle of Plassey: National Portrait Gallery London — Wikimedia Commons

Results of the Battle of Plassey

Judged by its results, the battle of Plassey is considered as one of the memorable battles in Indian history. Its results were deep and far reaching which transformed the subsequent history of India.

Following are some of the significant result of battle of Plassey:

- **Puppet nawab :** The battle resulted in the rule of puppet Nawab of Bengal. Siraj-ud- Daula , the last independent Nawab was replaced by Mir Jaffar. The new Nawab was sovereign in theory but not in practice. He became a protégé of the company. He occupied the throne as a tenant - at-will of the company. This proved true when Mir Jaffar was replaced by Mir Qasim at the will of Calcutta Council.

- **Increase in the prestige of the Company :** The prestige of the company increased both in India and in its home country. It had played the most important part in the removal of the Nawab and putting its own nominee, Mir Jaffar on the throne. It also brought about a great change in the position of the company. From the position of mere traders in Bengal, the English became now the king-makers of Bengal.
- **Territorial gain to company :** The battle resulted in the extension of the British territories around Calcutta and financial gain as well. Mir Jaffar granted to the company the territory of twenty-four Parganas. Thus, their settlement at Calcutta became more prosperous. Their trade increased. Moreover the trade privileges enjoyed by the company became more secure.
- **Impact on Anglo-French Conflict in Deccan :** The battle of Plassey immensely impacted the ongoing Anglo-French conflict in the Deccan. It placed at the disposal of the English the men and resources of the Bengal which were used in Carnatic wars. it was from Bengal that Clive sent Col. Forde who captured Northern Circars from the French. Thus the battle of Plassey enabled the English triumph over the French during the third phase of the Anglo-French hostilities in Deccan.
- **Paved the way for subsequent revolution in Bengal :** When Jaffar was made Nawab of Bengal after the battle of Plassey , it was considered a first revolution in Bengal. Mir Jaffar however became a puppet in the hands of Calcutta council. Soon the council members began to feel dissatisfied with Mir Jaffar and decided to replace Mir Jaffar by his son-in-law Mir Qasim. Thus the battle of Plassey prepared the way for the second revolution in Bengal.

Plassey's Victory was Incomplete and Fragile

The battle of Plassey was a mere skirmish and British victory was due more to treachery than to the superiority of British arms. The British in Bengal were looking for strengthening their trade through privileges and territories. This was achieved with the battle of Plassey. They got territories around Calcutta and their settlement became prosperous. They were able to make an independent ruler of Bengal as a puppet ruler. So, with Plassey, British got a firm footing in the soil of Bengal.

Yet Plassey's victory was not decisive. There were several factors and forces at play at that time which made company's position fragile and vulnerable. Firstly after the1760 revolution, Bengal came under the rule of Nawab Mir Qasim who did not want to be a puppet at the hands of Calcutta Council. He attempted to be independent from Company through his reforms. He abolished custom duties and attempted to modernize the army by employing Europeans. It threatened the Calcutta council and company's trade. Secondly, Marathas were at its pinnacle when the Plassey victory took place. The battle of Panipat happened only after four years of Plassey . They were already a formidable enemy to the British. If Panipat did not happen, the English would be routed first from Deccan and then from east. They would be waging much costlier and ferocious battles with Marathas than a skirmish like Plassey. Fourthly, French were in more cordial relations with the native rulers of Deccan including Marathas than the English. The French and Marathas alliance would have proved fatal for the east India's company's existence in Indian territories. Therefore, British were cautious of not meddling with Marathas. Even the Nawab of Bengal was apprehensive of Marathas than the English. Lastly, till 1750, English were at the receiving end in the Anglo-French struggle in Deccan. It was only after the victory of Plassey, the English position in Deccan became stronger due to the resources and men of Bengal.

Of course the credit for conquering Bengal goes to Clive who won Plassey through treacherous means. After his strategic siege of Arcot in 1751, Clive planned another strategy to wage a war against the unpopular Nawab of Bengal, Siraj-ud-Daula. Clive had sensed the weak political conditions prevailing in Bengal when he along with Admiral Watson were sent to Calcutta to recapture the fort and English settlements attacked by Siraj-ud-Daula. They were successful in their attempt to do.

In Calcutta, Clive drove Siraj's army and made a treaty with him, the treaty of Alinagar in January 1757. Clive became a part of the great conspiracy against the Nawab. Clive decided that the best way to secure the Company's interests in Bengal was to replace Siraj with a new nawab. Therefore he joined hand with the leading conspirators which included Mir Jaffar, Rai Durlabh, Ominchand, Jagat Seth and several officers in the Nawab's army. A treaty was drawn between the British and Mir Jaffar to raise him to the throne of the Nawab in return for support to the British in the field of battle and the bestowal of large sums of money upon them as compensation for the attack on Calcutta. Omichand, demanded money for keeping this conspiracy a secret, Clive deceived him by a fake treaty.

The confrontation came on 23rd June, 1757, in Plassey. He had won the battle even before its start by entering into a conspiracy. With a force of just 3000 soldiers, Clive was able to defeat Siraj-ud-Daula's 50,000 soldiers. The height of treachery is noteworthy that the Clive's army did not waste a single shot as per order of their commanders Mir Jaffar and Rai Durlabh. Clive with an army less than one sixteenth of the Nawab's won the battle. In fact, it was the treachery that won.

The Second Revolution of 1760

Removal of Mir Jaffar

Mir Jaffar's treasury was soon emptied by the demands of the Company's officials for presents and bribes. By 1759, Mir Jafar felt that his position as a subordinate to the British could not be tolerated. He started encouraging the Dutch to advance against the British and to eject them from Bengal. Clive, however, initiated immediate offensive operations by land and sea and defeated the Dutch in 1759. In 1760, when Mir Jaffar hesitated to fulfil all their expectations, they forced him to leave the throne in favour of his son-in-law, Mir Qasim, resulting in the second political revolution in Bengal. Mir Qasim rewarded his benefactors by granting the Company the *Zamindari* of districts of Burdwan, Midnapur and Chittagong and giving handsome presents to the higher British officials.

Mir Jafar — Wikimedia Commons

Mir Qasim

Unlike previous Nawabs, Mir Qasim did not want to become a puppet in the hands of the British. He wanted to remove his dependence on the English. He fulfilled all the demands of the British and began to work on administrative reforms.

Mir Qasim did following reforms and changes:

- The misuse of privileges given to the company and private trade carried out by the servants of the company adversely affected the revenue of the state. Moreover, the burden of paying duties fell on native merchants which deteriorated their position and trade. Therefore Mir Qasim abolished duties on Indian goods. By doing this he put the English and Indian merchants on an equal footing in matters of trade. The Nawab could not impose duties on the goods of the company but he was certainly free to abolish duties on the goods of all.
- He began to train his army on modern lines by appointing Europeans in the court. Factories for the manufacture of arms were started.
- He changed the capital from Murshidabad to Mongher, a place near the border of Bihar. The main reasons for the change of capital were that Murshidabad had become the hotbed of controversies and intrigues. Also, he wanted to keep a distance from the Calcutta council.
- He removed all his rivals and suppressed the rebellion zamindars

The British could not tolerate the independent attitude of the Nawab. They British did not like the reforms made by the new Nawab.The abolition of duties enraged members of Calcutta council because it affected their private trade also. The Nawab refused to reimpose duties on Indian goods. Therefore they made false charges against Mir Qasim and planned to attack him.

Events Leading to Battle of Buxar, 1764

- Ellis, the agent of the company at Patna, suddenly seized the city, but was immediately recaptured by the Nawab's troops.
- Ellis and other Englishmen were imprisoned and their territories were seized.
- The Calcutta council issued a proclamation of dethroning Mir Qasim and reinstating Mir Jaffar.
- The Nawab refused to care for it. The English marched towards Patna.
- Battle of Geriah was fought between English and Nawab in which Nawab was defeated.
- The English captured capital Mongher.

The battle of Buxar (1764) and the Third Revolution

Mir Qasim fled to Oudh, where the ruler Shuja-ud-Daula rendered help to him. The Mughal Emperor, Shah Alam II, who was residing there, too came for help. The combined forces of Oudh, the Mughals and the Nawab of Bengal attacked the British in Buxar in 1764. Sir Hector Monroe advanced with company's troops and defeated the combined forces of Oudh and Bengal at the battle of Buxar in 1764. The battle was a fiercely contested battle and the troops of Mir Qasim offered a determined resistance. The superiority of the Brithsh arms was proved. Mir Qasim made one more attempt but was defeated at Kara. Mir Qasim fled away while Shuja-ud-Daula of Oudh and Mughal emperor Shah Alam II surrended to the English.

The battle of Buxar is termed as the third revolution, resulting in complete conquest of Bengal by the Company and cementing their supremacy in Bengal.

Comparison of Battles of Plassey and Buxar

Historians have expressed different views regarding the importance of these battles.

Following are the reasons for the importance of the battle of Buxar:

- The battle of Buxar was a fierce and hotly contested battle.
- It completed the conquest of Bengal
- The Nawab of Oudh, the Nawab of Bengal and the Mughal Emperor Shah Alam II were defeated.
- Oudh became a friendly buffer state between the company's possessions in northern India and other powers of northern India.
- The Mughal emperor Shah Alam became the dependent of the company.

Some historians give more importance to the battle of Plassey due to following reasons:

- It was more difficult to defeat Siraj-ud-Daula than to defeat Mir Qasim if dissident forces had not raised their head.
- At the time of battle of Plassey English were not well established in Bengal.

Towards de jure master of Bengal – The Treaty of Allahabad (1765)

The battle of Buxar ended with the Treaty of Allahabad in 1765. After the battle, Clive arrived and made the treaty with Nawab Shuja-ud-Daula of Oudh and the Mughal emperor Shah Allam II.

Its terms were:

- The Mughal emperor Shah Alam II recognized British power by granting the East India Company the *diwani* or revenue rights of Bengal, Bihar and Orissa, thus making the Company the virtual rulers of Bengal.
- The emperor was also forced to pay a war indemnity of five million rupees.
- The Nawab of Oudh got back his territory of Oudh. But he gave the districts of Karra and Allahabad to the Company, which were later given to the Mughal emperor.
- The company supported Nawab Shuja-ud-Daula of Oudh by providing a subsidiary force for external defence. However, the Nawab had to pay for the services and maintenance of this force
- Shah Alam II became a pensioner. The company agreed to give him a 26 lac rupees a year.

Significance of the treaty of Allahabad

The treaty of Allahabad was very important for several reasons:

- The grant of Diwani by the Mughal emperor made the position of the company legal in the provinces of Bengal and Bihar. Since 1757 they had been de facto masters of Bengal but now they became its de jure masters.
- The Nawab of Oudh became a dependent ally of the company.
- Oudh became a friendly buffer state between the company's possessions in northern India and other powers in northern India like the Marathas.
- With Oudh as a friendly buffer state, it was easy for the company to introduce the policy of ring fence in northern India.
- The titular Mughal emperor became a prisoner of the company.

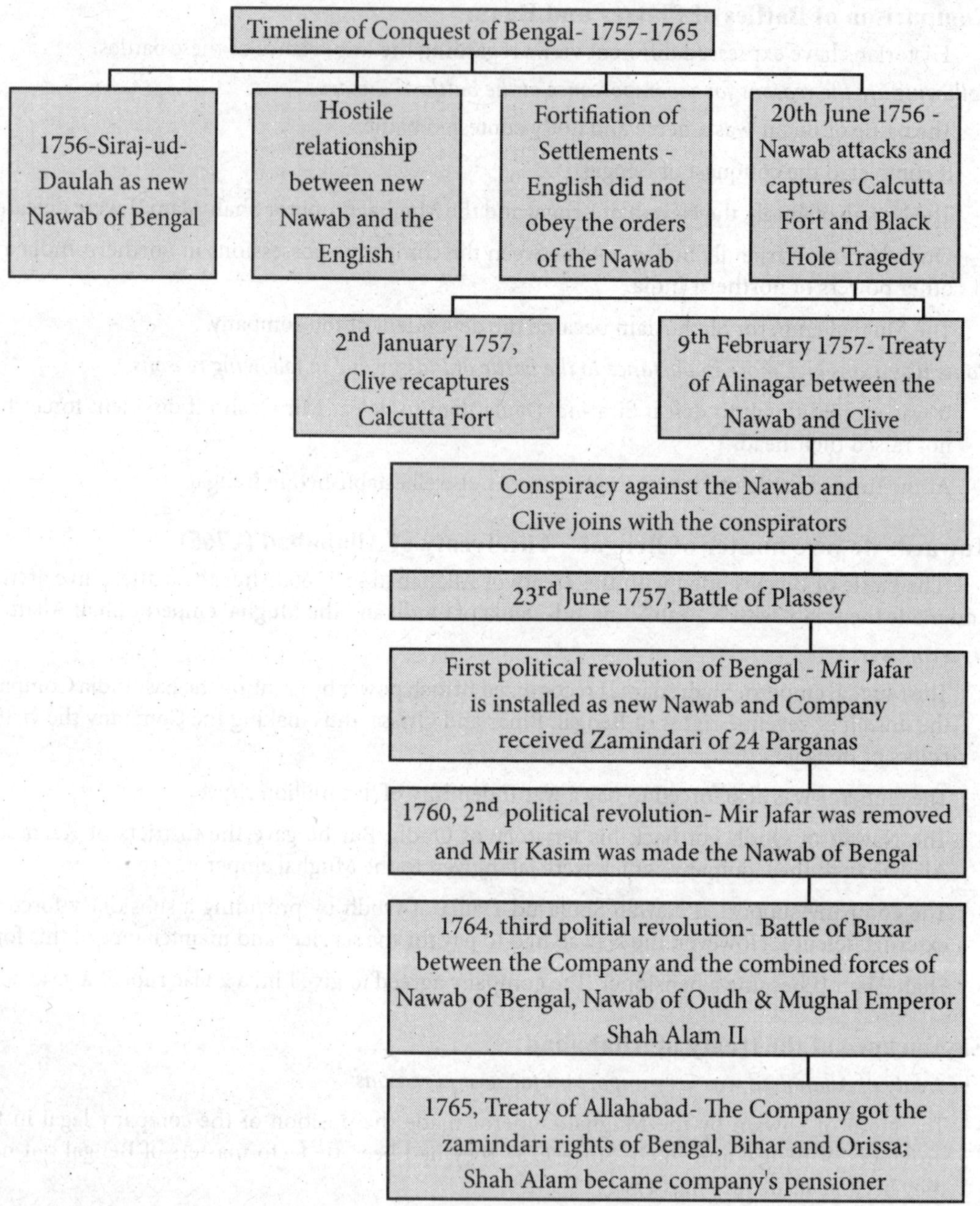

Heralding the Company's Rule and Dual System in Bengal

With a single stroke, the Treaty of Allahabad heralded the establishment of the rule of the East India Company in India. The victories at Plassey and Buxar secured a permanent foothold for the British East India Company in the rich province of Bengal, and secured its political ascendancy in the entire region. The conquest of Bengal also changed the nature of the Company from a trading organisation to an emerging political force in the subcontinent.

Robert Clive was made the governor of Bengal, and he introduced the dual or double government system.

Clive divided the function of government between the Nawab and the Company as Nizamat and Diwani in the following way:

- Nizamat administration: The internal administration or territorial jurisdiction, mainly judicial and police functions, was given to the Nawab. The Nizamat, under the Nawab, was actually carried out by the company's nominees Muhammad Raza Khan and Shitab Rai Khan
- The Diwani or fiscal administration was carried out by the company. The company also controlled military and foreign affairs.

Dual system arrangement made the Nawab completely dependent on the Company for finances, and made the Company the virtual ruler of Bengal by handing it military and revenue power. The Company collected revenue and paid fixed annual sums of Rs. 32 lakhs for the expense of Nizamat. The real power was in the hands of the company, because the deputy Nawabs, who exercised Nizamat functions in actual practice, were the Company's nominees. Thus, the Nizamat was controlled by the company indirectly.

Later, the Nawab of Bengal was forced to hand over the responsibility of judicial administration to the Company in 1793, thus completing the transfer of power from the Bengal Nawabs to the East India Company.

The Dual system proved to be the most defective in many ways. The most glaring defect of Clive's dual system of administration was that power was divorced from responsibility. The Nawab was responsible for administration but had no real power. The company controlled the revenue as well as the army. Under these circumstances, the administration began to grow bad. The zamindars, the officials, and the company's servants tyrannized the people. In 1769-70, there was a severe famine in Bengal, and about one-third of the population died. The company remained a passive spectator and did nothing to improve the condition of the starving masses.

An Era of Economic Loot and the Corruption in the East India Company

The conquest of Bengal led to the beginning of the economic loot of India. The Company's employees looted Bengal's wealth and resources through private trade and corrupt practices. Lord Clive, when he returned to England in 1760, had earned a fortune of 3 lac pounds and a rent of 27 thousand pounds per year.

Great Bengal Famine of 1770 — Wikimedia Commons

In 1769–1773, Bengal suffered its worst famine. This famine was so ruinous that every 1 out of 3 people in Bengal, including Bihar and Orissa, died and the population of 30 million was reduced to 10 million.

The immediate reason for this famine was that the rains were insufficient and the company, which was now the Diwan of the region, increased the land tax in April 1770. However, historians and scholars alike agree that it was the rampant corruption in the Company in Bengal that aggravated the famine.

Robert Clive : The Founder of the British Empire in India

Major-General Robert Clive (25th September, 1725 – 22nd November, 1774), also known as Clive of India, was a British officer claimed to have established the military and political supremacy of the East India Company in Bengal. He is credited with securing India and its wealth for the British crown. Clive began his career as a 'factor' or 'writer' in the service of the East India Company and reached Madras in 1744. He was given access to the governor's library, where he became a prolific reader.

Role in Carnatic War

The turning point in his career came during Second Carnatic War. The fortunes of the English have fallen very low. French had established themselves in Hyderabad and secured Northern Circars. Many allies of the English had sided with the French. During this juncture, Clive's strategic planning helped boost the morale of the English. He went with 200 European and 300 Indian troops and captured Arcot in 1751. The siege of Arcot gave a severe blow to the French power. Carnatic Nawab Chanda Sahib was defeated and fled. English were able to put their nominee Muhammad Ali on the throne of Carnatic. In 1753, he went back to England.

The Conquest of Bengal

Clive was again sent to India as Governor of Fort St. David in 1755 and made Lt. Colonel. After coming to India, he along with Admiral Watson, were sent to Calcutta where the Nawab Siraj-ud-Daula had captured the fort of Calcutta.

He successfully recovered the fort and made peace with the Nawab. Clive came to know the unstable political situation of Bengal and joined the conspiracy with the dissidents. He made false charges against the Nawab and declared war against him. He masterminded the battle of Plassey through treacherous means. The victory in the battle of Plassey gave him the credit of setting up the British rule in Bengal.

First Governorship of Bengal

Clive was the Governor of Bengal from 1757 to 1760. During this period, he defeated the Dutch, sent Col. Forde from Bengal to participate in Third Carnatic War.

Second Governorship of Bengal

Clive was away from India from 1760 to 1765. During this period, Bengal was conquered in the battle of Buxar. He returned in 1765 and soon made the treaty of Allahabad.

Reforms

Clive made significant civil reforms and military reforms. In the civil reforms the most significant were the abolition of private trade in the company. It resulted in the neglect of the Company's work. The employees of the Company were ordered not to carry private trade. Under the military reforms, Clive abolished the system of double bhatta or field allowance, of the military officers. Now the allowance was to be only during the war time.

Dual Government

This was the most significant measure of Clive as a governor of Bengal. The company acquired the Diwani rights of Bengal, Bihar and Orissa in 1765. Thus, it got the control over the revenue of these provinces. Clive divided the function of government between the Nawab and Company. The territorial jurisdiction, or Nizamat, was entrusted to Nawab. Army and foreign affairs did not come under Nizamat, since it was under the control of the company. The Diwani or Fiscal administration was carried out by the company .So, this system of dividing the functions of government into Diwan and Nizam has been called Clive's system of Dual Government. In the dual system, power came in the hands of company and responsibility fell on the Nawab.

The Nizamat under the Nawab was actually carried out by two deputy Nawabs , Muhammad Raza Khan for Bengal and Shitab Rai Khan for Bihar. These two deputy Nawabs were appointed on the advice of Company.The Company collected revenue and paid fixed annual sums of 32 lakhs for the expense of Nizamat. Therefore the real power was in the hands of the company because deputy Nawabs, who exercised Nizamat functions in actual practice, were Company's nominees. Thus the Nizamat was controlled by the company indirectly. There were several reasons for adopting dual system such as : the company feared that assumption of responsibility would consume profits; lack of sufficient number of administrators in the provinces; to avoid jealousy from European powers and to prevent any political revolution in Bengal, the company did not take the direct responsibility in the acquired territories.

The Dual system proved most defective in many ways. The most glaring defect of Clive's dual system of administration was that power was divorced from responsibility. Nawab was responsible for administration but he had no real power. The Company controlled the revenue as well as the army. Under these circumstances the administration began to grow bad. The zamindars, the officials and the company's servants tyrannised over the people. In 1769-70, there was a severe famine in Bengal and about one third population died. The company remained a passive spectator and did nothing to improve the condition of the starving masses.

Impeachment and death

Clive left India for the last time in February 1767. In 1772, Parliament opened an inquiry into the Company's practices in India. Clive's political opponents turned these hearings into attacks on Clive. He defended himself by stating "I stand astonished at my own moderation" and the vote to censure Clive for his actions failed. Later in 1772, Clive was appointed Lord Lieutenant of Shropshire, his birthplace.

There was a large famine in Bengal between 1769 and 1773, where the population of Bengal declined by a third. It was argued that rampant corruption in the Company in Bengal was to blame for the famine. The debates in the parliament and the revelations reduced Clive's political fortunes considerably.

Clive continued to be involved in ongoing Parliamentary discussions on Company reforms, during which General John Burgoyne, one of Clive's most vocal enemies, pressed the case in 1773 that some of Clive's gains were made at the expense of the Company and the government. Clive again made a spirited defence of his actions, and closed his testimony by stating "Take my fortune, but save my honour." The vote that followed completely vindicated Clive, who was commended for the "great and meritorious service" he rendered to the country. Immediately thereafter, Parliament began debating the Regulating Act of 1773, which significantly reformed the East India Company's practices.

On 22nd November, 1774, Clive committed suicide, aged forty-nine, at his Berkeley Square home in London. There was no inquest on his death and it was variously alleged he had stabbed himself or cut his throat with a penknife or taken an overdose of opium, while a few newspapers reported his death as due to an apoplectic fit or stroke. He was buried in St Margaret's Parish Church at Moreton Say, near his birthplace in Shropshire.

Clive was awarded an Irish peerage and was created Baron Clive of Plassey; he bought lands in County Limerick and County Clare, Ireland. One of these lands near Limerick City was named Plassey. Following Irish independence, these lands became state property. In the 1970s a technical college, which later became the University of Limerick, was built at Plassey.

The Anglo-Mysore Wars – 1767-1799

Anglo- Mysore wars are referred to a series of wars fought during the last three decades of the18th c., between the kingdom of Mysore on the one hand, and EIC represented chiefly by Madras Presidency, the Maratha confederacy and the Nizam of Hyderabad on the other hand.

The British intervention in the state of Mysore was primarily to protect their commercial interests in the South and to curb the growing power of the rulers of Mysore—Hyder Ali and Tipu Sultan. Annexation of Mysore state became urgency for the company due to Tipu Sultan's strong alliances with foreign powers, mainly French, and his modernisation measures.

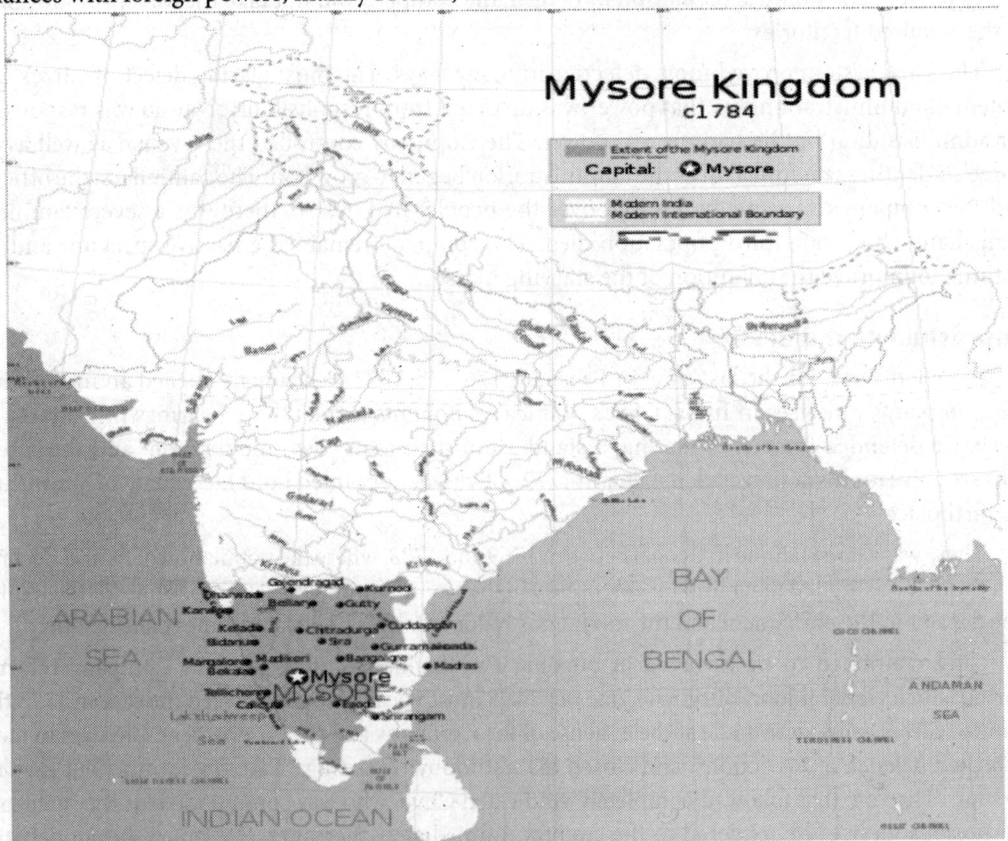

Map showing the state of Mysore, Nizam's territories and the state of Arcot — Wikimedia Commons

Hyder Ali and the First Anglo-Mysore War (1767-1769)

Hyder Ali, (1721-22) was a brave Indian warrior, who became the *de facto* ruler of Mysore in the second half of the 18th century. He rose by dint of his ability. He started his career as an ordinary soldier in the Mysore army and became the commander or Faujdar of the fort of Dindigul in 1755 CE. Soon he rose to the position of commander-in-chief. He was virtually the ruler by 1761CE. The Hindu ruler of Mysore, Krishnaraja Wodeyar II (1734 to 1766) died in 1766, and Hyder Ali usurped the power.

Hyder was credited with having been the first Indian to form a corps of Sepoys armed with fire rockets. Hyder Ali had territorial disputes and differences with the Nizam of Hyderabad and the Marathas. He made peace with these powers and waged war on the British in Madras. Thus began the First Anglo-Mysore War, where the British were humiliated, and they signed the Treaty of Madras with Hyder Ali in 1769.

Following were the Political conditions of the Deccan when Hyder came to power in 1761

- Bengal was under the control of EIC
- French were defeated in Carnatic wars
- Nizam was in financial crisis and dependent on British support
- Arcot or Carnatic was the dependency of EIC
- Marathas were defeated at Panipat and were weak.

Following are the Causes and Main Events of First Mysore War

The jealousy and hatred of Nizam of Hyderabad and Marathas and suscipicon of English towards Hyder Ali were the main cause of the war.

The Nizam and Marathas made an alliance against Hyder. However, Nizam joined with Hyder Ali against the English in ongoing Carnatic War. The English troops defeated the combined army of Hyder and Nizam at Changama Pass and Trincomali in 1767.

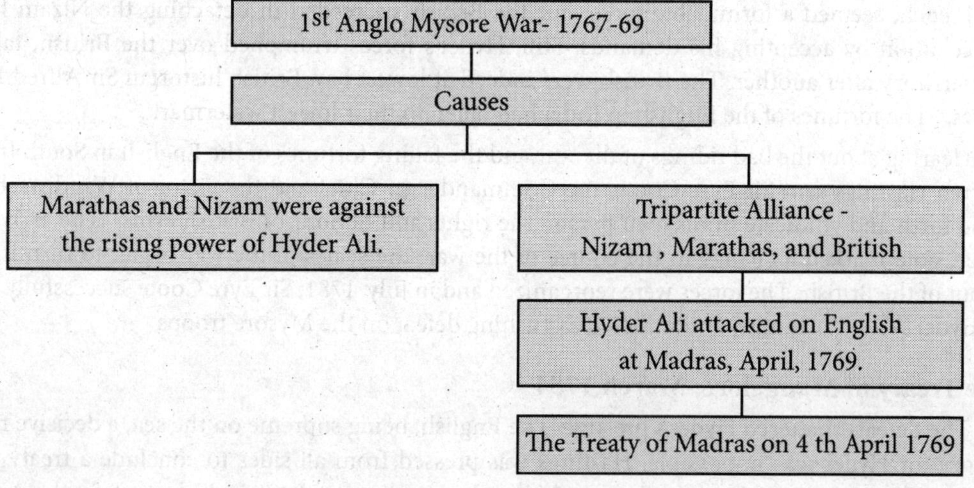

The English came to terms with the Nizam by the treaty of Masulipatnm in 1768. Therefore, Nizam, Marathas and the British made an alliance against Hyder Ali. Left alone, Hyder with his own army attacked Madras. The English were not in readiness to fight and therefore agreed to sign a treaty out of fear. British made peace with Hyder by signing the treaty of Madras in 1769. Hyder Ali practically dictated the terms of the treaty.

As per the Treaty of Madras, both parties agreed to return the areas won by each other, and Madras government committed itself to help Hyder Ali if he was attacked by any power. Later on, the clause of the Madras treaty to render help to Hyder Ali in case of attack put the Madras government in difficulty. In 1770 the Marathas invaded Mysore, and Hyder Ali demanded help. The English did not help him. It lowered their prestige and Hyder Ali now became a bitter enemy of the English.

The Second Anglo-Mysore War (1780-1784)

The second Anglo- Mysore war took place during the time of Warren Hastings.

Following are its causes:

- When the Marathas attacked Mysore in 1770, Hyder Ali asked the British for help, but they did not turn up. The result was that all the territories of Hyder Ali were confiscated by the Marathas. Hyder waited for an opportunity to strike against the British.
- The capture of Mahe by the British, a French settlement under the protection of Hyder Ali, acted as one of the most important causes for the outbreak of the Second Anglo- Mysore War. This was a period when the British where facing opposition and resentment from almost every quarter. Outside India also, France, Spain, Holland and revolting American colonies had combined against the English. The French sought to utilize this opportunity to recover their lost holdings.

Events

In 1774, the first Anglo-Maratha war began. This made the Marathas anxious to secure the friendship of Mysore against the British. Hyder too, accepted the Maratha's offer of friendship so that he could wreak vengeance upon the dissembling British. The Nizam who had already been resentful of British actions was also made a party. The Triple Alliance, combined with the aid of the French, seemed a formidable force; but the British succeeded in detaching the Nizam from the coalition by accepting his demands. Still, Hyder's forces triumphed over the British, taking one territory after another. The British were indeed at lowest bay. British historian Sir Alfred Lyall writes, "The fortunes of the English in India had fallen to their lowest watermark."

Hearing about the bad tidings of the war and the falling fortunes of the English in South India, Warren Hastings sent Sir Eyre Coote, the Commander-in-Chief and the victor of Wandiwash "to stand forth and vindicate in his own person the rights and honour of British arms." The arrival of Eyre Coote marked a change in the course of the war; the scales of the war began to turn in the favour of the British. The forces were reorganized and in July, 1781, Sir Eyre Coote successfully held up Hyder Ali at Portonovo and inflicted a crushing defeat on the Mysore troops.

The Treaty of Mangalore, March,1784

The defeats shattered Hyder's prestige. The English, being supreme on the sea, a decisive naval victory for Hyder was impossible. Hastings was pressed from all sides to conclude a treaty with the Marathas at any cost because that would be advantageous to the British interests in the Anglo-

Mysore War. Thus the war with the Marathas was terminated by the 'Treaty of Salbai' signed on 17th May, 1782. On 7th December, 1782, Hyder Ali died of cancer. Eyre Coote also died in 1783 in broken health in Madras. Hyder Ali earned fame in Indian history as a relentless foe of the British Company. He was succeeded by his son Tipu Sultan at that critical time. He was the worthy son of a worthy father. He conducted the unfinished war of his father with equal determination. However, both the sides were war-weary and in favor of a truce. Thus, the Second Anglo-Mysore War ended with the treaty of Mangalore, in March, 1784.

According to Warren Hastings, this treaty (Mangalore) was most shameful and humiliating. But he was forced to accept it. British historian Lyall remarked, "with the termination of the war, ended the only period in the long contest between England and the native powers, during which our position in India was for a time prolonged struggle uninjured, though not unshaken, is a result due to the political intrepidity of Warren Hastings". Similarly, another historian writes, 'if Warren Hastings would not be there at the helm of affairs the British dominion would have ended before it had started'.

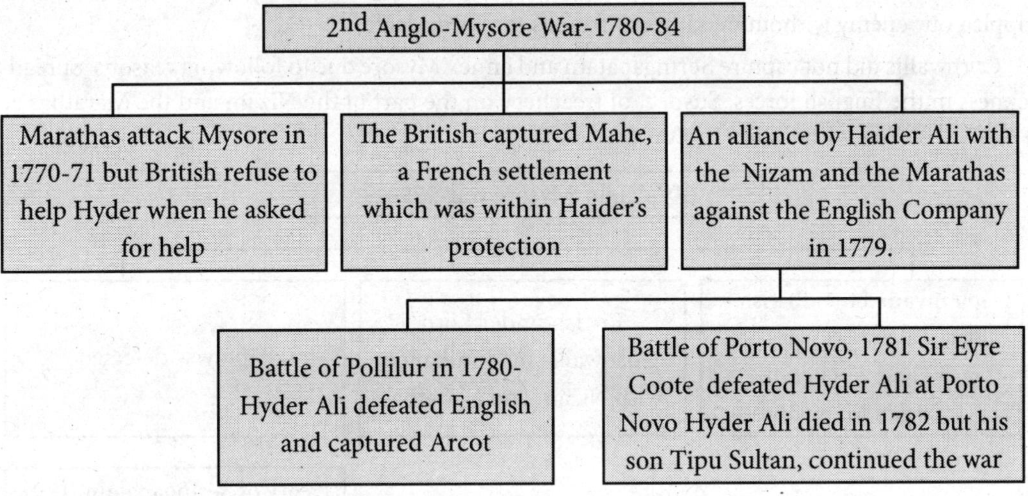

The Third Anglo-Mysore War(1790-92) and the Treaty of Seringapatam

This war took place during Cornwallis' time, who was suspicious of Tipu Sultan's alliance with the French. Tipu was a French ally. He had employed Europeans to train his army and had friendly relations with the French government.

Tipu had not given up hostility with the English and was carrying on negotiations with the French.

Causes

In 1789, Tipu invaded the British-allied state of Travancore because he had differences with the Raja of Travancore. This was a violation of the treaty of Mangalore. Thus, the outbreak of the Third Anglo-Mysore War was a corollary of the violation of the Treaty of Mangalore by Tipu Sultan.

Events

Cornwallis did not like Tipu's actions, but according to Pitt's India Act he could wage only a defensive war. This prevented Cornwallis to declare war on Mysore. Cornwallis got the opportunity to wage war against Tipu by helping Nizam in retrieving his territories from Mysore. Cornwallis made an alliance with the Nizam and the Marathas and started the war against Tipu.

Due to the on-going French revolution, Tipu did not receive any aid from his French ally. The triple alliance of the Marathas, the Nizam and the British collectively attacked Tipu's army.

Treaty of Seringapatam

The resultant war lasted three years and was a resounding defeat for Mysore. In 1792, the Treaty of Seringapatam was signed; Tipu had to surrender half of his territories. He also agreed to pay three and a half crores of rupees and to surrender two sons as hostages.

This war brought valuable territories to the British. The war indemnity was equally divided between the allies. Cornwallis summed up the defeat of Tipu Sultan saying, "we have effectively crippled our enemy without making our friends too formidable".

Cornwallis did not capture Seringapatam and annex Mysore due to following reasons: Spread of sickness in the English forces, Suspect of treachery on the part of the Nizam and the Marathas and likelihood of War with France in Europe.

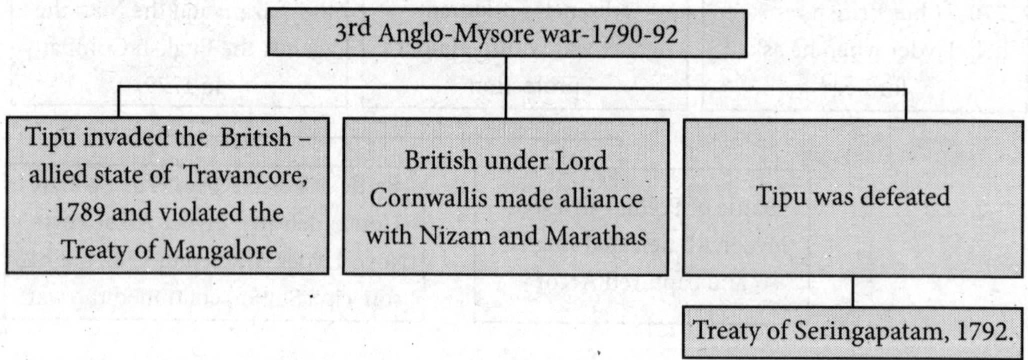

The Fourth Anglo-Mysore War(1799) and the Death of Tipu Sultan

This war took place in the time of Lord Wellesley, who was determined to annex Mysore and put an end to the power of Tipu Sultan.

Causes

Although the British had taken half of the territories of Mysore, Tipu Sultan had rebuilt significantly and Mysore was once more a prosperous place. He wanted to get back his territories and to achieve that, was carrying on negotiations with the French and Zaman Shah of Kabul. Tipu wanted to have allies to expel the English from India.

Wellesley was not prepared to tolerate this. The British East India Company knew that Mysore was the only thing standing between it and the total domination of India. Wellesley made charges on Tipu of making alliances with the foreigners and violating the previous treaty.

Events

The war broke out in 1799. In the beginning of May, 1799, the British and their allies surrounded Seringapatam, the capital of Mysore. The British army supported by Nizam's subsidiary army was under the command of Arthur Wellesley. Tipu Sultan had just 30,000 defenders matched against 50,000 attackers. On May 4, the British broke through the city walls. Tipu Sultan rushed to the breach, and was killed defending his city.

Results

Much of Tipu's territories were annexed by the British, the Nizam and the Marathas. The remaining core, around Mysore and Seringapatam, was restored to the Wodeyar dynasty, whose forefathers had been the actual rulers before Hyder Ali became the de facto ruler. The state of Mysore was brought under subsidiary alliance system.

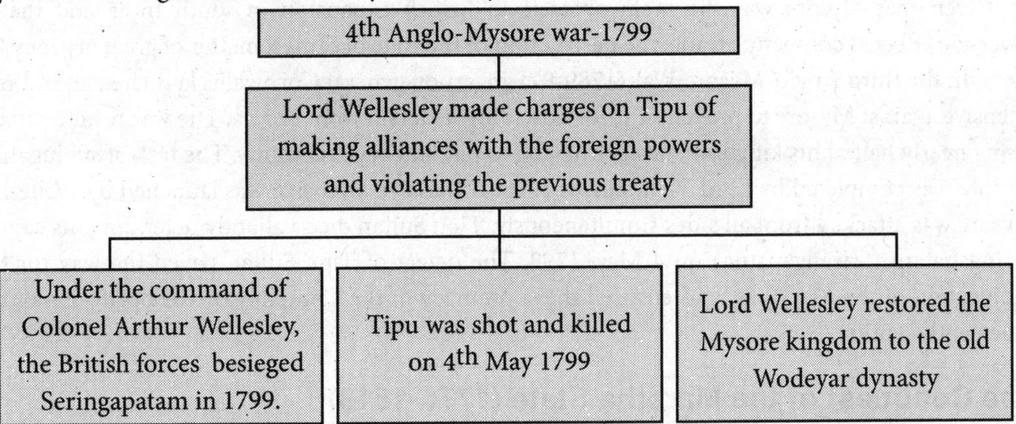

Mysore, under Hyder and Tipu Sultan, was a threat to the British in the second half of the 18th c. The Company had to engage in four large-scale wars (the four Anglo-Mysore wars) for over thirty years, from 1766 to 1799, to subjugate Mysore. The relentless struggle of Hyder Ali, and more so of Tipu Sultan, against the Company had assumed epic proportions and the contest between the British and Mysore became fierce.

Hyder Ali, in his life time waged two formidable wars against the British and defeated them, but Tipu Sultan lost the third and fourth wars and perished. His destruction came mainly on account of the administrative and economic measures that he introduced in his kingdom to augment and modernize the economy. His economic measures to make Mysore participate in foreign trade, attempts to commercialize the agriculture economy, building up of a navy, opening trade centres and emporia in west Asia, attempts to learn the secrets of Europe's progress and modernization-all went against British colonial interests in India and hence a grand plan by the British East India Company to liquidate him completely and dismantle the kingdom of Mysore and the infrastructure that was built by him. Napoleon Bonaparte, who was then in power in France, had just begun preparing for an invasion of Egypt, announcing his intention to significantly expand the French colonial empire in Africa and Asia. The possibility of an alliance between Tipu Sultan and Napoleon against the British was sought to be pre-empted by sending troops to invade Mysore in 1798.

Besides, Tipu Sultan was more aware than many of his contemporaries in Asia of trends in global politics. For this reason, he attempted to forge international alliances by sending embassies to Turkey and France. His relationship with France became more cordial after the revolution in which his sympathies lay with the Jacobins. He also became a member of the 'Jacobin Club' though it was a political move to enlist the support of France in his struggle against the British.

Mysore state controlled the profitable trade of the Malabar Coast from where British purchased spices. Tipu Sultan had blocked the exports of sandalwood, cardamom and pepper from the ports. He had also restricted the local merchants to trade with British. Tipu enjoyed his vast trade relations with the Durrani Afghans,the Ottoman Turks,the Ceylon kings, apart from those in the Indian Subcontinent This funnelled a lot of money into his coffers helping him fight the British in the third Mysore War.

Given that Mysore was the main obstacle to British expansion in south India and that it adversely affected company's trade, the destruction of the state became a matter of great urgency for them. In the third Anglo-Mysore War (1789-92) governor-general Cornwallis launched an indirect offensive against Mysore to prevent it from extending its territory in Kerala. The war resulted in his losing nearly half of his kingdom, besides having to pay a heavy indemnity. The task of subjugating Mysore was completed by Lord Wellesley in 1798. A massive offensive was launched by Wellesley. Mysore was attacked from all sides simultaneously. Tipu Sultan died valiantly defending his capital Seringapatam (Srirangapatna) on 4 May, 1799. The defeat of Tipu Sultan paved the way for the subjugation of the Marathas, and ensured the supremacy of the Company by the beginning of the nineteenth century.

The Conquest of the Maratha State (1776-1818)

The British intervention in the Maratha State in the mid eighteenth century was primarily driven by the commercial interests of the company in Gujarat and Bombay. This motivated the British to play a more interventionist role in the region. The volatile political situation among the Maratha chiefs paved a favourable ground for political intervention by the British. The conflicts between the Marathas and the British that took place from 1776 to 1818 are known as the Anglo-Maratha wars. The East India Company successfully annexed and conquered the territories of the Maratha chiefs through these wars.

Peshwa Madhav Rao (1761-1772)

After the debacle in the battle of Panipat, Peshwa Balaji Baji Rao died out of shock in 1761. He was succeeded by his son Madhav Rao, who was just a sixteen year old boy. His uncle Raghunathrao or Raghoba acted his regent until he came of age. Madhav Rao is considered as the last of the great Peshwas .

Under him the Marathas gradually recovered from the debacle of 1761. When Madhav Rao became Peshwa, the greatest danger to the Marathas came from the expanding powers of Nizam of Hyderabad and Hyder Ali of Mysore. He successfully subdued these powers. In 1763, Madhavrao defeated Nizam of Hyderabad at the battle of Rakshasbhuvan. He carried on a successful war against Hyder Ali of Mysore and subdued Rajputana and also demanded tribute. In a short period of eleven years, Madhav Rao did the magnificent work of recovering the lost Maratha territories and restoring once again the lost Maratha prestige and pride. Unfortunately in 1772, at the age of 28, Madhav Rao died all of a sudden. His untimely and sudden death came as a serious blow to Maratha people. In the untimely death of this great Peshwa began, the gradual decline and downfall of the Marathas. If he had not died so young he would have done wonders for the Marathas. Grant Duff rightly observes, 'the plains of Panipat were not more fatal to the Marathas empire than the early end of the excellent prince.'

The Maratha Confederacy

The Third battle of Panipat (1761) gave a severe blow to the mighty power of Marathas. After the battle, the young Peshwa Madhavrao brilliantly regained the Maratha power and prestige. But his sudden death in 1772 made the task of rebuilding Maratha power remains incomplete. The successors of Madhav Rao were weak and incompetent. Peshwa became a titular head and power was shared by Maratha chiefs of various confederacies. During the time of Peshwa Balaji Baji Rao, Maratha confederacy got consolidated. In a bid to effectively manage the large empire, semi-autonomy was given to the strongest Maratha *Sardars* or chiefs from the leading Maratha families. These leading Maratha families—Scindias, Holkars, Bhonsles, and Gaekwads—extended their conquests in northern and central India, and in the process became more independent. Consequently, the semi-autonomous Maratha states came into being in far flung regions of the empire. Five distinct Maratha ruling families, besides the ruler of Maharashtra i.e. the Peshwa came into prominence in the mid eighteenth century. These families took the shape of the Maratha confederacy by giving nominal allegiance to Peshwa.

The following is the brief description of the Maratha confederacy:

1. The Gaekwads of Baroda

The rule of the Gaekwad chiefs began when the Maratha general, Pilaji Rao Gaekwad, conquered Baroda from the Mughal Empire in 1721. The Gaekwads were granted Baroda as a fief by the Peshwa. After the rule of the Peshwas was weakened at the third battle of Panipat, the Gaekwads, along with several powerful Maratha clans, established themselves as virtually independent rulers of Baroda, only recognizing the nominal authority of the Peshwas.

2. The Holkars of Indore

The Holkar dynasty ruled over Indore in Central India as an independent member of the Maratha Empire. The dynasty was founded by Malhar Rao, who joined the service of the Peshwas in 1721, and quickly rose to the rank of Subedar. He was acknowledged as one of the five virtually independent rulers of the Maratha Confederacy. He was succeeded by Rani Ahilyabai Holkar (1767-1795), his daughter-in-law. Rani Ahilyabai was known for patronizing art and architecture in her state.

3. The Scindias of Gwalior

The Scindias were the rulers of the Gwalior State, which was a part of the Maratha Confederacy in the 18th and 19th centuries. The dynasty was founded by Ranoji Scindia. His successors include Jayajirao, Jyotibarao, Dattajirao, Jankojirao, Mahadji and Daulatrao Scindia. The Scindia state of Gwalior became a major regional power in the latter half of the 18th century. Ranoji Scindra's successor, Mahadji Scindra(1730 – 1794) was a great ruler of Scindra dynasty. He was a brilliant Maratha leader and as long as he was alive the Maratha power was at a height. He established the Maratha dominance in the northern India. In 1794, Mahadji Scindra died. Within a decade Maratha rule disappeared from the north of India because his nephew Dalulat Rao was not as good as his uncle. Through Mahadji Scindra, the treaty of Salbai in 1782 was negotiated.

4. **The Bhonsles of Nagpur**

The Bhonsles were the prominent ruling clan of the Maratha Empire. The most prominent member of this clan was Shivaji, the founder of the Maratha Empire. His successors ruled as Chhatrapatis from their capital at Satara. In addition to the Bhonsles of Satara, rulers of the Bhonsle clan established themselves at Nagpur in Maharashtra in the 18th century. Raghuji Bhonsle was the founder of this dynasty. There were eight rulers in the line and they were a leading power in the 18th-century Maratha confederacy.

First Anglo Maratha war (1776-1782)

Causes

The sudden death of Madhavrao Peshwa in 1772 caused a succession dispute. Narayanrao, the brother of Madhavrao, became Peshwa of the Maratha Empire. Though the new Peshwa was a competent man, he came under the influence of his infamous uncle Raghunathrao or Raghoba. Raghunathrao or Raghoba, assassinated him in a conspiracy. Owing to the absence of any legal heir, Raghunath Rao was declared the new Peshwa. However, he was opposed by a powerful lobby led by the great Maratha Statesman and chief minister, Nana Phadnavis (1742- 1800). Narayanrao's widow, Gangabai, gave birth to a posthumous son whose name was Madhav Rao Narayan. Nana Fadnavis lobbied with the Maratha leaders and declared Madhav Rao Narayan (1774-95) as the legal heir to the throne. Under the leadership of Nana Phadnavis, a Regency Council known as Barobhai was formed. The Regency Council took charge of the Maratha administration after removing Raghunathrao and nominating the minor son of Narayanrao, Madhav Rao Narayan, as the new Peshwa.

Under these circumstances, Raghoba felt weak and sought the help of the Bombay Government. The Bombay government found a golden opportunity in intervening in the internal feud of the Maratha kingdom. The Bombay government evaded the provisions of the Regulating Act, which had placed Bombay and Madras presidencies under the control of Governor-General of Bengal-in-Council, and made the treaty of Surat with Raghoba in on 6th March, 1775. In compliance with the treaty of Surat, Raghunathrao ceded the territories of Salsette and Bassein to the Bombay government, along with part of the revenues from Surat and Bharuch districts. In return, the British promised to provide Raghunathrao with 2,500 soldiers. The governor-general and the members of the council condemned this step of the Bombay Government. The group at Poona under the chief minister also condemned the treaty.

Governor General Warren Hastings wanted to consolidate control over the newly acquired province of Bengal at first, and then try expanding British trade in India, but the Company authorities in Bombay were not ready to lose this opportunity. They wanted to protect their commercial interest and continued to support Raghoba for Peshwaship. Warren Hastings was overruled by the majority in the council. The inevitable consequence of the Surat Treaty was the First Anglo-Maratha War. The company now had to wage a long and costly war with the Marathas and their ally Hyder Ali.

Events

The First Anglo-Maratha War began in 1776. The combined forces of the English under General Keating and Raghunathrao defeated the Maratha forces in the beginning. In 1779, the British army sent from Bombay was defeated by the Marathas. They were forced to surrender Raghoba and gave up all the territories acquired since the outbreak of hostilities. Warren Hastings however, did not approve this agreement between Marathas and Bombay government. He continued the war with the Marathas. Thus, the hostile relationship between the Bombay council and the Calcutta council made the war inevitable.

The war continued for seven years. The British were successful in putting pressure on the Maratha forces, led by Mahadji Scindia. However, due to Anglo-Mysore war against Hyder Ali, it became difficult for the British to continue wars on two different fronts against two formidable enemies. Moreover, Hastings was very apprehensive of the formation of an anti-English coalition by the Indian powers. Realizing the complexity of the situation, Hastings bribed Bhonsle of Nagpur to leave Maratha coalition. He proposed peace to Mahadji Scindia. Scindia accepted the proposal and accordingly the Treaty of Salbai was signed between the British and Marathas on 17th May, 1782.

According to the treaty, the British agreed not to give any further support to Raghunathrao and recognized the Peshwaship of Madhu Rao Narayan. The English company kept Salsette and Bassien with them. This treaty resulted in a peaceful period of twenty years for the Marathas and the British.

Significance of the Treaty of Salbai

Different views have been expressed regarding this treaty. Dr. Smith and Mr. Keene have regarded it as a landmark in the history of India. Smith says that the English became the controlling though not the paramount, power in India. However, many historians considered this treaty as no gain to British. They only got Salsette. This was a long and costly war with no material and strategic advantages. It only secured peace with the Maratha confederacy for about 20 years. Warren Hastings described the peace of Salbai as a, "Successful negotiation of peace in the most desperate period of his distress."

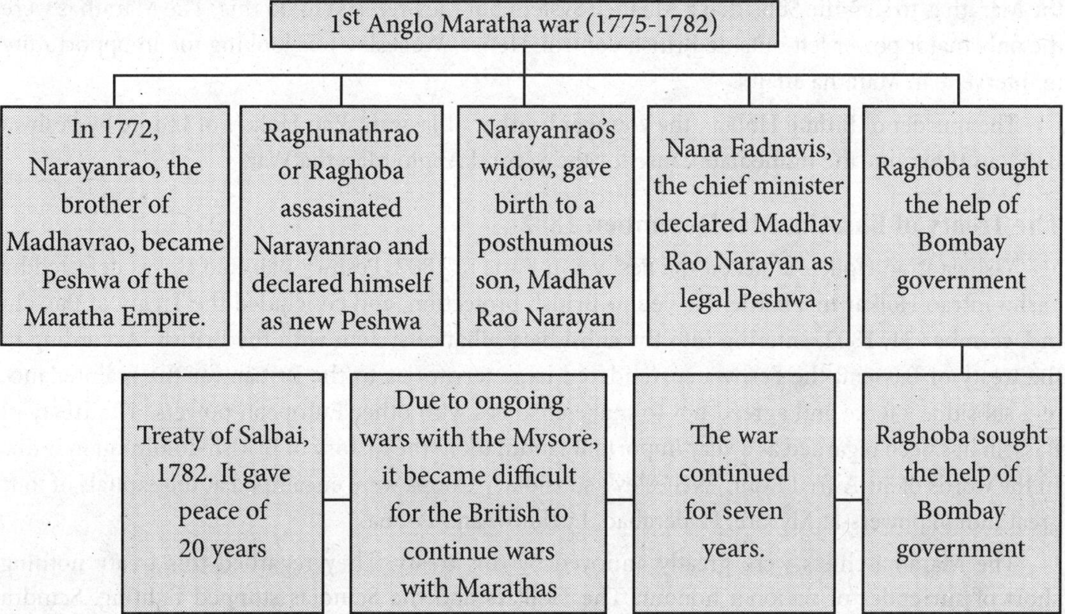

The Second Anglo-Maratha War (1803-1805)

Nana Fadnavis
— Wikimedia Commons

Nana Phadnavis (1742-1800) or Bạlaji Janardan Bhanu, was an influential minister and statesman of the Maratha Empire during the Peshwa administration in Pune. He was called 'the Maratha Machiavelli' by the Europeans. Nana Fadnavis practically ran the affairs of Maratha state. His position was opposed by Mahadji Scindia. In 1794, Mahadji Scindia died and thus Nana Fadnavis administered the Maratha affairs with undisputed authority.

The young Peshva Madhav Rao Narayan got impatient of the control of Nana Fadnavis and committed suicide. In 1796, Baji Rao II, who was son of the retired British nominee Raghunath Rao, was made next Peshwa who was hostile to Nana Fadnavis. In 1800, Nana Phadnavis died. According to Captain Palmer, 'in the death of Nana Fadnavis, departed all the wisdom and moderation in Maratha politics'. The unity in the Maratha confederacy began to disintegrate. The remaining Maratha veterans Yashwant Rao Holkar of Indore and Daulat Rao Scindia of Gwalior were hostile to each other.

The second Maratha war was fought in the time of imperialist governor general Lord Wellesley (1798-1805). The unity in the Maratha confederacy began to disintegrate. Daulat Rao Scindra and Jaswant Rao Holkar contested for power and wanted to control Peshwa Baji Rao II. Peshwa finally came under the influence of Scindra.

Cause

In 1798, Lord Wellesley became the new governor general. He was an imperialist and wanted the Marathas to sign the Subsidiary Alliance System but they refused to do this. The Marathas were the only major power left outside British control. Hence, Wellesley was looking for an opportunity to intervene in Maratha affairs.

The murder of Bithuji Holkar, the younger brother of Jaswant Rao Holkar of Indore by Peshwa Baji Rao II became the immediate cause for the Second Anglo Maratha War.

The Treaty of Bassein, 31st December, 1802

Yashwantrao Holkar attacked the Peshwa in Pune in 1802. Peshwa Baji Rao II was defeated by Yashwantrao Holkar in a battle. He fled to British protection, and concluded the Treaty of Bassein in December 31, 1802, entering into the subsidiary alliance system with the British. According to the treaty of Bassein, the Peshwa surrendered large territories to the British for the maintenance of a subsidiary force and agreed not to make alliances with other European powers. The treaty of Bassein has been regarded as a very important landmark in the history of British dominion in India. In the words of Sir Alfred Lyall, 'Wellesley's subsidiary troops were encamped at the capitals of four great Indian powers-at Mysore, Hyderabad, Lucknow and Poona.'

The Maratha chiefs were greatly annoyed by this treaty. They regarded this treaty nothing short of surrender of national honour. The Holkars and the Scindias stopped fighting. Scindra and Bhonsle combined but Holkar and Gaekwad remained aloof. Scindra and Bhonsle were asked by the English to withdraw troops to the north of the Narmada River but they refused. This led to war.

Events

The Second Anglo-Maratha War started in August, 1803. Under Major-general Arthur Wellesley and General Lake's aggressive war strategy, the Maratha forces were completely routed on every front. Scindia and Bhonsle were defeated by the British, and all the Maratha leaders lost large parts of their territory to the British. Raghuji Bhonsle II was compelled to sign the Treaty of Deogaon with the British. By the terms of the treaty, Bhonsle ceded Balasore and Cuttack of Orissa and the entire region in the western banks of the Wardha River to the British. On December 30, 1803, Daulat Rao Scindia signed the treaty of Surji-Arjangaon with the English. On 27th February, 1804, Scindia accepted the Subsidiary Alliance of the English. Thus the second Anglo- Maratha war ended with these treaties with Bhonsle and Scindra.

Significance of the War

The English gained heavily from the Second Maratha war. Munro exclaimed, 'we are now complete masters of India and nothing can shake our power, if we take proper measures to confirm it.' The two powerful Marathas, Scindia and Bhonsle, were completely crippled by the English. It cleared the path of English towards establishment of their political paramountcy over Indian states.

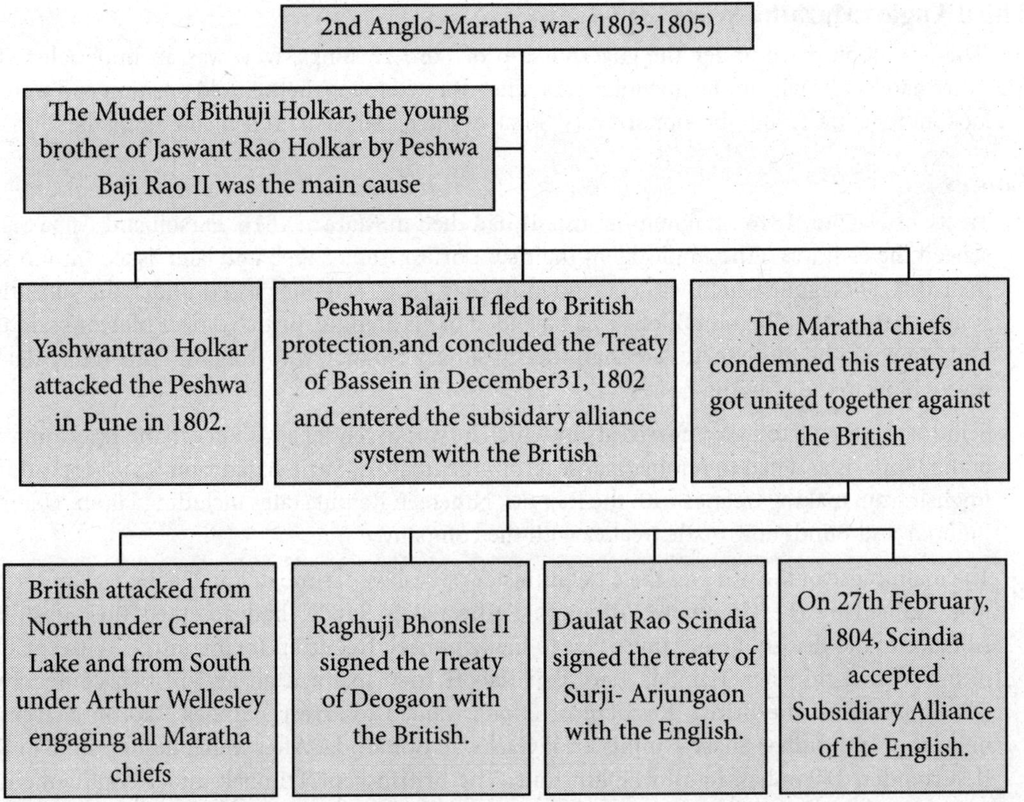

War with Holkar (1804-1806)

Jaswant Rao Holkar had not joined Scindra and Bhonsle but decided to exchange arms with the English. He formed an anti-British confederacy of the Indian powers and started a war against them. He plundered the territories of Jaipur and Wellesley declared war because Jaipur was an ally of the English. Holkar successfully defeated British generals like Col. Monson and Lord Lake. Jaswant Rao Holkar's success compelled the Court of Directors in London to direct Wellesley to leave India in 1805. The Court of Directors thought that the English Company's burden of debt had increased owing to the aggressive policy of Wellesley. Under these circumstances, Lord Cornwallis was sent to India in 1805 CE for a second time. He opened negotiations with the Marathas but Cornwallis died in Oct. 1805. Sir George Barlow came as the new Governor General in India, who followed a policy of non-interference. On January 7, 1806, Barlow signed a peace treaty with Holkar. Holkar gave up all claims to the territories north of the river Chambal. And British relinquished their claim over Kooch, Rampura, Bundelkhand, Tonk, Bundi, and many Rajput states. Gwalior was returned to Scindia.

Significance

Sir Barlowe's conciliatory policy had given the Marathas more than they expected. However, they could not attain much out of the contemporary messy situation. The Marathas were reaching their end and the countrywide empire of the Marathas was a thing of the past. They were now a hollow canopy. Only a jerk was needed to bring the downfall of Maratha confederacy. This happened after 15 years when the fourth and final Anglo Maratha war took place.

Third Anglo- Maratha War (1817-1818)

This war took place under the governorship of Lord Hastings, who was an imperialist. The Marathas had lost heavily in the previous wars. They wanted to regain their old position and were on the lookout for some favourable opportunity. Some of them had been even encouraging the Pindaris.

Causes

- Treaty of Nagpur, 1816 : Raghuji Bhonsle II had died in Marach 1816. Parsoji and Appa Saheb started the civil war . The English lent their support to Appa Saheb and later asked him to sign the treaty of Nagpur which was concluded in May 1816. Nagpur passed under the subsidiary system, a thing that Raghuji Bhonsle had avoided in his lifetime. British officer Malcom said that nothing could be more fortunate than the subsidiary alliance with Nagpur. This treaty dealt a severe blow to the Maratha power.
- Scindra was forced to sign a new treaty by which he was to render assistance in the extermination of the Pindaris and had to remove clauses from the treaty of Surji-Arjangaon which forbade the English from making treaties with the Rajputs. Nineteen Rajput states including Jaipur, Udaipur, Jodhpur and Bundi now made treaties with the company.
- The main cause of the war was the chief minister of Peshwa, Trimbak Rao Dabhade, a notorious man wanted by the Company. Although Peshwa Baji Rao II had accepted the Subsidiary Alliance of the British, he became eager to make himself free from their control. With the help of his trusted minister Trimbak Rao, Baji Rao II tried to form an anti-British confederacy. But Elphinstone, the British Resident of Poona wanted to arrest Trimbak Rao on charges of murder of Gangadhar Shastri, minister of Gaekwad of Baroda. After much hesitation, Baji Rao II surrendered Trimbak Rao to Elphinstone. The British kept Trimbak under confinement in

their fortress at Thana. This incident dealt a serious blow to the dignity of the Peshwa and he was out for revenge against the British. An attempt was made by the Peshwa to unite Maratha chiefs. Some Martha chiefs contacted the Pindaris, the Pathans and others to join them and strengthen their cause.

Events

The collective army of the Maratha chiefs attacked the British Residency at Poona and on 5th November, 1817, the Third Anglo-Maratha War began. Col. Burr collected forces and defeated Peshwa at Kirki in 1817. The Peshwa fled southwards and took with him the Raja of Satara. He was defeated at Koregaon and Ashti.

Appa Saheb Bhonsle in the meantime revolted at Nagpur but was defeated in the battle of Sitabaldi in 1817. Malhar Rao Holkar II's forces also revolted, but were defeated in the battle of Mahidpur, in Indore. He was compelled to sign the treaty of Mandsore.

Results

The Peshwa was eventually captured and placed on a small estate at Bithur, near Kanpur. He merely retained the title of Peshwa and given the pension of 8 lacs of rupees annually. Most of his territories were annexed and became part of the Bombay Presidency. The Maharaja of Satara was restored as the ruler of his territory as a princely state. In 1848, this territory was also annexed by the Bombay Presidency under the Doctrine of Lapse policy of Lord Dalhousie. The defeat of the Bhonsles and Holkars resulted in the acquisition of the Maratha kingdoms of Nagpur and Indore by the British. These chiefs were completely reduced to vassalage. Along with Gwalior from Scindia and Jhansi from the Peshwa, all of these territories became princely states acknowledging British control. Thus the whole Maratha confederacy was dissolved. The head of this confederacy was removed and other members were completely reduced to submission. They never again challenged the British. The breakup of the Maratha confederacy made the British the paramount power in India.

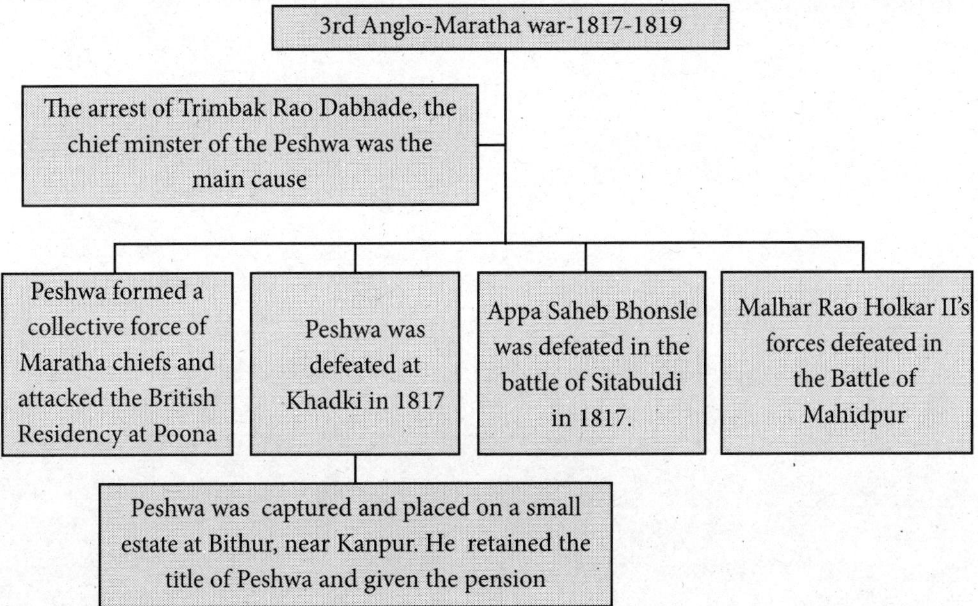

Previous Years' Questions

1. **How the East India Company did became the de jure power in India? (2009)**
2. **"The Battle of Plassey that decided the fate of Bengal was won by Clive through intrigues." Explain. (2014)**
3. **"Plassey did not complete the British conquest of India. Had the English been convincingly defeated in any subsequent battle in India, then (the battle of) Plassey would have remained as a minor episode in the history of India." (2014)**
4. **Why Mysore was considered a threat by the British to their possessions and mercantile interests in the south? Do You think that Tipu Sultan's posturing became his undoing? (2009)**
5. **The British "fought the First Maratha War in a period when their fortunes were at the lowest ebb". Comment. (1998).**
6. **"The Maratha polity disintegrated through internal stress." Critically examine. (2017)**

The British Conquest of Indian States (1818–1856)

Sindh

Strategic Importance of Sindh

Sindh occupies a strategic position of great importance. It is situated on the lower banks of the Indus River and extends to the Arabian Sea. It lay on the route from British India to Afghanistan through the Bolan Pass. During the opening years of the 19th century, Sindh was ruled by a number of Talpur tribes who had come from Baluchistan. The Amirs of Talpur dynasty ruled its most important states – the Khairpur, the Mirpur, and the Hyderabad. The Amir of Khairpur claimed nominal sovereignty over the other two kingdoms.

Anglo-Sindh Relations (1809–1843)

- **Relations with Amirs :** The relations with Amirs of Sindh started in the time of Lord Minto (1807–1813). During this time, the political situation in Europe was highly critical due to the Napoleonic Wars. Napoleon Bonaparte of France who was at the zenith of his power, defeated the Russians and came to terms with them by the Treaty of Tilsit in 1807. The British feared the French invasion of India. Hence, Lord Minto sent ambassadors to Afghanistan, Sindh, and Persia. A friendly treaty was made with the Amirs of Sindh in 1809 CE. The significant clause of the treaty was: They were not to permit French troops to pass through Sindh and were not to permit to settle in their territory.
- **Expansionist Policy of Ranjit Singh :** When Maharaja Ranjit Singh of Punjab started expanding his empire towards North-west, the British planned to annex Sindh and bring it under their influence. Both Ranjit Singh and the British wanted to have their control over Sindh. By controlling Sindh, Ranjit Singh wanted to have access to the sea trade.
- **Alexander Burnes Mission :** In 1831, Alexander Burnes went up the Indus River to go to Lahore with presents for Maharaja Ranjit Singh. The underlying idea was to know the commercial value of Sindh. When Burnes was passing through Sindh, a Sindhi remarked, 'Sindh is now gone, since the English **have** seen **the river...**'
- **Treaty of Friendship :** In 1832, the British made a treaty with the Amirs of Sindh. Accordingly, the river and roads of Sindh could be used by the merchants and traders of the Company, but no armed vessels or military stores were to be passed through Sindh.

- **British Resident at Hyderabad :** Ranjit Singh was again contemplating conquest of Sindh between 1834 and 1836. The Company practically took the Amirs of Sindh under its protection by warning Ranjit Singh. The Amirs in return for their protection reluctantly agreed to have a British resident at Hyderabad.
- **Policy of Lord Auckland towards Sindh :** The British policy under Lord Auckland (1836–42) towards Sindh sank to a low level. The British wanted to attack Afghanistan to replace Dost Muhammad by Shah Shuja on the throne of Kabul. A Tripartite Treaty was made between the English, Shah Shuja, and Ranjit Singh. Maharaja Ranjit Singh objected to the passing of British troops through Punjab. So it was decided by the British to march British troops through Sindh. It was in violation of the 1832 Treaty. Amirs were also asked to pay a large sum of money to Shah Shuja as a tribute. Amirs were not paying their tribute to Shah Shuja since his expulsion from Afghanistan. This was an unreasonable demand since in 1833, Shah Shuja had taken back all his claims from Sindh. Still, in 1839, Amirs were forced to pay three lakhs of rupees a year for the subsidiary force to be kept in Sindh. Sindh was made the base of operations for attacking Afghanistan.
- **Lord Ellenborough (1842–44) :** Under him, the First Afghan War was won. He decided to annex Sindh and wanted to find a pretext to achieve this object. He levelled a vague and a baseless charge of disaffection against the Amirs. In 1842, the sixty-year old General Sir Charles Napier (1782–1853) was sent with full civil and military powers. He soon made a new treaty and asked the Amirs to accept it. According to the new treaty, the Amirs were asked to cede some territory in lieu of subsidiary, to provide fuel to British steamers navigating the Indus, and to give up the right of coining money. This last provision amounted to loss of sovereignty and greatly shocked the Amirs.

Factors Influencing the British Policy Towards Sindh

Following were the three major factors that influenced the British policy towards Sindh:

- **Commercial value of River Indus :** British found River Indus highly valuable for their trade with Punjab and north-west India.
- **The expansion policy of Raja Ranjit Singh towards west :** There was a possibility that Sindh could be occupied by Ranjit Singh which they never desired.
- **The fear of French attack on India :** This fear induced the English to extend their frontiers in the north-west up to the natural boundary of India.

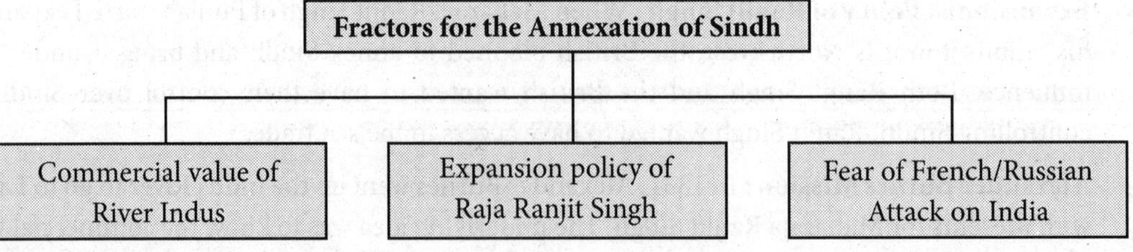

Annexation of Sindh, 1843

An angry mob attacked the British residency and the English declared war on the Talpur Amirs of Sindh in 1843 CE. Two battles were fought between the troops of Amirs and the English. These were: the Battle of Miani (February 1843) and the Battle of Hyderabad (March 1843).

General Sir Charles James Napier (1782–1853)

He was a general of the East India Company and the British Army's Commander-in-Chief in India. In 1842, at the age of 60, Napier was appointed Major General of the Indian army within the Bombay Presidency. Governor General Lord Ellenborough sent Napier to the Sindh Province for the purpose of quelling the insurrection of the Muslim rulers who had remained hostile to the British Empire following the First Anglo-Afghan War. Napier's campaign against these chieftains resulted in the Anglo-Sindh War. Two battles were fought –the Battle of Miani and the Battle of Hyderabad–that finally led to the subjugation of Sindh in 1843.

Regarding the annexation of Sindh, Napier wrote, "we have no right to seize Sindh, yet we shall do so, and a very advantageous, useful, humane piece of rascality it will be."

Annexation of Sindh was highly condemned both by pro-British historians and nationalist historians. The annexation of Sindh is considered as an act of high-handedness and an act of aggression by the British.

The Anglo-Sikh Relations

Raja Ranjit Singh (1780–1839) and Anglo-Sikh Relations (1800–1809)

Punjab was a part of the Afghan empire. In the late eighteenth century, the Sikhs began their struggle against the Afghans. They were divided into semi-autonomous confederations known as *misls*. Maharaja Ranjit Singh, born in 1780 in the Sukerchakia misl, united these *misls* and established the independent Sikh empire around 1799 with its capital Lahore. Ranjit Singh became Maharaja in 1801 and earned the title 'Sher-e-Punjab'.

Raja Ranjit Singh of Punjab — Wikimedia Commons

At its peak, the Sikh empire extended from the Khyber Pass in the west to western Tibet in the east, and from Mithankot in the south to Kashmir in the north. It was the last major region of the subcontinent to be conquered by the British.

Before 1799, no one could even dream that Ranjit Singh would become the master of Punjab. Within forty years, he created an extensive kingdom by his personal qualities. British historian Cunningham has rightly observed, 'Ranjit Singh found the Punjab a waning confederacy, a prey to the factions of its chief pressed by the Afghans and Marathas and ready to submit to English supremacy. He consolidated the numerous petty states into a kingdom, he wrested from Kabul its fairest provinces and gave the potent English no cause for interference.'

The most significant achievement of Raja Ranjit Singh was his successful defence of his kingdom against the Afghans. The North-west frontier, the Punjab and Kashmir, would have been lost to India but for Ranjit Singh. It was Ranjit Singh's superb Sikh army or military monarchy which saved these regions of India. The army created by Ranjit Singh was the toughest force which the British in India ever faced.

During his lifetime, Ranjit Singh did not interfere with the British policies. Ranjit Singh realised the British power and did not confront with them. Ranjit Singh's first contact with the English was established in 1800 with the Yusuf Ali Mission.

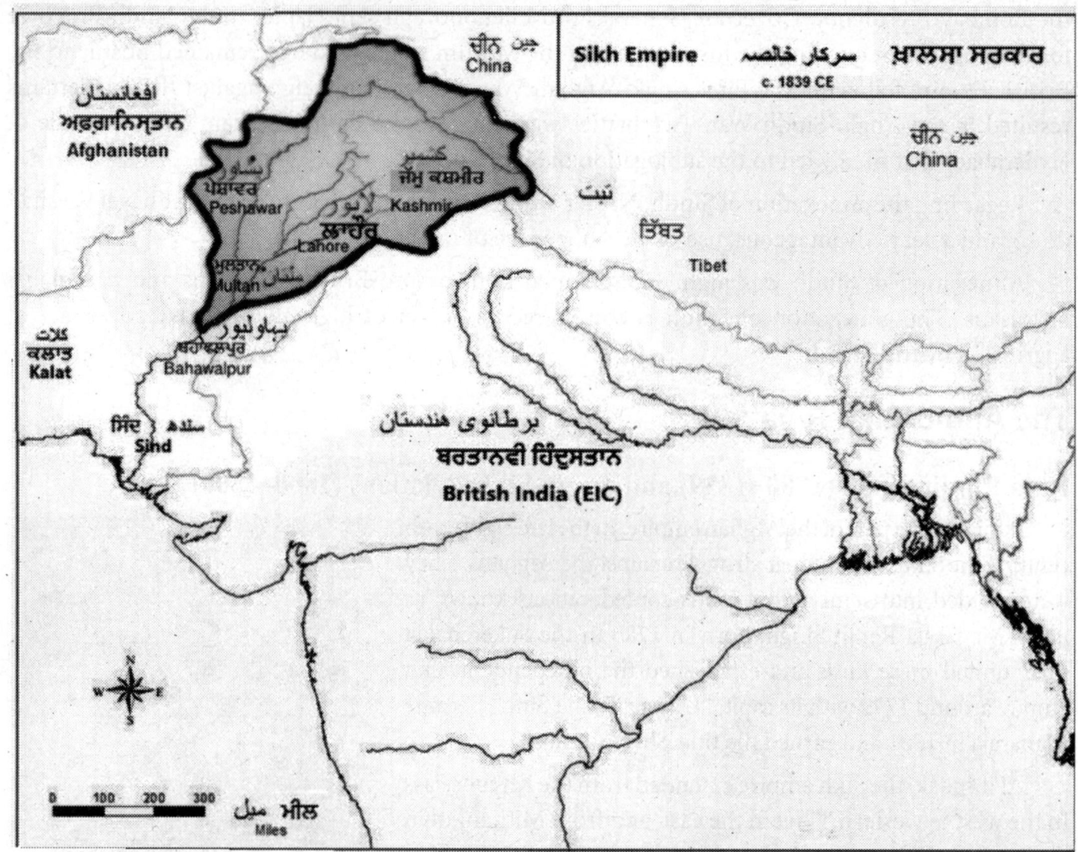

The boundaries of Sikh Empire under Maharaja Ranjit Singh — Wikimedia Commons

Yusuf Ali Mission (1800)

There were rumours that Afghan ruler Zaman Shah was preparing to attack India. The British began to feel anxious about the safety of their possessions. They sent Yusuf Ali with presents to request Ranjit Singh not to help Zaman Shah in case of an attack on India. Ranjit Singh accepted the English proposal but the situation soon changed. Zaman Shah soon got involved in domestic troubles in Afghanistan and the possibility of his invasion vanished. The English then recalled Yusuf Ali.

Agreement between Ranjit Singh and General Lake (1806)

The English came in closer contact with Ranjit Singh in 1805 on the issue of Maratha leader Jaswant Rao Holkar. Holkar who was defeated by the British during the Second Anglo-Maratha War had taken shelter in Punjab. General Lake came in his pursuit up to the river Beas. Ranjit Singh had gone to conquer Multan and Jhang, but came to Amritsar on learning about Holkar's arrival. Ranjit

Singh was advised not to come in conflict with the English by helping Holkar. Therefore, Ranjit Singh politely told Holkar that he would not be able to help him against the English. General Lake and Ranjit Singh concluded an agreement in January, 1806 CE.

Its terms were:

- Ranjit Singh was to force Holkar to leave Amritsar immediately.
- The British were to withdraw their troops from Punjab.
- The English were not to attack Ranjit Singh's territory if he remained friendly towards them.

Many scholars criticised Ranjit Singh for making such an agreement with the British.

But his policy of remaining friendly with the British is justified on the following grounds:

- Ranjit Singh was not strong enough to fight against the English at this time.
- He did not wish to make Punjab the battlefield for the Marathas and the English.
- Holkar was already defeated and an alliance with him would not have been useful.

Negotiations with Sir Charles Metcalfe (1807)

The agreement between Ranjit Singh and General Lake did not contain any clause regarding the eastern limit of the territory of Ranjit Singh. Therefore, Ranjit Singh continued his expeditions towards east, mainly in Malwa. The chiefs of Malwa requested the English for protection but did not get any help. Meanwhile, the strengthening position of Napoleon Bonaparte of France in Europe and fear of Franco-Russian invasion in India made the British to negotiate a friendly treaty with Ranjit Singh. Lord Minto, therefore, sent Sir Charles Metcalfe to negotiate the treaty. Sir Metcalfe put forward the terms of the treaty. Ranjit Singh, however, put two conditions. First, the British would not interfere in case he was involved in war with the Amir of Kabul. Second, he must have control over the Sikh State of Malwa. Metcalfe could not agree to the second condition and Ranjit Singh broke off the negotiations. Ranjit Singh led his third expedition into Malwa and captured many areas. Metcalfe protested but Ranjit Singh did not care.

The Treaty of Amritsar (1809)

Meanwhile, there was a change in European politics favourable to the British. In 1809 CE, Napoleon got involved in the Peninsular War and the fear of Franco-Russian attack vanished. The British attitude towards Indian rulers stiffened. In Punjab, Raja Ranjit Singh was a cause of worry to the British who continued to expand his empire towards east. Charles Metcalfe told Ranjit Singh that the territory up to the left bank of the river Sutlej had been under the protection of the Scindias before the Second Maratha War. These territories had come under the protection of the English when Scindia was defeated and renounced claim to the territory. At the same time, English troops marched to Ludhiana to make a demonstration of force. Ranjit Singh was conscious of his weak position and therefore, signed the Treaty of Amritsar in 1809 CE.

The clauses of the Treaty of Amritsar were as follows:

- River Sutlej became the boundary line between the territories of the British and those of Ranjit Singh. Ranjit Singh was not to acquire territories on the left bank of the River Sutlej.
- Ranjit Singh had a few places on the left bank of the river Sutlej. He was to keep only a limited number of troops to maintain peace there.

- The British were not to interfere in the affairs of Ranjit Singh, north of the river Sutlej.
- The British and the Maharaja were to maintain friendly relations with each other.

Significance of the Treaty of Amritsar

This treaty is of great historical significance. According to this treaty, Ranjit Singh was free to expand his kingdom to the west of river Sutlej and the British to the east of river Sutlej. Although the terms of the treaty prevented Singh from any further territorial expansion south of the Sutlej, they also permitted him complete freedom of action to the north of it. This enabled him to gain control of areas such as Peshawar and Kashmir. The Treaty of Amritsar was a diplomatic defeat for Ranjit Singh. He had a great desire to rule over all the Sikhs. The Treaty of Amritsar shattered his cherished dream of establishing a vast Sikh empire. He could not unite all the Sikhs under his flag.

According to Dr. N.K. Sinha, 'the Treaty of Amritsar was a diplomatic defeat for Ranjit Singh. He had to put his pride in the pocket and eat a humble pie ... his failure to absorb the cis-Sutlej states was a tragedy of Sikh militant nationalism and the success of the cis-Sutlej Sikhs with the date of the British government marked the disruption of the great creation of Guru Govind Singh.'

The treaty was advantageous to the British in several respects:

- **Victory from military and diplomatic points of view :** The demonstration of the British force at Ludhiana was one of the reasons which humbled down Ranjit Singh and made him sign the treaty. It greatly raised the prestige of the British in India.
- **Territorial gain :** The frontier of the British dominion in India was pushed from the Jamuna to the Sutlej River and the whole of Malwa came under their control.
- **It helped the British to make conquests elsewhere :** Now the English did not have to fear the hostility of the Sikh ruler and they could fearlessly wage wars in other parts of India. It enabled them to defeat the Gurkhas of Nepal and win the Third Maratha War.
- **It brought the British too near to Lahore :** The British, as a result of the treaty, came very near to Lahore and could easily watch the movements of Ranjit Singh and carry on intrigues. Their design on the Lahore kingdom became more definite and they were quite familiar with Punjab politics by the time of Ranjit Singh's death in 1839.

Ranjit Singh and Anglo-Sikh Relations from 1809–1839

The Anglo-Sikh relations were not friendly from 1809 up to 1812. Ranjit Singh considered the Treaty of Amritsar a humiliation for himself. However, he obeyed the terms of the treaty and did not expand his territories on the left bank of river Sutlej. He remained suspicious of British intensions. A small fort was built at Phillaur on the right bank of the Sutlej to serve as a watch tower, and it was under the charge of Mohkam Chand. He gave shelter to the deserters from the British forces.

The relations began to improve after 1812 and remained friendly with the British. The reason was that both sides were busy with their own affairs. The English were fighting against Nepal, Pindaris, Marathas, Burma, and Bharatpur. Ranjit Singh on the other hand, was busy conquering Multan, Derajat, Kashmir, and Peshawar.

After 1828, the British relations with Ranjit Singh began to get strained, though outward friendship was maintained.

Several events strained their relations:

- Syed Ahmed led the Afghan revolt in Peshawar from 1827 to 1831 against Ranjit Singh. The English did not help Syed Ahmed, but connived at the help given by its subjects. This was resented by Ranjit Singh.
- **Burn's Mission (1831) :** In the wake of fear of Russian invasion in central Asia, Alexander Burns went with presents from the King of England for Ranjit Singh. He travelled via the Indus River and told Lord William Bentinck about the importance of Sindh. Ranjit Singh wanted to discuss the question of Sindh with the British but William Bentinck refused even to consider this question.
- **British commercial treaty with the Amirs of Sindh :** In 1832, Lord William Bentinck made a commercial treaty with the Amirs of Sindh but kept Ranjit Singh in the dark. Ranjit Singh regarded this as the beginning of British influence over Sindh.
- **Sikh forces made to withdraw from Shikarpur :** Ranjit Singh wanted to get Shikarpur due to its great commercial importance. A tribe living near Shikarpur occupied the Sikh outpost. The Sikhs captured Shikarpur but the British forced Ranjit Singh to withdraw his troops from there.
- **British occupation of Ferozepore :** The British occupied Ferozpore in 1835 and built a cantonment after three years.
- **Tripartite Treaty :** Ranjit Singh, the English, and Shah Shuja of Afghanistan made a tripartite Treaty with the object of removing Dost Muhammad from the throne of Kabul and giving it to Shah Shuja. Ranjit Singh did not agree to let British troops pass through Sindh.

Anglo-Sikh Wars

The First Anglo-Sikh War (1845–1846)

After Ranjit Singh's death in 1839, there was chaos and confusion in Punjab. Finally, his youngest son, Duleep Singh, was put on the throne with Rani Jindan, his mother, as his regent. This political instability in Punjab offered an ideal opportunity to the British to conquer Punjab. Two Anglo-Sikh Wars took place. The first war took place in 1845 and lasted till 1846.

Following are the causes of the First Anglo-Sikh War:

- **British policy of encirclement :** The British had been following a policy of encirclement since 1830. The Sikhs had occupied Shikarpur and the British had forced Ranjit Singh's troops to withdraw from there. The Amirs of Sindh were forced to have a British resident at Hyderabad in 1838. Thus, a barrier had been created against Sikh expansion in Sindh. In Punjab, British occupied Ferozepore in 1835 and established a cantonment in 1838. The Sikhs felt that this policy of encirclement was being followed by the British with the ultimate idea of conquering Punjab.
- **Annexation of Sindh :** The Sikhs resented the British annexation of Sindh in 1843.
- **British military preparations :** The British, after the death of Ranjit Singh, began to increase the strength of their forces near the river Sutlej. The Sikhs resented these military preparations of the British.

- **Appointment of new resident Major Broadfoot at Ludhiana :** Clark was succeeded by Major Broadfoot as the British resident at Ludhiana. He was a hot-headed man and declared that the territories of the Sikhs on the left bank of the Sutlej were under the protection of the Company. The Sikhs were irritated and felt that war with the British was inevitable.
- **Anarchy in Punjab and the policy of Sikh Durbar :** There was anarchy in Punjab after the death of Ranjit Singh in 1839. First, his son Kharak Singh succeeded but died in 1840. Naunihal Singh, the son of Kharak Singh, was put on the throne but died from an accident. Sher Singh, another son of Ranjit Singh, got the throne with the help of the Khalsa army. Sher Singh was murdered. Finally, Duleep Singh, the youngest son of Ranjit Singh, was put on the throne with his mother Rani Jindan appointed as his regent. Lal Singh and Teja Singh became ministers. The Khalsa army had become very powerful and dangerous to Lahore Durbar. The Sikh Sardars encouraged the army to attack British territories hoping that the victory of the Khalsa army would divert its attention.
- The Khalsa army, encouraged by Lahore Durbar, crossed the river Sutlej. Thereupon, Lord Hardinge declared war and proclaimed the annexation of Sikh territories on the left bank of the Sutlej.

Four fierce battles were fought between the British and the Sikhs. These were the Battle of Mudki, Battle of Ferozeshah, Battle of Aliwal, and Battle of Subraon. The East India Company army was commanded by Sir Hugh Gough, the Commander-in-Chief of the Bengal Army, and was accompanied by Sir Henry Hardinge, the British Governor General of Bengal. The Sikh army was commanded by Tej Singh and Lal Singh.

The Sikhs fought with the valour of heroes, the enthusiasm of crusaders and the desperation of zealots. The British forces crossed the Sutlej and occupied Lahore. The war concluded with the Treaty of Lahore being signed on 9th March, 1846. The English army occupied Lahore and dictated the terms.

Treaty of Lahore

The following were the provisions of the Treaty of Lahore:

- The territories lying to the south of the river Sutlej were given to the Company.
- The Sikh committed to pay 1.5 crore rupees to the Company as war indemnity.
- The Company was given control over the mountainous areas between the Beas and the Indus River, which included Kashmir and Hazarah.
- Rani Jindan Kaur was made the Regent of the State and Lal Singh was appointed the *Wazir* of the Maharaja Duleep Singh.
- The treaty also limited the Sikh army to a specified number.
- Sir Henry Lawrence was appointed as the Resident of Lahore.
- The British imposed a heavy war indemnity amounting one and half crores rupees on the Lahore Durbar.

Lord Hardinge did not annex Punjab due to following reasons:

- The existence of a Hindu state between Afghanistan and British India would have been advantageous to the company.
- A lot of money was required for spending on the newly acquired province.
- The English had some regard for the memory of Raja Ranjit Singh who had been faithful throughout.

The Second Anglo-Sikh War (1848–49)

This war was fought in the time of Lord Dalhousie.

The Second Anglo-Sikh War took place between 1848 and 1849 CE. The interference of the British through the British resident became the cause of the war. However, the immediate cause was the rebellion of Mulraj, Governor of Multan, against the Company. This provided the new Governor General, Lord Dalhousie, a chance to interfere in the affairs of Punjab and annex Punjab to the British Empire. This war was the most dreadful and fiercest war that the British had to fight in India.

Let's study the causes of Second Anglo-Sikh War in brief:

- **Humiliation of the First Sikh War :** The Sikhs considered their defeat in the first war a great humiliation. The Sikhs wanted to restore the fallen fortunes of their kingdom.
- **Treatment meted out to Rani Jindan :** Rani Jindan was suspected of having intrigued against the British at Lahore. She was exiled to Benaras. Her pension was reduced, and she was kept on a strict watch by the British. This was very much resented by the Sikhs.
- **Revolt of Mulraj :** Mulraj became the governor of Multan in 1844. He was asked by the Lahore Durbar to pay the succession duty of thirty lakhs. He expressed his inability to pay that amount. To escape the huge payment to be made to the British, Mulraj expressed his willingness to resign, but the British resident did not accept his demand. In Multan, the soldiers murdered two British officers who had come to replace Mulraj with the new governor. Soon, many joined the rebels including the veterans of the First Sikh War. Thus, the general uprising of the Sikhs started. Lord Dalhousie declared war on the Sikh state.

Two major battles were fought, one at Chillianwala in 1849 and the other in Gujarat (Punjab). In the Battle of Chillianwala, the British suffered heavy losses. Sir Hugh Gough who commanded the British army was criticised for his strategy and it was decided to send Sir Charles Napier to supersede him.

The Second Battle at Gujarat, under the command of Sir Charles Napier, was decisive. Afghans, under the leadership of Akram Khan, the son of Dost Muhammad, joined the battle on the side of the Sikhs. The Battle of Gujarat is called the 'Battle of Guns' due to the heavy use of guns. After this battle, Punjab was annexed by Lord Dalhousie on 29th March, 1849. Duleep Singh, the minor son of Ranjit Singh, and his mother, Rani Jindan, were pensioned off and sent to England, and the British took away the famous Kohinoor diamond.

Sir John Lawrence became the first Chief Commissioner of Punjab to look after the administration of Punjab. Therefore, Punjab became a British province. Patiala and some other small states retained their rulers after recognizing the sovereignty of the British.

Annexation of Punjab has been bitterly criticised by many English scholars on the following grounds:

- The English permitted the Multan rebellion to spread. They wanted it to become a general uprising of Sikhs to find an excuse to annex Punjab.
- Lahore Durbar had not taken part in the uprising.
- The conduct of the British was responsible for provoking Mulraj, the Governor of Multan.
- The murder of two British officers at Multan was no justification for annexation.

Till Raja Ranjit Singh's death in 1839, the British followed a non-interference policy with the state of Punjab. However, within ten years of following Raja Ranjit Singh's death, Punjab was annexed by the British. The annexation of Punjab to British dominions in India in 1849 by Lord Dalhousie finally put an end to the sovereignty of the Sikhs over north-western India. It was the last of the Indian states to be included in British dominion. Internal dissensions and unstable political conditions gave Lord Dalhousie a pretext to wage a final war on Punjab.

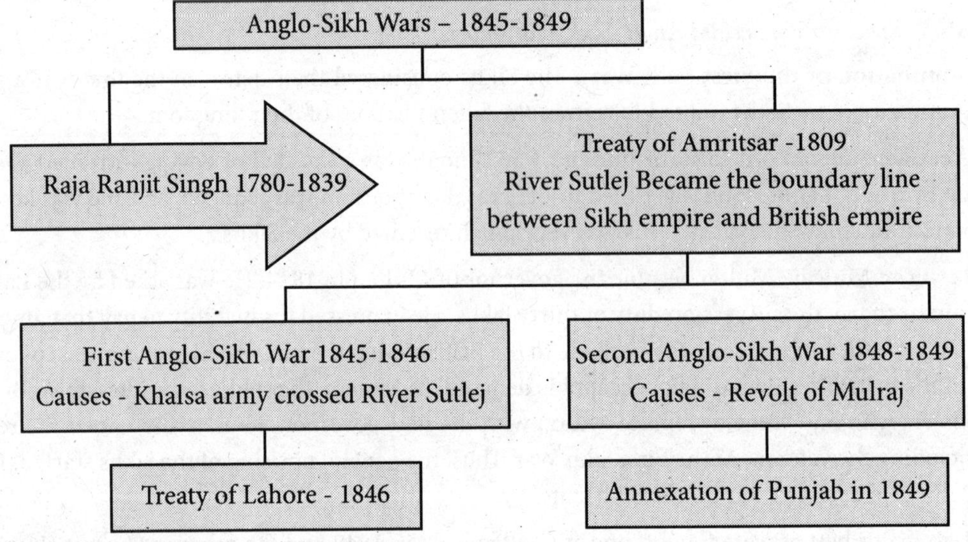

Conquest of Burma (1824–1885)

The British came in conflict with the Burmese government thrice in the 19th century. These three conflicts resulted in the defeats of the Burmese and the whole of Burma passed into British hands. Burma remained a part of India till 1937, when it became a separate country. Britain used Burma as a buffer zone between India and the rest of Asia.

First Burma War (1824–1826)

This war took place during the tenure of Lord Amherst. He was compelled to wage war against Burma when the ruler of Burma occupied many Indian territories of north-eastern regions.

The north-eastern frontier was very important for the British Empire for its territorial expansion. The eastern boundary of Bengal, in which the district of Chittagong was included, was very 'ill-defined and variable'. The Burmese rulers had conquered all the independent states of

Arakan, Pegu, and Tenasserim and unified Burma with the capital Ava. By the beginning of the 19th century, Burmese were conquering and annexing the British territory of eastern Bengal. In 1813, the Burmese pushed their frontiers up to Surma valley. The advance of the Burmese on the Chittagong frontier made an ultimate collision with the British inevitable. When the British were engaged with the large-scale campaign against Marathas and Pindaris, the King of Ava in 1818 sent a letter to Lord Hastinge demanding the surrender of Chittagong, Dacca, Murshidabad, and Kasim Bazar.

In 1822 CE, Burmese General Maha Bandula, captured Assam. Manipur was also captured by the Burmese. Lord Amherst tried to establish peace with the Burmese, but the Burmese government did not pay any attention. War became inevitable. Lord Amherst declared war on March 5, 1824.

In the war, the British government decided to be defensive. The main blow was to be struck by sea on Rangoon. Rangoon was captured on 11th May, 1824. Negotiations for peace started and in 1826, the Treaty of Yandabo was concluded.

Its most important provisions were the following:

- The Burmese government had to pay a heavy war indemnity.
- The Burmese gave the provinces of Arakan and Tenasserim to the British.
- The Burmese were not to interfere in Assam, Cachar, Jaintia, and Manipur. These places, thus, passed under the control of the Company.
- A commercial treaty was to be concluded between the Company and the Burmese government.
- A British resident was to be posted at Ava.

The First Burma War put an end to Burmese aggression. The rich provinces of Arakan and Tenasserim were secured. Assam, Cachar, Jaintia, and Manipur came under the British control.

Second Burma War (1852–1853)

The Second Burma War was fought in the time of Lord Dalhousie in 1852. The following were the causes:

- Lord Dalhousie feared that France or some other European power might establish itself in Burma.
- The English merchants were ill-treated by the Burmese government. They complained to Lord Dalhousie about the bad treatment meted out to them by the Burmese government. Dalhousie wanted an excuse to go to war with Burma. He took up the cause of the English traders. He captured a ship belonging to the Burmese King. This led to the exchange of gunfire and Lord Dalhousie declared war.

The British forces were sent under General Godwin. Martaban and Rangoon were captured. This was followed by the occupation of Prome. Thus, the whole of Lower Burma fell into the hands of the British in the Second Burma War. The Upper Burma was cut off from the sea. The Second Burma War is condemned by many. Lord Dalhousie is criticised for his act of annexing Lower Burma without any strong reasons.

Third Burma War (1885)

This war was fought in the time of Lord Dufferin. The following are the important causes:

- Upper Burma was still independent. The Burma King was anti-British and adopted a stern attitude towards them.
- The Burma King began commercial treaties with the French government. France was trying to establish influence in Upper Burma. Lord Dufferin wanted to root out any possibility of French influence by occupying Upper Burma.
- The King of Burma imposed a heavy fine on Bombay Burmah Trading Corporation and imprisoned its officers. Lord Dufferin sent an ultimatum making certain demands but it was rejected by the King. It led to war.
- The Burmese were not prepared for the war. The British forces made a swift attack. The Burmese were defeated. Their King was sent to India and Upper Burma was annexed.

Previous Years' Questions

1. **Annexation of Punjab was part of a broad formation after the exit of Maharaja Ranjit Singh." (2015)**
2. **Briefly trace the relations of Maharaja Ranjit Singh with the English from 1800 to 1809.**

   Solution : See under Anglo-Sikh Relations
3. **"Punjab's fate after Ranjit Singh was foredoomed as the impulse of neo-Victorian Imperialism was bound to overwhelm it". Elucidate. (2010)**

   Solution : Briefly write about the Anglo-Sikh relations during the time of Raja Ranjit Singh and discuss the Anglo-Sikh wars.
4. **Sir Charles Napier said, "We have no right to seize Sind, yet we shall do so, and a very advantageous, useful, humane piece of rascality it will be." Comment. (2000)**

5 CHAPTER

British Paramountcy Rule In India and Their Relations Towards Indian States

Paramountcy Policies of the British

The East India Company's rule in India began effectively after the conquest of Bengal. However, more than governance, the main interest of the Company in India was territorial expansion and commercial gains. These imperial interests were vividly reflected in the policies adopted by its Governor-Generals towards Indian states.

The Policy of Ring Fence (1765–1813)

In its initial period of consolidation from 1757 to 1813, the primary concern of the East India Company was to safeguard its territories. Therefore, the Company adopted a policy of keeping friendly or buffer states on the borders of its territory. The Company undertook to defend the territories of friendly Indian states, but did not interfere in their internal administration. The rulers of the states were considered sovereigns and the Company negotiated treaties with them on a footing of equality. The defence of the neighbouring states was the defence of their own territory. William Lee-Warner, British Historian and Civil Servant, had called this policy as the 'Policy of Ring Fence'. Under this policy, the Company was not concerned with what happened to the native states outside the Ring Fence.

The Company was not yet strong enough to interfere in the internal affairs of the Indian states. More specifically, the English Company neither had the strength nor the resources to defeat the Indian states. It was still not the only important power in India; the Marathas, the Nizams, and the French were the other powers.

The English had become de facto masters of Bengal as a result of the Battle of Plassey in 1757. In another battle in 1764, the Battle of Buxar, the Company became the *de jure* ruler of Bengal, Bihar, and Orissa. Clive came as a Governor of Bengal for a second time, and soon made the Treaty of Allahabad in 1765. Oudh was returned to Nawab Shuja-ud-Daula. The Company undertook the defence of Oudh and the Nawab was to pay for the expenses of the British troops stationed in his territory. This was done to safeguard the Company's possessions in the newly acquired provinces of Bengal and Bihar. The defence of Oudh was to be the defence of the Company's possessions in northern India. The sovereignty of Oudh's Nawab in internal affairs was not interfered with. Thus, Oudh became a protected state or a buffer state between the Company's possessions in northern India and the Maratha territories in northern India.

To safeguard the Company's southern possessions, the defence of Carnatic became crucial. The struggle with the French in the Deccan had resulted in the establishment of Muhammad Ali on the throne of Carnatic in 1754. The defence of the Carnatic was to be the defence of Madras. Carnatic became a Ring Fence State from Madras. It became a protected State or Buffer State between Madras and Mysore. In 1799, Tipu Sultan was killed. Considerable territories of this kingdom were annexed. The new ruler of Mysore, Krishna Rao, accepted the Subsidiary System. As a result, Carnatic was no more needed as a Ring Fence State and was annexed by Wellesley in 1801 CE. Mysore itself became a protected state between the Company's possessions on the Coromandel Coast and the Maratha territories in the Deccan.

Defects of Ring Fence Policy

The policy of Ring Fence had the following defects:

- The Company from the military point of view had to start a war without having secured efficient allies. In 1789, Tipu Sultan attacked the state of Travancore, an ally of the Company. Lord Cornwallis was forced to make alliance with the Nizam and the Peshwa in 1790. Treaties of friendship and alliance were concluded with rulers of Coorg in 1790 and Cochin in 1791, taking them under British protection for securing their cooperation against Tipu. When Tipu was defeated, half of his territory was taken away and divided among the English, Marathas, and Nizam.
- Sometimes two powers, both friendly to the English, came into conflict with each other. The relations of the Company with the Nizam were more intimate and older than the Marathas. In 1789, Cornwallis had agreed to help the Nizam, except when he was at war with a power in alliance with the Company. In 1775, the Marathas demanded Chauth and went to war with the Nizam. Sir John Shore refused to help the Nizam on the grounds that the Marathas were on friendly terms with the Company. He was defeated by the Marathas in 1795 at Kharda that resulted in a strained relationship between the Nawab and the English. The Nawab began to employ the French to train his troops.

Ring Fence Policy Under Robert Clive or Lord Clive (1725−1774)

Robert Clive, the founder of the British Empire in India, used foul and fair means to promote the interests of the Company. He is credited with establishing Company rule in the south and in Bengal. Clive served as Governor of Bengal twice. In his first governorship from 1757 to 1760, Clive subdued the power of the Mughal ruler, the Nawab of Oudh, and made the Nawab of Bengal a puppet in the hands of the English. Clive made a settlement with Nawab Shuja-ud-Daula of Oudh and the Mughal Emperor Shah Alam II through the Treaty of Allahabad in 1765. With this treaty, the Nawab of Oudh not only became a dependent ally of the Company, but it also became a friendly buffer state between the Company's possessions in northern India. Moreover, Clive secured Diwani of Bengal, Bihar, and Orissa which made the position of the English legal in those provinces. East India Company's position now became *de jure*. Clive showed great wisdom in not annexing Oudh but making it only a dependent state. Clive decided not to annex Oudh for reasons such as the lack of enough administrators to govern a big province like Oudh, and the opposition of the Directors of the Company for acquiring new territories. He made the titular Mughal Emperor a prisoner of the Company by making him the Company's pensioner.

Ring Fence Policy Under Warren Hastings (1772–1785)

Warren Hastings, National Portrait Gallery London — Wikimedia Commons

If Clive was the founder of the British Empire in India, Warren Hastings was its organiser. Under him, the rule of the Company strengthened. Warren Hastings served as Governor of Bengal from 1772 to 1774. Later, with the passing of the Regulating Act of 1773, he became the Governor-General of Bengal from 1774 to 1785. However, the Regulating Act of 1773 had created a Council that was hostile to the Governor-General of Bengal, and very often he was forced to act against his wishes.

Ring Fence policy was continued by Warren Hastings and friendship with Oudh was strengthened by the Treaty of Banaras in 1773.The treaty was signed between the Nawab of Oudh and Warren Hastings to help the Nawab defeat the Rohillas who were considered a threat to Oudh. The combined forces of Oudh and the Company defeated the Rohillas and Rohilla territory was plundered by the Nawab's forces. Warren Hastings conferred the conquered territories on the Nawab of Oudh instead of retaining them.

Warren Hastings accepted the proposal of waging war against Rohillas for two reasons. Firstly, he wanted to strengthen the position of the buffer state of Oudh against the Marathas. He found that if Oudh is strengthened, the Company's territories will remain secured from the Marathas in northern India. Second, the Nawab had promised to pay forty lakhs of rupees to the Company in the war against Rohillas. The Company was in need of money. However, Warren Hastings' Rohilla War was heavily criticised by historians and it became a main issue of Warren Hastings' impeachment in 1786. Warren Hastings' attack on the Rohillas was criticized as an unnecessary interference in the affairs of native states. This was against the policy of the Company. Eventually, Warren Hastings resigned and left India in 1785.

Warren Hastings, confronted with the task of safeguarding British territories, generally followed the policy of a Ring Fence in his wars against the Marathas and Mysore. The Pitt's India Act of 1784 laid down that the Home Government should not approve of the intervention of her officers in India in the internal affairs of the Indian states. When the Bombay government entered into the Treaty of Surat in 1775 with Raghunath Rao in the First Anglo-Maratha War, the Bengal government under Warren Hastings did not approve this step of the Bombay Government. But still, Warren Hastings wanted to attain peace on honourable terms. Bombay government's army got defeated by the Marathas and they were compelled to surrender all the acquired territories. To save the prestige of the Company, Warren Hastings continued the war that resulted in the capture of lost territories. Warren Hastings bribed Bhonsle to break the coalition of Indian power against the British. This Indian coalition included the biggest powers like Hyder Ali of Mysore and the Nizam of Hyderabad. Separate peace was made with Scindia who persuaded the Marathas to come to terms with the English. Hence, this resulted in the Treaty of Salbai in 1782 which saved the English from further conflict with the Marathas. It gave peace for twenty years between the Marathas and the British. According to the treaty, the British retained the forts of Broach and Salsette.

Warren Hastings saved the vulnerable position of the Company in the Second Anglo-Mysore wars in which Hyder Ali, and later Tipu Sultan, fought with great determination against the British. In a critical situation, when Hyder Ali defeated English forces, Warren Hastings signed the Treaty of Salbai with the Marathas in 1782. This left Hyder Ali alone without any help from the Marathas. Meanwhile, Hyder Ali died but the war continued under his son Tipu Sultan, with equal strength and aggression. Warren Hastings was forced to come to terms with Tipu Sultan and signed the Treaty of Mangalore in 1784. By signing of this Treaty of Mangalore, Warren Hastings, in fact, saved the British from Tipu's assault, who with the help of the French, would have ended the British dominion in India.

However, these two wars, i.e., Second Anglo-Mysore War and First Maratha war, proved very costly to the Company, and Warren Hastings adopted unfair methods to get money. This involved him in difficulties with the Raja Chait Singh of Banaras. The Raja of Banaras was a fuedatory of the Nawab of Oudh. In a treaty of 1775, it was agreed that the Raja of Banaras would pay an annual tribute of rupees twenty-two lakhs to the Company. But Warren Hastings extracted a huge amount of additional money from the Raja without the Company's knowledge. He violated the treaty of 1775 in which it was stated that the Raja Chait was to pay only twenty-two lakh rupees annually as revenue to the Company and no extra demand of money were to be made.

Some British Governor-Generals and Their Annexation Policies

Lord Cornwallis (1738–1805)

Lord Cornwallis succeeded Hastings as the Governor-General of India, after Sir John Macpherson became the temporary Governor-General in the interim. Lord Cornwallis is best known for his reforms. According to historian Jerry Dupont, Cornwallis was responsible for "laying the foundation for British rule throughout India and setting standards for the services, courts and revenue collection that remained remarkably unaltered almost to the end of the British era."

Lord Cornwallis – National Portrait Gallery, London — Wikimedia Commons

The major reforms for which Lord Cornwallis is known are in the areas of the judiciary and revenue administration. He abolished the old system of giving land to the highest bidder and introduced the Zamindari system or the Permanent Settlement system. We will study Cornwallis' reforms in detail in the ensuing chapter.

Cornwallis followed a relatively less expansionist policy. He had been sent to India with instructions to avoid conflict with the native states. With the notable exception of the Third Anglo-Mysore War, Cornwallis managed to keep the Company out of military conflicts during his tenure. According to Pitt's India Act of 1784, the Governor-General could wage only a defensive war. However, Cornwallis could not adhere to the Company's policy of non-interference in the case of Mysore. Tipu Sultan, the ruler of Mysore, was hostile to the English and had strengthened his alliance with the French. Cornwallis made an alliance with the Nizam and made a defensive attack on Tipu Sultan of Mysore. The British defeated Tipu Sultan and signed the Treaty of Seringapatam, by virtue of which half of the dominion of Tipu was taken away and divided among the British, the Marathas, and the Nizam.

Sir John Shore (1751–1834)

Sir John Shore succeeded Lord Cornwallis as Governor-General of India in 1793 and remained in office till 1798. He rigidly followed the policy of non-interference. It consisted of non-interference into the internal affairs of the native states. The Marathas took advantage of this and attacked the Nizam in 1795. The Nizam requested the English for help but Sir John Shore did not agree to help him. The Nizam, being dissatisfied with the Company policy, began to employ French officers to train his troops. Thus, the policy of non-interference followed by Sir John Shore proved to be a total failure for the Company. Major native powers like the Nizam, the Marathas, and Tipu used this policy to their advantage and strengthened their relationship with the French. The French influence in the courts of these rulers increased and the English began to seem like a decaying power. As a result, Sir John Shore was called back in 1798 CE.

Lord Wellesley (1760–1842) – The Subsidiary Alliance System

The next large-scale expansion of British rule in India occurred during the Governor-Generalship of Lord Wellesley (Marquess Wellesley) who came to India in 1798. The tenure of Lord Wellesley is especially significant in the consolidation of British power in India. During this period, France under Napoleon Bonaparte, was a great threat to the British Empire. Thus, Wellesley reversed the erstwhile policy of non-intervention, adopting an aggressive policy intended to remove all French influence in India and to make the British the paramount power.

Lord Wellesley
— Wikimedia Commons

Non-intervention policy had lowered the prestige of the British in India and the French began to increase their influence in the court of Indian rulers and encouraged the British enemies – the Nizam, the Marathas and Tipu Sultan of Mysore. Wellesley realized the gravity of the French influence and decided to combat it. To achieve his political aims, Wellesley relied on three methods – the system of Subsidiary Alliance, outright war, and the assumption of the territories of previously subordinate rulers. The direct conquest on Indian states was carried out by taking over the entire administration of the kingdom and leaving the ruler with the title and pension.

Wellesley, however, was known largely for introducing the Subsidiary Alliance System. This system was an alternative to direct annexation. Under Subsidiary Alliance system, the rulers of the allying Indian states were compelled to accept a British force within their territory and to pay a subsidy for its maintenance. This alliance also provided that the Indian ruler would agree to the posting of a British Resident in his court, would not employ any European in his service without the approval of the British, and would not negotiate with any other Indian ruler without consulting the Governor-General. In return, the British would defend the ruler from his enemies. In reality, by signing a Subsidiary Alliance, an Indian state virtually lost its independence. Wellesley signed his first Subsidiary Treaty with the Nizam of Hyderabad. The Nawab of Oudh was already an ally of the Company and there were no foreigners in his service. He was also made to accept the Subsidiary Alliance system, which strengthened the British control over Oudh.

Lord Wellesley tried to force this Subsidiary Alliance on Tipu Sultan of Mysore, who never accepted it. The British army attacked and defeated Tipu in 1799; who died on 4th May, 1799, defending his capital. Nearly half of Tipu's dominion was divided between the British and the Nizam. A reduced portion of Mysore was restored and placed under a ruler and a Subsidiary Alliance was imposed on him. In 1801, Lord Wellesley forced a new treaty upon the Nawab of Carnatic compelling him to cede his kingdom to the Company in return for a pension. The Madras Presidency was created by attaching Carnatic to territories seized from Mysore, including the Malabar. The territories of the rulers of Tanjore and Surat were taken over and their rulers were given pensions.

Wellesley then turned his attention to the Marathas. Wellesley had repeatedly offered a Subsidiary Alliance to the Peshwa and to Scindia. When on 25th October, 1802, Holkar defeated the combined armies of the Peshwa and the Scindia, Peshwa Baji Rao II signed the Subsidiary Treaty at Bassein in 1802 to seek British help. However, the treaty was not accepted by other Maratha chiefs, leading to the Third Anglo-Maratha War. The British army led by Arthur Wellesley defeated the combined forces of Scindia and Bhonsle twice. Both Scindia and Bhonsle became the Subsidiary allies of the British. The ruler of Baroda and rulers of several Rajput states also entered into the Subsidiary Alliance.

Some of the merits of the Subsidiary Alliance System were that native rulers became dependents of the Company; the French and other European influences were averted, ending foreign influences, and increased the resources of the Company. Thus, Wellesley ended French influence at the courts of native rulers within a period of seven years.

Wellesley's policy of Subsidiary Alliance was an extension of Ring Fence Policy—which sought to reduce Indian states to a position of dependence on the British Government in India. Major powers such as Hyderabad, Oudh, and the Marathas came under British influence. Thus, British supremacy was established. In the treaties concluded before Wellesley, there was the spirit of equality between the native state concerned and the Company. Wellesley's treaties show that the Company was more important than the native states' concerns and was assuming the position of predominance and superiority.

Impact of Subsidiary System on the Native Rulers

The Subsidiary System impacted the native states adversely in the following ways:

- The subsidy demanded from the native rulers was too heavy. The native rulers had very little left for spending on the welfare of their subjects.
- The Subsidiary System was sometimes made an instrument of seizing territory from the native states. The Nawab of Oudh was paying subsidy regularly but even then, Wellesley forced him to give up a part of his dominion.
- The system resulted in the internal decay of native states. The native rulers used to take an interest in governing their kingdoms because of the fear of rebellion and invasion. Now, the paramount power promised to guard them against both these dangers. Hence, they became negligent in the work of administering their territories and began to lead lives of ease and corruption.
- The administration system deteriorated due to the Subsidiary System. The Company could not interfere in their internal affairs. The only remedy was to end the rule of the native princes. Coorg and Oudh were annexed in 1834 and 1856 on grounds of misgovernment.

In the meantime, the British statesmen and Directors of the Company felt the need to check further expansion to put an end to their expenses. Wellesley was therefore recalled from India and the Company made peace with Maratha chiefs like Holkar and Scindia by giving back their territories.

Lord Wellesley was succeeded by Lord Cornwallis who resumed the policy of non-intervention. However, he died in 1805 and the senior member of the Governor-General's council, Sir George Barlow, was appointed the Governor-General between 1805 and 1807. He rigidly followed the policy of non-intervention. He was followed by Lord Minto (1807–1813). He too followed his predecessor's policy of non-intervention but was forced to modify it in certain circumstances. The only exception in the time of Lord Minto was the Treaty of Amritsar with Maharaja Ranjit Singh which brought the territories situated between the Yamuna and the Sutlej River under the protection of the Company.

Policy of Subordinate Isolation (1813–1857)

A new policy towards the Indian states was adopted by Marquess of Hastings which historian Lee-Warner has called as the policy of 'Subordinate Isolation'. The terms of this policy, to some extent, lay in the policy of Subsidiary Alliance of Lord Wellesley, yet there was one marked difference between the two. Wellesley's idea was to end danger to the British territories by concluding Subsidiary Alliances. He had not very clearly enunciated the doctrine of the paramouncty over the Indian states. Lord Hastings' policy of Subordinate Isolation asserted the British paramountcy over the Indian states clearly. Marquess of Hastings clearly realized that the policy of non-intervention would not work. The native states had taken advantage of the policy of non-intervention followed by his predecessors. The Nepalese had begun to encroach upon the British territory. The Pindaris were creating havoc in central India and the Marathas were growing restless. Peshwa Baji Rao II was anxious to get rid of the Treaty of Bassein of 1802 and was trying to become the head of the Maratha confederacy once more. Hence, Hastings waged wars with the Gurkhas and defeated them. The Pindaries were exterminated and the Marathas were routed in the Third Anglo-Maratha War in 1818.

The new policy of Subordinate Isolation aimed at controlling the external aspect of the sovereignty of the native states, but left the internal aspect of their sovereignty intact. The Company acquired complete control over the foreign policy of the native states. Indian rulers were not to have any direct relations with any foreign power or even with one another. They were, however, left completely free in domestic matters. They were absolute within their territories. The native states surrendered all forms of external sovereignty and retained full sovereignty in internal administration. British Residents were transformed from diplomatic agents of a foreign power to executive and controlling officers of a superior government.

There was trouble in Indore in 1835, but the Company did not interfere. When Sindh and Punjab were conquered, the treaties with the states like Khairpur, Bahawalpur, and Kashmir contained this stipulation about non-interference in their internal affairs.

Following were the defects of the policy of Subordinate Isolation:

- The fear of rebellion and invasion had been a great check on the native rulers before they came under the British protection. Now, the Company was to protect them against both these dangers. The rulers felt safe and at the same time, they knew that the Company would not interfere. Hence, they stopped taking interest in administration and the condition of the people under their rule began to deteriorate.
- The paramount power could not interfere even in case of misrule. Hence, the remedy was annexation of misgoverned states. Lord William Bentinck annexed Coorg on this account in 1834. Oudh was annexed by Lord Dalhousie in 1856 on the grounds of maladministration. Lord Dalhousie's Doctrine of Lapse was a measure to end the rule of native states. He made extensive use of this method to extend the British territories.

Lord Hastings or Marquess of Hastings (1732–1818)

Governor-General Lord Hastings (1774–1785) reversed the policy of non-intervention and started the era of Subordinate Isolation. The next important expansion of British dominion took place during the tenure of Governor-General Lord Hastings. His three predecessors had followed the policy of non-intervention. However, he felt the policy had greatly lowered the prestige of the Company and the Indian powers had begun to feel that the British were in decline in India. The British faced trouble from every side. The *Gurkhas* of Nepal were trying to expand at the cost of the British territories. The *Pindaris*, allies, and agents of the Marathas, had been emboldened by the policy of non-intervention. The Marathas had begun feeling restless and wanted to recover their lost territories.

Hastings first turned his attention towards Nepal. They were defeated and forced to make the Treaty of Sugauli in 1816. The English obtained the territories of Kumaon and Garhwal from the war.

Next, the Pindaris, who had made life miserable for the people in central India, were exterminated. This is considered as one of Hastings' greatest achievements.

The Marathas had been cowed down by Wellesley but had not been completely crushed. In 1817, the Maratha chiefs made a desperate last attempt to regain their independence and old prestige under the leadership of the Peshwa. However, Lord Hastings struck back with characteristic vigour. Thus, the Third Anglo-Maratha War broke out. Hastings compelled Scindia to accept British suzerainty and defeated the armies of the Peshwa, Bhonsle, and Holkar. The Peshwa was dethroned and pensioned off. His territories were annexed to the Bombay Presidency, and Holkar and Bhonsle accepted Subsidiary Alliances. To preserve Maratha pride, the small kingdom of Satara was founded out of the Peshwa's land and given to the descendants of Shivaji. The Rajputana states, which had been dominated for several decades by Scindia and Holkar, now accepted British supremacy.

Thus, by 1818, the entire Indian subcontinent, except Punjab and Sindh had been brought under British control.

Lord William Bentinck (1774–1839)

After Lord Hastings, Lord Amherst (1823–1828) became the Governor-General. During his time, the First Burmese War broke out, concluding with the Treaty of Yandabo in 1826. Lord Amherst was succeeded by Lord William Bentinck in 1828. He was the most liberal of all the Governor-Generals. He sincerely believed that the welfare of the governed should be the first concern of the rulers. Beside this, William Bentinck was a product of the liberal and progressive ideas of that period.

Governor-General of India, William Bentinck — Wikimedia Commons

By 1830, the East India Company had become the paramount ruler. The entire Indian subcontinent came under British rule. However, the Company was on the verge of bankruptcy and was about to lose the right to trade with India.

William Bentinck's Impact as Governor-General

The advent of Lord William Bentinck as Governor-General ushered in a new era. Bentinck's immediate instructions were to rescue the Company from its financial difficulties. He adopted a number of measures such as: a reduction in the salaries and allowances of military officers, the abolition of double allowance to troops, changing the language of the courts from Persian to English, and encouragement of Indians educated in English in the British bureaucracy at the clerical level.

These reforms turned the Company's deficit into a surplus. The result of his efforts was the renewal of the East India Company's government by the Charter Act of 1833, whereby Bentinck became the first Governor-General of India.

The social reforms by William Bentinck made his name immortal in the history of British India. These included the abolition of *Sati*, the suppression of thugs, and the prevention of female infanticide. Bentinck was greatly distressed with the practice of *Sati*. Therefore, he became a crusader against it and promulgated Regulation XVII on 4th December, 1829, prohibiting and criminalising the practice of Sati. Those who practiced *Sati* could now be punished by courts of law.

The introduction of English education was a significant event of Lord Bentinck's administration. He appointed a committee headed by Lord Macaulay for the promotion of education. Macaulay emphasised on the promotion of European literature and science through the English medium to the people of India. The Government Resolution in 1835 made English the official and literary language of India. In the same year, William Bentinck laid the foundation for the Calcutta Medical College.

William Bentinck was succeeded by Sir Charles Metcalfe (1835–1836). During his time, negotiation for the Treaty of Amritsar with Maharaja Ranjit Singh took place. Lord Auckland became the next Governor-General in 1836. The most important event of his time was the First Afghan War. He was succeeded by Lord Ellenborough (1842–1844). His time is marked by the event of the annexation of Sindh in 1843. The next Governor-General was Lord Hardinge (1844–1848), during whose time the First Anglo-Sikh War broke out.

The Marquess of Dalhousie or Lord Dalhousie (1812–1860)

Lord Dalhousie succeeded Lord Hardinge in 1848. He is considered as one of the greatest Governor-Generals of India. Dalhousie was an expansionist and an imperialist. He believed that British rule was definitely superior to the misrule of the native states. He wanted to expand British territories in India. Like Wellesley, he too adopted every fair and foul method to expand the boundaries of the British Empire. He followed these measures to achieve his objectives – the Policy of the Doctrine of Lapse, expansion by conquest, expansion on grounds of maladministration, expansion on account of default in payment, and expansion by abolishing titles and pensions.

Lord Dalhousie
— Wikimedia Commons

Lord Dalhousie, in 1848, was appointed as the Governor-General of India. He was the youngest man ever to be appointed to the post. He was only 36 at that time. His term ended in 1856. A year after he left India, the Indian Mutiny occurred. His policies of annexation were partly blamed for the mutiny.

Dalhousie's Doctrine of Lapse

The most important tool of Dalhousie's policy was the Doctrine of Lapse or the Law of Succession. Under this doctrine, when the ruler of a protected state died without a natural heir, his state was not to pass to an adopted heir as sanctioned by the age-old tradition of the country. Instead, it was to be annexed to British India, unless the adoption had been clearly approved earlier by the British authorities. Lord Dalhousie applied this principle in the states of Jaitpur and Sambalpur in Orissa, Baghat near Simla, Jhansi in Bundelkhand, and Satara and Nagpur in Maharashtra.

Dalhousie also refused to recognise the titles of many ex-rulers or refused to pay their pensions. Thus, the titles of the Nawabs of Carnatic and of Surat and the Raja of Tanjore were discontinued. Similarly, after the death of Peshwa Baji Rao II, Dalhousie refused to pay the pension to his adopted son, Nana Sahib.

Similarly, to satisfy Britain's growing demand for cotton, he took away the cotton producing province of Berar from the Nizam in 1853. Thus, by 1857, the British had largely completed the task of extension and consolidation of their Empire in India.

Annexation through Wars

In another measure, Lord Dalhousie annexed the state of Punjab in 1849, Lower Burma in 1852, and Sikkim in 1853 through waging wars. Annexation on the grounds of maladministration was carried out in the state of Oudh. The ruler of Oudh, Nawab Wajid Ali Shah was known for indulgence in pleasure, and his officials were corrupt and inefficient. Lord Dalhousie annexed the state in 1856 on charges of maladministration. In reality, Oudh was a potential market for British goods, and so, Dalhousie wanted to bring it under British control. No other Governor-General of India could match the extent of territories that Lord Dalhousie had taken over. He incorporated Indian territories to the empire which were nearly twice the area of England and Wales. Several historians attribute the 1857 revolt to the imperialist measures of Lord Dalhousie.

Policy of Subordinate Union (1857–1935)

The policy of Subordinate Isolation came to an end with the 1857 revolt. The native princes, in spite of their legitimate grievances due to the policy of Lapse and Annexation, had stood by the paramount power in those days of adversity. They had given proof of their loyalty. Hence, a new policy was adopted towards the Indian states which has been called by British historian and author of Native States of India (1910), Lee-Warner, as the policy of Subordinate Union. According to him, this policy of Subordinate Union extended up to 1919, but even afterwards, the same policy was continued up to 1947. The Crown took over Indian territories in 1858 and that was the beginning of the new policy.

Following were the chief features of the policy of Subordinate Union:

- After taking over Indian territories by the Crown, the policy of extending British territories was given up. The Queen's proclamation of 1858 clearly stated, 'We desire no extension of our territorial possessions.' The policy of 'Lapse and Annexation' was discarded. The Indian princes could adopt children on the failure of natural heirs. Lord Canning issued in 1860, at Her Majesty's wish, a series of circulars to the rulers of the important states that gave concessions for the right of adoption. The British government honoured this commitment and did not annex states. Hence, the states of Baroda and Manipur were not annexed, in spite of reports of misgovernment in Baroda and rebellion in Manipur.

- The policy of non-intervention was given up. The intervention had been an exception before 1858. Henceforth, intervention in the affairs of native state became a regular and normal feature. This was due to several reasons such as: to prevent gross misrule as seen in the cases of Baroda and Manipur, to settle disputed successions, to suppress inhuman practices, to prevent rebellion in the state, and for developmental activities like roads, communication system, irrigation works, for implementation of welfare schemes, government policies, etc.
- There was a policy of establishment of direct relations between the Crown and the Princes. The Crown in 1858 succeeded to the place and position of the East India Company as well as the honour and prestige of the defunct Mughal Empire. It was symbolic of the new policy that Queen Victoria by the Royal Titles Act of 1876 assumed the title of the "Empress of India". It lowered the status of the Indian princes. From their former position of allies, they sank to the position of dignified subjects of Her Imperial Majesty.
- All the Indian states were reduced to the same level. The old distinction between the allied and the feudatory states and between dependent and protected states was removed. Indian states, whether big or small, were made to realize that they were all equal in the eyes of the paramount power.
- The government began to get more and more cooperation from the rulers of the native states. The troops of Indian states and the British troops together fought against the frontier tribes. The British government, after 1906, began to look more and more towards the rulers of states to check the rising tide of nationalism in India. The establishment of the Chamber of Princes in 1920 was symbolic of the further development of this policy of cooperation. The Butler Committee of 1927 emphasised that the relationship of the Indian States was with the Crown and not with the Government of India. It was meant to widen the gulf between British India and the Indian States.

Queen Victoria
— Wikimedia Commons

The Cabinet Mission declared in 1946 that the British would not pass on paramountcy to the Indian government but it would come to an end. The paramountcy ended when India became independent in 1947.

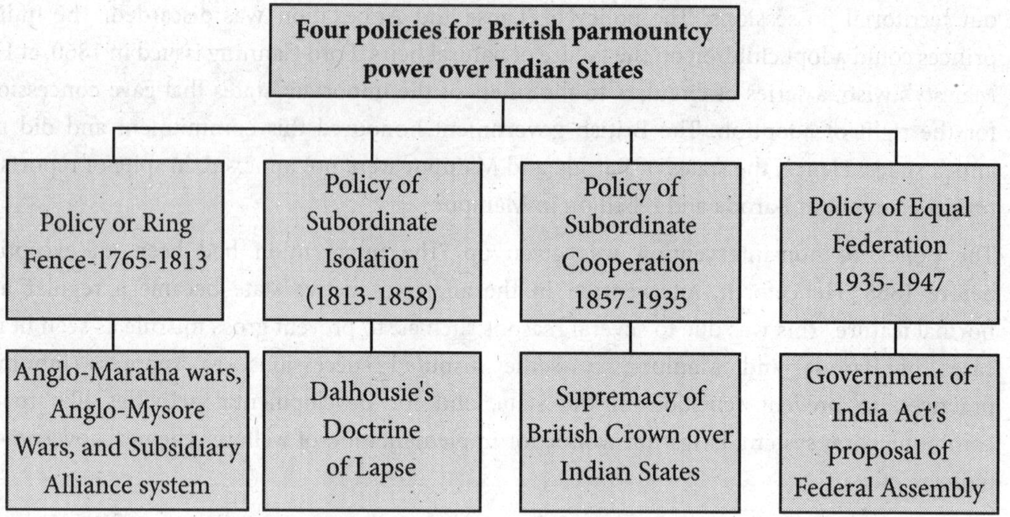

The expansion and consolidation of the British dominion was achieved in a span of one hundred years, i.e., 1757 to 1857, by using the tools of war and diplomacy. However, the two most important tools employed by East India Company that established the paramount power of the Company were Subsidiary Alliance and Doctrine of Lapse.

Thus, these policies were clever tools employed by the British to acquire Indian states to set up their dominion in India. Rabindranath Tagore has rightly stated in these words, "Darkness settled on the face of the land, then the weighing scales in the merchant's hand changed into the imperial sceptre".

Previous Years' Questions

1. **Describe the expansion and consolidation of the British Empire under its various Governor-Generals.**
2. **What do you mean by Subsidiary Alliance? How did it help to consolidate the British Empire in India?**
3. **Discuss the steps taken by Lord Hastings to extend British power in India.**
4. **What do you mean by the Doctrine of Lapse? Which states were made a part of the British Empire under this Doctrine?**
5. **"The British endeavored as far as possible to live within a Ring-Fence and beyond that they avoided intercourse with the chiefs." Comment. (1987)**
6. **"The British policy towards Indian States in 1818-1858 was one of isolation and noninterference tempered by annexation." Comment. (1996)**

CHAPTER

Administrative and Economic Changes Under East India Company (1757–1857)

Introduction

Administration became a major function for the East India Company. Since it was still a commercial organisation, the main objectives of British administration were to increase the profits of the company, while simultaneously maintaining the hold of the British dominion on India. Maintaining law and order in the areas under its control, exercising adequate checks on the Board of governors of the company and its employees, were the other objectives.

The Period Upto 1772

In the periodup to 1772, the Company was comparatively free to pursue its commercial and administrative policies in India. The period was one of plunder by the East India Company, resulting in a famine in Bengal in 1769-70. The officials of the company were making huge personal profits in India, while the Company was in huge losses and in deep dept. The financial condition of the Company became worse as a result of the First Mysore War. In order to escape bankruptcy, the company applied for a loan from the British government. A secret committee was appointed and it reported that the financial condition of the Company was in doldrums.

The servants of the Company were generally poor when they came to India. But they became very rich by the time they returned back to their country. This was because they were getting costly presents from Indians and carrying on private trade. On returning to England, they lived like petty princes and were popularly known as '*Naboobs*'. Banking on their ill-gotten wealth, many elected themselves to the House of Parliament.

Two parliamentary committees were set up by the British Parliament which was highly critical of the Company. It remarked, 'such a scene of tyranny and plunder has been opened up, as makes one shudder'.

The Period of Regulation and Control–1772-1853

The Company had been established to carry on trade with India and had acquired considerable territories by 1773. In other words, the Company, from the position of mere traders, had become a governing body. Thus the character of the Company had undergone a change. The British parliament now wanted to have a hand in supervising the Company's affairs.

Concerns of Britain

In order to supervise the East India Company's affairs, the British government was faced with manifold issues and concerns. The main concern before the British government was how to put an end to the growing monopoly of the Company, and how to define the relationship of East India Company and its possessions with the British government. Another issue was how to control the company's authorities and its large number of officials and soldiers working for it in far away India. The question of providing a single centre of control over far spread British possessions in Bengal, Madras and Bombay was also causing great concern. Many political thinkers and statesmen of Britain were afraid that the company and its powerful rich officials would lower the standard of morality of England and increase corruption in British politics. The seats in the House of Commons were bought by the Company for its agents. It was feared that the Company, with the help of money brought from India, might achieve dangerous supremacy in the British government.

The relationship of the East India Company with the British government was closely connected in Britain. English parliamentarians were politically ambitious and English merchants were commercially greedy. Fabulous wealth brought home by the officials of the Company caused jealousy in Britain. British statesmen wanted to put an end to the monopoly of trade held by the Company. They became critical of the way the Company administered Bengal.

Constitutional changes under East India Company

The British government decided to control the Company's Indian administration in the interest of Britain's influential elite class. The Company was allowed to continue with its monopoly of trade with the east. The Directors of the Company were given the control of Indian administration.

After 1772, the period of regulation and control by the British government on the affairs of the Company began. The British government passed various Acts. The Regulating Act of 1773 was the beginning of the British government's control on the Company's affairs.

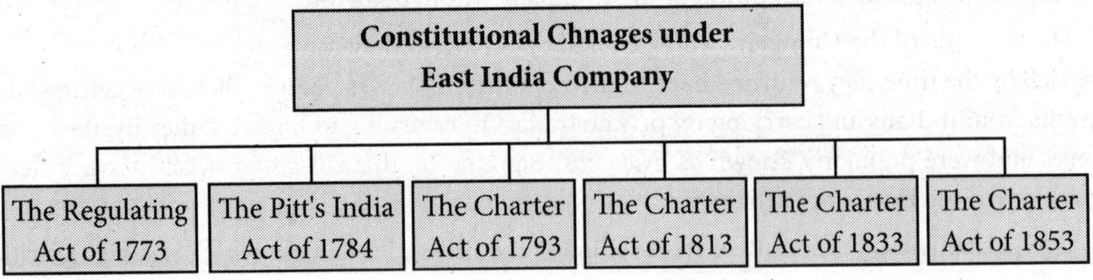

The Regulating Act of 1773

Circumstances leading to this Act:

- The dual administration of the company led to maladministration
- The officials of the company indulged in malpractices
- The company was in huge dept and appealed to the British government for help
- There was a lot of criticism of the working of the company in the British parliament.

Importance and Certain Provisions

The Regulating Act was the beginning of the control of the British government on the affairs of the company The Act made changes in the constitution of the Company at home i.e. in England, and Company's positions in India were brought under British government control.

Following were its provisions:

- The changes were made in the constitution of the court of Directors of the Company. It was required that it should submit to the British government all communication about civil and military affairs received from Bengal and revenues of India.
- In the field of executive government, the status of Governor of Bengal was raised to Governor General. His council would consist of four members. Warren Hastings was made governor general of Bengal. The councillors were to hold office for five years and could be removed before the expiry of the term only by the King.
- The governor general was bound by the decision of the majority of the council. He was given a casting vote in case of a tie.
- The governor general in council was given the power to superintend and control the presidencies of Madras and Bombay in matters of war and peace.
- The governors of Madras and Bombay were required to send regularly to the governor general, information connected with government, revenues or interests of the company.
- The governor general in turn was under the direct control of court of directors and kept it fully informed of the affairs concerning the interests of the company.
- However, the governors of Bombay and Madras could act without consulting the governor general-in-council in case of emergency.
- The Act also provided for the establishment of a Supreme Court.

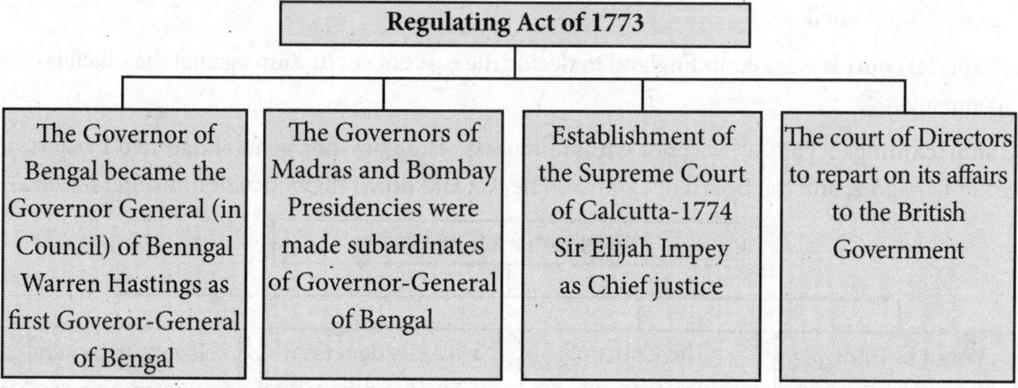

Shortcomings of the Act

The Regulating Act failed to achieve the desired results on account of its serious shortcomings:

- First, the governor general had no power to overrule the hostile majority of his council who united against him. He was at the mercy of the council as three members could combine and outvote the governor general

- Second, the governor general of Bengal in council was given control over presidencies, but the governors of these presidencies could act without consulting the former in case of emergency. Therefore, governor general's control over governors of Bombay and Madras proved inadequate.
- Third, the British parliamentary control was inadequate and ineffective.
- The jurisdiction of the Supreme Court was not clear.
- The Supreme Court had little knowledge about Indian customs and rites.

The Pitt's India Act of 1784

To remove the major shortcomings of the Regulating Act, the Pitt's India Act was passed in 1784. The Pitt's India Act of 1784 tried to remove the shortcomings of the previous Act. This Act was named after William Pitt, the prime minister of Britain of that time.

Following provisions were made under this Act:

- The functioning of the company came under the complete purview of the British parliament.
- The company was placed in complete subordination to the British government.
- The Board of Control consisting of Secretary of State, Chancellor of the Exchequer and four other Privy Councillors, was created.
- The Board of Control was to have comprehensive powers of supervision and control over Indian affairs.
- The number of members of the councils of governor general was reduced from four to three.
- The presidencies of Bombay and Madras were to be under greater control of the governor general-in-council.
- A special court was set up in England to decide the cases of corruption against the officials of the company.

Shortcomings : The Act was not without defects. The governor general had two masters, the court of Directors, and the Board of Control. The Act laid down the policy of non-intervention.

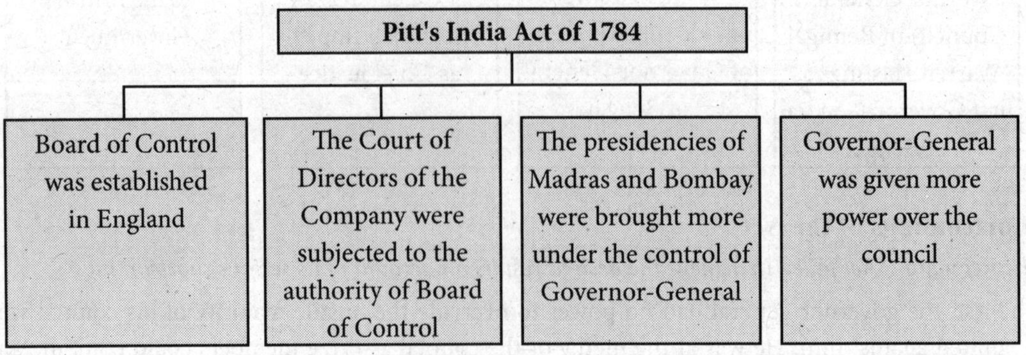

The Charter Act of 1793

- The next Act was passed in 1793 as the Charter Act of 1793.The Act allowed the company to continue with the possessions of territories for the next twenty years.

Important provisions of this Act were:

The payments of the members of the board of control and their staff was to be made out of Indian revenues;

- The councils of governor general and governors of Bombay and Madras were not to have more than three members each;
- A regular code of all regulations that could be enacted for the internal government of the British territory in Bengal was framed. The regulation applied to the rights, persons, property of the Indian people and it bound the courts to regulate their decisions by the rules and regulations contained therein.
- The Act of 1793 thus laid the foundation of government by written laws and regulations in British India in place of the personal rule of the past rulers. The concept of a civil law enacted by a secular human agency and applied universally, was an important change.

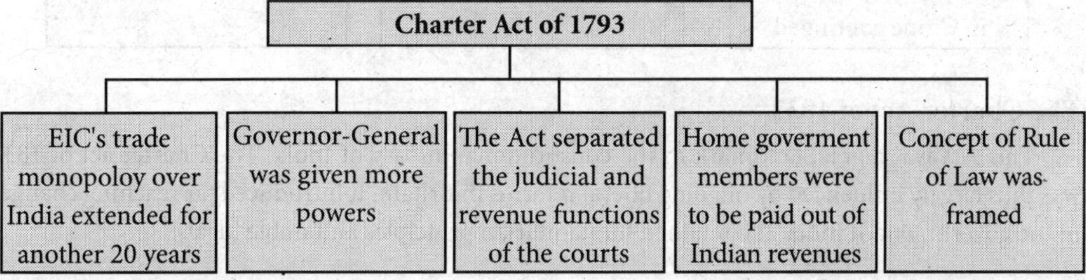

The Charter Act of 1813

Twenty years after the Charter Act of 1793, the charter of the Company was renewed in the Charter Act of 1813. This Act was passed with a great deal of controversy.

Important reasons for the controversy were:

(a) Great demand for abolishing the trade monopoly of East India Company,

(b) War with Napoleon that had adversely affected the trade

(c) Trading classes wanted that the company's monopoly of trade with India should be abolished, and

(d) Missionaries wanted that the company should take active steps for the propagation of Christianity.

It was under these circumstances that the Charter Act of 1813 was passed.

Important provisions of this Act were:

- The charter was renewed for twenty years, trade with India excepting in tea, was thrown open to other traders,

- British merchants and missionaries could come to India and settle here only by getting a licence from the court of directors,

The company was to keep its territorial and commercial accounts separately,

- One lakh of rupees a year was to be spent on the education of Indians.

Significance : The Act was important in several respects. The Charter Act of 1813 abolished the Company's monopoly of trade with India. Trade with India was thrown open to all British merchants. Most importantly, the provision for spending one lakh of rupees on education made the Company responsible for imparting education to the natives.

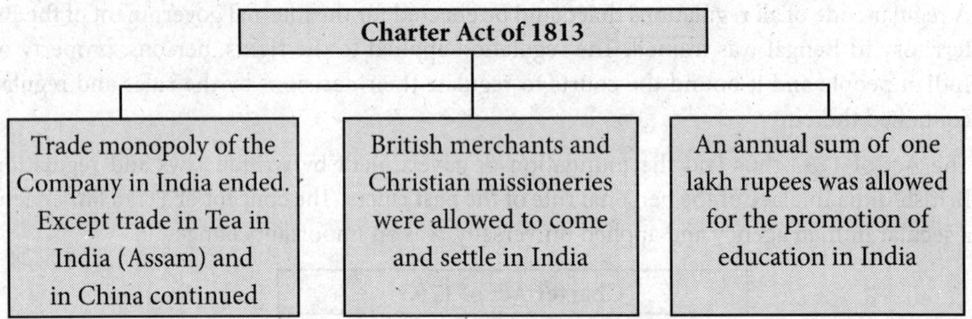

The Charter Act of 1833

This Act was a great landmark in the constitutional history of India. The Charter act of 1833 was thus largely influenced by ongoing liberal reforms in Britain. It introduced far reaching changes in the government of India. It contained humanitarian principles and noble ideals.

Some of the important provisions of this Act were:

- The Company's monopoly of trade with China came to an end.
- The territories and the revenues of India were granted to the Company for twenty years.
- This Act made the Governor General of Bengal the Governor General of British India and all financial and administrative powers were centralised in the hands of Governor General-in-Council. Thus, with the Charter Act of 1833, Lord William Bentinck became the "First Governor General of British India".
- The Act provided for the codification of law in India. A law commission was appointed under Lord Macaulay; the Act empowered the governor general in council to make laws for all the people living in India; the Act threw open government services to all, irrespective of religion, place of birth, descent or colour.
- It was this Act which declared "No native of India shall by reason of his religion, place of birth, descent or colour be disabled from holding any office under the company". Due to this Act, the Indian Penal Code and the Codes of Civil and Criminal Procedure came into existence.

Charter act of 1833 is the watershed in the administrative and constitutional history of India because of the following reasons:

- **Centralization of administration :** Governor General of Bengal was made the Governor General of India with the entire civil and military powers. Other governor generals were made subordinate to him and their legislative powers were taken away.
- **End of commercial activities of East India Company :** Its privilege in tea and trade with China were taken away and it was made a purely administrative body. Company was to rule over India in the name of British crown. Moreover, other British companies were allowed to freely trade with India.
- **An attempt to introduce open competition for civil service :** Indians could now enter into civil service on the basis of merit. But the exam was much difficult for any Indian as compared to the British.
- **Separation of power :** For the first time executive and legislative function of governor general council were separated. 6 new members were added to the council for legislative purpose. This is to function as mini-parliament for law making.
- **Codification of Law :** Law commission was established under Macaulay to codify all laws that needed to be placed before British parliament.

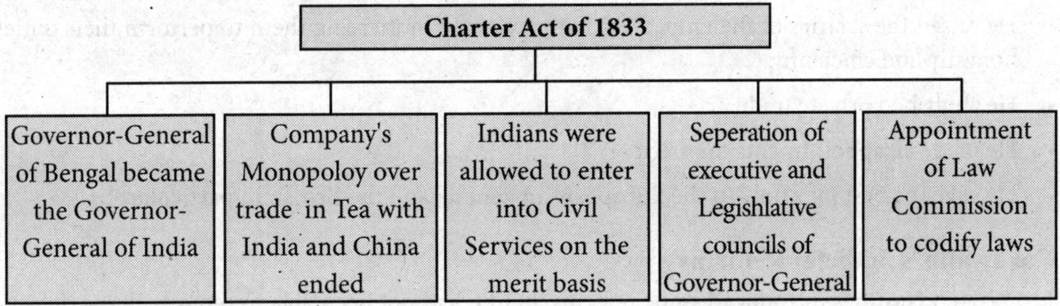

The Charter Act of 1853

This Act was the last in a series of the Charter Acts.

Significant provisions of this Act were:

The charter was not renewed for a definite period. The Company was to hold the territories in India as a Trust for His Majesty until Parliament should direct otherwise; the number of directors was reduced from 24 to 18 and 6 of these to be appointed by the Crown; the Act made provision for the appointment of Lt. Governor for Bengal; the Law Member was made a full member of governor general's executive council; the Act created a Legislative Council of India.

The Charter Act of 1853 gave indications of the fact that the Company's rule would not last a long time. The charter was not renewed for a definite period. However, the Act marked the beginning of a parliamentary structure of government for India. The Legislative Council was clearly distinguished from the Executive Council.

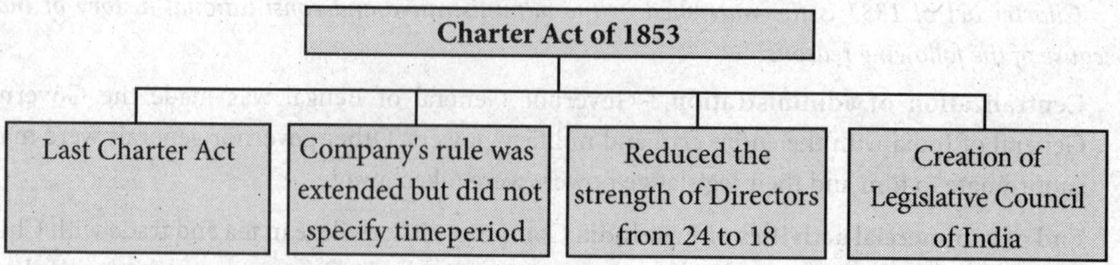

Administrative Changes and Reforms

Initially, the company's officials combined two functions viz, trading as well as performing administrative duties. With the acquisitions of several territories in India, it was not possible to combine these two functions. Besides performing these functions, the employees of the company indulged in private trade also and earned huge profits. They resorted to all sorts of unfair means to amass wealth. They were tempted to do so as they received very meagre salaries. The situation continued during the period of Clive and Warren Hastings.

Beginning of Administrative Reforms

In 1786, Lord Cornwallis succeeded as the governor-general of India. He was the first governor-general of India to introduce administrative reforms.

Following were the important reforms made by him:

- He raised the salaries of the employees with a view to motivating them to perform their duties honestly and efficiently.
- He abolished private trade
- He made all appointments on merit
- He gave the best jobs only to the Europeans in general and the British in particular.

Cornwallis's Judicial Reforms

Warren Hastings introduced some reforms, but he had not been able to remove all the defects. It was left for Cornwallis to carry out further reforms. Cornwallis found judicial system highly defective and he introduced many reforms in this department in 1787, 1790 and 1793. These reforms improved criminal as well as civil justice.

Criminal courts : The lowest criminal court was of *Daroga*. He was authorized to arrest the offenders and release them on bail. The next court was the district court. More serious cases were taken up in district court. It was held by European magistrate. Serious cases were tried in the circuit courts which consisted of at least two covenanted servants of the company. The appeal could be taken to *Sadr Nizamat Adalat* at Calcutta. Appeals against its decisions were taken to governor general in council.

Civil courts : The court of Registrars could try cases up to 200 rupees while the courts of *Munsifs* and *Ameens* could try cases up to 500 rupees. Appeals could be taken to a district court. It also tried cases in the first instance of more than 500 rupees. The appeals could be taken to a provincial court. There were four provincial courts at Calcutta, Murshidabad, Dacca and Patna. Its decisions were final in cases of up to 1000 rupees.

Cornwallis made the following judicial changes:

- Court fees paid by the litigants were abolished.
- Lawyers were to charge only moderate fees.
- Government regulations were published in one volume.
- Revenue functions were separated from the judicial functions.

Police Reforms : the police functions were performed by the Zamindars till the time of Cornwallis. They were expected to maintain peace and order in the areas. Lord Cornwallis took away the police power of the Zamindars. Each district was divided into small areas and each of these areas was placed under a *Daroga*. He was in charge of the police force of that area and maintained peace and order. The work of the *Daroga* in a district was supervised by the district magistrate.

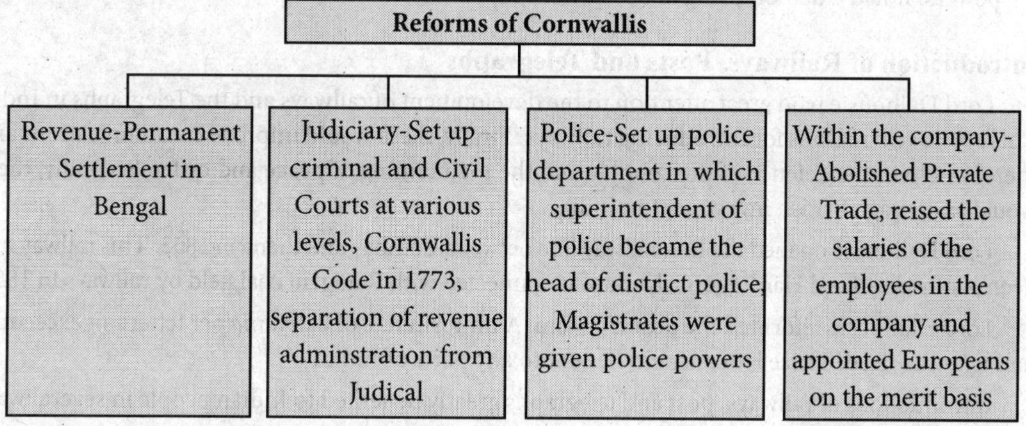

Reforms of Lord Dalhousie

Lord Dalhousie was not only a great conqueror and annexationist, but also a great administrator and reformer. Most of the departments of the government felt the impress of his master hand. He had two objective in introducing reforms in India. Firstly, he wanted to improve the condition of people under British rule in India. He appears to have believed that the rulers must justify their power by discharging the duties of governing efficiently. Secondly, he wanted to promote British interests in India. His capacity to work was immense. He mastered the Indian problems in a remarkably short span of time. Sir Richard Temple says, 'As an imperial administrator, he had never been surpassed and seldom equalled by any of the illustrious men whom England has sent forth to govern India.'

The reforms of Lord Dalhousie can be studied under several heads:

The administrative reforms : The administrative reforms aimed at centralisation and raising the efficiency of the work of government.

The most important of these reforms were as follows:

- **Proper demarcation of departments :** Lord Dalhousie began to carry on administration on modern lines. He properly demarcated the spheres of different departments and began to divide the work of government properly among them.

- **Appointment of Lieutenant Governor for Bengal :** A Lieutenant-Governor was appointed for Bengal so that the Governor-General of India could devote his whole time to the work of central government
- **Introduction of nonregulation system :** He organized a nonregulation system for the province. Each of the non-regulation provinces was under a chief commissioner responsible to the governor general in council. The system of non-regulation provinces was devised for the sake of economy. This system made no distinction between civil and military administration. It meant economy of personnel. The three presidencies of Calcutta, Bombay and Madras were regulation provinces. Punjab, C.P., Oudh and Burma were non regulation provinces.
- **Concentration of functions in the person of district magistrate :** The district magistrate was to exercise executive, judicial and revenue power. It is against the theory of the separation of powers. It had a demoralising effect on the people.

Introduction of Railways, Posts and Telegraphs

Lord Dalhousie paid great attention to the development of railways and the Telegraphs in India. There were two reasons for introducing railways. Firstly, these would improve communications and thereby help in the defence of the country and the maintaining of peace and order. Secondly, these would encourage British investment in India.

Lord Dalhousie opened the first railway line between Bombay and thana in 1853. This railway had been planned by Lord Hardinge. Calcutta was connected with Raniganj coal field by railways in 1854.

Lord Dalhousie reformed the postal system. A uniform rate of half *anna* per letter not exceeding half *tola* was fixed. These letters could be sent to any parts of India.

Introductions of railways, post and telegraphs greatly benefited to Indian people in several ways

Commercial Reforms

Lord Dalhousie wanted to benefit the British manufacturers and followed a free trade policy in their interests. All the ports of India were declared free ports. All obstacles in the way of British investment in India were removed. The Indian cottage industries suffered heavily. Even the coastal trade of India greatly fell into the hands of English capitalists.

Establishment of Public Work Department

Public Work Department was under the charge of military members before the time of Dalhousie. These members were primarily interested in matters of military department and the work on the civilian side was generally neglected. Lord Dalhousie separated Public Works Departments. This Department seriously took up the work of extending public utility works. Old roads were repaired and new ones were constructed. Grand Trunk Road was completed. It connected Calcutta with Peshawar. The Ganges Canal was constructed and Bari-Doab Canal in the Punjab was planned. These canals did much to improve agriculture. Some steps were taken for the preservation of historical buildings.

Educational Reforms

Lord Dalhousie paid attention to the development of education. Educational reforms were introduced by the Sir Charles Wood's Despatch of 1854.

It made the following recommendations:

- Universities were to be set up in the presidency towns. These were to be examining bodied just like the London University.
- Intermediate and degree colleges were to be affiliated to these universities.
- Education was to be provided in vernaculars in the high school and Anglo-vernacular schools to be set up.
- There was to be a department of education in every province.
- Training institutions were to be started for training the teachers.
- Private enterprise in the sphere of education was to be encouraged.
- There was to be a Director-General of Education for India to coordinate the educational activities of different provinces.

Criticism of Lord Dalhousie's Reforms

Lord Dalhousie introduced reforms with the idea of promoting British interests and to improve the conditions of the people of India. These reforms were meant for the good of the people, but he did not take into consideration the conservative temperament of the people. That is why his reforms were misunderstood. The telegraph was looked upon as something magical by the conservative people. The introduction of railways was considered by many as a means of spoiling religion, since people of all religion had to travel together. The motives of Lord Dalhousie cannot be questioned, but in introducing reforms he did not take into consideration the conservative mindset of the people, and it became one of the causes of the 1857 revolt.

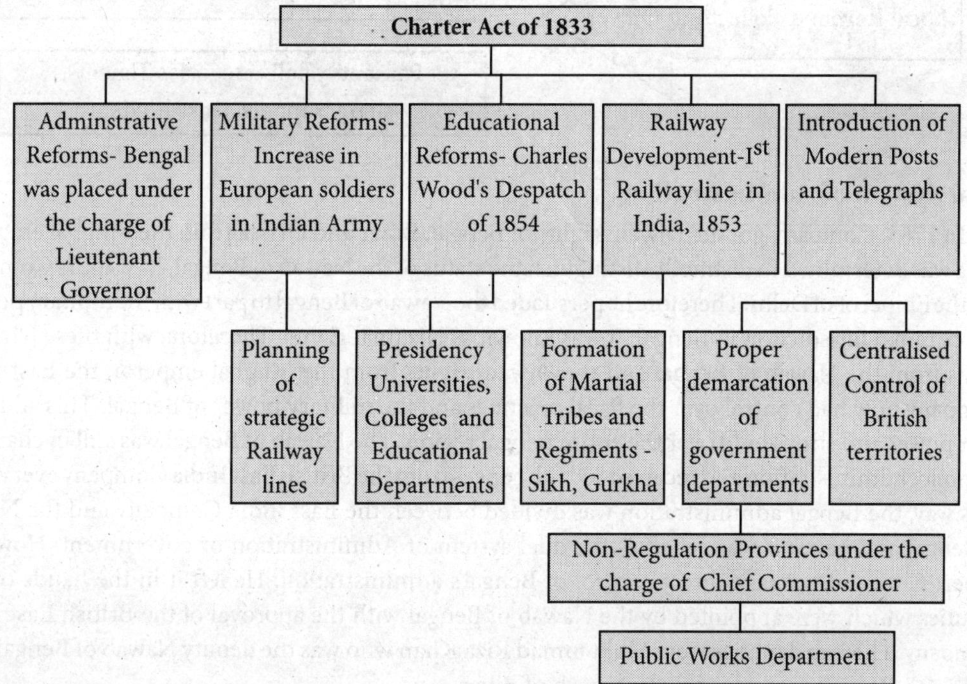

Changes In Economic Structure : 1757-1857

Land Revenue Administration

One of the major changes introduced by the Company in the Indian economy was in land revenue administration.

In later Mughal period, the cultivators paid a fixed share of the produce of land either in kind or in cash to the zamindars who were collectors of revenue. They kept one-tenth for themselves and deposited the rest in the state treasury. Thus the zamindars were not originally the owners of land, but only middlemen between the cultivators and the government. Before the British revenue system a symbiotic relationship existed between the local tax collectors and villages. In due course, the system tended to become hereditary. When a person inherited zamindars, he had to pay succession fee.

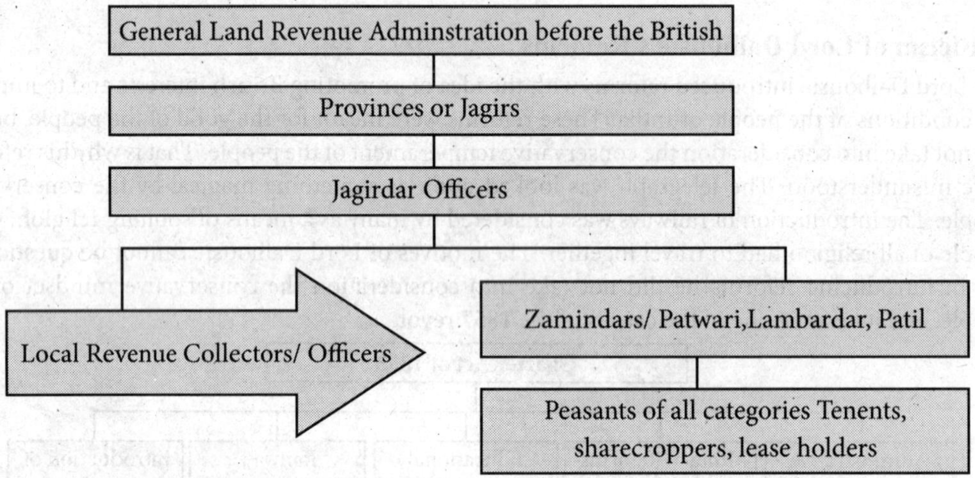

Dual System of Administration

In 1765, Company got the Diwani rights of Bengal, Bihar and Orissa from the Mughal emperor. Clive was determined to distinctly distinguish the status of the Nawab of Bengal, East India Company and the Emperor of Delhi. Therefore he persuaded the Nawab of Bengal to part with the military powers and criminal jurisdiction in Bengal. It was known as Nizamat rights. Therefore, with these Nizamat rights from the Nawab of Bengal and the Diwani rights from the Mughal emperor, the East India Company now had control over the fiscal revenues and the military power of Bengal. This added to their power and stronghold over the entire Bengal region. The Nawab of Bengal was still in charge of the police administration and received 53 lakh rupees from the British East India Company every year. This way, the Bengal administration was divided between the East India Company and the Nawab of Bengal and hence it was called as the dual system of Administration or government. However, Robert Clive did not take direct control of Bengal's administration. He left it in the hands of two deputies which were appointed by the Nawab of Bengal with the approval of the British East India Company. The two deputies were Muhammad Riza Khan who was the deputy Nawab of Bengal, and Raja Sitab Roy who was the deputy Nawab of Bihar.

The dual administration system was very beneficial for the British because the direct result of such a governing system was that the while the British had all the power in the region, they did not have any of the responsibilities. Civil and police responsibilities rested with the deputy Diwans which were appointed by the Company's directors.

Dual system had various disadvantages and led to the ultimate breakdown of Bengal's administration. Power was divorced from the responsibility. The British were in possession of power and money whereas the Nawab had neither power nor money. He had only the responsibility of running the administration. The Nawab failed to manage the administration smoothly with a small annual grant of rupees 50 lakhs only. The company tried to improve its own lot by the revenue it collected from Bengal, Bihar and Orissa. The Nawab could not do any work of public utility due to paucity of fund. The Nawab also had no power to enforce law. As a result, lawlessness prevailed in most parts of Bengal.

The poor administration in Bengal led to rapid increase of private trade. The servants of the East India Company carried on trade and commerce privately without paying any tax. They earned a lot of profit out of this illegal trade. But, on the other hand, the merchants of Bengal suffered a lot, because they were over burdened with tax. Thus, the Dual Government dealt a terrible blow to the local trade and commerce.

The local peasants suffered huge losses due to the unreasonable tax structure which proved to be a huge burden on the farmers. There was considerable decline in the agricultural industry. Local handlooms businesses were all but destroyed and trade had become way too costly for the local merchants to continue.

The dual administration proved disastrous for the people of Bengal. Neither the Company nor the Nawab cared for their welfare. The Company's servants now had the whole of Bengal to themselves and their oppression of the people increased greatly. This is evident from the words of Clive, who says: I shall only say that such a scene of anarchy, confusion, bribery, corruption, and extortion was never seen or heard of in any country but Bengal; nor did such and so many fortunes acquire in so unjust and rapacious a manner'. The abuses of the 'dual' government and the drain of wealth led to the impoverishment and exhaustion of Bengal province.

In 1770, Bengal suffered from a famine which in its effects proved one of the most terrible famines known in human history. People died in lakhs and nearly one-third of Bengal's population fell victim to its ravages. Though the famine was due to failure of the rains, its effects were heightened by the Company's policies.

The Bengal famine of 1770 or *Chhiattorer monnontór,* meaning the Famine of '76 in Bengali, was a catastrophic famine between 1769 and 1773 that affected the entire population of Bengal. The famine is estimated to have caused the deaths of over 10 million people, reducing the population to thirty million in Bengal, which included Bihar and parts of Orissa.

In the words of Prof. Ramsay Muir, "'The Dual System of Government was a complete failure from the outset. In the first place, the abuse of the private trade reached a greater height than ever. In the second place, the demands of the Company for the increase led to gross oppression of the peasantry."

Warren Hastings and Abolition of Dual System, 1772

The most urgent task before Warren Hastings was setting the administrative system in order. Clive's Dual System had been a total failure, plunging Bengal into administrative chaos. The Court of Directors instructed him that the Company must **"stand forth as Dewan"**, and take over the Civil administration directly in the hands of the Company. This was, in the words of Warren Hastings, "implanting the authority of the Company, and the Sovereignty of Great Britain, in the constitution of the country".

Warren Hastings put an end to this system in 1772, and the Company took over the administration work directly.

He appointed English collectors for revenue collection and revenue administration, who were to be assisted by native officers. The right of revenue collection was given to the highest bidders for five years. The great defect of this system was that high bids were offered and the bidders could not afford to pay that amount later. In 1777 the system of bidding for the collection of land revenue was again made annual. This system was also defective because of its precarious tenure. Hastings brought the servants of the Company under control and discontinued the annual tribute payable to the Mughal Emperor Shah Alam II. He also cut down the annual allowa1nce of Nawab of Bengal.

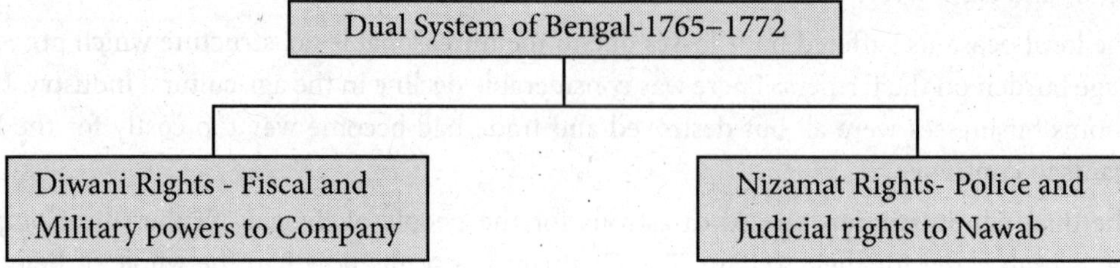

Permanent Rule for Collection of Land Revenue or Permanent Settlement System

Lord Cornwallis, who followed Warren Hastings, as Governor General of Bengal was sent with specific instructions to improve the land revenue to be collected from Bengal. Cornwallis on his arrival found agriculture and trade decaying, and zamindars sinking into poverty and money lenders the only flourishing class in the country.

An Act in Britain's parliament was passed in 1784 that required the Court of Directors to end the system of annual settlement and make permanent rules for the collection of land revenue. The Directors asked Cornwallis to make a settlement with the zamindars for ten years, and it was to be made permanent if found satisfactory. From 1786 to 1789, Sir John Shore carried out enquiries into the question of revenue collection. In 1789, a settlement was made for ten years with the zamindars. Cornwallis wanted to make the existing settlement permanent, but asked to wait for the data and results. Parliament accepted the viewpoint of Cornwallis and the existing settlement was made permanent in 1793 in provinces of Bengal, Bihar, Orissa and Varanasi.

Following were its features:

- The settlement was made with the zamindars who were recognised owners of land for which they had been previously collecting revenue.

- They had to pay a fixed annual amount to the government and it was not to be increased later on.
- The realized amount would be divided into 11 parts. 1/11 of the share belongs to zamindars .
- The share of the government was fixed at about $10/11^{th}$ of what a zamindar received at that time. He could keep the rest as his collection fee.
- The zamindars were absolved or free of the burden of paying succession fees or obtaining permission for selling their lands.
- Zamindars were recognized as owner of the lands. Zamindars were given the rights to collect the rent from the peasants.

Merits of Permanent Settlement of Bengal

Historians have expressed mixed viewpoints regarding permanent settlements of Bengal. According to Marshman, 'it was bold, brave and a wise measure. Under the great influence of this territorial charter, which for the first time created indefensible rights and interests in the soil, population has increased, cultivation has been extended and a gradual improvement has become visible in the habits and comforts of the people'. R.C.Dutt has supported the settlement in these words, 'if the prosperity and happiness of a nation be the criterion of wisdom and success, Lord Cornwallis' permanent settlelement of 1793 is the wisest and most successful measure which the British nation had ever adopted in India'.

Following were its merits:

- **Ultimately beneficial to zamindars :** The permanent settlement was beneficial to the zamindars in the long run. The produce of land increased in course of time, but the share of the state was permanently fixed. Thus the increased produce of land in course of time went as a share to the landlords. They become the most prosperous class of Bengal in course of time.
- **The produce from land increased :** The zamindars, before 1793, had not been taking interest in cultivating and improving the productivity of the land. They were not sure that it would remain with them at the time of next settlement. The permanent settlement created the proprietary rights of the zamindars in land, and they began to improve it. Fixed tenure encouraged investment in land. It finally encouraged flow of capital to land. The quality of land improved and it added to the prosperity of Bengal.
- **Helped in industrialization at a later stage :** The zamindars became rich in course of time due to greater income from land. They were able to save a good deal of money. Later on, they invested in industry. Thus, permanent settlement in the long run helped in industrialization.
- **Created a class of loyal zamindars :** The permanent settlement created a class of loyal zamindars in Bengal. The zamindars were recognized owners of land and the land revenue was permanently fixed. The zamindars knew that a new government would not honour permanent settlement and would enhance land revenue. Hence it was in their economic interest that the British should continue to rule. Thus permanent settlement strengthened the roots of the British government. It is quite well known that the zamindars of Bengal remained loyal to the British government during the mutiny of 1857.

- **Income of government became definite :** The income of the government from land revenue before 1793 was not definite. Under the system of collecting revenue through highest bidder, the government was not able to realize all the money agreed to by the zamindars at the time of bidding. The budget of the government was naturally upset. The permanent settlement assured the government of a definite income. If now the zamindars did not pay, his land could be sold.

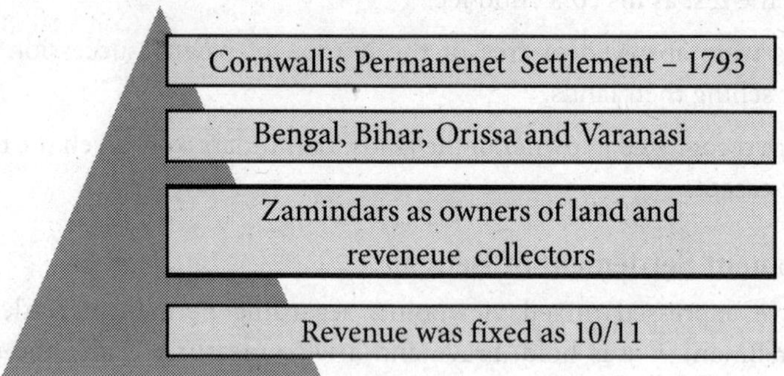

Demerits of Permanent Settlement

Following were its main defects:

- **Immediate ruinous effect on zamindars :** The immediate effect of permanent settlement on the zamindars was ruinous. The land revenue demanded from them was too high at that time. Many of them could not realise that amount from the cultivators and their land were sold. Thus, many zamindars were ruined.
- **Ignored the interest of the cultivators :** The permanent settlement looked only to the zamindars. It did not take into consideration the actual tillers of the soil. No substantial steps were taken to safeguard their interest. The zamindars began to extort too much money from them. Lord Cornwallis expected that the zamindars would keep registers of their tenants and would grant *pattas* specifying the rent. Cultivators could go to a civil court if the rules were violated by the zamindars. The zamindars did not keep the registers and their *pattas* were very rarely granted. Thus, in actual practice, the cultivators were at the mercy of the zamindars.
- **Created a class of absentee zamindars :** The permanent settlement created a class of absentee zamindars. Most of them stopped living in their lands. They built palatial residences in cities and began to live lavish life. Their agents collected rent from the tenants and sent the same to the zamindars in cities. Lord Cornwallis hoped that the Bengal zamindars would become a class like English landlords who lived on their lands. Actually, he created a class of zamindars very much resembling Irish landlords who did not stay on their land and whose agents tyrannically collected revenue.
- **Heavy taxation of non agricultural class :** The amount of revenue to be collected by the government from the zamindars was fixed but the expenses of the administration of the province increased with the passing of time. The deficit had to be partly made good by taxing non agricultural class more heavily. Thus the non agricultural classes of Bengal later on had to pay more, while the zamindars enjoyed a privileged position by paying less.

- **Ignored the ultimate interests of the state :** The settlement proved not in the interest of the British State in due course of time. The produce of the land increased in course of time due to better methods of cultivation and other factors but the amount to be charged by the government could not be increased. The whole of the increased produce from land went into the pockets of the zamindars. In other words, the government at a later period got only about 25% of what the zamindars collected. It had to suffer an annual loss of more than 4 crores of rupees a year.

Mahalwari and Ryotwari Settlements

The British soon introduced the Mahalwari and the Ryotwari settlements. The new systems took into account the increases in production. The State revenue share was revised at regular intervals. Also, apparently the settlements aimed at betterment of the peasants conditions.

Ryotwari Settlement

The Ryotwari settlement was devised by Capt. Alexander Read and Sir Thomas Munro at the end of 18th century. The latter, i.e. Sir Thomas Munro, introduced Ryotwari in Madras Presidency when he became the governor of Madras in 1820. Later, it was introduced in Bombay presidency. This system was already prevalent in various parts of the southern region. Under this system, the peasants or Ryots were directly responsible to the government without any intermediaries in the form of zamindars. The system was devised by Capt. Alexander Read and Sir Thomas Munro at the end of the 18th century and introduced by the latter when he was governor (1820–27) of Madras Presidency.

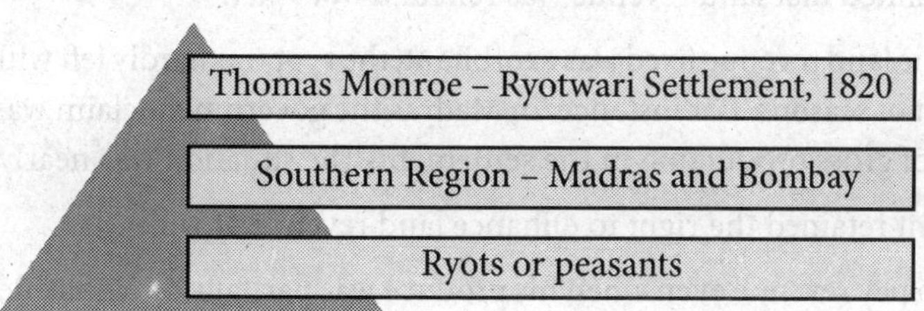

So, instead of creating a stable body of landowners and intermediaries as seen in permanent settlement, the new system proceeded to make a revenue settlement directly with the ryots or cultivators, not permanently, but temporarily without any need of creating the 'parasitic' zamindars and fostering growth through direct assessments.

Under this system, ryots were placed directly under the state who were recognised as the proprietors of land i.e., they could sublet, mortgage or transfer by gift or sale. Indulgence towards eviction of ryots from land had been rejected so long as they paid the revenue demand. Being a temporary one, the ryotwari settlement varied between 20 and 40 years.

In theory, as the ryotwari system bypassed intermediaries, it was a better arrangement from the point of the Ryots as it appeared to favour 'peasant proprietorship' rather than the permanent zamindari settlement. Under this system, the ryot was brought directly under the state.

Further, being the proprietor of land, it was expected that the ryots would make permanent improvement of land. The ryotwari system was hailed by the alien administrator as the precursor of stability and peace in the countryside.

This arrangement thus helped to win over the cultivating classes to the support of British rule. Finally, elasticity of land revenue under this settlement was considered to be a boon to the ryots, since revenue demands could be reduced according to the exigencies of the situation. This is because the system ensured the benefit of revenue increase in future in the event of extension of cultivation and/or the price rise of crops.

Though, apparently the settlement seems just, in reality the large numbers of zamindars were replaced by one giant landlord, the State. The land revenue was exorbitant; from 46 to 50 percent of the gross produce and revised upwards every 20 to 30 years.

The principle feature of ryotwari system was the direct collection of the land revenue from each individual cultivator, or ryot, by government agents. For this purpose, all holdings were measured and assessed according to crop potential and actual cultivation. The settlement under the Ryotwari system was not made permanent. It was revised periodically after 20 to 30 years when the revenue demand was usually raised.

The advantages of this system were the elimination of middlemen, who often oppressed villagers, and an assessment of the tax on land actually cultivated and not merely occupied.

However, peasants suffered under this system in several ways:

- It took away peasant ownership. The peasant soon discovered that the large number of zamindars had been replaced by one giant zamindar— the state—and that they were mere government tenants whose land was sold if they failed to punctually pay land revenue. In fact, the government later openly claimed that land revenue was rent and not a tax.
- In most areas the land revenue fixed was exorbitant; the ryot was hardly left with bare maintenance even in the best of seasons. For instance, in Madras the government claim was fixed as high as 45 to 55 per cent of gross production in the settlement. The situation was nearly as bad in Bombay.
- The government retained the right to enhance land revenue at will.
- The ryot had to pay revenue even when his produce was partially or wholly destroyed by drought or floods.

Mahalwari Settlement

Governor General Lord William Bentinck laid the basis of the mahalwari system in 1833. It was first adopted in Agra and Oudh and later extended to the Punjab and parts of central India.

Under the *mahalwari system*, the revenue settlement was to be made village by village with the heads of families; collectively claiming to be the landlords. The whole village was treated as a unit and the village lands were held jointly by the village communities. While the ownership of land was collective, the period of settlement, fixation of land revenue, etc., used to differ in different mahalwari areas resulting in different types of mahalwari system.

Initially, the land revenue share of the State was as high as 83 percent of the gross produce, but later it was revised downwards to 66 percent of the gross produce.

The new agrarian relations stabilized the government revenues but, however, reduced the peasant to abject poverty. Now, land became saleable, mortgageable which undermined the structure of the rural society.

The worst evil was the emergence of money-lenders and thereby the rural indebtedness. Another important development was the commercialization of agriculture which had some merits, but at the cost of food grains.

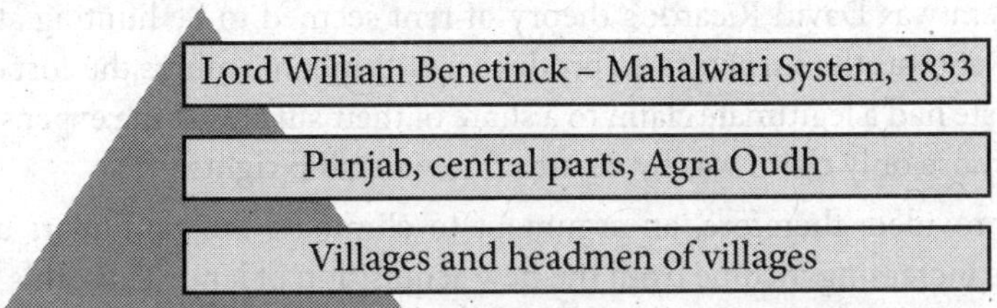

The ultimate structure which emerged in the agricultural sector can be termed as semi-feudal and semi-colonial in character. Increase in agricultural productivity as anticipated, was not achieved, as the landlords indulged in making quick money, like in trade rather than investing in agriculture.

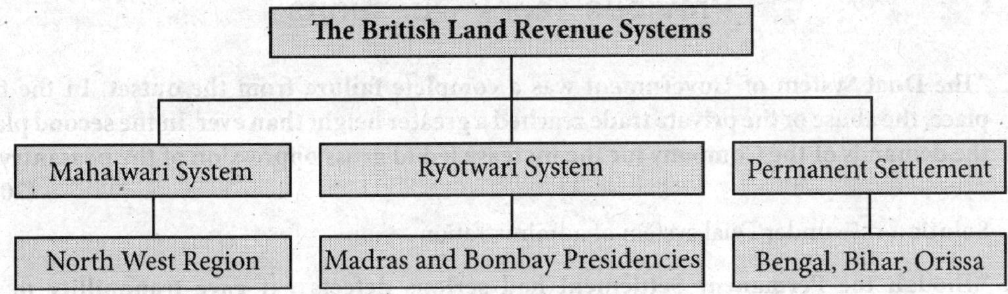

Influence of Economic Ideas in Shaping the Land Revenue Policy in India

Economic ideas played a very important role in shaping the Indian land revenue policy during early British rule. Two schools of economic thoughts primarily influenced the British government in shaping the land revenue policy in India. These were: Physiocrats in Permanent Settlement, and Utilitarians in Ryotwari settlement. Physiocrats were a group of 18th century Enlightenment French economists who believed that the wealth of nations was derived solely from the value of "land agriculture" or "land development" and that agricultural product should be highly priced.

Since 1770, i.e. even before Cornwallis arrived, a number of company officials and European observers like Alexander Dow, Henri Patullo were advocating for land tax to be permanently fixed. Despite their various ideological orientation, they shared a common faith in the Physiocratic school of thinking that assigned primacy to agriculture in a country's economy.

Alexander Dow in his book *History of Hindustan* introduced the idea of permanent settlement. This idea was elaborated by Henri Patullo, an economist. The idea of reorganising zamindars as proprietors of land on a permanent basis was put forward by Philip Francis, also an economist.

Eventually, permanent settlement was introduced by Lord Cornwallis in Bengal and Bihar in 1793 which recognised zamindars as the landlords.

In 1798, when Wellesley came to India, he gave orders for extension of permenent settlement to Madras Presidency. Here the problem was to find a sizeable zamindar class as in Bengal. However, an alternative was sought and polygons were recognised at zamindars.

However, there was a growing disillusionment with permanent settlement, as it provided no means to raise the income of government.

This was also the time when the Utilitarian idea had begun to influence policy planning in India. Among them was David Ricardo's theory of rent seemed to be hunting at a revision of the existing system. Rent was the surplus farm produce, i.e. its income minus the cost of production and labour, and the state had a legitimate claim to a share of their surplus at the expense of unproductive intermediaries, whose only claim was by virtue of no wnership rights.

The theory provided, therefore, an argument to eliminate the zamindars and appropriate a larger share of the increasing income from the new acquisition of land. Thus, this led to the shaping of a new revenue settlement, mainly ryotwari system.

Previous Years' Questions

1. **"The Dual System of Government was a complete failure from the outset. In the first place, the abuse of the private trade reached a greater height than ever. In the second place, the demands of the Company for the increase led to gross oppression of the peasantry." (2014)**

   Solution : see under Dual system of administration

2. **"Though the Permanent Settlement had serious defects , it gave tranquillity to the countryside and stability to the government".(2009)**

   Solution : See under merits of Permanent Settlement

3. **What role did economic ideas play in the early phase of British rule in the shaping of land tenure policy? 2010**

4. **''In many ways, Lord Dalhousie was the founder of modern India". Elaborate.(2015)**

   Solution : See under Dalhousie's reforms

7 CHAPTER

Impact of The Economic Policy of The British Rule in India

Introduction

The British colonial rule in India brought fundamental changes in the Indian economy. It profoundly changed India's pattern of production and consumption that enormously benefitted Britain in several ways, but left India bleeding and drained of its resources. British colonial exploitation consequently resulted in India's drain of wealth, exploitation of its resources, destruction of traditional crafts and industries, and mass impoverishment of the peasantry. Starting by making profits from trade with India, the British finally made India a major market for goods manufactured in Britain and a source of raw materials for their British factories.

Phases of Colonial Exploitation in India

Colonial exploitation was carried on broadly through the following three phases:

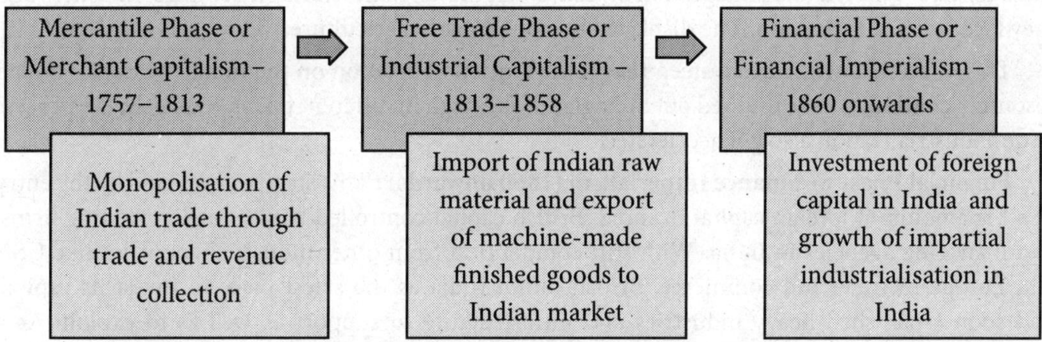

Mercantilist Phase or Merchant Capitalism (1757–1813) : In this phase, the East India Company after its victory in Bengal, began to monopolise the trade in India. The surplus Indian revenues were used to buy Indian finished goods to be exported to England. The main objective of the East India Company was to buy as much Indian goods as possible at the cheapest possible price and sell their goods in Britain and other foreign countries so that substantial profits could be made. The reckless and anarchic attempts to increase the purchases adversely affected the traditional Indian export industry, particularly the cotton industry. The government forced the textile weavers to sell their products below market prices. Many strict regulations were passed which reduced the weavers to the status of indentured labourers and gave them a life of abject poverty.

To exploit the wealth of India through taxes, new revenue settlement policies were introduced such as zamindari, mahalwari, and ryotwari systems. According to Professor Habib, during the latter half of the eighteenth century, the total British imports from India increased from 12 per cent to 24 per cent, and the British exports to India increased from 6.4 per cent to only 9 per cent of the total British exports.

Free Trade Phase or Industrial Capitalism (1813–1858) : The phase of Merchant Capitalism gave way to the phase of Industrial Capitalism towards the beginning of the 19th century. Now the emphasis shifted from revenue collection and trade to new forms of surplus appropriation. Indian economy was now geared to serve the interests of industrial England. India was converted into a source of raw material and a market for British manufactured goods. Due to the Industrial Revolution, Britain witnessed tremendous industrial growth. Now East India Company's objective was to accumulate the wealth of India in terms of raw material and money. British industrial policy made India not only the exporter of raw material, but also the consumer of British industrial goods.

Charter Act of 1813 ended the monopoly of the East India Company, and British Government opened trade with India for everyone. Emerging British capitalist class and British industries were in need of foreign markets and raw materials. To satisfy the interests and needs of British capitalists and British industrialists, the British government, through the Charter Act of 1813, turned India as a subordinate trading partner, as a market to be exploited, and as a dependent colony to supply raw materials.

The need for raw materials and markets for industrial goods resulted in the formation of a free trade policy. In this policy, Indian goods entered Britain with huge tariffs and British goods entered India for free. This led to disintegration of traditional Indian handicrafts and cottage industries and they faced virtual extinction. The displaced workers took to agriculture.

This phase also witnessed a steep rise in the burden of taxation on the Indian peasants. Indian resources continued to be drained out to England, although in different forms. Similarly, the process of de-industrialization also got accelerated.

Financial Phase or Finance Imperialism (1860 onwards) : This stage was marked by the entry of a big amount of foreign capital in India. British capital controlled banks, foreign trading firms, and managing agencies in India. With stiff competition from other industrial countries like USA and Europe in trade and commerce, British found India as the safest place to invest its capital, and soon established heavy industries and infrastructure to support as well as to exploit. As a result, India started getting industrialised, but only on foreign capital. All the major industries like Railways, Jute, Irons, and Steel (with the exception of cotton textiles) were being run by British capital. Its result was a further drain of wealth, as all the profits made on British capital were going back to England. There was a rush of foreign investment in India, mainly lured by high profits and availability of cheap labour and raw materials. The banking system was introduced in the form of Avadh Commercial Bank in the year 1881 CE. Home grown industries came into existence in the form of Tata Iron and Steel in 1907.The industrial policy grossly neglected the native industries. The rise of an industrial capitalist class and a working class became an important feature of this phase.

British Economic Policy After Industrial Revolution in England

Below we discuss some of the British policies which hindered India's path of economic development:

British Land Revenue Policy : The growth of a new land system in India affected India's economic and social life tremendously. We have already discussed land revenue policies in the previous chapter. Here, we will briefly see the economic impact of these policies in India. In 1793, Lord Cornwallis introduced Permanent Settlement in Bengal and neighbouring areas. Under this system, zamindars were given the hereditary rights to collect revenue on behalf of the British government and the peasants lost their ownership rights over the land, which in the past belonged to them.

Another totally different land revenue system called ryotwari settlement evolved in large parts of Bombay and Madras, which subsequently extended to North-Eastern and North-Western India. Under this system, each peasant holding a plot of land was recognised as the landlord and was made directly responsible to the State for the annual payment of land revenue. The conditions of the peasants under the ryotwari system deteriorated due to the high revenue.

Another land tenure system known as mahalwari was adopted in Punjab and nearby regions. In this, all villagers collectively deposited land revenue to the British government. In this land revenue settlement, the villagers and individual peasants suffered from excessive rent and exploitation from moneylenders.

In all the land revenue settlements, the land rents fixed were excessive and were instrumental in the destruction of the traditional village economy. In the zamindari system, the new landlords or zamindars, were made the masters of the village communities, while the ryotwari system cut through the heart of the village communities by making a separate arrangement between each peasant cultivator and the State.

Therefore, according to scholars Mishra and Puri, 'Due to defective land tenure system, virtually no investment was made in agriculture and the farm technology remained backward. Moreover, the size of holdings and the system of distribution of agricultural produce went against any improvement in agricultural production.'

British Polices of Industry and Commerce : British rule ruined the Indian economy through its industrial and commercial policies which favoured the British industries at the cost of the Indian economy. After the Industrial Revolution in England around 1760's, the political influence of the British capitalist and industrialist class increased. At the instance of this newly emerged class, the British government levied protective tariffs on Indian manufacturers, making their imports in England difficult.

Until 1813 CE, Indian cotton textiles sold to the British markets was about half the prices of the British cotton. Thus, the British government felt it necessary to levy protection. It banned the use of Indian products. So, in the words of British scholar Wilson, 'Had this not been the case, had not such prohibitory duties and decrees existed, the mills of Paisley and Manchester would have been stopped in their outset, and could scarcely have been again set in motion, even by the power steam. They were created by the sacrifice of the Indian manufacture'.

Similarly, a deliberate policy was pursued to destroy other industries in India. The Court of Directors opposed the use of Indian ships in trade between England and India, which not only obstructed India's export to Britain, but also caused a serious setback to the Indian shipping industry, thereby serving the twin purposes of the British.

With the development of railways, iron and steel industries were developed in Western European countries and in the UK. Hence, in India too, this would have been easily possible, had the policy of the British government been positive in this regard. But India lost this opportunity due to the negative approach of the government.

Another setback the Indian economy received through the British policy was commercialisation of agriculture for the supply of raw materials to British manufacturers. It led into two negative consequences for the Indians. First, it led to shortage of foodgrains, especially during famine. In fact, according to historians, the British created famine in India through its inhuman policies. Second, the machine-manufactured British goods flooded into Indian markets; thus destroying Indian cottage and handloom industry.

These are the important policies of the British Empire through which it exploited India. India could not oppose it. She was the mute spectator to her own destruction by some foreign power. The famous historian Wilson mentions, "Had India been independent, she would have retaliated, would have proposed prohibitive duties upon British goods, and would thus have preserved her own productive industry from annihilation".

Development of Railways and its Impact

With the advent of Industrial Revolution in Britain and other western countries, the industrial and finance capitalist phase of exploitation started in the Indian colony. The colonial government tried to develop India as a supplier of raw material and market for its manufactured goods. It was necessary to integrate the Indian economy with that of the mother country. Thus, railway development began in India in 1853 for serving colonial interest. Huge investments were made so that the railways reach nooks and corners of the country. By 1905 CE, 45000 km of railways had been laid out.

This was done for the following reasons:

- To propel the unequal free trade
- To help strengthen administration in the countryside
- To move the army

The private investment in railways was guaranteed an assured return of 5% from the government. Private investment was also assured risk-free return at public risk. Mobilising resources such as coal to meet the power requirements for industrial goods through railways only resulted in drain of wealth for India. India also became a massive importer of rail coaches, engines, etc. Due to this heavy investment and attention to the railways, many other crucial sectors were neglected. For example, the agriculture sector saw no investment, which gradually turned unproductive to the point that it led to many famines. National leader Tilak called the railway investments as 'decorating another's wife'.

Indian people did not benefit much from railways and remained grossly at loss. People in India were only seen as a means to develop the railway infrastructure and as a market for the finished goods from raw materials. The focus was on assuring returns to the private capital at the risk of public efforts. The public continued to be used as labour and also, the income and taxes in their name were also used to meet the trade interests.

Not only railways, but also, many of the infrastructure projects such as laying of roads and telegraphs were deliberately planned and implemented at the cost of the public to reap private benefits.

It was only after independence that service to the public became the objective of the railways.

However, there were certain unintended benefits of the railways to the public at large. It provided for better connectivity for the masses. Various feeder roads were developed around the railways and flow of modern ideas helped in raising the national consciousness.

Therefore, it can be said that while the Railways are often seen as one of the biggest contributions of the British regime, in reality, they were designed to support and enhance the unequal distribution of trade between India and Britain, with the larger aim of economic surplus extraction.

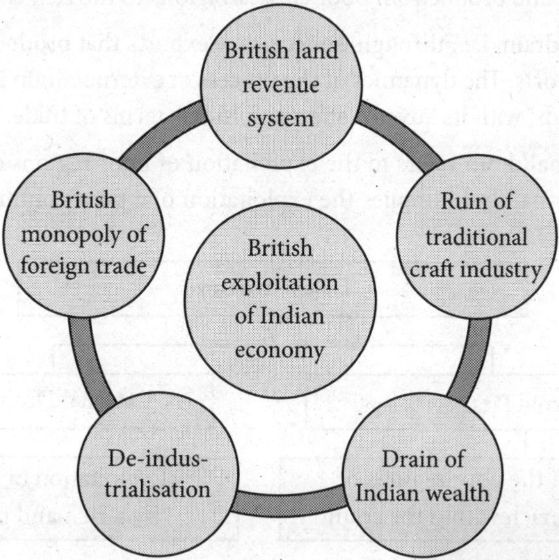

British Policy of Drain of Wealth from India

The constant flow of wealth from India to England for which India did not get adequate economic or commercial benefits or material gains has been described by Indian national leaders and thinkers as 'Drain of wealth of India'. Dadabhai Naoroji was the first person to say that internal factors were not the reasons for poverty in India. Poverty was caused by colonial rule that was draining Indian wealth and prosperity. While explaining the British economic exploitation of India, Dadabhai Naoroji put forward the 'Economic Drain Theory' in his book *"Poverty And Un-British Rule in India"* published in 1867. Dadabhai pointed out that the drain of wealth and capital from the country was responsible for the absence of development of India. The theory stated that the major components of drain were in the

Dadabhai Naoroji, 'The Grand Old Man of India' — Wikimedia Commons

form of salaries and pensions of civil and military officials, along with interests and loans taken by the Indian government from abroad. Other components were profits from foreign investment in India, shipping payments, and banking and insurance services which restricted the growth of Indian enterprise in these services. According to him, "The drain consists of two elements – first, that arising from the remittances by European officials of their savings, and for their expenditure in England for their various wants both there and in India: from pensions and salaries paid in England, and second that arising from remittance by non-official Europeans."

Thus, according the Naoroji, the economic resources of India were drained in two ways:

- Through internal drain, i.e., through the transfer of purchasing power by means of taxation, interest payments, and profits from poor classes/regions to the rich classes/regions.
- Through external drain, i.e., through unnecessary exports that produced no equivalent returns in the form of imports. The dynamics of the process of external drain is functionally related to a net transfer of funds, with its adverse effects on India's terms of trade.

Thus, while internal drain refers to the exploitation of poor regions or individuals by the rich within a country, external drain implies the exploitation of a poor country by a rich and powerful country.

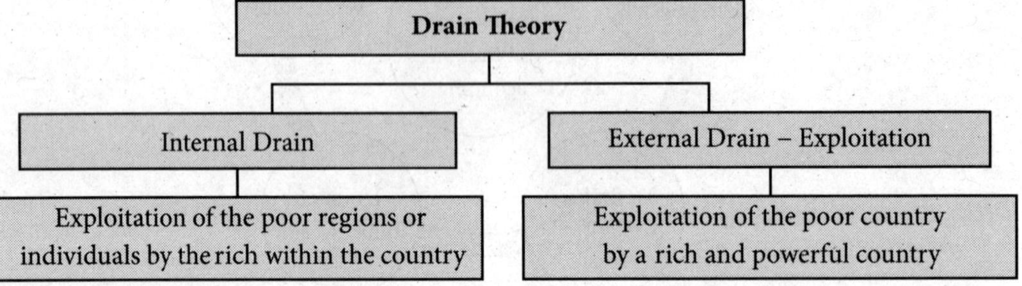

Following were the constituents of 'Drain of Wealth':

- The money extorted by company servants from various rulers, zamindars, and merchants as well as the common man was sent to Britain.
- The duty-free trade provided to the British manufacturers gave them a competitive edge over the Indian traders. These subsidies were also financed from the Indian treasury.
- The remittances and salaries along with other incomes sent to England by Company officials working in India.
- 'Home charges' were the cost of salaries and pensions of the Company officials in India, which were charged on the treasury of India.
- Hefty interests were paid to these British investors leading to drain of wealth.

Following Dadabhai, Indian national economist, Romesh Chunder Dutt, or R.C. Dutt, also pointed out the concept of drain of wealth in his book "Economic History of India" published in 1902, blaming British policies for Indian economic ills. These policies hampered income and employment potential within India.

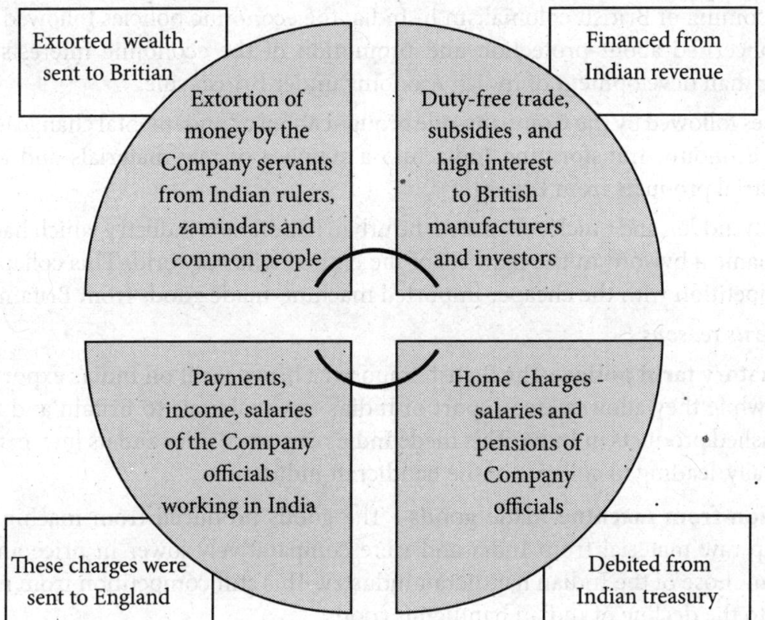

All scholars agreed that drain of wealth retarded and checked capital formation in India.

Naoroji suggested the following measures to remove India's poverty and to reduce the drain:

- Indians and Englishmen should be paid equal salary for the same type of job. Regarding the British employed in India and the Indians employed in England, he suggested that a fair and reasonable apportionment between the two should be made.
- British were getting high salaries and so they should not be paid any pension.
- No country could invade India through the sea, and so she should not be charged for the maintenance of the Indian Navy.
- Indians should be given due representation in the government, and foreign capital should come, but not the foreign capitalist who took everything from India.

Romesh Chunder Dutt
— Wikimedia Commons

Impact Of British Economic Policy In India

Following were some of the significant impacts of the economic policy of the British in India:

Ruin of Indian Handicraft Industry

Prior to British colonial rule, India was well known for its handicraft industries dealing with cotton and silk textiles, metal and precious stone works, etc. These products manufactured in India had a worldwide market due to the fine quality of material used and high standards of craftsmanship employed in the exported products.

With the coming of British colonialism in India, the economic policies followed by the British were more concerned about protection and promotion of the economic interests of their own country rather than development of Indian economy under British rule.

The policies followed by the Company rule brought about a fundamental change in the structure of the Indian economy, transforming India into a supplier of raw materials and a consumer of finished industrial products from Britain.

There was a sudden and quick collapse of the urban handicrafts industry which had for centuries made India's name a byword in the markets of the entire civilized world. This collapse was caused largely by competition with the cheaper imported machine-made goods from Britain.

Following were its reasons:

- **Discriminatory tariff policy :** The British imposed a heavy tariff on India's export of handicraft products, while they allowed free export of India's raw materials to Britain and free import of British finished products in India. This made India's export costlier and its international demand fell drastically, leading to collapse of the handicraft industry.
- **Competition from machine-made goods :** The goods produced from machines were made from cheap raw material from India and were comparatively lower in price and superior in quality than those of the Indian handicraft industry. This stiff competition from machine-made goods led to the decline of Indian handicraft goods.
- **Downfall of princely states :** Princely states and the traditional aristocratic class were the great patrons of handicraft goods. They used to patronise Indian handicraft industry. As a result, Indian handicraft industry gained international fame. With the domination of British power, princely states and Indian aristocracy were ruined. Consequently, Indian handicraft industry got ruined due to lack of patronage and protection.

The impact of the British rule has been summed up by R.C. Dutt : 'While machine made cotton goods from England ruined the weavers, machine made twist ruined the spinners. Between 1818 and 1836, the export of cotton twist from England to India rose 5,200 times.

The same process could be traced in respect of silk goods, woollen goods, iron, pottery, glass, and paper.

The effects of this wholesale destruction of the Indian manufacturing industries on the economy of the country can be imagined. In England, the ruin of the old handloom weavers was accompanied by the growth of the new machine industry. But in India, the ruin of the millions of artisans and craftsmen was not accompanied by any alternative growth of new forms of industry. The old populous manufacturing towns, Dacca, Murshidabad, Surat, and the like were in a few years rendered desolate under the 'Pax Britannica' with a completeness which no ravages of the most destructive war or foreign conquest could have accomplished.

De-industrialisation

India was the most industrialised country in the true and modern sense of the term before the advent of colonial rule. Further, India's traditional village economy was characterised by Marx as the "blending of agriculture and handicrafts".

The British government in India systematically slaughtered the village economy which was the backbone of the handicraft industry also. As a result of British policies of land revenue, industry, and commerce, Indian handicraft industries slipped away from its pre-eminence and its decline started at the turn of the 18th century and proceeded rapidly almost to the beginning of the 19th century. This process came to be known as 'de-industrialisation'— a term opposite to industrialisation.

Britain experienced 'industrialisation' in the mid-18th century and India experienced 'de-industrialisation' at the same time. The process of de-industrialisation of India began with the gradual disappearance of the handicraft industry, mainly the cotton industry. India's cotton industry was the best in the world before 1800. Machine-made textile goods of Britain, however, did the great damage to this Indian industry since 1750. Other affected industries were jute handloom weaving of Bengal, woolen manufactures of Kashmir, silk manufacture of Bengal, hand-paper industry, glass industry, lac, bangles, etc.

Indian handicraft industry was a rural industry and its decline is also termed as 'ruralisation' of India. D. R. Gadgil attributed the decline in handicrafts to three causes.

These were:

(i) Disappearance of the court culture and old aristocracy

(ii) The establishment of an alien rule with the influx of many foreign influences that such a change in the nature of government meant

(iii) The competition from machine-made goods

In the second half of the 19th century, British government set up modern industries like railways that led to the emergence of the modern industrial sector in urban India. However, this modern industrial sector was on a smaller scale and could not provide employment to as many people as were displaced from the traditional handicraft industry. Industrial sector arrested the economic growth of India due to the unfavourable colonial industrial policy.

Poverty and Famines in British India

A major characteristic of British rule in India and the net result of the British economic policies was the prevalence of extreme poverty among its people. The poverty of the people found its expressions in a series of famines which ravaged all parts of India in the 18th, 19th, and first half of the 20th century.

The following table gives a list of major famines that occurred under British rule from 1765–1947:

Year/s	Famine	Territory/Territories	Mortality
1769-1770	Great Bengal Famine	Bihar, Western Bengal	2–10 million
1783-1784	Chalisa famine	Delhi, Western Oudh, Eastern Punjab region, Rajputana, and Kashmir	Approx. 11 million people died
1791-1792	Doji bara famine or Skull famine	Hyderabad, Southern Maratha country, Deccan, Gujarat, and Marwar	Approx. 11 million
1837-1838	Agra famine of 1837–1838	Central Doab and trans-Jumna districts of the North-Western Provinces (later Agra Province), including Delhi and Hissar	Around 0.8 million

1860-1861	Upper Doab famine of 1860–1861	Upper Doab of Agra, Delhi, and Hissar divisions of the Punjab	2 million
1865-1867	Orissa famine of 1866	Orissa and Bihar, Bellary and Ganjam districts of Madras	1 million (Orissa) and approximately 4–5 million in the entire region
1868-1870	Rajputana famine of 1869	Ajmer, Western Agra, Eastern Punjab	1.5 million
1876-1878	Great Famine of 1876–1878 (also Southern India famine of 1876–1878)	Madras and Bombay	Approx. 6.1 to 10.3 million
1896-1897	Indian famine of 1896–1897	Madras, Bombay Deccan, Bengal, United Provinces, Central Provinces, parts of Punjab (Bagar)	5 million, and from other contemporary estimates 12–16 millions
1899-1900	Indian famine of 1899–1900	Bombay, Central Provinces, Berar, Ajmer, Punjab (Bagar tract)	Approx. 3 to 10 million
1943-1944	Bengal famine of 1943	Bengal	Approx. 2.1 to 3 million

The Bengal Famine of 1769–70

During the early rule of East India Company, India suffered its first dreadful famine – the Bengal famine of 1769–70 – which claimed a third of the population of the province. No substantial measures were adopted by the Company.

Famines Under British Raj

When the British Crown assumed the governance, a series of famines rocked all parts of India. The first of these famines occurred in western Uttar Pradesh in 1860–61, followed by the famine of 1865–66 in Orissa, and the famine of 1868–70 affecting UP, Bombay, Punjab and Rajputana.

Famine Commissions

The occurrence of such devastating famines at regular intervals ultimately forced the British to formulate Famine Commissions.

First Famine Commission, 1878

Following the Great famine of 1876–78, the Government appointed a Commission under the presidency of Sir Richard Strachey to formulate general principles and suggest preventive measures. The Commission recommended the adoption of certain basic principles. The Commission basically recommended State interference in food trade in the event of famine.

The government accepted in general the Commission's recommendations. In 1883, the Provisional Famine Code was formulated which formed the basis for provincial famine codes which were formulated subsequently. The code prescribed precautions to be taken in ordinary times and instructions to be followed during organization of a relief campaign. Besides, the code also detailed the duties of all those concerned when the famine actually began.

Second Famine Commission, 1897

The next great famine occurred in 1896–97 and affected almost every province in varying degrees of intensity. Following this famine, a Commission was appointed under the presidency of Sir James Lyall, the ex-Lieutenant Governor of Punjab. The Commission adhered largely to the views expressed by their predecessors suggesting some alterations which were designed to impart greater flexibility. This Commission recommended the development of irrigation facilities.

Third Famine Commission, 1900

Lord Curzon appointed a Commission in 1900 under the Chairmanship of Sir Anthony (Later Lord) McDonnel to re-evaluate and recommend changes in the report of the previous Commission, based on the findings of the recent famine. This Commission recommended that the official machinery dealing with a famine must work round the year so that the scarcity of food grains could be controlled well in time.

The Commission emphasised the benefits of a policy of "moral strategy", early distribution of advances for purchase of seed and cattle, and sinking of temporary wells. It also advocated the appointment of a Famine Commissioner in a province where relief operations were expected to be extensive.

Most of the recommendations of the Commission were accepted and before Curzon left India, he had taken various measures to prevent and combat famine. The next great famine to have ravaged India was the Bengal famine of 1943 which took a heavy toll of life.

The root cause of the famine of 1943 lay in a series of crop failures that Bengal experienced from 1938 and due to conditions created by the Second World War. The government import of rice from Burma stopped and trade and movement of food grains was dislocated owing to the Second World War. This famine was more of a man-made disaster than an act of God.

A Famine Inquiry Commission also known as the Woodhead Commission, was appointed in 1944 to investigate and inquire about the causes and factors for the 1943 Bengal famine. It declined to blame the British government as a cause for the famine. Rather, the Commission emphasised the natural, rather than man-made factors as causes of the famine.

Thus, the recurrences of famines under British rule were the consequences of pursuance of exploitative colonial policies by the British.

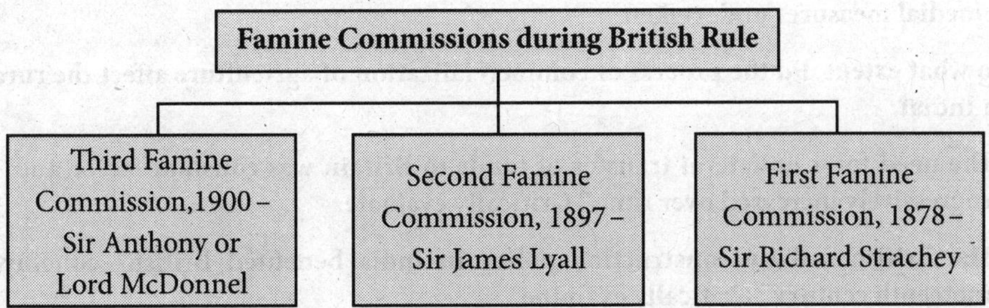

Views On Economic Exploitation During The British Rule In India

Most of the Indian scholars attribute India's backwardness and economic stagnation in the 19th and 20th centuries to the British colonial rule. Although there is unanimity on the issue of colonial exploitation by the Indian scholars, they differ in their approaches. Let's study the views and approaches of both Indian scholars and British scholars on the issue of economic exploitation and backwardness of India during the British rule.

Colonial view or approach : Most British scholars attribute economic stagnation during the British period due to overpopulation, religion, caste, social attitude, value system, and other social institutions. Their approach is called as colonial approach.

Nationalist leaders and scholars' views : Nationalist scholars Like Jadunath Sarkar, S. Chandra, R.C. Dutt, and leaders like Naoroji and Ambedkar, rejected the explanation of British administrators and writers of colonial schools with regard to India's economic underdevelopment, and strongly argued with logical explanations and evidences that the economic policies of the British rule in India were primarily responsible for the country's economic backwardness. According to these scholars, the British rulers of India consciously shattered the country's economy, appropriated her wealth and drained it out to England, and created all possible obstacles to its development.

The nationalists concluded that the decay of traditional industries, inadequate development of modern industries, and increasing dependence of the people on agriculture during the British period were largely due to the overall impact of British policies.

Political leaders and thinkers like Jawaharlal Nehru have argued that India was in a transitional phase of progress before the advent of the British and the capitalist development might have taken place in this country, if she could have escaped the colonial exploitation in the eighteenth and nineteenth centuries.

However, economist D.R. Gadgil disagreed with this argument as according to him, a number of factors which acted in India's pre-capitalist economy would not have permitted its development along the capitalist path.

Previous Years' Questions

1. **"Railway development in India provides an interesting instance of private enterprise at public risk". (2010)**
2. **Critically examine the impact of the famine policy on rural India. Describe the official remedial measures undertaken. (2008)**
3. **To what extent did the process of commercialization of agriculture affect the rural scene in India? (2010)**
4. **"The need for a unilateral transfer of funds to Britain was constant factor and, in fact, progressively increased over time." Critically evaluate. (2011)**
5. **"The British railway construction policy in India benefited British economy in the nineteenth century." Critically examine. (2017)**

Social and Cultural Policy Under The East India Company Rule : 1757–1857

Introduction

Initially, the British government's attitude was that of non-interference in India's social, cultural, and religious matters. However, gradually it became necessary for the British administrators to inculcate indigenous practices and customs in administration and judiciary and also to introduce some 'useful' Western education. However, it was only after 1813, that measures were employed to transform the Indian society and to implement education. The Charter Act of 1813 was the beginning towards the British government's move for transforming India's social and cultural landscape. The main reasons attributed for this approach were the impact of the industrial Revolution and the French Revolution, followed by the enlightenment Western thinking that opened new vistas for human progress.

The Need for Transforming Indian Society

By the beginning of the nineteenth century, the industrial capitalists of Britain began to concentrate on Indian markets. They demanded a certain level of modernisation in India for the facilitation of capital investments. The Industrial Revolution, which had begun in the middle of the eighteenth century, and the consequent growth of industrial capitalism, was rapidly changing various aspects of British society. The rising industrial groups wanted to make India a big market for their machine-manufactured goods. This could not be accomplished merely by adhering to the policy of non-interference. It required the partial transformation and modernisation of Indian society which would create demands for Western goods. And so, in the words of the historians Thompson and Garratt, "the mood and methods of the old brigandage were changing into those of modern industrialism and capitalism."

Liberal Thinking in Britain

At the same time, new liberal thinking in Britain was replacing the old imperialist attitudes and manners. The eighteenth and nineteenth centuries witnessed a great ferment of new ideas in Britain and Europe which influenced the British outlook towards India and its problems. All over Europe "new attitudes of mind, manners, and morals were appearing". The great French Revolution of 1789 with its message of liberty, equality, and fraternity generated powerful democratic sentiments and unleashed the force of modern nationalism. The three outstanding thoughts of this period were (a) rationalism, or faith in reason and science, (b) humanism, and (c) doctrine of progress.

The impact of these new thoughts was also felt in India and to some extent, affected the British notions of colonial governance.

Schools of Thought – Orientalists, Utilitarians, Evangelists

Three ideologies dominated the new thinking in the early 19th century: Orientalism, Evangelism, and Utilitarianism. Following is a discussion on these schools of thought:

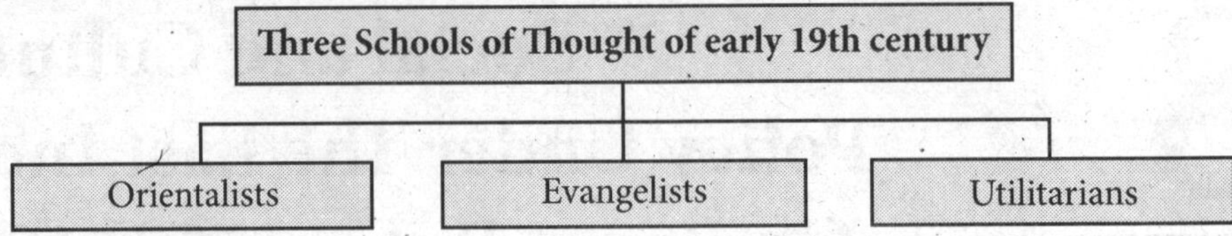

The Orientalists

The Orientalists stressed on the distinctiveness of the indigenous cultures and civilisations, mainly Eastern. They favoured in propagating and maintaining indigenous culture and heritage. Many Orientalists respected and admired Indian philosophy and culture and proposed to introduce Western ideas and philosophy in India very cautiously and gradually.

Orientalists pleaded for the safeguard of cultural traditions with minimum interference in socio-religious traditions. They argued that peace would promote the trade and it would be to Britain's advantage. They advocated that introduction of Western ideas and concepts should be as few as possible.

Many Orientalists began to take interest in the study and understanding of India's culture and its past. This serious study of the past of India became inevitable as the British East India Company authorities decided that it was essential for the officers of the Company to be proficient about Indian culture and civilisation to be able to rule them properly.

Orientalists believed that Indian civilisation had reached its epic in the past and then declined. They wanted to study the ancient texts and rules of India to understand the civilisation as they felt this could form the basis of future development of India. The British wanted to show Indians the grandeur of the past so that the latter would feel new respect for the British. The British, by doing this, would become guardians of Indian culture and also its masters.

Interest in Indian culture and heritage started with William Jones, a judge at the Supreme Court of Calcutta. Jones was a linguist who knew Greek, Latin, and Arabic and spent hours on studying Sanskrit and other intricacies of the language. He also started exploring other articles on ancient Indian laws, culture, practices, traditions, and philosophy. With like-minded Englishmen, he started the Asiatic Society of Bengal in 1784. The society undertook research into the past of Indian culture and civilisation. Along with William Jones, Wilkins, H.T. Colebrooke, H.H. Wilson, and Max Muller were the well-known Orientalists of the *Asiatic Society*.

Sir William Jones
— Wikimedia Commons

The British needed Indian scholars to teach them Sanskrit and ancient laws which the British believed would form the basis of British rule in India. Translations of the important Sanskrit classics were carried by Orientalists of the *Asiatic Society*. Lord Warren Hastings, who himself was an Orientalist, not only patronised the *Asiatic Society* but also desired to reconcile the British rule with the Indian institutions. In order to translate the vision of Hastings, a well-known Orientalist, Nathaniel Halhed prepared 'A Code of Gentoo Laws' with a view to ensure stability to the acquisitions of the British in India.

Educational institutions for the learning of Indian culture, languages, and customs were set up for British administrators. Warren Hastings opened Calcutta Madrasa, and Jonathan Duncan formed Sanskrit College in Varanasi. To encourage further the study of the past of India, Wellesley established the Fort William College at Calcutta in 1800 CE. The focus of the Fort William College was imparting scholarship in Indian languages to the students to enable them to become good administrators.

The representatives of the Oriental line of thinking in India were such British officials as Jeremy Bentham, Mountstuart Elphinstone, Metcalfe, Thomas Munro, and John Malcolm. These officials emphasised on purposeful and useful governance. Under the influence of these officials, the British government began to reshape and restructure its various administrative and economic policies.

The British, influenced by Orientalist thinking, believed that Indians ought to be educated in Sanskrit and Persian instead of languages alien to them. Thus, the Orientalists favoured stability over development. Owing to the efforts of these Orientalists, by the middle of the 19th century, interest in the past culture of India had become deep-rooted and spread to various parts of Europe.

Orientalists advocated that introducing reforms in the judiciary and landed property could solve the problems of India. They believed that modern laws could be instruments of change and through enactment of laws, Indian society could be transformed into a modern society. As a result, many officials of the Company proposed for a series of laws and penal codes to make India 'civilised' and improved.

The Orientalist outlook, which was generally regarded as conservative remained influential in England as well as in India for a long time. In fact, the majority of British officials in India were generally of Oriental thinking.

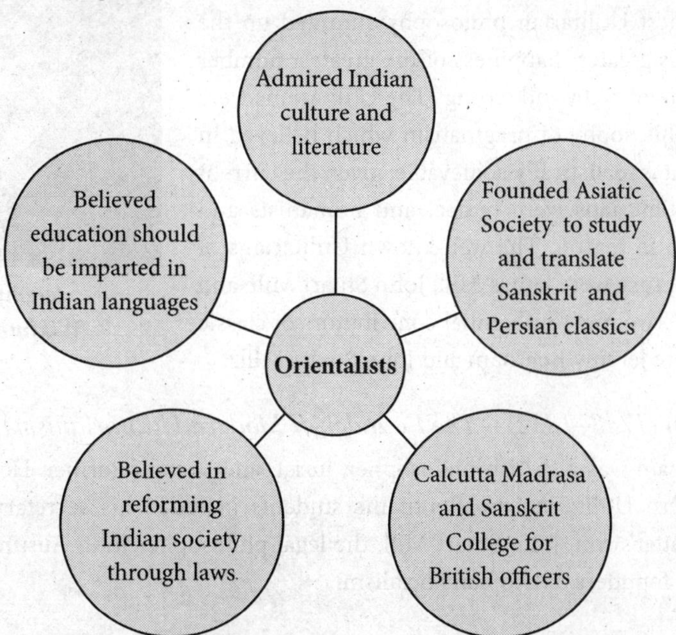

The period of Orientalism can be said to begin from 1773 during the governorship of Lord Warren Hastings and lasted till 1832. Orientalism proved to be a strategic tool to serve the infant British administration in the beginning and then to justify the colonial rule on Indians.

For British administrators and colonists, Oriantialism was certainly not for love and appreciation of Indian culture. When Hastings became Governor-General in 1773, the bureaucratic machinery of East India Company was corruption-ridden and incompetent because of lack of knowledge of native customs and culture. Thus, the only way to improve the administration was to learn and appreciate the languages, culture, and customs of the natives. Fort William College in Calcutta was set up by Lord Wellesly with this objective of learning the cultures and customs of the Indians. Judge William Jones established the *Asiatic Society* to understand and learn the customs and heritage of India. It initiated serious research and studies on India's culture and history that benefitted British imperialists in forming laws and legislations.

Orientalism also helped colonists to morally justify the colonialism. Scholars like Max Muller established the relationship between Indo-European family of language and came out with the Aryan Migration Theory which developed the kinship between British and Indians. British historians working on India's past also stressed that once the golden Indian civilisation got degenerated, British rule could revive it.

Utilitarianism

Utilitarianism is a theory that emphasises that the proper course of action is the one that maximises utility or maximizing total benefit and reducing suffering or the negatives. Jeremy Bentham (1748–1832), the founder of the modern greatest Utilitarian philosophy summed up the philosophy as 'it is greatest happiness of the greatest number that is the measure of right and wrong.' The Utilitarians were inspired by the philosophy of pragmatism which believed in choices to do what is realistically achievable, given the current situation. The Utilitarians were radical and humanists and had a strong faith in reason. The well-known Utilitarians of the nineteenth century were James Mill, John Stuart Mill, and Jeremy Bentham. Two most influential contributors of classic Utilitarianism were Jeremy Bentham and John Stuart Mill.

Jeremy Bentham
— Wikimedia Commons

Jeremy Bentham (1748–1832) – The Founder of Modern Utilitarianism

Jeremy Bentham was a British philosopher, jurist, and social reformer. He is regarded as the founder of modern Utilitarianism. Bentham's students included his secretary and collaborator James Mill, the latter's son, John Stuart Mill, the legal philosopher John Austin, as well as Robert Owen, one of the founders of Utopian Socialism.

Jeremy Bentham in his book 'A Fragment on Government', argued that 'it is the greatest happiness of greatest number that is the measure of right and wrong". Following him in the Indian context, James Mill justified the colonial power presence in India and imperial Utilitarian liberal policy.

John Stuart Mill

Another Utilitarian was John Stuart Mill (1806–1873), the son of James Mill and a British philosopher, political economist, and civil servant. He was an influential contributor to social theory, political theory, and political economy. He has been called 'the most influential English-speaking philosopher of the nineteenth century'. Mill's conception of liberty justified the freedom of the individual in opposition to unlimited State control. He was a proponent of Utilitarianism, an ethical theory developed by Jeremy Bentham. Mill was also a Member of Parliament and an important figure in liberal political philosophy.

James Mill John Stuart Mill — Wikimedia Commons

John Stuart Mill in his book 'Utilitarianism', stated, 'In the golden rule of Jesus of Nazareth, we read the complete spirit of the ethics of utility. To do as one would be done by, and to love one's neighbour as oneself, constitute the ideal perfection of Utilitarian morality.' According to both Bentham and Mill, Utilitarianism is only considered to be a hedonistic approach, if the results of an action do not directly cause a negative impact on others.

Utilitarianism was influential in political philosophy. Bentham and Mill believed that a Utilitarian government was achievable through democracy. Mill thought that despotism was also justifiable through Utilitarianism as a transitional phase towards more democratic forms of governance. As an advocate of liberalism, Mill stressed the relationship between Utilitarianism and individualism.

British Utilitarians' Principles in India

The nineteenth century Britain witnessed the rise of the philosophy of Utilitarians that had the most powerful influence on the administration of India.

The Utilitarianism philosophy believed in the maxim of greatest good and generalising it in measurable terms. However, in the context of India, English Utilitarianism had a different hue. In India, the British rulers claimed to be the benevolent masters of India.

They believed India to be civilised under the British footage. Indian civilisation was branded by most as backward-looking. The Englishmen took on themselves the task of taking India on a course of modernity. Indians were to be taught the virtues of self-government.

The English Utilitarianism in India took roots under such paternalistic attitudinal context. They saw Indian people held in bondage by despotic rulers, archaic economic relations, and by religion steeped in superstition. So, they set about to reform the Indians and the colonial system.

The three key areas they were especially interested in were the landed property, the law, and the administration. They favoured doing away with Permanent Settlement and gave their weight to the ryotwari system. Macaulay was appointed to organise the innumerable laws into easily intelligible codes. The most notable aspect of English Utilitarian was their ideas of administration in India. They favoured the notion of a strong centralised government with benevolent despotism.

By 1800, the conservative attitude of Orientalists was fast giving way to the Utilitarian attitude which was sharply critical of Indian society and culture. For Utilitarians, Indian institutions were corrupt and decadent, and Indian thought was narrow and unscientific. Utilitarian argued that Indians are despotic in nature.

Utilitarian approach was used by most of the officials and writers and statesmen of Britain to justify political and economic enslavement of India and to proclaim that it was incapable of improvement and must therefore, remain permanently under British tutelage.

Utilitarians started judging everything on the basis of their utility and functions. They started scrutinising every aspect of the culture and society in India. They scrutinised art, religion, culture, literature, and laws in India and they judged everything on the basis of their utility and contribution to social progress and where these things are located on the civilisation scale. In India, some of the British officials who came to India after 1820 were Utilitarian. Utilitarian school of thought was prominently represented by officials such as James Mill, Lord William Bentinck, and Lord Dalhousie. They were strongly supported by the reformers like Raja Ram Mohan Roy.

The Utilitarians wanted to make India a part of the modern progressive world of science and humanism and therefore, advocated the introduction of modern Western science, philosophy, and literature.

Utilitarian thinkers and administrators initiated social reforms in India through legislations and laws. Eradication of sati, widow remarriage, and lots of other reforms had been introduced in Indian society with the help of laws. Later, all these laws were criticised by lots of post-colonial thinkers on grounds of gender and patriarchy. The Utilitarian philosophy also influenced the views of Dalhousie in creating All-India departments with single heads.

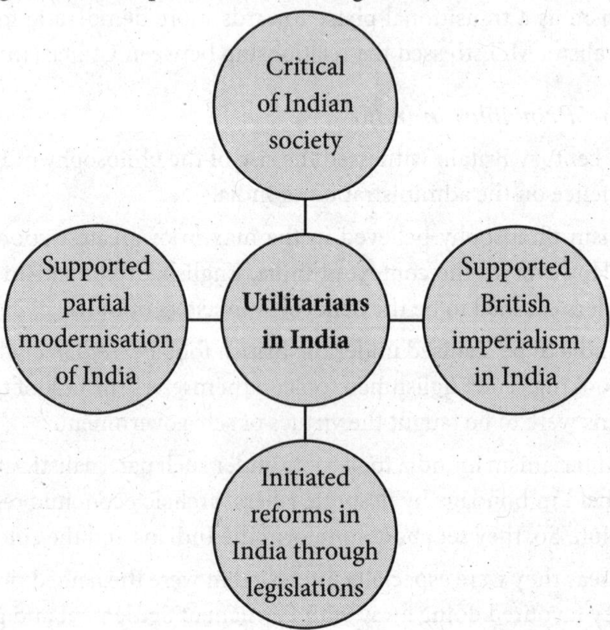

The most important advocate of Utilitarian principles and its applications in India was James Mill, the author of *The History of British India,* published in 1818. James Mill (1773–1836) was a Scottish historian, economist, political theorist, and philosopher. He was a founder of classical economics. His influential book *The History of British India* contains a complete denunciation and rejection of Indian culture and civilisation. *The History of British India* obtained a great and immediate success.

THE

HISTORY

OF

BRITISH INDIA

BY JAMES MILL, ESQ.

IN THREE VOLUMES.

VOL. I.

LONDON:

PRINTED FOR BALDWIN, CRADOCK, AND JOY,

PATERNOSTER ROW.

1817.

James Mill's book – 'The History of British India' — Wikimedia Commons

As James Mill took charge of East India Company in London, he started guiding policies towards India according to Utilitarian principles. In *The History of British India*, for the very first time, he argued that people like Sir William Jones created a myth about India's glorious past. He denied all glorious interpretation of India's cultural, spiritual, and traditional richness. He emphasised the weakness, and stagnant condition of Indian society, and established the fact that to bring progress in Indian society, India needed a change.

James Mill served for East India Company for almost seventeen years (1819–1836) and he achieved the highest post in East India Company. James Mill was highly influenced with the idea of Scottish Enlightenment which advocated scientific precision as a true measure of degree of civilisation of that society. He set himself the task of ascertaining India's true state in the scale of civilisation. He also disputed William Jones's claim that Hindus had a glorious past. Rather, he argued that the Hindus did not possess and never had possessed a "high state of civilisation". Hindus, according to Mill, were rather rude people who had made a 'but few of the earliest steps in the progress to civilisation'. He blamed that in India, there existed a hideous state of society which was inferior to the British feudal age. He immensely criticised the priest craft, superstitions, and despotism present in Indian society. In this background, he even argued that Hindus had become the most enslaved humane race. To bring change in Indian society and push it to the path of progress, James Mill suggested "Light taxes and good laws" which was basically Jeremy Bentham's idea.

James Mill argued that only through scientific codification of law, wholesome revolution in Indian society could be brought about. He argued that only through legislation, this change is possible. Only legislation could bring change in the caste-ridden, culturally backward, ritualistic, and static society. He argued that legislation could be an agent of change. Legislation could bring scientific, rational, and individualistic changes in Indian society. James Mill did not even consider about absence of Indian representation during these legislations. Mill was highly dualistic in his approach about this idea of change through legislation and his justification about this one-way process of legislation. Indian representatives were not there during enactment of these legislations.

Though James Mill supported the idea of representation and participation in England, he denied these opportunities in India. He argued that good governance in India could only be promoted through the British government and its colonial policy. British colonial Acts and legislations, according to him, would bring people out from the bondages of priesthood and despotism, and lead Indian masses on the path of life of their choices.

Evangelicalism

Evangelicalism was a Protestant Christian movement of England in the 18th century which emphasised on promoting Christian values to the masses. The Evangelists were critical of the Indian society and condemned it as 'barbaric'. They desired to 'civilise India'.

The influential members of the Evangelicalism were Wilberforce and Charles Grant. They favoured the spread of Christian faith to the East and advocated that "India will reform herself as a flower to the Sun". Charles Grant propagated the policy of assimilation of India into the great civilising mission of Britain. Charles Grant supported the idea of a civilising mission that would lead to reforming the degenerative Indian society, as well as material prosperity of the East India Company.

The missionaries regarded Christianity to be a superior religion and wanted to spread it in India through Westernisation which, they believed, would destroy the faith of the natives in their own religion and culture.

The Evangelists therefore :

(i) Supported the scientific approach propagated by Utilitarians, as they believed the approach would help in undermining the native culture and beliefs.

(ii) Supported the Imperialists, since law and order and the British supremacy were essential for their propaganda.

(iii) Sought business and the capitalist support holding out the hope to them that the Christian converts would be better customers of their goods.

They supported a programme of Westernisation in the hope that it would eventually lead to the country's conversion to Christianity. They thought that the light of Western knowledge would destroy people's faith in their own religions and lead them to welcome and embrace Christianity. They, therefore, opened modern schools, colleges, and hospitals in the country.

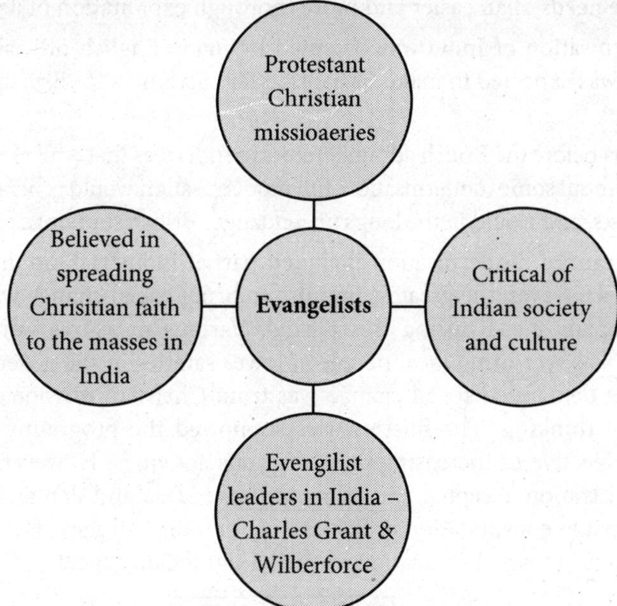

Charles Grant

Charles Grant (1746 – 31 October 1823), was a British politician and an influential officer in the Company. He was motivated by the Evangelical Christianity and championed the causes of social reform and Christian mission, particularly in India. He served as Chairman of the British East India Company, and also as a Member of Parliament.

Grant saw the Indian society as not only heathen, but also as corrupt and uncivilised. He was appalled by such native customs as exposing the sick, burning lepers, and *sati*. He believed that Britain's duty was not simply to expand its rule in India and exploit the subcontinent for its commercial interests, but to civilise and Christianise.

In 1792, Grant wrote the tract "Observations on the State of Society among the Asiatic Subjects of Great Britain." This famous essay pleaded for education and Christian mission to be tolerated in India alongside the East India Company's traditional commercial activity. It argued that India could be advanced socially and morally by compelling the Company to permit Christian missionaries into India. In 1797, Grant presented his essay to the Company's Directors, and then later in 1813, along with the reformer William Wilberforce, successfully to the House of Commons. These efforts resulted in granting permission to Christian missionaries in India in the Charter Act of 1813.

The 'Colonial Modernisation' of India

Predominantly, the ruling elements in the British Indian administration were imperialistic and exploitative. They would accept new ideas and adopt reformist measures only if, and to the extent, that did not come into conflict with commercial interests and enabled economic penetration of India and the consolidation of British rule. The Government feared that too much modernisation might generate forces hostile to their interests. Thus, it was thought to be appropriate to opt for partial modernisation — introducing it in some respects and blocking it in others, in other words, a 'colonial modernisation'. They thought that the modernisation of India had to occur within broad limits imposed by the needs of an easier and more thorough exploitation of its resources.

Thus, the modernisation of India was accepted by many English officials, businessmen, and statesmen because it was expected to make Indians better customers for British goods and reconcile them to the alien rule.

The basic dilemma before the British administrators in India was that while British interests in India could not be served without some modernisation, full modernisation would generate forces which would go against their interests, and would in the long run, endanger British supremacy in the country.

The British program of modernisation included partial industrialisation and a social change in the Indian society. However, the greatest impulse to bring social change was from the financial deficit that the Company faced during this period. Various measures were taken to curb the deficit. One of them was recruiting local people at lower salaries in the government departments. Another element that demanded social change was from Christian missionaries who propagated the Evangelist line of thinking. The missionaries supported the program of imparting Western education with the objective of increasing their religious activities. However, the ruling elements in the British administration accepted and adopted those ideas and demands which enabled the economic penetration and consolidation of British rule in India. All these factors culminated into a social and cultural policy in which education formed a significant aspect.

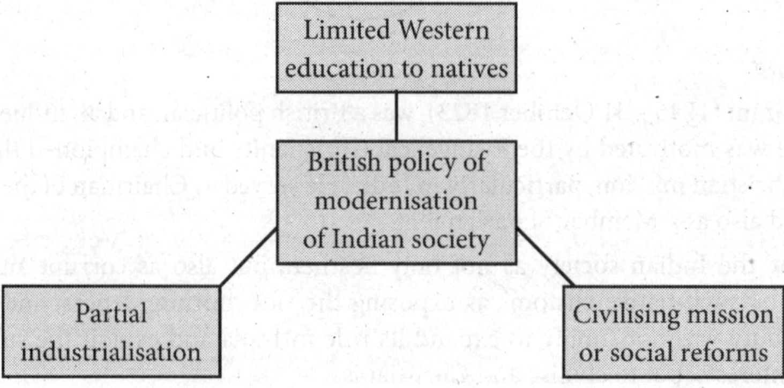

Charter Act of 1813 and Introduction of Modern Education

Before the nineteenth century, the British government did not take interest in imparting education. The major focus of the East India Company was on revenue administration. Education was hardly the concern of the British government. However, private organisations, individuals, and missionaries had already initiated the educational works in India. In 1781, Warren Hastings set up the Calcutta Madrasa for the study and teaching of Muslim laws and related subjects. In 1791, Jonathan Duncan started a Sanskrit College at Varanasi, where he was the Resident, for the study of Hindu Laws and Philosophy. Lord Wellesley founded the Fort William College in 1800 for making the Company employees aware of Indian languages for the sake of administration. But these educational institutions were designed to provide a regular supply of qualified British officers to help the Indian administration of the Company. These educational institutions were the initial attempts by the Company to impart educational activities in India. These attempts were purely an act of individual enterprise.

By the beginning of the nineteenth century, Christian Missionaries and their supporters and many humanitarians soon began to exert pressure on the Company to encourage and promote Western education in India. Indian reformer Raja Ram Mohan Roy fervently advocated the study of Western knowledge, which was seen by them as "the Key to the treasures of scientific and democratic thought of the modern West."

Under such strong pressure, the Charter Act of 1813 was passed which included a clause on education. It required the Company to spend rupees 1 lakh annually for encouraging learned Indians and promoting the knowledge of modern sciences in India.

The 43rd clause of the Charter Act of 1813, empowered the Governor-General to appropriate "a sum of not more than one lakh rupee in each year out of the surplus territorial revenues for the revival and improvement of literature and the encouragement of the learned natives of India, and for the introduction and promotion of a knowledge of the sciences among the inhabitants of the British territories in India". The 43rd clause of this Act was important, as for the first time, dissemination of education was laid down as the State responsibility.

Also, the Charter Act of 1813 allowed the entry of Christian missionaries to India to carry out their educational and religious activities.

Debate on the Nature of Western Education in India

The education policy of the British government was the outcome of debates between the Orientalists, the Evangelists, and the Utilitarians. The arguments put forward by these schools of thought resulted in shaping the education policy in India.

A few British officials took keen interest in indigenous education and learning. These officials were generally the Orientalists due to their interest in Indian arts and culture learning. The Orientalists endeavoured to set up educational institutions wherein indigenous education was imparted.

In the second decade of the nineteenth century, the British government began to take responsibility on imparting education in India. This was evident in the Charter Act of 1813, which allowed the government to spend 'a sum of not less than one lakh of rupees in each year out of the surplus territorial revenues for the introduction and promotion of knowledge of the sciences among the inhabitants of the British territories in India'. This clause was largely the result of Orientalists' efforts that, for a long time was agitating for more funds for the revival and improvement of classical learning in India. But, for a long period, the stated amount could not be utilised for the promotion of education. In the third decade of the nineteenth century, concern for promoting education resurfaced. The British government, now, began to take concrete steps towards the formulation of the education policy in India.

As mentioned, the education policy of the British government was the outcome of debates between the three prominent schools of thought of the time namely, the Orientalists, the Evangelists, and the Utilitarians. The arguments put forward by these schools of thought resulted in shaping the education policy in India.

The Orientalists were among the earliest group of British officials who took keen interest in Oriental studies. They emphasised more on indigenous learning in the education system. They argued that indigenous knowledge would help and enable the British, particularly the ruling elements, in understanding the 'native' culture and society.

In contrast to the Orientalists, the Evangelists favoured imparting Western knowledge in India. This school of thought was largely backed by Christian missionaries whose main objective was proselytisation. They argued that by imparting Western knowledge, the natives would be able to understand Christian values and Christian faith.

The most influential intellectual group of the nineteenth century was the Utilitarians. They believed in purposeful education. Uttilitarians were in favour of imparting Western education to the upper section of the society for the consolidation of the British Empire. They argued that by educating a section of the society, the government could employ Western educated natives not only on subordinate positions but in fewer wages.

The well-known Utilitarians of the nineteenth century like James Mill, John Stuart Mill, and Jeremy Bentham translated the philosophy of pragmatism in the field of education. According to them, education should be purposeful and useful.

The Utilitarians supported their views on the following grounds:

- First, by educating a section of the society, the government could employ Western educated natives not only on subordinate positions but in fewer wages. By this measure, the government could overcome its financial deficit.
- Second, Western education would help in regeneration of the Indian society which was infested with superstitions and inhuman customs. James Mill firmly believed that 'Indian society was decadent and the key to its regeneration lay in the introduction of Western knowledge and science'. In a letter to the Governor-General of India, Mill explained his position towards selective education in the following sentences. 'General education is my panacea for the regeneration of India. The ground must be prepared and the jungle cleared away before the human mind can receive, with any prospect of real benefit, the seeds of improvement'.

The debate between Orientalists, Evengelists, and Uttilitarians paved the way for the formation of the education policy. William Bentinck became the Governor-General of India by the Charter Act of 1833. He was a firm believer in Utilitarian principles. He believed that it was English education alone which could cure Indian society of its various evils. Under his Governor-Generalship, a general committee of public instruction was formed to undertake the work on education. It is interesting to know that most of the members of this committee were either backed by Evengelists or Utilitarians. Interestingly, there were hardly any takers of the Orientalists ideas. The President of the General committee was Lord Macaulay whose main interest was the promotion of English law and English culture.

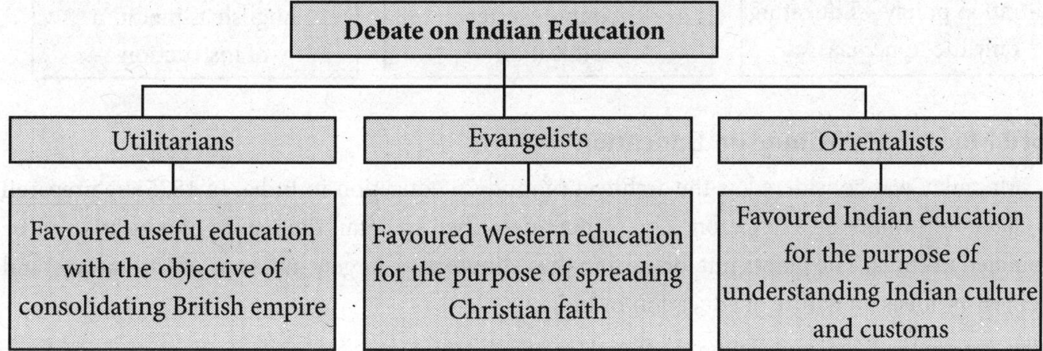

Education Policy During Colonial Rule

Role of Lord Macaulay

Thomas Babington Macaulay, 1st Baron Macaulay (1800 - 1859), was a British historian and conservative politician. He played a major role in introducing English and Western concepts to education in India. He supported the replacement of Persian by English as the official language, the use of English as the medium of instruction in all schools, and the training of English-speaking Indians as teachers.

Lord Macaulay
— Wikimedia Commons

In his view, Macaulay divided the world into civilised nations and barbarism, with Britain representing the high point of civilisation. In his Minute on Indian Education of February 1835, he observes, 'It is, I believe, no exaggeration to say that all the historical information which has been collected from all the books written in the Sanskrit language is less valuable than what may be found in the most paltry abridgement used at preparatory schools in England'. He was wedded to the Idea of Progress, especially in terms of the liberal freedoms. He opposed radicalism while idealising historic British culture and traditions.

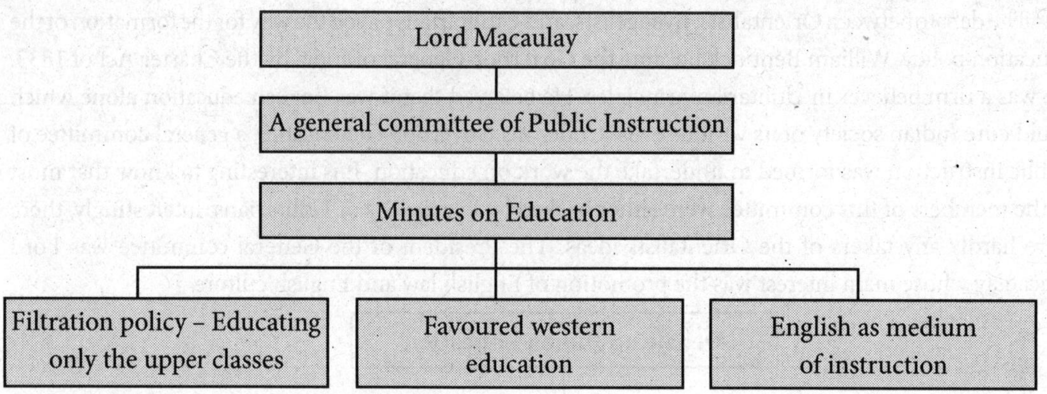

Lord Macaulay's Minute on Education

Macaulay was considered as the architect of modern education in India. In 1835, he prepared an elaborate Minute on Education. The Minute described in detail the nature of education to be promoted in India. The points put forward in this Minute were largely in favour of Utilitarians' and Evengelists' ideas on nature of education in India.

Following are the important claims made in Macaulay's Minute:

1. Lord Macaulay's Minute supported the promotion of Western literature in India. This was argued by Maculay in the following words, 'a single shelf of a good European library was worth the whole native literature of India'.
2. The Minute favoured English as a medium of instruction in schools. Macaulay supported this point on the grounds that 'the dialects commonly spoken among the natives of this part of India contain neither literary nor scientific information....English stands pre-eminent among the languages of the West....Whoever knows that language has already access to all the vast intellectual wealth which all the wisest nations of earth have created and hoarded in the course of ninety generations'.
3. Lord Macaulay was in favour of selective education. This, he claimed in his classical comments that, to form a class who may be interpreters between us and the millions whom we govern, a class of persons Indian in blood and colour, but English in taste, in opinions, in morals and intellect'.

In fact, Macaulay proposed for the filtration policy in education. The filtration theory meant the coming down of education or knowledge from the top to the bottom, i.e., from the higher class people to the lower classes or the general people.

William Bentinck, the Governor-General of India, approved Lord Macaulay's Minute on Education in Education Resolution of March 1835. This was a historic resolution on education. By passing this resolution, a central policy on education came into effect.

Issue on the Medium of instruction

Two approaches developed on the issue of medium of instruction in schools. One approach was to impart Western education in English at the secondary level. This approach was largely adopted in the Bengal Presidency. In Bombay Presidency, vernaculars were adopted as the medium of instruction. This approach was known as 'Downward Filtration Theory'. The architect of this theory was Mount Stuart Elphinstone (1779–1859), the Governor-General of Bombay Presidency. The 'Downward Filtration Theory' meant that education and modern ideas were supposed to filter or radiate downward from the upper classes. This policy of the Bombay government to encourage vernaculars as the medium of instruction was observed in a report of 1840–41 which stated that, 'knowledge must be drawn from the stores of the English language, the vernaculars must be employed as the media of communicating it, and Sanskrit must be largely used to improve the vernaculars and make them suitable for the purpose'. This approach was responsible for the growth of vernacular schools and vernacular literature all across the presidency.

Downward Filtration Theory

The Company favoured downward filtration policy in education primarily because it could not provide education to the entire masses. So it decided to educate only a few. But this 'few' were the people of the upper classes, because they alone could grab the opportunity for English education. This policy continued till the very end of the British rule, although it was officially abandoned in 1854.

The downwards filtration theory had the following three chief characteristics:

1. To educate only the upper class people in order to give them higher posts in the administration with a view to strengthen the roots of the British Empire in the country.
2. When the upper class people would receive English education, their culture would be improved and the general public would accept them as their models. As a result, the lower class people would also be educated after being influenced by the upper class people.
3. To educate the upper class people who might undertake the responsibility of educating the general people.

In 1839, the General Committee of Public Instruction again repeated the stand that education would be given only to the upper class people who should shoulder the responsibility of educating their countrymen.

In 1844, English became the official language and it was declared that people having knowledge of English would be preferred for public employment. This helped the spread of English education in India. The Government's policy of opening a few English schools and colleges instead of a large number of elementary schools led to the neglect of education of the masses.

Education Policy of the British Government in India (1854–1902)

The educational policies during the period of 1854 and 1902 were formulated by two main documents only – the Despatch of 1854 and the Report of the Indian Education Commission, 1882. Here, we will see Sir Wood's Despatch of 1854.

Wood's Despatch, 1854

In 1854, Sir Charles Wood, the President of the Board of Control sent his recommendations known as "Wood's Despatch of 1854" to India, reorganising the whole structure of education. Wood's Despatch is considered as a Magna Carta in the history of English education in India. The Wood's Despatch laid the foundations of the modern education system.

Its recommendations were the following:

1. To form a separate education department
2. To establish three universities in Calcutta, Bombay, and Madras presidencies
3. To take adequate measures for the teachers and the teaching process
4. To reform the government schools and colleges
5. To establish new middle schools
6. To start grants-in-aid in private schools
7. To improve the native primary schools
8. To expand women education, mass education, progress in vernacular language, and to set up centres of teachers' training
9. To increase the number of government schools arranged for inspection and to initiate secular education system, etc.

Wood's Despatch rejected the Filtration Policy. Under its recommendation, 'University of Calcutta' was founded in 1857. Later, Punjab (1882) and Allahabad (1887) universities were founded. Graded educational institutions were established in hierarchy starting with school educational institutions to colleges and universities.

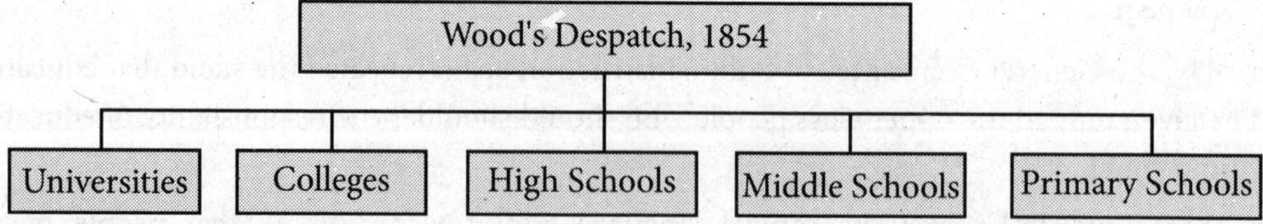

Colonial Education: The General Characteristics

The education system introduced by the British was consistent with the colonial objectives. The education which was imparted mainly in the English schools was alien to indigenous culture. No attempt was made in the school curriculum to assimilate indigenous knowledge and language. The knowledge imparted in colonial schools therefore had very little to do with the society and culture of the colonised people. Schools mainly served as a mechanism for securing a new social place and new culture or in other words, Westernizing people. English schools therefore, became sites of alienation. School system reflected the power and need of the colonists. Its curriculum was designed so as to create a section of the society. The curriculum was based on Utilitarian principles and was inherent with the zeal of the civilising mission. The Utilitarian natures of Western education qualified pupils for employment, mainly in government services and the capitalist economy. Therefore, the training given in schools was according to the needs and requirements of the colonial empire. In India, English education qualified people for lower and middle level administrative jobs.

The formal education introduced by the British was distinct from the indigenous education in terms of structure, approach, and aims. In the indigenous system, formal education was imparted in institutions such as schools. There were non-formal ways of imparting education which has been discussed in the previous chapter. However, with the advent of the English education system, the scope of non-formal education decreased tremendously because the British institutionalised the whole education system.

Western schools worked as a capitalist institution. As the capitalist forces made headway, the formal schools turned into training grounds for skilled labourers. The capitalist forces paved the ground for the emergence of institutions that supported capitalism. English schools were one of those institutions. Here, the school functioned as an institution which produced skilled labourers for material output and enabled men and women to face the competitive market.

Western education was a doorway for enhancing financial and social status. According to Martin Carnoy, 'when the individual goes to school, he or she has access to a larger slice of the economy and social pie, provided that everybody else has not gone to school along with him.' This also implied less accessibility to material resources compared to people educated in non-Western schools. Thus, the divide between English schools and vernacular schools was quite sharp. The beneficiaries of English education was the upper section of the society as this section could afford this type of education. This Western educated section of the society was generally employed in middle and lower grades of government services. Employment in such positions was considered as a mark of social status.

Social Reforms Under The East India Company – Abolition of Sati

The intellectual debates among the contemporary British thinkers on the Indian issue not only resulted in formulation of an education system on the Western lines, but also initiated a series of social reforms in the Indian society. The most important among them was the abolition of *sati*. According to the British, the practice of widow burning or *sati* was widespread in the Bengal Presidency and in some parts of western and southern India. *Sati* had become the central issue in Britain and among the Evangelists who were desperately trying to enter India. Many Indian reformers also joined along with British liberals on the issue of *sati* and demanded its abolition. It took the British more than 30 years to abolish *sati*. The Court of Directors left the issue to the discretion of the Governor-General. The Evangelists tried to prevent this practice with the support from missionaries in India. Raja Ram

Mohan Roy's writings convinced the Company's administrators that *sati* was not an integral part of the Hindu religion. When Lord William Bentinck took up the question of *sati*, he found that the abolition had been recommended by the judges of the criminal courts. Reassured by the majority view, he passed Regulation XVII on December 4, 1829 'declaring the practice of *sati* or burning alive the widows of Hindus, illegal and punishable by criminal courts'. Similar legislative measures were enacted later in the Bombay and Madras Presidencies.

Sati was virtually stopped in the Princely States through the rulers' cooperation. However, nearly thirty more years had to pass before it could be declared illegal in these states.

Previous Years' Questions

1. **"James Mill, the apostle of Utilitarian philosophy, proposed a revolution of Indian society through the weapon of law' solely. But in actual policy framing, other influences and considerations weighed much more than the colonial State." Elucidate. (2015)**

   Solution : See under James Mill

2. **"Sprung from paternalism, the English Utilitarian philosophy as introduced in India rejected its human warmth between rulers and the ruled." (2008)**

3. **"Orientalism produced knowledge of the past to service the needs of the Colonial States." Elucidate. (2011)**

Resistance, Uprisings, and The Revolt of 1857

Introduction

By 1857, the East India Company had become a paramount power exercising its direct rule over 63 per cent of the Indian Territory and 78 per cent of the population of the Indian subcontinent. However, the British penetration of India did not take place smoothly. People of India of various levels, by and large, resisted the British domination.

The subaltern groups, mainly peasants and tribal communities across India, were the first to express their resentment against the British hegemony. The resistance was in the form of movements or civil disturbances targeted against the authority of the British to regain their territories and identity. There were nearly forty major uprisings prior to the 1857 revolt all across India. These uprisings can be categorised into religious uprisings, peasants' uprisings, tribal uprisings, and uprisings in the army.

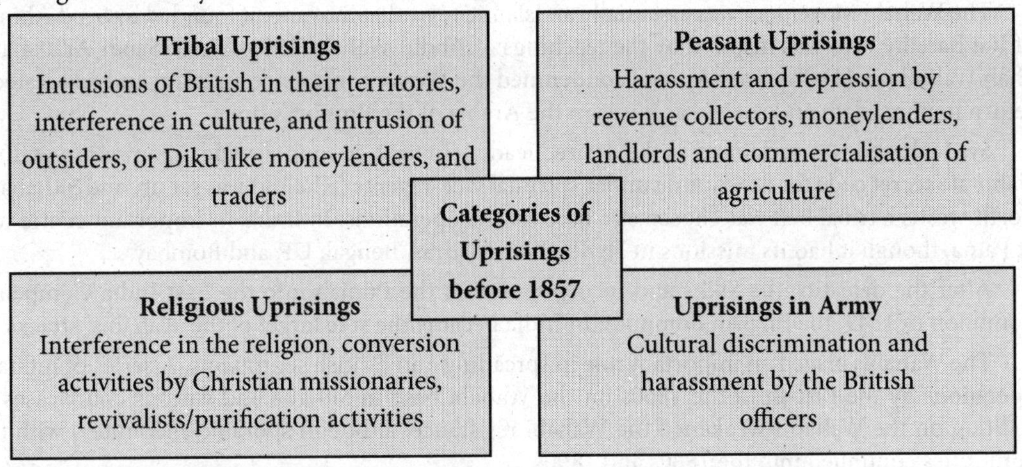

Religious, Peasant, and Tribal Uprisings – (1760s–1850s)

Religious Uprisings

The chief reasons for religious uprisings against the British were the interference in people's religion and beliefs, conversion activities of the Christian missionaries, and uprisings due to purification and revivalist activities by religious leaders.

Faqir and Sanyasi Uprisings (1763–1800)

In the series of uprisings of the period, the Faqir and Sanyasi Rebellions of 1763–1800 need to be mentioned as the first one. They were mainly religious uprisings. The Faqir Uprising took place in the Bengal region. *Faqirs* or Muslim mendicants lost their rights and privileges of charity and protection under local zamindars due to British annexation of Bengal. *Faqirs* revolted against the British under the leadership of Majnu Shah and Chirag Ali. The Faqirs were finally brought under control at the beginning of the nineteenth century. Similarly, the *Sanyasi* Uprising took place in Bengal around 1770–1800. The immediate cause of the rebellion was the restrictions imposed on the pilgrims' visiting the holy places. Famous Bengali novelist Bankim Chandra Chatterjee's *Anandamath* was based on the *Faqir-Sanyasis* rebellion which included national song '*Vande Matram*'. Till 1800, the conflict between the British forces and the sanyasis and fakirs became a common feature.

Rishi Bankim Chandra Chattopadhyay (1838–1894)

He was a Bengali writer, poet, and journalist. He was the composer of India's national song 'Vande Mataram', originally a Sanskrit hymn personifying India as a mother goddess and inspiring the freedom fighters during the Indian Freedom Movement. One of the many novels of Bankim Chandra was 'Anandamath', published in 1882. It was a political novel which depicts a Sanyasi army fighting the British soldiers. The book calls for the rise of Hindu nationalism to uproot the foreign British rule and attain self-rule. The novel was also the source of the song 'Vande Mataram' which was set to music by Rabindranath Tagore. It is now the National Song of India. The plot of the novel is loosely based on the Sanyasi Rebellion. The novel first appeared in serial form in *Bangadarshan*, the literary magazine that Bankim founded in 1872.

Wahabi Movement

The Wahabi Movement was essentially an Islamic revivalist movement founded by Syed Ahmed of Rai Bareilly who was inspired by the teachings of Abdul Wahab (1703–87) of Saudi Arabia and Shah Waliullah of Delhi. Syed Ahmed condemned the Western influence on Islam and advocated a return to pure Islam and society as it was in the Arabia of the Prophet's time.

Syed Ahmed was acclaimed as the desired leader (Imam). A countrywide organisation with an elaborate secret code for its working under spiritual vice-regents (Khalifa) was set up, and Sithana in north-western tribal belt was chosen as a base for the operations. In India, its important centre was at Patna, though it had its missions in Hyderabad, Madras, Bengal, UP, and Bombay.

After the defeat of the Sikhs and incorporation of the Punjab into the East India Company's dominion in 1849, the English dominion in India became the sole target of the Wahabis' attacks.

The Wahabis played an important role in spreading anti-British sentiments. A series of military operations by the British in the 1860s on the Wahabi base in Sithana and various court cases of sedition on the Wahabis weakened the Wahabi resistance, although sporadic encounters with the authorities continued into the 1880s and 1890s.

Faraizi Revolt (1838–1857)

The Faraizis were the followers of a Muslim sect founded by Haji Shariat-Allah of Faridpur in Eastern Bengal. They advocated radical religious, social, and political changes. Shariat-Allah's son Dadu Mian (1819–60), organised his followers with an aim to expel the English intruders from Bengal. The sect also supported the cause of the tenants against the zamindars. The Faraizi disturbances continued from 1838 to 1857. Most of the Faraizis joined the Wahabi ranks.

Mappilla Uprising (1836–1854)

Between 1836 and 1854, the Mappilla uprising of Kerala posed a great challenge to the British administration. These are the descendant of the Arabs and converted Muslims. Majority of them earned their living by working as daily agricultural labourers, petty traders, and fishermen. They rebelled against the British for their brutal behaviour.

The reasons for Mappilla rebellion were the transfer of land to independent owners, over-assessment, illegal taxes, forceful eviction from land, and hostile attitude of the government. The religious leaders kindled unity among the Mappillas and they rose against the British government. Between 1836 and 1854, there were 22 uprisings against the government in Malabar and the participants were from the lower strata of the society.

It was a prolonged movement, which the government subdued with great difficulty.

Kuka Revolt

The Kuka Movement was founded in 1840 by Bhagat Jawahar Mai (also called Sian Saheb) in western Punjab. After the British took over Punjab, the movement transformed from a religious purification campaign to a political one.

Its basic tenets were abolition of caste and similar discriminations among Sikhs, discouraging the eating of meat and taking of alcohol and drugs, and encouraging women to step out of seclusion. In 1872, one of their leaders, Ram Singh, was deported to Rangoon.

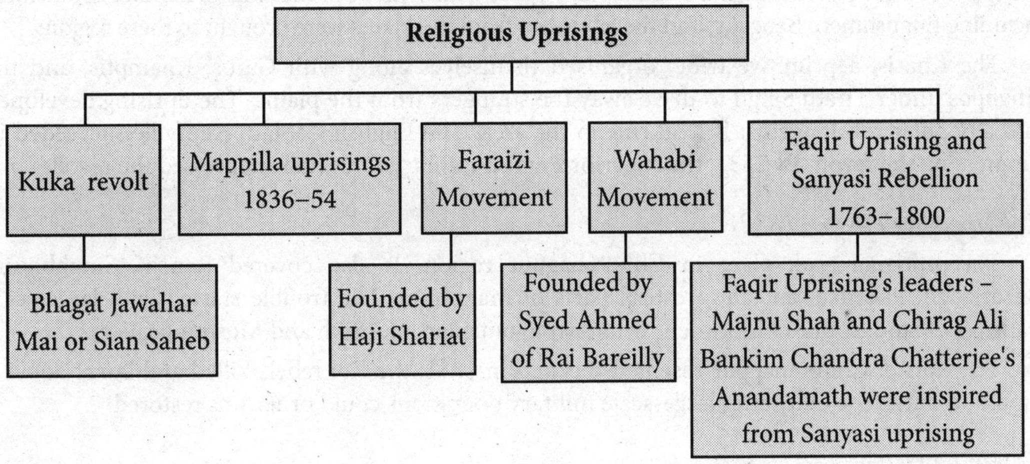

Tribal Uprisings

Tribal movements were the outcome of the imposition of a new land revenue system, increasing control of government over forest lands, and exploitation by landlords, timber traders, and moneylenders.

The tribals had been living peacefully and in harmony with nature for hundreds of years in their own forests. The British came and introduced many changes in their way of life and also introduced outsiders into their turf. This reduced them to the status of labourers and debtors from masters of their own land. The uprisings were basically against this unwelcome intrusion, and a fight for their independence. Scholar K. Suresh Singh observes, "The tribal insurrections were the most militant outbreaks and they revolted more often and far more violently than any other community, including the peasants in India".

Chief factors attributed to tribal resistance was interference in their sociocultural life, exploitation by outsiders (Diku), like moneylenders, displacements from their habitat, imposition of new farming and revenue policies, and reducing them to the lowest status in the mainstream society.

The British introduced moneylenders into the tribal areas which led to severe exploitation of the local tribals. They became bonded labourers under the new economic system.

The tribal societies had a system of joint ownership of land which was replaced by the notion of private property.

There were restrictions imposed on the use of forest produce, on shifting agriculture, and on hunting practices. This led to loss of livelihood for the tribals.

A Forest Department was set up in 1864 by the government mainly to control the rich resources of the Indian forests. The Government Forest Act of 1865 and the Indian Forest Act of 1878 established complete government monopoly over the forested land.

The work of the Christian missionaries also led to social upheaval in tribal society and this was also resented by them.

Following are some of the significant tribal uprisings that took place before the 1857 revolt :

Khasi Uprising—(1765–1833)

After having occupied the hilly region between Garo and Jaintia Hills, the East India Company wanted to build a road linking the Brahmaputra Valley with Sylhet. For this, a large number of outsiders including Englishmen, Bengalis, and the labourers from the plains were brought to these regions.

The Khasis, a primitive tribe, organised themselves along with Garos, Khamptis, and the Singhpos under Tirath Singh to drive away the strangers from the plains. The uprising developed into a popular revolt against British rule in the area. The English Captain Neufville succeeded in suppressing the revolt. By 1833, the superior English military force had suppressed the revolt.

Kol Uprising (1831–1832)

This uprising took place in Chhotanagpur region. It also covered Ranchi, Singhbhum, Hazaribagh, Palamau, and the western parts of Manbhum. The trouble started with large-scale transfers of land from Kol headmen (Mundas) to outsiders like Sikh and Muslim farmers.

The Kols of Chhotanagpur resented this and in 1831, the Kol rebels killed and burnt about a thousand outsiders. Only after large-scale military operations could order was restored.

Kandh Uprising (1837–56)

This covered Ghumsar, China-ki-Medi, Kalahandi, and Patna. Under Chakra Bisoi, the Kandhs retaliated against the British efforts to put an end to the Kandhs' practice of human sacrifice. The Britain first tried persuasion, and later used force to stop the evil practice. The Kandhs fought with *tangis* (a sort of battle axe), bows and arrows, and even swords.

Ahom Revolt (1828)

The British had pledged to withdraw after the First Burma War (1824–26) from Assam. But, after the war, instead of withdrawing, the British attempted to incorporate the Ahom's territories in the Company's dominion. This sparked off a rebellion in 1828 under the leadership of Gomdhar Konwar. Finally, the Company decided to follow a conciliatory policy and handed over Upper Assam to Maharaja Purandar Singh Narendra and part of the kingdom was restored to the Assamese king.

Pagal Panthis Revolt

Karam Shah was the founder of the Pagal Panth—a semi-religious sect having influence in the northern districts of Bengal. Tipu, the son and successor of Karam Shah, initiated the revolt. He was motivated by both religious and political motives and took up the cause of the tenants against the oppression of the zamindars. Tipu captured Sherpur in 1825 and assumed royal power. The insurgents extended their activities to Garo Hills. The area remained disturbed in the 1830s and 1840s.

Munda Revolt

For over three decades, the Munda Sardar of Chhotanagpur had been struggling against the destruction of their system of common landholdings by the intrusion of jagirdars, thikadars (revenue farmers), traders, and moneylenders. During the last decade of the nineteenth century, the Mundas rose under Birsa Munda in a religious movement or rebellion ("ulgulan") with an agrarian and political content.

They aimed to establish a Munda rule in the land by killing thikadars, jagirdars, rajas, and hakims. To bring about the liberation, Birsa gathered a force of 6,000 Mundas armed with swords, spears, battle-axes, and bows and arrows. Birsa was, however, captured in 1900 and he died in jail the same year. The primary reason for the revolt of the Mundas was the new policy of farming for outsiders and the revenue and judicial policies. It was suppressed by the British with the massive support of the British military force.

Bhil Uprisings (1818–1831)

The Bhils, an aboriginal tribe concentrated around Khandesh, revolted against their new masters, the East India Company, fearing agrarian hardships and the worst under the new regime. One of their leaders was Sewaram. The Bhils revolted in 1818–19, and again in 1825, 1836, and 1846. Between the period of 1818 and 1831, the Bhils of Khandesh ravaged the plains to show their anger against the occupation of their territory by the British in 1818. In spite of the use of force and conciliatory measures, the Bhils could not be suppressed.

Koli Uprisings (1829–1848)

The Kolis living in the neighborhood of Bhils rose up in rebellion against the Company's rule in 1829, 1839, and again during 1844–48. They resented the imposition of the Company's rule which brought with it large-scale unemployment for them and the dismantling of their forts.

Ramosi Uprisings (1822–1829)

The Ramosis, the hill tribes of the Western Ghats, had not reconciled to the British rule and the British pattern of administration. They rose under Chittur Singh in 1822 and plundered the country around Satara. Again, there were eruptions in 1825–26 and the disturbances continued till 1829.

The disturbance occurred again in 1839 over deposition and banishment of Raja Pratap Singh of Satara, and disturbances erupted in 1840–41 also. Finally, a superior British force restored order in the area.

Poligars' Revolt

The Poligars of Dindigal and Malabar rose up against the oppressive land revenue system under the British during 1801–06. Sporadic rising of the Poligars in Madras Presidency continued till 1856.

Santhal Rebellion (1855–56)

The last of the tribal uprisings before the 1857 revolt was the Santhal rebellion of 1855–56. The Santhals inhabited the districts of Birbhum, Banlarua, Murshidabad, Palkur, Damka, Bhaglapur, and Purnea. The Santhals of Rajmahal Hills resented the oppression by revenue officials, police, moneylenders, and landlords—in general, by the "outsiders' (whom they called diku). The Santhals under Sido and Kanhu rose up against their oppressors, declared the end of the Company's rule, and asserted themselves as independent in 1854.

It was only in 1856 after extensive military operations that the situation was brought under control. Sido died in 1855, while Kanhu was arrested in 1866. A separate district of Santhal Parganas was created by the Government to pacify the Santhals.

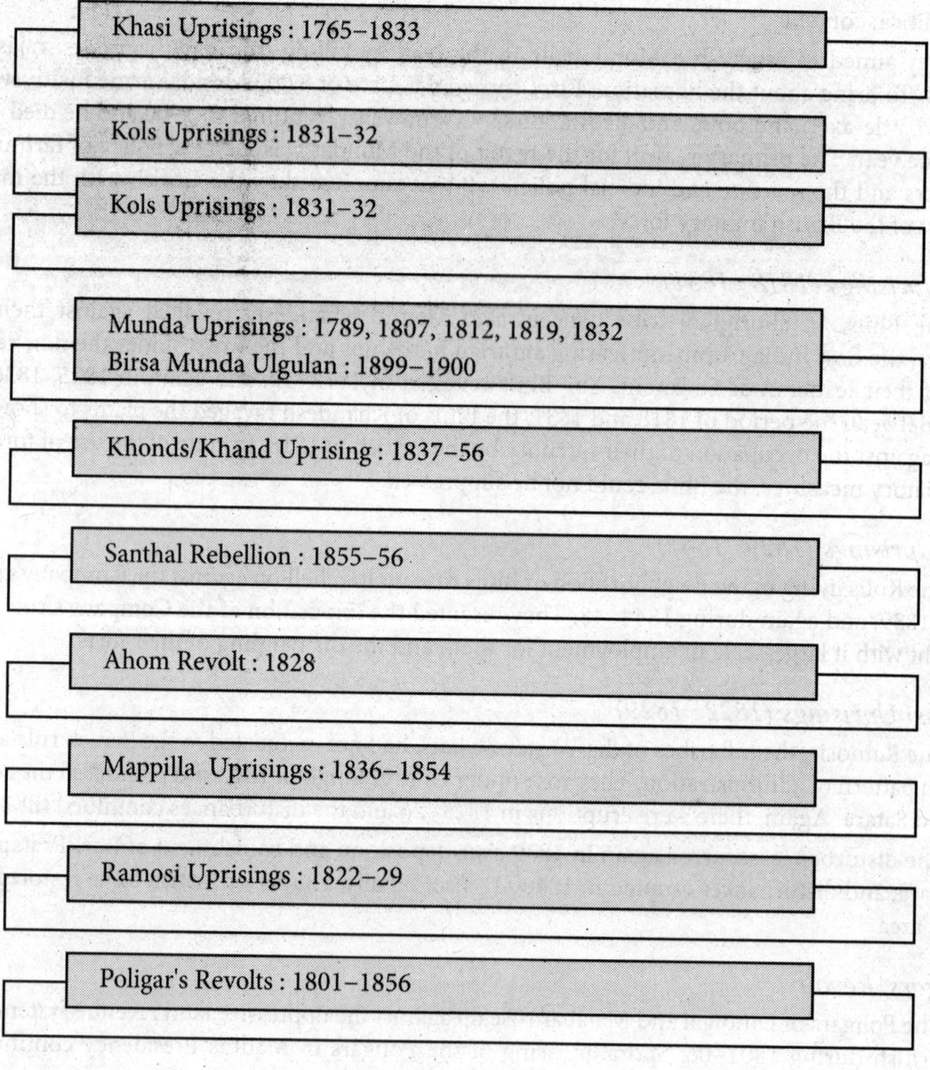

Peasant Uprisings

Main reasons attributed to peasants' uprisings were the harsh treatment by revenue collectors, moneylenders, landlords, and commercialisation of agriculture.

Following were some of the important peasant uprisings of the 19th century:

Revolt in Rangpur and Dinajpur 1783

The establishment of the British control over Bengal and their various land revenue policies brought unbearable hardship for the common man. The harsh attitude of the revenue collectors and their exactions became a regular feature of peasant life. The peasants of Rangpur and Dinajpur districts of Bengal rose in revolt in the year 1783 against the harsh and inhuman attitude of Debi Singh, the revenue contractor. It was because he and his agents created a reign of terror in these districts by beating and flogging the peasants. The peasants appealed to the government seeking justice but the silence and apathy of the government made the peasants revolt under the leadership of Dirjinarain. They formed the government of their own and stopped payment of revenue. The government, with great difficulty, suppressed the revolt.

The Indigo Movement of Bengal, 1859

The Indigo Movement in Bengal was a significant peasant uprising against the British. Indigo, a source of blue dye, was in huge demand in Europe's booming textile industry in the late 18th and 19th century. It was called 'blue gold'. The British established commercial cultivation and production of indigo in India as early as 1777. By 1788, most of the production of indigo originated in Bengal. The system became highly exploitative when the indigo planters, mainly Europeans, were accorded permission to own the land. At that time, there were two systems of cultivation of indigo – **Nij system** and **Ryoti System**. Under the *Nij system*, the European planters produced indigo directly on land which they directly controlled. They either owned the land or took it on hire to cultivate indigo with hired peasants. Under Ryoti system, the planters forced the ryots or peasants to sign an agreement, so that they could get loans or advances called *Dadon* from planters to grow indigo. However, one term of this agreement was that the ryot would cultivate indigo on at least 25% of the land. The loan made the people indebted. Soon, the peasants started losing landholdings due to poor yield and dept traps. These conditions resulted in a rebellion in 1859–60 in eastern parts of Bengal.

The revolt began as the peasants stopped paying rents. In March 1859, the revolt became more organised when thousands of ryots in Bengal refused to grow indigo. They attacked the indigo factories with whatever weapons they had. Women joined the revolt and fought with pots, pans, etc. The resistance was met with pressure from planters but farmers took pledge that they would not take advance and would not be bullied by the *lathiyals* of planters.

The key leaders of this revolt were Biswas Brothers of Nadia – Digambar Biswas and Bishnu Biswas, Kader Molla of Pabna, Rafique Mondal of Maida, and many more.

The revolt began from Govindpur village in Nadia district of Bengal where the Biswas brothers gave up indigo cultivation. This was followed by a struggle with the *Lathiyals* and revolt spread in many parts of Bengal. Strikes, legal actions, violence, social boycott of planters, etc. were some of the tools used in the revolt.

The Bengali intelligentsia played a significant role by supporting the peasants' cause through print media and supporting them in legal battles. Outstanding among them was Harish Chandra Mukerji, editor of the *Hindoo Patriot* and Din Bandhu Mitra who wrote the play *Nil Darpan* based on indigo peasant resistance.

Peasants' unity, Hindu-Muslim Unity, and support from Bengal intelligentsia made the revolt more effective. Finally, Indigo Commission was appointed which held the planters guilty, and criticised them for the coercive methods they used with indigo cultivators. The Company asked ryots to fulfill their existing contracts, but also told them that they could refuse to produce indigo in future. This was a big relief for the peasants and gradually the plantations of indigo came to an end in Bengal.

The quantum of violence in Indigo Revolt has been a subject of debate. Some historians consider that the Indigo Revolt was largely non-violent and was carried out on the path of *satyagrah* a which was later adopted by Gandhi. However, there was violence in ruthless suppression of the revolt by police, zamindars, and planters. Through their armed lathiyals, force was used by the planters in the form of kidnapping, illegal confinement, attacks on women and children, looting, demolition of houses, and destruction of crops.

Indigo Rebellion took the shape of a political movement and helped in arousing national sentiment against the alien British rulers among peasants.

Indigo Revolt was significant for an organised peasant resistance against the British planters that saw the involvement of intelligentsia and use of legal machinery for making the resistance effective. The Indigo Rebellion can be termed as the first form of resistance of the countryside against the British in economic and social terms. Unlike the spontaneous revolt of the soldiers in the Sepoy Mutiny, this countryside revolt evolved over the years and, in the process, rallied different strata of society against the British.

For the first time, resistance against the oppressive rule of the British was carried in an organised manner. There was complete discipline and unity among the peasants. Leadership was provided by conscious-minded ryots, zamindars, and moneylenders and a sense of complete Hindu-Muslim unity was present.

The Play *Nil Darpan*

Nil Darpan, meaning the Indigo Planting Mirror, was a Bengali play written by Dinabandhu Mitra in 1858–1859. The play portrayed the oppression of peasants by indigo planters. The play was central to Nilbidraha, or Indigo Revolt of 1859 in Bengal. The play has captured the entire scenario of Indigo Rebellion by showing how farmers refused to sow indigo in their fields as a protest against exploitative farming under the British Raj. It was also essential to the development of theatre in Bengal and influenced Girish Chandra Ghosh, who, in 1872, established The National Theatre in Calcutta where *Nil Darpan* was staged.

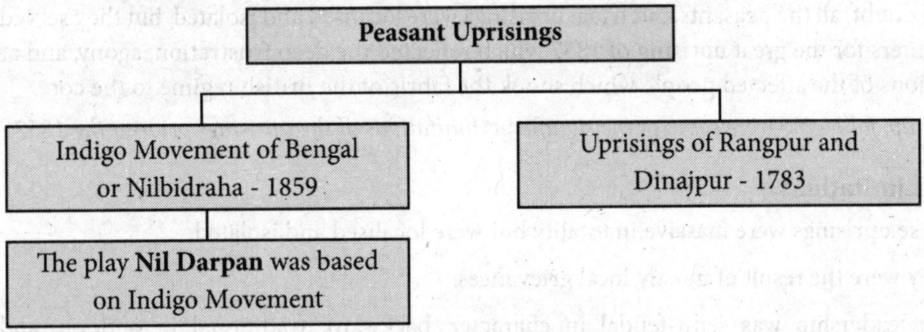

Army Rebellions

The dissatisfaction among the Indian soldieries or sepoys, in fact, had a long history. Before 1857, there were instances of Sepoy mutinies which were quickly suppressed.

Following were the two significant mutinies that took place before 1857.

Vellore Mutiny, 10 July 1806

In 1806, the *sepoys* at Vellore mutinied, but were crushed with terrible violence. The mutineers seized the Vellore Fort and killed or wounded 200 British troops. The immediate causes of the mutiny was resentment felt towards changes in the sepoy dress code – Hindus were prohibited from wearing religious marks on their foreheads and Muslims were required to shave and trim their beards.

Barrackpore Mutiny of 1824 (1st Mutiny)

During the First Anglo-Burmese War, November 1–2, 1824, sepoys revolted against the order to go to Rangoon to participate in the First Anglo-Burmese War. The sepoys revolted under the leadership of Binda.

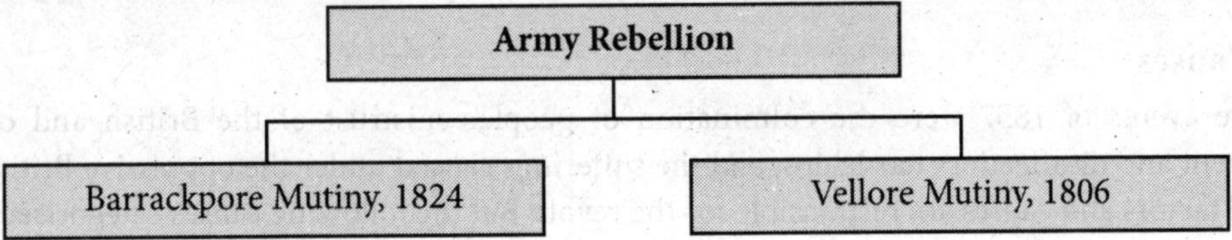

Limitations of Pre-1857 Uprisings

A critical examination of the pre-1857 peasant and tribal uprisings reveal that they did not emerge in a 'full-blown form'. It is because the consciousness of the insurgence and rebellion was limited in perspective and mostly, it was shaped by their vision of the past and what they have forgone by the annexation of the British.

One of the significant reasons cited by the scholars for these uprisings was the urge to recover their past from the newly established political power. Here, the past refers to their identity as reflected in their livelihood and the land on which their forefathers had been living for ages. What this movement of peasants and tribal risings lacked is the awareness of the need for integrating consciousness of all those adversely affected by the British colonial policies.

No doubt, all the peasants and tribal uprisings were localised and isolated, but they served as the forerunners for the great uprising of 1857 which reflected the deep frustration, agony, and anger of all sections of the affected people which shook the fabric of the British regime to the core.

To sum up, following were some of the significant limitations of the uprisings prior to the 1857 revolt:

Main Limitations

i. These uprisings were massive in totality but were localised and isolated.

ii. They were the result of mostly local grievances.

iii. The leadership was semi-feudal in character, backward, traditional in outlook, and their resistance represented no societal alternative.

iv. These rebellions were centuries-old in the form of ideological-cultural content.

v. The less recalcitrant of these were pacified through concessions by the authorities.

On the whole, however, these rebellions were able to establish valuable traditions of local resistance to authoritarianism.

The Revolt of 1857

We now know that popular discontent was widespread under the British rule. The British followed the policy of suppression and repression to crush such popular discontent arising in the form of revolts and resistance. However, uprisings or revolts prior to 1857 were in a small scale and confined to a place and to a group. The revolt of 1857, or the *Sepoy Mutiny,* according to the British was distinctive. It was not confined to a place and a group. The revolt began at a particular place and spread rapidly like a fury all across north India and parts of central India. Thus, 1857 is considered by historians not as a small uprising, but as a major revolt that shook the foundation of the British Empire in India.

The Causes

The events of 1857 were the culmination of people's mistrust of the British and of their discontent and disaffection, hardships, and the sufferings caused under the oppressive British rule. Several factors and causes are responsible for the revolt. But the following causes categorised under various heads, viz. economic, political, religious, social, judicial, and army are considered largely responsible for the outbreak of the 1857 revolt.

Economic Causes

The most important cause of popular discontent was the economic exploitation of India by the British. The economic policy of the British adversely affected every section of the Indian society. Both peasants and landlords or zamindars were pushed by the British to produce more to appropriate the maximum revenue. The peasants suffered due to high revenue demands. The various revenue settlements were designed to benefit the government and displayed total disregard for the cultivators. In case of failure to pay the revenue amount, the lands of the zamindar were taken away by the government. A large number of zamindars were thus dispossessed of their lands and estates as part of this policy.

Artisans and craftsmen were ruined by the large-scale influx of cheap British manufactured goods into India. Consequently, the country was reduced to poverty as traditional handicrafts and industries were ruined. Many people were rendered jobless and there was overcrowding in the agrarian sector.

The British exploited the economic resources of India to their advantage and drained her wealth by crippling the Indian trade and industry. The Company and its employees made huge profits. Almost all trade and commerce had gone into foreign hands. Under the British, India turned into a colonial economy to serve the British capitalist interests.

Political Causes – Annexation of Awadh

The British policy of territorial annexations led to the displacement of a large number of rulers and chiefs. The policies of Subsidiary Alliance and Doctrine of Lapse angered the ruling sections of the society. The native rulers resented the policy of Doctrine of Lapse adopted by Dalhousie. He annexed many states on the basis of this doctrine. Consequently, political dissatisfaction increased among the native rulers. Rani Lakshmi Bai and Nana Saheb became bitter enemies of the British and led to the revolt in their respective territories.

The annexation of Awadh, on grounds of misgovernment, was greatly resented. The Nawabs of Awadh had always been loyal to the British. The annexation was widely seen as a blatant act of back-stabbing by the British. It deeply hurt the sentiments of the Company's sepoys because most of them came from Awadh.

In 1856, on the pretext of misgovernment, Awadh was annexed and its king Wajid Ali Shah was dethroned and exiled to Calcutta. The British had thought that Wajid Ali Shah was an unpopular ruler. They were wholly mistaken. When he left his beloved Lucknow, thousands of his subjects followed him to Kanpur singing songs of lament.

The annexation did not just displace the Nawab, it also dispossessed the local officers like the taluqdars of the region. The countryside of Awadh was dotted with the estates and forts of the taluqdars who, for many generations, had controlled land power in the rural world.

The dispossession of taluqdars meant the breakdown of an entire social order. The ties of loyalty and patronage that had bound the peasants to the taluqdar were disrupted. Under the British rule, peasants were directly exposed to over-assessment of revenue and inflexible methods of collection. The peasants realised that in times of hardship, the revenue demand would not be reduced and neither would the collection be postponed. Also, they would be deprived of loans and contributions that the taluqdars had provided during the times of festivals and crisis.

These grievances of the peasants were carried over directly into the sepoy lines because a vast majority of the sepoys were largely recruited from the villages of Awadh. This link between the sepoys and the rural world was important. When the sepoys mutinied, they were quickly joined by their brethren from the villages. Thus, the mutiny became a rebellion.

Social and Cultural Causes

The social reforms introduced by the British were looked down with suspicion. Reforms such as abolition of *sati*, legalisation of widow remarriage, and Western education of women were looked upon by the natives as interference in their social customs. In 1850, the government passed

'The Caste Disabilities Removal Act'. The objective of this Act was to remove the Hindu right of inheritance and law of property. The Act was considered as a 'blow to Hindu Law'. The Act was passed to help the Christian missionaries in their proselytising activities.

The social discrimination faced by the Indians due to the British attitude of racial superiority created resentment among people of India. Also, Indians were excluded from well-paid, higher administrative posts.

There had been a growing suspicion among orthodox Hindus and Muslims that the British were trying to destroy their religion and culture through social legislations. The introduction of English and English-medium schools created a lot of unrest among the Mullahs and the Brahmins who were running indigenous schools and enjoyed respect among the common people. The Christian missionaries also indulged in attacking Hindu and Muslim religious beliefs. The introduction of the new law, which retained the right to inherit ancestral property even after conversion to Christianity, added to the conviction of the people that the government was determined to convert them to Christianity. The conversion of the young prince, Maharaja Duleep Singh of Punjab and the daughter of the Raja of Coorg, added fuel to the fire. Preservation of religion became a rallying cry in the revolt which was seen as a war of religion by the sepoys as well as those in the countryside.

Military Causes

Indian soldiers formed seven-eighths of the total British troops in India. But they were looked upon as inferior beings and treated with contempt by their British officers. They were paid much less than the British soldiers. All avenues of the promotions were closed to them as all the higher army posts were reserved for the British. Indian soldiers were discontent with the behaviours and attitudes of the British officers. The bulk of the sepoys of the East India Company were upper caste Hindus from the north-western provinces and Oudh. Nearly one-third came from Oudh, thus forming a homogeneous group within the army. Most of the soldiers were enraged due to the annexation of Oudh by the British on grounds of maladministration.

Lord Canning issued the General Service Enlistment Act by which all recruits to the Bengal Army were expected to serve anywhere in India or outside India. This affected the scruples of Indian sepoys of high castes about crossing seas. They thought it would spoil their caste.

Immediate Cause: The Greased Cartridge

The introduction of the Enfield rifle in the army set the stage for the revolt. The cartridges of the gun were covered with a greased paper cover. This greased cover had to be bitten off before the cartridge could be loaded into the rifle. The news spread that the grease was made of cow and pig fat. Both Hindus and Muslims were enraged and protested against using the greased cartridges. The introduction of the greased cartridge fell as a spark on a volcano that was about to burst. Hence, it is said, 'The great rising of 1857 was not the result of a chance cause only. The greased cartridge merely precipitated the crises'.

Planning and Organisation of the Revolt

It is not clear whether the Revolt of 1857 was spontaneous, unplanned, or the result of a careful and secret organisation. The people or leadership involved in the revolt have left behind no significant records. Many scholars have denied that any careful planning went into the making of the Revolt. They point out that not a scrap of paper was discovered before or after the Revolt indicating an organised conspiracy, nor did a single witness come forward to make such a claim.

Some historians and writers have asserted that the Revolt was the result of a widespread and well-organised conspiracy. They pointed to the circulation of chapattis and red lotuses, seditious propaganda by wandering sanyasis, *faqirs*, and madaris.

The historians say that many of the Indian regiments were carefully linked in a secret organisation which had fixed 31 May 1857 as the day when all of them were to revolt.

It is also said that Nana Saheb and Maulvi Ahmed Shah of Faizabad were playing leading roles in this conspiracy. Popularly, Nana Saheb is regarded as the brain of the rebellion, Rani Laxshmi Bai its nerve centre, and Ramchandra Pandurang Tope, better known as Tatya Tope, its forceful heavy hand.

Beginning and Spread of the Revolt

Mangal Pandey – The First Martyr

Usually, the beginning of the revolt is attributed to the Meerut mutiny. However, even before the outbreak at Meerut, the sepoys of 19th and 34th Native Infantry at Barrackpore protested against greased cartridges. In fact, the first soldier to protest against using the greased cartridges was Mangal Pandey. He belonged to the 34th Infantry stationed at Barrackpore. Mangal Pandey refused to use the cartridges and was subsequently hanged. The 19th and the 34th Infantries were disbanded and the sepoys of the two regiments returned to their distant homes in Oudh to spread the story of greased cartridges and the martyrdom of Mangal Pandey.

Mangal Pandey
— Wikimedia Commons

Meerut: The Epicentre of the Revolt

Meerut, the largest military cantonment, became the centre of the revolt. Here, Indian soldiers who refused to touch the new cartridge were court-marshialled and sentenced for 10 years' imprisonment.

On May 10, 1857, soldiers of the 3rd Bengal Native cavalry, galloped to the jail and released all the prisoners. This was followed by loot and plunder of British houses and families. Massacre of the British began in full fury. These sepoys marched to Delhi and proclaimed old Bahadur Shah Zafar as the emperor. Bahadur Shah, in turn, under the instigation and perhaps the pressure of the *sepoys*, soon wrote letters to all the chiefs and rulers of India urging them to organise a confederacy of Indian states to fight and replace the British regime.

The proclamation of Bahadur Shah Zafar as the emperor transformed the revolt into a legitimate war. Many Indian leaders proclaimed their loyalty to the Mughal emperor considered as the traditional symbol of unity.

Mutineers in other places followed the pattern set by Meerut soldiers – killing British officers, plundering and looting British houses, and burning government offices.

Soon, the mutiny spread in other places, joined by civil population under a leader or a chief, thus, transforming the revolt into a war. The common people joined the mutineers. It was the wide participation of the peasantry and the artisans which gave it real strength as well as the character of a popular revolt, especially in the areas at Uttar Pradesh and Bihar.

Following is the sequence of the spread of the revolt:

- On 29th March, Mangal Pandey revolted
- On May 10, 3rd Native Cavalry mutiny of sepoys at Meerut
- 11th May, Delhi was captured by the mutineers
- On 13th May, Bahadur Shah II proclaimed as new Mughal Emperor
- On 20-23, May , Part of 9th Native Infantry mutiny at Agra
- On 30th May, Oudh rose in mutiny
- On 30th May, Mutinies at Mathura and Lucknow
- 31 May, Rohilkhand and Bharatpur Army mutinies
- 5 June, Cawnpore 2nd Cavalry mutinies
- 6 June, Mutiny at Allahabad

Centers and Leaders of the Revolt

There were six main centres of the revolt – Kanpur, Lucknow, Bareilly, Jhansi, Gwalior, and Arrah in Bihar.

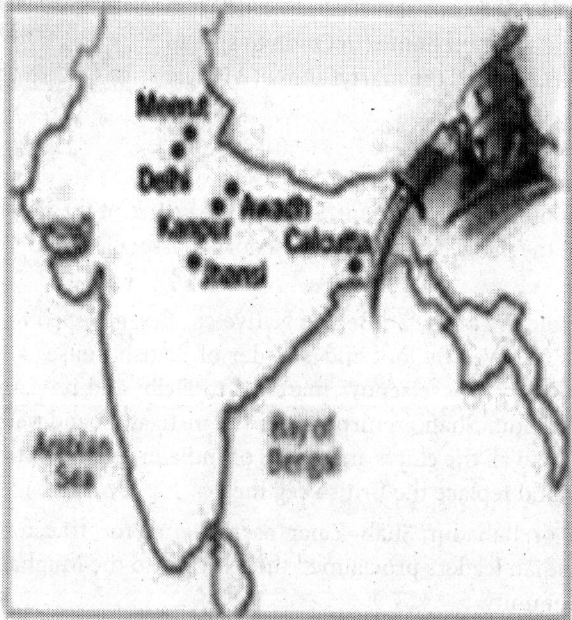

Main centres of the Revolt* — *Wikimedia Commons

- **Lucknow, the capital of Oudh :** The mutinous sepoys were joined by the disbanded soldiers from the old Oudh army. Begum Hazrat Mahal took up the leadership of the revolt. She had proclaimed her young son, Birjis Qadr, as the Nawab of Oudh.

Nana Saheb
— Wikimedia Commons

- **Kanpur :** The revolt was led by Nana Saheb, the adopted son of Peshwa Baji Rao II, the last Peshwa of Poona. He accepted Bahadur Shah as the emperor of India and declared himself to be a Subedar or governor of Bahadur Shah. Nana Saheb joined the revolt primarily because he was deprived of his pension by the British. He was supported by his two lieutenants – Tantia Tope and Azimullah Khan. Nana Saheb expelled the English from Kanpur with the help of the sepoys and proclaimed himself as the Peshwa.

Rani Lakshmibai
— Wikimedia Commons

- **Jhansi :** Here, the leadership was provided by Rani Lakshmibai, one of the significant leaders and a historical figure of the revolt. After her husband's death, Lakshmibai became the regent of her adopted son. However, the British refused to recognise him as the ruler and annexed Jhansi. She received help from Tantiya Tope. The combined efforts of Rani and Tantia Tope saw the capture of Gwalior. Rani Lakshmi bai was very brave and fearless. She fought very bravely with the British forces and died on the battlefield on 17th June 1858.
- **Arrah in Bihar :** Here, the revolt was led by Kunwar Singh. He was a ruined and discontented zamindar of Jagdishpur near Oudh. Nearly 80 years old, Kunwar Singh was perhaps the most outstanding military leader and strategist of the Revolt.
- Maulavi Ahmadullah of Faizabad was another outstanding leader of the Revolt. When the general Revolt broke out in May, Maulavi Ahmadullah emerged as one of its acknowledged leaders in Oudh. After the defeat at Lucknow, he led the rebellion in Rohilkhand where he was treacherously killed by the Raja of Puwain who received Rs 50,000 as a reward by the British.
- At Delhi, the nominal and symbolic leadership belonged to the Emperor Bahadur Shah, but the real command lay with a Court of Soldiers headed by General Bakht Khan who had led the revolt of the Bareilly troops and brought them to Delhi. The Emperor Bahadur Shah was perhaps the weakest link in the chain of leadership of the Revolt.

Suppression of the Revolt

After a bitter and prolonged fighting, the British captured Delhi on September 20, 1857. This was a severe blow to the mutineers. Bahadur Shah was captured and exiled to Rangoon. One by one, all the great leaders of the revolt fell. Nana Saheb was defeated at Kanpur. Tantia Tope escaped into the jungles of central India where he carried on a bitter and brilliant guerrilla warfare until April 1859, when he was betrayed by a zamindar friend and captured while asleep. He was put to death after a hurried trial on 15 April, 1859.

General Neil
— Wikimedia Commons

The Rani of Jhansi died on the battle field on June 17, 1858. Kunwar Singh sustained a fatal wound in the battle and died on 27 April 1858 at Jagdishpur.

The revolt lasted for one and a half years in a small measure. By the end of 1859, the British authority over India was fully established. John Lawrence, Outram, Havelock, Neil, Campbell, and Hugh Rose were some of the British commanders who earned military credit from Britain in the course of the revolt of 1857.

Reasons for the Failure

Many reasons are attributed for the failure of the 1857 revolt.

Following are some of the significant reasons for its failure :

- **Uprising was localised :** The revolt did not embrace the entire country. It did not spread to south India and most of western India like Sindh and Rajputana, and Central and Eastern Bengal remained calm. The Gurkhas helped the British government in suppressing the rising. Dost Muhammad of Afghanistan made no attempt to exploit the disturbed condition of India. Punjab gave a lot of help to the British government in disarming Bengal troops at Lahore, Mardan, and Peshawar. The troops sent from Punjab under Nicholson conquered Delhi.
- **Loyalty of Indian princes :** A large number of rulers of Indian states and landlords did not join the movement. On the contrary, many Indian rulers gave active support to the British in suppressing the revolt. Scindia and Holhar remained loyal, although some of their troops revolted. Sir Dinkar Rao and Sir Salarjung maintained peace in Gwalior and Hyderabad territories. The rulers of Nabha, Patiala, Jind, and Kapurthala not only maintained peace and order in their states, but they also lent their forces to the British to put down the rising. Governor-General Canning later remarked that these rulers and chiefs "acted as the breakwaters to the storm which would have otherwise swept us in one great wave."
- **Lack of support of merchants and educated people :** In most of the cases, villagers who joined the mutineers, attacked mainly moneylenders and their superiors. The merchants in general also became unfriendly to the rebels as the rebels demanded heavy money from them to buy equipment. Also, merchants wanted peace in the law and order situation. The educated Indians too did not support the movement.

- **Vested interest of the leaders :** The leaders of the revolt were largely dispossessed rulers who supported the revolt for their vested interests. They lacked a forward- looking programme for the revolt. Nana Saheb was interested in getting back his position of Peshwa, Rani Lakshmi Bai's concern was limited to her State of Jhansi, and dispossessed zamindar Kunwar Singh joined the revolt to get back his estate. Similarly, Bahadur Shah Zafar found a hope of re-establishing Mughal rule among the mutineers
- **Lack of discipline and arms :** The rebelled soldiers were short of modern weapons to fight with the mighty and modern British army. The organisation of the rebels was very poor and lacked unity of command and discipline. The rebel units did not have a common plan of action, or authoritative heads, or centralised leadership. The revolt was planned throughout the country on May 31, 1857, but it broke out prematurely. As a result, the operation of the revolt remained incomplete.
- **Rising confined to urban areas :** It remained confined to a few cities. The people of villages did not generally take part in it. Hence, it could not assume the character of a general and popular movement. If the rising had spread to the villages, it would have become very difficult for the British government to control the situation.
- **British lines of communication remained intact :** The mutineers did not care to disrupt British lines of communication. Roads and telegraph lines were not interfered with. The British could send supplies and instructions without interruption.
- **International situation :** The international situation had become favourable to the British in 1857. The Crimean war had been won and there was no Russian danger at this time. The war with Persia had also ended. The British forces were free for service in India.
- **Personal jealousies amongst the mutineers :** Mutineers failed to evolve unity of action. They were suspicious and jealous of one another and often indulged in suicidal quarrels. For example, the Begum of Oudh quarrelled with Maulavi Ahmadullah and the Mughal princes fought with the sepoy-generals.

Views on the Nature of the Revolt

Many historians and scholars have given divergent views on the nature of the revolt. For the British it was a mere Sepoy Mutiny, which was later exploited by a few groups to create law and order problems. For nationalists such as V.D. Savarkar, it was nothing less than the "Indian war of Independence". However, there is also a balanced approach to the understanding of the revolt. Initially, the revolt was a Sepoy Mutiny without any plan or conspiracy, which got flared up with the support from the deposed Rajas and landed zamindars/taluqdars along with the rural peasantry. The revolt invariably was inclined towards going back to the feudal structure of the society, with provincial rulers functioning with considerable autonomy, but acknowledging the Mughal emperor. Hence, the revolt had the military and feudal aspects with traditional overtones.

The British Views

The British, in general, categorised the revolt as mutiny of soldiers. Contemporary English scholars, Sir John Lawrence and Marshman were of the view that it was a Sepoy Mutiny, as the sepoys refused to use the greased cartridges of the Enfield rifles and opposed the move. Marshman called it as 'the savage mutiny of a hundred thousand sepoys'. Another English scholar L.E.R. Reese viewed it as a religious war against Christianity. J.R. Holmes expressed the opinion that it was a conflict between civilisation and barbarism. Sir James Outram, W. Taylor, and others are of the view that it was a conspiracy hatched by the Hindus and the Muslims against the British.

Nationalist Views

Contesting the British interpretation as that of Sepoy Mutiny only, the nationalist historians and in particular V.D. Savarkar in his banned book, 'The Indian War of Independence of 1857, published anonymously in 1912, argues that it was the First War of Indian Independence inspired by the lofty ideal of self-rule by Indians through nationalist upsurge. Asoka Mehta, another national leader, tried to bring out the national character of the events of the year in his book 1857–*The Great Rebellion*. He expressed the view that the revolt was national in character. Bishewswar Prasad observes "as the end of the alien rule was the essential object and the chief purpose and in this sense the revolt of 1857 may be termed a national war for freedom, though the sentiment of nationalism in the modern sense had not taken deep roots in the soil of India at that movement".

Rational Views

Dr. Tara Chand in his book *History of Freedom Movement in India*, comes to the conclusion that certainly, it would be inappropriate to call it mutiny, but it is also historically not sound to title it as the National War of Independence. However, many disagreed that it was a major revolt, as it was confined to a region, only few rulers participated, and it lacked nationalism. Historian R.C. Majumdar concludes that it is difficult to avoid the conclusion that the so-called First National War of Independence of 1857 is neither the first, nor national, nor a war of independence, as it was not pre-planned and was limited to certain pockets in North India.

Surender Nath Sen is of the view that: "The mutiny became a revolt and assumed a political character when the mutineers of Meerut placed themselves under the King of Delhi and a section of the landed aristocracy and civil population declared in his favour. What began as a fight for religion ended as a war of independence, for there is not the slightest doubt that the rebels wanted to get rid of the alien government and restore the old order of which the King of Delhi was the rightful representative".

The Marxist's Views

The uprising of 1857 was viewed as a struggle of the soldiers and the farmers against feudal bondage. The soldiers were disturbed by the unethical rules and regulations regarding their service conditions and repressive religious conspiracy, whilst the peasants' agitation was driven by the idea that the British are involved in a mechanism which is based on exploitation, repression, and wrongful accumulation of capital. In fact, the Indian soldier was a peasant in uniform and wanted to throw away the feudal domination infused by the British authorities. On the whole, one may look at the revolt as a product of the accumulated discontent of the people against the foreign government.

Scholars and many alike feel that it is difficult to make a generalisation of the 1857 event as the response of the people varied from one area to another and as such, it is argued that the revolt of 1857 was not one movement but a collection of many movements. The nature of the 1857 event has become so emotive that it gave scope to multiple perspectives.

Constitutional and Administrative Changes After 1858

The 1857 revolt, though failed and crushed by the superior military force of the British, was a significant event of far-reaching consequences in the history of British rule in India. After the suppression of the revolt, several significant structural changes in the Indian subcontinent were introduced. These changes were announced through the Government of India Act, 1858 and Queen Victoria's Proclamation of 1858. The Queen's Proclamation was announced at a *Darbar* held at Allahabad in 1858. The Queen's Proclamation remained the basis of Indian administration up to 1917. The changes proclaimed through Government of India Act, 1858 can be studied under several headings:

Constitutional Effects

1. **End of East India Company's rule :** The most significant result of the mutiny was the transfer of power from a trading company, i.e., The East India Company to a sovereign power of Britain, by the Government of India Act of 1858. Under the Government of India Act, 1858, India came under the direct control of the British Crown and British Parliament. Thus, the rule of the East India Company came to an end. It marks the end of an era of mercantile capitalism and early colonial rule and the beginning of direct imperial hegemony of the British Crown. This change, according to many scholars, was formal rather than substantial. All real power had already passed from Court of Directors to the President of the Board of Control. The Charter Act of 1853 had reduced the number of Directors from 24 to 18, and out of these, six were nominees of the Crown. The Charter Act of 1853 had prepared the way for the assumption of the Government of India by the Crown by not renewing the Charter of the Company by 20 years. It stated that the Indian territories were to remain under the Company in trust for the Crown until the Parliament should determine otherwise. The Act of 1858 completed the process.

2. **The Secretary of State :** In the place of the President of the Board of Control, the Secretary of State for India was appointed. The Secretary of State for India was assisted and helped by a 15-member body of India Council. Out of the fifteen, eight were appointed by the Crown and the rest were to be appointed by the Court of the Directors.

3. **Change in designation of Governor-General :** The designation of the Governor- General of India was changed to Viceroy. He was to be called Governor-General of India so far as the administration territories directly under him, but he was to be known as Viceroy in relation to the rulers of Indian States.

4. **Honouring of previous treaties :** In case of the rulers of the Indian states, the Crown made a categorical announcement that all the treaties and agreements entered into by the East India Company will be honoured and respected and it made it clear that no renewal was necessary.

5. **Change in policy towards Indian States :** The British Crown gave up the policy of subordinate isolation and advocated a policy of subordinate union in respect of native states. The administrative apparatus in India was centralised effectively due to the improvement in communications. They gave up the idea of the ruthless expansionist policy of their territorial boundaries in and outside India. The existence of native states was guaranteed, but their rights were limited and defined. The rulers were not to have relations with any foreign power or with each other except through the British. Limit was placed on their armed forces. The rulers were to have full control over internal affairs of their States, but the British government could temporarily take charge of administration in case of anarchy or disturbance in any State or part of it.

6. **Centralisation of Administration :** The Act of 1858 centralised the administration more than before. The control of the Secretary of State for India over the Viceroy was greater than the control of the President of the Board of Control over the Governor-General before 1858. This was due to the improvement in the means of communication.

Changes in the Army

1. **Amalgamation of the troops of Crown and Company :** Before the revolt of 1857, the army of the British in India was divided into two major divisions – King's forces and Company's troops. As a result of the revolt, the two forces were united and called King's forces and one-third of it was to consist of the Europeans.

2. **Artillery placed exclusively in British hands :** The artillery section was exclusively kept under the British. The idea was that the sepoys could not hope to revolt successfully without artillery.

3. **Increase in the number of European troops :** The low proportion of European forces in India had been one of the causes of the mutiny. It had encouraged the native sepoys. It was now laid down that at least one-third of the army in India must consist of Europeans.

4. **Increased expenditure on Army :** As a consequence of more European soldiers in the army, the expenditure on the army doubled up. The emoluments of European soldiers were now four or five times than those of a sepoy.

5. **Disbanding of Bengal Army :** The Bengal Army was virtually abolished. Soldiers from Avadh, Bihar, Central India, and South India who had first helped the British conquer India but had later taken part in the Revolt of 1857, were declared to be non-martial. They were no longer taken in the army on a large scale. They reduced the Brahmins from the army and recruited Gurkhas, Sikhs, Jats, and Rajputs of the Punjab.

Religious, Judicial, and Diplomatic Changes

Queen Victoria's proclamation of 1 November, 1858 guaranteed freedom of faith and equal treatment to all Indians. The Queen made it clear that there was to be no distinction between one individual and another on the pretext of race, religion, sex, and creed.

The British Crown agreed to provide employment to the Indians in the bureaucratic structure of the times, which was denied previously. In the sphere of the judiciary, the Sadar courts and Crown's Supreme Court were amalgamated into High Courts which were established in the Presidency towns of Madras, Bombay, and Calcutta. In the sphere of diplomatic ties between India and Britain, now there was a change and the British began to show greater interest in the internal development of India than in foreign affairs.

Divide and Rule Policy

The unity displayed by Hindus and Muslims during the Revolt of 1857 had disturbed the foreign rulers. They were determined to break this unity so as to weaken the rising nationalist movement.

After 1858, the British consciously followed the policy of 'Divide and Rule' by turning the princes against the people, province against province, caste against caste, group against group, and, above all, Hindus against Muslims. Immediately after the Revolt, the British repressed Muslims, confiscated their lands and property on a large scale, and declared Hindus to be their favourites. However, after 1870, this policy was reversed and an attempt was made to turn upper class and middle class Muslims against the nationalist movement.

'Divide and Rule' policy was applied among the educated section of the society too. The dependency of educated Indians on government service led to keen competition among them for the available government posts. The Government utilised this competition to foment provincial and communal rivalry and hatred. It promised official favours on a communal basis in return for loyalty and so played the educated Muslims against the educated Hindus.

Previous Years' Questions

1. **"The Revolt of 1857 seemed to call the very presence of the British into question. What it did not do was reverse these changes". (2007)**
2. **"In terms of administrative structure, the Government of India Act of 1858 meant more continuation than change." Do you agree? Substantiate. (2010)**
3. **"In 1857, the rebel sepoys showed a remarkable centripetal tendency to congregate at Delhi." Do you agree? Substantiate. (2011)**
4. **"Tribals revolted more often and far more violently than any other community including peasants in India." Elaborate. (2011)**
5. **"The Indigo Revolt of 1859–60 holds a very significant place in our history of national liberation movement. For the first time in the history of our anti-colonial struggle, its two independent currents—spontaneous peasant resistance and constitutional agitation in defence of the peasantry—came into mutual contact." (2015)**
6. **"The annexation of Awadh shook the loyalty of the sepoys, as it was for them an ultimate proof of untrustworthiness of the British." (2009)**
7. **"The military, feudal and traditional overtones of the Revolt of 1857 were overshadowed by its nationalist or proto-nationalist character." (2014)**
8. **"The tribal and peasant rebellion laid the foundation of the revolt of 1857."Comment. (2001)**

10 CHAPTER

Indian Renaissance and Reformative Movements of The Nineteenth Century

Introduction

The social and religious movements of the nineteenth century are popularly termed as the 'Indian Renaissance', which preceded the political struggles, and are considered as a necessary precursor to the Indian nationalism. Indian nationalism, hence, was the outcome of the renaissance of the nineteenth century. Indian Renaissance first emerged in Bengal and soon spread to other parts of the country. Stalwart figures of the Bengal Renaissance were Raja Ram Mohan Roy, Keshab Chandra Sen, Dayanand Saraswati, Ramakrishna Paramahamsa, and Vivekananda. Indian Renaissance was marked by sociocultural and intellectual movements.

The main objective of the Indian Renaissance movement was to regenerate Indian society and culture in the wake of Western condemnation and Western influence. Indian Renaissance tried to modernise religion by discarding irrational rituals, false doctrines, and monopolistic priestcrafts. It contributed immensely in reforming the degenerative society of that time through crusades against inhuman customs and practices. Thus, social and religious reforms were central to Indian Renaissance which were spearheaded by conscious-minded individuals and intellectuals.

Reform Movements of The 19th Century

The mid-nineteenth century of India is identified largely by the emergence of various social reformative movements. The beginning of these movements found expression in the first half of the century with socialcultural awakening and consciousness. Indian society of this period was condemned for its backwardness. Customs like Sati, child marriage, infanticide, caste system, and orthodox religious practices had brought overall degeneration in the society. Many Indians realised that social and religious reforms are essential for the development of the country. The impact of the advanced Western ideas and culture and increased awareness of the contemporary world led to greater awareness among educated Indians about the backwardness and degeneration of the society. Simultaneously, these individuals were highly conscious of the rich Indian culture and thought. Hence, the socio-religious reform movements of this period had a two-fold objective–to reform and eradicate degenerative customs and practices and to inculcate self-pride and consciousness towards the rich ancient Indian culture.

In the first half of the nineteenth century, the reform movements largely focused on eradicating evil practices and customs. The reformers of this period were highly critical of the Indian society and favoured Western ideas and culture. Prominent reformers of this period were Raja Ram Mohan Roy (1772–1833), Ishwar Chandra Vidyasagar (1820–1891), and Henry Vivian Derozio (1809–1831). However, the second half of the nineteenth century saw reformers like Swami Vivekananda and Swami Dayanand Saraswati, along with reformers like Mahadev Govind Ranade who were educated and highly conscious of their cultural roots. These reformers initiated movements against child marriage and widowhood and promoted women's education. But these reforms were carried within the existing sociocultural setting. Unlike reformers of the early nineteenth century, late nineteenth century reformers were in favour of promoting Indian culture and thought.

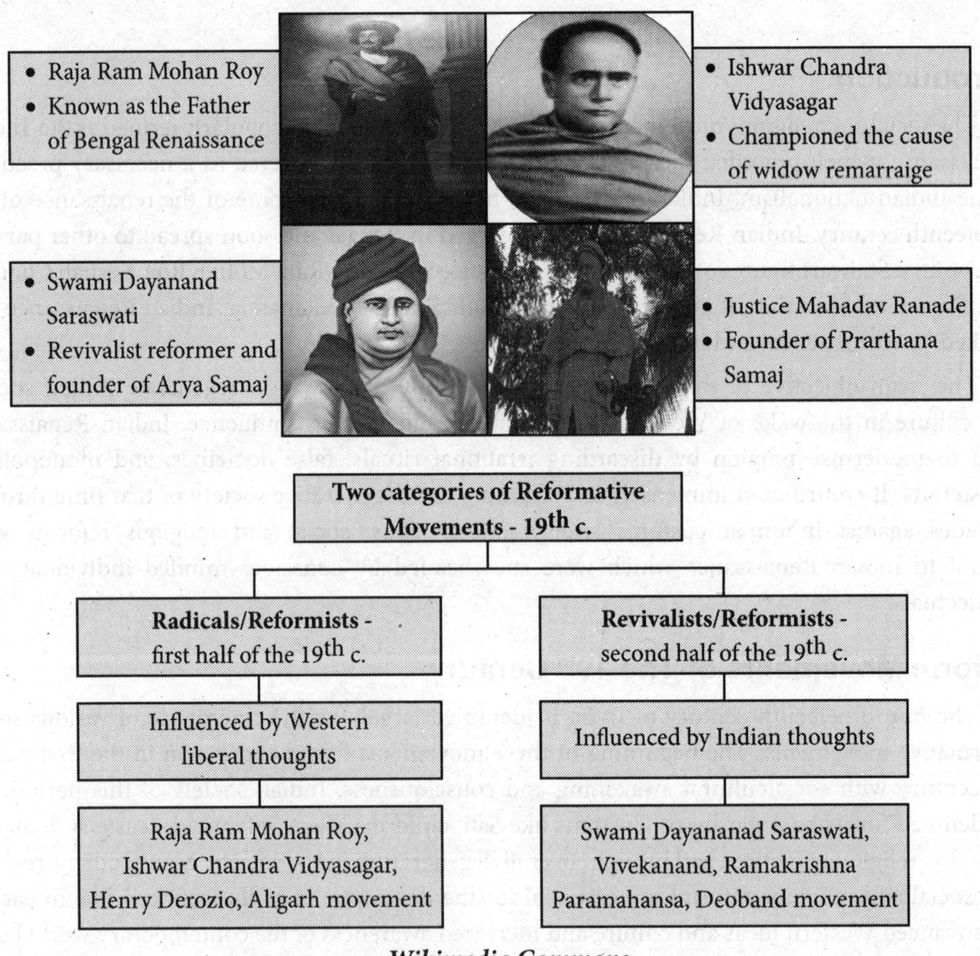

— *Wikimedia Commons*

Hindu Renaissance or Neo-Hinduism

In response to the influence of Western thoughts and challenges posed by Christianity, the Hindu thinkers of the nineteenth century advocated universal aspects of Hinduism and redefined Hinduism as a universal religion devoid of rituals and idol worship. Western scholars and critics termed this as 'Neo-Hinduism' in which Hindu thinkers and reformers such as Raja Ram Mohan Roy, Ramakrishna, Vivekananda, and later Gāndhi and Aurobindo Ghose, and religious reform movements such as the Brahmo Samāj and Arya Samaj redefined and propagated Hinduism as a universal religion. The main 'Neo-Hindu' stance was derived from the redefinition of Hindu Dharma as an essentially universal, ethical 'religion' or sadharana Dharma, based on principles of non-violence (ahimsa) and compassion, as opposed to the traditional ritualistic religion. 'Neo-Hinduism' stands for revival of Hinduism and is associated with Indian Renaissance.

Intellectuals responsible for Indian Renaissance advocated for simple, humanistic, and rational Hindu Dharma against the degenerative Hindu beliefs, practices, and doctrines. Hinduism as a universal religion was advocated by Raja Ram Mohan Roy who founded the Brahmo Samaj, Ramakrishna and his disciple Swami Vivekananda (who organised the Ramakrishna Mission), Sri Aurobindo Ghosh, Mahatma Gandhi, and Sarvepalli Radhakrishna.

In recent scholarly writing, the term Neo-Hinduism is generally used to describe Hindu thinkers who typically:

- have been concerned with the relationship between religion and nationalism
- have been exposed to Western ideas and education, and have confessed to having undergone a crisis of confidence in the value of Hinduism
- have voiced a critical attitude to the worship of images
- have been willing to re-interpret concepts and traditional philosophies, particularly Advaita Vedanta, in the light of new circumstances and influences external to Hinduism
- have been committed to organised, practical service to humanity

Social and Ideological Basis of the Reform Movements

The nineteenth century Indian society in general had reached a degenerative state shrouded with religious superstitions and social obscurantism. Caste system, untouchability, and social practices like Sati, infanticide, and widowhood had weakened the Indian society. Hinduism had lost its fundamental essence. It was associated more with idol worship, unnecessary rituals, and magical chants and superstitions and beliefs.

The spread of Western liberal education along with the socio-economic policies of the British were instrumental in creating an educated class of people who were aware and conscious of the degenerative state of Indian society. It was this class that was responsible for questioning the social ills of that time and for giving a new direction to Indian society. This was the emerging 'Middle Class' of the 19th century India which comprised of professionals and intellectuals.

The newly emerging professionals and intellectuals pioneered the 19th century socio-religious reform movement. The professional class of this period emerged from the people employed in the government and non-government services. It consisted of middle rank professionals such as doctors, teachers, journalists, and lawyers, as well as businessmen. The long association of this class with the colonists brought in them distinct changes in taste, fashion, and attitudes. Similarly, the traditional as well as Western-educated intellectuals of this period pioneered in bringing transformation through literary activities that eventually led to a renaissance type movement, particularly in Bengal. This section of the society–the middle class of professionals and contemporary intellectuals were predominantly the non-bourgeois social base for the reform movements of this period.

Ideologically, these movements were largely based on the principles of rationalism, religious universalism, and humanism. These principles became important intellectual criteria which gave the reform movements an ideological unity. Social relevance was judged by a rationalist critique. Raja Ram Mohan Roy upheld the principle of causality linking the whole phenomenal universe and demonstrability as the sole criterion of truth. This outlook enabled them to adopt a rational approach to tradition and evaluate the contemporary socio-religious practices from the standpoint of social utility and to replace faith with rationality.

Many reformers in varying degrees discarded the principle of authority in religion and evaluated truth in religion by the criteria of logic, reason, or science. Swami Vivekananda held that the same method of investigation which applies to other sciences should form the basis on which religion is to justify itself. Although some reformers tended to appeal to faith and ancient authority to reinforce their appeal, an overall rational and secular outlook was very much evident in posing an alternative to prevalent social practices.

The social reform movements were also an embodiment of a new humanitarian morality which included the notion that humanity and moral values are ultimately for human progress. An emphasis on the individual's right to interpret religious scriptures in the light of human reason and human welfare and a general attack on priestly domination of religious practices underlined the humanist aspect of religious reform movements.

Characteristics of the Reform Movements

Following were the common features evident among the reformers and their reformist organisations of this period:

(1) All the reformers propagated the idea of one God and the basic unity of all religions. Thus, they tried to bridge the gulf between different religious beliefs.

(2) All the reformers attacked priesthood, rituals, idolatry, and polytheism. The humanitarian aspect of these reform movements was expressed in their attack on the caste system and the custom of child marriage.

(3) The reformers attempted to improve the status of women in the society. They all emphasised the need for female education.

(4) By attacking the caste system and untouchability, the reformers helped to unify the people of India into one nation.

(5) The reform movements fostered feelings of self-respect, self-reliance, and patriotism among the Indians.

Reformers and Reformist Organisations

The 19th century social reform movements could broadly be classified into two categories: the reformist movements like the Brahmo Samaj, the Prarthana Samaj, the Aligarh movement, and the revivalist movements like Arya Samaj and the Deoband movement.

Raja Ram Mohan Roy (1772–1833) and the Brahmo Samaj

Raja Ram Mohan Roy is regarded as the 'Father of Indian Renaissance'. A scholar of English, French, Greek, Hebrew, and Latin languages, Raja Ram Mohan Roy was well acquainted with Hindu philosophy and philosophic thoughts of Jainism. Later on, he made an intensive study of Western thought and culture.

In 1814, Raja Ram settled in Calcutta and dedicated his life to the cause of social and religious reform. Here, he founded *Atmiya Sabha* in 1814 with an objective of propagation of the monotheistic doctrine of the ancient Hindu scriptures. Along with Dwarkanath Tagore, he founded the *Brahmo Sabha* in 1828, which began the Bengal Renaissance of the 19th century. This religious society was based on the twin pillars of rationalism and the philosophy of the Vedas. The Brahmo Samaj emphasised human dignity, criticised idolatry, and denounced social evils like *Sati*. It was one of the most influential religious reformist movements responsible for the making of modern India.

Raja Ram justified his views by the light of reason and humanitarian principles. He accepted the Upanishads as his authority and declared the fact that man can realise the spiritual goal of his life by means of meditation of the divine and not by sacrificial rituals. His aim was to promote monotheistic worship and adoration of the 'One Eternal Immutable God' with the abolition of caste system and inhuman social practices. Although the Brahmo Samaj was firmly rooted in the Vedas, the Upanishads, and the Brahma Sutras, it inculcated modern humanist ideas.

As a Universalist, Raja Ram stands for the solidarity of religions. He advocated a rational approach to religions based on the comparative study of the scriptures of other religions with a view to discover the fundamental unity of all religions. He showed how the essential values of the great Indian heritage were to be preserved and how the non-essentials were to be discarded. According to him, the Universal Religion can be formed by the assimilation of the common truths of Hinduism, Islam, Christianity, and other faiths.

His greatest contribution was the abolition of the *sati* system, which was the cruel practice of burning the Hindu widow on the funeral pyre of her dead husband. In 1818, he launched a crusade against *sati*. He was devastated by the experience of seeing his own sister-in-law being forced to commit *sati*. He personally visited the Calcutta cremation grounds to persuade widows against immolation, formed watch groups to do the same, and wrote and disseminated articles to show that it was not required by scriptures. He organised a movement against the practice of *sati* and helped William Bentinck to pass a law banning the practice. On 4th December, 1829, the practice of *sati* was formally banned in the Bengal Presidency. It was the first successful social movement against an age-old social evil.

Ram Mohan Roy was a pioneer of Indian journalism. He himself published journals in Bengali, Persian, Hindi, and English to educate the public on various current issues. One notable magazine was the *Sambad Kaumudi*. It was the most important journal brought out by Rajaram. It covered topics such as freedom of press, induction of Indians into high ranks of service, and separation of the executive and judiciary. Roy published magazines in English, Hindi, Persian, and Bengali.

Ram Mohan Roy was one of the earliest propagators of modern Western education. He looked upon it as a major instrument for the spread of modern ideas in the country. He was associated with the foundation of the Hindu College in Calcutta, which later came to be known as the Presidency College.

Raja Ram Mohan Roy — Wikimedia Commons

In 1830, Ram Mohan Roy travelled to England. At the time, Roy was an ambassador of the Mughal emperor Akbar II, who conferred on him the title of *Raja* to lobby in the British government for the welfare of India. He was sent to England by the Mughal Emperor Akbar II as his envoy and to ensure that the Lord Bentinck's regulation banning the practice of *Sati* was not overturned.

Roy died in Britain at Stapleton, Bristol, on 27th September 1833.

Debendranath Tagore and Tattvabodhini Sabha

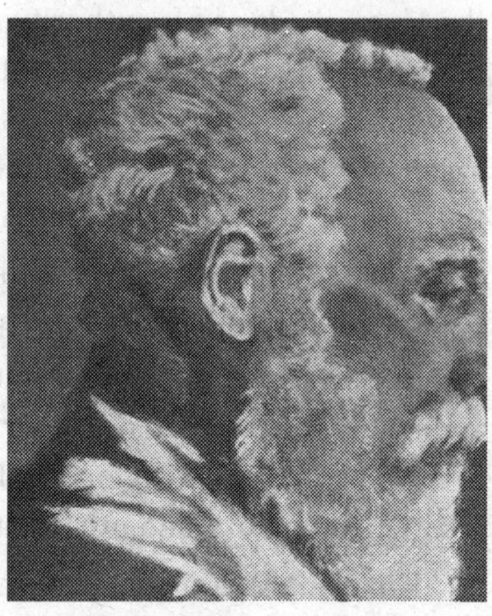

Debendranath Tagore — Wikimedia Commons

Debendranath Tagore, the father of Rabindranath Tagore, was responsible for revitalising the Brahmo Samaj. Under him, the first step was taken to convert the Brahmo Samaj into a separate religious and social community. He represented the best in traditional Indian learning and the new thought of the West.

In 1839, he founded the Tattvabodhini Sabha to propagate Ram Mohan Roy's ideas. He promoted a magazine to do a systematic study of India's past in Bengali language. The Samaj actively supported the movements for widow remarriage, the abolition of polygamy, women's education, and the improvement in the condition of the peasantry. Two prominent members of Tattvabodhini Sabha were Akshay Kumar Datta and Ishwar Chandra Vidyasagar. This Sabha continued till 1859.

Keshab Chandra Sen (1838–84) and New Brahmoism

The next phase of the Brahmo movement is dominated by K.C. Sen who spread the Brahmo movement in south and other parts of the country. Under K.C. Sen's leadership, Brahmo Samaj became an all India movement. In 1866 CE, Brahmo Samaj got divided into two divisions - Adi Brahmo Samaj under Debendranath Tagore and New Brahmo Samaj or New Brahmoism under Kesab Chandra Sen.

New Brahmoism is a movement started by a new set of radicals from the fold of Brahmoism under the leadership of Keshab Chandra Sen with the aim to modernise the Hindu society. K.C. Sen carried on an intensive programme of social reform of the Samaj. He set up schools, organised famine relief, and propagated widow remarriage. In 1861, Keshub Chandra Sen established Indian Mirror, the first Indian Daily in English.

Keshab Chandra Sen
— Wikimedia Commons

Influenced by the spirit of Christianity, K.C. Sen introduced Christian rituals of baptism and Western methods in his New Brahmoism. As a result, he alienated himself from the main Samaj and from the Hindu society.

The New Brahmoism activities led to the formation of the Indian Reform Association in 1870 CE and the enactment of the Special Marriage Act of 1872 validating inter-caste marriage or legalising marriages performed according to Brahmo Samaj rites.

In 1878, intellectuals of this period opposed K.C. Sen and set up a new Samaj called as Sadharan Brahmo Samaj on the lines of Ram Mohan Roy.

However, the Brahmo Samaj movement was not successful in attracting the masses, because it was an intellectual movement inspired by Western ideals.

Phases of Brahmo Samaj

It was the earliest reform movement which was greatly influenced by Western ideas. It heralded the Bengal Renaissance. It underwent various phases:

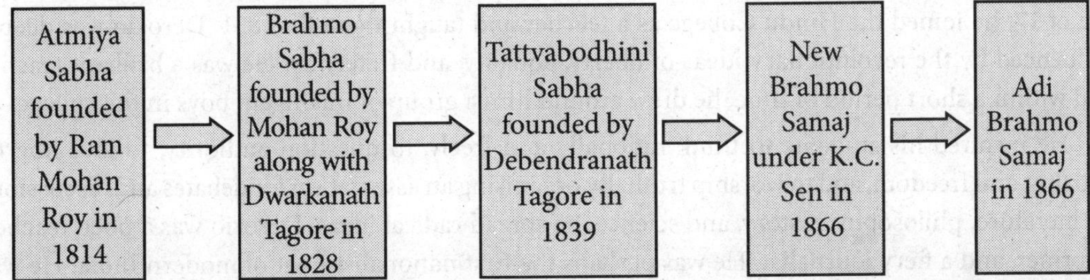

Ishwar Chandra Vidyasagar and Movement Against Widowhood

Ishwar Chandra Vidyasagar
— Wikimedia Commons

Ishwar Chandra Vidyasagar, a towering personality of the mid-nineteenth century, was born in a poor Brahmin family of Bengal in 1820. He was a renowned Sanskrit scholar and became the Principal of the Sanskrit College in 1851. The Sanskrit College conferred on him the title of 'Vidyasagar' because of his profound knowledge of Sanskrit.

Pandit Ishwar Chandra Vidyasagar was both a scholar and a reformer. He was a great humanist and had deep sympathy for the poor and the oppressed. He dedicated his entire life to the cause of social reform which he thought was necessary for modernising India. By admitting non-Brahmin students to the Sanskrit College, he dealt a severe blow to the prevalent caste system.

Vidyasagar was a staunch supporter of women's education and helped Drinkwater Bethune to establish the Bethune School, the first Indian school for girls, in 1849. As an Inspector of Schools, Vidyasagar opened a number of schools for girls in the districts under his charge.

Vidyasagar's greatest contribution lies in the improvement of the condition of widows. Despite opposition, Vidyasagar openly advocated widow remarriage. Soon, a powerful movement in favour of widow remarriage was started. At last, after a prolonged struggle, the Widow Remarriage Act was passed in 1856. Through his efforts, twenty-five widow remarriages took place. He also spoke vehemently against child marriage and polygamy.

Vidyasagar contributed enormously to the growth of the Bengali language and contributed to the evolution of the modern prose style in Bengali. He wrote a Bengali primer, 'Barna Parichay', which is used even today. Through his writings, Vidyasagar made the people aware of the social problems and thus, helped the growth of nationalism in India.

The Young Bengal Movement

The establishment of the Hindu College in 1817 was a major event in the history of Bengal. It played an important role in carrying forward the reformist movement that had already emerged in the province. A radical movement for the reform of Hindu Society, known as the Young Bengal Movement, started in the college.

Its leader was Henry Vivian Derozio, a teacher of the Hindu College. Derozio was born in 1809. He was of mixed parentage – his father was Portuguese and his mother was Indian. In 1826, at the age of 17, he joined the Hindu College as a teacher and taught there till 1831. Derozio was deeply influenced by the revolutionary ideas of liberty, equality, and fraternity. He was a brilliant teacher and within a short period of time, he drew around him a group of intelligent boys in the college.

He inspired his students to think rationally and freely, to question authority, to love liberty, equality, and freedom, and to worship truth. By organising an association for debates and discussions on literature, philosophy, history, and science, he spread radical ideas. Derozio was a poet, teacher, reformer, and a fiery journalist. He was perhaps the first nationalist poet of modern India. He was removed from the Hindu College because of his radicalism and died soon after, at the age of 22 due to illness.

The movement started by Derozio was called the Young Bengal Movement and his followers were known as the Derozians. The movement took place in late 1820s and 1830s. They condemned religious rites and the rituals, and pleaded for eradication of social evils, female education, and improvement in the condition of women. Derozians were inspired and excited by the spirit of free thought and were highly critical against the existing social and religious structure of the Hindu society. One scholar characterised the Young Bengal Movement in the following words:

"The Young Bengal movement was like a mighty storm that tried to sweep away everything before it. It was a storm that lashed society with violence, causing some good and perhaps naturally, some discomfort and distress."

Prominent Derozians and Young Bengal Group members who left a distinct mark in Calcutta society of the 1830s and 1840s were: Krishna Mohan Banerjee (1813–1885), Tarachand Chakraborti (1805–1855), Sib Chandra Deb (1811–1890), Hara Chandra Ghosh (1808–1868), Ramgopal Ghosh (1815–1868), Ramtanu Lahiri (1813–1898), Rasik Krishna Mallick (1810–1858), Peary Chand Mitra (1814–1883), Dakshinaranjan Mukherjee (1818–1887), and Radhanath Sikdar (1813–1870).

The Young Bengal Group formed associations for debates and discussions on burning social and political issues. Prominent among them were Academic Association and Society for the Acquisition of General Knowledge. These associations of the Young Bengal Group were forerunners of later organisations such as the Landholders' Society, British India Society, and British Indian Association.

Henry Louis Vivian Derozio — Wikimedia Commons

The young Bengal group remained unsuccessful in generating any change in the society as their ideas were pro-Western and too advanced to flourish. Yet, they carried forward Ram Mohan's tradition of educating the people on social, economic, and political issues.

The Young Bengal movement started with radical ideas which directly challenged the existing societal practices. Their open social rebellion and sprit of free thinking had great potential to influence the masses.

However, the same attitude alienated them from the masses and hence, they failed to make any distinctive and permanent impression in matters of religious and philosophical thoughts.

However, the blind reliance and faith on English education, their rationalism, and scientism without taking into the cognizance of local society and culture proved fatal to their efforts. The society, as a whole, could not connect with their Western ideals and styles.

Swami Dayanand Saraswati and the Arya Samaj

After Brahmo Samaj, the next significant socio-religious reform movement was carried by Arya Samaj founded by Swami Dayanand Saraswati (1824–1883).

Dayanand Saraswati, was born in Tankara, Gujarat, into a Brahmin family in 1824, as Mool Shankar. He met Swami Virajanand at Mathura and became the disciple of Virajanand. There he studied Vedas. He developed a profound belief in Vedas and Vedic philosophy.

Swami Dayanand wanted to regenerate Hinduism on the basis of the Vedic philosophy. So he propagated the motto "Back to the Vedas." He believed in the divinity of the Vedas and opposed idol worship. According to him, the solution to human misery and salvation is found in the Vedas. Asserting that the Vedas made no mention of untouchability, child marriage, and the subjugation of women, Swami Dayanand attacked these practices vehemently.

In 1863, Swami Dayanand started preaching his doctrine of 'One God'. He questioned the meaningless rituals, decried polytheism, and image worship, and denounced the caste system. He wanted to purify Hinduism and attacked the evils that had crept into the Hindu society.

Dayanand began the 'Shuddhi' movement which enabled the Hindus who had accepted Islam or Christianity to return to Hinduism, their original faith. Dayanand published his religious commentaries in Hindi so as to make the common people understand his thoughts. *The Satyarth Prakash* was his most important work in which he described the historical, doctrinal, and ethical aspects of the Vedic life.

For propagating Vedic philosophy and its implication on daily life, Swami Dayanand founded the Arya Samaj which has produced eminent national leaders, freedom fighters, and philanthropists. The first Arya Samaj was founded in 1875 and then in 1877 at Lahore. Since then, a network of Arya Samaj branches has come up in India and in other countries as well. The Arya Samaj founded by Dayanand worked for widow remarriage and education of women. The Arya Samaj made significant contributions to the fields of education and social and religious reforms. Arya Samaj educational institutions put great emphasis on compulsory primary education, adult education, and education of girls and women. These institutions, to a large extent, carried the social reforms like untouchability and child marriage. Emphasis of these educational institutions is on the *gurukul* system of education.

After his death, his followers had established the Dayanand Anglo Vedic Schools, first in Lahore, and then in other parts of India. Gurukuls were also established to propagate traditional ideals of education. A network of educational institutions had been set up in the country which is known as Dayanand Anglo-Vedic (D.A.V.) schools and colleges. The objective of these educational institutions is to provide a happy blending of the modern scientific approach of the West and the spiritual philosophy of the East. Later, the Arya Samaj got involved in the national movement through Gadharists, or the Gadhar movement activists. Prominent Gadhar leaders such as Pandit Lekh Ram, Lala Har Dayal, and Swami Shraddhan (also known as Mahatma Munshi Ram) were from the Arya Samaj.

Swami Dayanand was a revivalist social religious reformer who advocated Vedic Hinduism and Hindu culture without getting swayed by Western ideas and culture.

Dayanand gave a terrible blow to Lord Macaulay's idea on English education. For the revival of India's glory, Dayanand put emphasis on the Vedic education which was based on morality. Equality of treatment in the educational institutions was advocated by Dayanand. Emphasis was to be laid down on character-building of the pupils championing the moral-based education.

The Shuddhi Movement introduced by Dayanand was to bring back the individuals to Hinduism who were either voluntarily or involuntarily converted to other religions like Islam or Christianity. 'Shuddhi' or purification was imparted to those who sought their way back to Hinduism and the Samaj did an excellent work in penetrating the various strata of society, taking back the depressed classes into the folds of Hinduism.

Dayananad Saraswati — Wikimedia Commons

Dayanand Saraswati also contributed to the growth of democracy and national awakening. It is said that "political independence" was one of the first objectives of Dayananda. Indeed, he was the first man to use the term "Swaraj." Swami Dayanand Saraswati's Arya Samaj brought about changes in the religious perception of Indians.

Dayanand was an ardent champion of nationalism. He injected a sense of pride and dignity in every Indian by unfolding the glorious cultural heritage of this land before them. "India for the Indians" was his doctrine. He wanted to get rid of the European influence. For the first time, he had uttered the word "Swaraj" and put emphasis on "Swadeshi" or self-reliance.

Sri Ramakrishna Paramahamsa, Vivekananda, & Neo-Vedanta

Ramakrishna Paramahamsa

Sri Ramakrishna Paramahamsa was one of the greatest saints of modern India. Ramakrishna was born in a poor Brahmin family of Bengal. He showed a religious bent of mind from his childhood. He had no formal education, but his discourses were full of wisdom. He was the chief priest of the Kali temple at Dakshineswar near Calcutta. People from all walks of life visited Dakshineswar to listen to his discourses.

Sri Ramakrishna Paramahamsa — Wikimedia Commons

Ramakrishna Paramahamsa was a man with a liberal outlook. He firmly believed that there was an underlying unity among all religions and that only the methods of worship were different. God could be approached by any form of worship as long as it was done with single-minded devotion.

Different religions were all different roads to reach the same God. He believed that service to man was service to God, for man was the embodiment of God on earth. As man was the creation of God, man-made divisions made no sense to him.

Ramakrishna Paramahamsa was a great teacher who could express complicated philosophical ideas in a simple language for everyone to understand. He believed that religious salvation could be attained through renunciation, meditation, and devotion.

Ramakrishna derived wisdom neither from any book or scripture, nor from any prophet, but directly from the eternal fountainhead of all knowledge and wisdom. He is revered and recognised by all as the prophet of universalism and harmony of religions. In his view, realisation of God is considered to be the ultimate goal of human life.

Standing on the basis of his rich and varied spiritual experience, Ramakrishna declared that all creeds, Hindu, Islamic, Christian, or of any other denomination, are so many distinct paths leading to the same goal, namely the realisation of God. He stated "God can be realised through all paths. All religions are true. The important thing is to reach the roof. You can reach it by stone stairs or by wooden stairs or by bamboo steps or by a rope." He stressed that every individual is a part of God. Therefore, according to him "service to man means service to God."

Ramakrishna approached different religions not as a scholar but as a devotee. By realising the great truths of different religions, he demonstrated in practice that there is nothing but unity, and that all men are the children of the same Reality, whether it is called by different names. His faith in the fundamental realisation of unity that exists among religions has universal importance. His spirit of finding out unity in the world of diversity is evident in his following statement: "Exactly as water can exist in a liquid, solid and invisible form.....As water is called by different names, in different languages, so different religions call God by different names like Hari, Siva, Allah, Christ etc., but all denote the same God".

Mahatma Gandhi expressed the essential practical character of Ramakrishna' s thoughts and his personal vision of Truth as follows: "The story of Ramakrishna Paramahamsa' s life is a story of religion in practice ... His sayings are pages from the Book of Life."

Swami Vivekananda and the Ramakrishna Mission

Narendra Nath Dutta, better known as Swami Vivekananda, was the most illustrious disciple of Sri Ramakrishna. He was born in Calcutta in January, 1863. He graduated from the Scottish Church College and was well-versed in Western philosophy. Vivekananda was a man of great intellect and possessed a critical and analytical mind. At the age of eighteen, Vivekananda met Sri Ramakrishna. This meeting transformed his life completely. After the death of Sri Ramakrishna, he became a 'sanyasi' and devoted his life to preaching and spreading Ramakrishna's message to the people. His religious message was put in a form that would suit the needs of the contemporary Indian society.

Vivekananda proclaimed the essential oneness of all religions. He condemned the caste system, religious rituals, ceremonies, and superstitions. He had a deep understanding of Hindu philosophy and travelled far and wide to spread its message. At the Parliament of World Religions in Chicago (1893), Vivekananda spoke about Hindu religion at length.

His brilliant speech on Hindu philosophy was well received. American newspapers described him as an 'Orator by Divine Right'. He delivered a series of lectures in the USA, England, and in several other countries of Europe. Through his speeches, Vivekananda explained Hindu philosophy and clarified the wrong notions that prevailed in Western countries about the Hindu religion and Indian culture.

In India, however, Vivekananda's main role was that of a social reformer rather than a religious leader. He propagated Ramakrishna's message of peace and brotherhood and emphasised the need for religious tolerance which would lead to the establishment of peace and harmony in the country.

He believed that it was the social responsibility of the influential people to take care of the downtrodden. With his clarity of thought and the deep understanding of the social problems of India, Vivekananda undoubtedly left a deep mark on the Indian intelligentsia as well as on the masses. At a time when the nation was in despair, he preached the gospel of strength and self-reliance. Vivekananda died at the age of 39.

In 1897, Vivekananda founded the Ramakrishna Mission to propagate social welfare. It laid emphasis not on personal salvation but on social good and social service. The Ramakrishna Mission stood for religious and social reform based on the ancient culture of India. Emphasis was put on the essential spirit of Hinduism and not on rituals.

Rendering social service was the primary aim of the Ramakrishna Mission. It believed that serving a human being was the same as worshipping God. The Mission opened a chain of schools, hospitals, orphanages, and libraries throughout the country. It provided relief during famines, earthquakes, and epidemics. A *math* or monastery was established in *Belur* near Calcutta. The *Belur math* took care of the religious developments of the people.

Swami Vivekananda
— Wikimedia Commons

Vivekananda's Views

Vivekananda's interpretation of Vedanta gave a new lease of life to traditional Hinduism. Hindu religion with a new interpretation and vigour established its greatness in the cultural firmament of India.

On Education and Society

Vivekananda rightly realised education as the manifestation of the perfection already in man. According to him, the real education is that which enables one to get employed or earn livelihood and it helps in life-building, man-making, and character-making. As knowledge is inherent in man, the external world only gives suggestions.

Education provides a better standard of life to the society. If the social life of the country will improve, it will be a boon to national life. So Vivekananda in his teachings had attached great significance to the role of education in society-building. According to him, Indian society has its own fundamental characteristics. We should not be blind imitators of the West. Our own individuality and uniqueness will help us to be the pioneers in every front.

Swami Vivekananda was the first to understand the importance of Indian culture in comparison with Western culture. If the West is materialistic and ahead in science and technology, India is rich in its heritage and spiritual education. Knowledge of both the cultures is essential for the growth of humankind and nation-building. India can help the West by lending its spiritual knowledge and the West can help India by disseminating science and technical education. He saw that science is not contradictory to the eternal spiritual principles, which is the foundation of Indian culture. Both science and eternal principles of dharma are concerned with truth. Science seeks truth in the physical world, whereas dharma seeks truth in the spiritual realm.

To Vivekananda, mother tongue is the right medium for mass education. But he prescribed the learning of English and Sanskrit also. While English is necessary for mastering Western science and technology, Sanskrit leads one into the depths of our vast store of classics.

Vivekananda, in his scheme of education, meticulously includes all those studies, which are necessary for the all-around development of the body, mind, and soul of the individual. Vivekananda, in his plan for the regeneration of India, repeatedly presses the need for the eradication of poverty, unemployment, and ignorance. He says, "We need technical education and all else which may develop industries, so that men, instead of seeking for service, may earn enough to provide for themselves, and save something against a rainy day." He feels it necessary that India should take from the Western nations all that are good in their civilisation. However, just like a person, every nation has its individuality, which should not be destroyed. The individuality of India lies in her spiritual culture. Hence, in Swamiji's view, for the development of a balanced nation, we have to combine the dynamism and scientific attitude of the West with the spirituality of our country. The entire educational program should be so planned that it equips the youth to contribute to the material progress of the country as well as to maintaining the supreme worth of India's spiritual heritage.

On Service to Mankind

A humanist to the core, he regarded **"Jiva as Shiva".** It is through the service of 'Jiva' or human being, 'Shiva' or God can be attained. His call to the people was "Go, all of you, wherever there is an outbreak of plague or famine, or wherever the people are in distress, and mitigate their sufferings. I do not believe in a God or religion that cannot wipe the widow's tears or bring a piece of bread to the orphan's mouth. If we want to rejuvenate India, we must work for them. So as long as the millions live in hunger and ignorance, I hold each man a traitor."

Ideas on Nationalism

Vivekananda was a patriotic monk. He had genuine feelings of love and attachment for the land and people of the land. He specially inspired the young masses to free India from the foreign yoke. In his own words, "What our country now wants are muscles of iron and nerves of steel and granite wills that nothing can resist. Only the young men can play an active role in this regard and on their shoulders rests the future of the land."

"Arise, Awake, and Stop not till the goal is reached", he declared. The intense feelings for the country, attachment for the soil, and closeness to its people inspired the monk to spread the spirit of nationalism. Setting the example of the American revolutionaries who had already tasted the fruits of freedom, Vivekananda indirectly instilled into the minds of the Indian people the inspiration for the freedom struggle.

On Religion and Ethics

Being a socio-religious reformer, Vivekananda gave a new touch to the ongoing reformist movement. He said, "We want to lead mankind to the place where there is neither the Veda, nor the Bible nor the Koran; yet this has to be done by harmonising the Vedas, the Bible and the Koran. Mankind ought to be taught that religions are but the varied expressions of THE RELIGION."

Thus, he believed in the harmonious existence of all religions. Religions should be free from dogmas and superstitions to make human beings more rational. The social evils of child marriage, widowhood, lack of education, etc. can be removed only through a rational approach. The work must proceed from the bottom and not from the top.

Other Reform Movements

Annie Besant and the Theosophical Society

The Theosophical Society was founded in 1875 at New York by a Russian spiritualist, Madam Helena Blavatsky and an American, Colonel H.S. Olcott. The society was greatly influenced by the Indian doctrine of Karma and Hindu Philosophy. Later on, they came to India and established the Head Office of the society at Adyar near Madras in 1882.

The term 'Theosophical' implies a system of philosophy which aims at attaining spiritual happiness through deep knowledge of the self. The society wanted to blend together the best principles of Hinduism and Zoroastrianism. The society believed in one God and condemned the social as well as racial discrimination. It accepted the doctrine of transmigration of the soul and preached the universal brotherhood of man.

The Theosophical Society reached the climax of its glory under the leadership of Mrs. Annie Besant (1847–1933). Annie Besant was an Irish lady who had settled in India and adopted Hinduism. She worked for the regeneration of Indian culture and propagation of education. A free thinker and a captivating orator, she remained the President of the Theosophical Society of India from 1907 till her death. She had a deep insight to understand the needs of the masses of India and prepared a national scheme of education based on the fundamental principles of Indian culture. During the national movement, she urged the students to be conscious of the glory of the country.

Annie Besant was the founder of the Central Hindu College in Banaras, which later developed into the Banaras Hindu University. Annie Besant herself made India her permanent home and played a prominent role in Indian politics. In 1917, she was elected as President of the Indian National Congress. She edited several journals for the task of national awakening. She established Women's Indian Association which later on came to known as All India Women's Conference–an organisation for the upliftment of women. She wrote a number of books on Hindu philosophy and translated the Bhagavad Gita into English.

Syed Ahmed Khan and the Aligarh Movement (1817–1898)

The socio-religious reform movement among the Muslims emerged late. Most Muslims feared that Western education would endanger their religion as it was un-Islamic in character. During the first half of the 19th century, only a handful of Muslims had accepted English education.

The Muhammedan Literary Society, established by Nawab Abdul Latif in 1863, was one of the earliest institutions that attempted to spread modern education. Abdul Latif also tried to remove social abuses and promote Hindu-Muslim unity.

Sir Syed Ahmad Khan
— Wikimedia Commons

The most important socio-religious movement among the Muslims came to be known as the 'Aligarh Movement'. It was organised by Syed Ahmad Khan (1817–1898). He is considered as the most outstanding figure among the Muslims.

Syed Ahmad Khan was born in 1817 into a Muslim noble family and had joined the service of the Company as a judicial officer. Syed Ahmed Khan was firmly convinced that the Muslims could progress only with the education of modern scientific thoughts. He urged the people to develop a critical and rational outlook. He considered the Koran to be the sole authority of Islam but was keen for the progress and advancement of the Muslim society. He urged his Muslim fellowmen to give up medieval customs. He advocated the removal of purdah among women and pleaded for the spread of education among Muslim women. He also condemned the practice of polygamy and early divorce among the Muslims. He realised that the Muslims had to adapt themselves to the British rule. So Syed Ahmad advised Muslims to embrace Western education and take up government service.

In 1864, he founded the Scientific Society to translate English books on science and other subjects into Urdu. He also started an English-Urdu journal through which he spread the ideas of social reform. Through his initiative was established the Mohammedan Anglo-Oriental College in 1875, which later developed into the Aligarh Muslim University. It helped to develop a modern outlook among its students. This intellectual movement is called the Aligarh Movement.

As a social reformer, Syed Ahmad Khan campaigned against the purdah system, polygamy, and the Muslim system of divorce. He emphasised the need for removing irrational social customs while retaining the essence of Islam and encouraging a rational interpretation of the Koran.

Syed Ahmad Khan believed that the interest of the Muslims would be best served through cooperation with the British Government. It was only through the guidance of the British that India could mature into a full-fledged nation. So he opposed the participation of the Muslims in the activities of the Indian National Congress.

The promotion of Science and modern education among Muslims remained the first task throughout his life. Syed Ahmed Khan drew around him a band of dedicated followers which collectively came to be known as 'Aligarh School'. Among the important ones were Chiragh Ali, Altaf Hussain Hali (Urdu Poet), Nazir Ahmed , Maulana Shibli Nomani, and Khuda Baksh. Collectively, they worked for bringing social reforms among Muslim communities.

Deoband School Movement

It was a revivalist movement whose twin objectives were:

(i) to propagate the pure teaching of the Koran and the Hadis

(ii) to keep alive the spirit of Jihad against the foreign rulers

Under the leadership of Muhammad Qasim Nanautavi (1832–80) and Rashid Ahamd Gangohi (1828–1905) was founded the school at Deoband in the Saharanpur district of the UP in 1866. The object was to train religious leaders for the Muslim community. The education was in original Islamic religion.

Deoband School did not prepare its students for government jobs or worldly careers but for the preaching of Islamic faith. Deoband School attracted students not only from all parts of India, but from the neighbouring Muslim countries also.

The Ahmadiyya Movement

The movement is considered one of the most influential and important Muslim socio-religious movements in India. The movement was started by Mirza Ghulam Ahmad in Punjab in 1889. It was a liberal reform movement among Muslims in India. It was based on the principles of universal religion of all humanity and opposed Jihad or religious war against non Muslims.

The main targets of the Ahmadiyya movement were Ulemas of Deoband and the Ahl-i Hadith.

Mirza Ghulam Ahmad strongly spoke against the increasing influence of the Christian missionaries in Punjab. Mirza Ghulam Ahmad and his followers described themselves as a distinct religious community. They also claimed themselves to be the only upholders of `true Islam`.

Jyotirao Govindrao Phule and Depressed Class Movement

Jyotirao Govindrao Phule (1827–1890), was a prominent social figure in Maharashtra. Born in the Mali caste, Phule emerged as a champion of the oppressed sections of the society. He was the first Indian to start a school for the untouchables in 1854. He also fought for improving the condition of women. He started a school for the education of girls of the lower castes and founded an association called the Satyashodhak Samaj.

Jyotirao Govindrao Phule
— Wikimedia Commons

People from all castes and religions were allowed to join the association. He was opposed to the domination of the Brahmins and started the practice of conducting marriages without Brahmin priests. He wrote a book called 'Gulamgiri' in which he championed the cause of the lower castes' movement.

Historian Sumit Sarkar points out: "The anti-Brahmin toxin was first sounded in Maharashtra in the 1870s by Jyotiba Phule with his book, Gulamgiri (1872) and his organisation, the Satyashodhak Samaj (1873) which strongly pleaded for saving the lower castes from the hypocritical Brahmins and their opportunistic scriptures."

The Prarthana Samaj

In 1867, the *Prarthana Samaj* was founded by Dr. Atmaram Pandurang in 1867 under the influence of Brahmo leader Keshab Chandra Sen with an aim of religious reforms in Maharashtra. Mahadev Govind Ranade and R.G. Bhandarkar were the two great leaders of this Samaj.

Mahadev Govind Ranade
— Wikimedia Commons

The *Prarthana Samaj* in Maharashtra played the role of the Brahmo Samaj of Bengal. It attacked the caste system and the predominance of the Brahmins, campaigned against child marriage and the purdah system, preached widow remarriage, and emphasised on female education. In order to reform Hinduism, Ranade started the Widow Remarriage Association and the Deccan Education Society. In 1887, Ranade founded the National Social Conference with the aim of introducing social reforms throughout the country. Ranade was also one of the founders of the Indian National Congress. The activities of the Prarthana Samaj spread to south India through the efforts of the Telugu reformer, Veeresalingam.

Pandita Ramabai and the Women's Movement

Pandita Ramabai
— Wikimedia Commons

The broad objectives of social reform movements of the 19th century were caste reform, improvement in the status of women, promoting women's education, and eradication of social practices such as *Sati*, widowhood, and child marriage. In the earlier phase of the social reform movement, the initiatives came largely from male reformers like Raja Ram Mohan Roy.

However, very few women reformers were visible in the 19th century that took up the cause of women's upliftment. One name that comes prominently among the early women reformers was Pandita Ramabai (1858–1922). She was a social reformer, a champion for the emancipation of women, and a pioneer in education. She acquired a reputation as a Sanskrit scholar.

Ramabai resolved to spend her life attempting to better the status of women in India. She founded Arya Mahila Samaj. The purpose of this institution was to promote the cause of women's education and deliverance from the oppression of child marriage. In an address to Lord Ripon's Education Commission in 1882, she declared with fervour, "In ninety-nine cases out of a hundred, the educated men of this country are opposed to female education and the proper position of women. If they observe the slightest fault, they magnify the grain of mustard-seed into a mountain, and try to ruin the character of a woman." She suggested that teachers be trained and women school inspectors be appointed. Further, she said that as the situation in India was that women's conditions were such that only women could medically treat them, Indian women should be admitted to medical colleges.

In 1883, Ramabai received a scholarship to train as a teacher in England. During her time there, she converted to Christianity and joined the Anglican Church. Ramabai combined her Christian ideals with her Indian culture to promote change in India. She also lectured across America on the plight of women and child widows in India. She wrote a book, *The High Caste Hindu Woman.* Ramabai dedicated this book to Dr. Anandibai Joshi, the first Indian woman to earn a medical degree. More than 10,000 copies of this book were sold in America, the profits from which were used to give shelter to the destitute women in India.

In 1889, she had started a home-cum-school in Bombay which she named as Sharda Sadan, which was later changed to Mukti Mission.

Reform Movements in South India

Following are some of the earliest prominent reformers from the south and their organisations:

- **Kandukuri Veeresalingam (1848–1919) :** He pioneered the movement in support of widow remarriage and girls education in Andhra. Veeresalingam was influenced by the Brahmo Samaj and established a number of schools for girls as well as a widow home. He started a social organisation called Hitakarini Samajam.

- **Chembeti Sridharalu Naidu :** He founded the Veda Samaj in Madras in 1864. It advocated discarding of caste distinctions and promotion of widow remarriage and women's education. It condemned the superstitions and rituals of orthodox Hinduism and propagated belief in one supreme God.

Sree Narayana Guru — Wikimedia Commons

The Sree Narayana Dharma Paripalana Yogam (SNDP) Movement

SNDP was a movement of the backward class of Kerala called Ezhavas led by Sri Narayana Guru Swamy in 1903 .The Ezhavas were a caste of toddy-tappers in Kerala.

Sree Narayana Guru formed a program of action known as the 'SNDP Yogam' for the depressed classes in Kerala. The movement was successful, resulting in upward social mobility of backward classes and shift in power distribution from upper castes to lower castes.

The Self-Respect Movement

Periyar E.V. Ramaswamy (1879–1973), a social reformer from Tamil Nadu, was the leader of the Self-respect movement. Known as 'Father of the Dravidian Movement', Periyar started the Self-respect movement in Tamil Nadu in 1925. Its main goal was to improve upon the socio-economic conditions of the low caste Tamils.

Periyar — Wikimedia Commons

It had two aims :

1. Demanding more concession for lower classes in education and improving their social status
2. Achieving 'Swayam Maryada', or self-respect

Periyar was anti-Brahmin and pro-British. He attacked the Brahmins and Hindu religion and upheld the Dravidian culture. He founded the 'Dravidar Kazhagam' party or later DMK which became the dominant Dravidian political party of Tamil Nadu.

Previous Years' Questions

1. **"Though Sri Ramakrishna became the prophet of neo-Hinduism, he never claimed to have founded any new religion." Elaborate. (2014)**

2. **"The first point to note is the continuing importance of religion and philosophy as vital ingredients in the modern Indian Renaissance. Indeed, there is as much reason for regarding it as a reformation as there is for treating it as a Renaissance." Critically examine. (2013)**

   Solution : See under Indian Renaissance

3. **"Swami Dayanand's philosophy represents both elements of extremism and social radicalism". Substantiate. (2015)**

4. **Swami Vivekananda opined that "We should give our ancient spirituality and culture and get in return Western science, technology, methods of raising the standards of life, business integrity and technique of collective effort." (2013)**

5. **"Young Bengal left little distinctive or permanent impression on the plane of religion and philosophy." Critically evaluate. (2011)**

6. **"Sri Narayana Guru's was a major intervention in the social reform movement from a subaltern perspective." Critically examine. (2017)**

11 CHAPTER

Growth of Nationalistic Consciousness and Foundation of Indian National Congress

Introduction

After the 1857 revolt, a sense of national consciousness among Indians became conspicuous with growing disillusionment of the British rule. With the exception of a few with vested interests, the entire people of India lost faith in the British rule. The very nature of the British rule with its expansionist, exploitative, imperialistic, and oppressive designs created hatred among Indians. Indians now firmly believed that British rule was a stumbling block to their overall development–cultural, economic, educational, intellectual, political, social, and spiritual.

Contributing Factors for the Growth of National Consciousness

The growth of nationalism was not the result of any single factor. It was the product of a number of factors operating during the period extending over several decades. To quote A.R. Desai, "Indian nationalism was the outcome of the new materialistic conditions created in India and the new social forces which emerged as a result of the British conquest. It was the outcome of the objective conflict of interests, the interest of Britain to keep India politically, economically subjected to her, and the interest of the Indian people for a free political economic and cultural evolution of the Indian society, which was intruded by the British rule."

Following are some of the significant factors that led to the growth of Indian nationalism:

British Imperialism

British imperialism was the most important factor which contributed to the rise of nationalism in India. The centralised administrative structure and policies of the British made the geographical unification of the country possible. Before the advent of the British, the people of the south and north-east usually remained separated from the rest of India, except for some short intervals. British imperialism made the people think as one nationalised centralised administrative machinery. The modern judiciary and lucrative employment opportunities in British Indian Services also played an important role.

Contact with the West

The establishment of British rule in India made closer relations with the Western world possible. These contacts with the European countries influenced the Indians immensely. Nationalism and liberalism were the dominating ideologies in the nineteenth century Europe. Indians imbibed the ideas of nationalism and liberalism from the Western countries, particularly from Germany, Italy, Greece, and Belgium. Besides this, the ideas and ideologies of the contemporary liberal Western thinkers, namely Burke, Bentham, Mill, Spencer, Rousseau, and Voltaire also influenced the thought processes of educated Indians which helped in igniting nationalistic feelings for their own country.

Impact of English Education

There was a rapid growth of English education in India, especially after the revolt of 1857. The second half of the nineteenth century was a golden age of Liberalism in Europe, particularly England. The study of the political classics of English literature from Milton to Mill planted in the minds of English-educated Indians the seeds of liberalism in its two aspects—nationalism and democracy.

Western-educated Indians gradually became conscious of the contemporary happenings and the current affairs of the world and those around them. Though the British introduced English language in India, it was for their own selfish interests. English education was mainly needed to serve the purpose of producing Indians with clerical grades in various government departments at low wages and also to strengthen their rule in India. However, it became a significant agent in the growth of national consciousness among the English-educated Indians. English education also facilitated people of different provinces to come close to one another in the form of lingua franca. Thus, it helped in raising national feelings and political consciousness among the Indians.

Modern Means of Communication and Transportation

The introduction of telegraphs and railways in 1852 and 1853 respectively, gave India a swift means of transport and communication.

The modern means of communication shattered the age-old isolation of Indian villages and the people of remote parts had the opportunity of coming closer to each other. They also promoted trade and commerce and helped people of different regions to develop social and intellectual intercourse. Its growth quickened the pace of the nationalist movement in the country.

Contribution of Vernacular Literature and Intellectuals

The vernacular literature of this period played a crucial role in spreading national consciousness and awakening. Novels, plays, poems, and stories written in various Indian languages greatly helped in national awakening. The novel *Anandamath* and the composition *Vande Mataram* of Bankim Chandra became a great source of inspiration to the people. Vast literature produced by Bhartendu Harishchandra in Hindi, Vishnu Chiplunkar in Marathi, Subramaniya Bharati in Tamil, Rabindranath Tagore in Bengali, and Altaf Hussain Hali in Urdu, helped in stirring the hearts of the Indian people and filled their minds with the ideals of freedom. The scholarly writings of Dadabhai Naoroji and R.C. Dutt touched the conscience of the intellectuals and made them aware of the exploitative nature of the British economic policies. Also, the study of India's past by the British scholars, indologists, and archaeologists like Max Mueller, John Marshall, and R.G. Bhandarkar helped profoundly to bring to light the richness of the ancient heritage of India. These scholars revealed to the people of India the splendour of the Sanskrit language and also inculcated among them a feeling of pride in their past and their faith in the future. People began to feel proud of India's past glory and its rich culture.

Growth of Indian Press

As A.R. Desai opined, "the printing press played a big role in the History of people in their national awakening, in their progressive ideas and in their being drawn as active forces into great social, political and cultural movements".

The first newspaper in India was the *Bengal-Gazette* started in 1780 by James Augustus Hicky. It laid the foundation of the Indian Press. It was followed by the several influential journals and newspapers such as *Bengal Journal, Calcutta Chronicle, Madras Courier*, and *Bombay Herald.* By the 19th century, press emerged out as an important medium, not only for the dissemination of information on various problems, but also as a mouthpiece for generating social and national consciousness.

Ram Mohan Roy was also acclaimed as the 'Father of vernacular journalism in India'. He was a staunch advocate of the freedom of press. Ram Mohan Roy published two papers, *Sambad Kaumudi* in Bengali and *Mirat-ul-Akbar* in Persian, which was propagating the case for social reform.

Dadabhai Naoroji edited *Rast Goftar* and Ishwar Chandra Vidyasagar started *Shome Prakash.* In 1890, an English weekly, the *Indian Social Reformer*, was started in Bombay to propagate social reforms.

Newspaper and magazines served as a powerful media for mass awakening, infusing political ideas, and arousing patriotic sentiments. Editors like Bal Gangadhar Tilak of *Kesari* and *Mahratta* and Lala Lajpat Rai of the *Bande Mataram* and *The People*, suffered deportation due to their critical views on British rule in India. Newspapers like the *Indian Mirror, Bombay Samachar, The Hindu Patriot, The Amrit Bazar Patrika, The Hindu*, and *The Kesari*, tremendously influenced the people of India and thus, left an indelible mark on the political life of the country.

By the end of the 19th century, about 500 newspapers and journals in Indian languages and English were started in different parts of country. Initially, the newspapers of Madras and Bombay were on good terms with the government, whereas, those of Bengal were antagonistic to the government. During the 19th century, the newspapers largely concentrated on issues relating to the Indian society, and by the third quarter of the 19th century, they acquired a nationalistic tone, and by that time most of the English journals were run by Indians themselves.

The British Government passed many Acts from time to time to impose censorship over the Indian Press. In spite of the suppression, the Press played the role of awakening the people to the need for reform and became one of the instruments in the growth of nationalism.

The vernacular press in the nineteenth century India served not just as newspapers but more importantly as views-papers. In the 19th century, the main task before the press was the generating of awareness and propagation of nationalist ideology. The press played as the chief instrument for arousing, mobilising, and consolidating nationalist public opinion.

Even the work of the National Congress was accomplished largely through the vernacular press. Its resolutions and proceedings had to be propagated through newspapers. The influence of the press extended far beyond its literate subscribers. It was not just confined to cities and large towns.

In the 19th century, press played the heroic role of a freedom fighter against the colonial exploitation. Newspapers were published as a national service and public views were propagated through them. It played an important role in enlightening the masses on government policies and works.

The vernacular press, despite many odds and restrictions (such as Licensing Regulations of 1823, Registration Act of 1867, and Vernacular Press Act of 1878), continued preaching the lessons on nationalism and aroused the sentiments of the masses.

HICKY's
BENGAL GAZETTE;
OR THE ORIGINAL
Calcutta General Advertiser.

A Weekly Political and Commercial Paper, Open to all Parties, but influenced by None.

59 From Saturday March 3d to Saturday March 10th 1781. No. VII

From the LONDON GAZETTE EXTRAORDINARY.

Bengal Gazette – The first Indian newspaper — *Wikimedia Commons*

Social Reform Movements

Religious and social reformers namely Raja Rammohan Roy, Keshab Chandra Sen, Debendranath Tagore, Ishwar Chandra Vidyasagar, Swami Dayanand Saraswati, Ramakrishna Paramhamsa, Vivekananda, and others had left a tremendous influence on the people of India. They were responsible for generating self-consciousness and social and cultural awareness among the people of India. Revivalist reformers like Dayanand Saraswati and Vivekananda upheld Indian philosophy and culture. This instilled in Indians a sense of pride and faith in their own culture. The cultural and ideological struggle taken up by the socio-religious movements helped to build up national consciousness. They, thus, paved the way for the growth of nationalism.

Discrimination Against Indians

From the beginning, there was massive discrimination shown by the British towards Indians in every field, starting from recruiting Indians into British government services. No Indian was given high positions. The British did not trust the Indians and their sincerity.

The Proclamation of Queen Victoria in 1858 declared that Indians, henceforward, would be appointed to high posts on the basis of their merit irrespective of their caste, religion, or race. But this policy was never implemented.

The British policy of discrimination, exploitation, and unjust treatment created a great discontent and unrest among the educated people of India. They started taking active part in the national movement with the aim of driving away the British altogether from India.

Economic Exploitation by the British

The primary objective of the British rule in India was the economic exploitation. They took away raw materials from India and brought here their manufactured goods. The policy of economic exploitation ruined the Indian industries; and the British were taking away the wealth of India to their country.

Their free trade policy proved ruinous for Indian trade and industries. Indian industries failed to compete with those of the British because the British had all the advantages and privileges on their side. Moreover, the British officials working in India had become a drain on the Indian resources.

The economic system of India was moulded according to the needs of the people of England. Thus, the interests of the Indian people were completely ignored. This created hostile relations among Indians of all levels towards the British

Anti-Indian Policy of Lord Lytton

The period from 1870 to 1884 was extremely tumultuous and was seen as the beginning of the growth of Indian nationalism. The several acts of omission and commission in the time of Lord Lytton accelerated the nationalist movement. Lord Lytton held his famous Delhi Darbar in 1877 at a time when the entire country was under drought and famine.

Most of the import duties on British textile imports were removed to please the textile manufacturers of England. Indians interpreted the action as proof of the British desire to ruin the small but growing textile industry of India. In 1878, the Arms Act was passed, which disarmed the Indians. It appeared that it was an attempt by the government to weaken the whole nation.

Lord Lytton
— Wikimedia Commons

The Second Anglo-Afghan War cost the Indian treasury a lot. Lytton passed the Vernacular Press Act in 1878. The people belonging to all walks of life condemned the discriminatory provisions of the Act. It has been pointed out that the Act was a retrograde and ill-conceived measure injurious to the future progress of India.

At the same time in 1878, the government announced new regulations reducing the maximum age limit for sitting in the Indian Civil Service Examination from 21 years to 19. All these measures created a widespread discontentment among the Indians. Anti-Indian administration of Lord Lytton helped to intensify discontent against the foreign rule.

Ilbert Bill Controversy

During the viceroyalty of Lord Ripon, a controversy arose concerning the Ilbert Bill. Ripon tried to pass a law to enable the Indian district magistrates and sessions judges to try the Europeans in criminal cases. The Europeans in India organised a vehement agitation against the Bill, which was drafted by Ilbert, the law member of Ripon's government.

They poured abuses on Indians. Lord Ripon became the target of agitations. The Europeans declared that even the most highly educated among the Indians were unfit to try the Europeans. In the end, the government bowed before the Europeans. The Indians became conscious of the degradation to which foreign rule had reduced them. It increased racial bitterness, and led to the growth of national discontent.

Early Political Associations (1838–1885)

After 1857, several political associations came up for the first time, for taking up their respective causes to the British government and promoting a sense of national awakening among the people.

Important characteristic features of early 19th century political associations were:

- They were founded and dominated by the wealthy aristocratic class.
- They were local or regional in character.
- Their major demands included administrative reforms, association of Indians with the administration, and spread of education.

The political associations of the second half of the nineteenth century came to be increasingly dominated by the educated middle class—the lawyers, journalists, doctors, teachers, etc. and they had a wider perspective and a larger agenda.

The Indian National Congress cannot claim to be the first political organisation in India. There were around six important political associations all over India before the foundation of the Indian National Congress in 1885. Important political associations before the Indian National Congress were: The Zamindari Association or Landholders' Society (1838), East India Association, London (1866), Poona Sarvjanik Sabha (1870), Indian Association, Calcutta (1876), Madras Mahajan Sabha (1884), and Bombay Presidency Association (1885).

The Zamindari Association

The Zamindari Association, which was later renamed Landholders' Society, was established in 1838 by Dwarkanath Tagore, Prasanna Kumar Tagore, Radhakanta Deb, Ramkamal Sen, and Bhabani Charan Mitra. It has been described as "the first organisation of Bengal with a distinct political object." The society virtually became defunct after the death of Dwarkanath Tagore. This association was founded to safeguard the interests of the landlords. Although limited in its objectives, the Landholders' Society marked the beginning of an organised political activity and use of methods of constitutional agitation for the redressal of grievances.

It sent a petition to the British Parliament demanding inclusion of some of its suggestions to be included in the renewed Charter of the Company, such as :

(i) Establishment of a separate legislature of a popular character

(ii) Separation of executive from judicial functions

(iii) Reduction in salaries of higher officers

(iv) Abolition of salt duty and stamp duties

These were partially accepted when the Charter Act of 1853 provided for the addition of six members to the Governor-General's Council for legislative purposes.

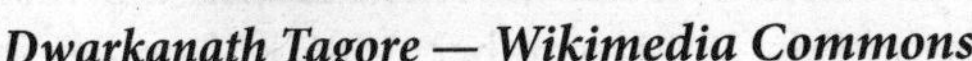

Dwarkanath Tagore — Wikimedia Commons

Prasanna Kumar Tagore — Wikimedia Commons

East Indian Association, London

Dadabhai Naoroji — Wikimedia Commons

Dadabhai Naoroji (1825–1917), popularly known as "Grand Old Man of India", organised East Indian Association in London, primarily for two objectives—first, to organise discussions on the plight of the Indian people and second, to influence British public opinion to promote the welfare of the Indians. Later on, Dadabhai organised branches of this association in prominent cities of India.

Poona Sarvjanik Sabha

Poona Sarvajanik Sabha was founded by Justice M. G. Ranade in 1870 to represent the people's views to the government. The Sabha provided many prominent national leaders including B.G. Tilak. It organised the Swadeshi movement during the national movement.

Indian Association, Calcutta

One of the distinctive political associations of this time was the Indian Association, Calcutta. It was formed by Surendranath Banerjee (1848–1925) and Ananda Mohan Bose in 1876 and became the forerunner of the Indian National Congress. Majority of the early associations failed to transform as a national political association. However, Indian Association worked towards forming a national level political body. Indian Association's aims were to first create strong public opinion in the country and to unify people on a common political program. It opened several branches in and outside Bengal.

Surendranath Banerjee — Wikimedia Commons

The Indian Association of Calcutta was the most important of pre-Congress associations and aimed to:

(i) Create a strong public opinion on political questions

(ii) Unify Indian people on a common political program

Branches of the association were opened in other towns and cities of Bengal and even outside Bengal. The membership fee was kept low in order to attract the poorer sections to the association.

Before the Congress came into existence, the Indian Association may very well claim to be the British Majesty's Permanent Opposition. It organised All-India agitations against the British government's orders such as Vernacular Press Act of 1878 and reduction of the age limit from 21 to 19 years for Indians in Civil Service exams. Indian Association was the first to hold a National Conference, from December 28 to 30, 1883. It was the first conference of the people in which representatives from all parts of India were invited. In 1885, the second sitting of the Indian Association was held in Calcutta. It met for three days, on December, 25, 26, and 27, 1885. While Surendranath and his friends were organising the Conference in Calcutta, Allen Hume, a British Civil Servant, founded another all-India level organisation on 28th December, 1885 in Bombay. It was named the Indian National Congress. Its first conference was held in Bombay with 72 delegates in attendance. Hume assumed office as the General Secretary, and Womesh Chandra Bonnerjee of Calcutta was elected President. Thus, the Indian National Congress was inaugurated excluding its rival, the Indian Association and Surendranath Banerjee.

Madras Mahajan Sabha

The first organisation in the Madraṣ Presidency to agitate for the rights of Indians was the Madras Native Association which was established by Gazulu Lakshminarasu Chetty in 1849. This organisation did not survive for long and was eventually disbanded. In May 1884, S. Ramaswami Mudaliar and P. Anandacharlu established the Madras Mahajana Sabha. P. Rangaiah Naidu was elected President of the Sabha with R. Balaji Rao as its Secretary. In September 1885, the Sabha in collaboration with the Bombay Presidency Association and the Indian Association sent a delegation to England.

Bombay Presidency Association

Bombay Presidency Association was organised by Pherozshah Mehta, K.T. Telang, and Badruddin Tyabji for promoting public interests.

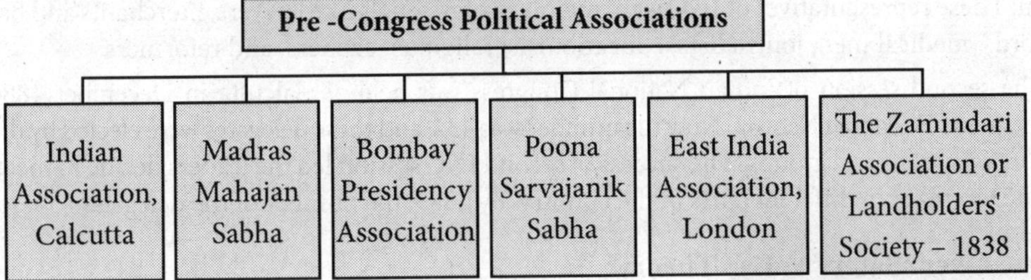

The Indian National Congress (INC)

Although the origin and its nature of work remained controversial, the Indian National Congress played the most prominent role in shaping Indian nationalism. The Congress was founded in the era of undisputed British supremacy. Factors like patronage of British authorities, existence of Anglo-Indians, and a rising Indian educated class led to the acceptance and survival of the Congress in the late nineteenth century.

A.O. Hume
— *Wikimedia Commons*

On the suggestion of a retired British civil servant, Allan Octavian Hume (1829–1912), the Congress was created. Allan Octavian Hume, the founder of Indian National Congress, 1885, was a renowned ornithologist and horticulturalist in British India. Hume has been called "the Father of Indian Ornithology".

A.O. Hume wanted to set up an all-India organisation of educated Indians to prevent a recurrence of the 1857 outburst. Hume viewed that the emergence of educated class should be accepted as a political reality and timely steps should be taken to provide a legitimate outlet to the grievances of this class and satisfy their ambitions. The scheme of formatting an Indian political body was prepared in Simla in early 1885 and Lord Dufferin took the leading part in it.

In May 1885, Hume secured the Viceroy, Lord Dufferin's approval to create an 'Indian National Union', which would be affiliated with the government and act as a platform to voice Indian public opinion.

Hume had toured the country and persuaded political leaders in Bombay, Calcutta, and Madras to meet at a national conference planned at Poona. The meeting of representatives from all parts was planned at Poona during the Christmas holidays but owing to the outbreak of cholera in the town, it was shifted to Bombay.

On 28 December 1885, the Indian National Congress representatives met at Gokuldas Tejpal Sanskrit College in Bombay with 72 delegates in attendance from all parts of India. Hume assumed office as the General Secretary, and Womesh Chandra Bonnerjee of Calcutta was elected President. Besides Hume, two British ers were the members of the founding group, William Wedderburn and Sir John Jardine. The other members were mostly Indians from the Bombay and Madras Presidencies.

The Congress was attended by such eminent leaders as Dadabhai Naoroji, Pherozeshah Mehta, S. Subramania Iyer, Dinshaw Wacha, Kashinath Trimbak Telang, P. Ananda Charlu, Gopal Ganesh Agarkar, M. Veeraraghavachariar, G. Subramania Iyer, N. G. Chandavarkar, and Rahmatullah Sayani. These representatives of INC were mainly professionals like lawyers, merchants and bankers, landlords, medical men, journalists, educationists, religious teachers, and reformers.

The second session of Indian National Congress was held at Calcutta in December 1886. The President was Dadabhai Naoroji. Now the number was 434, and these delegates were elected by different local organisations and groups. The success of second INC session led the leaders decide to meet every year in December in different parts of the country. By 1889, the number of the delegates rose to 2000.

Debate Over 'Safety Valve' Theory

This theory originated from William Wedderburn's biography of Hume published in 1913. He wrote that in 1878, Hume came across seven volumes of secret reports showing discontent among the lower classes and conspiracy to overthrow the British rule. He met Lord Dufferin and they decided to form an organisation with educated Indians serving as a safety valve by opening up a communication between rulers and the ruled, thus preventing mass revolution. Hume's involvement in the formation of INC gave rise to a lot of controversy regarding the origins of the Congress. Hume and his friends were convinced that the growing restlessness in the country could be directed into a constitutional channel to prevent a 1857-type outburst.

Hume and Lord Dufferin together decided to establish an organisation with educated Indians that would serve as a safety valve by opening up a line of the rulers and the ruled and would thus, prevent a mass revolution.

According to the theory, Congress was envisioned as a 'safety valve' that will prevent anti-British agitations in India and help in maintaining a cordial relationship between the British government and the enlightened Indians. Hume wanted to create a forum which was under the supervision of the British and which should let the British government know the demands of the Indian people. He wanted to prevent another nationwide outbreak like the 1857 revolt.

The following arguments were put forward to the safety valve theory :

- A. O. Hume and other British thought that the educated Indians may become leaders of the Indian public and organise a rebellion against the government. So, if the government itself provides them a platform to raise their voice, it may be possible to stop such nuisance.

- A. O. Hume had a series of meetings with Lord Dufferin, the Viceroy.
- He also lobbied with some other people such as Sir James Caird, Lord Ripon, John Bright, etc.
- A large number of British in India such as Sir William Wedderburn, George Yule, Charles Bradlaugh, etc., supported A.O. Hume.

The safety valve theory or the conspiracy theory that originated from William Wedderburn's biography of Hume, was for a long time, subscribed to by all shades of historians.

The theory was believed by the nationalist historians and the imperialist historians to discredit the Congress. The Marxist historians developed a conspiracy theory from this. Historian R.P. Dutt argued that Congress was born out of a conspiracy of the British to end any possibilities of an uprising and bourgeois leaders were a part of it.

In 1888, Dufferin openly criticised the Congress for representing a "microscopic minority". Thus, historians like Sumit Sarkar have rejected the theory of the safety valve. Bipan Chandra made an analogy in these words, "if Hume and other English liberals hoped to use Congress as a safety valve, the Congress leaders hoped to use Hume as a lightning conductor".

'Safety valve' theory has been discarded now. But still, the contribution of British cannot be disregarded in creation of the first all-India political party in which majority of the people were Hindus. The Muslims took Congress negatively in the beginning but there were leaders such as Badruddin Taybji who were active leaders. The contribution of the British in the foundation of this organisation was accepted and verbalised by Gopal Krishna Gokhae in 1913 as follows:

"No Indian could have started the Indian National Congress…if an Indian had come forward to start such a movement embracing all-Indians, the officials in India would not have allowed the movement to come into existence. If the founder of the Congress had not been an Englishman and a distinguished ex-official, such was the distrust of political agitation in those days that the authorities would have at once found some way or the other to suppress the movement".

Congress: A Loyalist Party

The Congress had very modest beginnings. It held its sessions all over India once a year, usually in the month of December. The Congress was not intended to be a political party like the Liberals or Conservatives in England. In the initial years, the Congress leaders did not want the Congress to function as a political party. W.C. Bonerjee, the President of the first Congress, made it clear at the very outset that it was not "a nest of conspirators and disloyalties". Instead, INC was an annual gathering of representatives of different regions speaking on behalf of their respective people pertaining to social, economic, educational, or political nature. The aim of the gatherings were to enable all the earnest participants to become personally known to each other in the cause of national progress and to discuss and decide upon the political operations to be undertaken during the ensuing year.

INC met annually on Christmas days in different cities of India. Due to holidays in schools and law courts, the Congress could attract a large gathering of the elite class.

Each year the Congress sessions were held in different towns, normally in capital towns of a presidency or province. It was Gandhi who directed to have its sessions in villages and small towns so as to involve all in the national stream. In the first ten years, the Congress met twice at Bombay, Calcutta, Madras, and Allahabad and once in Lahore and Nagpur.

INC was a British loyalist party. Its members were thoroughly loyal and consistent well-wishers of the British Government. They simply sought autonomy in internal affairs under the British suzerainty. Dadabhai Naoroji in his speech to the Congress advised his countrymen in these words, "In dealing with Englishmen make up your mind deliberately, speak clearly and work perseveringly. Then and then alone can you hope to be listen to". W.C. Bonerjee in his presidential address said that "All that we desire that the basis of the government should be widened and that the people should have their proper and legitimate share in it."

From the beginning, the INC tried to eliminate regional differences. "Development and consolidation of those sentiments of national unity" would be the basic objective.

Therefore, following were the aims and objectives of the Congress in its initial years:

- To promote the feeling of national unity; to weld India into a nation; to help create an Indian people–to meet the imperialist charge that Indians were not a people or nation but a mere grouping of hundreds of diverse races, languages, castes, and religions.
- To create a national political platform or program on which all Indians could agree and which could serve as the basis for all-India political activity.
- The politicisation of the people and the creation of public interest in political questions and the training and organisation of public opinion in the country.
- The creation of an all-India political leadership. Such a leadership on a country-wide level did not exist in the 1880s. Allied to this was the need to train a common band of political workers or cadre to carry on political work.

W.C. Bonerjee
— Wikimedia Commons

The Moderate Phase (1885–1905)

The period from 1885–1905 is known as the era of Moderates. During this period, the Congress was guided by early nationalists who were called the Moderates on account of their cautious, cooperative, and peaceful approach. Moderates distinguished themselves from the neo-nationalists of the early twentieth century who were referred to as the Extremists.

Moderates were the supporters of British institutions and British sense of justice. They desired self-rule for India but they were not prepared to break up ties with Britain. They initiated Liberal Nationalism. Early nationalists were staunch believers in 'liberalism' and 'moderate' politics. They believed that their main task was to educate the people, to arouse national and political consciousness, and also to create a united public opinion on political consciousness.

The Moderate leaders believed that political connections with Britain were in India's interest at that stage of history and that the time was not ripe for a direct challenge to the British rule. Therefore, it was considered to be appropriate to try and transform the colonial rule to approximate to a national rule.

The national leaders like Dadabhai Naoroji, Pherozshah Mehta, W.C. Bonnerjee, S.N. Banerjea, D.E. Wacha, and Gopal Krishna Gokhale dominated the Congress during this period.

Social Composition of Moderates or the Early Nationalists

The founding members of INC belonged to the educated middle class. They had got English education and had firm faith in the British providence. They belonged to a class which was Indian in blood and colour but British in tastes, in opinions, in morals, and in intellect. They were supporters of British institutions. They believed that what India needed was a balanced and lucid presentation of her needs before the Englishmen and their Parliament.

Majority of the Moderate leaders were high caste Hindus, except a few Muslim leaders like Badruddin Tyabji. Muslim participation began to decline dramatically after 1889. Their social composition inevitably resulted in social orthodoxy as social questions were not raised in the Congress sessions till 1907.

With this narrow social base, the early nationalists were not able to penetrate down to the lower masses. Their movement did not have a wide appeal. The area of their influence was limited to the urban community.

They wanted to keep their movement restricted to the upper middle class as they were of opinion that people in general were not educated enough to understand the basic need of the hour.

Methods of Moderate Nationalists

The Moderates believed in constitutional methods and agitations within the confines of law. The Moderates believed that the British basically wanted to be just to the Indians but were not aware of the real conditions.

Most of the Moderates came from the English-speaking upper classes of the society. They believed in constitutional methods for getting their demands accepted. They believed that since their demands were moderate, they would be accepted by the government. They hoped that by peaceful methods of persuasion, they would be able to get their demands accepted. They had faith in the British government and believed that the British rule could be reformed from within.

Therefore, if public opinion could be created in the country and public demands be presented to the Government through resolutions, petitions, meetings, etc., the authorities would concede to these demands gradually.

To achieve these ends, they worked on a two-pronged methodology – one, create a strong public opinion to arouse consciousness and national spirit and then educate and unite people on common political questions; and two, persuade the British Government and British public opinion to introduce reforms in India on the lines laid out by the nationalists.

For this purpose, a British Committee of the Indian National Congress was established in London in 1899 which had India as its organ. Dadabhai Naoroji spent a substantial portion of his life and income campaigning for India's case abroad. In 1890, it was decided to hold a session of the Indian National Congress in London in 1892, but owing to the British elections of 1891, the proposal was postponed and never revived later.

Moderates' methodology of working was labelled as 'petitions, prayers and persuasion' to the British government. They resorted to constitutional agitation method. They sent a delegation to England to convince the government regarding the requirements of the Indians. They held meetings, criticised the government through the press, drafted and submitted memorials and petitions to the government, and worked to influence the British Parliament and British public opinion. They believed in piecemeal reforms and subscribed to the philosophy of gradualism. Later, Extremists criticised Moderates and called their way of working as 'method of mendicancy'.

Their main demands were :

- Freedom of speech and expression;
- Expansion of welfare programs;
- Promotion of education;
- Reduction of land revenue;
- Recruitment of Indians to high posts in the administration;
- More powers for the Legislative Councils and more Indian members in these Councils;
- Holding the Civil Services exams in India as well;
- Change in the economic priorities of the government so as to benefit Indian industries;
- Reduction of government expenditure on administration.

These demands suggest that the early Nationalists of Congress acted as a spokesman of every interest and section of the people.

After 1887, the Moderates'-led Congress started a campaign of agitation against the various acts, omissions, and commissions of the government by means of public meetings, pamphlets, and leaflets.

This led the government to reverse its policy towards the Congress. Dufferin ridiculed it as representing only a 'microscopic minority of the people'.

In 1900, Lord Curzon announced to the Secretary of State that "the Congress is tottering to its fall, and one of my great ambitions, while in India, is to assist it to a peaceful demise."

Major Achievements of the Moderates

Following are the significant achievements of early nationalists :

Economic Critique of British Imperialism

The most notable achievements of the Moderates were their systematic and factual criticism of the economic policy of the British rulers through the press and various publications. Dadabhai Naoroji, R.C. Dutt, Dinshaw Wacha, and others, carefully analysed the political economy of British rule in India, and put forward the "Drain Theory" to explain British exploitation of India.

They highlighted the evil consequences of the exploitative economic policies of the British rulers pursued in all the three important areas of trade, industry, and finance. They vehemently opposed British economy. Naoroji's book, *Poverty and Un-British Rule in India*, and R.C. Dutt's book *The Economic History of India in the Victorian Age*, Digby's work *Prosperous India*, and Lajpat Rai's *Unhappy India*, provided a graphic picture of heavy taxation, costly wars, discriminatory tariff policy, neglect of industries, enormous export of India's raw materials, recurring famines, growing national debt, occurrence of epidemics, rising death rate, heavy foreign capital investment, and the unending huge drain of India's wealth to England. About the drain of wealth, Dadabhai caustically remarked, "The English stand sentinel at the front door of India... and carry away by the back door, the very treasure they stand sentinel to protect.'

They opposed the transformation of a basically self-sufficient Indian economy into a colonial economy. Thus, the Moderates were able to create an all-India public opinion that British rule in India was the major cause of India's poverty and economic backwardness.

POVERTY AND UN-BRITISH

RULE IN INDIA

BY

DADABHAI NAOROJI

LONDON

SWAN SONNENSCHEIN & CO., LIM.

PATERNOSTER SQUARE

1901

Naoroji's book, 'Poverty and Un-British Rule in India', and R.C. Dutt's book 'The Economic History of India in the Victorian Age', provided a graphic picture of British exploitation of India. – Wikimedia

To mitigate the deprivation characterising Indian life, the early nationalists demanded severance of India's economic subservience to Britain and development of an independent economy through involvement of Indian capital and enterprise.

The early nationalists demanded reduction in land revenue, abolition of salt tax, improvement in working conditions of plantation labourers, reduction in military expenditure, and encouragement to modern industry through tariff protection and direct government aid.

Constitutional Reforms and Propaganda in Legislature

Legislative councils in India had no real official power till 1920. Yet, work done by the early nationalists helped the growth of the national movement. The Imperial Legislative Council constituted by the Indian Councils Act (1861) was an important body designed to disguise official measures as having been passed by a representative body.

Indian members who were nominated were very few in number (in the thirty years from 1862 to 1892 there were only forty-five Indians). Most of them were wealthy, landed, and with loyalist interests. Only a handful of political figures and independent intellectuals such as Syed Ahmed Khan, Kristodas Pal, V.N. Mandlik, K.L. Nulkar, and Rash Behari Ghosh were nominated.

The early nationalist demands for constitutional reforms were centred on expansion of councils—i.e., greater participation of Indians in councils and reform of councils, i.e., more powers to councils, especially greater control over finances.

Due to Moderates' agitation for constitutional reforms, the Indian Councils Act was passed in 1892. Although the Act increased the number of non-official members in various legislative councils in India, Moderates remained highly dissatisfied with the Act. They became more vocal and increased their agitation for more constitutional reforms with the objective of self-rule in India. Leaders like Dadabhai Naoroji, Gopal Krishna Gokhale, and later Lokamanya Tilak began the demand of self-government like the self-governing colonies of Canada and Australia. Also, leaders like Pherozshah Mehta and Gokhale put government policies and proposals to severe criticism.

Other Major Achievements of the Moderates were :

- They evolved a common economic and political programme.
- They paved the way for close interaction of Indian leaders on national matters.
- They helped in popularising the basic concepts of democracy, civil liberties, freedom of the press, and finally they worked for promoting national unity irrespective of caste, religion, or region.
- Freedom of the press and worked for promoting national unity.
- They mounted pressure on the government to separate judiciary from the executive.

An Evaluation of the Early Nationalists

(i) They represented the most progressive forces of the time.

(ii) They were able to create a wide national awakening of all Indians having common interests and the need to rally around a common programme against a common enemy, and above all, the feeling of belonging to one nation.

(iii) They trained people in political work and popularised modern ideas.

(iv) They exposed the basically exploitative character of colonial rule, thus undermining its moral foundations.

(v) Their political work was based on hard realities, and not on shallow sentiments, religion, etc.

(vi) They were able to establish the basic political truth that India should be ruled in the interest of Indians.

(vii) They created a solid base for a more vigorous, militant, mass-based national movement in the following years.

(viii) However, they failed to widen their democratic base and the scope of their demands.

Failure and Weakness of The Moderates

The national movement under the Moderates suffered from armchair discussions, resolutions and appeals, and ineffective methods. The programmes were not action-oriented; with the result that the masses had no contribution to make.

Following are reasons that contributed to the failure of Moderates:

- The nationalistic work spearheaded by the Moderates was confined to 'paper work' or Constitutional means which consisted of passing resolutions, petitions, and prayers to the government.
- Their programs were not action-oriented with the result that the masses had no contribution to make.

- The Indian Councils Act, 1892 brought dissatisfaction to the Congress, particularly to the emerging Extremists group.
- The Moderates' leaders like Dadabhai Naoroji demanded Swaraj or self-government within the British Empire like the self-governing colonies in Canada and Australia.
- Too much attachment to rationalism and Western ideals almost alienated the Moderates from the masses in India. Despite their high idealism, they failed to create a solid mass base for their movement.
- There was emergence of a new and younger group within the Indian National Congress which was sharply critical of the ideology and the methods of the old leadership.
- The basic weakness of the Moderates lay in their narrow social base. Their movement did not have a wide appeal. The area of their influence was limited to the urban community. As they did not have the support of the masses, they declared that the time was not ripe for throwing out a challenge to the foreign rulers. That was likely to invite pre-mature repression. The Moderate leaders did not realise the enormous reserve of power behind the government. If the Congress were to do anything as you suggest, the government would have no difficulty in throttling it in five minutes. However, it must not be presumed that the Moderate leaders fought for their narrow interests. Their programmes and policies championed the cause of all sections of the Indian people and represented nation-wide interests against colonial exploitation.

Historian Bipan Chandra has opined that the Moderates failed because of their wrong beliefs. They failed to realise that there existed conflict of interest between the rulers and the ruled. They attached too much importance to the British sense of justice and fair play. They failed to keep pace with the yearnings and aspirations of the people.

Methods And Working of The Moderates in The Indian National Congress

For twenty years, the Indian National Congress was dominated by Moderate leadership who did not want the Congress to function as a political party. Instead, the INC was an annual gathering of representatives of different regions speaking on behalf of their respective people pertaining to social, economic, educational, or political nature. INC met annually in Christmas days in different cities of India. In the first ten years the Congress met twice at Bombay, Calcutta, Madras, and Allahabad and once in Lahore and Nagpur.

For twenty years, the Indian National Congress was dominated by Moderate leadership who did not want the Congress to function as a political party. Instead, the INC was an annual gathering of representatives of different regions speaking on behalf of their respective people pertaining to social, economic, educational, or political nature. INC met annually in Christmas days in different cities of India. In the first ten years the Congress met twice at Bombay, Calcutta, Madras, and Allahabad and once in Lahore and Nagpur.

As a staunch believer in constitutional methods, the Congress proceedings were organised in the most orderly and efficient manner. A strict parliamentary procedure was observed in moving, discussing, and passing the resolutions.

The holding of the annual session of the Congress was a significant method of its propaganda. The Congress leaders had trust in the essential sense of justice and kindness of the British nation. But, they were all under illusion that the British rule in India would be beneficial. So, their aim was to educate the Indian public and make it conscious of its rights.

The means chosen by them to achieve the ends were very well within the constitutional limits. They had an absolute faith in the effectiveness of peaceful and constitutional agitation.

The National Congress took pride in the British connection and regarded the British government not as an antagonist, but as an ally. The Moderate Congress leaders were aware of the fact that India was a nation in the making. They had consistently worked for the development and consolidation of the idea of national unity irrespective of region, religion, or caste.

During the early years, the Moderates appealed for self-rule for India. They favoured gradual reforms and their demands also remained moderate. Their objectives were confined to seeking an autonomy in internal affairs under the British suzerainty.

They made a modest beginning in this direction by promoting close contacts and friendly relations among the people from different parts of the country. The economic and political demands of the Moderates were structured with a view to unify the Indian people on the basis of a common political program.

Previous Years' Questions

1. **"The 'safety valve thesis' does not adequately explain the birth of the Indian National Congress in 1885." (2014)**

   Solution : See under 'The debate over Safety Valve theory'

2. **Analyse the social composition of the early Congress leadership. (2009)**

3. **Discuss the extent to which the Indian Renaissance movement contributed towards the rise of nationalist consciousness. (2010)**

4. **"Politics remained for the bulk of the Moderates very much a part-time affair. The Congress was not a political party, but an annual three-day show..." Elucidate. (2014)**

5. **"The vernacular press in the nineteenth century was both newspaper as well as 'views-papers' that enlightened the dormant masses." (2008)**

6. **Examine the economic and social factors which led to the rise of Indian nationalism in the second half of the nineteenth century. (2001)**

12 CHAPTER

The Extremists' Phase (1900–1919)

Introduction

The closing decades of the 19th century witnessed the emergence of a younger section within the Indian National Congress. The emergence of the younger section of leaders added a new vitality and gave a new dimension to the policies and programmes of the Indian National Congress. They were critical of the ideology and methods of the old leadership. They were called the Extremists. Extremist ideals mainly guided the second phase of the Indian National movement from 1900 to 1919.

Rise of The Extremist Groups

Following are the factors for the rise of Extremist groups from the last decades of the 19th century:

Famine and Plague

The closing years of the nineteenth century witnessed the growing resentment among the people against British rule on account of widespread famines and plagues and British indifference. It affected about 20 million people in different parts of India. While the people were starving, the government celebrated the Jubilee of Queen Victoria. The Jubilee celebration at such a time was considered an act of callousness on the part of the government. The failure to check plagues infuriated people to such an extent that the revolutionary Chapekar Brothers - Damodar Hari Chapekar, Balkrishna Hari Chapekar, and Vasudeo Hari Chapekar assassinated W.C. Rand, the Plague Commissioner of Pune.

The Statue of Chapekar Brothers in Chinchwad, Pune — Wikimedia Commons

Political Events from 1892 to 1899

The political events from the years 1892 to 1905 also disappointed nationalists and forced them to think of more radical methods. The Indian Councils Act of 1892 was a complete disappointment. It did not give anything substantial to the Indians and even the Moderates were not pleased with it. Many people felt that the policy of appeals and prayers was a sign of weakness. Aurobindo Ghosh labelled the Moderates' persuasive policy as 'policy of mendicancy'. B.G. Tilak remarked, 'Political rights will have to be fought for. The Moderates think that these can be won by persuasion. We think that they can only be obtained by strong pressure.'

Reactionary Rule of Lord Curzon

In 1899, Lord Curzon became the next Governor-General/Viceroy of India. He was an imperialist and was against the rising wave of nationalism in the country. The imperialist policies followed by Lord Curzon during his tenure from 1899–1905 gave a further fillip to the Extremist movement in India. Lord Curzon was a staunch advocate of an efficient administration and strong opponent of the administration of the Indian Association because he had no faith in the capacity of Indians to rule them.

He, therefore, enacted a number of measures which evoked strong resentment from the Indians and helped the Extremist leaders to exploit the situation. These included:

- The Calcutta Corporation Act of 1899, which reduced the number of elected representatives in it
- The Indian Universities Act of 1904 which placed Calcutta University under the most complete governmental control and further restricted Press freedom.
- Partition of Bengal, 1905

Lord Curzon
— Wikimedia Commons

In his Calcutta University Convocation address, Curzon described the highest ideal of truth as essentially a Western concept, which hurt the pride of educated Indians.

Reacting to the Calcutta Corporation Act, Surendranath Banerjee said, "He (Curzon) has built better than he knows he had laid broad and deep foundations of our national life; he has stimulated those forces which contribute to the upbuilding of nations, he has made us a nation and the most reactionary of Indian viceroys will go down to the posterity as the architect of Indian life."

Thus, Curzon's measures were the sparks needed by the Extremists to take over the Congress to challenge the colonial rule.

Rising Unemployment Among Educated Youth

The development of higher education was very lopsided. Professional education in general, and industrial and technical education in particular, remained neglected. There were fewer avenues of self-employment for the educated and thus, they faced unemployment. Added to this was the lack of avenues in services, and when employed, they received very low salaries as compared with their counterpart

Europeans. Thus, the economic plight of the educated Indians made them look critically at the British rule. The anti-British policy of Lord Curzon led to all the more bitterness and discontentment. The view of Lord Curzon was, 'The highest ranks of all civil employment must, as a general rule, be held by Englishmen.' Primary and technical education was also not making any progress.

National Pride and Self-Respect

The Extremist nationalists drew inspiration from India's past, invoked the great episodes in the history of the Indian people, and tried to infuse national pride and self-respect among them. The rich history of India was revived by them, especially with regard to Hindu history and ideologies. Leaders like Bipin Chandra Pal and Aurobindo Ghosh were influenced by the Neo-Vedantic movement of Swami Vivekananda and Dayananad Saraswati's revivalist reforms.

Impact of International Events

The Russo-Japanese War of 1905, in which a big country like Russia was very badly defeated by a small nation like Japan, encouraged and inspired the educated youth of this period. There was a feeling that British power is declining and other countries like Germany and US are the emerging powers of the world. All these encouraged the Extremist elements.

Inspiration From Other Countries

Extremists also drew its inspiration from the revolutionary doctrines of the West. The struggles for independence by America, France, Italy, and Germany had revealed to the Indians that freedom could be achieved not by constitutional methods, but by revolutionary methods. The Indian leaders also remarked that 'History does not record any instance when an empire might have been conceded by the rulers. You will have to fight for your right'. The Indians thus, lost faith in legislation and constitutional means and they resorted to violence.

Failure of Moderates

Moderate politics reached a dead end as most of their demands remained unfulfilled and this was certainly a major reason behind the rise of extremism. This increased the anger against colonial rule and this anger was generated by the Moderates themselves through their economic critique of colonialism.

The failure of the Moderates' methods, i.e., to work through constitutional means brought forth a section of the young leaders who were dissatisfied with the achievements of the Congress. They lost all faith in the British sense of justice and constitutional methods. These were Extremists as they believed in the approach of confrontation with the British government. The British rule was no longer held as progressive.

These Extremists contemned and criticised the Moderates' approach of reconciliation. They were firmly convinced that India could not make any progress under the exploitative and oppressive British regime. Three new leaders of the Congress who questioned the Moderates and British rule in India were Bal Gangadhar Tilak, Bipin Chandra Pal, and Lala Lajpat Rai. They called for strong political action such as strikes and Boycotts. Through nationalist publications and popular festivals, they tried to spread political awakening and patriotic feelings among the people. Bal Gangadhar Tilak called for the attainment of Swaraj. He declared – "Swaraj is my birthright and I must have it". The newspaper, *Kesari*, became the mouthpiece of the new group of leaders. Soon, this newly emergent trend came to dominate the Congress.

— ***Wikimedia Commons***

Moderates and Extremists – The Differences

The following were the significant differences between the Moderates and Extremists:

Moderates

Faith in British Government

The Moderates, in general, were loyal to the British and had full faith in their rule. Their aims were generally to have representation in the British government and minor reforms in the administrative and economic structure. They had faith in the goodwill and sympathy of the English people. Liberals were attached to rationalism and Western ideals and were alienated from Indian thoughts.

Believed in Constitutional and Legal Methods

Their methods were constitutional which involved sending petitions, prayers, and resolutions to the government for consideration and implementation. They believed in conciliation and passive methods and were against active resistance like Swaraj and Boycott propagated by Extremists. They hoped that they could get their requests accepted to, without any substantial sufferings and sacrifices.

Narrow Social Base

Moderates' social base was narrow and limited. They usually consisted of influential landlord class or zamindars and upper middle classes in towns. The Moderates believed that people of India were not yet fit for self-government. Moreover, the Moderates confined their activities to the small section of intelligentsia and assigned a passive role to the masses.

Ideological Inspiration

They were influenced by Western liberal thoughts and European history. They highly believed that political connections with Britain were in India's social, political, and cultural interests. In fact, early nationalists were patriots but did not play the role of a martyr.

The Extremists

Objective of Extremists

For Extremists, the ultimate goal was to attain Swaraj or self-rule. However, the meaning of Swaraj differed within Extremist leadership. For Tilak, 'Swaraj' meant Indian control over the administration within the British Empire. For Bipin Chandra Pal, 'Swaraj' meant freedom from British rule. For Aurobindo Ghosh, 'Swaraj' meant self-rule within the parameters of British rule.

Believed in Confrontation and Resistance

They believed that constitutional methods had failed to deliver anything. Unlike Moderates, they did not believe in passive resistance. They believed in confrontation and resistance. They believed that national problems could be solved by agitation. They propagated Swadeshi and Boycott as important weapons for active resistance. They were convinced that without hardships and sufferings, salvation of India was not possible. The Extremists were prepared to follow the path of active resistance. They had immense faith in the masses and made them active partners in the national struggle.

No Faith in British Rule

The British rule was considered as a curse by the Extremists. The Extremists believed that the Indians were fully competent to handle their own affairs. They strongly reacted to imperialist policies of the British. They opposed the idealisation of Western culture by the liberals.

Broad Social Base

Unlike Moderates, the social base of Extremist was broad and wide. They represented urban masses and rural people.

Ideological Inspiration

Ideological inspiration was Indian history, cultural heritage, national education, and Hindu traditional symbols. Hence, leaders like Tilak revived the Ganapati and Shivaji festivals to arouse the masses. They wanted to inculcate pride in India's glorious culture to generate the spirit of nationalism. They invoked goddesses Kali or Durga for strength to fight for the motherland. Aurobindo was very much attracted by the teachings of Dayanand Saraswati who was hardly influenced by any ideas from the West. He credited Dayanand with more definite work for the nation than any other reformer. Bankim Chandra, Dayanand, and Vivekananda had thus prepared the ideological ground on the basis of which the Extremists drew up their political programme.

Radical Methods of Extremists

The Extremists began to emerge as a strong force by the end of the 19th century. Extremist nationalists infused national consciousness among the Indian people. Extremists were guided by four principles – swarajya, swadeshi, boycott of foreign goods, and national education to make the Indians aware. They declared Moderates' methods of arguments and appeals as futile, and gave programmes of action such as the 'boycott' in which the power of the masses of the people could be felt by the British ruling nation. Regarding the efficacy of the boycott of British goods, Lala Lajpat Rai said, 'the logic of losing business is more likely to impress this nation of shopkeepers than any argument based on the ethics of justice.'

The Extremist leaders reacted violently to the repressive measures of the British and decided to follow certain specific methods to demoralise the British administrators and paralyse the British administration in India before they were totally ousted from the country. These methods included swadeshi, boycott, national education, and involvement of the masses.

Economic boycott of foreign goods and use of home-made products was one of the major objectives of Boycott and Swadeshi movements. This was designed in order to encourage Indian industries and provide people with opportunities for work and employment. According to Lala Lajpat Rai, the actual aim behind boycott of British goods was to cause financial loss to the British manufacturers. This would secure their sympathy, thereby cancelling the partition of Bengal. Economic boycott proved a powerful instrument against economic exploitation by foreigners. It was also considered that the newly-rising Indian manufacturing units would freely provide funds for the Congress, thereby strengthening it. This is the spiritual significance of the boycott movement. Prominent leaders of Extremists groups such as Bal Gangadar Tilak, Lala Lajpat Rai, and Bipin Chandra Pal carried vigorous propaganda to propagate these programmes during the partition of Bengal agitation in 1905.

The resolution of swadeshi, boycott, and national education were accepted in the annual session of the Congress at Calcutta in 1906 just after the partition of Bengal. It was realised that swadeshi and boycott were complementary. One would not succeed without the other.

Another instrument of the Extremists was national education. The national leaders recommended national universities and colleges, independent of government control, all over the country. The Bengal National College was established at Calcutta by the Bengal Council of National Education. A large number of national schools sprang up in East Bengal. In Punjab, many educational institutions of national character were established under the supervision of the DAV Society. Many educated Indians resigned from government jobs and joined as teachers in nationalist schools and colleges with a very small salary. Aurobindo, for example, become the Principal of the Bengal National College founded in 1906.

The Extremists wanted to widen the base of their movement by bringing the common masses into their fold. The nationalist movement was no longer confined to a few intelligent people but the message of liberty and nationalism spread to the peasant class, irrespective of caste, creed, and sex.

The Extremists also encouraged co-operative organisations. Voluntary associations were set up for rural sanitation, regulation of fairs, and pilgrims gathering for providing relief during famines and other natural calamities.

Cooperative movement was implemented in order to create a strong sentiment among the people. It was basically a type of training for them. The Extremists, through this, wanted to cover the whole country with a network of active political organisations.

All Extremist leaders were united in realising the evils of foreign rule. They were together in demanding some degree of independence from colonial monopoly. Extremism was a practical strategy to meet a scrupulous situation. They also advocated democracy, constitutionalism, and progress. Their aim was to highlight the negative role of the colonial rule. The Extremists were successful in giving new slogans to the Indian nationalist movement–non-cooperation, passive resistance, mass agitation, self-reliance, and so on. They changed nationalism to 'service and suffering for the nation'.

Extremist Leaders – 'Lal, Bal, Pal'

Bal Gangadhar Tilak (July 23, 1856 – August 1, 1920)

***Bal Gangadhar Tilak* — Wikimedia Commons**

Popularly known as Lokmanya Tilak, Bal Gangadhar Tilak is considered as the 'Father of Indian Unrest'. He is recognised as the most outstanding among the leaders of the new group due to his powerful intellect, robust political realism, indomitable will, and self-sacrifice. Tilak was deeply influenced in his early days by such stalwart nationalists as Chiplunkar and Agarkar. Since childhood, Tilak had an intolerant attitude towards injustice and he was truthful and straightforward in nature. He was among India's first generation of youth to receive a modern, college education. Along with his classmate Agarkar and great social reformer Vishnushastri Chiplunkar, Bal Gangadhar Tilak founded "Deccan Education Society" to impart quality education to India's youth. The very next year after the Deccan Education Society was founded, Tilak started two weeklies, *Kesari* and *Mahratta*. *Kesari* was a Marathi weekly while 'Mahratta' was an English weekly. Soon, both the newspapers became very popular. In his newspapers, Tilak highlighted the plight of the Indians. He gave a vivid picture of the people's sufferings and of actual happenings. Bal Gangadhar Tilak joined the Indian National Congress in 1890. He was a member of the Municipal Council of Pune, Bombay Legislature, and an elected 'Fellow' of the Bombay University. Tilak was a great social reformer. He issued a call for the banning of child marriage and welcomed widow remarriage. However, when Age of Consent Act in 1891 was introduced by the government, Tilak resented any interference by an alien government into the domestic and private life of the people.

Through the celebrations of Ganapati Festival and the birthday of the Shivaji, he organised the people. In 1897, Bal Gangadhar Tilak was charged with writing articles instigating people to rise against the government and to break the laws and disturb the peace. He was sentenced to rigorous imprisonment for one and a half years. Tilak was released in 1898. After his release, Tilak launched the 'Swadeshi Movement'. His slogan "Swaraj is my birthright and I shall have it" inspired millions of Indians. A big 'Swadeshi Market' was opened in front of Tilak's house. Tilak was arrested on the charges of sedition in 1908. After the trial, Tilak was sentenced to six years of imprisonment in Mandalay (Burma). Tilak spent his time in prison by reading and writing. He wrote the book 'Gita Rahasya' while he was in prison. Tilak was released on June 8, 1914. After his release, Tilak tried to bring the two factions of the Congress together. But his efforts did not bear much fruit. In 1916, Tilak decided to build a separate organisation called the 'Home Rule League'. Its goal was swaraj. Tilak went from village to village, and explained the aim of his League to the farmers and won their hearts.

Lala Lajpat Rai (January 28, 1865 – November17, 1928)

Lala Lajpat Rai was one of the foremost leaders who fought against British rule in India. He was popularly known as 'Punjab Kesari (Lion of the Punjab)'. Lala Lajpat Rai joined the Government College at Lahore in 1880 to study Law. While in college, he came in contact with patriots and future freedom fighters like Lala Hans Raj and Pandit Guru Dutt. The three became fast friends and joined the Arya Samaj founded by Swami Dayanand Saraswati. Lala Lajpat Rai was one of the three most prominent Hindu Nationalist members of the Indian National Congress, i.e., Bal Gangadhar Tilak and Bipin Chandra Pal. They formed the Extremists faction of the Indian National Congress, as opposed to the Moderates, led first by Gopal Krishna Gokhale. Lalaji actively participated in the struggle against partition of Bengal. Lalaji was arrested on May 3, 1907 for creating "turmoil" in Rawalpindi. He was put in Mandalay jail for six months and was released on November 11, 1907. Lalaji believed that it was important for the national cause to organise propaganda in foreign countries to explain India's position because the freedom struggle had taken a militant turn. He left for Britain in April 1914 for this purpose. At this time, the First World War broke out and he was unable to return to India. He went to USA to galvanise support for India. He founded the Indian Home League Society of America and wrote a book called *Young India*. The book severely indicted British rule in India and was banned in Britain and India even before it was published. He was able to return to India in 1920 after the end of World War I. After his return, Lala Lajpat Rai led the Punjab protests against the Jallianwala Bagh Massacre and the Non-Cooperation Movement. He was arrested several times. He

Lal Lajpat Rai
— Wikimedia Commons

disagreed with Gandhiji's suspension of Non-Cooperation movement due to the Chauri-Chaura incident, and formed the Congress Independence Party, which had a pro-Hindu slant. In 1928, the British Government decided to send the Simon Commission to India to discuss constitutional reforms. The Commission had no Indian member. This greatly angered the Indians. In 1928, when the Commission came to India, there were protests all over India. Lala Lajpat Rai himself led one such procession against the Simon Commission. While the procession was peaceful, the British Government brutally lathicharged the procession. Lala Lajpat Rai received severe head injuries and died on November 17, 1928.

Bipin Chandra Pal (1858 – 1932)

Bipin Chandra Pal was a teacher, journalist, orator, writer, and librarian. But above all, he was the one of the three famous national leaders of the "Lal Bal Pal" trio who comprised the Extremist wing of the Indian National Congress. Bipin Chandra started a magazine, *New India*, which aimed to be, as he put it, "intensely national in spirit, breathing the deepest veneration for the spiritual, moral and intellectual achievements of Indian civilisation and distinctly universal in aspiration". In 1904, he presided over the Bombay session of the Congress. Pal annoyed the British move to partition Bengal in 1905, through his paper, *Bande Mataram*. Aurobindo Ghosh joined as an editor of *Bande Mataram*, and the two leaders developed a special bond.

Bipin Chandra Pal
— Wikimedia Commons

In 1907, Pal was jailed for refusing to give evidence against Aurobindo in a sedition case. After he was released from jail, he went to England, in 1908, and lived there for three years.

Bipin Chandra Pal recognised the positive outcome of the British kingdom, but at the same time, upheld India's federal idea. He was a staunch radical in both public and private life. He was also among the first who openly rebuked Mahatma Gandhi and his followers for their sympathetic attitude towards the British government. It was, however, his coalition with pan-Islamism during the Khilafat movement due to which he was cast off from the Congress till his death in 1932. With the other two members—Lala Lajpat Rai and Bal Gangadhar Tilak—Bipin Chandra Pal doled out a number of Extremist measures like boycotting goods made by British, burning Western clothes, and organising lockouts in the British-owned businesses and industrial concerns to get their message across to the foreign rulers. Since he was a member of the Brahmo Samaj, he championed the cause of social reforms in the Hindu society. One of the earliest causes that Pal vocally took up was that of the harsh treatment meted out to workers at Assam's tea plantations.

Other Political Happenings in Nationalism

Emergence of Sri Aurobindo Ghosh (1872–1950): The Secret Revolutionary

Aurobindo Ghosh was a philosopher, poet, and eminent nationalist. Sri Aurobindo came to the active politics when Moderates were failing. He demanded total freedom from British rule and propagated the idea of 'Independence' instead of 'Swaraj'. He believed that the nation had the right to obtain its freedom from foreign rule by any means possible. According to him, the existing condition of the government in India suffered from corrupt Western influences. To escape it, she must get rid of these conditions and seek refuge in her own superior civilisation.

Aurobindo provided the following outline to attain Swaraj or independence from foreign rule:

(i) to win Swaraj or independence for India from British rule

(ii) to ensure that the Swaraj when gained would be a Swadeshi Swaraj and not an importation of the European variety.

The movement for Swaraj found its first expression in an outburst for Swadeshi sentiment directed not merely against foreign goods, but against foreign habits, dress, manners, and education and sought to bring the people to their own civilisation.

Sri Aurobindo Ghosh
— Wikimedia Commons

Aurobindo supported non-cooperation and passive resistance to the British rule but in private, he was involved in secret revolutionary activities and helped build the revolutionary atmosphere in the country. In 1905, Aurobindo edited the English newspaper, the *Bande Mataram*. It was a mouthpiece of Extremist ideology. The paper influenced the minds of young people towards creating a revolution.

In Bengal, Aurobindo got in touch with revolutionaries and inspired young revolutionaries such as Bagha Jatin, Jatin Banerjee, and Surendranath Tagore. He was also instrumental in the formation of several youth clubs including the Anushilan Samiti. In April 1910, Aurobindo Ghosh secretly moved to Pondicherry to start a new life of a yogi.

Personality Clash Between Tilak the Extremist and Gokhale, the Moderate

The earlier clash between the Moderates and Extremists reached to its highest point in the personality clashes between two stalwarts of the period – Tilak from the Extremist group and Gopal Krishna Gokhale from the old group, or Moderates.

Both Tilak and Gokhale hailed from Poona. Tilak was militant, an Orientalist who would use any stick to beat the government with. He wielded a powerful pen and exerted great influence on public opinion through his mouthpiece – the *Mahratta* and the *Kesari*.

Gopal Krishna Gokhale (1866 – 1915), was a senior leader of the Indian National Congress and the founder of the *Servants of India Society*. He was the first Indian leader who followed the principles of non-violence and social reform much before Gandhi used these principles in India's struggle for independence. Gokhale was a mentor to Mahatma Gandhi in his formative years. In 1912, Gokhale visited South Africa at Gandhi's invitation. As a young barrister, Gandhi returned from his struggles against the Empire in South Africa and received personal guidance from Gokhale, including a knowledge and understanding of India and the issues confronting common Indians.

By 1920, Gandhi emerged as the leader of the Indian independence movement. In his autobiography, Gandhi calls Gokhale his mentor and guide. Gandhi also recognised Gokhale as an admirable leader and master politician, describing him as '*pure as crystal, gentle as a lamb, brave as a lion and chivalrous to a fault and the most perfect man in the political field*'.

Gokhale had wonderful mastery over Indian financial problems, was at his best in the Imperial Legislative Council, and an expert in exposing the hollow claims of the government. He had established at Poona the 'Servants of India Society' with a view to training a band of dedicated workers who were expected to give their all to the service of the motherland. The members of the Society had to take an oath of poverty and had to observe a strict code of conduct. They were given only a subsistence allowance and had to perform hard duty.

The difference between Gokhale and Tilak may be traced back to an earlier period. There had been an intense clash of personalities at Poona from the beginning of the nineties of the last century. A quarrel ensured between Tilak and G.G. Agarkar, although they had been co-workers in the Deccan Education Society. Ultimately, Tilak was pushed out of the Society. Thereafter, there had been a constant tussle between the followers of Tilak on the one hand and his opponents on the other. The opponents rallied round Mahadev Govind Ranade and Gokhale, backed in Congress affairs by Pherozeshah Mehta from Bombay.

Gokhale enjoyed the support of the Congress establishment. As the Moderates were losing their popularity and the Extremists were capturing the imagination of the country because of the growth of the new spirit, the conflict between the two contending groups in Maharashtra and Poona also became more pronounced. There was ferment all over India. The 'Bande Mataram' under Aurobindo was not only challenging the right of the British Government to rule India, but also the right of the veteran leaders to speak for India.

Outside Bengal, Tilak was the first to recognise the potential of the ferment in Bengal. The Partition of Bengal was to him not so much a British blunder as an Indian opportunity to build up strength. He extended support to the anti-partition movement and encouraged the emerging

Extremist leaders in Bengal. Gokhale had seen this alliance growing since the Benaras Congress (1905). This Tilak–Pal alliance caused a deep concern not only to the Government, but also to many Congress Leaders. Tilak was regarded as a dissident, if not a rebel. Pherozeshah Mehta, D.E. Wacha, and the whole Bombay Group distrusted him since the controversies raging in the 1890s. The differences were partly temperamental. For at least 15 years, there had been a Cold war between the Congress establishment headed by Mehta on the one hand, and Tilak on the other.

Previous Years' Questions

1. **"Politics remained for the bulk of the Moderates very much a part-time affair. The Congress was not a political party, but an annual three-day show..." Elucidate. (2014)**
2. **Discuss the extent to which the Indian Renaissance movement contributed towards the rise of nationalist consciousness. (2010)**

The Partition of Bengal and Beginning of National Movement-1905–1918

Introduction

The advent of the 20th century witnessed the beginning of an organised mass movement against the British rule. British government's controversial policies launched under the governorship of Lord Curzon compelled the Congress to rise up in agitation. The period from 1905 to 1918 witnessed the first phase of the national movement.

Lord Curzon's Administrative Policy

Lord Curzon (1859–1925), was the Governor-General and Viceroy of India from 1899 to 1905. He was a British Conservative statesman. As a representative of the Conservative Government, Lord Curzon was expected to serve the British Empire. Eloquent, masterful, and energetic, Curzon followed aggressive imperialist policies in India.

Thus, the five years of Lord Curzon's rule (1900–1905) were full of reactionary measures that shocked the entire country and marked the beginning of a new phase in the nationalist movement.

No Governor-General since the time of Lord Dalhousie had made changes on such a vast scale, though some of the changes were resented by the Indians.

Some of the notable events during his administrative tenure were as follows:

Famine and Plague

The regime of Lord Curzon saw the worst famine in 1899–1900. The areas affected by this famine were Punjab, Rajputana, Baroda, Bombay, Central Province, Berar, Hyderabad, and Gujarat. The sufferings of the people were intensified by the simultaneous outbreak of cholera and malaria. One million people are said to have perished in British territory alone and over 6 million sterling were spent on famine relief.

MacDonnel Commission was appointed by Curzon in 1901 and it made the following recommendations:

- Government should take steps to prevent demoralisation among the people.
- Government should take assistance of non-official agencies.
- More railways should be constructed.
- Agriculture banks and co-operative credit societies should be established.
- There should be greater irrigation facilities.

Reforms in Agriculture

Following were the agricultural reforms carried under Curzon's administration:

- Punjab Land Alienation Act was passed in 1900 to check transfers of lands from agriculturists to non-agriculturists in Punjab.
- Agricultural or Zamindara Banks were to be started.
- Co-operative credit societies were to be encouraged.
- Imperial Department of Agriculture was created.
- Agricultural Research Institute was established at Pusa.
- Construction of Upper Jhelum, Upper Chenab, and Lower Bari Doab Canals was started in Punjab.
- Extension of the period of settlement by the Land Resolution of 1902.

Police Reforms

Lord Curzon set up a Police Commission under Sir Andrew Frazer in 1902–03. On the basis of recommendation of this commission, a basic structure of Indian domestic intelligence developed and remained almost the same till 1947. He attached the Department of Criminal Intelligence (DCI) to the Government of India while setting up the *Criminal Investigation Departments (CIDs)* in the provinces of British India.

Ancient Monuments Preservation Act, 1904

One of the most remarkable Acts passed during the times of Lord Curzon was the Ancient Monuments Preservation Act of 1904. This Act made it an offence to do any injury to the protected monuments. This Act also established the Archaeological Department which was to collect the historical documents of importance, conduct excavations, and bring the ancient historical information to light.

Relationship with INC

During Lord Curzon's tenure as Governor-General, attitude of the Government of India towards the Indian National Congress had become increasingly hostile. From 1888, i.e., after the fourth session of INC, the government adopted a hostile attitude towards the Congress. The government servants were forbidden to take any part in the proceedings of the Congress. Conservative Secretary of State for India, George Hamilton, wrote to Lord Curzon in 1899, suggesting how to counter the Congress.

The British came to look upon the Congress as a great menace to the security of their Indian Empire. Hence, the Indian National Congress became almost a nightmare with the British politicians.

The British attitude became even more hostile to the Congress under Lord Curzon whose greatest ambition was to assist the Congress to a peaceful demise which he declared in 1900, "the Congress is tottering to its fall and one of my great ambitions, while in India, would be to assist it to a peaceful demise."

Controversial Reforms of Lord Curzon

Curzon's glorious administrative record was largely marred by three controversial policies. These were:

- Calcutta Corporation Act, 1899
- The Indian Universities Act, 1904
- Partition of Bengal, 1905

Calcutta Corporation Act, 1899

Lord Curzon got an opportunity to curtail the sphere of local self-government in India. A Bill to reduce the powers of the Calcutta Corporation was before the Bengal Legislative Council. It was the result of agitations carried on by Anti-Ripon Organisation of Anglo-Indians and Europeans. Considerable powers of the Calcutta Corporation were to be transferred to the executive. The corporation, however, was to retain elected majority. Lord Curzon called this measure a clumsy dualism. This Bill was changed according to his wishes and passed in 1899 and became a law in 1900. It reduced the number of the members of Calcutta Corporation from 75 to 50. The reduction of 25 was only in the case of elected members who were mainly Indians. Thus, the nominated members, mainly the British, came to have a majority in the Calcutta Corporation. According to S.N. Banerjee, the Act marked the extinction of local self-government in Calcutta.

The Indian Universities Act, 1904

The Indian universities and the colleges were slowly becoming a cradle of propaganda against the Government. To bring the universities under control, Lord Curzon appointed the Raleigh Commission under Sir Thomas Raleigh. The Raleigh Commission had only one Indian member, Syed Hussain Belgrami. When the Hindus protested about this, Justice Guru Das Banerjee was called from the High Court of Calcutta and made a member. This commission submitted its report in 1902 and this was followed by the introduction of a Bill called Raleigh Bill. When the Raleigh Bill became an Act, it was called Indian Universities Act, 1904.

The Act, however, aimed at reforming the University of Calcutta and its relations with other educational institutions. Under the Indian Universities Act, government nominees, mainly Europeans, were made predominant on the governing bodies of schools and colleges. The governing bodies of the universities, i.e., Senates and Syndicates, were to be reconstituted. The size of the Senates was reduced. The number in the Senate could be minimum 50 and maximum 100. Each of them would hold the office for 6 years.

The Governor-General was now empowered to decide a University's territorial limits and also affiliation between the universities and colleges. The Indian Universities Act made the universities and colleges completely under the Government control. However, for better education and research, a grant of Rs. 5 lakh per year for 5 years was also accepted. This was the beginning of university grants in India which later became a permanent feature in the structure of Indian education.

Curzon's education reforms were interpreted by the nationalists as an attempt to keep the educational institutions under tight imperial control and to suppress the rising nationalistic tide in the universities and colleges across the country.

The Partition of Bengal, 1905

The most controversial administrative reform of Lord Curzon was the partition of Bengal in 1905.

Following were the reasons behind the partition of Bengal:

- The Presidency of Fort William which comprised of Bengal, Bihar, Orissa, and Assam was considered too large to be administered. The entire province of Bengal had a population of 78 million. East Bengal was largely backward in comparison to West Bengal. The countryside of East Bengal was cut off by rivers and creeks and suffered from piracy in the waterways. The government thought that by splitting, the eastern districts would be governed effectively.
- The Eastern Bengal roughly comprised of Manipur, Assam, Chittagong, and Rajshahi with its capital at Dhaka. The administration was left under a lieutenant-governor with a legislative council and board of revenue, but the jurisdiction was under the High Court of Calcutta.

The Partition of Bengal was also an administrative need with three main objectives:

Firstly, to relieve the government of Bengal from the extra administrative burden and to ensure more efficient administration in the outlying districts.

Secondly, the government desired to promote the development of backward Assam (ruled by a Chief Commissioner).

Thirdly, the government felt the urgent necessity to unite the scattered sections of the Oriya-speaking population under a single administration.

In 1903, a proposal was prepared to separate Chittagong Division and the districts of Dhaka and Mymensingh from Bengal and add them up with the Assam Province. This proposal met with an overwhelming opposition from all strata of the society; from rich landlords and poor landless farmers, from political leaders and labour classes as well, as from both Hindus and Muslims alike. The protest meetings, processions, pamphlets, and newspaper articles amply voiced the general public opinion opposing even the idea of separating people by geographical boundaries.

However, it was the imperialistic motives of Lord Curzon in the splitting of Bengal which created havoc. Curzon witnessed the rising tide of nationalism in Bengal. He wanted to crush this and in order to do that, Curzon planned to crush the solidarity among Bengali people. In East Bengal, the backward Muslim majority would pose no danger to the British, as the new privileges granted to them would make them loyal to the British government. At the same time, in West Bengal, the Bengalis would cease to be a majority after it would be attached with Bihar and Orissa. Calcutta, the centre of the new-found nationalism would lose its importance, as the Bengali Hindus with their advanced political awareness would be a minority in the new province of Bengal.

Lord Curzon, who vehemently opposed the Congress and the nationalists, had once written to the Secretary of State for India that:

"I would dig the grave of the Indian National Congress before leaving office......One of my greatest ambitions in India is to assist it (Congress) to a peaceful demise..."

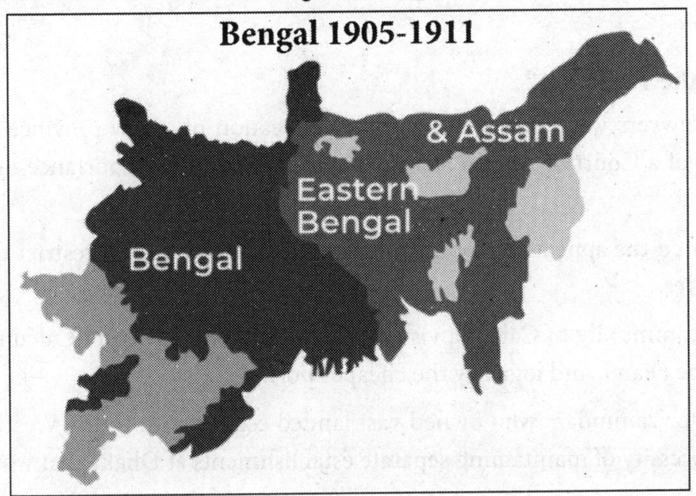

Map showing the partitioned Bengal : West Bengal and East Bengal (period 1905–1911)
— Wikimedia Commons

So in 1905, the British decided to redraw Bengal's boundaries and divided it on the basis of language and religion :

- One was Western Bengal, with a population of 54 million, of which 42 million would be Hindus and 9 million Muslims with Calcutta as the capital. This part of Bengal was to have 17 million Bengalis and 37 million Hindi and Oriya speakers.
- The other was Eastern Bengal and Assam with a population of 31 million of which 18 million would be Muslims and 12 million Hindus with Dhaka as their capital.
- The territory to be transferred from Bengal to the new province consisted of the districts of Chittagong and Dhaka divisions, and those of Rajshahi division except Darjeeling and the district of Malda.

The primary motive behind the partition plan was to weaken the unity of Bengal, to check the growth of nationalism, and to germinate the idea of communal disharmony in Bengal.

Curzon explained the political purpose to his superiors in London, " Bengal united is a power", he wrote, "that power was to be broken by partition." Calcutta, the capital city of the British Government, was seen as a hotbed of politics with anti-British feelings.

Curzon also planned to make Dacca as the capital of Muslim Viceroys and kings. Thus, it was clear that the British Government was stimulating Muslim communalists to counter the Congress and the national movement. Both the Congress and the Extremists branded partition as a policy of 'Divide and Rule'.

The decision for the Partition of Bengal was announced in July, 1905. The partition took effect on 16th October, 1905. Bengal got divided into two parts – the Hindu majority 'Bengal' comprising of Western Bengal, Bihar, and Odisha and the Muslim majority "East Bengal and Assam" with its capital as Dacca.

Who Opposed the Partition?

- The Calcutta lawyers were apprehensive that the creation of a new province would mean the establishment of a Court of Appeal at Dacca and diminish the importance of their own High Court.
- Journalists feared the appearance of local newspapers, which would restrict the circulation of the Calcutta Press.
- The business community of Calcutta visualised the shift of trade from Calcutta to Chittagong, which would be nearer, and logically the cheaper port.
- The landlords or zamindars who owned vast landed estates both in the West and East Bengal foresaw the necessity of maintaining separate establishments at Dhaka that would involve extra expenditure.
- The educated Bengali Hindus felt that it was a deliberate blow inflicted by Curzon at the national consciousness and growing solidarity of the Bengali-speaking population.
- The Indian National Congress leadership viewed the partition as an attempt to 'Divide and Rule'.
- Opposition to the partition was supported by Sir Henry John Stedman Cotton who had been Chief Commissioner of Assam.
- Congress insisted that the Government could separate the Non-Bengali speaking areas (Bihar or Orissa) rather than splitting the Bengali speaking area. The new West Bengal made the Bengali people a minority in their own country because now the population of Hindi and Oriya speaking people was 37 million while the population of Bengali speaking people was only 17 Million.

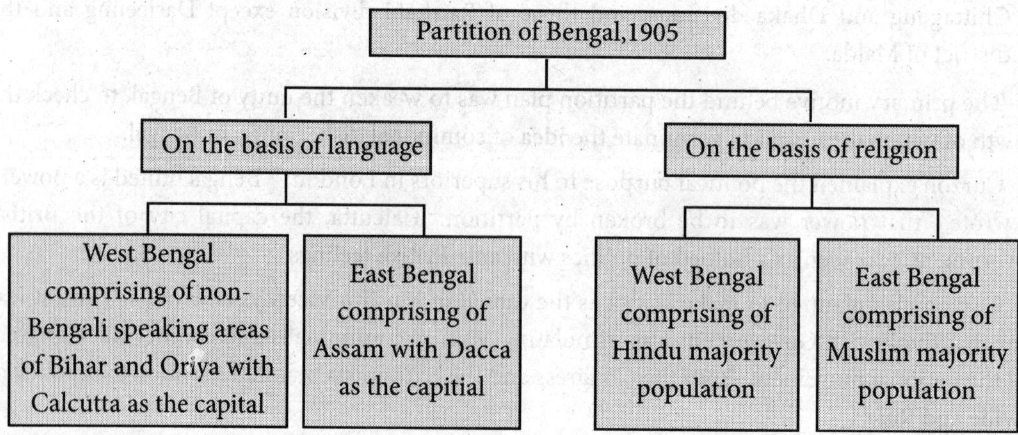

Anti-Partition Agitation

The partition evoked fierce protest in West Bengal, especially in Calcutta, and gave a new fillip to Indian nationalism. The resistance to the partition of Bengal practically shook the foundations of the British Empire in India. The partition stirred an anti-British movement that involved non-violent and violent protests. One of the greatest programmes that sprang from the anti-Bengal agitation was the program movements of Boycott, and Swadeshi.

A large number of people took the vow that so long as the Partition was not undone, they would reject all foreign goods. Boycott of foreign goods necessitated the demand of Swadeshi or indigenous goods. It was out of this necessity that the Swadeshi movement was born. Along with the bonfire of the foreign cloth, the weavers in villages as well as the Indian mill-owners were encouraged to produce cloth. Historian Dr. R. C. Majumdar rightly pointed out that: "The Boycott was the negative, the Swadeshi the positive aspect of the same idea."

During the agitation period, the Moderates' leadership of Surendranath Banerjee, K.K. Mitra, and Prithwishchandra Ray continued with their methods of petitions' writing to the Government, public meetings, memoranda, and propaganda through pamphlets and newspapers such as *Hitabadi, Sanjibani,* and *Bengalee.* Their objective was to exert pressure on the Government through an educated public opinion in India and England to prevent the unjust partition of Bengal from being implemented. However, ignoring these modest protests, the Government announced partition of Bengal in July, 1905. Within days, protest meetings were held in small towns all over Bengal.

It was in these meetings that the pledge to boycott foreign goods was first taken. The INC meeting held at Calcutta Town hall on 7 August, 1905 under the Presidentship of Gopal Krishna Gokhale passed a resolution to abstain from purchases of British products so long as 'Partition resolution is not withdrawn'. Gokhale declared "the true Swadeshi movement as both a patriotic and an economic movement. The idea of Swadeshi, or one's own country, is one of the noblest conceptions that had ever stirred the heart of humanity". After this, nationalist leaders dispersed to other parts of Bengal to propagate the message of boycott of Manchester cloth and Liverpool salt.

October 16, 1905, the Day of Mourning

October 16, 1905, the day when the partition formally came into force, was observed as a day of mourning throughout Bengal. People fasted, bathed in the Ganga, and walked barefoot in processions singing 'Bande Mataram'. On the suggestion of Rabindranath Tagore, a Raksha Bandhan ceremony was observed all over Bengal. People tied *Rakhis* on each other's hands as a symbol of unity of the two halves of Bengal. Later in the day, Surendranath Banerjee and Ananda Mohan Bose addressed huge gatherings.

Soon, the movement was dominated by the Extremists' leadership — in Poona and Bombay under B.G. Tilak, in Punjab under Lala Lajpat Rai and Ajit Singh, in Delhi under Syed Haider Raza, and in Madras under Chidambaram Pillai.

Swadeshi and Boycott Movement

Boycott of the British goods appealed to the Indian masses. The educated Indians knew the economic evils of the British rule. The Indian markets at that time were flooded with the finished goods manufactured in England by Indian raw materials. The Swadeshi movement therefore, was a challenge to the British Government. People started burning the British cloth and throwing away foreign goods. People were induced to use home-made goods and cloth everywhere.

The idea of Swadeshi soon turned into a great enterprising idea. Soon, Indian industrialists and manufacturers got an opportunity to develop indigenous business. This resulted in the establishment of Swadeshi textile mills, soap and match factories, tanneries, banks, insurance companies, and shops. These enterprises were based more on patriotic zeal than on business acumen.

The nationalists of all hues took inspiration from songs written by Rabindranath Tagore, Rajnikant Sen, Dwijendralal Ray, Mukunda Das, Syed Abu Mohammad, and others. Tagore's *Amar Sonar Bangla* written on this occasion was later to inspire the liberation struggle of Bangladesh and was adopted by it as its national anthem.

In the field of painting, Abanindranath Tagore broke the domination of Victorian naturalism over Indian art and took inspiration from Mughal, Ajanta, and Rajput paintings. Nandalal Bose, who left a major imprint on Indian art, was the first recipient of a scholarship offered by the Indian Society of Oriental Art, founded in 1907.

In science, Jagdish Chandra Bose, Prafulla Chandra Roy, and others pioneered original research which was praised the world over.

The Extremists' Programme

The partition of Bengal gave the Extremists a wider stage to attract millions of people across the country. The Extremist nationalists led by Tilak, Lajpat Rai, Bipin Chandra Pal, and Aurobindo Ghosh wanted the movement to be taken outside Bengal to other parts of the country and go beyond a boycott of foreign goods to become a full-fledged political mass struggle with the goal of attaining swaraj.

But the Moderates, dominating the Congress at that time, were not willing to go that far. However, a big step forward was taken at the Congress session held at Calcutta (1906) under the presidentship of Dadabhai Naoroji, where it was declared that the goal of the Indian National Congress was 'self-government, or Swaraj'.

Emboldened by Dadabhai Naoroji's declaration at the Calcutta session of 1906 that self-government or *swaraj* was to be the goal of the Congress, the Extremists gave a call for passive resistance in addition to Swadeshi and boycott which would include a boycott of government schools and colleges, government service, courts, legislative councils, municipalities, and government titles so as to, as Aurobindo put it, "make the administration under present conditions impossible by an organised refusal to do anything which will help either the British commerce in the exploitation of the country or British officialdom in the administration of it".

The Extremists tried to transform the anti-partition and Swadeshi movement into a mass struggle and gave the slogan of India's independence from foreign rule.

Lokamanya Tilak preached non-cooperation with the government in all sectors. In 1902 at Poona, he said, "You must realise that you are a great factor in the power with which the administration of India is controlled. You are yourself the great lubricants which enabled the gigantic machinery to work so smoothly. Though down-trodden and neglected, you must be conscious of your power of moving the administration impossible, if you but choose to make it". This statement of Tilak created a long-lasting effect on the minds of the people irrespective of any caste, creed, and religion. The Extremists, thus, emphasised on the process of putting an end to the economic exploitation by the British and on getting a larger share for Indians in the administration of their own country.

It is to be noted that a distinct difference was seen in Bengal and Maharashtra during the anti-partition agitation. In Bengal, the agitation was economic in character but the Swadeshi movement was carried with religious fervour in Maharashtra.

In Maharashtra, the Swadeshi mood led to the revival of religious and political festivals such as Ganapati and Shivaji, which was already pioneered by Tilak.

Therefore, Extremists, through the following programs, widened the scope of Swadeshi and Boycott movement in the following ways:

- **Boycott of foreign goods :** This included boycott and public burning of foreign cloth, boycott of foreign-made salt or sugar, refusal by priests to ritualise marriages involving exchange of foreign goods, and refusal by washermen to wash foreign clothes. This form of protest met with great success at the practical and popular level.
- **Public meetings and processions :** These emerged as major methods of mass mobilisation and simultaneously, as forms of popular expression.
- **Corps of volunteers or 'samitis' :** Samitis such as the *Swadesh Bandhab Samiti* of Ashwini Kumar Dutta (in Barisal) emerged as a very popular and powerful method of mass mobilisation. These *samitis* generated political consciousness among the masses through lectures, swadeshi songs, physical and moral training to their members, social work during famines and epidemics, organisation of schools, training in Swadeshi crafts, and arbitration courts.
- **Setting up of co-operative organisations :** The Extremists encouraged co-operative organisations. Voluntary associations were set up for rural sanitation, preventive police duties, and regulation of pilgrims' gathering for providing relief during famines and other national calamities. Arbitration committees were established to take up civil and non-cognizable disputes in villages and small towns so as to expose the imperialistic and inhuman behaviour of the British administration. Extremist leader Bipin Chandra Pal was entrusted with the work of co-operative movements in India.

- **Use of traditional popular festivals and fairs :** The idea was to use such occasions as a means of reaching out to the masses and spreading political messages. For instance, Tilak's Ganapati and Shivaji festivals became a medium of swadeshi propaganda not only in Western India, but also in Bengal. In Bengal also, the traditional folk theatre forms were used for this purpose.
- **Self-reliance or 'atmashakti' :** This implied re-assertion of national dignity, honour, confidence, and social and economic regeneration of the villages. In practical terms, it included social reform and campaigns against caste oppression, early marriage, dowry system, consumption of alcohol, and other vices.
- **Programme of national education :** The formation of the national education system was a significant outcome of the Bengal agitation. The Extremists emphasised the national scheme of education boycotting the government-controlled universities and colleges all over the country.

  The Extremists advocated for the establishment of National Universities independent of government control. A large number of National Schools came up in East Bengal. The Bengal National College, inspired by Tagore's 'Shantiniketan', was set up with Aurobindo Ghosh as its Principal. A Bengal Institute of Technology was set up for technical education and funds were raised to send students to Japan for advanced learning. In Punjab, the DAV movement made considerable work by establishing schools and colleges of national character. Soon, national school and colleges sprang up in various parts of the country. Education was to be imparted through the medium of vernaculars. On August 15, 1906, the National Council of Education was set up to organise a system of education—literary, scientific, and technical—on national lines and under national control.
- **Swadeshi or indigenous enterprises :** The Swadeshi spirit also found expression in the establishment of Swadeshi textile mills, soap and match factories, tanneries, banks, insurance companies, shops, etc. These enterprises were based more on patriotic zeal than on business acumen.
- **Impact on cultural sphere :** The nationalists of all hues took inspiration from songs written by Rabindranath Tagore, Rajnikant Sen, Dwijendralal Ray, Mukunda Das, Syed Abu Mohammad, and others. Tagore's *Amar Sonar Bangla* became a classic that inspired generations to come. Renowned painter Abanindranath Tagore broke the domination of Victorian naturalism over Indian art and took inspiration from Mughal, Ajanta, and Rajput paintings. Nandalal Bose, who left a major imprint on Indian art, was the first recipient of a scholarship offered by the Indian Society of Oriental Art, founded in 1907. In science, Jagdish Chandra Bose, Prafullachandra Roy, and others pioneered original research which was praised the world over.

Extent of Mass Participation

One of the noteworthy features of the Bengal agitation was the mass participation of young men and women. Students came out in large numbers to propagate and practice Swadeshi, and to take a lead in organising picketing of shops selling foreign goods. The police adopted a repressive attitude towards the students. Schools and colleges whose students participated in the agitation were to be penalised by disaffiliating them or stopping of grants and privileges to them.

Students who were found guilty of participation were to be disqualified for government jobs or for government scholarships, and disciplinary action—fine, expulsion, arrest, scholarships, etc. was to be taken against them.

Women, who were traditionally home-centred, especially those of the urban middle classes, took active part in processions and picketing. From now onwards, they were to play a significant role in the national movement. Among women, Sarala Devi Chaudhurani, the niece of Rabindranath, was the most active. She was the founder of the first women's organisation in India, the *Bharat Stree Mahamandal* in Allahabad in 1910.

Thus, the social base of the movement expanded to include certain sections of the zamindars, the students, the women, and the lower middle classes in cities and towns. An attempt was also made to organise political strikes in British-owned concerns such as East Indian Railway.

Historian Bipan Chandra writes, "With the start of the Swadeshi movement at the turn of the century, the Indian national movement took a major leap forward. Women, students and a large section of the urban and rural population of Bengal and other parts of India became actively involved in politics for the first time". It indicates how the social base of the movement increased.

But the movement was not able to garner support of the Muslims, especially the Muslim peasantry; because of the conscious government policy of 'Divide and Rule' helped by overlap of class and community at places. To further government interests, the All-India Muslim League was propped up in 1907 as an anti-Congress front and reactionary elements like Nawab Salimullah of Dacca were encouraged.

Factors for the Failure of the Swadeshi Movement

Some of the factors that led to the failure of the Swadeshi movement were:

- Termination, or annulment of the partition of Bengal which took place in 1911. Main reason for termination was to curb the menace of revolutionary terrorism. In 1911, in the Grand Durbar at Delhi, the king Emperor George V himself announced about the creation of the province of Bengal containing all the Bengali speaking people of both Eastern and Western Bengal. Bihar and Orissa was declared as a separate state on the same day. It was decided to shift the capital from Calcutta to Delhi as a concession to the Muslims, as it was associated with Muslim glory, but the Muslims were not pleased.
- The movement failed to create an effective organisation or a party structure. It threw up an entire gamut of techniques that came to be associated with Gandhian politics—non-cooperation, passive resistance, filling of British jails, social reform, and constructive work—but failed to give these techniques a disciplined focus.

- The movement was rendered leaderless with most leaders either arrested or deported by 1908, and with Aurbindo Ghosh and Bipin Chandra Pal retiring from active politics.
- The Moderate-Extremist dispute over the pace of the movement and techniques of struggle reached a deadlock at the Surat session of the Indian National Congress in 1907 where the Congress party split with serious consequences for the Swadeshi Movement.
- The movement aroused the people but did not know how to tap the newly released energy, or how to find new forms to give expression to popular resentment.
- The movement largely remained confined to the upper and middle classes and zamindars, and failed to reach the masses—especially the peasantry.
- Non-cooperation and passive resistance remained mere ideas.
- It became difficult to sustain a mass-based movement at a high pitch for too long.

Significance of Anti-Partition Agitation

Despite its gradual decline and failure, the movement was a turning point in modern Indian history for the following reasons:

- Hitherto untouched sections—students, women, and some sections of the urban and rural population—participated. All major trends of the national movement, from conservative moderation to political extremism, from revolutionary terrorism to incipient socialism, from petitions and prayers to passive resistance and non-cooperation, emerged during the Swadeshi movement.
- The movement was not confined to the political sphere alone, but encompassed art, literature, science, and industry also.
- People were motivated to take bold political positions and participate in new forms of political movements.
- The Swadeshi campaign undermined the hegemony of colonial ideas and institutions.
- Moderates' techniques and thinking proved absolutely wrong and outdated in the Bengal agitation.
- The future struggle was to draw heavily from the experience gained from the Bengal agitation.

The Rise of Militant Nationalism

The Extremists' line of thinking paved the way for the rise of militant nationalism that existed along with the national movement. A section of the Indian youth lost their faith in active resistance propagated by the Extremists in the National Congress. Movements like Swadeshi and Boycott were unconvincing to them. They were convinced that the British would have to be physically expelled from India. In a general sense, they believed in violent activities to fulfil their goal.

The partition of Bengal in 1905 led to the increase in militant activities and proliferation of secret societies. These secret societies propagated extreme nationalism, patriotism, and spirit of sacrifice. The militants or revolutionaries took resort to methods that created terror and obstruction in the British government. Some of these were: Organising into secret societies, distribution of revolutionary literature, organising secret mobs, taking oaths and pledges for the freedom of the country, physical training, weapon training and making bombs, killing of oppressive British officers, looting government treasuries, establishing revolutionaries' societies abroad, creating sedition among the Indian soldiers of the British army, and study of religious scriptures to infuse a spirit of bravery. The Swadeshi movement lost its vitality and vigour but still the fire of rebellion was alive in the shape of militant nationalism. Militant nationalism was mostly active in Bengal, Maharashtra, and Punjab.

Factors Contributing to the Rise of Extremism

Extremism or militant nationalism became a predominant philosophy of Indian nationalism from 1905 to 1917.

Many factors contributed to the rise of extremism or militant nationalism.

1. The Moderate-led movement had failed to yield results.
2. The divisive tactics of the Governments of both the Bengals had embittered the nationalists.
3. The government had resorted to suppressive measures which included atrocities on students—many of whom were given corporal punishment; ban on public singing of Bande Mataram; restriction on public meetings; prosecution and long imprisonment of Swadeshi workers; clashes between the police and the people in many towns; arrests and deportation of leaders; and suppression of Freedom of the Press.
4. The Calcutta Corporation Act of 1899, and Indian Universities Act of 1904, along with the partition of Bengal in 1905, accelerated the extremist movements.

Militants were fuelled with an immense sense of patriotism from the Extremists' programs of corps of volunteers of 'Samitis', Swadeshi songs, physical and moral training for their members, social work during famines and epidemics, organisation of schools, training in Swadeshi crafts and arbitration courts, use of popular festivals and meals to reach out to the masses, and spreading political massages. The idea of self-reliance or 'atmashakti' was popularised by the militant nationalists. This implied re-assertion of national dignity, honour and confidence, and social and economic regeneration of the villages. In practical terms, it included social reforms and campaigns against caste oppression, early marriage, dowry system, and consumption of alcohol.

Prominent Revolutionary Leaders/Terrorist Activities/Secret Societies

The revolutionaries targeted to assassinate unpopular British officials and thereby, kindle patriotic spirit and sustain the pace of the nationalist movement. *Following were some of the prominent revolutionary leaders and their revolutionary societies and activities:*

Chapekar Brothers

The first political murder of Europeans was committed at Poona on 22nd June 1897 by the Chapekar brothers, Vinayak Damodar Savarkar and Balkrishna Savarkar. Mr. Rand, Chairman of the Plague Committee of Poona, was murdered. The Chapekar brothers were caught, convicted, and hanged.

Prafulla Chaki and Khudiram Bose

In Bengal, the militants approached and motivated people through revolutionary literature in the form of poems, prose, and press. This played a significant role in mobilising people. In April 1908, Prafulla Chaki and Khudiram Bose threw a bomb on the carriage which they believed to be occupied by Kingsford, the unpopular judge of Muzaffarpur, but the attempt misfired and it killed two English ladies. Prafulla Chaki shot himself dead with the feeling of guilt for killing two innocent women and the other accused Khudiram Bose, was tried and hanged. Both of them had become popular heroes and earned a permanent place through folk songs composed in the praise of their selfless sacrifice. Khudiram Bose (1889 - 1908) was one of the youngest revolutionaries of India. At the time of his hanging, he was 18 years old.

Savarkar Brothers

Among the Marathi revolutionaries of this period (1900–1919), the names of Savarkar brothers—Vinayak Savarkar and Ganesh Savarkar comes to the forefront. They founded the *Abhinav Bharat Society*. Vinayak Savarkar went to London where he lectured on the events of 1857 which he called India's First War of Independence.

Sardar Ajit Singh

The revolutionary group in Punjab was led by Sardar Ajit Singh. He was an early protester in the Punjab region who challenged British rule, and openly criticised the Indian colonial government. In 1907, he was deported to Mandalay Jail in Burma along with Lala Lajpat Rai.

Madanlal Dhingra

Madanlal Dhingra (1887–1909) was a young revolutionary who worked outside India. In England, he was in contact with prominent revolutionaries of this period. In 1909, he shot dead an English officer in England. At his trial in a court in England, he told the judge, "the only lesson required in India at present is to learn how to die and the only way to teach it is by dying ourselves. Therefore, I die."

Madam Bhikaji Cama

The first prominent revolutionary woman to work outside India was Madam Bhikaji Cama. She was from a Parsi business family. She operated the revolutionary activities from Paris for over 30 years. In 1907, she unfurled the flag of India's freedom at the International Socialist Congress held at Stuttgart, Germany.

Revolutionary Terrorist Activities

Two of the most spectacular revolutionary terrorist activities of this period were the unsuccessful attempts under the leadership of Rash Behari Bose and Sachin Sanyal to assassinate the Viceroy, Lord Hardinge, who was wounded by the bomb thrown at him while he was riding an elephant in a state procession, and the assassination of Curzon while in London by Madan Lal Dhingra. These types of revolutionary terrorist activities took place in important centres abroad. The most famous revolutionary terrorists acting abroad were Shyam Krishna Verma, V.D. Sarvarkar, and Hardayal in London, and Madame Cama and Ajit Singh in Europe.

Revolutionary Secret Societies

Very soon, secret societies of revolutionaries sprang up all over the country. Of such secret societies, the famous ones of long-standing credit were Anushilan Samiti and Jugantar. Between 1908 and 1918, nearly 186 revolutionaries were killed or convicted for sedition.

Anushilan Samiti

Anushilan Samiti was one of the most active secret revolutionary organisations in pre-independence. The organisation was very active in manoeuvring its revolutionary operations throughout the undivided Bengal region. Anushilan Samiti means "Self-Culture Association" and followed the teachings of 'Sahitya Samrat' Bankim Chandra Chattopadhaya, Swami Vivekandanda, and Aurobindo Ghosh. Operations of the Anushilan Samiti were controlled under the pretext of suburban fitness clubs or 'Akharas'.

In the initial phase, Anushilan Samiti was established in 1902 in Kolkata under the headship of Pramathanath Mitra, a barrister and a patron of revolutionary movements. Sri Aurobindo and Deshabandhu Chittaranjan Das were made the Vice-presidents of the Samiti. Noted revolutionist Surendranath Tagore became the treasurer. The partition of Bengal in 1905 led the Anushilan Samiti to take up full-time extremism programs. The partition of Bengal was considered the chief reason behind the terrorist activities of Anushilan Samiti. In 1906, a Bengali weekly namely Jugantar (New Era) was published by the members of the Samiti. The Calcutta Anushilan Samiti and the Dhaka Anushilan Samiti were unionised on the lines of the secret societies of Russia and Italy. Under Jatindranath Banerjee of Calcutta, Anushilan Samiti undertook military training in the army of Maharaja of Baroda along with Barindra Kumar Ghosh, younger brother of Aurobindo Ghosh. Calcutta Anushilan Samiti in its beginning was confined to only physical and moral training of the members. The revolutionary activities of Calcutta Anushilan Samiti started taking off from 1907. It was Surya Sen, or 'Masterda', who carried on probably the last radical terrorist act in East Bengal. He was a member of the Dhaka Anushilan Samiti as well as the Jugantar group. On April 18, 1930, Masterda and his followers coordinated the Chittagong armory raid. This incident of Anushilan Samiti was unusual for the organisation. Masterda was arrested and hanged till death on 12th January, 1934. Anushilan Samiti was merged with the Congress.

Previous Years' Questions

1. **"The Anti-Partition Agitation (1909) had an economic character in Bengal unlike the Extremist Agitation in Maharashtra which had a religious character." Examine. (2014)**
2. **'At the dawn of the twentieth century Lord Curzon, the Viceroy of India, was full of hostility towards the Indian National Congress and he confidentially reported to the Secretary of State in November 1900: "My own belief is that the Congress is tottering to its fall, and one of my greatest ambitions while in India is to assist it to a peaceful demise". Examine. (2013)**
3. **"India after 1905 had new interests and objectives and compelled new lines of policy."Comment. (1996)**
4. **Explain "Constructive Swadeshi" Characterize by atmashakti (self-reliance), which propelled the Swadeshi Movement in Bengal. (2016)**

14 CHAPTER

National Movement During The First World War (1907–1918)

Introduction

One of the significant outcomes of the partition of Bengal was extremism in the Indian National Movement. Extremists' group in the Indian National Congress dominated the Congress and the national movement. As a result, Indian National Congress suffered a great setback during the period 1905–1916 on two accounts - one, rise in differences between the Extremists and Moderates that resulted in split in the Congress at its Surat Session in 1907 and second, the constitutional reforms of 1909. The First World War period also witnessed significant developments that further strengthened the Indian National Movement.

The Tussle Between Moderates and Extremists and Surat Split, 1907

Difference In Ideology

In the first five years of the 20th century, the Congress sessions had been presided over by the Moderate leaders. The programs of Extremists like Swadeshi and Boycott, and national education sent alarm bells to the Moderates and they feared extremist domination in the Congress. In December 1905, at the Banaras session of the Indian National Congress presided over by Gopal Krishna Gokhale, the Moderate–Extremist differences came to the fore. The Extremists wanted to extend the Boycott and Swadeshi Movement to regions outside Bengal and thus, start a nationwide mass movement. Therefore, Extremists wanted a strong resolution supporting their program at the Banaras session.

The Moderates, on the other hand, were not in favour of extending the movement beyond Bengal and were totally opposed to boycott of councils and similar associations. They advocated strictly constitutional methods to protest against the partition of Bengal. As a compromise, a relatively mild resolution condemning the partition of Bengal and the reactionary policies of Curzon and supporting the swadeshi and boycott programme in Bengal was passed. This succeeded in averting a split for the moment.

However, at the Calcutta session of the Congress in December 1906, the Extremists wanted either Tilak or Lajpat Rai as the President, while the Moderates proposed the name of Dadabhai Naoroji, who was widely respected by all the nationalists. Finally, Dadabhai Naoroji was elected as the President and as a concession to the Extremists, the goal of the Indian National Congress was defined as 'swaraj' or self-government but within the British dominion. A resolution supporting the programme of swadeshi, boycott, and national education was passed.

The Extremists, emboldened by the proceedings at the Calcutta session, gave a call for wide passive resistance which included boycott of schools, colleges, legislative councils, municipalities, and legal professions. The two sides seemed to be heading for a confrontation. While the Extremists were excited for the acceptance of their program, the Moderates saw in the forthcoming constitutional reforms, an opportunity to realise their dream of Indian participation in the administration.

Dr. Rash Behari Ghosh - President of Surat Session of Congress, 1907 — Wikimedia Commons

In the next year, the Congress session at Surat on December 27, 1907, witnessed an open and ugly confrontation between the Moderates and the Extremists. Here, the Extremists first tried to push the candidature of Lala Lajpat Rai for Presidentship of Congress and the Moderates pitched Dr. Rash Behari Ghosh for the President position. Lala Lajpat Rai however stepped down and allowed Dr. Rash Behari Ghosh to become the President of the session.

The real trouble started when the Moderates tried to repudiate the programs of the Extremists accepted in the 1906 session. This was not acceptable to the Extremists. As a result, open clashes took place. The session was suspended and the Extremists were excluded. This marked a complete split in the Congress. The Congress was now dominated by the Moderates who lost no time in reiterating the Congress commitment to the goal of self-government within the British Empire and to constitutional methods only to achieve this goal.

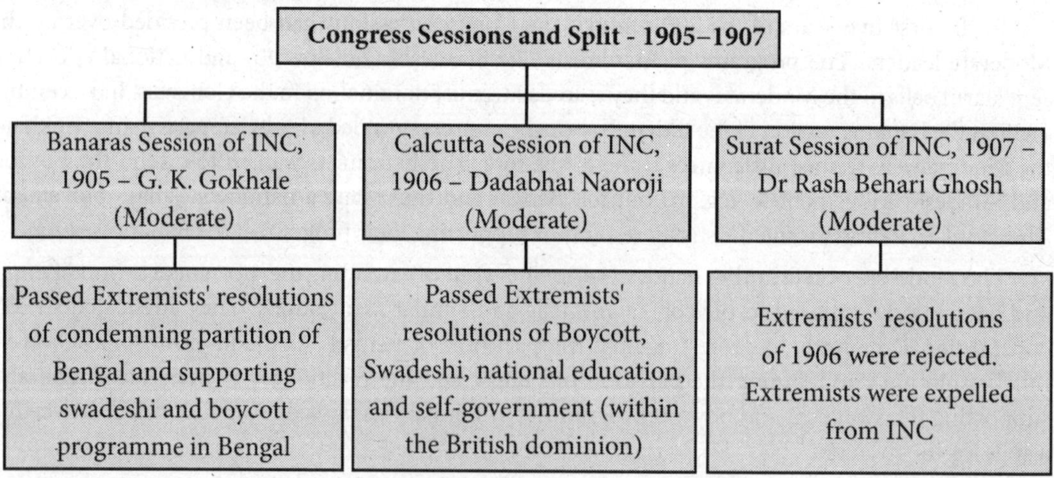

Decline of the Extremists' Movement

After the Surat Split, the British Government launched a massive attack on the Extremists. Between 1907 and 1911, five new laws were enforced to check anti-government activity. These legislations included the Prevention of Seditious Meetings Act, 1907; The Newspapers (Incitement to Offences) Act, 1908; Criminal Law Amendment Act, 1908; and the Indian Press Act, 1910.

But much of the frustration and anger of the Swadeshi movement got channelised into revolutionary activities. On April 30, 1908, two revolutionaries – Prafulla Chaki and Khudiram Bose – threw a bomb onto a carriage in Muzzaffarnagar in order to kill the unpopular chief Presidency Magistrate Douglas Kingsford, but by mistake killed two women in the carriage instead. Chaki committed suicide before he was caught, while Bose was hanged.

Revolutionary Khudiram Bose
— Wikimedia Commons

In his newspaper *Kesari*, B.G. Tilak defended these revolutionaries and called for immediate Swaraj. Tilak was arrested and tried on the charge of sedition. Muhammad Ali Jinnah, then an up-and-coming lawyer, defended him. Tilak was sent to prison for six years in Mandalay, Burma. While in the prison, he wrote the *Gita Rahasya*.

In May 1907, Lala Lajpat Rai and Sardar Ajit Singh of Punjab were deported to Mandalay without trial. Lala Lajpat Rai was released after about 6 months and he left for abroad. Aurobindo and B.C. Pal retired from active politics.

The Extremists were not able to organise an effective alternative party to sustain the movement. The Moderates, who still controlled the Congress, dominated the Congress session at Madras in 1908 and did not condemn the arrest of the Extremist leaders. The Extremists were left with no popular base or support, especially as the youth rallied behind the Moderates. After 1908, the national movement as a whole declined for a time. For the next eight years, the Congress remained a divided house.

Constitutional Reforms of 1909

Indian Councils Act of 1909 or Morley-Minto Reforms of 1909

In 1909, the government of India introduced constitutional reforms with a view to please the Moderate leaders (mainly the Muslims minorities), and to strengthen their position in the Congress. These reforms were named after Lord Minto, the Viceroy of India, and Lord Morley, the Secretary of the State for India, who formed the bill through the British Parliament. The reforms were mainly characterised with the provision of separate electorates for the minority (mainly Muslims). Loyalist Muslims led by Agha Khan, met Lord Minto in 1906 and demanded separate electorates for the Muslims. Their demands were accepted through the provision of 'separate electorates' for Muslims which became a contagious provision of the 1909 reforms.

The Main Provisions Of The Reforms Of 1909

i. The number of elected members in the Imperial Legislative Council and the Provincial Legislative Councils was increased. In the Provincial Councils, non-official majority was introduced, but since some of these non-officials were nominated and not elected, the overall non-elected majority remained.

ii. In the Imperial Legislative Council, of the total 68 members, 36 were to be the officials and of the 32 non-officials, 5 were to be nominated. Of the 27 elected non-officials, 8 seats were reserved for the Muslims under separate electorates, i.e., only Muslims could vote here for the Muslim candidates, while 6 seats were reserved for the British capitalists, 2 for the landlords, and 13 seats came under the general electorate.

iii. The elected members were to be indirectly elected. The local bodies were to elect an electoral college, which in turn would elect members of provincial legislatures, who in turn would elect members of the central legislature.

iv. Besides separate electorates for the Muslims, representation in excess of the strength of their population was accorded to the Muslims. Also, the income qualification for Muslim voters was kept lower than that for Hindus.

v. Powers of legislatures both at the centre and in the provinces were enlarged and the legislatures could now pass resolutions, ask questions, and vote separate items in the budget, but the budget as a whole could not be voted upon.

vi. One Indian was to be appointed to the Viceroy's Executive Council. Satyendra Sinha was the first to be appointed in 1909.

The reforms fell short of popular expectations. The Extremists termed the Moderates as 'old fossils' and the reforms as 'ingenious fraud'. The reforms of 1909 afforded no answer to the Indian political problem. Lord Morley made it clear that colonial self-government as demanded by the Moderates was not suitable for India, and he was against the introduction of Parliamentary or responsible government in India. He said, "if it could be said that this chapter of reforms led directly or necessarily to the establishment of a Parliamentary system in India, I for one, would have nothing at all to do with it."

The British refused the Indian demand for 'swaraj'. The Congress opposed the creation of separate electorates for the Muslims. This system of separate electorates for the Muslims sowed the seeds of the policy of communalism. In a statement, Lord Morley, the Secretary of the State, confessed, "Please remember, in granting separate electorates we are sowing the dragon's teeth and the harvest will be bitter." Hence, this statement of Lord Morley reflected the concerns and difficulties with the introduction of separate electorates in Indian politics.

The Minto-Morley reforms in 1909 also sowed the seed of alienation and hatred between Hindus and Muslims in India. The Hindu-Muslim rift was to turn into major communal riots, first for the partition, and then at the time of actual exodus of people from across the boundaries.

The concept of a separate electorate is considered by historians as a well-planned move from the British government to weaken the national movement which till then was flourishing with larger Hindu-Muslim unity.

Annulment or Cancellation of The Partition of Bengal, 1911

In 1911, a Grand Durbar was held at Delhi in the honour of King Emperor George V. It was during this Delhi Darbar, that the Emperor George V announced the cancellation of the partition of Bengal and the creation of the province of Bengal containing all the Bengali speaking people of both Eastern and Western Bengal. Bihar and Orissa was declared as separate states.

Also, the Government of India announced the shifting of the Capital from Calcutta to Delhi as a concession to the Muslims, as it was associated with Muslim glory, but the Muslims were not pleased.

Delhi Darbar, 1911 — Wikimedia Commons

India During The First World War

In 1914, the First World War began. India, being a colony of the Britain, bore the brunt of the war. India contributed massively to the British war effort by providing men and resources. About 1.3 million Indian soldiers and labourers served in Europe, Africa, and the Middle East, while both the Indian government and the princes sent large supplies of food, money, and ammunition.

In World War I, the Indian Army fought against the German Empire, East Africa, and on the Western Front. At the First Battle of Ypres, Khudadad Khan became the first Indian to be awarded a Victoria Cross.

Indian Bicycle Troops at the Battle of Somme — Wikimedia Commons

Response of Nationalists and Princely States During the War

The news of the war was received enthusiastically by the native princes, the political bourgeoisie, and the educated middle-classes alike, with pledges of imperial loyalty and support. The movement for self-rule in India had aggravated as leaders such as Annie Besant and Bal Gangadhar Tilak launched the Home Rule League in 1916 and used India's war contributions to demand self-government within the empire.

To Annie Besant, the war was the ideal opportunity for India to demonstrate its loyalty and support to the empire, and thus earn the right of self-government. Gandhi, who was raising an Ambulance Corps in London in 1914, threw himself wholeheartedly into the recruitment drive on his return to India in 1915. He argued that "We should send our men to France and Mesopotamia. We are not entitled to demand *Swaraj* till we come forward to enlist in the army".

Princely States formed one-third of India and were in alliances and partnerships with the British Raj. They made vast offers of money, troops, labourers, hospital ships, ambulances, motorcars, flotillas, horses, food, and clothes.

The Indian support given to Britain's cause surprised the establishment in Britain. *The Times* wrote: "The Indian empire has overwhelmed the British nation by the completeness and unanimity of its enthusiastic aid." Pleased by India's massive war contribution to Britain, the Secretary of State, Edwin Montagu made a declaration in 1917, "the progressive realisation of responsible self-government" would be the aim of British rule in India.

Anti-Colonial Activities during the War

However, during the Great War, Bengal and Punjab remained the hotbeds of anti-colonial activities. There were two revolutionary organisations working from abroad which caused a considerable deal of imperial panic during the war years – the first was the Ghadar party and the second was the Indian Independence Committee.

Chempakaraman Pillai
— Wikimedia Commons

Virendranath Chattopadhyay
— Wikimedia Commons

The Berlin Committee, later known as the Indian Independence Committee, was an organisation formed in Germany in 1914 during World War I by Indian students and political activists with the support from Germen Foreign Office, Ottoman Turkey, and Irish Republican Movement.

Some of the important members of the Berlin Committee included Virendranath Chattopadhyaya (alias Chatto), Chempakaraman Pillai, and Abinash Bhattacharya.

Madan Lal Dhingra (1883–1909) — Wikimedia Commons

Both these organisations – the Ghadar party and the Indian Independence Committee – were considered as a part of the so called 'The Hindu–German Conspiracy' – a series of plans between 1914 and 1917 by radical Indian nationalist groups to attempt a Pan-Indian rebellion against the British Raj during World War I.

During this period, 'India House' in North London rapidly became a hub for prominent overseas Indian revolutionaries. Nationalists of the India House played a significant role in the Hindu-German Conspiracy. Members of India House also published an anti-colonialist newspaper, *The Indian Sociologist*. Some of the significant Indian revolutionaries associated with the India House were Vinayak Damodar Savarkar, Bhikaji Cama, V.N. Chatterjee, Lala Har Dayal, V.V.S. Aiyar, M.P.T. Acharya, and P.M. Bapat. Nationalists like Shyamji Krishna Varma promoted nationalist views among Indian students in Britain.

In 1909, a member of the India House, revolutionary Madan Lal Dhingra, assassinated Sir W.H. Curzon Wyllie, political aide-de-camp to the Secretary of State for India.

The Delhi Conspiracy Case

The Delhi Conspiracy case, also known as the Delhi-Lahore Conspiracy, 1912 refers to a conspiracy to assassinate the then Viceroy of India, Lord Hardinge, on the occasion of transferring the capital of British India from Calcutta to New Delhi.

Hatched by the underground Indian revolutionaries in Bengal and in Punjab, headed by Rash Behari Bose, the conspiracy culminated in the attempted assassination on 23 December, 1912 when a homemade bomb was thrown into the Viceroy's *Howdah* when the ceremonial procession moved through the Chandni Chowk of Delhi. However, the assassination attempt failed as the Viceroy received minor injuries and safely escaped.

1912 Assassination attempt On Lord Hardinge — Wikimedia Commons

The Komagata Maru Incident, 1914

This was a major racist and discriminatory international episode towards Indians during the war period that further incited anti-colonial feelings among the Indians. The Canadian government had passed exclusionist laws to stop Indians' Immigrations or 'Brown Invasion'.

The 'Komagata Maru' was a Japanese streamliner chartered by an affluent businessman, Gurdit Singh, to bring Indian immigrants to Canada. The ship's route departed from Hong Kong, stopped in Japan, and then headed to Canada. Its passengers included 376 Indians, all Punjabis, among whom 340 were Sikhs, 12 were Hindus, and 24 were Muslims.

The ship was eventually turned back at Vancouver where landing was refused, and terminated eventually at Calcutta. The ship returned to Calcutta on 27 September and was stopped by the British.

The passengers were put under guard and the ship was allowed to dock in Budge Budge, Calcutta. The British believed that the passengers were law breakers and political agitators. When the police sought to arrest the persons it viewed as leaders of the group, there was resistance followed by a riot. The police fired shots and 19 passengers were killed. Baba Gurdit Singh, who was one of the persons the British wanted to arrest, escaped with some other persons. Most of the remaining passengers were either arrested or sent back to Punjab. Baba Gurdit Singh later surrendered to the police.

The Komagata Maru incident became a media sensation, and drew plenty of attention from the public at large. The incident was widely criticised by nationalists living abroad. The Ghadar party used this incident to recruit more members to increase its anarchist activities. Therefore, Koamagata Maru incident triggered more anti-colonial activities in India.

The 'Komagata Maru' Steamer — Wikimedia Commons

The Ghadar Party Movement

Ghadar which means 'rebellion', was a revolutionary party formed by the Indians residing abroad. The Ghadar party for the liberation of India was formed by the Indians who had gone overseas. Most of the members of the party were Punjabi Sikh peasants and ex soldiers, who had faced the brunt of economic and racial discrimination. They had gone to other countries for livelihood. The leaders of the party were however, educated Hindus and Muslims.

Some of the important leaders of the party were Lala Hardayal, Mohamed Barakatullah, Bhagwan Singh Gyanee, Jawala Singh, Kartar Singh, Ram Chandra, V.G. Pingle, Rash Behari Bose, Sachin Sanyal, and Sohan Singh Bhakna. The party was founded in 1913 at Stockton in America, with Sohan Singh Bhakna as the President and Hardayal as Secretary.

The Ghadar party was pledged to wage revolutionary war against the British rule in India. The party carried on its propaganda in an Urdu weekly 'The Ghadar' which carried the caption '*Angrezi Raj Ka Dushman*'. It used to make appeals to people for joining its activities. In a short period of time, the party became the supreme organisation of immigrant Indians residing in Canada, Indo-China, Japan, Philippines, Malaya, Singapore, Mexico, and USA.

The party made an attempt to create a mutiny in the British army on February 21, 1915. Prominent leaders of the Ghadar party like Rash Behari Bose, Sachin Sanyal, Ganesh Pingle, and Baghi Kartar Singh prepared a master plan for the mutiny in the British army. Unfortunately, the British authorities came to know of these plans and took immediate action. The rebellious regiments were disbanded and their leaders were either imprisoned or hanged. Almost all leaders of the Ghadar Party in Punjab were arrested. Later, they were tried in the Lahore Conspiracy Case.

Following is a summary on the failed February mutiny of the Ghadar party and the trial of the Ghadarists in the Lahore Conspiracy Case.

The February Mutiny of Ghadar Party, 1915 : With the extensive support from German and the Irish republican movement, plan to stimulate unrest in the British Indian Army from Punjab to Singapore was made by the *Ghadar* Party. The plan was to be executed in February 1915 with the aim of overthrowing the Raj from the Indian subcontinent.

The February mutiny by the Ghadar party was ultimately thwarted when the British intelligence infiltrated the Ghadarite movement and arrested the key figures. Mutinies in smaller units and garrisons within India were also crushed.

The Lahore Conspiracy Case : The Lahore Conspiracy Case trial also known as the *First Lahore Conspiracy Case*, were the trials held in Lahore in the aftermath of the failed Ghadar conspiracy in 1915. The trial was held by a Special tribunal constituted under the Defence of India Act. Out of a total of 291 convicted conspirators, 42 were executed, 114 got life sentences, and 93 got varying terms of imprisonment. 42 defendants in the trial were acquitted. The uncovering of the conspiracy also saw the initiation of the Hindu German Conspiracy trial in the USA. Later on, the British government for the safety purposes, enacted the Defence of India Regulations Act, 1915.

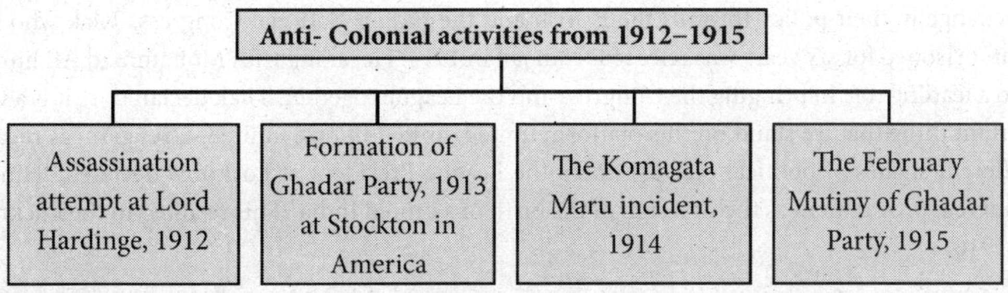

The Unity of Moderates and Extremists

Two significant developments of the war period were: unity between the Moderates and the Extremists, and agreement between the Muslim League and the Congress.

The growing nationalist feeling in the country led to the unification of the Moderates and the Extremists. In 1914, B. G. Tilak was released, and he picked up the threads of the movement. The Moderates, after the death of Gopal Krishna Gokhale in 1915, became leaderless and at the same time, there was some change in the attitude of the Extremists' leader Tilak. To assure the Moderates, Tilak declared, '... I have no hesitation in saying that the acts of violence which have been committed in different parts of India are not only repugnant to me, but have, in my opinion, unfortunately retarded to a great extent, the pace of our political progress.'

The 31st Session of the Congress was held at Lucknow in 1916. It was presided over by Ambika Charan Majumdar, who was a prominent lawyer and was actively associated with the Congress since its birth. After a lapse of about 10 years, both the Moderates and Extremists were united again which was a good sign for the national movement. In his address the Congress President declared, 'If the United Congress was buried at Surat, it is reborn at Lucknow in the garden of Wajid Ali Shah. After nearly 10 years of painful separation and wanderings through the wilderness of misunderstandings the brother had at first met brothers'.

In this session, the Congress and the Muslim League came closer to each other and they signed the historic Lucknow Pact. Thus, this session of 1916 cemented the friendship between the Congress and the Muslim League and promoted goodwill between the Hindus and the Muslims.

Muslim League and The Lucknow Pact

In December 1906, Muslim delegates from all over India met at Dhaka for the All India Muslim Educational Conference. Taking advantage of this occasion, Nawab Salimullah of Dhaka proposed the setting up of an organisation to look after the Muslim interests. The proposal was accepted that resulted in the foundation of All-India Muslim League on December 30, 1906.

Like the Indian National Congress, the Muslim League conducted its annual sessions and put their demands to the British government. It was viewed by the British as a loyalist, communal, and conservative political organisation. Initially, they enjoyed the support of the British. Their first achievement was the separate electorates for the Muslims in the Minto-Morley reforms.

During the First World War, Turkey, which was regarded as the stronghold of Islam, faced the onslaught of Britain and its allies. The Muslims in India felt greatly disturbed. There was thus, a great change in their policy towards the British and the Indian National Congress. Tilak who had been imprisoned for six years was released from jail in 1914. He, along with Mohammad Ali Jinnah, played a leading role in bringing the Congress and the League together. Tilak declared,' ...it is a very important thing that we stand on this platform united, united in race, united in religion, as regards all different shades of political creed.' Jinnah, the League President at Lucknow declared, 'Hindu-Muslim reapproachment as the first sign of the birth of a united India.' This resulted in the Lucknow Pact, 1916.

Main Clauses of the Lucknow Pact

The main clauses of the Lucknow Pact were:

- There shall be self-government in India.
- Muslims should be given one-third representation in the central government. There should be separate electorates for all the communities until a community demanded for joint electorates.
- System of weightage should be adopted.
- The number of the members of Central Legislative Council should be increased to 150.
- At the provincial level, four-fifth of the members of the Legislative Councils should be elected and one-fifth should be nominated.
- The strength of Provincial legislative should not be less than 125 in the major provinces and from 50 to 75 in the minor provinces.
- All members, except those nominated, were to be elected directly on the basis of adult franchise.
- No bill concerning a community should be passed if the bill is opposed by three-fourth of the members of that community in the Legislative Council.
- Term of the Legislative Council should be five years.
- Members of Legislative Council should themselves elect their President.
- Half of the members of Imperial Legislative Council should be Indians.
- Indian Council must be abolished.

The Home Rule Movement

The period from 1909 to 1915, witnessed a vacuum in the mass movement due to British suppression, lack of Extremists' leadership, and role of Congress as a directionless body.

The World War period brought frustration and disillusionment in the Indian masses. Besides, there was no mass movement or political agitation or protest against the government. The Home Rule movement filled up this vacuum and prevented the mass movement from derailing. The Home Rule movement combined and balanced the best ideas of the Extremist, Moderates, and Radicals.

The Indian Home Rule Leagues were organised on the lines of the Irish Home Rule League and they were represented by Annie Besant and B.G. Tilak.

In September 1915, Annie Besant launched the Home Rule League, modelling demands for India on the Irish model. She clearly gave a signal of fighting for a change. For the first time, India saw a political party that was to work all year round, unlike the Congress which croaked once a year.

In the next year 1916, Tilak also reorganised his supporters. When the war was near closing, Bal Gangadhar Tilak, Annie Besant, Mohammad Ali Jinnah, Joseph Baptista, G. S. Khaparde, and Sir S. Subramania Iyer, all came together under the umbrella of the All India Home Rule League. The demand was self-government within the British Empire for all of India.

The Home Rule had two divisions:

- Indian Home Rule League under Tilak. (Joseph Bapista was the first President of the Indian Home Rule League established in April 1916.)
- Home Rule League under Annie Besant.

Joseph Baptista - The First President of Indian Home Rule League — Wikimedia Commons

Factors Leading to the Movement

(i) A section of nationalists felt that popular pressure was required to attain concessions from the government.

(ii) The Moderates were disillusioned with the Morley-Minto reforms.

(iii) People were feeling the burden of wartime miseries caused by high taxation and a rise in prices, and were ready to participate in any aggressive movement or protest against the government.

(iv) The War, being fought among the major imperialist powers of the day and backed by naked propaganda against each other, exposed the myth of white superiority.

(v) Tilak was ready to assume leadership after his release in June 1914, and had made conciliatory gestures to reassure the Government of his loyalty, and to the Moderates that he wanted, like the Irish Home Rulers, a reform of the administration and not an overthrow of the Government. He also said that the acts of violence had only served to retard the pace of political progress in India. He urged all Indians to assist the British Government in its hour of crisis.

(vi) Annie Besant, the Irish theosophist based in India since 1896, had decided to enlarge the sphere of her activities to include the building of a movement for Home Rule on the lines of the Irish Home Rule League.

The Home Rule Movement was the Indian response to the First World War in terms of bringing administrative reforms and political awareness by replacing aggressive nationalism. Both Tilak and Besant realised that the section of a Moderate-dominated Congress as well as full cooperation of the Extremists was essential for the movement to succeed. Although Besant failed to get the Congress to approve her scheme of Home Rule Leagues, the Congress did commit itself to a program of educative propaganda and to a revival of local-level Congress committees.

Many of the Moderate Congressmen who were disillusioned with Congress inactivity, and some members of Gokhale's Servants of India Society also joined the agitation. The League aimed to convey to the common man the message of Home Rule as self-government. It carried a much wider appeal than the earlier mobilisations did and also attracted the hitherto 'politically backward' regions of Gujarat and Sindh.

The main aim of the Home Rule movement was to promote political education to the masses and to establish self-government within the British Empire.

Means and Methods Adopted

The aims of the movement was to be achieved by promoting political education and discussions through public meetings, organising libraries and reading rooms containing books on national politics, holding conferences, organising classes for students on politics, propaganda through newspapers, pamphlets, posters, illustrated post-cards, plays, religious songs, etc., collecting funds, organising social work, and participating in local government activities.

Therefore, Home Rule movement shifted the emphasis of the mass protest from the educated elite to the masses which resulted in the Moderates' decline. It created an organisational link between the town and the country, which was to prove crucial in later years when the national movement became a mass movement.

It prepared the masses for the politics of the Gandhian style.

The Home Rule agitation was later joined by Motilal Nehru, Jawaharlal Nehru, Bhulabhai Desai, Chittaranjan Das, Madan Mohan Malaviya, Tej Bahadur Sapru, and Lala Lajpat Rai.

In 1920, the All India Home Rule League elected Mahatma Gandhi as its President that led the League to merge with the Indian National Congress.

The Significant Contribution of the Home Rule Movement

(i) The movement shifted the emphasis from the educated elite to the masses and permanently deflected the movement from the course mapped by the Moderates.

(ii) It created an organisational link between the town and the country, which was to prove crucial in later years when the movement entered its mass phase in a true sense.

(iii) It created a generation of ardent nationalists.

(iv) It prepared the masses for politics of the Gandhian style.

(v) The August 1917 declaration of Montagu and the Montford reforms were influenced by the Home Rule agitation.

(vi) Tilak's and Besant's efforts in the Moderate-Extremist reunion at Lucknow (1916) revived the Congress as an effective instrument of Indian nationalism.

(vii) It lent a new dimension and a sense of urgency to the national movement.

It can be concluded that the Home Rule League (HRL) had more impact on the Indian national movement than contemporary movements like Ghadar. The Home Rule movement was not in direct confrontation with the colonial government. On the other hand, Ghadar movement was localised to a few provinces like Bengal and Punjab and involved a few sections with a lot of revolutionary zeal and underground activities.

Home Rule League or HRL, brought about a major transition in the objective of the movement. Earlier, the objectives were a greater role for Indians in the institutions of State in the Moderate phase. The Home Rule movement put self-government as the objective to be pursued by the movement and not less than that. Tilak's League put up the question of Swaraj along with the demand for the formation of linguistic states and vernacular education. His demand for Home Rule was made on a wholly secular basis. Besant's League enlarged the sphere of her activities to include the building of a movement for Home Rule on the lines of the Irish Home Rule League.

The Congress under the Moderates' phase was not willing to expand the organisational reach and strength. The Moderates opposed the branches of the Congress in the village level and district level. The Home Rule movement independently expanded, even to the remote places. This organisational expansion was the major achievement of the Home Rule League.

The promotion of political education and scholarly discussion was promoted under HRL.

They established libraries containing material on national politics, organised classes for students on politics, printed and circulated pamphlets, collected funds, organised social work, took part in local government activities, and arranged political meetings and lectures

Due to its reach, many new sections of the people came into contact with national politics through library movements and magazines. Many people got aware of the ill-effects of the colonialism. It helps in strengthening the notion of "We are Indians". These strengths were later exploited in the Gandhian Phase.

HRL was most effective in bringing the Congress leaders and the Muslim League together. It was seen in the Lucknow Pact which provided cooperation between the Congress and the Muslim League. During this period, there were negligible contentious issues left between leaders of any political group fighting against British Imperialism.

Due to the Home Rule movement, the British government was forced to decide a change in policy and adopted a conciliatory posture. The demand for Home Rule or self-government could no longer be treated as seditious after the Montagu Declaration.

HRL was therefore the Indian response to the First World War in a less charged but a more effective way.

Thus, the Home Rule League made great transitions in terms of objectives and organisational strength of the national movement and nation-building.

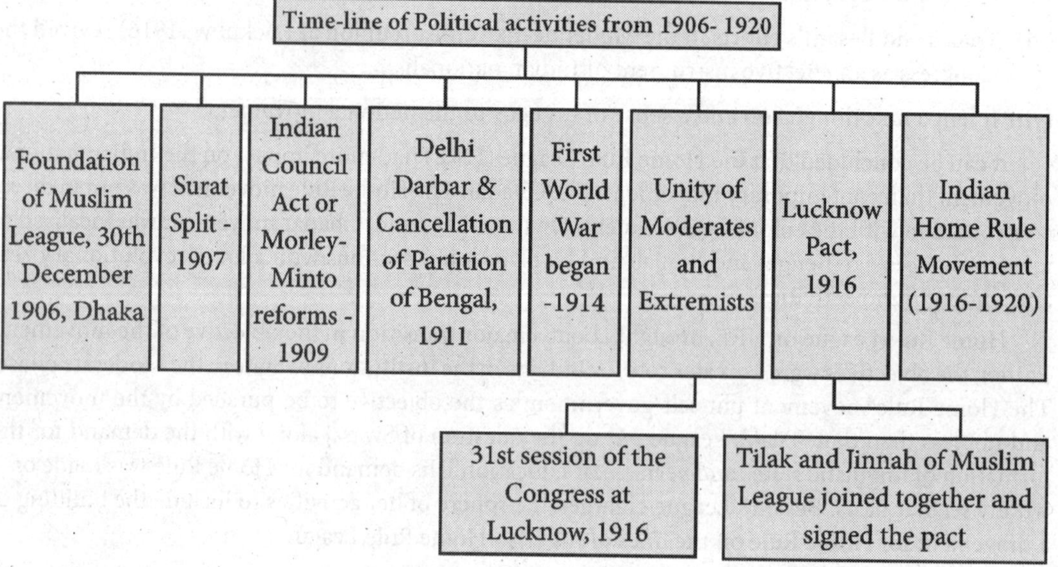

Previous Years' Questions

1. **"Please remember, in granting separate electorates we are sowing the dragon's teeth and harvest will be bitter." (Morley) (2009)**
2. **"The Home Rule League Movement, led by Lokamanya Tilak and Annie Besant, was less charged but more effective compared to other movements of the time". Examine how and why. (2000)**
3. **"India after 1905 had new interests and objectives and compelled new lines of policy." (1996)**
4. **Trace the factors which led to a split in the Indian national Congress in 1907. What was its impact on the course of the nationalist movement? (2003)**

15 CHAPTER

National Movement Under Mohandas Karamchand Gandhi : 1915–1919

Background

The national movement spearheaded by the Extremists got a new dimension with the coming of Mohandas Karamchand Gandhi in 1915. Often considered as the Father of the Indian National Movement and later 'Father of the Nation', Gandhi before coming to India, had spent 21 years in South Africa working against racial discrimination. It was there that he created his concept of 'Satyagraha', a non-violent way of protesting against injustice. While in India, Gandhi first related himself with the masses by adopting a simplistic lifestyle and virtues of truth and non-violence.

Born on 2nd October 1869 in Porbandar, Gujarat, Gandhi became the principle leader of Indian national struggle and leader of the masses. In 1915, Gandhi returned to India permanently. He was already perceived as a reputed leader and a leading Indian nationalist. He joined the Indian National Congress and was introduced to Indian issues, politics, and the Indian people primarily by Gopal Krishna Gokhale. Gokhale was a key leader of the Congress Party and belonged to the genre of Moderates. Gandhi took Gokhale's liberal approach and transformed it according to the Indian requirements and situations.

Gandhi in South Africa (1893–1914)

In 1893, Gandhi proceeded to Natal, South Africa in relation with a case involving his client, Dada Abdullah. When Gandhi arrived in 1893, the issue of Indian immigration was a hot topic, and from the outset, he became aware of the racial discrimination directed at Indians living in Durban. Indentured Indian labour had started arriving in the then Natal (now KwaZulu-Natal) from 1860 onwards to work on the sugar plantations, and many of these labourers stayed on for economic reasons. This increase in the Indian population gave rise to growing opposition on the part of the white colonists, particularly when Indian traders also started arriving in the province.

M.K. Gandhi as barrister in South Africa — Wikimedia Commons

While traveling by train to Pretoria, Gandhiji experienced his first taste of racial discrimination. He was thrown off a train at Pietermaritzburg after refusing to move from the first class to a third class coach while holding a valid first class ticket. "It was winter," Gandhi was to write in his autobiography, and "the cold was extremely bitter. My overcoat was in my luggage, but I did not dare to ask for it lest I should be insulted again, so I sat and shivered". He says he began to think of his "duty": ought he to stay back and fight for his "rights", or should he return to India? His own "hardship was superficial", "only a symptom of the deep disease of colour prejudice."

The Natives Legislative Assembly Bill of 1894 proposed a bill that intended to remove Indians from the voters' roll. Indian merchants appealed to Gandhi to stay and fight the legislation on their behalf. Gandhi decided to stay in South Africa to organise the Indian workers to enable them to fight for their rights. Gandhi followed the Moderates' methods. He started a signature campaign and presented it to the government. To unite different sections of the Indians, Gandhi set up the Natal Indian Congress and started a paper 'Indian Opinion'. Moderates' methods of signature campaign and petitions failed in its objective of stopping the government from disfranchising Indians. In 1896, a law was passed disqualifying Indian voters. However, Natal Indian Congress became a driving force behind the *satyagraha* campaigns between 1906 and 1913 in South Africa.

Gandhi in 1901 attended the Calcutta session of the Indian National Congress and had the satisfaction of seeing his resolution on South Africa pass with acclamation. He was however disappointed with the Congress. He felt that Indian politicians talked too much but did little.

The Transvaal Registration Act, 1907 and Passive Resistance or Satyagraha

The government in Transvaal passed the Asiatic Registration Act in 1906 amid massive protest by the Indians. This Act made it compulsory for Indians to carry at all times certificates of registration with their fingerprints. It was at this juncture that Gandhi officially used the satyagraha campaign. Gandhi was convinced that the method of protest, petition, and prayer which he had sedulously pursued for nearly fourteen years had failed.

Gandhi termed the Asiatic Registration Act as 'Black Act' and formed the Passive Resistance Association to conduct the campaign. Gandhi encouraged Indians and other Asians to burn their identity documents. The Indians made a bonfire of their registration certificates and decided to defy the ban on immigration to the Transvaal.

Great March from Newcastle to Transvaal and other protests

Gandhi led the great march of 2,200 Indian coal miners and sugar plantation workers across the border to the Transvaal, i.e., from Newcastle to the Transvaal border – a distance of over 40 miles. This great march was a forerunner to the famous Salt March in India in 1930. The march started on 6 November, 1913 and had in its ranks 127 women, 57 children, and some 2037 men. Gandhi was first arrested on 27 December 1907 for failing to register and staying in the Transvaal.

A second major satyagraha campaign was initiated in 1913 in protest against a £3 tax that was being imposed on ex-indentured Indians. A poll tax of three pounds was imposed on all ex-indentured Indians, i.e., staying in South Africa after expiry of their contracts.

Fuel was added to the fire by a Supreme Court order which invalidated all marriages, not conducted according to Christian rites and by the Registrar of Marriages. By implication, Hindu, Muslim, and Parsi marriages were illegal and children born out of such marriages, illegitimate. The Indians treated this judgement as an insult to the honour of their women and many women were drawn into the movement because of this indignity. During this campaign, Gandhi's wife, Kasturba, was arrested while attempting to cross the border into Transvaal by train with a group of women in protest against their marriages being declared invalid.

As the protest continued, the number of Indian prisoners swelled to some 155 and the authorities had to put tents up in the yard to accommodate them.

The 1913 protest actions led to a meeting between Gandhi and General Jan Smuts (colonial secretary and education secretary). General Smut agreed to encourage voluntary registration in exchange for the legislation being dropped. When Smuts failed to keep his word, the *satyagraha* campaign gained in intensity and spread.

Eventually, through a series of negotiations involving Gandhi, Governor-General Lord Hardinge, C.F. Andrews, and General Smuts, an agreement was reached by which the Government of South Africa conceded the major Indian demands relating to the poll tax, the registration certificates, and marriages solemnised according to Indian rites, and promised to treat the issue of Indian immigration in a sympathetic manner.

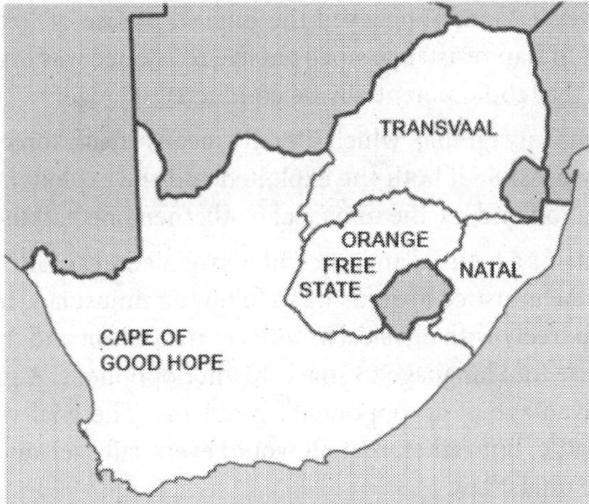

Gandhi led the Great March from Newcastle to Transvaal — Wikimedia Commons

Community Settlements

Influenced by the Hindu religious book, the Bhagavad Gita, Gandhi wanted to purify his life by following the concepts of *Aparigraha* (non-possession) and *Samabhava* (equability). A friend gave him the book, *Unto This Last*, by John Ruskin, and Gandhi became excited about the ideals professed by Ruskin. The book inspired Gandhi to establish a communal living community called 'Phoenix Settlement' just outside of Durban in June, 1904. The Settlement was an experiment in communal living, a way to eliminate one's needless possessions and to live in a society with full equality. Gandhi moved his newspaper, *The Indian Opinion*, established in June 1903 and its workers to the Phoenix Settlement as well as his own family a bit later.

Gandhi's second communal settlement in South Africa was the 'Tolstoy Farm', a small colony 21 miles from Johannesburg set up around 1910. The Tolstoy Farm was meant to house the families of the Satyagrahis and to give them a way to sustain themselves.

Indian Ambulance Corps and Stretcher Bearer Corps

With the outbreak of the Boer war in 1899, Gandhi enlisted 1100 Indians and organised the Indian Ambulance Corps for the British. He argued that Indians could not demand their rights as British citizens if they were not willing to show loyalty to the Empire.

In 1906, during the Zulu rebellion in Natal, Gandhi again offered his help to the Government and organised a Stretcher-Bearer Corps.

In 1915, Lord Hardinge awarded *Kesar-e-Hind* medal for his services in the Zulu and Boer wars, but later he returned these medals to Viceroy Chelmsford in 1920.

Gandhi's Technique of Satyagraha

Satyagraha is a philosophy and a practice within the broader category generally known as non-violent resistance or civil resistance. Someone who practices satyagraha is known as 'satyagrahi'. Satyagraha theory influenced Martin Luther King Jr's and James Bevel's campaigns during the Civil Rights Movement in the United States and Nelson Mandela's struggle in South Africa under Apartheid.

Gandhi developed the concept of satyagraha in late 1906. The English translation of 'satyagraha' is passive resistance. However, Gandhi believed the English phrase of "passive resistance" did not represent the true spirit of Indian resistance since passive resistance was often thought to be used by the weak and was a tactic that could potentially be conducted in anger.

Gandhi chose the term "satyagraha," which literally means "truth force." Since Gandhi believed that exploitation was only possible if both the exploited and the exploiter accepted it, if one could see above the current situation and see the universal truth, then one had the power to make change.

In practice, satyagraha was a focused and forceful non-violent resistance to a particular injustice. A satyagrahi would resist the injustice by refusing to follow an unjust law. In doing so, he/she would not be angry, would put up freely with physical assaults to the person and the confiscation of his/her property, and would not use foul language to smear his/her opponent. A practitioner of satyagraha also would never take advantage of an opponent's problems. The goal was not for there to be a winner and loser of the battle, but rather, that all would eventually see and understand the "truth" and agree to withdraw the unjust law.

Its basic tenets were :

- A satyagrahi was not to submit to what he considered as wrong, but was to always remain truthful, non-violent, and fearless.
- A true satyagrahi would never bow before the evil, whatever the consequence.
- He should be ready to accept suffering in his struggle against the evil doer.
- This suffering was to be a part of his love for truth.
- Even while carrying out his struggle against the evil doer, a true satyagrahi would love the evil doer; hatred would be alien to his nature.
- Only the brave and strong could practise satyagraha, which was not for the weak and cowards, and even violence was preferred to cowardice.

Gandhi's Sources of Inspiration

Gandhi himself said, "Three moderns have left a deep impress on my life and captivated me. Raychandbhai by his living contact, Leo Tolstoy by his book, *The Kingdom of God is Within You*, and Ruskin by his *Unto This Last*. Besides these three personalities, Gopal Krishna Gokhale and the *Bhagavad Gita* and the *Bible* were lifelong sources of inspiration for Gandhi.

Shrimad Raychandbhai or Shri Rajchandra

He was a spiritual guide to Gandhi. Gandhi enjoyed the closest association with him. Gandhi implicitly believed that Raychandbhai would never willingly lead him astray and in turn, Raychandbhai would always confide in Gandhi his innermost thoughts. In Gandhi's moments of spiritual crisis, as in South Africa, Raychandbhai was Gandhi's refuge.

Gopal Krishna Gokhale

He was Gandhi's political guru. Gokhale seemed like the Ganga to Gandhi where one could have a refreshing bath in the holy river. Gokhale embodied the goal of spiritualising (i.e., values of life) in politics and Gandhi steadfastly adhered to it by enriching it. It is significant to remember that Gandhi has devoted seven chapters exclusively to Gokhale in his autobiography. Finally, on his return from South Africa to India in 1915, Gandhi looked upon Gokhale as his political guide whenever Gandhi was in difficulty, and that took a great load off Gandhi's mind.

Leo Tolstoy

Both Tolstoy and Gandhi worshipped in the common shrine and the same heroes – i.e., Buddha's *Light of Asia*, Socrates, Mohammed, *Upanishads*, and the *Bhagavad Gita*. Both of them were not mere philosophers, but teachers of humanity who endeavoured hard to practise what they preached. Gandhi described himself with characteristic candour as Tolstoy's disciple in his letters to Tolstoy. Tolstoy wrote to Gandhi emphasising the almost pivotal significance of Gandhi's satyagraha in South Africa. Tolstoy was the prophet of the latter half of the nineteenth century and Gandhi of the first half of the twentieth century. Finally, Tolstoy's *The Kingdom of God is Within You* overwhelmed Gandhi. It left an abiding impression on Gandhi. Tolstoy manifested independent thinking, profound morality, and truthfulness.

John Ruskin

This English thinker was perhaps the most powerful source of inspiration when Gandhi himself described Ruskin's book, *Unto This Last* as "the magic spell". Gandhi was offered Ruskin's book by Gandhi's intimate friend Mr. Polak, and Gandhi read it on his train journey from Johannesburg to Durban. The book gripped Gandhi so much that the teaching of the book appealed to Gandhi instantaneously and Gandhi paraphrased it into Gujarati as "Sarvodaya" (The welfare of all). *Gandhi learned the following teachings from this book* :

- The good of the individual is contained in the welfare of all;
- All have the same right of earning their livelihood from their work;
- That a life of labour is the life worth living.

Dr. Pranjivan Mehta, a long-time friend of Gandhi. The book written by Gandhi titled 'Hind Swaraj' was dedicated to him
— Wikimedia Commons

Bhagavad Gita

It made a deep impression on his mind. Gandhi regarded the *Gita* par excellence for the knowledge of Truth and it afforded him invaluable help in his moments of gloom. The *Gita* became Gandhi's lifelong companion and guide, especially the last eighteen verses of the second chapter of the *Gita*. Gandhi derived the Gospel of selfless action or duty from the *Gita*. His commentary on the *Gita* reflects his life and mission.

Bible

Gandhi used to read the *Bible*, especially "The New Testament" and "The Sermon on the Mount" which went straight to his heart. The compassion and renunciation of Jesus appealed greatly to Gandhi.

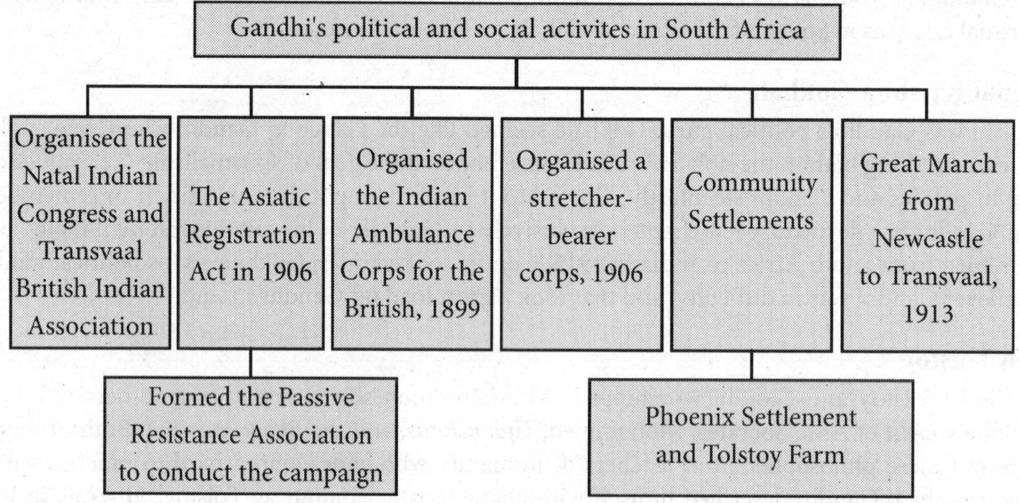

Gandhi's Return to India and his Satyagraha Experiments

Having spent 21 years in South Africa helping fight discrimination, Gandhi decided to return to India. However, when World War I broke out during his journey, Gandhi decided to stay in England and form another ambulance corps of Indians to help the British. Gandhi sailed to India in January 1915. A hero's welcome awaited Gandhi when he landed on January 9, 1915, at the Apollo Bunder in Bombay. He received a "Kaiser-I-Hind" gold medal in the King's birthday honours list of 1915.

Gandhi's struggles and triumphs in South Africa had been reported in the worldwide press. By the time he reached home in India, he was a national hero. Although he was eager to begin reforms in India, his political guru Gopal Krishan Gokhale advised him to wait a year and spend the time travelling around India to acquaint himself with the people and their tribulations.

In an attempt to understand and relate with the common masses properly, Gandhi began to dress like them, i.e., wearing a loincloth (dhoti) and sandals (the average dress of the masses). If it was cold outside, he would add a shawl. This became his wardrobe for the rest of his life.

Also, during this year of probation, Gandhi founded another communal settlement, this time in Ahmadabad and called it the Sabarmati Ashram. Gandhi lived in the Ashram for the next sixteen years, along with his family and several members who had once been part of the Phoenix Settlement.

M.K. Gandhi Wearing Simple Indian Dress
— Wikimedia Commons

When Gandhi came to India, he did not participate in the Home Rule agitation or in the negotiations which led to the Lucknow Pact between the Indian National Congress and the All-India Muslim League.

The Indian national scene dominated then by the Annie Besant-Tilak combination impressed the Government during the war. The Moderates did not like Gandhi's extra-constitutional methods of satyagraha carried out in South Africa. The Extremists did not like his loyalty to the British government during the war.

The Champaran Satyagraha, 1917

Gandhi's early experiments on satyagraha in India were carried in Champaran, a district in Bihar in 1917. The peasantry of this district was suffering from the European indigo planters who compelled them to grow indigo in their crop areas. The European planters had been forcing the peasants to grow indigo on 3/20 of the total land called *tinkathia system*. When towards the end of the nineteenth century, German synthetic dyes replaced indigo, the European planters demanded high rents and illegal dues from the peasants in order to maximise their profits before the peasants could shift to other crops. Besides, the peasants were forced to sell the produce at prices fixed by the Europeans.

Champaran peasant sufferings were brought to the notice first to the Bihar Provincial Congress Committee in 1914. It was in 1916 that the Indian National Congress, in its Lucknow session, discussed the peasant situation of Champaran. But, no action was taken.

Gandhi, who had returned from South Africa, wanted to test his non-cooperation movement and satyagraha techniques in India. Champaran seemed to be a suitable place for making such an experiment. A local leader, Ram Kumar Shukla persuaded Gandhi to come to Champaran. Joined by prominent local leaders – Rajendra Prasad, Mazhar- ul-Haq, Mahadev Desai, Narhari Parekh, and J.B. Kripalani, Gandhi reached Champaran in 1917. Gandhiji was very much disturbed by the abject poverty of the peasants. He expressed his feelings in the following words: "The peasants in Champaran are leading their lives like animals, suffering from all kinds of miseries."

The authorities ordered him to leave the area at once. The district officials threatened him with legal actions but Gandhi defied government orders and was willing to face trial and jail. Finally, the authorities retreated and permitted Gandhi to make an enquiry. Now, the Government appointed a committee to go into the matter and nominated Gandhi as a member.

Gandhi was able to convince the authorities that the *tinkathia* system should be abolished and that the peasants should be compensated for the illegal dues extracted from them. As a compromise with the planters, he agreed that only 25 per cent of the money taken should be compensated. Within a decade, the planters left the area. The Champaran Agrarian Act of 1918 was passed which accepted the demands of the peasants.

In this way, Gandhi had won the first battle of Civil Disobedience. One very important feature of the Champaran movement was that it was led by intelligentsia like Rajendra Prasad, Brijkishore Prasad, and Muzharul Haq. This provided strength and direction to the movement.

The Ahmedabad Mill Strike, 1918

Gandhi once again used satyagraha as a tool for fighting against injustice in the Ahmadabad Mill Workers Strike in 1918. He intervened in a dispute between mill owners of Ahmadabad and the workers over the issue of discontinuation of the plague bonus. Gandhi asked the workers to go on a strike and demand a 35 per cent increase in wages. The employers were willing to concede a 20 per cent bonus only.

Gandhi advised the workers to remain non-violent while on strike. After two weeks, when the strikers were losing the zeal, Gandhi warned the authorities that he would not touch any food till a settlement was reached. So after 21 days of strike, the mill owners finally agreed to give the workers a 35 per cent increase in wages. Ambalal Sarabhai and his sister, Anasuya Behn, were the main lieutenants of Gandhi in this struggle.

The Kheda Satyagraha, 1918

Immediately after the Ahmedabad Mill Workers Strike, Gandhi plunged into a satyagraha campaign in the Kheda district of Gujarat.

A famine had struck the Kheda district and a large part of Gujarat. However, the British government instead of providing relief from the taxes to the farmers not only insisted on full payment of taxes, but also increased the tax amount that was declared to take effect in that year. Gandhi organised villagers and volunteers from the region and began the campaign against the Bombay government. Using non-cooperation as a technique, Gandhi initiated a signature campaign where peasants pledged non-payment of revenue even under the threat of confiscation of land. A social boycott of *Mamlatdars* and *Talatdars* (revenue officials) accompanied the agitation. For five months, the administration refused, but finally in the end of May 1918, the Government gave way on important provisions and relaxed the conditions of payment of revenue tax until the famine ended.

Vallabhbhai Patel represented the farmers in negotiations with the British, who then suspended revenue collection and released all the prisoners. In the Kheda campaign, Gandhi provided the spiritual leadership and guidance. Organising other grassroot works were carried largely by the local leaders, mainly Sardar Vallabhbhai Patel, Narhari Parikh, Mohanlal Pandya, and Ravi Shankar Vyas. Later, these leaders became devoted Gandhians.

Effects of the Champaran, Ahmedabad, and Kheda Non-Cooperation Movement

- Gandhi demonstrated to the people the efficacy of his technique of satyagraha.
- He found his feet among the masses and came to have a surer understanding of the strengths and weaknesses of the masses.
- He acquired the respect and commitment of many, especially the youth.

The Landmark Year 1919

The year 1919 is considered as a landmark year in the history of British India for three outstanding events: the Government of India Act or the Montague-Chelmsford Reforms, the Rowlatt Act, and the Jallianwalla Bagh Massacre. These events unfolded into a biggest ever mass movement that commenced the second phase of the national movement under the leadership of Gandhi.

The Government of India Act, 1919 or Montford Reforms

The British government during the war had promised for responsible government, i.e., giving adequate political powers and responsibilities to the Indians. In 1917, Montague, the Secretary of State for India, declared in British Parliament about providing a responsible government in India. He was known to have put a statement in the British Cabinet which asked for "gradual development of free institutions in India with a view to ultimate self-government". Later, the words "ultimate self-

Edwin Montagu, the Secretary of State for India (1917–1922) — Wikimedia Commons

government" was removed from his statement and came out with what is now known as the 'Montagu Declaration'.

The Montagu declaration reads as: "Increasing association of Indians in every branch of the administration and the gradual development of self-governing institutions with a view to the progressive realisation of responsible government in India as an integral part of the British Empire". Although the key phrase "ultimate self-government" was removed, still another key phrase "responsible government" was added in this statement. It gave the inference for the first time that rulers are answerable to the public.

The declaration made the Moderates happy and they said "It is Magna Carta of India". Montague discussed his scheme of reforms with the Viceroy, Lord Chelmsford. These reforms in the form of a report were published in 1918. Based on this report, Government of India Act of 1919 was passed. The Government of India Act 1919 had a separate Preamble. This Preamble declared that the objective of the British Government is the gradual introduction of responsible government in India. Thus, this Act initiated the responsible governance in India and it covered a period of 10 years from 1919 to 1929.

One of the chief features of this Act was the introduction of the system of Dyarchy. Dyarchy means a dual set of governments – one is accountable, another is not accountable. The Act of 1919 made a provision for the classification of the central and provincial subjects. The provincial subjects were divided into two groups: One was reserved and another was transferred.

The reserved subjects were kept with the Governor and transferred subjects were given to the Indian ministers. Key subjects like the finance, law and order, police, and justice were called as reserved subjects which were brought under the direct control of the Governor of the province or with the central legislature. On the other hand, subjects like local self-government, education, and public health (known as transferred subjects) were put under the control of ministers who were responsible to the legislature.

Following is the detailed description of the Government of India Act, 1919:

Provincial Government and Dyarchy

Executive

(i) Dyarchy, i.e., rule of two—executive councillors and popular ministers—was introduced. The Governor was to be the executive head in the province.

(ii) Subjects were divided into two lists: "reserved" which included subjects such as law and order, finance, land revenue, irrigation, etc., and "transferred" subjects such as education, health, local government, industry, agriculture, excise, etc. The "reserved" subjects were to be administered by the Governor through his executive council of bureaucrats, and the "transferred" subjects were to be administered by ministers nominated from among the elected members of the legislative council.

(iii) The ministers were to be responsible to the legislature and had to resign if a no-confidence motion was passed against them by the legislature, while the executive councillors were not to be responsible to the legislature.

(iv) In case of failure of constitutional machinery in the province, the Governor could take over the administration of "transferred" subjects also.

(v) The Secretary of State and the Governor-General could interfere in respect of "reserved" subjects while in respect of the "transferred" subjects, the scope for their interference was restricted.

Legislature

(i) Provincial Legislative Councils were further expanded—70% of the members were to be elected.

(ii) The system of communal and class electorates was further consolidated.

(iii) Women were also given the right to vote.

(iv) The Legislative Councils could initiate legislation but the Governor's assent was required. The Governor could veto bills and issue ordinances.

(v) The Legislative Councils could reject the budget but the Governor could restore it, if necessary.

(vi) The legislators enjoyed freedom of speech.

Central Government and Dyarchy

Executive

(i) The Governor-General was to be the chief executive authority.

(ii) There were to be two lists for administration—central and provincial.

(iii) In the Viceroy's executive council of 8, three were to be Indians.

(iv) The Governor-General retained full control over the "reserved" subjects in the provinces.

(v) The Governor-General could restore cuts in grants, certify bills rejected by the Central Legislature, and issue ordinances.

Legislature

(i) A bicameral arrangement was introduced. The Lower House or Central Legislative Assembly would consist of 144 members (41 nominated and 103 elected—52 General, 30 Muslims, 2 Sikhs, and 20 Special) and the Upper House or Council of State would have 60 members (26 nominated and 34 elected—20 General, 10 Muslims, 3 Europeans, and 1 Sikh).

(ii) The Council of State had tenure of 5 years and had only male members, while the Central Legislative Assembly had tenure of 3 years.

(iii) The legislators could ask questions and supplementaries, pass adjournment motions, and vote a part of the budget, but 75% of the budget was still not votable.

(iv) Some Indians found their way into important committees including finance.

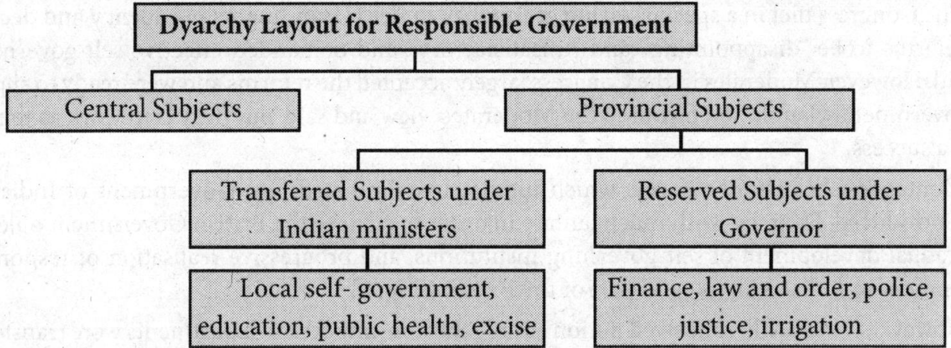

Other Salient Features of Government of India Act, 1919:

- This Act provided for the first time, the establishment of a Public Service Commission in India.
- The Act also provided that after 10 years, a statutory commission would be set up to study the working of the government. This resulted in the Simon Commission of 1927.
- It also created an office of the High Commissioner for India in London.

Merits of this Act

- Dyarchy introduced the concept of responsible government.
- It introduced the concept of a federal structure with a unitary bias.
- There was increased participation of Indians in the administration. They held some portfolios like labour, health, etc.
- For the first time, elections were known to the people and it created a political consciousness among the people.
- Some Indian women also had the right to vote for the first time.

Limitations of Montford Reforms of 1919

One of the major drawbacks of this reform was that the transferred subjects were to be handled by Indian ministers who were given responsibility without powers. Therefore, Government of India Act of 1919 failed to provide responsible government and adequate powers to Indians. The provincial ministers had no control over finances and over the bureaucrats, leading to constant friction between the two. Ministers were often not consulted on important matters too; in fact, they could be overruled by the Governor on any matter that the latter considered special.

Other limitations :

- This Act extended consolidated the communal representation.
- Franchise was very limited. It did not extend to the common man.
- The Governor-General and the Governors had a lot of power to undermine the legislatures at the centre and the provinces respectively.
- Allocation of the seats for the central legislature was not based on population but the 'importance' of the province in the eyes of the British, for instance, Punjab's military importance and Bombay's commercial importance.

The Congress met in a special session at Bombay under Hasan Imam's presidency and declared the reforms to be "disappointing" and "unsatisfactory" and demanded effective self-government instead. However, Moderates in the Congress largely accepted the reforms and were ready to support the government. Gandhi too favoured the Moderates' view and said 'our duty is to work as to make them a success'.

Montague-Chelmsford reforms which ultimately culminated into Government of India Act, 1919 introduced 'Dyarchy' with much fanfare in order to achieve the British Government objective of 'Gradual development of self-governing institutions, and progressive realisation of responsible government in India as an integral part of the British Empire'.

However, it was an ill-conceived notion as only the non-important departments were transferred to the ministers chosen by the masses. Even then, the Viceroy and provincial Governor had a veto on everything. Even the bills rejected by the majority could be passed with 'certificate' from the Viceroy/Governor.

Hence, though the concept of dyarchy was to de-centralise and transfer the government duties, it actually further eroded the responsibility of the government by not providing the autonomy (financial and administrative) to the ministers concerned.

Rowlatt Act, 1919

In the same year, i.e., 1919, the Governor-General Lord Chelmsford passed a bill for curbing the revolutionary activities or 'crimes' across the country. The Anarchical and Revolutionary Crimes Act commonly known as Rowlatt Act was passed on March 21, 1919. The Act was intended to enforce Martial law curtailing the freedom of peaceful assembly and restricting the Press.

Sir Sydney Rowlatt — Wikimedia Commons

On December 1917, the Governor-General appointed a committee of five members to find out the extent of the criminal conspiracies connected with revolutionary activities and to suggest new laws for their suppression. A British judge, Sir Sidney Rowlatt was the President. Based on the committee's recommendation, bills were framed and placed before the Governor-General. However, these bills contained controversial provisions like denying protection of law to the Indians. Still in the teeth of the opposition of all elected Indian members, the Anarchical and Revolutionary Crimes Act or Rowlatt Act, 1919 was passed in the imperial Legislative Council. All non-official Indian members of the council (i.e., those who were not officials in the colonial government) voted against the Acts.

This Act authorised the Government to imprison any person without trial and conviction in a court of law, thus enabling the Government to suspend the right of *habeas corpus* which had been the foundation of civil liberties in Britain. The Act also included provisions like restriction on movement of individuals, security for good conduct, and so on.

Therefore, on one side, the Government passed Montague-Chelmsford Reforms and on the other side, the Rowlatt Act seemed to play the part of the 'Carrot and Stick policy' of the colonial British.

Rowlatt Satyagraha

The Act came like a sudden blow to the people of India who had been promised the extension of democracy. A widespread public agitation began to take place across the country. Gandhi, in vain, appealed to the Viceroy to repeal the bill. When his appeal was ignored, he took the lead and started satyagraha. A campaign was organised and Gandhi made an all India appeal to observe hartal for a day. Gandhi was forcibly removed from the train and arrested. On the news of Gandhiji arrest, people committed acts of violence in Ahmadabad. Gandhi suspended the satyagraha on 18th April, 1919 as he felt that it was a 'Himalayan miscalculation' to call upon people to launch satyagraha without preparing them.

Jallianwala Bagh Massacre or Amritsar Massacre – April 13, 1919

Events in Punjab took a different turn in the month of April 1919. Lt. Governor, Sir Michael O' Dwyer terrorised Punjab by following ruthless suppression. He deported two prominent local leaders, Dr. Satyapal and Dr. Kitchlew. But things became worse with the arrival of Brigadier General Dyer who immediately established martial law that banned people's gathering.

Brigadier General Dyer
— Wikimedia Commons

On Sunday, 13 April 1919, the day of Baisakhi, the main Sikh festival, many villagers had gathered in the Jallianwala Bagh (garden) near the Harmandir Sahib in Amritsar. On hearing that a meeting had assembled at Jallianwala Bagh, Dyer went with fifty Gurkha and Baluchi riflemen, and without warning the crowd to disperse, blocked the main exits and ordered them to shoot at the crowd. Dyer continued the firing for about ten minutes, until the ammunition supply was almost exhausted. The casualty number estimated by the Indian National Congress was more than 1,500, with approximately 1,000 dead. Many people died in stampedes at the narrow gates or by jumping into the solitary well on the compound to escape the shooting. A plaque placed at the site after independence states that 120 bodies were removed from the well. The wounded could not be moved from where they had fallen, as a curfew was declared, and many more died during the night.

Jallianwalla Bagh memorial
Amritsar
— Wikimedia Commons

Reaction to the Jallianwalla Massacre

The entire nation was stunned. Rabindranath Tagore was so shocked that he renounced his Knighthood which had been conferred upon him by the government. Gandhi returned the *Kaiser-i-Hind* Gold medal given to him for his work during the Boer war. He was overwhelmed by the total atmosphere of violence and withdrew the movement on April 18, 1919 calling it a 'Himalayan Blunder'.

Sir Michael Francis O'Dwyer, the Lieutenant Governor of the Punjab in India from 1912 to 1919 endorsed General Reginald Dyer's action regarding the Jallianwala Bagh massacre and termed it a 'correct action'.

On 13 March, 1940, at the Caxton Hall in London, Udham Singh, an Indian independence activist who had witnessed the events in Amritsar and was himself wounded, shot and killed Michael O'Dwyer, the British Lieutenant-Governor of Punjab at the time of the massacre, who had approved Dyer's action and was believed to be the main planner. Dyer himself had died in 1927.

Hunter Committee Report

The Amritsar massacre was followed by martial law in Punjab that included public floggings and grave humiliations. The government of India appointed the Hunter Committee for the investigation of the Jallianwala incident. This committee had 7 members, viz. 4 British and 3 Indians.

Before the committee could publish its own report, the Congress put forward its own view. This view criticised Dyer's act as inhuman and also said that there was no justification in the introduction of the martial law in Punjab. But the Hunter Report, as expected, saw the things differently. Although it condemned most of the decisions taken by General Dyer, it agreed with the imposition of the martial law in Punjab. It also criticised the method of satyagraha adopted by Gandhi and held Gandhi partially responsible for the "deteriorated" law and order situation. The result was that Dyer was sent to England and was relieved of his command. But the rest of the things were as per the official opinion of the Government. This miffed Gandhi and he returned the Kaisar-I-Hind Gold medal. He said that the time has come when such blatant action of inhumanity could not be 'remedied' through the conventional political channels.

Previous Years' Questions

1. **"Montague-Chelmsford reform proposals introduced `dyarchy', but blurred the lines of responsibility." (2014)**
2. **"This retention of Rowlatt legislation in the teeth of universal opposition repeal is an affront to the nation. Its repeal is necessary to appraise national honour." (2015)**
3. **Discuss how the Satyagrahas of Gandhi removed the spell of fear among Indians and thus knocked off an important pillar of imperialism. (2017)**

16

CHAPTER

Non-Cooperation Movement and The Swarajists' Phase (1920–1930)

Introduction

The Jallianwala Bagh Massacre at Amritsar in Punjab became a turning point in the history of modern India as it made the national movement a mass movement under the leadership of Gandhi. Gandhi was horrified. He lost all faith in the goodness of the British government and declared that it would be a 'sin' to cooperate with the 'satanic' government. Protests against the British government spread all across the country. It is at this juncture Gandhi began the biggest mass movement in the country – the Non-Cooperation Movement.

Causes for the Start of the Non-Cooperation Movement

1. **Disillusion at the end of the war :** With the outbreak of the World War I, India enthusiastically participated in the War as a part of the British Empire. The British Government utilised India's wealth, money, and manpower for its own interests. About 1.25 million Indian soldiers fought on behalf of the British in different war fronts and many of them sacrificed their lives. They also donated about six crores and 21 lac pounds as war subscription. Indians expected that in return for their valuable service, the British Government would grant autonomy to them at the end of the War. But they were greatly disillusioned. This dissatisfaction was one of the causes of the non-cooperation movement by Gandhi.

2. **Home Rule movement :** Indians were disappointed to see the British government adopting repressive measures. In response to it, Tilak and Besant started the Home Rule movement. The Lucknow Pact had brought the Congress and the Muslim League closer together. The unity of the Extremists and Moderates in 1916 provided an environment of conducive politics. Under such circumstances, the Home Rule movement was launched, which was accepted by all political parties and political leaders. The Home Rule movement included the ideologies and actions of both Moderates and Extremists. It significantly contributed towards strengthening the demands for self-government and making the masses aware in political developments. Thus, Home Rule Movement prepared the ground for the non-cooperation movement.

3. **Economic distress caused by the World War I :** The war brought about great economic distress to the Indians. At the end of the war, the economic conditions took a turn for the worse. Prices shot up. Price of cloths, sugar, and other essential commodities began to soar. Foreign goods

began to be imported. Both the peasants and the workers suffered due to the impact of the war. However, the price of agricultural products did not increase. The workers being unemployed, had to live in miserable economic conditions.

4. **Montague-Chelmsford Act :** The Montford Act of 1919 could not satisfy the Congress. The actual scheme of reforms fell far short of the nationalists' demands. The proposed Dyarchy initially appealed to the Moderates but soon its drawbacks began to appear. The promise of self-government again remained unfulfilled.

5. **Rowlatt Act and Jallianwala Tragedy :** The passing of the Rowlatt Act and the Jallianwala Bagh tragedy gave a new turn to Indian politics. Gandhi became firm in the policy of non-cooperation. The Rowlatt Act was one of the greatest repressive measures from the British government. The Act culminated into the Jallianwala Bagh tragedy that shocked the nation. Gandhi and eminent national leaders, in protest, returned their honorary awards and medals bestowed on them by the British government. The entire nation rose in indignation against the government, and like a wild fire, there was a wave of agitation all over the country.

6. **Discontentment with the British rule :** The Montford Reforms and Jallianwala tragedy was like a 'stick and carrot policy' adopted by the British government. The appointment of the Hunter Commission for the investigation of the Jallianwala incident proved to be an eyewash. People became increasingly critical of the British rule. The economic situation of the country in the post World War I years had alarmingly worsened with a rise in prices of commodities, decrease in production of Indian industries, and increase in burden of taxes and rents. Politically, the scheme of Dyarchy failed to satisfy the rising demand of the Indians for self-government. Nationwide disillusionment with the British rule prevailed. Government policies and reforms exposed the brutal and uncivilised face of the foreign rule.

7. **The Khilafat movement :** Indian Muslims leaders too were disillusioned with the British rule. Many joined the Khilafat movement – a pan-Islamic, anti-British protest to protect Turkey from the control of allied forces in the aftermath of the First World War. Below is the detail description of the Khilafat movement.

The Khilafat Movement and Inclusion of Indian Muslims in Mass Agitation

During the First World War, Ottoman Empire, which was a German ally, had fought against the British. Turkey, which was a part of the Ottoman Empire, housed the seat of the Caliph – the revered head of the Muslims. Ottoman Empire was defeated in the war and was dismembered by the allied forces. When the War ended, the British took a stern attitude towards Turkey. This incensed Muslims all over the world. In order to save the revered office of Caliph from the western powers, Khilafat Movement began in all Islamic countries. Muslims in India too joined this pan-Islamic movement. The Khilafat movement was launched by Muslims in India to persuade the British government not to abolish the caliphate.

The general impression among the Muslims of India was that the western powers were waging a war against Islam throughout the world in order to rob it of all its power and influence. The Muslims of India launched the Tehrik-e-Khilafat.

The objectives were as follows :

1. To maintain the Turkish caliphate
2. To protect the holy places of the Muslims
3. To maintain the unity of the Ottoman Empire

There was absolute unanimity among the Indian Muslims. Though separated from Turkey by thousands of miles, they were determined to fight Turkey's battle from India.

Although the Khilafat issue was not directly linked to Indian politics, it provided the immediate background to the national movement and gave an added advantage of cementing Hindu-Muslim unity against the British. The Khilafat issue also paved the way for the emergence of radical nationalists among the younger generation of Muslims who were becoming increasingly critical of the British rule.

In early 1919, a Khilafat Committee was formed under the leadership of the Ali brothers—Shaukat Ali and Muhammad Ali—to force the British Government to change its attitude to Turkey.

The Ali Brothers — Wikimedia Commons

At the All-India Khilafat Conference, held in Delhi in November 1919, a call was made for boycott of British goods. The Khilafat leaders also clearly spelt out that unless peace terms after the War were favourable to Turkey, they would stop all cooperation with the Government. Khilafat movement received enormous support from Gandhi as he looked upon this as 'an opportunity of uniting Hindus and Mohammendans as would not arise in a hundred years'.

Although the Khilafat issue had the least concern with Indian politics, still Gandhi chose this issue for its first mass agitation against the British. So far, Muslims were not a part of any political agitation. They hadn't taken part in the Rowlatt Satyagraha. Therefore, to start a pan-India mass movement, the inclusion of Muslims was necessary.

Majority of the Muslim leaders were anti-Congress. But in Gandhi, they found an approachable leadership which was appealing to any section of the society. Thus, Khilafat leaders comfortably accepted his advice and his leadership.

Despite the Khilafat issue being religious in nature, Gandhi found in it an issue which could unite the Indian Muslim community which was divided into lines of regional, linguistic, class, and sectarian. This issue hence, brought the Muslim masses into the mainstream politics for the first time. It also witnessed the Hindu-Muslim unity in boycotting the public institutions and following other organisations.

The younger generation of Indian Muslim nationalist leaders like Maulana Azad, Mukhtar Ahmed Ansari, Hakim Ajmal Khan, Abbas Tyabji, Maulana Muhammad Ali, and Maulana Shaukat Ali supported Gandhi. The Muslim League also decided to give full support to the Congress and its agitation on political questions.

Congress and Khilafat Issue

The support of the Congress was essential for the Khilafat movement to succeed. However, Congress was not united in giving support to the issue of Khilafat. Tilak was opposed to having an alliance with Khilafat leaders and he was also sceptical of satyagraha as an instrument of politics.

There was opposition to some of the other provisions of Gandhi's non-cooperation program such as boycott of councils. Later, however, Gandhi was able to convince the Congress for his programme of political actions. The Congress felt inclined to support a non-cooperation programme on the Khilafat issue, since it was considered as a golden opportunity of Hindu-Muslim unity and to bring Muslim masses into the national movement. The Congress was losing faith in the constitutional struggle, especially after the Punjab incidents and the blatantly partisan Hunter Commission Report. Hence, Gandhi's programme of non-cooperation was unanimously approved by the Congress.

On March 10, 1920, Gandhi issued a manifesto. This manifesto was the first of its kind that included the idea of non-violent non-cooperation. Initially, it included only the issue of Khilafat. Thus, Gandhi's non-cooperation was the direct outcome of the Khilafat movement.

The Non-Cooperation Movement — Agenda and Programmes

By 'Non-Cooperation Movement', Gandhi meant a peaceful rebellion. In September 1920, the old veteran leaders of the Congress like Annie Besant, Motilal Nehru, and C. R. Das opposed the idea of Gandhi. However, he appealed to the Congress to adopt his policy of 'progressive, non-violent, non-cooperation' which the Congress could not deny.

On August 1, 1920, non-cooperation movement was launched. It was a coincidence that Bal Gangadhar Tilak passed away on the same day. The void was filled up by the leadership of Gandhi. Gandhi inaugurated the non-cooperation movement by returning his Kaiser-I-Hind gold medal, Zulu War medal, and Boer War medal with a letter to Lord Chelmsford, the Viceroy. The letter briefly stated his reasons for returning the medals and starting the non-cooperation movement.

On 4th September 1920, at a special session at Calcutta which was presided over by Lala Lajpat Rai, Gandhi said that if the non-cooperation movement gets successful, 'Swaraj could be attained in one year'.

In December 1920, the Congress met in the Nagpur Session. Chittaranjan Das moved the main resolution of non-cooperation.

A seven point program was approved which included:

1. Surrender of honorary posts and titles. The second phase could include mass civil disobedience, including resignation from government service, and non-payment of taxes.
2. Refusal to attend any government functions
3. Boycott of government schools, colleges, courts, and legislative councils
4. Boycott of foreign cloth and use of khadi. Also, practice of hand-spinning to be done
5. The promotion and maintenance of Hindu-Muslim unity
6. Refusal of civilian and military personnel to serve in Mesopotamia
7. Strict policy of non-violence to be adopted

Broadly speaking, non-cooperation had three objectives: settlement of the Khilafat issue, atonement for atrocities in Amritsar, and establishment of Swaraj or self-government.

The idea was to bring it close to the masses by using the vernacular languages and the numbers of delegates were fixed in proportion to the population. The above changes in the Nagpur session made the Congress party a people's party.

At this stage, some leaders like Mohammad Ali Jinnah, Annie Besant, G.S. Kharpade, and B.C. Pal left the Congress as they believed in a constitutional and lawful struggle. Jinnah was not convinced with the objectives of the movement and left the Congress after his association of 15 years with the party. Others like Surendranath Banerjee founded the Indian National Liberal Federation and played a minor role in national politics henceforward.

The Working of the Non-Cooperation Movement (1921–1922)

The non-cooperation movement was the first nationwide mass movement. The year 1921–22 witnessed an unprecedented mass movement in the nation's history, when there was a widespread unrest among all sections of the society. Boycott, mammoth meetings, **Khadi** making, picketing, and entering jails were the highlights of the movement.

Gandhi, accompanied by the Ali brothers, undertook a nationwide tour. In July 1921, the Ali brothers gave a call to the Muslims to resign from the Army as that was unreligious. The Ali brothers were arrested for this in September. Gandhi echoed their call and asked local Congress committees to pass similar resolutions to that effect.

Students' processions and boycott of schools and colleges became the order of the day. About 90,000 students left government schools and colleges and joined around 800 national schools and colleges which cropped up during this time. These educational institutions were organised under the leadership of Acharya Narendra Dev, C.R. Das, Lala Lajpat Rai, Zakir Hussain, and Subhash Bose (who became the principal of National College at Calcutta) and included Jamia Millia at Aligarh, Kashi Vidyapeeth, Gujarat Vidyapeeth, and Bihar Vidyapeeth. The leaders of the Indian movement started teaching in Indian educational institutions.

The boycott of the legal profession was heralded by the outstanding self-sacrifice of Pandit Motilal Nehru and C.R. Das who earlier enjoyed princely income. Their example was followed by a large number of lawyers. National leaders like C. Rajagopalachari, Rajendra Prasad, Sardar Patel,

C. R. Das, Motilal Nehru, M.R Jayakar, Saifuddin Kitchlew, Vallabhai Patel, T. Prakasam, and Asaf Ali left their legal practice and jumped into the full-fledged politics of the Congress. Some members of the Viceroy Executive Council followed suit. Sir Sankaran Nair resigned from the Viceroy's Council.

However, the objective of boycott of titles and honour, as well as government offices, was not fully achieved. Only a few resigned from their government jobs, including Subhash Chandra Bose, who resigned from the Indian Civil Service.

The Swadeshi concept became a household word. Khadi and Charkha became the symbol of the national movement. C.R. Das organised a large number of volunteers to sell *Khadi* in Calcutta.

In order to finance the non-cooperation movement, Tilak Memorial Swaraj Fund was started, to which money poured and within six months, nearly a crore of rupees was subscribed.

Heaps of foreign cloths were burnt publicly and their imports fell by half. Bonfire of foreign cloths became a common sight across the country. One such bonfire was lit on the 31th July 1921, in Bombay on the grounds of the Elphinstone Mills. Picketing of shops selling foreign liquor and of toddy shops was undertaken at many places.

A Congress Working Committee (CWC) of 15 members was set up to lead the Congress party. A 4 *anna* membership fee was prescribed so that more and more poor people could join the Congress. A hierarchy of village, taluka, and district level committees were formed so that Congress reached the grassroots. Provincial Congress Committees were reorganised on linguistic basis.

Congress volunteers created a parallel unofficial police force called Volunteer Corps.

All the Congress candidates withdrew from contesting elections for the councils. Their seats were filled up by non-congressmen.

People in various parts of the country joined the 'no-tax to Government' movement. In Bengal, Someshwar Prasad Chaudhary led the peasants in an anti-indigo cultivation. The *Tana-Bhagat* sect of Bihar boycotted the liquor. In Punjab, the Akali Movement which was originally for the reforms of Gurudwaras, got linked with the non-cooperation movement. In Andhra Pradesh, Alluri Sitaram Raju organised the tribals and linked with the Non-cooperation movement. In Midnapore of Bengal, a movement was led by Birendranath Sasmal against the Union Board of Taxes.

In Assam, strikes in tea plantations, steamer services, and Assam-Bengal Railways had been organised. J.M. Sengupta was a prominent leader in these strikes. The spirit of defiance and unrest gave rise to many local struggles such as Awadh Kisan Movement (UP), Eka Movement (UP), Mappila Revolt (Malabar), and the Sikh agitation for the removal of *Mahants* in Punjab.

Students started to boycott the Government or Government-aided institutions. The All-India College Students Conference held at Nagpur on 25th December, 1920 under the chairmanship of Lala Lajpat Rai accepted the proposal of boycott with great enthusiasm.

The most spectacular achievement of the boycott program was seen during the visit of the Prince of Wales to India on 17th November, 1921. He was greeted by the Indians with black flags. A countrywide *Hartal* or strike was observed, and more than 60,000 people were arrested.

Participation of the Muslims in the movement and the maintenance of communal harmony was also a great achievement of this movement. Muslim participation gave the movement a mass character.

Indian mill owners earned a good profit due to the programme of boycott. The import of sugar from England decreased considerably. The import of British cotton goods decreased from Rs. 6.7 crores to Rs. 2.8 crores within a period of six months. Likewise, the import of iron decreased to 50%.

Government Response

The Government denied the right of speech by proclaiming the Prevention of Seditious Meetings Act in the various parts of India. The Government arrested a large number of people all over the country. It declared the activities of Congress and the Khilafat volunteers illegal. It came down heavily on the protestors. Volunteer corps was declared illegal, public meetings were banned, the press was gagged, and most of the leaders barring Gandhi were arrested. Within a few days, prisons were filled with political prisoners. Camp prisons were then opened, but they too were filled in no time. Nearly 40 thousand Congress workers were in jail in December 1921, when the Annual Congress Session was held in Ahmedabad.

Talks between Gandhi and Reading, the Viceroy, broke down in May 1921 as the Government wanted Gandhi to urge the Ali brothers not to make anti-British speeches. In February 1922, Gandhi wrote to the Viceroy stating that, 'This lawless repression has made immediate adoption of Mass Civil Disobedience, unless the Viceroy declared a policy of non-interference with all non-violent activities for the redress of the Khilafat or the Punjab wrongs or for Swaraj'.

Finding no response from the Viceroy, on February 1, 1922, Gandhi threatened to launch civil disobedience from Bardoli in Gujarat if political prisoners were not released, and press controls were not removed. The whole of India watched with suspense.

Suspension of the Khilafat and Non-Cooperation Movements

The Chauri Chaura Incident and Suspension of the Movement, 1922

The Congress had asked all its workers or *Satyagrahis* to take a pledge to remain non-violent in word and deed. When the movement was at its height, violence occurred at Chauri Chaura, a small village in the Gorakhpur district of Uttar Pradesh on 5 February, 1922. On that day, a procession of 3,000 protesters had gathered to picket the liquor shop at the local market in Chauri Chaura. Armed policemen were dispatched to control the situation, while the crowd marched towards the market and started shouting anti-government slogans. With the situation getting out of control, the sub inspector ordered the police to open fire on the advancing crowd, killing three and wounding several others. In retaliation, the angry mob took to violence and burnt the police station causing the death of 22 policemen. In response to the police killings, the British authorities declared martial law in and around Chauri Chaura.

Shocked at the outrage, Gandhi went on a five-day fast. Gandhi felt that he had acted too hastily in encouraging people to go anti-British without adequately training the people to exercise restraint. He was disappointed that the movement had lost its non-violent nature. He decided to halt the movement, reasoning that the Indian people were ill-prepared and not yet ready to do what was needed from the movement. According to Gandhi, people had not learnt or fully understood the method of non-violence. Incidents like Chauri Chaura could lead to excitement and fervour, turning the movement generally violent. A violent movement could be easily suppressed by the colonial regime that could use the incidents of violence as an excuse to use the armed might of the state against the protestors.

On February 12, 1922, the Indian National Congress on the request of Gandhi, suspended the non-cooperation movement. It resolved to stop all activity that led to the breaking of law and instead to get down to constructive work, which was to include popularisation of khadi, national schools, and campaigning for Hindu-Muslim unity and against untouchability.

Many did not like the suspension of the movement. Nationalist leaders including C.R. Das, Motilal Nehru, Subhash Bose, and Jawaharlal Nehru expressed their bewilderment at Gandhi's decision to withdraw the movement. Indian communist leader M.N. Roy called for a general strike of Indian workers and termed the suspension as 'legalised murder'.

Contemporary historians and critics suggest that the movement was successful enough to break the back of British rule, and possibly potent enough in achieving the desire goal of Swaraj or self-rule. But many historians and Indian leaders of the time also defended Gandhi's judgment. If he had not stopped the movement, India could have descended into a chaotic rebellion which would have alienated common Indians and impressed only the violent revolutionaries.

Also, the situation in the country was unfavourable to the resort of civil disobedience. The country was heading towards violence and indiscipline in the Congress. Hence, Gandhi cannot be accused of sacrificing the interests of the country for his own principles. The Chauri Chaura incident was "really an index finger". The violence at Chauri Chaura was not committed by unknown people but by Congressmen. This weighed heavily on Gandhi. He had also been receiving news of indiscipline in the Congress ranks for quite some time. Thus, under these circumstances, Gandhi was unable to direct the organisation. Even Lajpat Rai, Motilal Nehru, and Jawaharlal Nehru who were critics of Gandhi's decision, later on admitted the wisdom of his decision of suspending the civil disobedience.

In March 1922, Gandhi was arrested and sentenced to six years in jail. He made the occasion memorable by a court speech "I am here, therefore, to invite and submit cheerfully to the highest penalty that can be inflicted upon me for what in law is deliberate crime, and what appears to me to be the highest duty of a citizen." Later, Gandhi was released in February 1924, on grounds of his ill health.

Phases of the Non-Cooperation Movement

The non-cooperation movement can be divided into four distinct phases from its beginning in January 1920 till its abrupt end in February 1922.

First Phase : In the first phase of the movement (January–March 1920), thousands of students left government schools and colleges. Around 800 national schools and colleges were opened to accommodate the students. The academic boycott was most successful in Bengal. In Punjab, it was headed by Lala Lajpat Rai. Many renowned and established lawyers like Motilal Nehru, C.R.

Das, Jawaharlal Nehru, C. Raja Gopalachari, Vallabhbhai Patel, Saifuddin Kitchlew, Asaf Ali, Rajendra Prasad, and T. Prakasam gave up their practice. Students, intellectuals, and other influential heads of the society were urged to take up the Charka (Spinning Wheel) program to promote nationalist products.

Second Phase : During the second phase (April–July 1921), subscriptions were collected for the "Tilak Swaraj Fund" in order to finance the movement with a target of one Crore rupees. The common public was encouraged to become members of the Congress. The Fund was oversubscribed and one crore rupees collected, but the target of membership reached only 50 lakhs. The Charka (Spinning Wheel) was distributed among the public. The Swadeshi concept became a household word. Khadi and Charka became a symbol of freedom.

Third phase : In the third phase (July–November 1921), bonfire of foreign cloths became common across the country. Foreign clothes were burnt publicly, reducing their imports by half. People resorted to picketing shops selling foreign liquors and toddy shops. The All-India Khilafat conference was held at Karachi on 8 July, 1921, where leaders called upon Muslim soldiers in the British Indian army to quit their jobs. Gandhi called for volunteers to fill the jail. The Khilafat Conference in Malabar incited so much communal feelings among the Muslim peasants (The Moplahs) that it took an anti-Hindu turn in July 1921. This uprising of the Muslims peasants against the Hindu Landlords came to be known as the Moplah Rebellion. The tour of the Duke of Connaught to India was boycotted. In a similar way, in November 1921, mass demonstrations were held against the Prince of Wales during his tour of India. The British government resorted to strong measures of repression. Many leaders were arrested. The Congress and the Khilafat Committees were proclaimed illegal.

Fourth Phase : The fourth phase and final phase (November 1921–February 1922) of the movement saw citizens choosing not to pay taxes in several regions. In December 1921, the Congress in its annual session at Ahmedabad affirmed its resolve to intensify the movement. On 1 February, 1922, in a letter to the Governor-General, Gandhi spoke of non-payment of taxes. Gandhi threatened to launch the civil disobedience from Bardoli, Gujarat, if the Government didn't release political prisoners and lift the press control imposed by the Rowlatt Act.

Barely a few days after this correspondence, the Chauri Chaura incident took place on 5 February 1922, which led to the suspension of the movement abruptly.

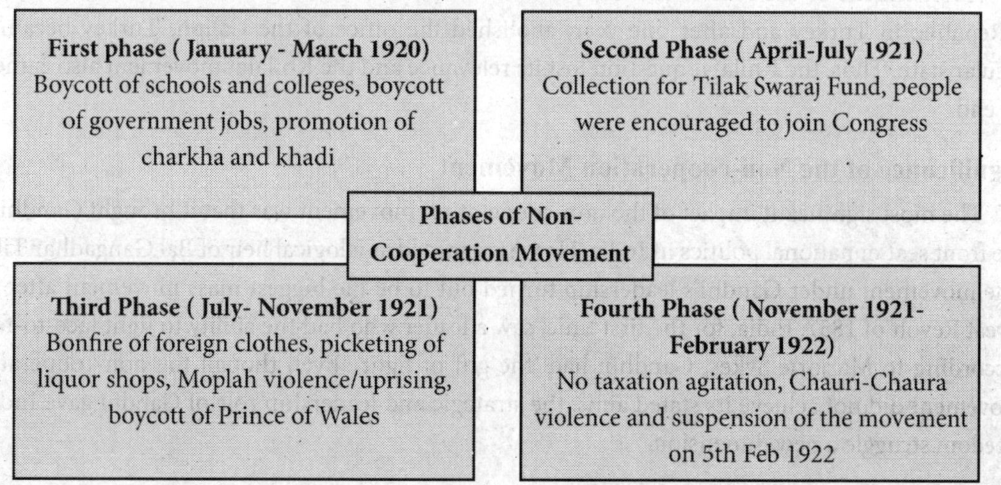

Moplah or Mappila Uprising and Hindu massacre, 1921

It was not Chauri Chaura alone that marked the only violent incident in the peaceful Non-cooperation and Khilafat movement. There were reports of revolts across the country which was directly connected with the ongoing national movements. One of the major revolts which occurred during this period was the Moplah uprising in the south. This uprising disturbed the Hindu-Muslim unity and became a factor for the decline of the Khilafat movement.

Moplah or Mappila uprising in the Malabar region of North Kerala was the outcome of the Khilafat movement which was anti-British. The Government had declared the Congress and Khilafat meetings illegal. The Khilafat meetings incited communal feelings among the poverty-stricken Muslims peasants of Northern Kerala known as Moplah or Mappila. Their protests turned out to be an anti-Hindu movement from August 1921 onwards. The Moplah peasants revolted against their local Hindu landlords' oppressive policies, which were in alliance with the British. Moplah uprising which began as a part of the Khilafat movement turned into communal riots. Hundreds of Hindus were massacred and their temples were destroyed in the riots. A pitched battle between the British regiment and the Moplahs killed several Europeans.

The leaders of this rebellion were: Variyankunnath Kunjahammed Haji, Seethi Koya Thangal of Kumaranpathor, and Ali Musliyar. Finally, the British forces suppressed the movement with great difficulty. The situation was under control by the end of 1921.

Decline of Khilafat Movement

Following were the reasons for the decline of the Khilafat movement:

Arrest of Ali Brothers : Treaty of Sevres, August 1920, hurt the Muslim sentiments in India and Ali brothers after coming back from England delivered a strong ant-British speech at Karachi after which they were arrested and imprisoned in September 1921. Their arrest gave a severe blow to the Khilafat Movement.

Abolishment of the seat of the Caliph : In October 1923, Mustafa Kemal Pasha established a Republic in Turkey and after one year, abolished the office of the Caliph. Turkey became a secular state. Thus, the Khilafat question lost its relevance and the Khilafat movement also came to an end.

Significance of the Non-cooperation Movement

The most significant impact of the non-cooperation movement was that it brought Gandhi on the front seat of national politics in India. He was regarded as a logical heir of Bal Gangadhar Tilak. The movement under Gandhi's leadership turned out to be the biggest mass movement after the Great Revolt of 1857. India, for the first time, saw a leader who had the ability to fight face-to-face. According to Marjorie Sykes, Gandhiji had 'the gift of fight'. Even though the non-cooperation movement did not achieve its stated aims, the strategic and leadership role of Gandhi gave India's freedom struggle a new dimension.

The Non-Cooperation movement unified the nation in an unprecedented feat of protest against the Government. Under Gandhi's leadership, this was a mass movement of the first of its kind in the world which included almost all the sections of the society. The ideals and programs of the movement were received with great enthusiasm, fervour, and zeal.

Undoubtedly, Congress became the party of the common man. Now it was with the widespread support of the average peasants, workers, and the intellectuals. Charkha and Khadi became the symbol of Indian nationalism.

Gandhi was able to see the real picture of India. He realised that the real power of India lay in the rural areas and not in urban areas. There was a need for general awakening of the masses to their political rights and privileges, and further, there was a total loss of faith in the system of government. People could realise that it was only through their own efforts that India could hope to be free. Hence, Congress was the only organisation which could properly direct national effort to gain freedom.

The movement also revealed that the communal problem was going to be a big problem and this problem of communalism could be solved only through mutual understanding amongst the national leaders.

The movement gave a new hope and methods to the common people and taught them to be fearless in their political pursuit. Gandhi made the idea and need for Swaraj a more popular notion, which in turn; created a new wave of patriotic enthusiasm. Satyagraha or protesting through passive resistance became the primary tool of the Indian freedom movement. Promotion of charkha and khadi as the symbol of Indian nationalism helped Indian handloom products gain recognition.

Charkha as a symbol of nationalism — Wikimedia Commons

Aftermath of the Non-Cooperation Movement

Disillusionment set in the ranks of Congress and others after the suspension of the non-cooperation movement and imprisonment of Gandhi. The Khilafat movement lost its momentum. Majority of the Khilafat leaders, the Ali brothers—Mohammed Ali and Shaukat Ali, soon became fierce critics of Gandhi and the Congress. Some Khilafat leaders such as Dr. Ansari, Maulana Azad, and Hakim Ajmal Khan became Gandhi followers. These leaders founded the Jamia Millia Islamia in 1920 to promote independent education and social transformation for Muslims. Abul Kalam Azad of the Khilafat movement remained a true Congressman. The communal harmony between the Hindus and Muslims deteriorated with the suspension of both the movements.

Gandhi's decision had given a sudden jolt to the Congress. The reasons for which it was started were the Jallianwallah Bagh tragedy, Swaraj, and issue of Khilafat volunteers. But none of them got a remedy. Gandhi's idea of 'Swaraj in one year' proved to be a bubble.

The boycott of the educational institutions was not accepted by many of the leaders such as Lala Lajpat Rai. Some leaders did not like the way it was started, many others did not like the way it was conducted, and most of them could not digest the sudden withdrawal. The people of Punjab (who were waiting for some wonders to happen that would punish those guilty of the Jallianwala massacre) and others were largely disappointed. Hence, the revolutionary activities in Punjab began to surface. Some new political outfits were born parallel to the Congress, because the Congress was left without any political program.

Although most Congress leaders remained firmly behind Gandhi, the disillusioned broke away. Motilal Nehru and Chittaranjan Das formed the Swaraj Party, rejecting Gandhi's leadership.

The Swarajists' Movement (1922–1928)

The suspension of the non-cooperation movement brought disillusionment and disappointment in the Congress ranks. There was no major programme to carry on. With the arrest of Gandhi in 1922, many Congress leaders continued the constructive or passive programme of the non-cooperation movement. As a result of the constructive work under the non-cooperation movement, Ashrams sprang up in many places where young men and women worked with tribals and lower castes and popularised the charkha and khadi. National schools and colleges were set up where students were trained in a non-colonial ideological framework. Significant work was done for Hindu-Muslim unity, removing untouchability, boycott of foreign cloth and liquor, and for flood relief. The constructive workers served as the backbone of civil disobedience as active organisers.

With the withdrawal of the movement, differences arose among the nationalist leaders. A debate started among them on what to do in the passive phase of the non-cooperation movement. Two groups emerged in the Congress – No-Changers and Pro-Changers.

No-Changers and Pro-Changers

After the suspension of the non-cooperation movement, most of the leaders of the Congress continue to pursue the constructive programme of the non-cooperation movement which included upliftment of the poor people by teaching them how to use charkha, denouncing untouchability, and making non-violence and Gandhian methods popular. These were called No-changers. This group was led by Sardar Vallabhbhai Patel, Dr. M.A. Ansari, C. Rajagopalachari, and Babu Rajendra Prasad. The No-Changers did not want any change from the non-cooperation policy.

However, there was a section of the leaders in the Congress who were not satisfied with the passive phase of the non-cooperation movement. They wanted to start the non-cooperation movement from 'above', i.e., in the legislative councils and assemblies and bring change. These leaders were Motilal Nehru, N. C. Kelkar, and C.R. Das. Leaders like C.R. Das, Motilal Nehru, and Ajmal Khan wanted to remove the plan of the boycott of legislative and council elections under the non-cooperation movement policy. They were of the opinion that by contesting elections of legislative councils, the nationalists could enter into government bodies and expose the weaknesses of these assemblies and use these as an arena of national struggle and to generate public awareness as well. They wanted, in other words, to 'end or mend' these councils, i.e., if the Government did not respond to the nationalists' demands, then they would obstruct the working of these councils. In association with some Khilafat leaders such as Huseyn Shaheed Suhrawardy, and some other leaders such as Subhash Chandra Bose and Vithalbhai Patel, they came to be known as Pro-Changers.

The Gaya Session of the Congress, 1922

In December 1922, the Gaya session of the Congress took place. C. R. Das was the President of the session who was leading the Pro-Changers. The No-changers' leader was C. Rajgopalachari. The differences over the question of council entry between the two groups of thought resulted in the defeat of the Pro-Changers' proposal of 'ending or mending' the councils at the Gaya session of the Congress. The outcome of this session was that these leaders got divided. C.R. Das resigned from the Presidentship of the Congress. The Pro-Changers announced the formation of the Congress – Khilafat Swarajya Party or Swaraj Party, with C.R. Das as the President and Motilal Nehru as one of the secretaries.

C.R. Das
— Wikimedia Commons

Motilal Nehru
— Wikimedia Commons

This group came to be known as the Swarajists as they wanted to carry out the struggle for Swaraj inside the government assemblies and councils. They were of the view that nationalists should contest the Legislative Councils election, enter them, obstruct government working, expose government weaknesses, and transform government seats into arenas of political struggle. This would, according to Swarajists, gradually prepare the country for the new round of mass struggle. The Swarajists argued that entering the councils would not negate the non-cooperation programme; in fact, it would be like carrying on the movement through other means. Their only intention was to use the councils as an arena of political struggle; they had no intention to use the councils as organs for gradual transformation of colonial rule.

The No-Changers who opposed the Swarjists' strategy of council entry, advocated concentration on constructive work and quiet preparation for continuation of the suspended civil disobedience programme. The No-Changers argued that parliamentary work would lead to neglect of constructive work, loss of revolutionary zeal, and political corruption, whereas constructive work would prepare everyone for the next phase of civil disobedience.

But at the same time, both sides wanted to avoid a 1907 Surat-type split and kept in touch with Gandhi who was in jail. Both sides also realised the significance of putting up a united front to get a mass movement to force the Government to introduce reforms. Keeping these factors in mind, a special session of the Congress held in Delhi in September 1923 accepted the views of the Swarajists.

Belgaum Session of Congress, December 1924

On 5th February 1924, Gandhi was released from jail due to health problems. He favoured the 'No-Changers' but wanted to stop a disastrous repeat of the Surat split of 1907. So he wanted conciliation and in November that year, he brought the strife between No-changers and Swarajists to an end.

Both the parties signed the joint statement and declared that Swarajists would work in the council on behalf of and as an integral part of the Congress. This decision was endorsed in the December 1924 Belgaum Session of the Congress in which Gandhi became the President of the Congress for the first and only time.

The Swarajists were allowed to contest elections as a group within the Congress. The Swarajist came out with their manifesto for elections to be held in November 1923. The manifesto took a strong anti-imperialist line. It promised that the Swarajists would wreck the sham reforms from within the councils.

Swarajists in Councils

In the election of November 1923, the Swarajists managed to do quite well. They won 42 seats out of the 101 seats in the Central Legislative Assembly. They got a clear majority in the Central Provinces. They were the largest party in Bengal and they fared quite well in Bombay and U.P., though not in Madras and Punjab because of strong casteist and communal currents.

Simultaneously, during 1923–24, Congressmen captured a large number of municipalities and other local bodies. C.R. Das became the Mayor of Calcutta (with Subhash Bose as his Chief Executive Officer), and Vithalbhai Patel, the President of Bombay Corporation, Vallabhbhai Patel of Ahmedabad Municipality, Rajendra Prasad of Patna Municipality, and Jawaharlal Nehru of Allahabad Municipality. The No-Changers actively joined in these ventures since they believed that local bodies could be used to promote the constructive programme.

With coalition partners, Swarajists started the politics of obstruction. They outvoted the Government several times, even on matters relating to budgetary grants, and passed adjournment motions. They made Dyarchy unworkable. They agitated through powerful speeches on self-government, civil liberties, and industrialisation. In 1925, the Swarajist leader Vithalbhai Patel was elected President of the Central Legislative Assembly. C. R. Das was elected as Mayor of Calcutta in 1924.

In the very first session, Motilal Nehru put forward the national demand for the framing of a new constitution, which would transfer real power to India. This demand was passed by 64 votes to 48. It was reiterated and passed in September 1925 by 72 votes to 45. The Government also had to face humiliation when its demands for budgetary grants under different heads were repeatedly voted out. On one such occasion, Vithalbhai Patel told the Government: 'We want you to carry on the administration of this country by veto and by certification. We want you to treat the Government of India Act as a scrap of paper which I am sure it has proved to be.'

By their activities, they filled the political vacuum at a time when the national movement was recouping its strength. They also exposed the hollowness of the Montford Reform Act of 1919. They demonstrated that the councils could be used creatively. The Swarajist activity in the legislatures became a centre of attraction in the press. Their agitation and speeches kept the political issues of the nation alive. People were thrilled every time the all-powerful foreign bureaucracy was humbled in the councils.

They did excellent work in the fields of education, sanitation, health, untouchability, and *khadi* promotion, won the admiration of friend and foe, and quite often aroused popular enthusiasm.

A noteworthy achievement of the Swarajists was the defeat of the Public Safety Bill in 1928 which was aimed at empowering the Government to expel undesirable and subversive foreigners suspected of spreading socialist and communist ideas.

Decline of the Swarajists' Movement

The Swarajists could not carry on with their coalition partners very far because of conflicting ideas, which limited their effectiveness. They failed to support the peasants' cause in Bengal and lost support among Muslim members who were pro-peasant. Many Swarajists came under the influence of power and politics.

By 1924, the Swarajists' position had weakened because of widespread communal riots and split among the Swarajists themselves. The Swarajists suffered a serious blow in the death of C.R. Das in 1925. Swarajist leaders like Lala Lajpat Rai, Madan Mohan Malaviya, and N.C. Kelkar advocated cooperation with the Government and holding of office wherever possible to protect the Hindu interests. They accused Swarajists like Motilal Nehru of being anti-Hindu.

By 1926, the Party began to break and many Swarajists walked out of the legislative assembly, first in March 1926 and then in January 1930. In 1930, the Swarajists finally walked out as a result of the Lahore Congress resolution on *Purna Swaraj* and the beginning of the Mass Civil Disobedience Movement in 1930.

Previous Years' Questions

1. **Explain the circumstances leading to the alliance between the Khilafat and Non-Cooperation Movements. Was it a politically wise step on the part of the Congress? (2007)**
2. **"M.K. Gandhi made a gross mistake in championing the Khilafat cause, an extra-territorial issue which cut at the very roots of Indian nationality." (2014)**
3. **'Many of us who work for the Congress program lived in a kind of intoxication during the year 1921. We were full of excitement and optimism… We had a sense of freedom and pride in that freedom'. (2013)**
4. **"Gandhi restrained mass movements, yet he retained his popularity among the masses." Comment. (2002)**

17 CHAPTER

The Rise of The Left Movement, Hindu Nationalist Ideology, and Demand For Complete Independence

The Post Non-cooperation movement witnessed the rise of several political organisations and associations opposing both the Congress and Gandhi's ways of working. These organisations and associations came broadly under two political ideologies – the leftist and the rightist. Like elsewhere, the left movement in India got inspiration from the Russian revolution. Till 1920s, the leftist ideology was limited to peasants and trade organisations. But with the sudden suspension of the non-cooperation movement, many disappointed leaders and people joined or rendered their support to the leftist groups. Subsequently, many socialist and communist parties came up that radicalised the national movement.

So far, we have read about the leftist parties which countered the Congress and Gandhi. But very little is known and as a result, inadequately written about the right-wing political organisations, often relegated as communal outfits or organisations that played an equally significant role in the national struggle. Rightists contributed in shaping a distinctive nationalist ideology that opposed both the Congress and the left ideologies. This chapter is about the emergence of leftists and right-wing organisations, post the non-cooperation movement, and their contribution in the national movement, mainly advocating for the complete independence from the British.

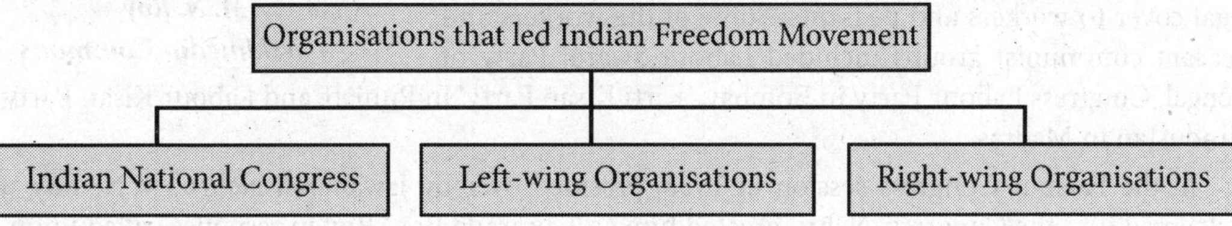

Emergence of Leftist Movement in India

In the late 1920s and 1930s, powerful left-wing group developed in India contributing to the radicalisation of the Indian National Movement.

The emergence and growth of the leftist movement was the result of a combination of factors:

- Success of the Russian Revolution of 1917
- Suspension of Non-cooperation movement
- Dissatisfaction with the Gandhian methodology
- Economic crunch caused by the two World Wars

The Russian Revolution of 1917 had a great impact on the minds of the Indian people. Many peasant and Labour parties sprang up that adopted communist ideology. With the failure of the mainstream national movement, communist parties began to emerge that sought alternate roads for their fight against imperialism and social-economic inequality. When the Non-cooperation movement turned out to be a failure, leftist parties started parallel agitation to counter the Congress-led passive resistance against the British.

Communist writings and publications strengthened the left movement in India. In Mumbai, S.A. Dange brought out a pamphlet, 'Gandhi vs. Lenin' and the first socialist weekly called *The Socialist.* In Bengal, Muzaffar Ahmad brought *Navyug* and later founded *Langal* in cooperation with Nazrul Islam. In Punjab, *Inquilab* was published by Ghulam Hussain and others. In Chennai, *Labour Kisan Gazette* was published by M. Singaravelu.

M.N. Roy and Communist Party of India (Tashkent), 1920

M. N. Roy
— Wikimedia Commons

The early founder of the communist party in India was Manabendra Nath Roy or M.N. Roy. Earlier, M.N. Roy was a member of the Revolutionary Organisation, Anushilan. He was very much influenced by the communist thoughts. His original name was Narendra Nath Bhattacharya. At the age of 20, he carried out a political dacoity to raise money for Anushilan. In 1920, he went to Russia to attend the Second Congress of the Communist International. Here, he founded the Communist Party of India in Tashkent. At the same time, a Berlin group was launched by Virendranath Chattophadhyaya, Bhupendra Dutt, and others. Thus, the Communist Party of India was launched in Tashkent in October, 1920. Thereafter, various communist groups were formed in various parts of India from 1922 to 1928. These communist groups essentially provided legal cover to workers and peasants. Some of the workers and peasant communist groups included Labour-Swaraj Party of Bengal, Congress Labour Party in Bombay, 'Kirti Kisan Party' in Punjab, and Labour Kisan Party of Hindustan in Madras.

In the Faizpur Congress session in 1936, presided over by Jawaharlal Nehru, M.N. Roy was welcomed into the Congress. Nehru greeted him as 'Comrade Roy'. Roy in response called upon all sections and segments of the political parties and groups including communists, trade unions, Kisan Sabhas, and youth organisations to join the Congress and build it up into a strong united front against imperialism and for attaining India's independence. He also spoke about his idea of a Constituent Assembly of India with a view to ultimately capture power. Roy did not want the Congress to be completely swayed away by the influence of Gandhi and of the bourgeois. The Congress, according to him, was a mass nationalist movement. It was not the party of any particular class.

The Peasant-Labour Movement

The labour movement was not far behind in its development. In the first half of 1920, there were approximately 200 labour strikes. Under the Presidentship of Lala Lajpat Rai, All India Trade Union Congress held its first session in October in Bombay.

In December 1928, a Conference of different labour kisan parties was called forth and they merged into the All-India Workers and Peasants' Party (WPP). Their aim was to work within the Congress and infuse in it a more radical orientation.

Their programme comprised

- Abolition of zamindari and redistribution of land,
- Development of the peasants' and workers' movement, and
- Raising the general standard of the masses.

Communist Party of India (CPI), 1925

The Communist Party of India (CPI) claimed its origin in December 1925, when a communist leader Satyabhakta organised all small organisations into one at the All India Conference of the Communists at Kanpur. The Presidentship of the All India Conference of Communists was given by Singaravelu Chettiar, a communist leader from the Madras Province. S.V. Ghate became the first General Secretary of CPI. This conference is known as the "formal" beginning of Communist Party of India in 1925, Kanpur.

With the agreement of supporting the national movement as encouraged by Lenin, the Communist Party of India (CPI) asked its members to join the ranks of the Congress and to form a strong Left-wing within it.

The left group of the Congress was represented by Jawaharlal Nehru who became the President of the Congress in 1936 and 1937. Subhash Bose too was the President in 1938 and 1939, reflecting the far reaching influence of the left ideologies within the Congress. In 1927, Jawaharlal Nehru attended the Brussels Congress of the Oppressed Nationalities and visited the Soviet Union. In 1928, Nehru with Subash Bose organised the Independence for India League to fight for complete independence.

Congress leftist leaders like Jawaharlal Nehru and Subhash Chandra Bose gave the communists an opportunity to thrust their perspective vis-à-vis Gandhian ideology.

Congress Socialist Party or CSP

Earlier, CPI declared the Congress as the class party of the bourgeoisie and all connections with it were broken. However, there was a shift in the communists' stand towards the Congress in 1934 when Congress Socialist Party or CSP was formed. CSP was formed in 1934 in Pune under the Chairmanship of Narendra Dev and Jai Prakash Narayan as its Secretary within the Congress. It was formed with the objective of moulding the Congress along socialist lines and consolidating the communists' movement. The communists were urged to support the ongoing national movements against imperialism. Many communists joined the Congress Socialist Party (CSP). Nehru and Bose supported the CSP from outside.

However, CSP could not really gain much headway working within the Congress. Neither could it leave the Congress at this point in time, as it would have weakened the CSP. Gradually, within the Congress, there emerged two camps on account of the growing socialist influence in the INC. Congress got divided along "Leftist" and "Rightist" lines. The leftist leaders like G. B. Pant, P. D. Tandon, and Jai Prakash exerted their influences on the local Congress executives to implement radical measures like removal of middlemen, cancellation of debts of peasants owed to the landlords, and regulation of land tax. This was criticised by the right-wing leaders like Sardar Patel.

The left influence was strongly visible in the second phase of revolutionary terrorism from 1922–1928. Significant revolutionary organisations of this period was *Hindusthan Socialist Association* and later *Hindusthan Socialist Republican Association* that conducted revolutionary activities under the zeal of communist ideology.

Many scholars and historians assert that with the emergence of powerful left-wing groups, the social economic agenda of the Congress got radicalised. The emergence of modern industries and factory system gave impetus to socialistic ideas in the Congress. It led to the growth of trade unions as they subsequently came under socialistic principles.

The left-wing of the Congress led by Jawaharlal Nehru imparted a socialist vision to the national movement which became the symbol of socialism and socialist ideas in India after 1929. The notion that freedom could not be defined only in political terms but must have a socio-economic agenda began increasingly to be associated with the national movement.

Nehru was able to declare *Poorna Swaraj* or Complete Independence as the goal of the Congress in its Lahore Session based on these socialist principles. Consequently, the Congress was forced to accept the programme and resolution on Fundamental Rights and Economic reforms to define what Swaraj would mean for the masses.

Socialist ideas became more popular during the 1930s as the world was engulfed by the Great Economic Depression. The foundation of the All India Students' Federation and the Progressive Writers' Association and the convening of the first All India States' People's Conference in 1927, were all inspired from the socialist ideology. The Left was also very active in the All India Women's Conference.

Aims and Objectives of Indian Communists

The communist party markedly differed from the Congress in terms of the national movement and economic development plans.

Following were the significant aims and objectives of the Indian communists:

- **Complete Swaraj or Independence :** The communists in India favoured complete independence of India not with the help of ahimsa or non-violence but with the use of violent methods. They wanted that all British factories should be confiscated and then nationalised. Furthermore, no compensation should be paid for confiscated lands and other properties of landlords and bourgeois classes.

- **Common ownership :** Communists aimed at an economic system in which there will be common ownership over all means of production and distribution. These will be used for the welfare of the masses. They favoured nationalisation of banks, railways, and all other major industries. All debts, according to them, should be cancelled. They also suggested that the minorities should have the right of self-determination and native states should be abolished and an All India Workers and Peasants Party should be created.

- **Against Gandhi's ideology :** Majority of the communists rejected the Gandhian philosophy of non-violence and Gandhi's passive methodology in the national movement. They were in favour of and expressed their desire for complete independence from the British. They criticised the Gandhian philosophy of Civil Disobedience movement for being not a struggle, but a manoeuvre of the Indian bourgeoisie to obtain concessions from imperialism. They believed that the Gandhian programme diverted the attention of the workers and peasants from their main struggle against the landlords and capitalists.

- **In favour of radical changes :** They wanted that radical changes should be brought in the Congress party programmes. They were critical of both the Congress and the Swaraj party. They pleaded that the Congress party should follow the policy of militant mass action and policy of surrender and compromise should be discarded.
- **Congress as bourgeois party :** They considered the Congress to be under the influence of bourgeois leadership from which it should be liberated. In 1926, the communists decided to work under the guidance of the Communist International or Comintern and some Communist leaders even attended the Sixth Congress of Communist International held in 1928.
- **Fight against bourgeoisie and Imperialism in India :** Communists decided to fight on two fronts for the country's freedom: National bourgeoisie on the one hand and British imperialism on the other. In *Communist International*, Indian communists took the resolution that, "The communists must unmask the national reformism of the Indian National Congress and oppose all the phases of the Swarajists and Gandhi's passive resistance."

Because of their negative approach towards Satyagraha, the communists lost the appreciation of the masses. After the *Meerut Conspiracy Case* against the communist leaders (1922–1928), the leftists were out of the national movement.

Conspiracy Cases Against Communists

The British Government became increasingly paranoid with the growth of the left movement in India. They grew alarmed at the increase in Left activities. From the period 1922–1928, the communists in India faced a series of conspiracy cases.

Three prominent conspiracy cases against the communists were:

- Peshawar Conspiracy Trial (1922–23)
- Kanpur Bolshevik Conspiracy Trial (1924)
- Meerut Conspiracy Trial (1929–33)

It was the *Meerut Conspiracy Trial Case* that attracted world-wide attention and after that, the communists were out of the national movement but the communist movement became much stronger.

The Meerut Trial Case

The *Meerut Conspiracy Case* was on Indian communists and trade unionists for organising an Indian Railway strike and establishing a branch of Communist International (Comintern) in India.

In March 1929, the government arrested 32 political and trade union leaders under the *Meerut Conspiracy Case* which dragged on for more than three years. These communists were defended by Jawaharlal Nehru, M. A. Ansari, and M. C. Chagla. 27 accused were sentenced to rigorous imprisonment while Muzaffar Ahmad, a communist leader from Bengal, was given life imprisonment.

The Meerut Conspiracy Case attracted the attention of the people in Great Britain so much so that a Manchester street theatre group, 'The Red Megaphones' in 1932 enacted a play titled 'Meerut' in England. The *Meerut Conspiracy Case* is a milestone that goes a long way in defining the history of the communist movement in India.

The government, however, did not favour the activities of the communists in India and in 1934, it imposed a ban on the functioning of the party. Communists now tried to infiltrate into the Congress party. They formed a socialist wing within the Congress known as the Congress Socialist Party (CSP).

Resurgence of the Socialist – Revolutionary Nationalism

Revolutionary nationalism was suppressed during the World War I. The sudden suspension of the Non-cooperation movement shattered the hopes of the Indian youths. They again began to believe that violent methods alone could free India. Revolutionary terrorism fired with socialist ideology thus resurfaced in the Indian freedom movement.

In 1924, at Kanpur, revolutionaries – Sachindranath Sanyal, Jogesh Chandra Chatterjee, Ram Prasad Bismil, and Chandra Shekhar Azad founded the Hindustan Republican Association (HRA). The aim of the HRA was to organise armed revolution to end the colonial rule and establish a Federal Republic of the United States of India. The Kakori train robbery was a notable act of mutiny by this group. A government treasury carried by a train was looted near the Kakori railway station near Lucknow. The government reaction was quick and hard. It arrested a large number of young men and tried them in the Kakori conspiracy case. Four of the conspirators, Ramprasad Bismil, Rajendranath Lahiri, Roshan Singh, and Ashfaqulla Khan were hanged, while four others were sent to the Andamans for life, and seventeen others were sentenced to life imprisonment. One powerful member, Chandrasekhar Azad, however managed to escape.

Though the Kakori case was a major setback to the revolutionaries, young men like Bijoy Kumar Sinha, Shiv Varma, and Jaidev Kapoor of U.P., and Bhagat Singh, Bhagwati Charan Vohra, and Sukhdev in Punjab soon reorganised themselves under the leadership of Chandrasekhar Azad. They were being influenced by the socialist ideas and the Bolshevik revolution. Finally, the young revolutionaries met at Ferozeshah Kotla Ground in Delhi on 9th and 10th September, 1928. They adopted socialism as their goal and changed the name of the party to Hindustan Socialist Republican Association (HSRA).

On 30th October 1928, Lala Lajpat Rai was severely injured while leading an anti-Simon Commission demonstration at Lahore. He died a little later. The death of this great leader was seen as a direct challenge by the leaders of the Hindustan Socialist Republican Association.

The first revolutionary act of the HSRA was the murder of Saunders, the Assistant Superintendent of Police. However, it was James A. Scott, who had lathicharged and wounded Lajpat Rai during the anti-Simon Commission protest march at Lahore on October 30, 1928.

On 8th April, 1929, Bhagat Singh and Batukeswar Dutt threw a bomb in the Central Legislative Assembly against the passage of the Public Safety Bill and the Trade Disputes Bill which would reduce the civil liberties of the citizens. They also threw red leaflets on the floor, which began with the slogan of a French revolutionary "It needs a loud voice for a deaf to hear".

Bhagat Singh
— Wikimedia Commons

The aim was not to kill anybody. The revolutionary leaders wanted that the people should become familiar with their movement and ideology. Bhagat Singh and Batukeswar Dutt were tried in the Assembly bomb case.

The revolutionaries were fearless by nature. They would enter the courtroom shouting slogans like 'Inquilab Zindabad' 'Down, Down with imperialism', and singing songs like 'sarfarosi ki tamanna ab hamare dil me hai' and '*Mera rang de basanti chola*'.

All these were reported in the newspapers and they won support from all over the country. Even those who had complete faith in non-violence became sympathetic towards the revolutionaries. On 23rd March 1931, Bhagat Singh, Sukhdev, and Rajguru were hanged, and a large number of revolutionaries were sent to the Andamans.

However, the revolutionary movement failed to achieve its objectives. With the death of Chandrasekhar Azad in a shooting encounter in a public park at Allahabad in February 1931, the revolutionary movement virtually came to an end in Punjab, U.P., and Bihar. Revolutionary Surya Sen's death also marked an end to the extremists' activity in Bengal. A large number of revolutionaries turned to Marxism.

The politics of the revolutionary nationalists had severe limitations. It could not mobilise the masses. In fact, it had no base among the people. They believed in individual heroism. The revolutionaries could not function under a central control and mostly worked in isolated groups. They could not withstand the repression of the colonial government. The non-violent movement led by Gandhi was more popular and proved more successful. The revolutionaries failed to gain the support of the common people of India and that remained the primary cause of their failure.

Moreover, Gandhi never approved of the revolutionary methods and their actions. There was a vast difference in the ideology and methodology between Gandhi, and revolutionaries like Sardar Bhagat Singh. Revolutionaries, especially Bhagat Singh, strongly believed in revolution and war. These revolutionaries infused in the masses a sense of patriotism and a determination to drive out the foreigners from their soil. The revolutionaries were inspired by the socialist ideologies and wanted to wage a war against the British by crippling the government's system. This was totally against Gandhi's ideology of Satyagraha in which there was no space for violence. Gandhi advocated non-violent principles in the mass movement for attaining Swaraj. As a result, revolutionaries like Bhagat Singh rejected Gandhi's passive ideology of non-violence.

Gandhi published the article titled 'The Cult of the Bomb' in *Young India* in 1930 in response to an assassination attempt on Lord Irwin by the revolutionaries. This attempt took place on December 23, 1929, when a special train carrying the Viceroy, Lord Irwin, was derailed by bombs just outside New Delhi. The Viceroy escaped unhurt. Gandhi thanked God for the Viceroy's narrow escape and condemned in his article 'The Cult of the Bomb' the revolutionaries for the act. It was in reply to Gandhi's article that Bhagwati Charan in consultation with Chandra Shekhar Azad wrote an article 'The Philosophy of the Bomb'. In this article, Bhagawati justified that independence could come only through armed struggle against the occupying power. While denouncing their cult of violence, Gandhi, an apostle of non-violence, unhesitatingly appreciated their feelings of intense patriotism and their self-sacrifice.

The Rise of the Hindu Nationalist Ideology

In the medieval period, the rise of Hindu consciousness was largely attributed first to the Islamic Invasions of India in the 8th and 12th century respectively; second, the establishment of Islamic rule under Delhi Sultanates and Mughals, and third, the Bhakti movement. The establishment of the Delhi Sultanate and later the Mughal rule was marked by a constant resistance among the Hindu rulers and Hindu population to accept completely the suzerainty of the Islamic rule. Some historians considered the emergence of Vijayanagar Kingdom in the Deccan as a reaction to the Islamic rule in the south. In the 17th and 18th century, the emergence of the Maratha state was considered as a reaction to the Islamic rule. However, Hindu consciousness in the medieval period is largely attributed to the Bhakti movement which gave a new dimension to the Hindu identity and Hindu ways of worship.

In the 19th century, the reformists like Swami Dayananad Saraswati through his Arya Samaj brought fundamental reforms in the Hindu religion and encouraged Hindu nationalism. Swami Vivekananda propagated Hinduism as a missionary religion by encouraging social service.

In the late 19th century, extremist leaders like Bal Gangadhar Tilak and Aurobindo Ghosh took inspiration from Hindu culture and Hindu religion and began to encourage nationalism and patriotism. These leaders were critical of the passive methodology of the moderate nationalists who were also loyalists of the British Empire. Extremists' leader Bal Gangadhar Tilak infused the spirit of Hindu nationalism among the people by encouraging Ganesh festivals and Shivaji Mahotsav.

The Rise of Hindu Mahasabha

The partition of Bengal on communal lines in 1905 and provisions for separate electorates for Muslims by Morley-Minto reforms of 1909, prompted the rise of political consciousness among the Hindus. In 1906, All-India Muslim League was founded in Dacca. In a short span, the league emerged as a largest political party representing Indian Muslims. It was successful in demanding a separate electorate for Muslims in the 1909 constitutional reforms. Similar efforts were made to form a national political association representing all sections of the Hindu community. While the National Congress party comprised largely of Hindu leaders, it posed as an All Indian Community's party and not a Hindu party.

The initial step to safeguard the interests of the Hindu community was taken with the foundation of the Punjab Hindu Sabha in 1909. In its first conference in October 1909, the Punjab Hindu Sabha criticised the National Congress for not representing the Hindus' interests and called for Hindu nationalist politics. Soon after, many such provincial Hindu Sabhas came up in the United Provinces, Bihar, Bengal , Central Provinces, Berar, and in the Bombay Presidency.

Efforts were made to bring together all the provincial Hindu sabhas under one umbrella organisation. Therefore, in December 1913, at its Ambala session, a resolution was passed by the Punjab Hindu Sabha to create an All India Hindu Sabha. The Conference proposed holding a general conference of Hindu leaders from all over India at the 1915 Kumbh Mela in Haridwar. Consequently, in April 1915, 'Sarvadeshak Hindu Sabha' was formed at the Kumbh Mela in Haridwar. Interestingly, Gandhi and Swami Shraddhanand were also present at the conference, and were supportive of the formation of the All India Hindu Sabha. The Sabha laid emphasis on Hindu solidarity and the need for social reform.

In its 1921 conference, the Sarvadeshak Hindu Sabha changed its name to Akhil Bharatiya Hindu Mahasabha. The conference was presided over by Manindra Chandra Nandi in which it proposed Mahasabha as a non-loyalist party to the British, and to strive for a united and self-governing Indian nation.

The earliest leadership to the Mahasabha was provided by the prominent nationalist, educationalist, and four times Indian National Congress President Pandit Madan Mohan Malaviya, who founded the Banaras Hindu University. Under Malaviya, the Mahasabha campaigned for Hindu political unity, for the education and economic development of Hindus, as well as for the conversion of Muslims to Hinduism. Another prominent Congress leader who supported the Hindu Mahasabha was Lala Lajpat Rai.

Vinayak Damodar Savarkar or Veer Savarkar
— Wikimedia Commons

One of the leading figures of Hindu Mahasabha was Vinayak Damodar Savarkar or Veer Savarkar (1883 – 1966), a revolutionary and a Hindu nationalist, who developed the Hindu nationalist political ideology. As a revolutionary, Savarkar founded a secret society known as Abhinav Bharat society (Young India Society) in 1904. This society was responsible for the assassination of eminent British officers in India. In 1909, Savarkar wrote 'The Indian War of Independence of 1857' in which he took the view that the Indian Mutiny of 1857 was the first expression of Indian mass rebellion against the British colonial rule. In 1910, on various charges, Savarkar was sentenced for life imprisonment and was detained in the Cellular Jail in the Andaman Islands. He was brought back to India in 1921 and kept in Ratnagiri jail. While in Ratnagiri Jail, he wrote Hindutva: Who Is a Hindu? 'Hindutva' meaning Hindu-ness became the popular Hindu political ideology of the Mahasabha. As a President of the Hindu Mahasabha, Savarkar endorsed the idea of India as a 'Hindu Rashtra'.

M. S. Golwalkar or Guruji Golwalkar
— Wikimedia Commons

Savarkar opposed the secularism of the Congress. Under Savarkar, the Mahasabha became a more intense critic of the Congress and its policy of wooing Muslim support. He criticised Gandhi's Wardha resolution of 'Quit India'. Savarkar wrote a letter titled 'Stick to your Posts', in which he instructed Mahasabha members who were serving in municipalities, local bodies, legislatures, and in the army to stick to their posts across the country, and not to join the Quit India Movement at any cost. Savarkar retired from the active politics in 1942 by resigning from the post of the President of the Hindu Mahasabha.

Influenced by the writings of Savarkar, a former member of Mahasabha, Keshav Baliram Hedgewar formed the Rashtriya Swayamsevak Sangh (RSS), a Hindu volunteer organisation in 1925. RSS abstained from the freedom movement but worked for cultural and spiritual regeneration of Hinduism.

One of the prominent ideologues of the RSS was Guruji Golwalkar, a Hindu nationalist thinker who put forward the concept of 'Hindu Rashtra'. Golwalkar spoke of cultural nationalism and a 'Hindu Rashtra' incorporating the ancient Hindu civilisational cradle as Akhand Bharat. Guruji Golwalkar succeeded Hedgewar as the General Secretary of RSS in 1940.

The Hindu Mahasabha did not support the Gandhian principles of Satyagraha and passive resistance methods. Mahasabha officially abstained from participating in the Civil Disobedience Movement of 1930 and the Quit India movement in 1942.

Demand for Complete Independence (1927–1928)

The leftist organisations and organisations like Hindu Mahasabha and RSS openly advocated for complete independence from the British Empire. Consequently, the young leadership within the Congress was motivated by the idea of complete independence as the goal of the national movement.

Following are the sequence of events that propelled the Congress to demand for complete independence:

The Simon Commission and Protests

The Government of India Act, 1919 had a provision that a commission would be appointed after 10 years to study the constitutional developments. In order to save its electoral defeat from the Labour Party, the then Conservative government in power in Britain appointed seven MPs to constitute the promised commission to examine the state of Indian constitutional affairs. Therefore, in March 1927, the conservative Government announced its decision to appoint the "Statutory Commission" in advance of the prescribed date, i.e., 1929. In 1928, the Indian Statutory Commission was formed and sent to India to study the constitutional reforms of 1919.

Staney Baldwin
— Wikimedia Commons

Prime Minister Stanley Baldwin was the conservative Prime Minister of UK who appointed the Simon Commission.

The commission was a group of seven British Members of Parliament under the chairmanship of Sir John Simon. One of its members was Clement Attlee, who subsequently became the British Prime Minister. It was commonly referred to as the Simon Commission after its chairman, Sir John Simon. The Indian leaders were not satisfied with the constitutional reforms introduced in the Government of India Act, 1919. Therefore, the commission was set primarily to inquire into the working of the Act of 1919 and to study what changes were needed for the establishment of a 'responsible government' in India.

Indians primarily objected to the composition of the commission which had all its seven members from the English community. No Indian was included in it. This sent a wave of anger against the commission throughout India. The Indian National Congress at its session passed a resolution 'to boycott the commission at every stage'.

The commission was boycotted by the Hindu Mahasabha and the Muslim League. The cry of 'Go back Simon' greeted its members from city to city. A complete *hartal* was observed in Bombay and other cities on February 3, 1928, the day the Simon Commission landed in Bombay. Many people turned out to greet the Commission with black flags.

The government of India resorted to repressive measures and the police lathicharged the demonstrators. At Lahore, a peaceful demonstration was subjected to repeated baton blows and Lala Lajpat Rai was severely beaten up by the blows. He died after 18 days on account of serious injuries. The death of Lala Lajpat Rai due to *lathi* blows generated the climate of revolutionary terrorist activities. It angered the youth and on December 17, 1928, three revolutionaries, namely Bhagat Singh, Azad, and Rajguru assassinated Saunders, the British police officer whom these revolutionaries thought was behind the lathi charge. They were the founders of a revolutionary outfit called Hindustan Socialist Republican Association.

Later, An All-India Committee for Cooperation with the Simon Commission was established which had many Indians with C. Sankaran Nair as Chairman.

The Nehru Report (1927–1928)

The Simon Commission paid two visits to India in 1928 and 1929. It submitted its two-volume Report in May 1930, which was later discussed at the Round Table Conference held in London. The Simon Commission proposed the abolition of dyarchy and the establishment of representative government in the provinces.

However, the report went unnoticed and the Secretary of State, Lord Birkenhead challenged the Indian leaders to draft a Constitution to which all parties would agree. Ahead of the Simon report, Pandit Motilal Nehru presented a report named as Nehru Report.

An all parties' conference was held in Delhi in February, 1928 under the chairmanship of Dr. M.A. Ansari which appointed a committee to draft a constitutional scheme. Pandit Motilal Nehru was appointed as the chairman of the committee during the third session of the All Parties Conference held at Bombay in May 1928. The report was placed in the annual session of the Congress held on 28th August, 1928 where it was accepted unanimously.

Some of the important features of the Nehru Report were as follows:

- India must be given Dominion status like Canada, Australia, and South Africa within the British Commonwealth.
- India would be a Federation, having a bicameral Legislature at the Centre.
- The Governor-General would be only the constitutional head with the same powers as the British Crown.
- There would be no separate electorate. It did provide for reservation of minority seats. It provided for reservation for seats for Muslims at the centre and in provinces where they were in a minority and not in Bengal and Punjab. Similarly, it provided for reservation for non-Muslims in the NWFP.
- There would be nineteen fundamental rights including the right to vote for men and women above 21 years of age, unless disqualified.
- There would be equal rights for men and women as citizens.
- There would be no state religion.
- The provinces would be created along linguistic lines.

- The language of the country would be Indian, written either in Devanagari (Sanskrit/Hindi), Telugu, Tamil, Kannada, Bengali, Marathi, or Gujarati in character. English usage to be permitted.

Thus, the Important recommendations of the report included demand for dominion status in which India would be a federation of linguistic provinces; the formation of responsible government with Dominion status; setting up of two houses of parliament, i.e., Senate and House of Representatives. It also directed that the Governor-General should act on the advice of executive council, and the statute should embody Fundamental Rights like freedom of speech, expression, and religion.

Response to the Nehru Report

The issue of communal representation proved controversial among the members of the Muslim League. In December 1927, many Muslim leaders met Motilal Nehru at Delhi and suggested a few proposals. These were accepted by the Congress at its Madras session.

These proposals were:

- 1/3rd representation of Muslims in the Central Legislature
- Representation of Muslims in Punjab and Bengal in proportion to their populations
- Formation of three new provinces with Muslim majority – Sindh, Baluchistan, and North-West Frontier Province (NWFP)

However, the Hindu Mahasabha was opposed to the formation of the new provinces and the communal representation in Bengal and Punjab. They pressed for a strictly unitary system. The report made concessions to the Hindu group by stating that joint electorates would be the system followed with reservation of seats for Muslims only where they were in a minority. Sindh would be created into a new province (by severing from Bombay) only after dominion status was granted and weightage would be given to the Hindu minority there.

At the All-party Conference held in Calcutta in 1928 to discuss the report, Jinnah made three amendments to the report:

- 1/3rd representation of Muslims in the Central Legislature
- Reservation to Muslims in Punjab and Bengal in proportion to their populations until adult suffrage was established
- Residual powers to be vested with the provinces and not the centre

However, the All Party Convention failed to accept the recommendation of the Nehru report. Jinnah's demands were not met. He put forth his fourteen point demands in March 1929. The Congress accepted the report only under pressure from Gandhi. The younger members led by Subhash Chandra Bose and Jawaharlal Nehru felt that acceptance of 'dominion status' was a step away from complete independence. It was decided that the British government should accept the report before December 21, 1929; otherwise the Congress would declare 'Poorna Swaraj' (Complete Independence) as their goal and launch a struggle for independence.

Jinnah's 14 Point Demand

The Fourteen Points were proposed by Muhammad Ali Jinnah as a constitutional reform plan to safeguard the political rights of Muslims in a self-governing India. Jinnah's aim was to get more rights for Muslims in self-governing India. He therefore gave his 14 points. These points covered all of the interests of the Muslims and in this, Jinnah stated that it was the "parting of ways" and that he did not want and would not have anything to do with the Indian National Congress in the future.

These 14 points were:

(i) The form of the future Constitution should be federal, with the residuary powers vested in the provinces.

(ii) A uniform measure of autonomy shall be guaranteed to all provinces.

(iii) All legislatures in the country and other elected bodies shall be constituted on the definite principle of adequate and effective representation of minorities in every province without reducing the majority in any province to a minority or even equality.

(iv) In the Central Legislature, Muslim representation shall not be less than one-third.

(v) Representation of communal groups shall continue to be by means of separate electorate as at present, provided it shall be open to any community at any time to abandon its separate electorate in favour of a joint electorate.

(vi) Any territorial distribution that might at any time be necessary, shall not in any way affect the Muslim majority.

(vii) Full religious liberty, i.e., liberty of belief, worship and observance, propaganda, association, and education, shall be guaranteed to all communities.

(viii) No bill or resolution or any part thereof shall be passed in any legislature or any other elected body if three-fourths of the members of any community in that particular body oppose it as being injurious to the interests of that community or in the alternative, such other method is devised as may be found feasible and practicable to deal with such cases.

(ix) Sindh should be separated from the Bombay Presidency.

(x) Reforms should be introduced in the North West Frontier Province and Baluchistan on the same footing as in the other provinces.

(xi) Provision should be made in the Constitution giving Muslims an adequate share, along with the other Indians, in all the services of the state and in local self-governing bodies having due regard to the requirements of efficiency.

(xii) The constitution should embody adequate safeguards for the protection of Muslim culture, education, language, religion and personal laws, as well as for Muslim charitable institutions.

(xiii) No cabinet, either central or provincial, should be formed without there being a proportion of at least one-third Muslim ministers.

(xiv) No change shall be made in the Constitution by the Central Legislature except with the concurrence of the State's contribution of the Indian Federation.

Notably, these fourteen points served as the basis of all the future agendas of the Muslim League.

Declaration of 'Poorna Swaraj' – 1930

In England, the Labour party authorised Lord Irwin, the Governor-General, to make a statement in India regarding the acceptance of the Simon proposal. Lord Irwin's declaration contained the following statement:

'I am authorised, on behalf of his majesty's Government, to state clearly.... that the natural issue of India's Constitutional progress... is the attainment of Dominion Status.'

In India, the declaration of Lord Irwin was welcomed by all the political parties. But the Conservative and Liberal Parties opposed it in the British Parliament.

A Congress session was immediately held at Lahore on December 29, 1929. The choice of Jawaharlal Nehru, an embodiment of youthful enthusiasm for independence, as President of the session, lent a special glamour to the vast assembled congressmen. The new Congress resolution was read as, 'The Congress declares that the word *Swaraj* in Article 1 of the Congress Constitution shall mean Complete Independence....'

The adoption of independence as the goal of India was accepted unanimously. As the clock struck midnight between December 31, 1929 and January 1, 1930, Pandit Jawaharlal Nehru came out in a solemn procession to the banks of the river *Ravi* and hoisted the tricolour flag of Indian independence.

The new working committee of the Congress met on 2nd January, 1930 and read a declaration prepared by Gandhi: 'We will withdraw as much as possible, all voluntary association with the British government, we will prepare for Civil Disobedience including non-payment of taxes, every Indian was to make a declaration of Complete Independence and take a pledge of loyalty to the Indian National Congress'. January 26, 1930 was celebrated as the Poorna Swaraj day or the First Independence Day, all over the country. The working committee met again from February 14–16, and authorised Gandhi to start the Civil Disobedience Movement.

Previous Years' Questions

1. **"At Karachi in 1931, the Congress defined what Swaraj would mean for the masses". (2007)**
2. **"The very idea of the bomb and the secret society and of propaganda through action and sacrifice were imports from the west". (2015)**
3. **"The emergence of left-wing group in the Congress radicalised its social and economic agenda." (2014)**

18 CHAPTER

Civil Disobedience Movement, Depressed Classes Movement & Constitutional Deliberations : 1930–1935

The prevalent political and social circumstances led to a change in the strategy of the National movement. On the other hand, National leaders urged Gandhi to start a mass movement that would hit the foundations of the British Empire, i.e., to defy British laws. The Civil Disobedience Movement – the biggest mass movement – was based on the essence of defying British laws. Under the spirited leadership of Gandhi, the Civil Disobedience Movement brought the unification of the country once again, resulting in awakening of the masses, and bringing politics within the arena of the common man.

Another significant development of this period was the rise of the Depressed Classes Movement or Dalit movement under the leadership of Dr. B.R. Ambedkar or 'Babasaheb'. Ambedkar led the Dalit movement which came in conflict with the Congress party and Gandhi's ideas and designs. Subsequently, it led to differences between Gandhi and Ambedkar on approaches and methods towards Dalit issues and their political identity.

Gandhi and The Civil Disobedience Movement

On 14–16 February, 1930, the Congress Working Committee met and authorised Gandhi to start the Civil Disobedience Movement. Gandhi's plan was to begin Civil Disobedience aimed at breaking the British salt tax. The reason given by Gandhi for defying the salt rule was that salt tax was a deeply symbolic choice, since salt was used by nearly everyone in India. Gandhi said, "Next to air and water, salt is perhaps the greatest necessity of life."

On 2nd March, 1930, Gandhi wrote to the Viceroy Lord Irwin, offering to stop the march if Irwin met eleven demands, including reduction of land revenue assessments, cutting military spending, imposing a tariff on foreign cloth, and abolishing the salt tax.

Gandhi wrote, "on the 11th day of this month, I shall proceed with such co-workers of the Ashram as I can take, to disregard the provisions of the salt laws. It is, I know, open to you to frustrate my design by arresting me, I hope that there will be tens of thousands ready, in a disciplined manner, to take up the work after me, and in the act of disobeying the Salt Act to lay themselves upon to the penalties of a law that should never have disfigured the statute book".

Gandhi made it clear that if the 11 points are ignored, the only way out was Civil Disobedience. The Viceroy ignored the letter and refused to meet with Gandhi. Gandhi thus began his historic mass movement from Dandi.

The Dandi March or the Salt March/Walk (12th March – 6th April, 1930)

Under the leadership of Gandhi, the Civil Disobedience Movement was launched on 12th March 1930. It began with the *Dandi March*. The march or walk was planned from the Sabarmati Ashram to Dandi, a small village on the Gujarat sea coast, where Gandhi decided to make salt in defiance of the Salt Law regulations as a symbol of protest. Gandhi wanted the Civil Disobedience Movement on the strict standards of *Satyagraha* and *Ahimsa*. For that reason, he recruited those people for the march who were trained in strict standards of Satyagraha discipline. The 24-day march was planned to pass through 4 districts and 48 villages. Gandhi sent scouts to each village ahead of the march so he could plan his talks at each resting place, based on the needs of the local residents. Events at each village were scheduled and publicised in the Indian and foreign press.

On 12th March 1930, Gandhi with 78 followers left the Sabarmati Ashram at Ahmedabad and made his way towards Dandi to break the salt law. After travelling for twenty-four days and covering a distance of three hundred and eighty-five kilometres, Gandhi reached Dandi on 6th April 1930. Here, Gandhi picked up a handful of salt from the sea and defied the salt law as a symbol of India's refusal to live under the British laws. Sarojini Naidu standing by his side cried "Hail Deliver". The touching scene signalled the beginning of countrywide waves of Civil Disobedience. The Dandi March thus signified the start of the Civil Disobedience Movement.

Gandhiji's energy at the age of 61 was amazing. Daily he walked 10 miles or more and addressed public meetings. The ashram routine of prayer, spinning, and writing up the daily diary was incumbent on every Marcher. Whenever Gandhi and his followers crossed a village, the villagers flocked from all sides, and sprinkled the roads with water and flowers. The peasants saw a frail figure with a *lathi* in hand walking with his followers pass them. Over 300 village headmen gave up their jobs. This slow march on foot, from village to village, inflamed the country-side and the nation with the spirit of patriotism.

Gandhi with his followers at the Dandi March — Wikimedia Commons

On 9th April 1930, Gandhi prepared a programme for the movement and instructed the people to manufacture salt in every village and do picketing in front of liquor and opium shops and work against abolition of untouchability. Students were asked to leave government schools and colleges. Employees were requested to resign from their services.

The movement spread in other parts of the country. In Tamil Nadu, C. Rajagopalachari led a similar march from Trichinopoly to Vedaranyam. In Gujarat, Sarojini Naidu led the protest. In the North-West Frontier Province, the movement was led by Khan Abdul Ghaffar Khan, popularly known as 'Frontier Gandhi'.

Frontier Gandhi - Khan Abdul Ghaffar Khan — Wikimedia Commons

Along with salt breaking law, activities like no tax campaign, no revenue and no rent (land tax) campaigns became very popular in different parts of India. No-tax campaign started at many places in Gujarat, Bihar, Bengal, and U.P. In the Central Provinces and in Bombay, in defiance of forest laws, people began to cut down timber. In Maharashtra, the Central Provinces, and Karnataka, satyagrahis organised peaceful violations of the forced laws. In certain parts of the country, people took control of the towns for a week and set up parallel government.

The Civil Disobedience Movement carried forward the unfinished work of the Non-Cooperation Movement. There were large-scale boycotts of schools, colleges, and offices. People stopped paying taxes, faced the batons and bullets of the police with supreme courage, and faithfully followed Gandhi's Satyagraha. Foreign goods were burnt in bonfires.

The Dandi March and the resultant Civil Disobedience campaign drew worldwide attention through widespread newspaper coverage. As reports and photographs of this extraordinary protest began to appear in newspapers across the world, there was a growing tide of support for India's freedom struggle. The thrashing of hundreds of non-violent protesters by the police at Dharasana Salt Depot became the centre point of the Salt Satyagraha. An English Lady, Miss Slade, saw how satyagrahis at the Dharasana Salt Depot were being treated by the police. She gave details in *Young India* about the injuries inflicted on the satyagrahis.

Dharasana Satyagraha

Dharasana Satyagraha was a protest against the British salt tax in May, 1930. Following the conclusion of the Salt March to Dandi on 6th April, Gandhi chose a non-violent raid of the Dharasana Salt Works in Gujarat as the next protest against British rule. Hundreds of satyagrahis were beaten by soldiers under British command at Dharasana. Gandhi was arrested before reaching Dharasana. After Gandhi's arrest, his successor Mr. Abbas Tyabji, ex-Justice of Baroda, marched towards Dharasana Salt Depot but he too was arrested. Mrs. Sarojini Naidu succeeded Abbas Tyabji.

On May 21, over 2,000 volunteers led by Ms Naidu and Imam Saheb raided the Dharasana Salt Depot, about 150 miles north of Bombay. Ms. Naidu led the volunteers in prayer and addressed them briefly: "Gandhiji's body is in jail but his soul is with you. India's prestige is now in your hands. You must not use any violence under any circumstances. You will be beaten but you must not resist, you must not even raise a hand to ward off blows." With Manilal, Gandhi's son in the forefront, the throng moved forward towards the salt pans, which were now surrounded with barbed-wire stockade and ditches filled with water, guarded by four hundred Surat police with half a dozen British officials in command.

Hundreds of Indian National Congress volunteers started marching towards the site of the Dharasana Salt Works. Several times, Naidu and the satyagrahis approached the Salt Works, before being turned back by police. At one point they sat down and waited for twenty-eight hours. Hundreds more were arrested.

Following was the account written by Mr. Miller, an American journalist, on the Dharasana Satyagraha:

"Suddenly at a word of command, scores of native police rushed upon the advancing marchers, and rained blows on their heads with steel-shod lathis. Not one of the marchers even raised an arm to fend off the blows. They went down like ninepins. From where I stood, I heard sickening whacks of the clubs on unprotected skulls... Those struck down fell sprawling, unconscious or writhing in pain with fractured skulls or broken shoulders. In two or three minutes the ground was quilted with bodies. Great patches of blood widened on their white clothes. The survivors without breaking ranks, silently and doggedly, marched on until struck down."

"Bodies toppled over in threes and fours, bleeding from great gashes on their scalps. Group after group walked forward, sat down, and submitted being beaten into insensibility without raising an arm to fend off the blows. Finally the policemen became enraged by the non-resistance, sharing, I suppose, the helpless rage I had felt at the demonstrators for not fighting back. They commenced savagely kicking the seated men in the abdomen and testicles. The injured men writhed and squealed in agony, which seemed to inflame the fury of the police, and the crowd again almost broke away from their leaders. The police then began dragging the sitting men by the arms or feet, sometimes for a hundred yards, and throwing them into the ditches... Hour after hour stretcher-bearers carried back a stream of inert, bleeding bodies."

The British government did not take first the campaign seriously. Many ridiculed the campaign. The *Statesman* wrote: 'The Mahatma could go on boiling sea water till Dominion Status was attained'. But before a month passed, the government realised the gravity and struck hard in a ruthless manner. As the movement intensified, the government resorted to severe repression. Repressive laws, mass arrests, torture, firings, lathi charges, and police excesses became common occurrences. But people continued to manufacture salt on the sea shores and laws were broken elsewhere systematically.

The Indian National Congress was declared an illegal body. Gandhi was arrested on 5th May, 1930 and sent to Yerwada Central Jail. The arrest of Gandhi infuriated the masses and they voluntarily expressed their solidarity with the movement. All the leading leaders were put inside jails. These arrests intensified the movement. The national flag, the symbol of the new spirit, now became a common sight even in remote villages.

Almost all sections of the people participated in varying degrees. One of the significant aspects of the movement was the mass participation of women. The movement is said to be the most liberating experience for Indian women. It provided an opportunity for them to participate in the public arena.

Historian Bipan Chandra observes "The Civil Disobedience Movement of 1930–31, then marked a critically important stage in the progress of the anti-imperialist struggle".

In fact, the Civil Disobedience Movement came to be synonymous with Indian freedom struggle and non-violence. It continued for almost a year, ending with the release of Mahatma Gandhi from jail and the discussions at the Second Round Table Conference with Viceroy Lord Irwin. The movement had a significant effect on changing British attitudes toward Indian independence and caused a huge number of Indians to aggressively join the freedom struggle for the first time.

B. R. Ambedkar and The Movement for Depressed Classes

Babasaheb Ambedkar

Babasaheb Ambedkar
— Wikimedia Commons

Bhimrao Ramji Ambedkar (1891 – 1956), an eminent national leader, economist, and jurist was born into a Mahar caste, which was treated as 'untouchable' in the society. His father was an army officer in the East India Company in Mhow district of Madhya Pradesh. From his childhood onwards, Ambedkar and his family faced mistreatment and subjugation from the upper caste communities. In the school, untouchable children were segregated and given little attention by teachers.

Ambedkar was the only child from his family who successfully completed high school. After matriculation, Ambedkar enrolled himself in the Elphinstone College in Bombay, thus becoming the first Mahar to do so. After completion of his college studies, Ambedkar took up a small job in the Baroda State Service where he faced untouchability. He had to leave the job immediately as his father became seriously ill and later died in 1913. Ambedkar's mentor Krishna Keshav, a Brahmin school teacher, introduced him to the visionary ruler of Baroda, Maharaja Sayajirao Gaekwad III. Sayajirao had announced a Baroda State Scholarship for three years for those wanting to study in Columbia University in the US.

Ambedkar was granted the Baroda State Scholarship for his postgraduate studies in Columbia University. He obtained MA in Economics in 1915 from Columbia University and in 1916, left for London for his further studies in the London School of Economics. In 1917, he joined the Baroda State Service but was forced to resign due to ill treatment he faced in the office on the grounds of untouchability. Ambedkar settled in Mumbai and started his legal profession in the Bombay High Court.

Movements for Justice for the Depressed Classes

While practising law, Ambedkar started his movement against untouchability and fight for justice for the Depressed Classes. He began to promote education to untouchables through an organization 'Bahishkrit Hitakarini Sabha', intended to promote education and socio-economic improvement, as well as the welfare activities to the Depressed Classes. He put up the case for separate electorate and reservation for Depressed Classes before a Committee which was preparing for the India Act of 1919. For the abolition of untouchability and promoting awareness among the Depressed Classes, he started many periodicals like Mooknayak, Bahishkrit Bharat, and Janata.

In 1923, Bombay Legislative Council had passed a resolution that public watering places, schools, markets, and temples should be open for the entry of untouchables. In spite of this resolution, depressed communities faced discrimination and harassment from the upper classes. Ambedkar launched several movements to implement these rights for the untouchables. In 1927, Ambedkar led the Mahad satyagraha to fight for the right of the untouchable community to draw water from the main public tank - the Chavdar Tank. The main objective of this satyagraha was to implement the resolution of the Mahad municipality which had declared public watering places open to untouchables. In March 1927, thousands of men and women along with Babasaheb, had assembled near the tank to assert their rights of drawing water. Offended upper caste people considered this action as trespassing and began to beat up the untouchables. Babasaheb Ambedkar called for another satyagraha at Mahad in which he appealed to lower caste Hindus not to follow Hindu Chaturvarna system and Hindu Shashtras. He stated, 'Unless the Chaturvarna system is destroyed, there is no hope for Hinduism, because this system hampers the development of the individual. So allow this social revolution that we are bringing about to unfold peacefully, do not oppose us, reject the Shastras and embrace justice.'

Many resolutions were passed in the Mahad satyagraha. One of them was to burn the Hindu text *Manusmriti* which holds women and Shudras in contempt and imposes immoral rules that amount to treating them as lower than animals.

Women took part in large numbers in the Mahad satyagraha. Ambedkar appealed to them to change their traditional ways of dressing which are all signs of being an untouchable. He said, 'The way you wear your saris is a sign of your being untouchable, you must wipe out that sign. You must begin the practice of wearing your saris in the same fashion that upper-caste women do, it will not cost you anything.'

The Mahad satyagraha generated a lot of political awareness among the men and women of the untouchable class.

In 1930, Ambedkar launched the Kalaram Temple Satyagraha in Nasik to assert the rights of temple entry for the untouchables.

Ambedkar launched a peasant rebellion against the *khoti* system prevalent in Konkan. The *khots* were the government revenue collectors, mostly Brahmins, Marathas, and Muslims, who exploited farmers and tenants by collecting four times the amount they remitted to the government. In 1937, Ambedkar tabled a bill in the Bombay Legislative Assembly aimed at abolishing the *khoti* system by creating a direct relationship between the government and the farmers.

Ambedkar felt the need to establish an organisation of volunteers to safeguard human rights amongst the Depressed Classes. Hence, the Samata Sainik Dal or the SSD was established in 1926. SSD played a significant role in promoting human rights and abolition of untouchability.

In 1936, Ambedkar founded the Independent Labour Party, which contested the 1937 Bombay election to the Central Legislative Assembly for the 13 reserved and 4 general seats, and secured 11 and 3 seats, respectively.

From 1930–1932, the Round Table Conferences were held in London to discuss the constitutional reforms in India. B. R. Ambedkar as a representative of Depressed Classes was an active participant to these conferences. In August 1932, Prime Minister Ramsay MacDonald announced the Communal Award which provided for separate electorates for various Indian communities, including Depressed Classes. Gandhi fiercely opposed the separate electorate for untouchables, saying he feared that such an arrangement would divide the Hindu community. However, Ambedkar favoured the provision of a separate electorate for the Depressed Classes, as according to him, political solutions like a separate electorate would work for the upliftment of the Depressed Classes.

However, after a series of negotiations, both Gandhi and Ambedkar agreed to a solution called the Poona Pact, thereby withdrawing separate electorate for Depressed Classes. The Poona Pact agreement gave the provision of reserved seats for the Depressed Classes within the general electorate.

Ambedkar's most popular books include *Annihilation of Caste* (1936) and *Who Were the Shudras?* (1946). These works are a critique of the Hindu caste system and gives details on exploitation of Dalits or untouchables in the oppressive caste system of India.

Upon India's independence on 15 August 1947, Ambedkar was appointed as independent India's first Law Minister. After some time, he was appointed as Chairman of the Drafting Committee of the Constituent Assembly to frame the Constitution of India.

In 1956, along with his five lakhs supporters, Ambedkar converted to Buddhism in a large public ceremony in Nagpur.

Round Table Conferences — (1930–1932)

The Round Table Conferences were a series of conferences organised by the British Government to discuss constitutional reforms in India as per the recommendation made by the Simon Commission Report. There were three Round Table Conferences that took place in London from 1930–1932. Efforts were made to persuade Gandhi to agree to participate in the proposed Round Table Conference at London as suggested in the Simon Commission. The negotiations failed, and the British Government decided to go ahead with the proposed Round Table Conference. Congress refused to attend the conference, but representatives of other parties like the Muslim League, and other parties, and the Princely States attended the conference at London in November 1930.

First Round Table Conference (1930–1931)

The first Round Table Conference started on November 12, 1930 at London, chaired by the British Prime Minister, Ramsay MacDonald of the Labour Party. There were fifty-seven political leaders from British India and sixteen delegates from the Princely States. In total, 89 delegates from India attended the Conference. However, the Indian National Congress kept away from the conference due to their participation in the ongoing Civil Disobedience Movement.

British Prime Minister, Ramsay MacDonald — Wikimedia Commons

The main issues discussed in the conference were: Federal Structure, Provincial Constitution, Minorities, Burma, North West Frontier Province, Franchise, Defence, and Services. The concept of forming an 'All-India Federation' became central to the discussion and well supported by all the groups. The conference also paid attention to Dr. B.R. Ambedkar's demand of a separate electorate for the 'Untouchables'. While winding up the first conference, the British Prime Minster declared that 'steps would be taken to enlist the cooperation of those sections of public opinion which had held aloof from the Conference'.

The Gandhi-Irwin Pact

It was felt that the British government would have to hold consultations with the Congress. Lord Irwin, the Viceroy of India appealed to the Indian people and released the Congress leaders from jail. Discussions between the Viceroy and Gandhi continued for 15 days and the Gandhi-Irwin Pact was signed on March 5, 1931.

Following were the provisions of the Pact:

(a) To withdraw all ordinances and pending prosecutions,

(b) To release all political prisoners, except those who were guilty of violence,

(c) To restore the confiscated property of the satyagrahis,

(d) To permit peaceful picketing of liquor, opium, and foreign cloth shops
(e) To permit the collection or manufacture of salt, free of duty, by persons residing within a specific distance of the sea shore
(f) To agree not to press for investigation into police excesses by the Congress
(g) To suspend the Civil Disobedience Movement, and
(h) To stop boycott and to participate in the Second Round Table Conference.

The Viceroy, Irwin however, turned down two of Gandhi's demands:
(i) Public inquiry into police excesses, and
(ii) Commutation of Bhagat Singh and his comrades' death sentence to life sentence.

Gandhi on behalf of the Congress agreed:
(i) To suspend the Civil Disobedience Movement, and
(ii) To participate in the next Round Table Conference.

Karachi Congress Session—1931

In 1931, the Congress met at Karachi. It approved the Gandhi-Irwin Pact. The session was presided over by Sardar Patel. The most significant contribution of the Karachi session was a resolution it passed on Fundamental Rights and Economic Policy.

Some important aspects of this resolution were:

- Basic civil rights of Freedom of Speech, Freedom of Press, Freedom of Assembly, and Freedom of Association,
- Equality before law,
- Elections on the basis of Universal Adult Franchise,
- Free and compulsory primary education,
- Substantial reduction in rent and taxes,
- Better conditions for workers including a living wage, limited hours of work, and protection of women and peasants,
- Government ownership or control of key industries, mines, and transport and protection of minorities.

Through the Karachi Resolution, the Congress for the first time defined what 'Swaraj' would mean for the masses. The resolution defined Swaraj for the masses as the basic civil liberties of equality, freedom of thought, expression, belief, faith, and worship. The Swaraj for the peasants was to mean reduction in the rent, and exemption in case of uneconomic holdings. For the workers, the Swaraj would mean the independence to work for limited hours and protection for women workers, in addition to the living wages. Thus, the Congress which was agenda-less a few years back had the most impressive agenda in hand now.

The Second Round Table Conference and the Suspension of the Civil Disobedience Movement

The Second Round Table Conference started on 7th September and lasted till December 1931. Major changes were witnessed in the Second Round Table Conference. These were: Congress representatives accepted the invitation to participate in the conference; Ramsay MacDonald now headed a National Government dominated by the Conservative Party; Britain faced a financial crisis that distracted the British Government from the conference.

The Gandhi-Irwin Pact opened the way for Congress participation in this conference. Gandhi was invited from India and attended as the sole official Congress representative accompanied by Sarojini Naidu and also Madan Mohan Malaviya, Ghanshyam Das Birla, Muhammad Iqbal, Sir Mirza Ismail (Diwan of Mysore), S.K. Dutta, and Sir Syed Ali Imam.

During the Conference, Gandhi claimed that the Untouchables were Hindus and should not be treated as a "minority"; and that there should be no separate electorates or special safeguards for Muslims or other minorities. These claims were rejected by the other Indian participants. He clashed with the leader of depressed classes, Dr. B. R. Ambedkar, over the issue of Untouchables as minority. The two eventually resolved the issue with the Poona Pact of 1932. At the end of the conference, Ramsay MacDonald undertook to produce a 'Communal Award' for minority representation.

Disappointed with the results, Gandhi returned to India on December 28, 1931. On December 29, the Congress Working Committee decided to resume the Civil Disobedience Movement.

In 1931, certain events like coming to power of Conservatives in Britain, replacement of the Viceroy, and execution of Bhagat Singh, created an atmosphere of dejection in Gandhi and other younger Indian leaders. The Congress decided to restart the movement in January 1932. As usual, the British government took stern steps to suppress the movement and in the meanwhile, the British Prime Minister announced Communal Award in 1932. The Civil Disobedience Movement continued up to 1934 and it was withdrawn in that year.

A file picture of the Second Round Table Conference — Wikimedia Commons

The Communal Award and Poona Pact, 24th September 1932

The Communal Award was made by the British Prime Minister Ramsay Macdonald on 16th August 1932, granting separate electorates to the Forward Caste, Lower Caste, Muslims, Buddhists, Sikhs, Indian Christians, Anglo-Indians, Europeans, and Dalits. The Untouchables were assigned a number of seats to be filled by election from special constituencies in which voters belonging only to the Untouchables could vote.

The Award was highly controversial and Gandhi, who was in Yerwada jail, fasted in protest against it. The Communal Award was supported notably by the leader of the Untouchables, Dr. B. R. Ambedkar.

Madan Mohan Malaviya summoned a conference of various castes and political parties, including Dr. B.R. Ambedkar, the leader of the Depressed Classes League. The conference finally arrived at an agreement in Poona on September 25, 1932, the sixth day of Gandhiji's fast.

A common electorate of all the Hindus was agreed upon, subject to two conditions –

1. First, 148 seats in different Provincial Legislatures were reserved for the Depressed Classes, in place of 71 as provided in the Communal Award.
2. 18% of the seats in the Central Legislature were reserved for the Depressed Classes.

This is called the Poona Pact. Electorates for other religions like Muslims, Buddhists, Sikhs, Indian Christians, Anglo-Indians, and Europeans remained separate.

The Third Round Table Conference

The Third and the last Round Table Conference started on November 1931 and lasted till December 24, 1932. Only forty-six delegates attended, since most of the main political figures of India were not present. The Labour Party from Britain and the Indian National Congress refused to attend.

In this conference, a college student Chaudhry Rahmat Ali proposed the name of the new land carved out from India for the Muslims – Pakistan.

From September 1931 until March 1933, under the supervision of the Secretary of State for India, Sir Samuel Hoare, the reforms recommended in the Round Table Conferences were proposed in the forthcoming Government of India Act, 1935.

The Government of India Act, 1935

In August 1935, Government of India Act was passed. This Act is considered as a mini constitution that formed the background for the Constitution of independent India. The Act was based on:

- Simon Commission Report
- The recommendations of the Round Table Conferences
- The White Paper published by the British government in 1933 (based on the Third Round Table Conference)
- Report of the Joint Select Committees

Objectives of the British Government Behind the India Act, 1935

- The federalism of the Indian Union as the main provision of the Act was designed to meet the aims of the Conservative Party who expected the Act to grant Dominion status to India.

- To win the support of Moderate nationalists to lead eventually to a Dominion of India.
- To retain British control of the Indian Army, Indian finances, and India's foreign relations
- To win Muslim support by conceding most of Jinnah's Fourteen Points
- To convince the Princes to join the federation with the following terms such as: Each Prince would select his state's representative in the Federal Legislature; there would be no pressure for the Princes to democratise their administrations or allow elections for state representatives in the Federal Legislature; the Princes would enjoy heavy privileges.
- Ensuring that the Congress could never rule alone or gain enough seats to bring down the government. This was done by over-representing the Princes, by giving every possible minority the right to separately vote for candidates belonging to their respective communities through separate electorate, and by making the executive theoretically, but not practically, removable by the legislature.
- That by giving Indian politicians a great deal of power at the provincial level, while denying them responsibility at the Centre, it was hoped that Congress, the only national party, would disintegrate into a series of provincial fiefdoms.

The main provision of the Act were broadly classified under two heads – central set-up and provisional set-up.

Central Set up – Formation of All India Federation

- All India federation was to consist of British India and the Princely States.
- The provinces in British India would have to join the federation but this was not compulsory for the Princely States.
- The federal legislature was to consist of two houses – Council of States or Upper House and the Federal Assembly or Lower House.

The federation could not be established until:

- The Upper House was to have 156 members from British India and not more than 101 from the Princely States;
- The Federal Assembly was to have 250 members from British India and 125 from the Princely States;
- The terms on which a state joined the Federation were to be laid down in the Instrument of Accession.

This federation never materialised because of the lack of support from the required number of Princely States.

Provincial Set-Up – Provincial Autonomy

- Abolition of provincial dyarchy and introduction of dyarchy at the centre.
- The Act gave more autonomy to the provinces.
- The number of provinces was now 11 with the creation of two new provinces, Sindh and Orissa; and Burma was separated from India.

- The Governor was the Head of the Executive.
- There was a Council of Ministers to advise the Governor. The ministers were responsible to the provincial legislatures who controlled them. The legislature could also remove the ministers.

Dyarchy at Centre

- The executive authority of the centre was vested in the Governor-General on behalf of the Crown.
- The federal subjects were divided into two-fold categories of *Reserved* and *Transferred* subjects.
- The Reserved list comprised of subjects such as administration of defence, external affairs, ecclesiastical affairs, and matters related to tribal areas. These subjects were to be administered by the Governor-General at his discretion with the help of three counsellors appointed by him. They were not responsible to the legislative.
- The administration of the transferred subjects was to be done by the Governor-General on the advice of the Council of Ministers whose number could not exceed 10. The Council of Ministers had to command the confidence of the legislature.
- However, the Governor-General could act contrary to the advice of the Council of Ministers if any of his 'special responsibilities' was involved in such act. However, in that case (when an act involved special responsibilities), the Governor-General would work under the control and direction of the Secretary of State.
- Further, the Governor-General was also responsible for the coordination of work between the two wings and for encouraging joint deliberations between the counsellors and the ministers.

Other Features of the 1935 Act

- A Federal Court was established at Delhi for the resolution of disputes between provinces and also between the centre and the provinces. It was to have one Chief Justice and not more than 6 judges.
- A Federal Railway Authority was set up to control Indian Railways.
- The Reserve Bank of India was established as per this Act.
- The Act also provided for the establishment of Federal, Provincial, and Joint Public Service Commissions.
- The Indian Council was abolished. The Secretary of State for India would instead have a team of advisors.
- This Act introduced direct elections in India for the first time. About 10% of the whole population acquired voting rights.
- The British Parliament retained its supremacy over the Indian legislatures, both provincial and federal.
- A controversial feature of the Government of India Act, 1935 was the safeguards and reservations provided in the Act, which would serve as checks and limitations on such undesirable tendencies which might lead to the failure of the responsible government in India.

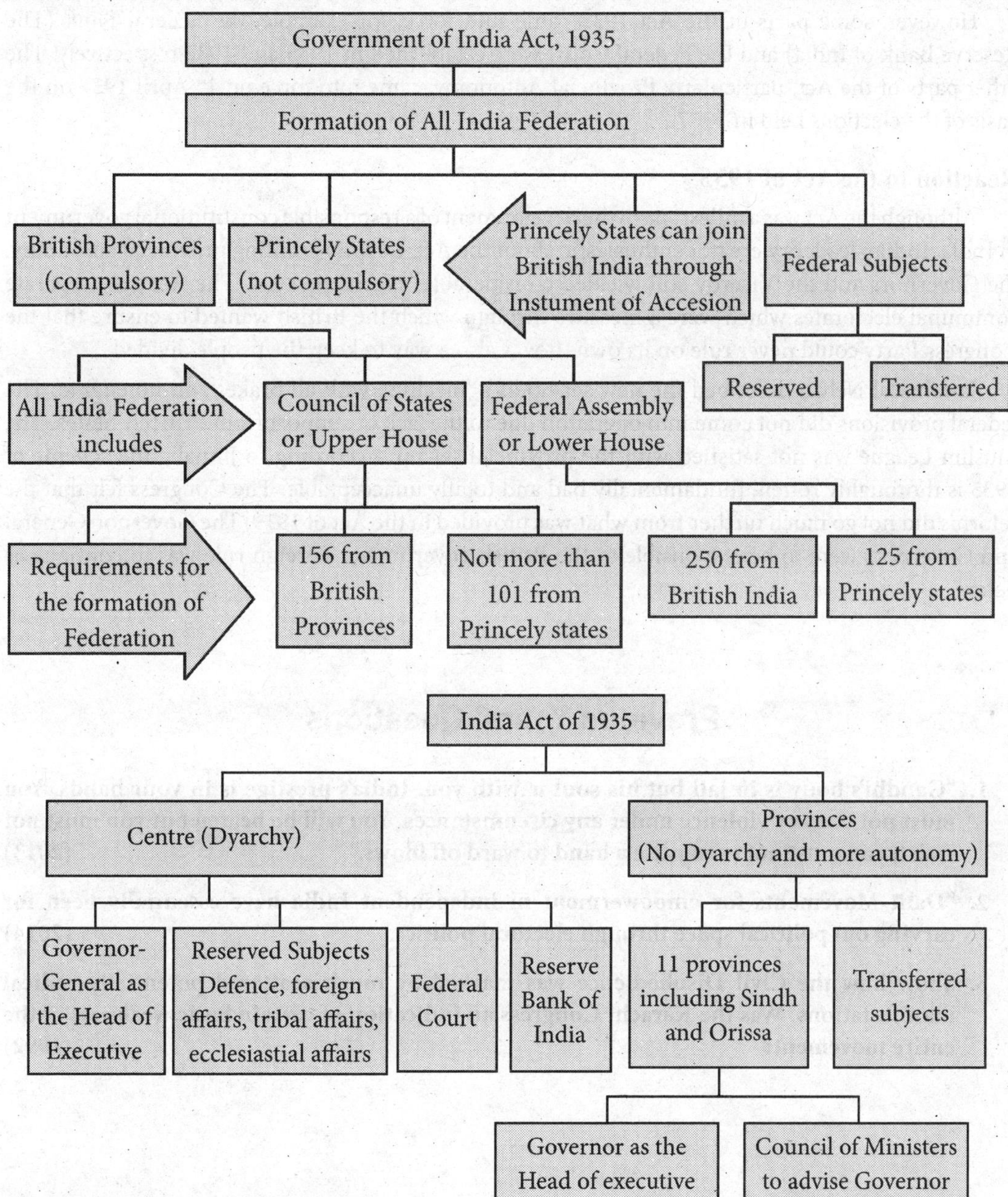

Implications of the Act of 1935

The proposal for setting up of the Federation of India did not materialise because the Act proposed that the federation could come into existence only if as many Princely States (which had been given option to join or not to join) were entitled to one-half of the states' seats in the Upper House of the federal legislature. Due to this, Central Government in India continued to be governed by the provisions of the Act of 1919.

However, some parts of the Act 1935 came into force, for example, the Federal Bank (The Reserve Bank of India) and the Federal Court were established in 1935 and 1937 respectively. The other parts of the Act, particularly Provincial Autonomy, came into force on 1st April 1937 on the basis of the elections held in 1937.

Reaction to the Act of 1935

Although the Act was a milestone in the development of a responsible constitutional government in India, Indian leaders were not enthusiastic about the Act. Despite granting provincial autonomy, the Governors and the Viceroy still wielded considerable 'special powers'. The Act gave separate communal electorates which were a measure through which the British wanted to ensure that the Congress Party could never rule on its own. It was also a way to keep the people divided.

Jawaharlal Nehru described the new set-up as a 'machine with all brakes and no engine'. The federal provisions did not come into operation due to the lack of support from Princely States. The Muslim League was not satisfied with the provincial set-up. According to Jinnah, 'the scheme of 1935 is thoroughly rotten, fundamentally bad and totally unacceptable'. The Congress felt that the reforms did not go much further from what was provided in the Act of 1919. The Governor-General and Governors were to be responsible to the British government. Foreign rule was to continue as before.

Previous Years' Questions

1. **"Gandhi's body is in jail but his soul is with you. India's prestige is in your hands. You must not use any violence under any circumstances. You will be beaten but you must not resist; you must not even raise a hand to ward off blows." (2013)**
2. **"Dalit Movements for empowerment in independent India have essentially been for carving out political space through electoral politics." (2014)**
3. **Show how the Civil Disobedience was marked by much scattered potentially radical manifestations. Was the Karachi Congress an indication of certain basic weakness of the entire movement? (1992)**

CHAPTER 19

The Leadership of Subhash Chandra Bose and National Movement During The Second World War

Introduction

We have discussed in previous chapters how Gandhi's pacific methods were increasingly challenged by Leftists and radical leaders. Subhash Chandra Bose was one such revolutionary leader who was known for his militant approach to the national movement and promoted socialist policies in the Congress. In fact, after the Civil Disobedience Movement, Gandhi's influence was eclipsed by the rising popularity of Bose both in the Congress and in the national movement for shifting to a radical approach.

Subhash Chandra Bose (1897 – 1945)

Subhash Chandra Bose (23 January 1897 – 18 August 1945) popularly known as 'Netaji' was the leader of the younger, radical wing of the Indian National Congress in the late 1920s and 1930s, rising to become Congress President in 1938 and 1939. Subhash Chandra Bose stood for hardliner socialism and complete independence against the British.

Netaji Subhash Chandra Bose
— Wikimedia Commons

Subhash Chandra was born in a wealthy and influential family in Cuttack, Odisha, then under the Bengal province in 1897. After completing his college education, Bose was sent to England to prepare for the Indian Civil Service. In 1920, he passed the Preliminary Civil Service Examination, but was reluctant to appear for the final exam after hearing of the national movement in India. In 1921, Bose resigned from his candidacy and hurriedly came back to India and joined the Indian National Congress.

Bose took charge of the Bengal Provincial Congress Committee and also started a newspaper called 'Swaraj'. In Bengal, Bose found his mentor in C.R. Das who was more receptive to his ideas than Gandhi . When C.R. Das became the Mayor of Calcutta in 1924, Bose worked as the CEO of the Calcutta Municipal Corporation. He was the President of the All India Youth Congress and also the Secretary of the Bengal State Congress. In 1930, he became the Mayor of Calcutta.

During the INC session of 1928, he gave himself the title of 'General Officer Commanding', much to the displeasure of the Moderate wing of the Congress. Expressing disgust against the activities of Bose, Gandhi had remarked that he is conducting "Bertram Mills Circus".

By 1935, Bose had made it clear that he would opt for methods other than the 'harmless' ahimsa and satyagraha to achieve his goals. He began meeting powerful leaders of Europe to determine the supporters for the Indian cause. Bose's visits to the Italian dictator and the strongest proponent of fascism, Benito Mussolini, had irked Gandhi to a greater extent.

Bose presented Mussolini with book 'Indian Struggle' in which he described the synthesis of Communism and Fascism to prevail over India following the exodus of the British.

Bose further opined that India would need a dictator who would rule this nation with an iron fist for at least 20 years following the independence.

Thus, Bose's hard-line approach towards the Independence movement and his leaning towards left ideology distanced him away from Moderate leaders of the Indian National Congress.

Congress Under Subhash Chandra Bose (1938–1939)

The Left influence had become predominant in the Congress since 1934. In May 1934, Acharya Narendra Dev, Jayaprakash Narayana, and Achyut Patwardhan, who were members of the Congress Working Committee, organised the Congress Socialist Party.

With the emergence of prominent Leftist leaders like Jawaharlal Nehru and Subhash Chandra Bose, the gap between the Leftists and Rightists widened within the Congress. Leftists were radical while Rightists were conservative and followers of Gandhi's ideology.

At the Haripura session in February 1938, Subhash Chandra Bose (with Leftist leaning) was unanimously elected President of the Congress. Bose outlined his policy as follows: "My term of office as the Congress President will be devoted to resist the unwanted federal scheme with all the peaceful and legitimate powers, including non-violence and non-cooperation if necessary and to strengthen the country's determination to resist this scheme".

Haripura session adopted two important resolutions:

- First, the people of Princely States were assured of moral support in their struggle against the rulers.
- Secondly, the Congress declared that India "could not be a party to an imperialist war" and "would not permit her manpower and resources to be exploited in the interest of British imperialism".

Subhash Chandra Bose formed the National Planning Committee, a forerunner of independent India's Planning Commission. The idea was to draw a comprehensive plan for economic development of India on the basis of industrialisation. It was against the 'Charkha' policy of Gandhi.

It was in the Haripura session when the differences between Gandhi and Bose surfaced over their attitudes towards the Great Britain. Subhash Chandra Bose was against the plan of the British to drag India into the Second World War. He was aware of the political instability of Britain and wanted to take advantage of it, rather than wait for the British to grant independence. This is evident from his statement: 'Britain's Peril is India's Opportunity'.

During this time, the split in the Congress camp between the Rightists and Leftists further widened. The former, i.e., Rightists were led by Rajaji and Vallabhbhai Patel and the latter, i.e., Leftists were led by Subhash Bose. The Rightists were not yet in favour of overthrow of the British government in India. The Leftists who stood for a bold policy thought for a national resistance against the foreign rule.

The differences between these groups came to a head over the election of the President of the next session of the Congress to be held in Tripuri in March 1939.

In 1939, Subhash Chandra Bose decided to stand again for the Presidentship – this time as the spokesperson of militant politics and radical groups. Putting forward his candidature on 21st January 1939, Bose said that he represented the 'new ideas, ideologies, problems and programme' that had emerged with 'the progressive sharpening of the anti-imperialist struggle in India.' The Presidential elections, he said, should be fought among different candidates 'on the basis of definite problems and programmes.'

Gandhian followers like Sardar Patel, Rajendra Prasad, J.B. Kripalani, and four other members of the Congress Working Committee issued a counter statement, declaring that the talk of ideologies, programmes, and policies was irrelevant in the elections of a Congress President since these were evolved by the various Congress bodies such as the AICC and the Working Committee, and that the position of the Congress President was like that of a constitutional head who represented and symbolised the unity and solidarity of the nation.

On behalf of Gandhi, the Rightists set up Dr. Pattabhi Sitaramayya as a rival candidate. Subhash Bose was elected on 29th January 1939 by 1580 votes against 1377. Gandhi declared that 'Pattabhi's defeat is my defeat'.

Bose branded Sardar Patel and the majority of the top Congress leadership as Rightists. He accused them of working for a compromise with the Government on the question of the federation. He also labelled them as 'Low Intellectuals' and 'Compromisers'. The Congress leaders resented such charges and many showed their disagreement with Bose by resigning from the working committee.

Bose could see no other way but to resign from the Presidentship. Nehru tried to mediate but to no avail. Bose could also not get the support of the Congress Socialists and the Communists at Tripuri. Subsequently in May, Subhash and his followers formed the Forward Bloc as a new party within the Congress. And when he gave a call for an all-India protest on 9th July against an AICC resolution, the Working Committee removed him from the Presidentship of the Bengal Provincial Congress Committee and debarred him from holding any Congress office for three years.

National Movement and Events During The Second World War

The Indian National Army or Azad Hind Fauj

After his removal from the Congress, Bose was placed under house arrest by the British before escaping from India in 1941. In 1942, the Indian National Army (INA) was formed by Rash Behari Bose and revived by Subhash Chandra Bose on October 21, 1943.

The aim of the army was to secure Indian independence from the British.

The idea of the INA was first conceived in Malaya by Mohan Singh, an Indian officer of the British Indian Army when he decided not to join the retreating British army and instead went to the Japanese for help.

Indian prisoners of war were handed over by the Japanese to Mohan Singh who then tried to recruit them into an Indian National Army. By the end of 1942, forty thousand men expressed their willingness to join the INA.

However, serious differences emerged between the Indian army officers led by Mohan Singh and the Japanese over the role that the INA was to play. Mohan Singh and Niranjan Singh Gill, the senior-most Indian officer to join the INA, were arrested by the Japanese.

The second phase of the INA began when Subhash Chandra Bose reached Singapore by means of German and Japanese submarines on 2nd July 1943, after meeting Hitler in Berlin. Subhash Bose set up two INA headquarters, one in Rangoon and the other in Singapore, and began to reorganise the INA. Recruits were sought from civilians, and funds were gathered. The INA was also at the forefront of women's equality and the formation of a women's regiment. The Rani of Jhansi regiment was formed as an all-volunteer women's unit to fight the British Raj as well as provide medical services to the INA.

On 6th July 1944, Subhash Chandra Bose in a broadcast on Azad Hind Radio addressed to Gandhi, said: 'Father of our Nation, in this holy war of India's liberation, we ask for your blessing and good wishes.'

One INA battalion commanded by Shah Nawaz along with the Japanese Army marched to the Indo-Burma front and participated in the Imphal campaign against the British. The failure of the Imphal campaign, and the steady Japanese retreat there, quashed the hopes of the INA liberating the nation.

Ideological differences between Gandhi and Subhash Chandra Bose

Though Gandhi and Subhash Chandra Bose wanted the emancipation of India from Colonial rule, they differed in their strategy and methods as well as the vision of what future programmes should be followed.

Subhash Bose was a fierce nationalist with socialistic zeal. He was inspired by the Extremist tradition and followed the footsteps of Aurobindo Ghosh. Bose was in contact with the leaders of the powerful European nations and had met the radical leaders like Mussolini and Hitler. He was convinced that with the alliance of these emerging powerful European nations, India could get independence from the British.

Gandhi was a Moderate nationalist and was inspired by leaders like Tilak and Tagore. His outlook towards the national movement was moderate rather revolutionary. Bose believed that Independence could be obtained only through a military war against the British. Contrary to this view of Bose, Gandhi believed in non-violent satyagraha and was convinced that the might of British colonial administration could be brought down only by mass mobilisation.

Gandhi and the Congress had adopted the strategy of struggle for the masses. He felt that mass struggle could not be sustained indefinitely since the masses had limited capacity for suffering. Bose was opposed to this strategy. He believed in continuing the struggle and criticised Gandhi for withdrawal of the non-cooperation movement.

Bose was inspired by fascism and communist authoritarianism. He felt that such a model could be adopted for Indian development. Rapid modernisation achieved by the Soviet Union Five-Year Plans appealed to him. Gandhi in contrast, was the proponent of village democracy and self-rule. He was in favour of cottage and village industries. Gandhi was a critique of mass production and viewed industrialisation itself with scepticism.

Despite their differences, both Gandhi and Bose had immense respect for one another. It was Gandhi who advised Bose to work under Deshbandhu Chittaranjan Das, a prominent national Congress leader from Bengal. Later, C.R. Das became Bose's greatest mentor. Under Das's guidance, Subhash Bose emerged as a youth educator, journalist, and commandant of the Bengal Congress volunteers. His activities led to his imprisonment in December 1921. In 1924, he was appointed Chief Executive Officer of the Calcutta Municipal Corporation, with Das as Mayor.

Gandhi called Bose as "Prince among Patriots". Bose called Gandhi as "The Father of our Nation" in a radio broadcast from Rangoon in 1944. On hearing the news about Bose's death, Gandhi was shocked and stated that Netaji's 'patriotism is second to none. His bravery shines through all his actions. He aimed high but failed. Who has not failed?'

Election of 1937 and Provincial Congress Ministries

At its 49th session held in Lucknow, the Congress party, despite opposition from the newly elected Jawaharlal Nehru as the Party President, agreed to contest the provincial elections to be held in 1937. There was general opposition to the Act of 1935. It criticised the Act's proposal for making All India Federation, safeguards, and Governor-General's overriding powers. The resolution of the Congress was "not to submit to this Constitution or to cooperate with it, but to combat it both inside and outside the legislatures so that it can be ended."

However, the provincial aspect of the Act of 1935 was largely accepted and the demand to contest election was well received by the Congress. Jawaharlal said, 'there was no choice but to contest the elections as it would educate the masses on the political policies and economic programmes of the party.' The Congress launched the Election campaign and its manifesto included "A demand for the Constituent Assembly". The main objective of contesting elections for the Congress was to combat the Act of 1935 by not cooperating with the British government.

In the same year 1936, Jinnah was elected President of the Muslim League. The Muslim League appointed a Central Parliamentary Board to direct the elections.

Under the provisions of the 1935 Act, provincial Assemblies' Elections were held in the winter of 1936–37. This was the first election in the Indian subcontinent in which a large number of Indians, i.e., approximately 30 million adults, were eligible to participate. Still, it was a limited Adult Franchise as the eligibility criteria was based on land ownership. There were two major political parties in the country besides multiple local parties – the Congress and the Muslim League. Both the political parties did their best to persuade the masses. Congress contested from the joint electorate while Muslim League from the separate electorate.

Elections were held in the eleven provinces – Madras, Central Provinces, Bihar, Orissa, United Provinces, Bombay Presidency, Assam, NWFP, Bengal, Punjab, and Sindh.

The results of the election of 1937 were in favour of the Indian National Congress. Out of total 1,585 seats, Congress won 707. There were 864 seats assigned as 'general' constituencies. Congress contested 739 and won 617 seats. Of the 125 non-general constituencies contested by the Congress, 59 were reserved for Muslims and in those, the Congress won 25 seats. Hence, the Congress failed to attract Muslim votes.

Even the All-India Muslim League which emerged as the second largest party could win just 106 seats out of 482 reserved seats for Muslims. In the United Province, it won only 27 out of 64 reserved seats for Muslims. The League offered to form coalition with the Congress, but the latter refused its offer.

In Punjab, the Unionist Party emerged as the winner under the leadership of Sikandar Hayat Khan. In Sindh, the largest party in reserved seats was Sindh United Party while in the general constituencies, it was was Sindh Hindu Mahasabha. In Bengal, the Krishak Praja Party under the leadership of A. K. Fazlul Huq won 36 seats and formed a coalition government with the support of the Muslim League.

The final results of the elections were declared in February 1937. The Indian National Congress emerged in power in eight provinces – the three exceptions being Bengal, Punjab, and Sindh. The All-India Muslim League failed to form the government in any province.

Congress formed its own ministries in seven provinces and coalition ministries in Assam and NFWP. Only Sindh, Bengal, and Punjab had no Congress ministries. The Congress did extremely well in their respective provinces. The people regarded the Congress ruled provinces as 'islands of self-rule where they could breathe freely and stand upright with dignity'.

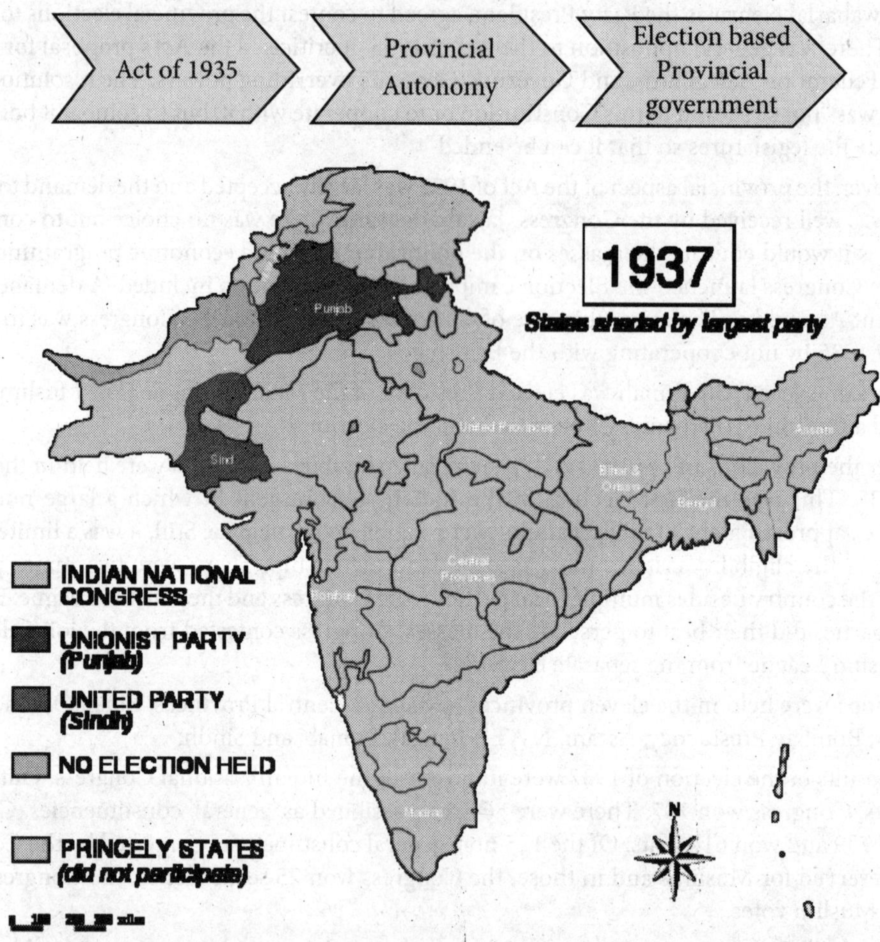

Map showing provinces ruled under Congress Party and other parties in 1937
— Wikimedia Commons

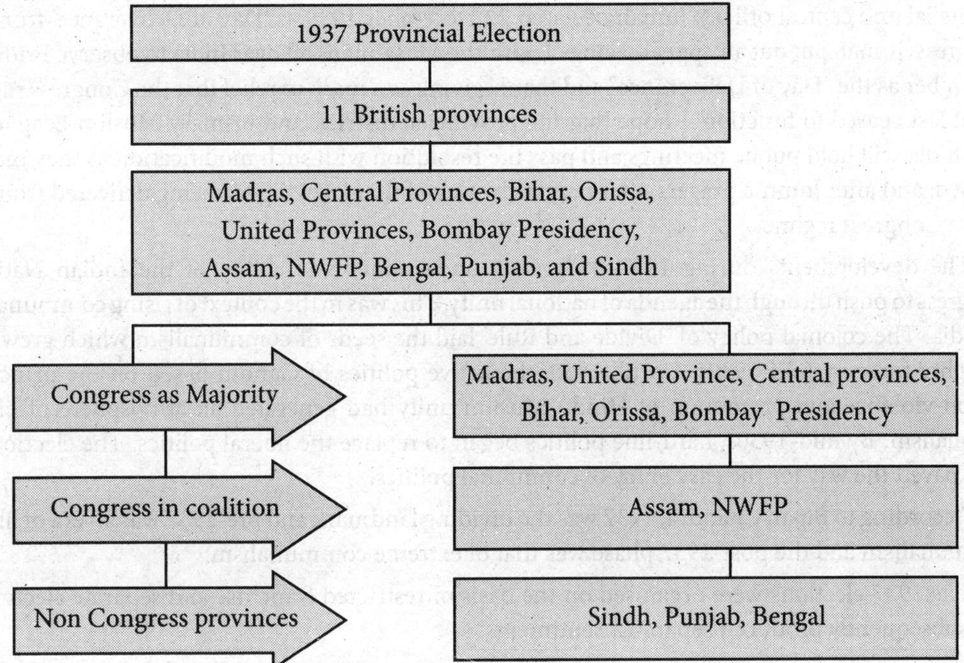

World War II and Resignation of Congress Ministries

On September 1, 1939, the Second World War began. Viceroy Linlithgow declared the news of India at war with Germany on 3rd September, 1939. The Congress objected strongly to the declaration of war without prior consultation with the Indians. The Congress Working Committee suggested that it would cooperate if there were a Central Indian National Government formed, and a commitment made to India's independence after the war. The Muslim League promised its support to the British, with Jinnah calling on Muslims to help the Raj by "honourable cooperation" at the "critical and difficult juncture," while asking the Viceroy for increased protection for Muslims.

Linlithgow refused the demands of the Congress. The Congress ministries resigned in October and November 1939, in protest against Viceroy Lord Linlithgow's action of declaring India to be a belligerent in the Second World War without consulting the Indian people.

Post-1937 – The Growth of Communal Politics

One of the significant phenomenons observed after the 1937 election, was the growth of communal politics. It is to be noted that many regional parties, including larger parties like the Muslim League, contested 1937 elections on the basis of separate electorates. Congress however, contested election in general constituencies.

After the 1937 election, the rift between the Congress and the Muslim League further widened. Jinnah openly declared, 'Muslims can expect neither justice nor fair play under the Congress government'. Majority of the Muslims accepted this view.

Muslim League under Jinnah was critical of the Congress rule. The resignation of the Congress ministries was celebrated. To celebrate the resignation of all members of the Congress party from provincial and central offices, Jinnah declared 22 December 1939 as 'Day of Deliverance' from the Congress. Jinnah put out an appeal saying: 'I wish the Musalmans all over India to observe Friday 22 December as the "Day of Deliverance" and thanksgiving as a mark of relief that the Congress regime has at last ceased to function. I hope that the provincial, district, and primary Muslim Leagues all over India will hold public meetings and pass the resolution with such modification as they may be advised, and after Jumma prayers offer prayers by way of thanksgiving for being delivered from the unjust Congress regime'.

The developments during 1937–39 greatly undermined the ability of the Indian National Congress to push through the agenda of national unity. This was in the context of rising communalism in India. The colonial policy of 'Divide and Rule' laid the seeds of communalism which grew into a mighty force by mid-1930s. Up till 1930, the active politics of Gandhi based on the principles of non-violence and promotion of Hindu-Muslim unity had generated an atmosphere of liberal nationalism. By mid-1930s, hard-line politics began to replace the liberal politics. The elections of 1937 paved the way for the easy entry of communal politics.

According to Bipan Chandra, 1937 was the dividing landmark and pre-1937 was an era of liberal communalism and the post-1937 phase was that of extreme communalism.

The 1937 elections were organised on the basis of restricted franchise and separate electorates that subsequently produced separatist sentiments.

However, the results were contrary to the expectations of communal-based parties and groups. Indian National Congress won with massive majority in the 1937 election. The Muslim League won only 109 seats from 492 reserved Muslim seats and only 4.8 percent of the overall Muslim votes, showing the lack of assistance for the Muslim League even amongst the Muslim inhabitants.

Similarly, hard-liner party Hindu Mahasabha fared miserably. It could acquire only 12 seats from 175 in Punjab. The landlord and moneylender parties too fared badly in the elections.

After 1937, the Congress prohibited communalists from functioning within the Congress organisation. It adopted a radical agrarian programme and supported peasant movements. This made landlords and moneylenders to shift their support to the communal parties.

They found that an open defence of their interests was no longer possible in the era of mass politics. It was now that the communal parties began to gather strength.

The Muslim League, led by Jinnah, turned to bitter opposition against the Congress. It began to spread the cry that the Muslim minority was in danger of being engulfed by the Hindu majority. It propagated the unscientific and unhistorical theory that Hindus and Muslims were two separate nations which could, therefore, never live together. The Hindu communalists echoed the Muslim communalists by declaring that the Hindus were a distinct nation and that India was the land of the Hindus.

Thus, the Two-nation theory was accepted by the separatists. Hindu Mahasabha stated that the country belonged only to Hindus and the Muslims should find their own home or should remain obedient to the Hindus. Muslim League stated that Pakistan was the only option to protect the interest of the Muslims.

In 1940, the Muslim League passed a resolution demanding partition of the country and the creation of a state to be called Pakistan after independence.

The August Offer

To persuade the Congress, Viceroy Lord Linlithgow offered the August offer.

Following were the main proposals of the August Offer:

- Dominion status as the objective for India.
- Expansion of the Viceroy's Executive Council.
- Setting up of a Constituent Assembly after the war where mainly Indians would decide the Constitution according to their social, economic, and political conceptions, subject to the fulfilment of the obligation of the Government regarding defence, minority rights, treaties with states, and All India Services.
- No future Constitution to be adopted without the consent of minorities.

The August Offer was rejected by the Congress. Nehru said, "Dominion status concept is dead as a door nail."

Cripps Mission, 1942

The Second World War broke out in 1939. The Congress demanded that it could help the war efforts of the government only if India was declared an independent country after the war. The negotiations between the Congress and the government failed. Therefore, the Congress ministries resigned in 1939.

World War II broke out on 1 September, 1939 when Nazi Germany invaded Poland. The Government of India immediately declared India to be at war with Germany without consulting the Congress or the elected members of the central legislature.

The All India Congress made several offers to cooperate with the British on acceptance of their demand of complete freedom to India after the war, but the British rulers gave no assurance. Gandhi now favoured individual *satyagraha* instead of Mass Civil Disobedience. This was because he felt that at this time, the mass movement would not be appropriate when Britain itself was dealing with a major crisis of war, but it was necessary to impress that India was not interested in the war. So, in October 17, 1940, Gandhi started the individual satyagraha. Vinoba Bhave was the first leader to offer *satyagraha*. Thousands were arrested. Gandhi suspended it on December 17, 1940.

In December 1941, Japan joined the war on the side of Germany and attacked Pearl Harbour. It soon overran the Philippines, Indo-China, Indonesia, Malaya, and Burma. Thus, the war was on India's doorstep.

England itself was under severe attack by the German bombing. The situation was becoming very grim for the British government. Now they thought of securing the cooperation of Indians in their war efforts. As the war situation worsened, President Roosevelt of the USA and President Chiang Kai-Shek of China, as also the Labour Party leaders of Britain put pressure on Churchill to seek the active cooperation of Indians in the War.

To secure this cooperation, the British Government sent to India in March 1942, a mission headed by a Cabinet minister Stafford Cripps, a left-wing Labourite, who had earlier actively supported the Indian National Movement.

Sir Stafford Cripps was sent to India with the following main proposals :

- India to have Dominion Status after the war;
- An elected body to be set up after the war to frame a new Constitution of India;
- Any province of India to have the right to reject the new Constitution and to have its own, if so desired;
- The Princely States to be represented in proportion to their population.

The Cripps' proposals were rejected by almost all sections of the society. The Congress objected to the provision for Dominion Status, the representation of the Princely States in the Constituent Assembly not by the people of the states but by the nominees of the rulers, and above all, by the provision for the partition of India. The British government also refused to accept the demand for the immediate transfer of effective power to the Indians and for a real share in the responsibility for the defence of India. According to the Congress, the proposal meant tearing India into pieces, each piece representing religions, majority power, vested-interest lobby, or autocratic Princely rule. Gandhi's comment on the Cripps declarations was; "It is a post dated cheque on a crashing bank." Muslims rejected it as the proposal of Pakistan was not approved.

Sir Richard Stafford Cripps
— Wikimedia Commons

To Protest government's decision of declaring India at war

Congress Ministries resigned - 1939

To secure India's support for the war

Viceroy's August Offer-
- Dominion Status
- Setting up of Constituent Assembly after the war

British government sent

Cripp's Mission, 1942-
- Dominion Status to India
- To frame Constitution for India
- Option to provinces to accept or reject the Constitution

The Quit India Movement, 1942

The failure of the Cripps Mission made the Congress leaders realise that Britain was not genuinely interested in granting even Dominion Status, when India was demanding complete independence. Churchill, the Prime Minister of Britain, had bluntly said, 'No Sir', to a question asked in the Parliament, whether the famous Atlantic Charter, promising the rights of man—liberty, equality, and fraternity to be enforced throughout the world—will be applicable also to India.

There was also a change in the attitude of Gandhi. He was earlier not in favour of initiating any mass movement because he 'did not seek to raise a free India from the ashes of Britain'. However, the threat of Japanese invasion of India and the incapacity of the British to defend India made Gandhi to change his stand.

On 14th July 1942, the Congress Working Committee met at Wardha and passed a resolution demanding Complete Independence from the British government. The draft was proposed for Civil Disobedience. The Quit India Movement or the August *Kranti* was launched on 8th August, 1942 in response to Gandhi's call of '*Do or Die*', at the Gowalia Tank Maidan, Mumbai. The All-India Congress Committee proclaimed a mass protest demanding what Gandhi called "an orderly British withdrawal" from India.

However, the movement proved to be controversial within the party. Prominent Congress national leader Chakravarti Rajagopalachari quit the Congress and so did some local and regional level organisers. Jawaharlal Nehru and Maulana Azad were apprehensive and critical of the call, but supported it under Gandhi's leadership. Sardar Vallabhbhai Patel, Dr. Rajendra Prasad, Dr Anugrah Narayan Sinha, and socialists like Asoka Mehta and Jayaprakash Narayana enthusiastically supported such a disobedience movement. Hindu Mahasabha protested 'Quit India call' by 'not resigning from their posts'.

The British responded quickly by imprisoning Gandhi. Within hours, all the members of the Congress Working Party were imprisoned without trial. The Congress was once again declared illegal. The news of these arrests left the country aghast, and a spontaneous movement of protest arose everywhere, giving expression to the pent-up anger of the people. Due to the arrest of major leaders, a young and relatively unknown Aruna Asaf Ali presided over the AICC session on 9th August and hoisted the flag.

Many national leaders went underground and continued their struggle by broadcasting messages over concealed radio stations, distributing pamphlets or *Patrikas,* and establishing parallel governments. The British had the support of the Muslims, the Communist Party, and the Princely States.

Despite lack of direct leadership, large protests and demonstrations were held all over the country. Mill workers went on strikes for a long time. At many places, protesters were involved in violent activities like making bombs and organising bomb blasts. In addition, government buildings were set on fire, electricity wires were cut off, and transport and communication lines were severed. People indulged in arson, murder, and sabotage.

The railways and the post and telegraph system came in for severe attack, and communications were disrupted. The government buildings became targets of attack. Students came out of colleges and schools. Peasants took the leading part in the revolt and so did the lower middle class. Industrial workers in many important centres declared strikes but they were mostly of short duration.

In many places, the rebels sieged temporary control over many towns, cities, and villages. British authority disappeared in parts of Uttar Pradesh, Bihar, West Bengal, Orissa, Andhra, Tamil Nadu, and Maharashtra. In some areas, the revolutionaries set up 'parallel governments'.

In general, the students, workers, and peasants provided the backbone of the revolt while the upper classes and the bureaucracy remained loyal to the Government.

However, Quit India Movement did not fit within the parameters of the Gandhian ideology of non-violence and satyagraha. Unlike the other two Gandhian movements – the Non-Cooperation and the Civil Disobedience Movement that was unleashed under the aegis of Mahatma Gandhi – the Quit India Movement was devoid of the Gandhian principles of satyagraha and non-violence. The movement captured the quintessence of a 'spontaneous' rising by the people.

Gandhi's wife Kasturbai Gandhi and his personal secretary Mahadev Desai died in those months. Gandhi went on a 21-day fast demanding for the release of the Congress leaders. He was released on account of his health in 1944.

In terms of immediate objectives, the Quit India movement failed because of heavy-handed suppression, weak coordination, and the lack of a clear-cut programme of action. However, it made the British government realise the difficulties in governing India in the long run and in the post-war, the question of granting powers to India became a major concern.

Post War Events

Red Fort Trials of INA Prisoners, 1945

The end of World War II witnessed the downfall of the Subhash Bose-led Indian National Army (INA). The sudden death of Bose in a plane crash contributed to its downfall. The issue which most caught the popular imagination was the fate of the members of the Indian National Army (INA), who were captured by the British during the war. Sentence to death was declared on eminent officers of the INA – Colonel Prem Sahgal, Colonel Gurbaksh Singh Dhillon, and Major General Shah Nawaz Khan. But under public and political pressure, these leaders were released. The INA prisoners were tried in the historic Red Fort Trials in 1945.

Bhulabhai Desai
— Wikimedia Commons

The Red Fort trials of captured INA officers provoked massive public outcries in support of their efforts to fight for Indian independence against the Raj. In November 1945, the first Red Fort trials began. But before that, INA agitation campaign started in many parts of the country. There were daily editorials hailing the INA men as the most heroic patriots and criticising the Government stand. One hundred and sixty political meetings were held in the Central Provinces and Berar alone in the first fortnight of October 1945 where the demand for clemency for INA prisoners was raised. INA Day was observed on 12th November and INA Week from 5 to 11 November, 1945. The defence of the INA prisoners was taken up by the Congress and leaders like Bhulabhai Desai, Tej Bahadur Sapru, K.N. Katju, Nehru, and Asaf Ali who appeared in court at the Red Fort trials.

Bhulabhai Desai well-remembered for his defence of the three Indian National Army soldiers

Royal Indian Navy (RIN) Mutiny – 1946

The Royal Indian Navy (RIN) mutiny took place in the aftermath of the Indian National Army (INA) Trials. The immediate cause of the RIN mutiny was dissatisfaction over the general conditions in the Navy. The RIN Mutiny began in Bombay, and spread throughout British India, covering 78 ships, 20 shore establishments, and 20,000 sailors. The mutiny also found widespread support among the people who were already discontent with the British establishment. Also, as the mutiny grew, members of the Royal Indian Air Force and the armed forces also joined in the rebellion. The revolt could have gone on longer and assumed larger proportions, if it were not for the opposition to the mutiny from the leading political parties of its time, the Indian National Congress and the Muslim League. Only the Communist Party of India lent its support to the mutineers. The mutiny showed the British that they could no longer trust the armed forces in India, and marked the end of their supremacy over the Indians.

The revolt began in Bombay and spread throughout British India, i.e., Karachi to Calcutta, and ultimately came to involve over 10,000 sailors in 66 ships and shore establishments.

Events Leading to Mutiny in RIN

On February 18, 1946, a section of non-commissioned officers and sailors known as Ratings, serving in the Royal Indian Navy, mutinied against the British Officers. The mutiny started as a strike by the ratings to protest against the hardships regarding pay, food, and racial discrimination.

In the same night, a Naval Central Strike Committee was created by the Ratings.

This committee was presided over by signalman M.S. Khan and vice president was telegraphist Madan Singh. The people of India were already fascinated by the heroic tales of the Indian National Army. So, the strikes and hartals spread from Bombay to Calcutta, Madras, and even Karachi. Mutineers took possession of some ships, mounted guns over there, and started firing.

The mutineers hoisted three flags tied together on the ships which they had captured – One of the Congress, one of the Muslim League, and the third Red Flag of the Communist Party of India. The mutiny was ended by intervention of Sardar Patel, who after a meeting with M. S. Khan made a statement of ending the strike. A similar statement was made by

Jinnah in Calcutta. The mutineers surrendered, but despite the assurances of the Congress and Muslim League, many mutineers were arrested, subjected to court martial, and dismissed from the services. Then violence broke out in Mumbai and over 200 people lost lives in this disturbance. The mutiny made an impression on the British, that it would be better to leave the country. On February 19, the second day of this mutiny, the Cabinet Mission was sent to India.

Previous Years' Questions

1. **In what ways did the Naval Mutiny prove to be the last nail in the coffin of British colonial aspirations in India? (2014)**
2. **Highlight the differences in the approach of Subhash Chandra Bose and Mahatma Gandhi in the struggle for freedom. (2016)**
3. **Do you think that the Quit India Movement was a Spontaneous Revolution? (2009)**
4. **"The developments during 1937–39 greatly undermined the ability of the Indian National Congress to push through the agenda of national unity." Comment. (2010)**

20 CHAPTER Constitutional Deliberations For Transfer of Power (1944–1947)

Introduction

Immediately after the end of World War II, a radical change in the attitude of Britain towards India was visible. Several factors contributed to this radical change. First and the foremost was the coming of the Labour government in Britain who always sympathised with India. In the general elections, Labour Party came to power in Britain. Lord Attlee, the Prime Minister, came to the conclusion that England could not hold on to India for a long time. During his tenure, a Cabinet Mission was sent and finally, Lord Mountbatten was appointed as Governor-General to complete the process of transfer of power in India.

The emergence of USA and USSR subdued Britain's dominating position in the world. After the Second World War, the USA and USSR emerged as the big powers that supported India's demand for freedom. Both these powers put pressure on Britain for India's independence. India's cause of freedom was advocated in the world. The Indian point was put forward before the conference at San Francisco which met to finalise the Charter of the United Nations. Britain's economy after the war was in shambles and the military strength too had reduced. Hence, its main concern was to tackle the crisis at home.

In India, the British government lost faith in the Indian Armed Forces. There were several revolts in the Royal Indian Navy, Army, and Air Force that shattered the confidence of the government in the Indian Armed Forces. The growing nationalist sentiment that reached a crescendo around the INA trials, developed into violent confrontations of the Indian Armed Forces with the authority in 1945–46. In 1946 in Bombay, the Royal Indian Navy (RIN) went on strike.

The Princely States who always sided with the British government faced the brunt of the freedom struggle. There were popular upsurges in several Princely States such as Hyderabad, Travancore, and Kashmir.

There was hardly an industry in India in which there was no large-scale labour unrest. The Peasant movement also acquired a fresh thrust after 1945. The Quit India Movement left the British authorities in a weak and fretful condition.

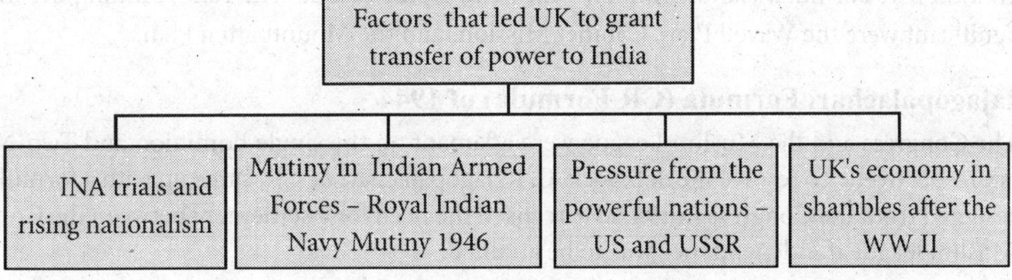

Bengal Famine (1943)

The early years of 1940s is marked with a devastating Famine of Bengal that wiped out more than three million people from Bengal. In 1943, Bengal was devastated by a massive famine. At least 3 million people died from starvation and malnutrition in this famine which was a largely a man-made disaster.

The mains reasons cited for this catastrophe were the World War II, the Japanese occupation of neighbouring Burma , damage to the local rice crop due to tidal waves, and a fungal disease epidemic.

Eminent agricultural scientist, Swaminathan, also blamed "panic purchase and hoarding by the rich, failure of governance, particularly in relation to the equitable distribution of the available food grains, disruption of communication due to World War II and the indifference of the then UK government to the plight of the starving people of undivided Bengal."

The Bengal famine of 1943 was largely a man-made famine. Dr. Gideon Polya, an Australian biochemist, has called the Bengal famine a man-made "holocaust."

In 1942, Japan seized Burma, which was an important rice exporter. The British purchased up massive amounts of rice and hoarded it. Dr. Gideon Polya noted that the "loss of rice from Burma and ineffective government controls on hoarding and profiteering led inevitably to enormous price rises. Thus, it can be estimated that the price of rice in Dacca (East Bengal) increased about four-fold in the period from March to October 1943. Bengalis having to purchase food (e.g. landless labourers) suffered immensely. Thus, it is estimated that about 30 percent of one particular labourer class died in the famine."

Many observers in both modern India and Great Britain blame Winston Churchill for this devastating famine. Churchill ordered the diversion of food away from India and towards British troops around the world. This worsened the starvation in Bengal. Shiploads of wheat from Australia which could have been delivered to starving Indians were instead transported to the British troops in the Mediterranean and the Balkans. Offers of food aid from Canada and the US were turned down by British colonial authorities under Churchill's leadership.

The famine only ended because in the ensuing year 1944, there was a good rice harvest in Bengal.

Constitutional Deliberations Before 1947

Several constitutional discussions and debates began from 1943 onwards to resolve issues related to the Constitution, partition, and later, transfer of power to India. Both the Indian leaders and the British held talks to resolve the deadlocks. The significant talks held among Indian leaders involved the CR Formula, Gandhi-Jinnah Talks, and Desai-Liaquat Ali Talks. Among the British, the significant were the Wavell Plan, Cabinet Mission, and the Mountbatten Plan.

C. Rajagopalachari Formula (CR Formula) of 1944

The Congress and the Muslim League were adamant on the single dominion and Two-Nation Theory respectively. To resolve the deadlock, C. Rajagopalachari or CR, came up with a formula. CR had resigned from the Congress in 1943. He realised the need for a settlement between the Congress and Muslim league if independence was to be attained.

Following were the proposals of the CR Formula:

- For the time being, i.e., till a provisional is formed, the Muslim League would support the Congress demand of complete freedom and single dominion.
- Once the war ends, a Commission would be appointed to demarcate the districts having a Muslim population in absolute majority and in those areas, plebiscite will be conducted on the basis of adult suffrage.
- All parties would be allowed to express their stance on the partition and their views before the plebiscite.
- If the plebiscite accepts separation, a mutual agreement would be signed to safeguard essential matters such as defence, communication and commerce, and for other essential services.
- In case of separation, the transfer of population would be on voluntary basis.

However, Jinnah rejected the CR Formula because separation could not be deferred till after independence. The idea of safeguarding essential services was useless; and thought that a plebiscite where both the Muslims and Hindus voted, contradicted the basic principle of Muslims being a distinct nation with an inherent right of self-determination.

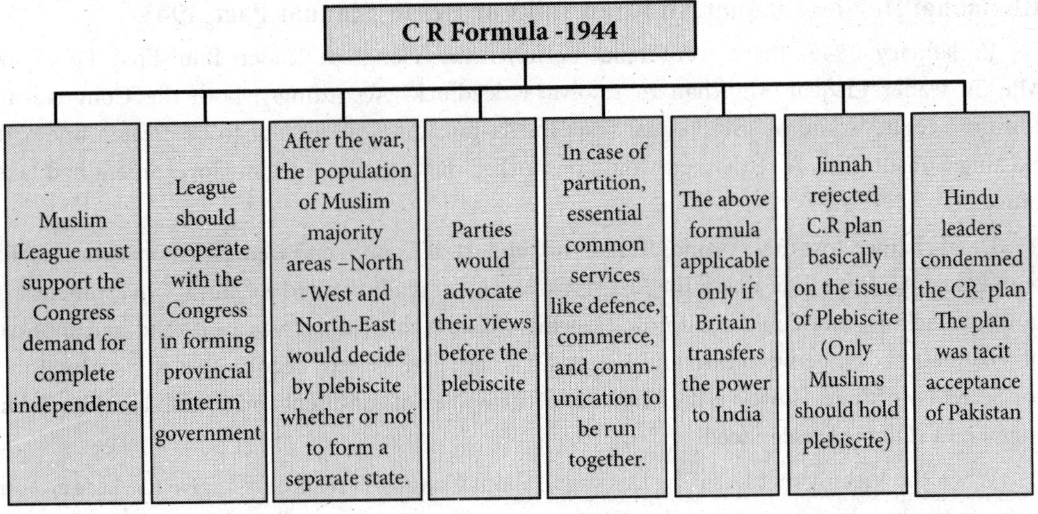

Gandhi – Jinnah Talks, 1944

Most of Congress leaders were still in jail but Gandhi was released on 5 May, 1944. He proposed to engage in talks with Jinnah on his Two-Nation theory. And, the CR formula was used as a basis of these talks. Gandhi and Jinnah met in September 1944. Negotiations continued for two years and ultimately failed.

In these talks, Gandhi proposed that only the Muslims living in Baluchistan, Sindh, NWFP, and parts of the Punjab, Bengal, and Assam, who desired to live in separation from the rest of India, should form the new state. But on this, Jinnah insisted that Pakistan should include all the six provinces based on the resolution of the Muslim League in 1940. He did not want to have a mutilated, moth-eaten Pakistan, similar to the way the Muslim leader Allama Mashriqi cried for Pakistan. Jinnah also rejected other suggestions such as Treaty of Separation to provide for common services, etc.

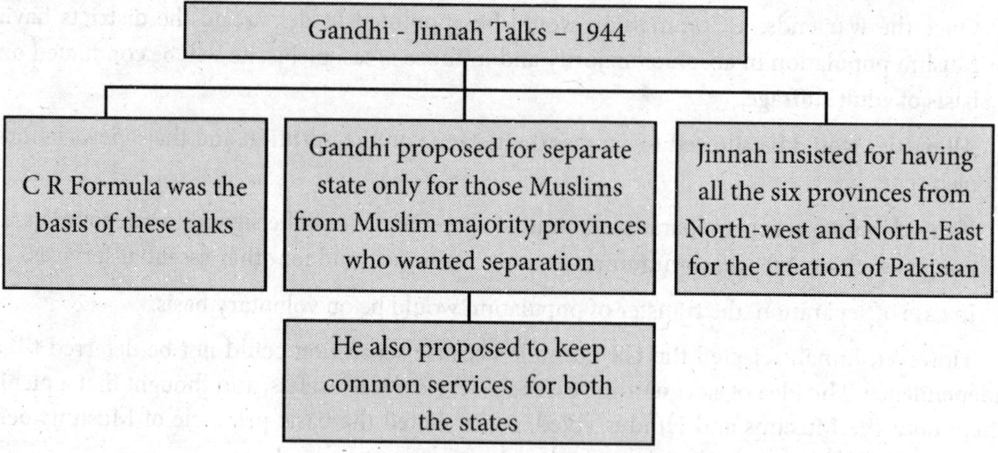

Bhulabhai Desai – Liaquat Ali Khan Talks or Desai–Liaquat Pact, 1945

In January 1945, there were talks between the Congress leader Bhulabhai Desai and Muslim leader Liaquat Ali Khan to resolve a deadlock. Accordingly, both the Congress and Muslim League would be given equal seats in the Interim Government to be created under the existing Constitution. A settlement would be worked out after the Interim Government had taken office.

Desai claimed that these proposals had the support of Gandhi and were based on informal talks with Liaqat Ali Khan, and that if the British Government really wanted a Central Government with political backing, they could get it now. He was confident that Jinnah was aware and had approved of what had passed between him and Liaqat Ali Khan. The Viceroy recommended its adoption to the Secretary of State. However, the Secretary of State was not confident and doubted that Bhulabhai might be a *stalking horse* indeed!

When the Viceroy met Desai, he was vague about Congress's readiness to give the League equal status in the interim Government. It was later rejected by Jinnah as well as the Congress.

The Talks failed because of Jinnah's rejection.

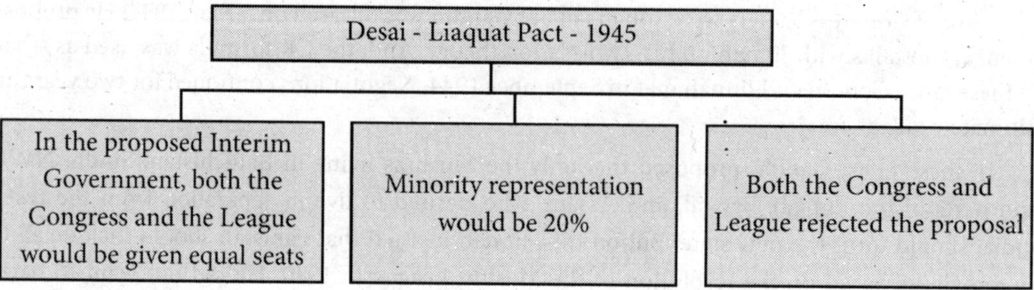

Wavell Plan, June 1945

In October 1943, the British Government decided to replace Lord Linlithgow with Lord Wavell as the new Viceroy of India. Wavell's most important task was to present a formula for the solution of the Indian problem which was acceptable to both the Congress and the Muslim League.

The Plan, commonly known as Wavell Plan, presented the following proposals:

- Viceroy's Executive Council would be immediately reconstituted and the number of its members would be increased. In that Council, there would be equal representation of high-class Hindus and Muslims.
- All the members of the Council, except the Viceroy and the Commander-in-Chief, would be Indians.
- Defense of India was to be in the hands of a British authority till power was transferred to the Indian hands.
- Viceroy would convene a meeting of the Indian politicians including the leaders of the Congress and the Muslim League so that they could nominate the names of the members of the new Council.
- If this Plan is approved for the Central Government, then the same type of popular ministries comprising of the political leaders would be formed in all the provinces.

Lord Wavell
— Wikimedia Commons

Wavell Plan, June 1945					
The Viceroy's Executive Council was to have all Indian members except the Viceroy and Commander-in- Chief	There would be equal represen-tations of high caste Hindus, Muslims, and other Indian communities	The Defence portfolio would be under British authority till power was transferred to India	External Affairs portfolio would be transferred to Indians	The Viceroy/ Governor-General would still have veto power but its use would be minimal	If this proposal was accepted for central government, similar councils would be formed in all provinces comprising of local leaders

In order to discuss the proposal with the Indian leaders, Wavell summoned a conference in Simla, the summer capital of British India on June 25, 1945.

Simla Conference, June 1945

In the summer of 1945, Lord Wavell organised the Simla Conference in order to solve the Constitutional tangle. Both the Congress and the Muslim League took part in the Simla Conference but the Conference could not succeed on account of the attitude of the Muslim League.

Maulana Abul Kalam Azad was the President of the Congress, while M.A. Jinnah was the Leader of the Muslim League. In the conference, Jinnah objected to the inclusion of any non-League Muslims in the Executive Council, with the claim that the Muslim League was the sole representative of Indian Muslims. According to him, the Congress had no right to nominate any Muslim in the Executive Council. He also demanded that in case of the division of votes and objections by the Muslim members, there should be a provision that the vote is cleared only by 2/3rd of the majority.

Wavell had given the Muslims, who constituted only about 25 per cent of the total population of India, 6 representatives in an Executive Council of 14.

National Leaders at Simla Conference — Wikimedia Commons

At the Simla Conference, the Muslim League acquired the weapon of veto, which it threatened to use or actually used in the coming years, till India was partitioned.

In the Wavell Plan, the Muslim League was in a powerful position, while in the Cripps Mission, the Congress was recognised as the only party to discuss with the government. Wavell Plan made the Muslim League the representative of Muslims in India. Jinnah's status was raised to equal of Gandhi and two representatives were created for the first time - one for India and the other for Pakistan. Since the League would not relent on its demands, Wavell dropped the plan.

The Wavell Plan and the Simla Conference was a watershed moment in India's struggle for Independence because the Wavell Plan and the Simla Conference adopted all the steps to prevent partition but met with failure. Hence, with the failure of the Wavell plan, Partition became inevitable.

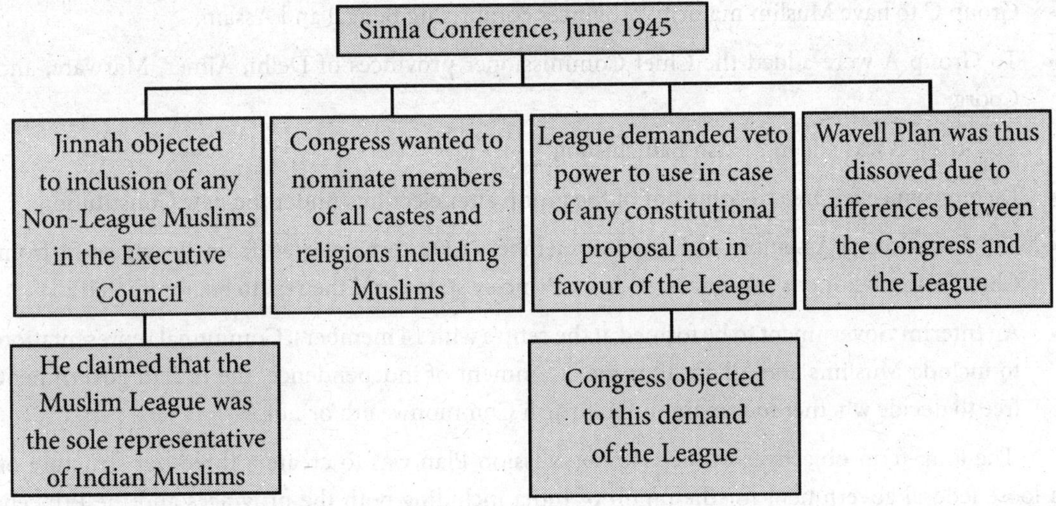

Cabinet Mission Plan, 1946

At the end of the Second World War in 1945, the Labour government was elected in Britain who was keen on giving independence to India without much delay. The Labour government sent a Cabinet Mission to India to find out ways for transfer of power to India. The Mission consisted of Lord Pethic Lawrence (Secretary of State for India), Sir Stafford Cripps (President of the Board of Trade), and A.V. Alexander (First Lord of the Admiralty).

The main objective of the Cabinet Mission was to find out ways and means for the peaceful transfer of power in India, to suggest measures for the formation of a Constitution-making machinery, and also to set up the Interim Government. Therefore, the plan was embedded with long-term and short-term objectives.

Prolonged discussions took place between the members of the Mission and with the Indian political parties. The mission spent some 3 weeks to discuss with the leaders of various political parties, but could not arrive at any agreed solution. So finally, it announced its own recommendations on May 16, 1946.

The key recommendations were:

- The formation of the Union of India embracing both British India and the Princely States;
- Immediate arrangement for drafting the future Constitution of India;
- Undivided India, thus turning down the demand of Pakistan of Muslim League.
- The union of India to deal only with Foreign Affairs, Defence, and Communication;
- The provinces to form regional groups and each group to determine the subjects to be taken in common;
- Group A to have Hindu majority provinces of Madras, Bombay, United Province (UP) , Central Province (CP) , Bihar, and Orissa;
- Group B to have Muslim majority provinces of Punjab, North-West Frontier Province (NWFP), and Sind;

- Group C to have Muslim majority provinces comprising Bengal and Assam;
- To Group A were added the Chief Commissioner provinces of Delhi, Ajmer, Marwara, and Coorg;
- To Group B was added British Baluchistan;
- Each province left free to come out of the group after elections under the new Constitution;
- The Constituent Assembly to have 389 members (292 to be elected from Provinces, 4 from Chief Commissioner's Provinces, 93 from Princely states, and the rest to be nominated);
- An Interim Government to be formed at the centre with 14 members; Communal representation to include Muslims and Sikhs; after the attainment of independence, the Indian government free to decide whether to remain in the British Commonwealth or not.

The long-term objectives of the Cabinet Mission Plan was to create a three-tier structure of a loose federal government for the union of India including both the provinces and the Princely States, with union government at the top, in charge of defence, communication, and foreign affairs. The Cabinet Mission Plan of 1946 therefore proposed for central federation – a strong Provincial Government with residual powers in its own hand and a weak Centre. The Princely states would retain all subjects and all residuary powers.

The short-term plan, on the other hand, was to create an Interim Government with the Congress and the Muslim League on board.

The Cabinet Mission recommended an undivided India and turned down the Muslim League's demand for a separate Pakistan. According to its recommendation, the British Indian Provinces and the territories should be divided into three groups. The Muslim majority provinces however, were given much autonomy, to run their own affairs. The plan, thus, accepted the demand of the autonomous state of Pakistan without formally dividing the nation.

Though the idea of accepting an undivided India thrilled the Congress, it was generally unhappy on various other issues. The Congress accepted the idea of a Constituent Assembly but rejected the scheme of the government having a weak centre and strong provinces.

The Congress Working Committee first approved of the Cabinet Plan but then Nehru retracted from the same by announcing that the Congress has agreed to nothing but participation in the Constituent Assembly. The short-term provisions of forming the Ministry, however, were accepted. Historians were of the view that the Congress was in much hurry to get the power into its own hands, even at the cost of increasing religious polarisation.

The country was under the tight grip of communal riots that created civil war-like conditions. Also, without forming the Constituent Assembly, the transfer of power was not possible as was made clear by the Mission. Hence, it is in this light, that the Congress, despite its disregard for the long-term federation, accepted the short-term plan to form the Interim Government, and later the Constituent Assembly.

Lord Wavell, the Viceroy of India, invited Jawaharlal Nehru to form the Interim Government on 2nd September, 1946. Communal riots broke out in Calcutta on 16th August, 1946 on the Direct Action Day called by the Muslim League.

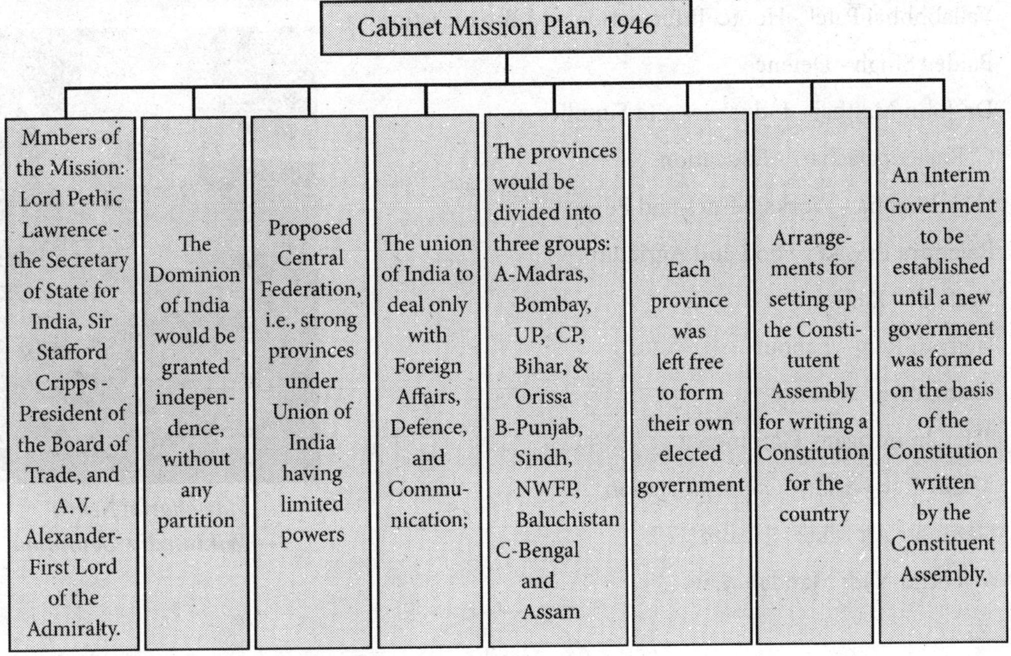

Direct Action Day, 16 August 1946

On July 27, the Muslim League Council met at Bombay where Jinnah reiterated the demand for Pakistan as 'the only course left open to the Muslim League'. Jinnah called the Muslims to resort to "Direct Action" to achieve the land of their dreams – "Pakistan".

Then 16 August, 1946 was fixed as the Direct Action Day and it turned into the "Great Calcutta Killing". This date started the week of "Long Knives" in which 6000 Hindus and Muslims stabbed, shot, and battered each other. Nearly 20 thousand were maimed and raped.

Amidst this situation of chaos and insanity, Mahatma Gandhi went to calm down the maddened rioters.

Interim Government, September, 1946

On 2nd September 1946, the newly-elected Constituent Assembly formed the Interim Government of India which existed till 15th August, 1947. The Executive Branch of the Interim Government was served by the Viceroy's Executive Council that was headed by the Viceroy of India. It was composed of 12 members, including 3 Muslims nominated by the Congress. It was for the first time since the coming of the British that the Government of India was in the Indians' hand. On 26th October, five nominees of the League joined the Government.

The portfolios of the composite fourteen-member government were as follows:

- Pandit Jawaharlal Nehru - Vice President of the Executive Council, External Affairs and Commonwealth Relations
- Vallabhbhai Patel - Home, Information and Broadcasting
- Baldev Singh - Defence
- Dr. John Matthai - Industries and Supplies
- C. Rajagopalachari - Education
- C.H. Bhabha - Works, Mines and Power
- Rajendra Prasad - Food and Agriculture
- Asaf Ali - Railways
- Jagjivan Ram - Labour
- Liaquat Ali - Finance
- T.T. Chundrigar - Commerce
- Abdur Rab Nistar - Communication
- Gazanfar Ali Khan - Health
- Jogendra Nath Mandal - Law

Jawaharlal Nehru
— Wikimedia Commons

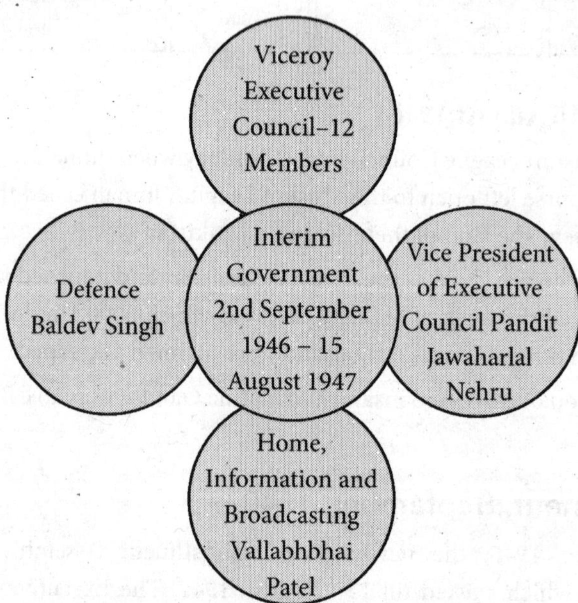

Constituent Assembly – December 1946

On the basis of the framework provided by the Cabinet Mission, a Constituent Assembly was constituted on 9th December, 1946. The Constitution-making body was elected by the Provincial Legislative Assembly constituting of 389 members who included 93 from Princely States and 296 from British India. The seats to the British Indian provinces and Princely States were allotted in proportion of their respective population and were to be divided among Muslims, Sikhs, and the rest of the communities. All sections of the Indian society got representation in the Constituent Assembly in spite of limited suffrage.

The first meeting of the Constituent Assembly took place on December 9, 1946 at Delhi with Dr Sachchidanand being elected as the interim President of the Assembly. However, on December 11, 1946, Dr. Rajendra Prasad was elected as the President and H.C. Mukherjee as the Vice-President of the Constituent Assembly.

However, the Muslim League demanded for a separate Constituent assembly for Muslims in India. So, the British declared that the decisions of the Constituent Assembly would not be valid in the Muslim majority areas. Thus, the working of the Assembly got virtually crippled.

Following were accomplishments of the Constituent Assembly:

- Framed the Constitution
- Enacted laws and was involved in the decision-making process
- Adopted the National flag on July 22, 1947
- Accepted and approved India's membership of the British Commonwealth in May 1949
- Elected Dr. Rajendra Prasad as the first President of India on January 24, 1950
- Adopted the National anthem on January 24, 1950
- Adopted the National song on January 24, 1950

The Constituent Assembly appointed 22 committees out of which eight were major committees and the others were minor committees. Among these eight major committees, the most significant was the Drafting Committee under the chairmanship of Dr. B.R. Ambedkar to prepare a Draft Constitution for India.

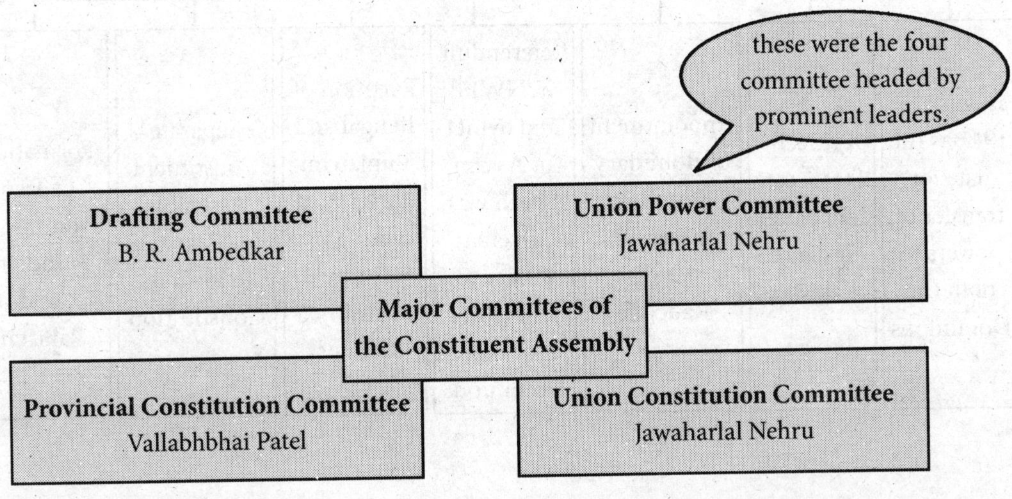

Process For Transfer of Power in 1947

Atlee's Declaration – February 20, 1947

The Prime Minister of Britain, Clement Atlee declared on February 20, 1947 in the House of Commons that the British would quit India after transferring power into the responsible hands not later than June 1948. The idea was that the Indians should settle their issues before that. He also announced the appointment of Lord Mountbatten as the New Viceroy in place of Lord Wavell.

The Mountbatten Plan – 3rd June, 1947

Lord Mountbatten replaced Lord Wavell as Viceroy of India in March 1947. His talks with the Indian leaders convinced him that partition of India was the only viable solution and he therefore put forward his plan on June 3, 1947. Mountbatten's scheme was to divide India but retain maximum unity. The country would be partitioned but so would Punjab and Bengal, so that the limited Pakistan that emerged would meet both the Congress and League's position to some extent.

The Mountbatten Plan sought to affect an early transfer of power on the basis of Dominion Status to the two successor states, India and Pakistan. The scheme was accepted by both the Congress and the Muslim League.

Lord Mountbatten
— Wikimedia Commons

Mountbatten Plan - 3rd June, 1947

- August 15, 1947 as the date for transfer of powers to both the Dominions
- Princely States can join either India or Pakistan
- Appointment of Boundary Commission under Sir Cyril Radcliffe
- Referendum in NWFP and Sylhet of Assam Sindh was given a choice to join either of the Dominions
- Partition of Bengal and Punjab on the basis of voting in Hindu - Muslim Groups
- Separate Constituent Assembly for Pakistan to form its Constitution
- Formation of Two Dominions – Indian and Pakistan

Components of the Mountbatten Plan

- India to be divided into two dominions – India and Pakistan.
- Bengal and Punjab will be partitioned and a referendum in NWFP (North-West Frontier Province) and Sylhet district of Assam would be held.
- Appointment of the Boundary Commission headed by Sir Cyril Radcliffe
- There would be a separate Constituent Assembly for Pakistan to frame its Constitution.
- The Princely States would enjoy the liberty to join either India or Pakistan or ever remain independent.
- August 15, 1947, was the date fixed for handling over power to India and Pakistan.

Indian Independence Act, July 1947

On the basis of the Mountbatten Plan, a Bill was introduced in the British Parliament on July 5, 1947 which was passed in both the Houses in July 18, 1947 that turned out as the Indian Independence Act. The Indian Independence Act became operative on August 15, 1947.

The Act contained the provisions like:

- India to be divided and the two Dominions of India and Pakistan to be established;
- The British government to have no control over the affairs of the Dominions;
- The Legislatures of the two Dominions to have full powers and all treaties and agreements entered upon by the Princely states to lapse.

Following were the main provisions of the Independence Act:

- The partition of the country into India and Pakistan would come into effect from 15th August, 1947.
- The British Government would transfer all powers to these two Dominions.
- The title of Viceroy was to be dropped and henceforth, he was to be called only Governor-General.
- A Boundary Commission would demarcate the boundaries of the provinces of Punjab and Bengal. The task of demarcating the boundaries of the two dominions was given to Sir Cyril Radcliffe.
- Till the framing of the new Constitutions by the Constituent Assemblies of these two Dominions, their Governments were to be carried on in accordance with the Government of India Act, 1935 with necessary modifications.
- The Act provided for the transfer of power to the Constituent Assemblies of the two Dominions, which will have full authority to frame their respective Constitutions.
- The office of the Secretary of State for India was to be abolished and the work was to be taken over by the Secretary of State for Commonwealth Affairs.

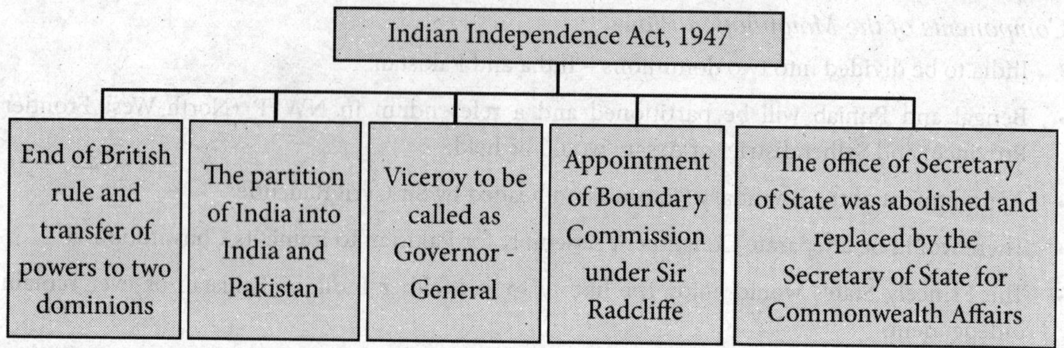

After the implementation of the Independence Act, the Indian Dominion got the following provinces: East Punjab, United Province, Bihar, West Bengal, Orissa, Bombay, Madras, Central Provinces, and Assam (exclusive of Sylhet district).

The territories of Pakistan included West Punjab, NWFP, Sind, East Bengal, Baluchistan, and Sylhet in Assam.

A vast majority of the Princely States joined India, while only a few adjoining states joined Pakistan. On 15 August, 1947, Lord Mountbatten became the Governor-General of the Indian Dominion, and Jinnah became the Governor-General of the Pakistan Dominion. Pandit Nehru was appointed the Prime Minister of India and Liaquat Ali Khan of Pakistan. The new system was brought into operation on August 14 in Pakistan and August 15 in India in the year 1947.

The speed at which the work of transfer of power was done made the prevailing conditions worse. The time period of seventy-two days, i.e., 3rd June to 15th August 1947, for the transfer of power and division of the country, proved disastrous. The country was faced with the unprecedented influx of displaced persons or refugees, particularly in the partitioned regions of Punjab and Bengal. Large-scale killings took place in East and West Punjab. Approximately, eight million people crossed the frontiers of India and Pakistan. Rehabilitation of such people was a huge task. Many relief camps were set up by the government for the refugees and many people extended help in the rehabilitation work.

The chaotic conditions that prevailed during the partition proved that the Mountbatten's Plan of peaceful transition was a failure. Many senior officials in India were of the opinion that peaceful division was a process that could have taken a few years, at the very least.

Indian National Congress accepted partition because of the prevailing dynamics in India, which made acceptance the only practical decision:

- **Failure of the Congress :** Jinnah was never in favour of Partition before as opposed to his stance later. He was, in fact, always avowed to serve some basic requirements to secure a dignified position at the centre. Pakistan was initially a bargaining lever to secure his chances. But the Congress was adamant to wield the centralised apparatus of the colonial state without the minimum intention to share power with the Muslim League.

- **Differences between the Congress and Muslim League :** Isolationist policy of the Muslim League coupled with the hateful nature of the Congress went a way forward towards the Two-Nation Theory. The Congress was not able to contain the spread of the growing hatred by granting the Muslim League the rights they wanted.
- **Hindus fundamentalists :** They were also responsible for the breakdown of the communal harmony. The issues of Fundamentalist parties like the Hindu Mahasábha (1915), Unionist Party, and others were overlooked by the Congress which proved to be a great mistake later on.
- **Communal violence :** The Congress failed to draw the Muslim masses into the National Movement. The prolonged communal violence in Bihar, Noakhali, and in Calcutta during Direct Action Day created a Civil War situation and partition seemed to be the only viable solution.
- **Failure of Constitutional proposals :** Failure of the Cripps Mission, Simla Conference, Cabinet Mission, and the Interim Government convinced the INC that the Muslim League will not relent. Also, the British had given virtual veto to the League at various stages of proposals.
- **Failure of Rajaji Formula :** CR devised a proposal for the Congress to offer the League the Pakistan based on the plebiscite of all the people in the regions where Muslims made a majority. Jinnah outrightly rejected the proposal as he wanted a full version of Partition.
- **Failure of Gandhi-Jinnah talks :** These talks were based on the CR formula. Jinnah did not accept anything short of an Independent Pakistan. Gandhi wanted the central federation to have control over reserved subjects like defence and foreign policies. This would mean more power to the Congress and Jinnah believed that this was against provincial autonomy. Jinnah opposed to Gandhi's ideas which claimed that the Congress was the representative of India and Muslims were not a separate nation.
- **Interim Government :** Its task was of assisting the transition of India from British rule to independence. It remained in place until 15 August, 1947. Muslim League leaders initially had opposed joining, but later joined the Interim Government only to obstruct. Jinnah was not at all in favour of the League's cooperation with the Congress. Liaquat Ali Khan, who was in charge of the finance department, rejected most of the bills and proposals.
- **Princely States :** With the declaration of the Partition of India, the 565 Princely States began weaving their dreams of Independence, which initially had their allegiance to the British Crown. As the message reached the Congress high command, they found it difficult to keep both the formation of Pakistan and Balkanisation of India; one had to let go, and Partition had become that necessary evil.
- **Mountbatten's role :** India was passing through a moment of terrible crisis of Communal War. Brutality and human sacrifice had reached beyond the limit. Under these circumstances, Mountbatten proposed a viable solution of peaceful partition. Sardar Patel readily accepted the idea of Partition proposed in the Mountbatten's Plan, and influenced Nehru to accept the same.

- **Jinnah's refusal to attend Constitution Assembly on December 9, 1946 :** Fearful of the thumping majority of the Indian National Congress in the Constituent Assembly, Jinnah declined the invitation of the Viceroy and instructed the representatives elected on the Muslim League ticket to keep out.

In view of all the above points, the Congress was left with nothing other than to accept the proposal of Pakistan. However, they were promised the maintenance of the integrity of India with peace, by Mountbatten, and it was better to have a larger India with uninterrupted mass killings.

Previous Years' Questions

1. **Discuss as to why the Congress accepted the partition of India in 1947. (2009)**
2. **"... instead of rejecting the plan (Cabinet Mission Plan), they (the Congress Leadership) resorted to a half-baked legalistic stratagem to reserve their position on its long-term arrangements and accepted its short-term provisions." Critically examine. (2014)**
3. **"The Royal Indian Navy Revolt was seen as an event which marked the end of the British rule almost as finally as Independence Day." Explain. (2015)**
4. **Explain why the efforts at finding solution to India's constitutional impasse failed during 1942-1946. (2017)**
5. **"The active participation of Aruna Asaf Ali in 1942 movement symbolized the role of women in India's freedom struggle." Comment. (2010)**

21 CHAPTER

Political Integration of Princely States Into The Indian Union

Introduction

The next immediate problem faced by India after the transfer of power was the integration of the Princely States. While the directly ruled British provinces were smoothly merged either with India or Pakistan, the Indian independence Act of 1947 did not give any clear solution for the numerous Princely States that covered a third of the area of the British Empire in India. They were left free to join either India or Pakistan or remain independent. At the time of independence, there were nearly 565 Princely States in India. The problem of amalgamating 565 independent states with a democratic self-governing India was difficult and delicate. But it was essential to save India from balkanisation, once the paramount power of the British Crown would lapse.

Apart from the Princely States, there were small territories owned by the French and the Portuguese. The French had five territories—Chandernagore, Pondicherry, Karaikal, Yanam, and Mahe. By 1954, all these colonies became an integral part of India. Portugal had five colonies—Goa, Daman, Diu, and Dadra and Nagar Haveli. Dadra and Nagar Haveli were liberated on August 2, 1954. Goa was liberated on December 19, 1961.

Princely States

On the eve of independence, Indian territories were divided into British Provinces and Princely States. British provinces were directly ruled territories either by the Governor, Lieutenant-Governor, or a Chief Commissioner. There were 17 British provinces at the time of independence. These were: Ajmer-Merwara, Andaman and Nicobar Islands, Assam, Baluchistan, Bengal, Bihar, Bombay, Central Provinces and Berar, Coorg, Delhi, Madras, North-West Frontier, Orissa, Panth-Piploda, Punjab, Sind, and United Province.

On the other hand, there were numerous Princely States of varying sizes which covered more than one-third of the territory of undivided India.

Relationship Between the British and the Princely States

Princely States shared a cordial and loyal relationship with the British. Majority of them extended military, financial, and logistical help to the British. Financial and military help rendered by states like Hyderabad, Gwalior, Patiala, and others during the 1857 Revolt and more importantly, during the First World War, made the British realise the significance of Indian states as a whole. They were regarded as partners, albeit subordinate, in the British imperial policy.

After their massive contribution to the First World War, the British provided them representation in the British imperial legislature. With the help of King George V, the Chamber of Princes or Narender Mandal or Narendra Mandal was established in 1920. The Chamber aimed to provide a forum in which the Indian rulers could voice their needs and aspirations to the British government.

An image of Chamber of Indian Princes or Narendra Mandal — Wikimedia Commons

The loyalty of the princes was sought to be closely secured through the award of honours and titles, as well as grand ceremonies in the form of Imperial Durbars. Thus, by the late 19th century, the Indian Princely States were closely identified with British rule.

The colonial regime had created a status hierarchy among the princes. The rulers of the largest states of Hyderabad, Kashmir, Mysore, Baroda, and Gwalior were each granted a 21-gun salute, while the smaller in the hierarchy were entitled with a 19-gun salute. The states with entitlement to 19 salutes included the Nawab of Bhopal, the Maharaja Holkar of Indore, the Maharana of Udaipur, the Maharaja of Kolhapur, and the Maharaja of Travancore.

Jayachamarajendra Wadiyar - The Ruler of Mysore — Wikimedia Commons

In major states, British residents were appointed who looked into the external affairs of the states and also kept a check on the powers of these states. Smaller principalities and Jagirs were brought under British agencies. So there was the Central India Agency which included 148 principalities, Gwalior Residency, Baluchistan Agency, Rajputana Agency, and Eastern States Agency. The British followed the policy of non-interference in the internal matters of the Princely States.

Some states like Baroda, Travancore, Cochin, Mysore, and Kolhapur had a reputation for being progressive states. Their rulers initiated educational endeavours and supported social reforms. Travancore and Cochin made impressive strides in the spread of literacy. Rulers of states like Maharaja Sayajirao Gaekwad of Baroda and Chhatrapati Shahu Maharaj of Kolhapur were the most progressive Indian rulers of this period. Both of them financially assisted Dr. B.R. Ambedkar in pursuing higher education abroad. Baroda, Mysore, Hyderabad, and Gwalior were some of the states that encouraged industrial development on a significant scale.

People's Movement in Princely States

The post-War period saw the emergence of People's movements in the Princely States demanding increasing popular participation in the administration of these states. These movements were largely led by the urban elites. Their major demand was the progressive introduction of representative institutions in the states. At the same time, there also emerged peasants' movements in Princely States, which were largely protests against enhanced land revenue demands besides exaction of feudal dues. A significant outcome of People's movements in the states was the emergence of popular organisations or Praja Mandals. The locals along with the Congress formed 'Praja Mandals' in various Princely States. In 1927, various Praja Mandals grouped together to form the 'All India States' People's Conference' in Bombay. From the 1930s onwards, the Congress started supporting the cause of this organisation. One of the earliest Praja Mandals was the Dakshini Samsthan Hitavardhak Sabha (The Society for the Promotion of the Interests of the People of South India) or the Deccan States' Subjects Conference in 1922. N.C. Kelkar and A.V. Patwardhan, the close associates of Tilak and Gokhale respectively, took the initiative in the establishment of this organisation.

British Attitude Towards Integration of Princely States

The attitude of the British was not aligned with the ideology of the Congress and the nationalists. In the Constitutional reforms carried out by the British government since the Act of 1935, Princely States were given the option of voluntary representation. In the Government of India Act of 1935, that proposed 'All India Federation', Princely States were given an option to join or opt out.

In the Wavell Plan (1945), it was declared that the Princely States would be independent even after India's independence. Cabinet Mission Plan (1946) reiterated that Princely States would remain independent post India's independence.

With the India Independence Act, 1947, the supremacy of the British Crown on Princely States lapsed. The British gave them the option to either join Indian – Pakistan dominions or remain independent. This decision was left to the rulers and not to the people. This was a serious problem and could threaten the very existence of a united India.

Important Faces and Facets of Integration of Princely States

Following were the events and eminent personalities whose strong leadership, coordination, and cooperation helped in the integration of several Princely States into the Indian union:

V.P. Menon

V.P. Menon - Veteran Civil Servant — Wikimedia Commons

V.P. Menon, a civil servant, political advisor, and Secretary to the Government of India in the Ministry of the States, played a crucial role in integration of Princely States to the Indian union. V.P. Menon turned the Bill of Indian Independence in India's favour with respect to the Princely States. It made their integration within the Indian state mandatory and not optional.

On Menon's suggestion, the Viceroy Mountbatten asserted to the Princely States that it is mandatory to the accede either to India or Pakistan and that the British government would not maintain diplomatic relations with those who chose to remain independent. This suggestion of Menon helped to arrive at a quicker political settlement with the Congress and a smoother transfer of power prior to the actual transfer scheduled for August 1947.

With the agreement of Nehru and Sardar Patel, the formula that the states would accede to India only with respect to defence, external affairs, and communications was devised. A separate States Department (States Ministry) was established by the Government of India in June 1947 to deal with matters related with the states. Meanwhile, Lord Mountbatten took the lead in persuading recalcitrant and suspicious princes to agree to this formula.

Sardar Vallabhbhai Patel

Sardar Vallabhbhai Patel - The Iron Man Of India — Wikimedia Commons

The lion's share of the credit of effecting this relatively seamless integration of these states, using a mixture of persuasion, conciliation, and coercion, goes to Sardar Vallabhbhai Patel, the Deputy Prime Minister, who was in charge of the Ministry of States, formed to deal with this knotty problem, and the Secretary of the Ministry, the veteran civil servant, V.P. Menon.

Sardar Vallabhbhai Patel handled effectively the integration of the Princely States with his diplomatic skills and foresightedness. Patel used social meetings and unofficial surroundings to engage most ruling elites. At these meetings, Patel stated that there was no inherent conflict between the Congress and the princely order. Nonetheless, he stressed that the princes would need to accede to India in good faith by 15th August, 1947. Patel invoked the patriotism of India's monarchs, asking them to join in the freedom of their nation and act as responsible rulers who cared about the future of their people. He proposed favourable terms for the merger, including creation of *privy purses* for the descendants of the rulers.

Lord Mountbatten

Loard Mountbatten
— Wikimedia Commons

The arrival of Lord Mountbatten gave an impetus to the process of decolonisation set in motion by Attlee's declaration. The princes expected much from the new Viceroy since he was a close relative of the British royal family.

Mountbatten was trusted by most of the princes and was a personal friend of many, especially the Nawab of Bhopal, Hamidullah Khan. Prime Minister Jawaharlal Nehru and Patel had asked him to become the first Governor-General of the Dominion of India. Following V.P. Menon's advice, Mountbatten declared that the Princely States had to join any of the Dominion, i.e., Pakistan or India according to their geographical location. He asserted that the British Government would not grant dominion status to any of the Princely States, nor would it accept them into the British Commonwealth, who chose to remain independent. Mountbatten pointed out that the accession of a predominantly Hindu state to Pakistan would violate the principle of the Two-Nation theory on which Partition was based, and was likely to cause communal violence in the State.

Congress Under Nehru

Prime Minister Jawaharlal Nehru
— Wikimedia Commons

The Congress stated that the Princely States were not sovereign entities, and as such, could not opt to be independent. They also stated that the Princely States must accede to either India or Pakistan. Nehru declared that any Princely State which refused to join the Constituent Assembly would be treated as an enemy state. The Indian National Congress advised all these Princely States to join the Constituent Assembly and surrender their army, communications, and foreign affairs initially.

The 'States' Department'

A new department called the 'States' department' under Sardar Patel was created in June 1947. Sardar Patel took charge of the Indian States Department and V.P. Menon became his Secretary and an official statement was made on 5th July, 1947. They dealt with matters arising between the Central Government and the Indian states. All states, except a few, acceded to the Indian union in accordance with an "Instrument of Accession", by which they acceded only three subjects – **Defence, External Affairs, and Communications**.

Assimilation Strategy of Integration (Patel Scheme)

The process of the integration of the Princely States was divided into three stages: in the first stage, V.P. Menon would meet the *Diwans* of these Princely States; in the second, Sardar Vallabhbhai Patel would meet the rulers; and in the third, Governor-General Mountbatten would meet these rulers for the last time.

Sardar Patel developed a scheme of assimilation and merger of small states. It was named as 'Patel Scheme'.

There were the following provisions under the Patel Scheme:

1. **Merger of small states with adjoining provinces :** About 216 states were merged with provinces adjoining them, e.g. merger of 24 states of Orissa, 14 states of the Central Province, Pudukkotah with Madras, etc. These merged states were included in Part A of the Constitution.
2. **Grouping of small states :** Many small states grouped themselves to form a big state with the rulers of the most important one becoming the Rajpramukhs, e.g. Union of Saurashtra, Patiala and East Punjab States Union (PEPSU), etc. These unions were called Part B States.
3. **Integration into Chief Commissioner's Provinces :** About 61 states which were small and backward were converted into centrally administered areas as Chief Commissioner Provinces and were called Part C States, e.g. Himachal Pradesh, Ajmer, Coorg, Cooch-Bihar, etc.

The rulers of these states were promised honourable positions and were assured of their rights and privileges. Of the states situated within the boundaries of the Dominion of India, about 565 states, except Junagadh, Hyderabad, Kashmir, and a few had acceded before the independence itself.

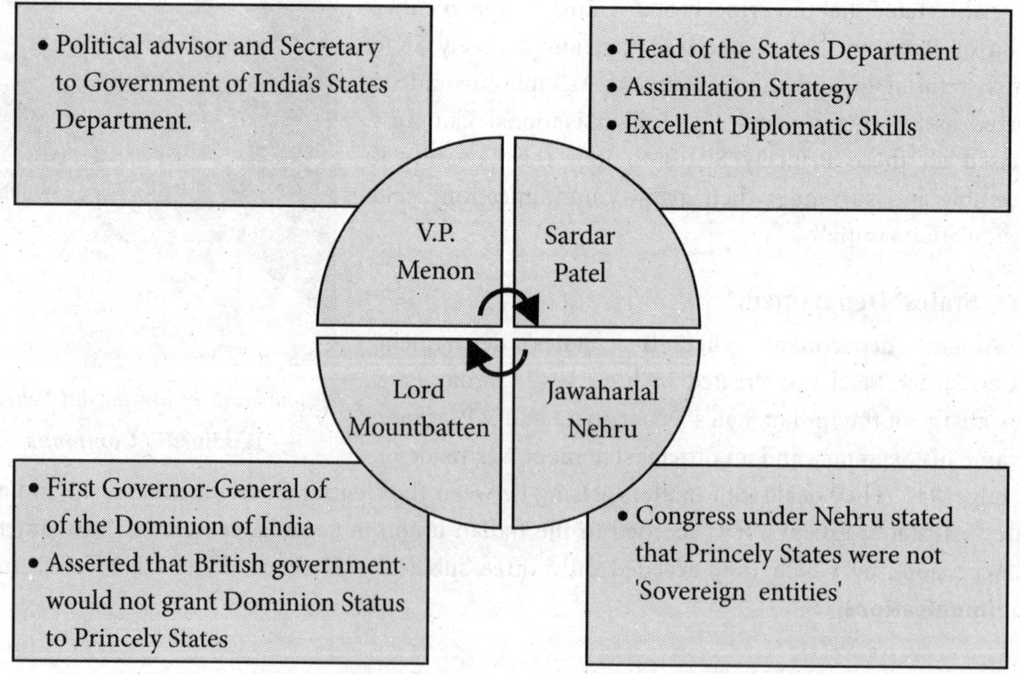

Attractive Treaties and Patel's Soft Skills

The most significant factor that led to the princes' decision to accede to India was the policy of Patel and Menon. Patel and Menon used all diplomatic skills to attract rulers.

Patel and Menon formed treaties that were designed to be attractive to the rulers of the Princely States. The official policy statement of the Government of India made by Patel on 5th July, 1947 not only emphasised the friendly attitude of the Indian Union towards Princely States, but revealed remarkable soft skills of Patel in developing trust and confidence among the states. The statement emphasised the unity of India and the common interests of the princes and independent India. Patel invited the states to join independent India "to make laws sitting together as friends than to make treaties as aliens". He reiterated that there would be no attempt to establish a relationship of domination over the Princely States. Unlike the Political Department of the British Government, it would not be an instrument of paramountcy, but a medium, whereby business could be conducted between the states and Government of India as equals.

Instruments of Accession

For the accession of states, the Government of India came out with two documents - the Standstill Agreement and Instrument of Accession. The Standstill Agreement was for maintaining the status quo. It confirmed for the time being the continuance of the pre-existing agreements and administrative practices. The Instrument of Accession was a legal document created in 1947 to enable each of the rulers of the Princely States to join the Indian dominion. By accepting the Instrument of Accession, the ruler of the Princely State technically or officially agreed to the accession of his kingdom to independent India.

The Instrument of Accession had many attractive safeguards that made many rulers to accede to India. For instance, the instrument would not bind the princes to the Indian Constitution as and when it was drafted. It guaranteed their autonomy in their areas. It guaranteed protection of rulers' extra-territorial rights. The instrument allowed the states to democratise slowly. Major states would not be forced to merge. They would remain eligible for British honours and decorations.

In return of their surrender of all power and authority, the rulers of major states were given privy purses guaranteed by the Constitution. The rulers were allowed succession to the *gaddi* or throne and retained certain privileges such as keeping their titles, flying their personal flags, and gun salutes on ceremonial occasions.

The amount of autonomy offered in the Instrument of Accession and other guarantees appealed to the Princely rulers. They found it as the best deal they could strike with the Indian dominion. Between May 1947 and the transfer of power on 15 August, 1947, nearly 560 states signed the Instrument of Accession.

States That Resisted The Integration

Some ambitious states like Hyderabad and Travancore were making preparations for an eventual independent status by establishing links with foreign countries, while others sought to use their links with the leading figures in British politics to safeguard their existence.

Border states like Jodhpur tried to negotiate better deals with Pakistan while Junagadh tried to accede to Pakistan. The Nawab of Bhopal was not ready to join the Constituent Assembly. Travancore, Hyderabad, and Kashmir declared that they intended to remain independent. However, the state of Travancore was handled diplomatically by V.P. Menon and its ruler agreed to accede to India. Therefore, major states that acceded before the Independence were Jodhpur, Bhopal, and Travancore.

Mountbatten's Plan to ensure that all states that lay surrounded by the Indian territory or did not have territories contiguous with those of Pakistan should be acceded to India failed. States of Junagadh, Hyderabad, and Jammu and Kashmir posed a challenge to the Government of India. None of them had acceded to India by August 15, 1947. Their rulers took advantage of the provisions of the India Independence Act, 1947 by which British control over them lapsed and was not replaced by any other external authority. These states declined to sign the Instrument of Accession by August 1947.

Junagadh

Junagadh, a predominantly Hindu state in Saurashtra (south-western end of Gujarat), was ruled by a Muslim Nawab. The state had 80% Hindu population and no common border with Pakistan. The Nawab announced his intention to join Pakistan though this state did not have any frontier with Pakistan. The rulers of the two states that were subject to the suzerainty of Junagadh—Mangrol and Babariawad—reacted to this decision by declaring their independence from Junagadh and acceding to India. The Indian government sent the military and called for a plebiscite to decide the question of accession. On 26 October, the Nawab and his family fled to Pakistan following clashes with the Indian troops. A plebiscite was conducted in February 1948, which was in favour of accession to India.

Kashmir

The issue of Kashmir proved to be very complex and thorny. The state of Jammu and Kashmir was ruled by Maharaja Hari Singh, a Hindu, although the state had a Muslim majority. Hari Singh was hesitant about acceding to either India or Pakistan. He signed a Standstill Agreement and announced that Kashmir intended to remain independent. Hari Singh's plan was opposed by Sheikh Abdullah, the popular leader of Kashmir's largest political party, the National Conference, who demanded his abdication.

Maharaja Hari Singh – Ruler of Jammu and Kashmir — Wikimedia Commons

Tribes from the North-West Frontier Province of Pakistan crossed the border and invaded Kashmir. Pakistani troops joined the invaders in the disguise of volunteers. The Maharaja of Kashmir wrote to India, asking for military assistance. India asked for the signing of the Instrument of Accession and setting up of an interim government headed by Sheikh Abdullah and plebiscite. The Hindu ruler signed the Instrument of Accession on October 26, 1947. The then Governor-General of India, Lord Mountbatten, accepted the accession with a remark, "it is my Government's wish that as soon as law and order have been restored in Jammu and Kashmir and her soil cleared of the invader, the question of the State's accession should be settled by a reference to the people." Lord Mountbatten's remark and the offer made by the Government of India to conduct a plebiscite or referendum to determine the future status of Kashmir led to a dispute between India and Pakistan regarding the legality of the accession of Jammu and Kashmir to India.

Indian troops secured Jammu, Srinagar, and the valley. Prime Minister Nehru declared a ceasefire and sought UN arbitration, arguing that India would otherwise have to invade Pakistan to stop the tribal incursions. The plebiscite however, was never held. On 26 January 1950, the Constitution of India came into force in Kashmir, but with special provisions made for the state. The northern and western portions of Kashmir came under Pakistan's control in 1947.

Hyderabad

The Muslim Nizam of Hyderabad, a predominantly Hindu state, surrounded by India, was determined to stay independent. The Hindu population rose in revolt against the Nizam's decision. The Nizam tried to suppress the agitation of the people for the merger with India. Having failed to persuade him, the Government of India took recourse to police action which resulted in the accession of the state to India.

Nizam of Hyderabad
— Wikimedia Commons

Ruler of Hyderabad

Hyderabad was a landlocked state where 87% of its population was Hindu. The ruler was Nizam Osman Ali Khan. Ittehadul Muslimeen (also known as Razakars) was a powerful pro-Nizam Muslim party which insisted that Hyderabad remain independent and stand on an equal footing with India and Pakistan. The Nizam prepared to enter into a limited treaty with special provisions such as guaranteeing Hyderabad's neutrality in the event of a conflict between India and Pakistan. India rejected this proposal. A temporary Standstill Agreement was signed maintaining the status quo between the Government of India and the Nizam of Hyderabad. However, the Ittehadul-Muslimeen, led by Kasim Rizvi, was strongly against Hyderabad coming to any agreement with the Indian government.

In the meantime, a People's movement in Hyderabad state against the Nizam's rule gathered force. Hyderabad Congress and the Communists were in the forefront of the movement. Hyderabad State Congress was pressing for its accession to and integration with India. It launched an agitation for the integration of the state. In the Telangana region, the peasantry with the support from the communists rose against the Nizam's rule. Women too joined the movement in large numbers. Hyderabad town was the nerve centre of this movement. The Nizam responded to the Telangana movement by using Razakars. They murdered, maimed, raped, and looted, targeting particularly the non-Muslim people. The Nizam attempted to approach the UN Security Council and the International Court of Justice to complain against the Government of India's measures against the state. In such a situation, the Central government gave order to the army to intervene in Hyderabad. On 13 September, the Indian Army was sent into Hyderabad under 'Operation Polo' on the grounds that the law and order situation in the state had threatened the peace of South India. The troops met little resistance by the Razakars and took complete control of the state between 13 and 18 September.

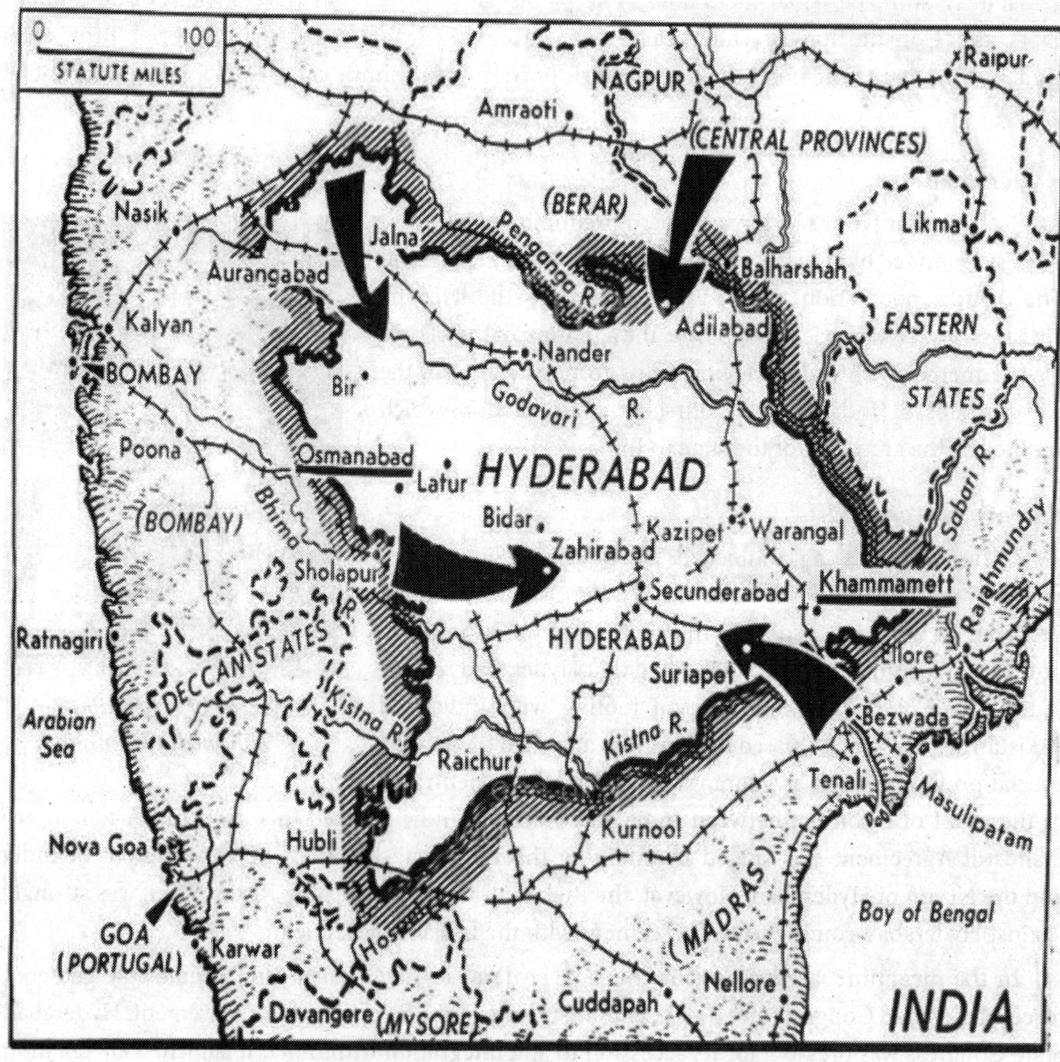

'Operation Polo' in Hyderabad State — Wikimedia Commons

Manipur

The Maharaja of Manipur signed the instrument of Accession with the Indian government on the assurance that the internal autonomy of Manipur would be maintained. Under the pressure of public view, the Maharaja held elections in Manipur in June 1948 and thus, the state became a Constitutional monarchy. Manipur was the first state to hold an election based on Universal Adult Franchise. The Government of India succeeded in pressurising the Maharaja into signing a Merger Agreement in September 1949, without consulting the popularly elected Legislative Assembly of Manipur. This caused anger and resentment among the people of Manipur whose consequences are still felt.

Challenge of Accession

Post-Independence, the Indian dominion had 11 provinces. These were: Ajmer-Merwara-Kekri, Andaman and Nicobar Islands, Bihar, Bombay, Central Provinces and Berar, Coorg, Delhi, Madras, Panth-Piploda, Orissa, and the United Provinces. On the other hand, Pakistan dominion had three provinces – Baluchistan, North-West Frontier, and Sindh and the three provinces of Punjab, Bengal, and Assam were partitioned between India and Pakistan.

It was a big challenge to integrate more than 500 Princely States into the Indian union. Sardar Vallabhbhai Patel, the Home Minister and his Secretary, V. P. Menon played a historic role in integrating these states into the Indian dominion.

Sardar Patel, through diplomacy, persuasion, and interpersonal communication led many princely rulers to accede to India. He invoked in them the sentiments of patriotism towards the motherland and gave them assurance for the security and autonomy in their internal affairs. He persuaded these rulers to surrender only communication and external affairs to the centre and participate in the progress of the nation. Many Princely States thus readily signed the "Instrument of Accession" before August 15, 1947.

The accession of the states of Junagadh, Manipur, Hyderabad, and Kashmir however proved difficult. But Sardar Patel's policy of diplomacy and pressure made these states' accession possible. The Junagadh issue was resolved after the plebiscite. Hyderabad was integrated with the help of the army. The Manipur king signed the "Instrument of Accession" with assurance that the internal autonomy of Manipur will be maintained. Kashmir joined India with the 'Special Status' mentioned in the Article 370 of the Indian Constitution.

Sardar Patel's friendly approach and masterful diplomacy appealed to many Princely States. They were ready to become a part of India on the basis of assurances given by Patel in the Instrument of Accession and public statements. For this historic role of integrating Princely States into the Indian union, Sardar Patel has always been remembered as the 'Iron Man of India'.

Thus, with great skill and masterful diplomacy and using both persuasion and pressure, Sardar Vallabhbhai Patel succeeded in integrating the hundreds of Princely States with the Indian Union.

Previous Years' Questions

1. **"With great skill and masterful diplomacy and using both persuasion and pressure, Sardar Vallabhbhai Patel succeeded in integrating the hundreds of Princely States with the Indian Union." (2007)**
2. **"The relations of the Native States, however conducted are essentially relations with the British Crown and not with the Indian Government." Comment. (1991)**
3. **"It is sometimes asked by Ruling Chiefs, as well as by the public in India and in Europe what our policy towards Native States is. I can tell you that the basis of the policy was laid in Queen Victoria's Proclamation of 1858 and repeated in the Coronation message of His Majesty the King Emperor." Comment. (1986)**
4. **Throw light on the nature of 'Instrument of Accession' and 'Standstill Agreement' signed by the Princely States with the Indian Union. (2017)**

CHAPTER 22

Legacy of The British Rule in India (Local Self-Rule, Civil Services, and Western Model of Education)

Introduction

The 200 years of British rule left some permanent imprints in the life of the Indians. The developments witnessed during the two centuries of British rule were not planned by the colonial rulers for the welfare of the Indians, but were merely an outcome of their larger aim of maintaining political and economic hegemony in India. Jawaharlal Nehru has rightly commented that "Changes came to India because of the impact of the West but these came almost in spite of the British in India. They succeeded in slowing down the pace of those changes."

Divergent Views of Scholars

Scholars have expressed divergent views about the legacy of the British rule in India. The British scholars and the Indian scholars hold different views relating to the contribution and legacy of the English to India. English scholars like Alfred Loyal, J.F. Stephen, and W.W. Hunter opined that the modernisation of India, growth of nationalism, efficient administration, modern education, law and order was the legacy of the English to the Indians. They even showered lavish praises on the British for converting India into a civilised nation. They did not pay any heed to the economic exploitation by the British.

But Indian scholars like Dadabhai Nauroji, R.C. Dutta, and many others, do not accept the views of the British scholars and historians. They evaluated the legacy of the British from a nationalistic point of view. They criticised the English as they disturbed the economic life of India. According to them, the British destroyed the flourishing handicrafts, trade, and commerce. They put obstacles in the way of modernisation by exploiting the rich economic resources of the country. They also spread the feeling of communalism among the Hindus and Muslims, which ultimately led to the partition of India.

However, the contribution of the British towards the modernisation of the country cannot be ignored. A noteworthy legacy of the British rule is the modernisation of the administrative system. The British are credited with setting up of a centralised system of administration and development of modern institutions, even though these were developed by the Imperial rulers for their own benefit. Two major areas of Indian administration which have been heavily influenced by the decades of British rule are Local Self-government and the System of Civil Services.

Local Self-Government In India

Local government refers to the administration of a particular locality by the government officials. Local self-government, on the other hand, refers to the administration of a locality by the representatives of the people.

The English East India Company introduced a highly centralised system of administration in its territories. Towards the end of the 17th century, urban self-government received its first attention. The first municipal corporation in India was established at Madras in 1687. Similar corporations were set up at Calcutta and Bombay in 1726. Acts of 1842, 1854, and 1856 provided for the establishment of municipal institutions in the towns of India and the appointment of Municipal Commissioners. Municipal committees sprang up in several towns of India. However, these Acts were non-obligatory and many cities remained without municipal committees. Also, these Acts did not establish the system of elections.

Lord Mayo's Resolution of 1870

After 1857, many factors combined together which fostered the growth and development of local government institutions. One of them was the Resolution of 1870 in the time of Lord Mayo (1869–1872), the fourth Viceroy and Governor-General of India. The resolution of 1870 in the time of Lord Mayo stressed the necessity of taking further steps to bring local interest and supervision to bear on the management of funds devoted to education, sanitation, public works, and likewise. These included the principle of elections.

The progress made in the sphere of local self-government as a result of the Resolution of 1870 was admitted by the Resolution on the Self-government of 1882. It stated that considerable progress has been made since 1870. A large income from local rates and cesses had been secured, and in some provinces, the management of income had been freely entrusted to the local bodies. Municipalities had also increased in number and usefulness.

Lord Ripon – The Father of Local Self-government in India

Lord Ripon (1880–1884) was appointed as the Viceroy of India by the then Liberal Party Prime Minister of England, Gladstone. Ripon was a Liberal democrat with faith in self-government. P.E. Roberts writes about Lord Ripon, "He was a true liberal of Gladstonian Era with a strong belief in the virtues of peace, laissez faire, and self-government."

During his time, the system of local self-government was elevated to the next stage of development. Ripon helped the growth of local bodies like the municipal committees in towns and the local boards in talukas and villages. Lord Ripon, therefore, is considered as the 'Father of Local Self-government in India'.

Lord Ripon was not prepared to accept the official view that the Indians were indifferent towards self-government. It was perhaps the desire of Ripon that power in India should be gradually transferred to the educated Indians. Lord Ripon believed that the aim of Local Self-government was to train the Indians to manage their own affairs themselves. Lord Ripon wrote, "What I want is a gradual training of the best, most intelligent, and influential men in the community, to take an interest and active part in the management of their local affairs."

Local Self-government Resolution of 1882

In 1882, Lord Ripon issued the famous resolution on Local Self-government. Prior to the changes introduced in 1882, the Government nominated the Municipal Commissioner. In rural areas there were committees to manage local affairs such as sanitation, repair and construction of roads, maintenance of ferries, education, etc. However, these local committees were all under official control. Their area of jurisdiction was too large. Committee members were not sufficiently acquainted with the needs of the people of different localities.

The resolution of 1882 addressed these obstacles through the following measures:

- In rural areas, District Boards and Local Boards known as *Tahsils* or *Taluk* Boards were set up. The members were to be elected by rent-payers rather than nominated by the Government. In towns, the municipalities' board members were to be partly elected and partly nominated.
- The Chairman of the committee was to be a non-official member. The nominated members should not be more than one-third of the total strength.
- The management of health, education, roads, and communications were to remain under the control of the local boards. The local bodies were given certain financial powers but the Government retained the powers of inspection.
- The provincial governments were instructed to maintain and extend a network of local boards in every district.
- The area of the jurisdiction of the local board was to be small, so as to secure the advantages of local knowledge and local interests on the part of the people.
- The system of elections was to be introduced wherever possible. The number of elected members was to be gradually increased.
- More district boards were to be set up. The numbers of municipal committees were to be increased and their powers were to be enhanced.

The control of the local bodies was to be exercised from without and not from within. It was to be exercised in the following ways:

- The sanction of the government was to be made necessary to legalise certain actions of the local bodies, e.g. levying the taxes.
- The power of absolute suppression was to be exercised only with the consent of the Government of India.
- The provincial governments were to be authorised to set aside the proceedings of local bodies or to suspend them temporarily in the case of crisis or neglect of duty.
- The approval of the local government was made necessary to validate the election of the Chairman and the former could disallow it.

The resolution of 1882 is a landmark in the history of local self-government in India and some writers have described it as the *Magna Carta* of Local Self-government.

It had the following merits:

- It provided opportunities to the people to equip themselves with the knowledge, experience, and work of the representative institutions.
- It laid down a clear-cut path for the progress of Local Self-government in the provinces.
- It made some definite and concrete proposals.
- It extended the principle of self-government even to the rural areas.

However, the scheme of Lord Ripon on Local Self-government could not be developed, as many were opposed to it.

Royal Commission on Decentralisation (1907–1909)

This commission made three important suggestions regarding Local Self-government in India:

- Special measures should be adopted for the revival and growth of village *Panchayats* in India,
- The control of the government over local bodies should be reduced, and
- The local bodies should have more sources of income.

The government agreed on the Commission's recommendation but it was never implemented.

Local Self-Government Under the Act of 1919

The Government of India Act of 1919 introduced the system of dyarchy in the provinces. Local Self-government became a transferred subject and was placed under an Indian minister responsible to the provincial legislature. The ministers tried to develop the system of Local Self-government in different provinces. Acts were passed to lower the franchise qualification and increase the elected element. Laws were passed to encourage the growth of village *Panchayats*. The ministers, however, had to face financial difficulties as finance was a reserved department.

Local Self-Government Under the Act of 1935

The Act of 1935 introduced provincial autonomy. Finance was no more a reserved department and the ministers for Local Self-government were able to get more money from the department.

Some further progress was made after the attainment of independence in 1947. The legislature of UP passed the Gaon *Hukumat* Act in 1948 with a view to encourage the development of village Panchayats. Several other provinces have also passed similar Acts since then.

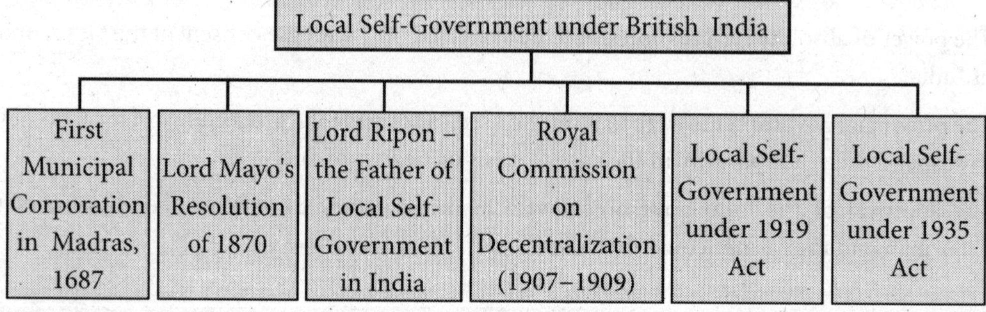

The Civil Services Administrative System

The Civil Services was introduced by the British to govern a vast country like India as they realised the fact that India cannot be governed properly unless it is backed by a strong and efficient Civil Service. They also made sure that those who enter into the Civil Service reflected the concerns of the imperial rulers and not that of ordinary people.

Both the Hindu rulers of ancient India and the Muslim rulers of the medieval period had their own systems of administration and recruited men to run it. But they had never followed a systematic system and pattern of recruitment and training of their employees. It was the British who for the first time in India, introduced the cadre-based Civil Services which eventually became the steel framework of the administrative machinery of British India.

Both under the East India Company and under the administration of the British Queen, the system of the Civil Services underwent changes and developed gradually through four distinct periods following the gradual changes in the nature, functions, and responsibilities of the Company.

Civil Services From 1650 to 1750 onwards

During this period, the primary concern of the East India Company was mainly trade, though occasionally and rarely, they had to deal with administration. During this period, the Company servants were generally visionary youths *"who were more hopeful than useful."* A four-graded regular Civil Service was introduced in this period. The four grades were *apprentices, writers, junior factors,* and *the senior factors* respectively. These graded servants required only one qualification—the quality of a good penmanship. Later on, they were required to have the knowledge of commercial accounts also. Moreover, a candidate willing to be appointed to any of the above four posts had to submit a petition for the same and obtain a nomination from any one of the Directors of the Company.

Civil Services From 1757 to 1858 onwards

When the British acquired large territories, administration of these territories became a problem largely due to shortage of English employees and lack of training. Therefore, a large numbers of Indians were employed to help in the work of administration. Only key positions and superior posts were manned by Englishmen. The system had two defects: Firstly, there was no arrangement to give training to the employees of the Company. Secondly, the salaries of the employees were low. This encouraged many English employees of the Company to get into private trade and illegal activities. The employees of the Company, in spite of the low salaries, used to be rich and were popularly known as Indian Nabobs in their home country.

Role of Lord Cornwallis

Lord Cornwallis made certain changes in the Civil Services of the Company. He stopped giving good jobs to the Indians as he did not consider them fit for this. These were now to be given only to Europeans. This decision was disadvantageous as Europeans charged high salaries.

This raised the expenditure of the Company. Indians disliked the ban on superior services on them.

Cornwallis took strong steps to end the evil of private trade by the servants of the Company. He persuaded the Directors to increase their salaries. The Charter Act of 1793 brought out the provisions of salary of the Company's employees and promotion rules. An important result of the reforms of Cornwallis and the legislation of 1793 was the complete exclusion of Indians from all the higher branches in the Civil Service. In 1817, Sir Thomas Munro remarked, 'There is perhaps no example of any conquest in which the natives have been so completely excluded from all share of the government of their country as in British India. Such a course would not render the character of the people worse, but our government more and more inefficient.'

Role of Lord Wellesley and Lord Bentinck

Lord Wellesley, with a view of providing training to young civil servants, established a college at Calcutta. Only the candidates nominated by the Directors were eligible for admission in that college. The principal subjects of study were languages, law, and history. The college was later closed. Later, a college at Haileybury was established in 1806.

Lord William Bentinck removed the ban on the giving of high jobs to the Indians. The Charter Act of 1833 gave legal effect to this decision.

Government of India Act of 1858

The Government of India Act of 1858 ended the patronage of the Court of Directors and threw open the Covenanted Civil Services to competition to be held in England. According to Sir John Strachey, 'the main object of the competition was to secure for the Indian Civil Service, young men who had received the best, the most liberal and the most finished education which England could afford'. The examination was to include most of the subjects of the honours schools of the universities of Great Britain and Ireland.

Civil Services from 1858 to 1919

The Queen's proclamation removed the ban on giving of high jobs to the Indians. A committee was appointed in 1860 by the Secretary of State for India to give effect to the pledge given in 1858. It recommended the holding of the competitive examination simultaneously in England and India to remove the injustice from which the Indians had suffered.

The Indian Civil Services Act, 1861

The Indian Civil Services Act of 1861 authorised the Government of India to appoint, in exceptional cases, non-covenanted servants to the covenanted posts. The special reasons for these appointments had to be given to the Secretary of State for India.

During this period, there were two defects in the competitive examination. First, the examinations were to be held in England. Second, the maximum age limit was fixed at 22 in 1860. It was further lowered to 21 years in 1866 and to 19 years in 1878. Up to 1870, only one Indian had successfully qualified for the Covenanted Civil Service.

Aitchison Commission

With the formation of the Indian National Congress in 1885, demands for relaxing rules for the examination were put forward. Lord Dufferin appointed a commission in 1886 under the Chairmanship of Sir Charles Aitchison. Hence, it came to be called Aitchison Commission. It reported against the simultaneous holding of Civil Service examinations in England and India. The reason given by it was that it would benefit only a few classes. The number of seats to be filled would be small and a large number of candidates would compete. The rejected candidates would become the centre of dissatisfaction in the country. It recommended the transfer of a number of posts to a lower service in each province to provide opportunities to the Indians as junior civilians. The services should be classified into imperial, provincial, and subordinate. Officers of the imperial and the provincial Civil Services were to hold all the important jobs.

Royal Commission on Public Services in India or Islington Commission

In 1912, another commission, the Islington Commission, for bringing reforms in Indian Civil Services was set up. This commission submitted its report in 1915. In 1917, Lord Montague, the Secretary of State for India, made the August Declaration, promising self-government to the Indians by stages. It implied that the Indians would have to be given a share in the administration and the report of Islington thus, became outdated.

Civil Services from 1918 to 1947

The Government of India Act of 1919 recommended that more and more Indians should be given administrative posts and the Civil Service examination should be simultaneously conducted in England and in India. The percentage of candidates to be recruited in India should be increased by one and a half percent every year.

The Lee Commission, 1923

The Lee Commission of 1923 recommended that the recruitment to the Indian Civil Service, Indian Police Service, the Indian Medical Service, the Indian Forest Service, and the Indian Service of Engineers should be made by the Secretary of State for India. Others members of All India Service could be recruited by the Indian government. It also recommended the establishment of the Public Service Commission in India.

The Government of India Act, 1935

The Government of India Act of 1935 provided many safeguards for the All India Services. The existing rights were guaranteed. The Governor-General and the Governors were to safeguard the legitimate interests of the services. No civil servant was to be dismissed by an authority and their salaries could not be reduced. Federal Public Service Commission and State Public Service Commissions were set up under this Act. When India became independent in 1947 with the transfer of power, the nomenclature of the Indian Civil Service was also changed into the Indian Administrative Service.

For more than 150 years, the main pillar of British imperialism in India was its Civil Service. It greatly helped the British imperialists to preserve law and order in the domain, especially in the period when the nationalist movement and militancy became the rule of the day. It also created a highly prestigious and privileged class in the society. Set in hierarchies, it created a separate class possessing strength and efficiency, who always remained aloof, exclusive, and class-conscious.

Development of Modern Education System Under The British

India had its own education system. The modern system of education came to be established in India during the British period and ruined the indigenous education system.

Early Educational Institutions

The Indian officers of the East India Company found difficult to comprehend the natives' laws, culture, and language. Therefore, on the insistence of these officers, the Court of Directors set up early educational institutions to cater to the needs of the Company's officers.

- **Calcutta Madrasa, 1781 :** Warren Hastings set up the Calcutta Madrasa for the study and learning of Persian and Arabic.
- **Sanskrit College, 1791 :** Jonathan Duncan, the British resident at Benares, set up a Sanskrit College at Benares for the study of laws, literature, and religion of the Hindus.
- **Fort William College, 1800 :** Lord Wellesley set up the Fort William College for the training of the civil servants of the Company in languages and customs of Indians.

Three Agencies for the Spread of Modern Education

The growth and development of Western education system in India happened by the following agencies: The British Government, Christian missionaries, and Indian intellectuals and reformers.

The British government's role in the spread of Western education was limited. It basically gave access to the upper classes on the basis of the Downward Filtration Theory.

Indian intellectuals and social reformers became a powerful agency in the spread of Western education both to the men and women.

The missionaries supported the spread of Western education in India primarily for their proselytising activities. They established many schools with education only being a means to an end which was Christianising and 'civilising' the natives. William Carey, also known as 'Father of Modern Missions', established Mission Schools in Bengal.

Formation of Educational Policy — The Charter Act of 1813

The development of modern system of education in India began with the Charter Act of 1813. The Act sanctioned a sum of Rs. 1 lakh towards education of Indians in British-ruled India. This Act also gave an impetus to the missionaries who were given official permission to come to India.

However, differences arose in the government over what kind of education should be offered to the Indians. British Liberal scholars belonging to the three different schools of thought, viz. Orientalists, Evangelists, and Utilitarians, initiated a debate on the kind of education to be imparted to the Indians.

The Orientalists preferred a traditional and indigenous education to be imparted to the Indians. Utilitarian and Evangelists wanted Indians to be educated in the Western style of education and be taught Western subjects.

There was confusion regarding the language of instruction. Some wanted the use of Indian languages or vernaculars, while others preferred English.

Bentinck had appointed Thomas Babington Macaulay as the Chairman of the General Committee of Public Instruction. In 1835, Macaulay presented his Minute on Indian Education which was accepted by the government.

Macaulay's Minute

Macaulay's Minute refer to his proposal of education for the Indians. According to him:

- English education should be imparted in place of traditional Indian learning because oriental culture was 'defective' and 'unholy'.
- He believed in the education of a few upper and middle class students.
- In course of time, education would trickle down to the masses. This was called Downward Filtration Theory.
- He wished to create a class of Indians who were Indian in colour and blood but English in taste and affiliation.

Policy of Downward Filtration Theory

Macaulay's Minute recommended the policy of Downward Filtration, i.e., educating only to selected few. This was accepted by the British in its Educational Policy.

Policy of Downward Filtration means educating only the upper classes because

- The British rulers needed educated employees to run the commerce and administration.
- The Government did not receive sufficient funds for educating the masses.
- After educating some people, the responsibility of educating the masses could be left to them.

After the formulation of the Education Policy in 1835, there was still no clarity on issues such as medium of instruction, aims, and other things.

The direction of Indian education remained uncertain during the next 22 years on the following issues:

1. **The Medium of Instruction :** It could not be decided whether the medium of instruction should be English or Indian languages.
2. **Aim of Education of the British Policy :** Whether education should be available to all or should be given to only a selected few.
3. **Type of Knowledge :** Whether to preserve and promote Oriental learning or to introduce Western knowledge, culture, and science.
4. **Agency of Education :** Whether the Government should assume direct responsibility of educating the Indians or the Indigenous system of education of the country was to continue.
5. **Role of Missionaries :** Whether the missionaries should be given a free hand in their educational practices or should the Company itself shoulder the total responsibility.

Educational Policies of the Government – Wood's Despatch and Hunter Commission

The educational policies during the period from 1854 and 1900 were formulated by two main documents – the Wood's Despatch of 1854 and the Report of the Indian Education Commission, 1882.

Wood's Despatch, 1854

Charles Wood's Despatch of 1854 was the first comprehensive document for promotion of modern education in India. It was considered as the 'Magna Carta' of English education in India. Wood's Despatch recommended to the Government of India to provide education to all Indians and not to a selected few.

Following were its main provisions:

- English was recommended as the medium of instruction for higher studies and Indian local languages at the school level.
- Emphasis was given on female and vocational education and on teachers' training.
- Education imparted in the government institutions was to be secular.
- A system of grants-in-aid was recommended for the institutions that satisfied certain conditions to encourage private enterprise.

Results of Wood's Despatch

- Graded schools were established in hierarchy as primary schools, middle schools, high schools, colleges, and universities.
- Universities were to be set up at Calcutta, Madras, and Bombay.
- Grant-in-aid schools came up in large numbers

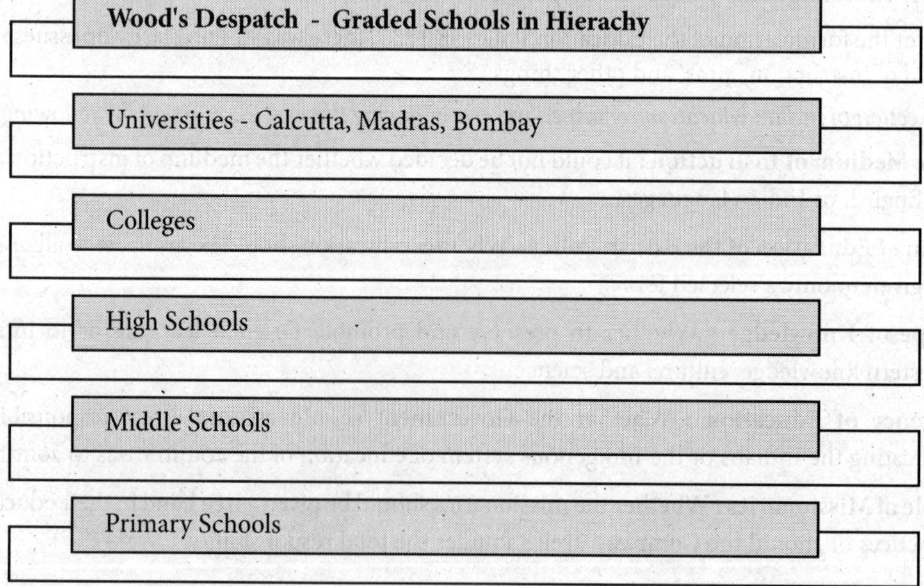

The Indian Education Commission or Hunter Commission (1882)

The Hunter Commission recommended decentralisation of Education, i.e., the complete withdrawal of Government's role from taking direct responsibility of education. There was transfer of all primary schools to the control of Local Self-government bodies such as municipalities and local boards. The Education Commission of 1882 was the first comprehensive document dealing exclusively with women education in India.

The major recommendations of the Hunter Commission were as follows:

- Elementary Education – Encouragement and support to indigenous schools for extending elementary education.
- Freedom to the management committees for choosing vernacular languages as a medium of instruction.
- Gradual transfer of all government secondary schools to local native management committees.
- Bifurcation of secondary education into two streams—one leading to the entrance examination of the universities and the other of a more practical character preparing the students for commercial jobs.

Results of the Hunter Report

The Hunter Report encouraged Indian private enterprise and awakened public enthusiasm for the cause of education for the first time in India. It resulted in the transfer of complete control of primary education to local boards and municipalities.

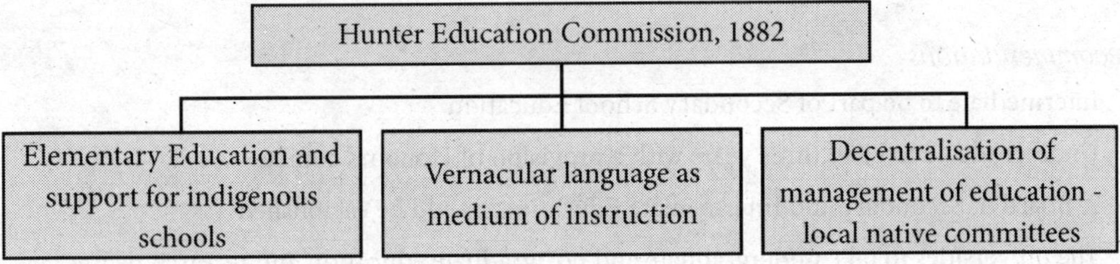

Other Educational Reforms

Lord Curzon's Educational Policy – Raleigh Commission

A new set of educational reforms came up during Lord Curzon's period. He wanted to improve the quality of higher education and also wanted to check the growth of nationalism. In 1901, Lord Curzon convened an educational conference at Simla. This was followed by the appointment of a Commission under the presidency of Sir Thomas Raleigh on 27 January, 1902 to enquire into the condition and prospects of the Universities in British India. The Commission submitted its report to the Government of India, and its recommendations were incorporated in the Universities Act of 1904.

Indian Universities Act, 1904

This Act was passed in 1904 based on the recommendations of the Raleigh Commission. According to this Act, the number of members of the governing body of the universities (senates), were reduced and government's nominees were appointed. In this way, universites came under the control of the government. People of India condemned this Act because it increased the government's control over the universities and reduced the number of Indians in the governing bodies. They saw it as an attempt to restrict education to a selected few and curb the sentiments of nationalism among students.

Government Resolution on Education Policy, 1913

This Resolution advocated three principles of educational policy:

1. The curricula of primary and secondary schools should be made more practical and useful;
2. Facilities of higher education should be provided in India so that Indian students may not have to go abroad;
3. Instead of increasing the number of existing institutions, their standard should be raised.

The First World War which broke out the next year delayed its implementation.

Calcutta University Commission or Sadler University Commission (1917–1919)

Calcutta University Commission was appointed by the Government of India in 1917 to inquire into the condition and prospects of Calcutta University under the Chairmanship of Dr. Michael Sadler, the Vice-Chancellor of Leeds University. This commission clearly separated the school education and college education and pioneered in introducing the 10+2+3 Pattern.

Recommendations

- Intermediate to be part of Secondary School Education
- Undergraduate to be of three years with a provision of Honours courses
- A Board of Secondary and Intermediate Education should be established
- The universities to take undergraduate and postgraduate education and research degrees
- The universities should have Departments of Education with provision of teaching "Education" as a subject at B.A. Level
- An Inter-University Board (IUB) should be established to coordinate the work of different Indian universities.

The recommendations of the Commission introduced a fresh outlook at university education in India and a number of new universities sprang up on the suggested lines.

Education under Dyarchy and End of Direct Responsibility for Education

The 1919 Montague-Chelmsford Reforms marked the end of direct colonial responsibility for education. The Department of Education was transferred to the control of popular ministries in the various provinces. The Central Government ceased to take direct interest in educational matters.

Financial difficulties prevented the provincial governments from taking up ambitious schemes of educational expansion or improvement. During this period, expansion of education was mostly made by philanthropic effort.

Central Advisory Board of Education (CABE), 1921

The need for a coordinating agency in the matter of education was immediately felt by the Central and provincial governments. The Central Advisory Board of Education (CABE) was established at the Centre in 1921 to offer expert advice on important education matters. Educational Commissioner with the Government of India was made the Chairman, and it included a number of eminent educationists, officials, and non-officials from the provinces.

The Hartog Committee, 1929

For improving education and bringing reforms, the Hartog Committee was appointed in May, 1928. Its Chairman, Sir Philip Hartog, made wide-ranging proposals for the development of both general and professional education. The Committee submitted its report in September, 1929.

Report of Hartog Committee

The main findings of this report was regarding the stagnation and wastage of present system of education due to rapid expansion of education that has resulted in the deterioration of quality. Education had become largely ineffective and wasteful.

The Report's recommendations were as follows:

- The immediate need was to improve the quality rather than increase the number of institutions.
- The Committee recommended the policy of consolidation and improvements by reducing the large extent of stagnation and wastage.
- The Committee highlighted that a policy of expansion resulted in wastage and stagnation and thus weakened the need for a rapid expansion of primary education, irrespective of quality.

However, the Report, like Macaulay's Downward Filtration Theory, stopped the progress of the growth of primary education.

The Abott-Wood Report (1937)

The absence of adequate and proper vocational education was being felt in India and the public was raising its demand for it since long. Therefore, the Government of India invited in 1936, two British experts to come to India and prepare a plan for vocational education in the country. These two experts were A. Abott and S.H. Wood. These two persons toured in Punjab, Delhi, and UP and prepared a report on vocational education within four months. On the basis of this report published in 1937, the Sargent Report of 1944 was published. The Sargent Report presented a more detailed plan of vocational education as compared to the Abott Report.

Following were its recommendations:

- Vocational education should be organised according to the needs of various vocational areas.
- Vocational education should be considered at par with literary and science education and its standard should be raised.

- For general and vocational education, there should be separate schools, as the purpose of the two is different.
- Skilful workers engaged in small industries should also be given proper vocational training.
- The Government should open vocational institutions in big cities and big vocational centres.

Post-War Plan of Educational Development or Sargent Plan (1944)

Due to absence of popular ministries during the period 1940–1946, the pace of educational progress slowed down. After the end of the Second World War, the Central Advisory Board of Education (CABE) in India published a comprehensive report on the "Post-War Educational Development in India" in the country.

The report was the first systematic and national level attempt to review the problems of education as a whole. It is also known after John Sargent, the then Educational Advisor to the Government of India.

Recommendation of the Sargent Plan

- Pre-primary education for 3–6 years age group;
- Free, Universal, and Compulsory elementary education for 6–11 years age group;
- High school education for 11–17 years age group for selected children, and a university course of 3 years after higher secondary;
- High schools to be of two types: (i) academic and (ii) technical and vocational;
- Adequate technical, commercial, and arts education with different curricula;
- Abolition of intermediate course;
- Development of adult education and liquidation of adult illiteracy;
- Stress on teachers' training, physical education, and education for the physically and mentally handicapped.

Sargent Plan was one of the most comprehensive schemes of education ever proposed by the British Government after the Wood's Despatch of 1854.

National Education Movement

National education movement emerged in the late 19th century and gathered momentum during the Bengal agitation of 1905.

Following were some of the main causes for its emergence:

- **Inherent defects in the British system of education :** British education was only for a selected few. It was limited to the upper strata of the society. The masses or common people were not benefitted by the then system of education. It was not national in character. It was anti-Indian as well as anti-democratic. The existing system of education failed to generate employment for the educated youth.
- **Rise of Extremists in the Congress :** Towards the end of the 19th century, the Moderates lost their hold in the Congress organisation as well as in the public mind. Extremists dominated the national arena and vehemently propagated nationalism. Extremists were not at all in a mood to tolerate any imperialist design in the arena of education.

- **National Education Policy under Lord Curzon :** The immediate cause of the National Education Movement was the anti-national educational policy followed by Lord Curzon.
- **Swadeshi Movement :** The Swadeshi Movement or the Bengal Partition Movement paved the way for the national education movement.

The National Education Movement underwent three distinct phases:

- First Phase (1906–1911)
- Second Phase (1911–1922)
- Third Phase (1930–1938)

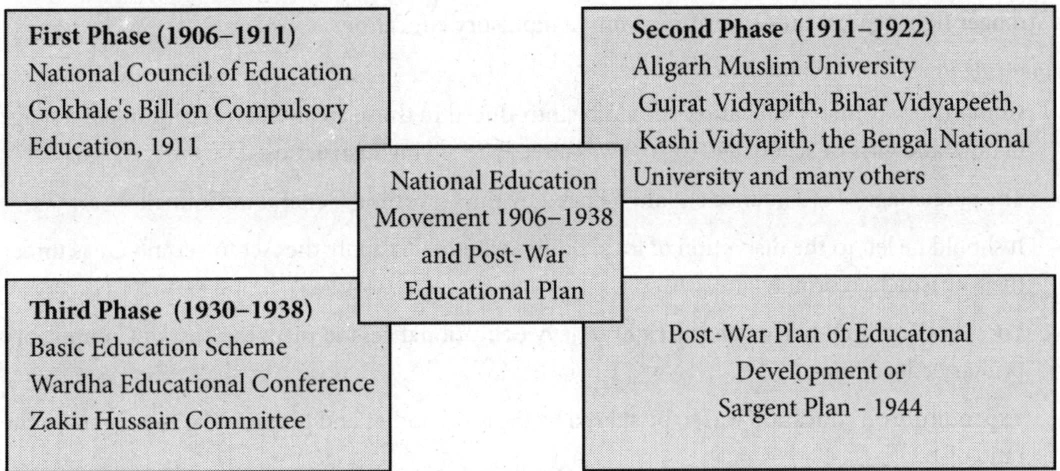

First Phase (1906–1911)

It coincided with the Swadeshi Movement or Boycott Movement. This phase was limited to the boundary of Bengal but had its echoes outside Bengal, particularly in Maharashtra and Punjab.

In the first phase of the National Education Movement, there were no clear-cut objectives and no clarity of thought. Absence of rationality was one of its peculiar characteristics.

The first phase was associated with the establishment of the National Council of Education at Jadavpur and similar other National educational institutions in the country. The birth of the National Council of Education was facilitated by the previous establishment of other educational institutions in Bengal and outside. Prominent educational institutions that were established prior to the National Council of Education were Kangri Gurukul in Haridwar by Swami Sradhhananda in 1902 and Arya Samaj's Gurukul system of education.

The Council chalked out a comprehensive plan for national education in Bengal. On 14th August, 1906, a memorable meeting was held in the Town Hall in Calcutta. It was presided over by Shri Ashutosh Chaudhury. It was attended by a large number of illustrious personalities of Bengal like Rabindranath Tagore and Sir Gurudas Banerjee.

Bengal National College and School were first set up at Bowbazar and these were shifted to Jadavpur later. Sri Aurobindo became its first Principal and Satish Chandra Mukherjee its first Honorary Superintendent. After the resignation of Sri Aurobindo, Satish Chandra became its Principal. "Society for the Promotion of Technical Education" was set up in 1906 by Taraknath Palit. "Society for the Promotion of National Education in Bengal" was also set up by Sir Gurudas Banerjee.

After 1910, the national political movement waned and with it, the national education movement also waned.

Gokhale's Bill, 1911

On 16th March, 1911, Gopal Krishan Gokhale presented a Bill in the Legislative Council to make a stronger fight against the Government for Compulsory education.

Following the recommendation of this bill:

- Compulsory primary education should be introduced in those areas where a certain percentage of boys and girls of school age (6–10) was already receiving instructions.
- The percentage of attendance should be fixed by the Governor-General in Council.
- It should be left to the discretion of local bodies whether to apply the Act to certain areas under their jurisdiction or not.
- Local bodies should be given the right to levy educational cess to meet the cost of Compulsory primary education.
- Expenditure on education was to be shared by the local bodies and provincial government in the ratio of 1:2.
- For the introduction of compulsion, the previous sanction of the Viceroy and the Governor respectively, were necessary.
- Compulsory primary education is intended to apply in the first instance only to boys, though later on, a local body may extend it to girls also.
- Guardians whose income is less than Rs. 10/- per month should not be asked to pay any fee for their ward.

Gokhale's Bill, the first ever attempt to introduce Free and Compulsory Primary education in our country, is a landmark in the history of education in India. Although the Bill was rejected, it focused the attention of the entire country on education. The Government could not entirely ignore the growing popular demand for the spread of mass education.

Second Phase (1911–1922)

The second phase of the movement was more extensive and widespread than the first phase as it was not limited to the Bengal Presidency only. The 2nd phase was more rational than the first one. It was more productive and fruitful than the 1st phase. It coincided with the Khilafat and Non-cooperation Movement. One of the programs of Non-Cooperation Movement was the gradual withdrawal of children from schools and colleges, aided or controlled by Government, and in place of such schools and colleges, the establishment of national schools and colleges in the various provinces.

The whole of India including Bengal, Maharashtra, Punjab, Gujrat, Andhra, and Bihar was practically involved in this phase of the movement. This phase witnessed proactive participation of the Muslims. Hence, the second phase of the National Education Movement originated in Aligarh. Both the teachers and students jointly protested against the non-national curricula and anti-national attitude of the British Government towards the Aligarh College. They set up the Jamia Millia Islamia which was national in character in 1920.

During the 2nd phase, a large number of schools, colleges, and universities came into being. These included the Aligarh Muslim University, the Gujrat Vidyapith, the Bihar Vidyapith, the Kashi Vidyapith, the Bengal National University, the Tilak Maharashtra Vidyapith, Quami Vidyapith, Andhra Vidyapeeth, and many more. The 2nd phase came to an end with the withdrawal of the Non-cooperation Movement.

Third Phase (1930–1938)

The Third phase of the National Education Movement coincided with the Civil Disobedience Movement launched by Gandhi in 1930. Though the physical existence of the National Education Movement practically came to an end with the termination of the Non-cooperation Movement, yet it resurged during and after the Civil Disobedience Movement.

This phase of the national education movement was more theoretical and abstract than practical. No concrete or creative step was taken during this phase. Still, the third phase was characterised by educational schemes and plans mainly enunciated by Gandhi by launching the scheme of Basic Education at Wardha. In this scheme, Gandhi advocated that primary education should be based on Indian traditional culture through the medium of the mother tongue. He expressed his views on education through a series of articles in 'Harijan' in July 31, 1937, which later on developed into the Wardha Scheme of Basic Education.

Wardha Educational Conference

All India National Education Conference was held in Wardha on 22nd and 23rd October, 1937.

After serious discussions, the following four resolutions were passed:

- In the opinion of this conference, Free and Compulsory education was to be provided on a nation-wide scale.
- The medium of instruction was to be the mother tongue.
- The process of education through this period should centre round some form of manual productive work suitable for the local conditions.
- The conference expected that the system of education will be gradually able to cover the remuneration of the teacher.

The conference then appointed a committee under the Chairmanship of Dr. Zakir Husain to prepare a detailed education plan and syllabus on the lines of the above resolutions.

Zakir Husain (3rd President of India) (1897–1969) – Wikimedia Commons

Zakir Husain Committee

- Free, Universal, and Compulsory education should be provided for all boys and girls between the ages of 7–14.
- This education should be imparted in the mother tongue of the child.
- All education should be craft-centric. The committee suggested spinning and weaving, cardboard and wood work, leather work, kitchen-gardening, agriculture, and fishery as obviously suitable crafts.
- In this craft-centred education, all the subjects to be taught were to be integrally related to the selected craft or the child's physical and social environment.

Previous Years' Questions

1. **The introduction of Western Education transformed India in unforeseen ways. (2021)**
2. **Examine the forces at work for the introduction of Western education in India. Analyse the thrust given to it by the Christian Missionaries. (2019)**
3. **How did the introduction of Community Development Program and Panchayati Raj promote welfare of rural India? (2019)**
4. **At different periods and at various levels, the National Movement assumed social, cultural and economic dimensions. Amplify. (1988)**

Appendix–I

The Arrival of the Europeans in India

The Portuguese

1498: Vasco da Gama reaches Calicut in India on 20th May

1502-03: Second trip of Vasco da Gama to India

1503-04: Alfonso de Albuquerque establishes the first Portuguese fort in Kochi during the fifth Portuguese India Armada

1505: Francisco de Almeida appointed as the first viceroy of Portuguese India (Estado da Índia)

1510: Portuguese conquer Goa to serve as capital of their Asian maritime empire

The Dutch

1602: The United East India Company of the Netherlands formed. Receives the sanction of the government to trade in the East Indies

1605: The Dutch set up their first factory in Masulipatnam in Andhra Pradesh

The French

1664: The French East India Company is formed and it receives permission to trade with India

1674: The French East India Company sets up a trading centre at Pondicherry

1742: Dupleix appointed as the governor general of all French establishments in India

The East India Company

1600: The East India company is formed in England on December 31. Elizabeth I grants a charter to the East India Company

1615-18: Thomas Roe is ambassador to the court at Agra, India of the Great Mughal emperor, Jahangir

1612: The East India Company establishes a factory at Surat

1640: The East India Company establishes a factory at Madras

1661: Charles II receives Bombay from Catherine of Braganza as part of her dowry; the East India Company establishes a factory at Bombay

1690: The East India Company establishes a factory at Calcutta

Foundation of the East India Company Rule

1746: The First Carnatic War between the British and the French

1751: Robert Clive seizes Arcot in Carnatic Wars

1756-63: The Seven Years War in Europe

1757: The Battle of Plassey. The British defeat Siraj-ud-Daulah, the Nawab of Bengal

1760: The Battle of Wandiwash–the British defeat the French in Carnatic Wars

1761: The Third Battle of Panipat. The Afghans under Ahmed Shah Abdali defeat the Marathas

1764: The Battle of Buxar–the British defeat Mir Kasim

1765: The Treaty of Allahabad. The British get Diwani Rights in Bengal, Bihar and Orissa

1767-69: First Mysore War.The British forced to concede a peace treaty, the Treaty of Madras in 1769 with Hyder Ali

1772: Warren Hastings appointed as Governor of Bengal

1773: The Regulating Act passed by the British Parliament

1774: Warren Hastings as first Governor General of Bengal Presidency

1775: The First Anglo-Maratha war

1780-84: Second Mysore War. The British defeat Hyder Ali

1782: The treaty of Salbai between the Marathas and the British

1784: Pitt's India Act

1786-93: Lord Cornwallis appointed as Governor-General of Bengal Presidency

1790-92: Third Mysore War between the British and Tipu Sultan

1793: Permanent Settlement of Bengal

1798: The Marquess Wellesley as the Governor General

1799: Fourth Mysore War. The British defeat Tipu in the Battle of Seringapatam. The Partition of Mysore

1802: Treaty of Bassein

1803-05: The Second Anglo-Maratha war

1804: The Mughal Emperor at Delhi is placed under British protection

1805: The Treaty of Amritsar

1813: The East India Company's charter is renewed, but its monopoly over Indian trade is abolished

1814-16: The Anglo-Gurkha war

1817-18: The Pindari war

1824-26: The First Burmese war

Consolidation of the East India Company Rule

1828: Lord William Wiilam Bentinck becomes the first Governor General of India – Foundation of Brahmo Samaj

1829: Regulation on the Prohibition of Sati

1831: Rise of Sikhs under Maharaja Ranjit Singh

– Mysore administration taken over by East India Company

1833: Renewal of Company's Charter and the abolition of the East India Company's trade

– Abolition of slavery throughout the British Empire

1835: The Education Resolution

1837: Suppression of Thugs

1838: Tripartite treaty between Shah Shuja, Ranjit Singh and the British

1839: Maharaja Ranjit Singh dies

1839-42: First Afghan war

1843: Gwalior war

1845-46: First Anglo-Sikh war

1848: Lord Dalhousie becomes the Governor-General

1848-49: Second Anglo-Sikh war and the annexation of Punjab

1849: Awadh annexed on grounds of maladministration

1852: Second Anglo-Burmese war

1853: First Railway line in India between Bombay and Thane

– Telegraph introduced in India

1857: Revolt of 1857

Crown's Rule in India

1858: British Crown takes over the Indian Government

1861: Indian Councils Act

– Indian High Courts Act and Indian Penal Code (IPC) introduced

1868: Railway line opened from Ambala to Delhi

1876–80: Lord Lytton as Governor General and Viceroy of India

1877: Delhi Durbar organised to proclaim Queen Victoria as the Empress of India

– Bengal hit by its worst ever famine

1878: Discriminative Vernacular Press Act promulgated

1881: Factory Act

– Rendition of Mysore, Mysore restored to its original Wodeyar rulers

1880–84: Lord Ripon as Governor General and Viceroy of India

– Resolution on Local Self Government, 1882

1885: Foundation of the Indian National Congress

1892: Indian Council Act to regulate Indian administration

1897: Plague in Bombay; Famine Commission

1899: Lord Curzon becomes Governor-General and Viceroy of India

National Movement

1905: The First Partition of Bengal comes into effect on October 8

– Swadeshi and Boycott Movement

1906: Formation of Muslim League at Dhaka

1907: Surat Split

– Extremists expelled from Congress

1908: Khudiram Bose executed on 30th April

1909: Morley-Minto Reforms

1911: King George V and Queen Mary hold Durbar in Delhi

– Cancellation of Partition of Bengal

– Imperial capital shifts from Calcutta to Delhi

– Attempt to assassinate Viceroy Lord Hardinge

1913: Educational Resolution of the Government of India

1914: First World War begins

– The Ghadar Party formed at San Francisco on 1st November

– Tilak released from jail

1915: Defence of India Act(DIRA)

1915: Gandhi returns to India

– Gopal Krishna Gokhale passes away on 19th February

1916: Home Rule Movement under Tilak and Anne Besant

1916: Unification of Congress

– Lucknow Pact between Congress and Muslim League

1917: The Champaran movement in Bihar

– Ahmedabad Mill Workers Strike

– Kheda Movement

1919: Montague-Chemsford reforms and introduction of Dyarchy

– Rowlatt Act and Rowlatt Act Satyagraha

– Jalianwalla Bagh massacre

Gandhian Movement

1920: The Khilafat Movement and Non-Cooperation Movement started

1921: Moplah (Muslim) rebellion in Malabar

– Census of India

– Visit of the Prince of Wales

1922: Congress makes Gandhiji sole leader of Bardoli Civil

– Disobediance Movement

– Outburst of violence in Chauri-Chaura leading to suspension of movement by Gandhiji

1923: Swaraj Party founded by C.R. Das and Motilal Nehru

1924: Gandhi presided as the president of the Belgaum session of the congress

1925: Death of C.R. Das

– Reforms Enquiry committee Report

– The Kakori Train Conspiracy Case in August

1927: Indian Navy Act

– Simon Commission appointed

1928: Simon Commission comes to India

– Boycott by all parties

– Nehru Report recommends principles for the new Constitution of India. All parties conference consider the Nehru Report

– Lala Lajpat Rai passes away on 17th November due to injuries

1929: Lord Irwin promises Dominion Status for India

- Bhagat Singh and Batukeshwar Dutt throw a bomb in the Central Legislative Assembly on 8th April
- Lahore session of the Congress asks for independence
- On the midnight of Dec. 31, Jawaharlal Nehru hoists National Flag at Lahore

1930: Dandi March or Salt Satyagraha and Civil Disobediance Movement

- First Round Table Conference

1931: Second Round Table Conference

- Irwin-Gandhi Pact
- Bhagat Singh, Sukh Dev and Rajguru executed on 23rd March

1932: Third Round Table Conference

- British Prime Minister Ramsay Macdonald announce the infamous "Communal Award" on 16th August

1934: Civil Disobedience Movement called off

Towards Freedom

1935: The Government of India Act

1937: Inauguration of Provincial Autonomy and formation of Congress ministries

1939: Second World War Begins

- Resignation of Congress ministries
- Observation of Deliverance Day on 22nd December by Muslim League
- Subhash Chandra Bose elected president of Tripuri session of the Congress
- Crisis between Gandhi and Subhash in Tripuri
- Subhash quits Congress and forms Forward Bloc

1940: Lahore session of the Muslim League passes the Pakistan Resolution in March

- Viceroy Linlithgow announces August Offer on 10th of August.
- Congress launches individual satyagraha movement on 17th October

1941: Japan enters the War

- Attack on Pearl Harbour
- Subhash escapes from prison and reaches Germany

1942: Cripps Mission

- Quit India Movement
- Formation of Indian National Army (INA)

1943: Bengal famine

- Lord Wavell becomes the Governor General of India

1944: Wavell calls Simla Conference in a bid to form the Executive Council of Indian political leaders on 25th January

- Gandhi-Jinnah talks break down on Pakistan issue

1946: The trial of the INA men

- Cabinet Mission in India (Aug. 19)
- The ratings of the Royal Indian Navy rise in open revolt (Feb. 18)
- Cabinet Mission announces its plan for an interim government and a constituent assembly
- Interim Government formed under Jawaharlal Nehru
- Constituent Assembly's first meeting
- Direct Action Day or Great Calcutta Killing (16th August)

1947: Lord Mountbatten appointed as governor general of British India

- 3rd June Plan of Lord Mountbatten for partition of India
- 18th July, the Indian Independence Act
- 15th August, India attains independence

Appendix II

Photo Credits

The photographs in the book have all been taken from the below mentioned copyright free links

Page 1.5 https://commons.wikimedia.org/wiki/File:Bahadur_Shah_I_and_his_Consort.png

Page 1.6 https://garystockbridge617.getarchive.net/amp/media/muhammad-shah-rangeela-of-mughal-0c9927

Page 1.7 https://picryl.com/media/akbar-ii-1806-37-f8d781

Page 1.7 https://snl.no/Bahadur_Shah

Page 1.13 https://commons.wikimedia.org/wiki/File:Iron_Fort_-_Bharatpur_India_%284609963201%29.jpg

Page 1.15 https://commons.wikimedia.org/wiki/File:Peshwa_Bajirao.jpg

Page 1.16 https://commons.wikimedia.org/wiki/File:MarathaEmpire1759.png

Page 1.17 https://commons.wikimedia.org/wiki/File:Sadashivrao_Bhau_Peshwa.jpg

Page 2.2 The Cape of Good Hope

https://commons.wikimedia.org/wiki/File:CapeHopeOverview.png

Page 2.2 Vasco da Gama

https://commons.wikimedia.org/wiki/File:Vasco_Da_Gama,_1525-50_ca._02.jpg

Page 2.3 Portuguese empire in India

https://commons.wikimedia.org/wiki/File:Map_of_Portuguese_India.png

Page 2.4 Portuguese governor

https://commons.wikimedia.org/wiki/File:Retrato_de_Afonso_de_Albuquerque_(ap%C3%B3s_1545)_-_Autor_desconhecido.png

Page 2.7 The Dutch East India Company

https://commons.wikimedia.org/wiki/File:17th_century_plaque_to_Dutch_East_India_Company_%28VOC%29,_Hoorn.jpg

Page 2.8	Evolution of the Dutch East Indies
	https://commons.wikimedia.org/wiki/File:Evolution_of_the_Dutch_East_Indies.png
Page 2.9	https://jenikirbyhistory.getarchive.net/amp/media/elizabeth-i-watching-defeat-of-spanish-armada-by-an-unknown-artist-16th-century-4841a7
Page 2.10	https://en.wikipedia.org/wiki/Battle_of_Swally#/media/File:Battle_of_Swally.jpg
Page 2.11	https://upload.wikimedia.org/wikipedia/commons/f/ff/SirThomasRoe.jpg
Page 2.13	https://commons.wikimedia.org/wiki/File:Fortwilliam1828.jpg
Page 2.14	https://commons.wikimedia.org/wiki/File:French_India_1741-1754.png
Page 2.15	https://snl.no/Joseph_Fran%C3%A7ois_Dupleix
Page 2.19	https://commons.wikimedia.org/wiki/File:Muhammad_Anwaruddin.jpg
Page 2.20	https://commons.wikimedia.org/wiki/File:Robert,_Lord_Clive,_Baron_of_Plassey_Wellcome_L0040164.jpg
Page 2.22	https://commons.wikimedia.org/wiki/File:Vandavasi_Fort.jpg
Page 2.26	https://commons.wikimedia.org/wiki/File:Anthony_Cardon_-_Sir_Eyre_Coote_-_B1977.14.9865_-_Yale_Center_for_British_Art.jpg
Page 3.2	https://commons.wikimedia.org/wiki/File:Siraj_ud-Daula.jpg
Page 3.5	https://picryl.com/media/robert-clive-and-mir-jafar-after-the-battle-of-plassey-1757-by-francis-hayman-e6aef7
Page 3.11	https://picryl.com/media/bengal-famine-image-002d6f?zoom=true
Page 3.14	https://commons.wikimedia.org/wiki/File:Indian_Mysore_Kingdom_1784_map.svg
Page 4.3	https://commons.wikimedia.org/wiki/File:Statue_of_Maharaja_Ranjit_Singh_in_Amritsar_26_September_2018.jpg
Page 4.4	https://commons.wikimedia.org/wiki/File:Sikh_Empire_tri-lingual.jpg
Page 5.3	https://garystockbridge617.getarchive.net/amp/media/warren-hastings-by-tilly-kettle-82d25e
Page 5.4	https://picryl.com/media/lord-cornwallis-eb6442
Page 5.8	https://upload.wikimedia.org/wikipedia/commons/7/7f/Lord-william-bentinck.jpg
Page 5.9	https://garystockbridge617.getarchive.net/amp/media/dalhousie-c413fa
Page 5.11	https://commons.wikimedia.org/wiki/File:Queen_Victoria_by_Bassano.jpg
Page 7.5	https://commons.wikimedia.org/wiki/File:Dadabhai_Naoroji_1889.jpg
Page 8.2	https://commons.wikimedia.org/wiki/File:Sir_William_Jones_von_John_Linnell.jpg
Page 8.4	https://upload.wikimedia.org/wikipedia/commons/c/c8/Jeremy_Bentham_by_Henry_William_Pickersgill_detail.jpg

Page 8.5 John Stuart Mill & James Mill
https://upload.wikimedia.org/wikipedia/commons/b/bb/JAMES_MILL_1773_-_1836_JOHN_STUART_MILL_1806_-_1873_Philosophers_lived_here_1814_-_1831.jpg

Page 8.7 https://upload.wikimedia.org/wikipedia/commons/6/66/History_of_British_India_1817_James_Mill.jpg

Page 8.13 https://commons.wikimedia.org/wiki/File:Thomas_Babington_Macaulay2.jpg

Page 9.13 https://commons.wikimedia.org/wiki/File:Mangal-pandey_1460075022-1.jpg

Page 9.15 https://commons.wikimedia.org/wiki/File:Peshwa_of_Kanpur.jpg

Page 9.15 https://upload.wikimedia.org/wikipedia/commons/4/46/1957_Rani_Laxmi_Bai_2.jpg

Page 10.2 https://upload.wikimedia.org/wikipedia/commons/6/6b/Raja_Ram_Mohan_Roy_%28%E0%A6%B0%E0%A6%BE%E0%A6%AE%E0%A6%AE%E0%A7%8B%E0%A6%B9%E0%A6%A8_%E0%A6%B0%E0%A6%BE%E0%A6%AF%E0%A6%BC%29_%E0%A6%85%E0%A6%A5%E0%A6%AC%E0%A6%BE_%E0%A6%B0%E0%A6%BE%E0%A6%9C%E0%A6%BE_%E0%A6%B0%E0%A6%BE%E0%A6%AE_%E0%A6%AE%E0%A7%8B%E0%A6%B9%E0%A6%A8_%E0%A6%B0%E0%A6%BE%E0%A6%AF%E0%A6%BC.jpg

Page 10.2 https://upload.wikimedia.org/wikipedia/commons/6/68/Ishwar_Chandra_Vidyasagar_oval.png

Page 10.2 https://commons.wikimedia.org/wiki/File:Justice_Ranade_CIE.JPG

Page 10.7 https://snl.no/Keshab_Chandra_Sen

Page 10.11 https://commons.wikimedia.org/wiki/File:Ramakrishna.jpg

Page 10.12 https://upload.wikimedia.org/wikipedia/commons/3/35/Swami-vivekananda.jpg

Page 10.15 https://upload.wikimedia.org/wikipedia/commons/f/fe/Sir_Syed_Ahmad_Khan.jpg

Page 10.18 https://commons.wikimedia.org/wiki/File:Pandita_Ramabai_Sarasvati_1858-1922_front-page-portrait.jpg

Page 10.19 https://upload.wikimedia.org/wikipedia/commons/0/03/Narayana_Guru.jpg

Page 10.19 https://upload.wikimedia.org/wikipedia/commons/2/2b/Periyar_SocialJusticeDay_2.jpg

Page 11.4 https://commons.wikimedia.org/wiki/File:Hicky%27s_Bengal_Gazette,_March_10,_1781,_University_of_Heidelberg.jpg

Page 11.6 https://upload.wikimedia.org/wikipedia/commons/f/f4/Robert_Bulwer-Lytton_by_Nadar.jpg

Page 11.7 https://upload.wikimedia.org/wikipedia/commons/2/24/Dwarkanath_Tagore.jpg

Page 11.7 https://commons.wikimedia.org/wiki/File:Prasanna_Tagore.jpg

Page 11.8 https://upload.wikimedia.org/wikipedia/commons/4/43/Surendranath_Banerjee.jpg

Page 11.9 https://upload.wikimedia.org/wikipedia/commons/5/54/A_O_Hume.jpg

Page 11.12 https://upload.wikimedia.org/wikipedia/commons/4/4a/WCBonnerjee.jpg

Page 11.15 https://upload.wikimedia.org/wikipedia/commons/2/2c/Poverty_and_Un_British_Rule_in_India1.jpg

Page 12.1 https://commons.wikimedia.org/wiki/File:Chaphekar_Brother%27s.jpg

Page 12.2 https://commons.wikimedia.org/wiki/File:George_Curzon2.jpg

Page 12.7 https://upload.wikimedia.org/wikipedia/commons/5/5f/Lokmanya_Gangadhar_Tilak.jpg

Page 12.8 https://upload.wikimedia.org/wikipedia/commons/1/13/Mahatma_Lala_Lajpat_Rai.jpg

Page 12.9 https://upload.wikimedia.org/wikipedia/commons/6/6e/Bipin_Chandra_Pal.jpg

Page 12.10 https://commons.wikimedia.org/wiki/File:Sri_aurobindo.jpg

Page 13.5 https://www.geeksforgeeks.org/partition-of-bengal-1905/

Page 14.2 https://commons.wikimedia.org/wiki/File:Rashbehari_Ghosh.jpg

Page 14.3 https://commons.wikimedia.org/wiki/File:Khudiram_Bose_1905.jpg

Page 14.5 https://en.wikipedia.org/wiki/Delhi_Durbar#/media/File:The_Nizam_of_Hyderabad_pays_homage_to_the_king_and_queen_at_the_Delhi_Durbar.jpg

Page 14.5 https://upload.wikimedia.org/wikipedia/commons/0/00/Indian_bicycle_troops_Somme_1916_IWM_Q_3983.jpg

Page 14.6 https://commons.wikimedia.org/wiki/File:Champakraman_Pillai.jpg
https://commons.wikimedia.org/wiki/File:Biren_Chattopadhyaya.jpg

Page 14.7 https://commons.wikimedia.org/wiki/File:Madan_Dhingra.jpg

Page 14.8 https://upload.wikimedia.org/wikipedia/commons/4/4a/Komagata_Maru_incident_VPL_6225_%2811243895045%29.jpg

Page 14.12 https://upload.wikimedia.org/wikipedia/commons/b/b6/Kaka_Joseph_Baptista.jpg

Page 15.1 https://upload.wikimedia.org/wikipedia/commons/f/ff/Gandhi_st.jpg

Page 15.3 https://upload.wikimedia.org/wikipedia/commons/3/39/Map_of_the_provinces_of_South_Africa_1976-1994_with_English_labels.svg

Page 15.5 https://commons.wikimedia.org/wiki/File:Pranjivan_Mehta.jpg

Page 15.9 https://commons.wikimedia.org/wiki/File:Edwin_Samuel_Montagu.jpg

Page 15.12 https://commons.wikimedia.org/wiki/File:Sir_Sidney_Arthur_Taylor_Rowlatt_(cropped).jpg

Page 15.13 https://en.wikipedia.org/wiki/File:General-Reginald-Dyer.jpg

https://upload.wikimedia.org/wikipedia/commons/2/24/The_Jallianwala_Bagh_memorial_in_Amrithsar_.jpg

Page 16.11 https://upload.wikimedia.org/wikipedia/commons/2/20/Charkha_at_Gandhi_Ashram.jpg

Page 16.13 https://upload.wikimedia.org/wikipedia/commons/2/24/Chittaranjan_Das_2.jpg

https://commons.wikimedia.org/wiki/File:MotilalNehru3.jpg

Page 17.2 https://commons.wikimedia.org/wiki/File:Mn_roy2.jpg

Page 17.6 https://commons.wikimedia.org/wiki/File:Bhagat_Singh_1929.jpg

Page 17.9 https://commons.wikimedia.org/wiki/File:Vinayak_Damodar_Savakar.jpg

Page 17.9 https://commons.wikimedia.org/wiki/File:M_S_Golwalkar.jpg

Page 18.2 https://commons.wikimedia.org/wiki/File:Marche_sel.jpg

Page 18.3 https://commons.wikimedia.org/wiki/File:Khan_Abdul_Ghaffar_Khan.jpg

Page 18.5 https://en.wikipedia.org/wiki/File:Dr._Bhimrao_Ambedkar.jpg

Page 18.7 https://en.wikipedia.org/wiki/File:J._Ramsay_MacDonald_LCCN2014715885_(cropped).jpg

Page 18.9 https://commons.wikimedia.org/wiki/File:Gandhi_in_London_meeting,_1931.jpg

Page 19.1 https://en.wikipedia.org/wiki/File:Subhas_Chandra_Bose_NRB.jpg

Page 19.6 https://commons.wikimedia.org/wiki/File:Indian_Provincial_Election_1937.svg

Page 19.10 https://en.wikipedia.org/wiki/File:Stafford_Cripps_1947.jpg

Page 19.12 https://www.google.com/search?q=bhulabhai+desai&source=lnms&tbm=isch&sa=X&ved=2ahUKEwidp4_joaj8AhWIzTgGHRGsCJ0Q_AUoAXoECAEQAw&biw=1366&bih=657&dpr=1#imgrc=aLF-E8XuiB1aUM

Page 20.5 https://commons.wikimedia.org/wiki/File:Archibald_Wavell2.jpg

Page 20.6 https://commons.wikimedia.org/wiki/File:Simla_conference.JPG

Page 20.10 https://commons.wikimedia.org/wiki/File:Jawaharlal_Nehru_1957_crop.jpg

Page 20.12 https://commons.wikimedia.org/wiki/File:Lord_Mountbatten_Navy_Allan_Warren.jpg

Page 21.2 https://commons.wikimedia.org/wiki/File:Chamber_of_Princes_1917.png

Page 21.2	https://commons.wikimedia.org/wiki/File:Court_portrait_of_Jayachamarajendra_Wadiyar_of_Mysore.jpg
Page 21.4	https://upload.wikimedia.org/wikipedia/en/1/10/V._P._Menon.jpg
Page 21.4	https://commons.wikimedia.org/wiki/File:Sardar_patel_(cropped).jpg
Page 21.8	https://commons.wikimedia.org/wiki/File:Hari_Singh_1931.jpg
Page 21.9	https://commons.wikimedia.org/wiki/File:NezamHaydarabad_(cropped_to_image_only).jpg
Page 21.10	https://commons.wikimedia.org/wiki/File:Operation_Polo_1948.jpg
Page 22.18	https://commons.wikimedia.org/wiki/File:President_Zakir_Husain_1998_stamp_of_India_(cropped).jpg

Recommended Reading

- *History of Modern India* — **Bipan Chandra**
- *India's Struggle For Independence* — **Bipan Chandra**
- *Nationalism and Colonialism in Modern India* — **Bipan Chandra**
- *Modern India : 1885-1947* — **Sumit Sarkar**
- *From Plassey to Partition: A History of Modern India, 2nd Edition* — **Sekhar Bandyopadhyay**
- *An Advanced History of Modern India* — **Sailendra Nath Sen**
- *A New Look At Modern Indian History: From 1707- to the Modern Times*
  — **B.L Grover & Alka Mehta**
- *The Anarchy: The East India Company, Corporate Violence and the Pillage of an Empire*
  — **William Dalrymple**
- *The History of Education in Modern India : 1757-1998* — **Suresh Chandra Ghosh**
- *Social Background of Indian Nationalism* — **A. R. Desai**
- *Congress and Classes : Nationalism, Workers and Peasants* — **Kapil Kumar**
- *The Economic History of India : 1857-1947* — **Tirthankar Roy**
- *A Brief History of Modern India, NCERT Class XI Modern India* — **Bipan Chandra**
- *A Brief History of Modern India* — **Rajiv Ahir**
- IGNOU material (especially on freedom struggle)